D1140557

THE HOODOO MAN

Also by Steve Harris

AdventureLand
Wulf

THE HOODOO MAN

Steve Harris

HEADLINE

First published in 1992
by HEADLINE BOOK PUBLISHING PLC

10 9 8 7 6 5 4 3 2 1

British Library Cataloguing in Publication Data

Harris, Steve
The Hoodoo Man.
I. Title
823.914 [F]

ISBN 0-7472-0518-3

Typeset by
Letterpart Limited, Reigate, Surrey

Printed and bound in Great Britain by
Ronald Clay Ltd, Bungay, Suffolk

HEADLINE BOOK PUBLISHING PLC
Headline House
79 Great Titchfield Street
London W1P 7FN

The Hoodoo Man
is dedicated
with love
to
Florence
of course!

Thanks are due to C.A. Vaughan for inspiration and countless other things! Porker Thomson for her Satanic Rites – keep that magic working! Twinkle Oakley for a nice'n'easy edit; Caroline (no relation) Harris for publicity and letting me bend her ear; Gary Dobbs for his support; Steve Crisp for another knockout illustration; all Headline's Louises; Anne Williams for spreading the word; Patrick and Mike for hearing the word; Lynn Curtis for her sharp copy editing; Sian Thomas and her team for doing their best; Colin Rowe for eagle-eyed continuity advice under duress; Marion L. for her support (and for promising lunch); Steve Andrews for the music; Steve Harris the younger, Graham and Rebecca, Scott & Stacey 'Arizona' Novis, Phil & Barb, Geoff & Sarah for being there; Tuesday Lobsang Rampa whose work made me wonder; and most of all, my readers, wherever and whoever you are. Thanks folks, I've been thinking about you all!

'I never think of the future; it comes soon enough' – *Albert Einstein*

'Everything turns out for the bad in the end' – *Suzie Anderson*

'Pineal Gland: Pineal body or gland. A conical gland of unknown function which lies in the upper part of the mid-brain. Said to be the site of the third eye in certain lizards; thought by Descartes to be the seat of the soul' – *New English Dictionary, 1932*

Chapter One
Ghosts and Bullets and People On Fire

1

Everything turned sour for fifteen-year-old Danny Crickett at two minutes past two on the afternoon of Thursday 21st of August 1958.

That was when his big brother Ray died and killed him.

The moments leading up to the event were burnt indelibly into his memory, of course, but he wouldn't realise until much later that he had not truly recovered with the healing of the wound.

A part of him did not survive.

2

The rot, as Danny would ruefully admit himself during the year-long echo of that Bad Day, had probably set in even earlier. Joey the budgie might have been the seed of it if you counted the pets as he had allergy – and Danny did – and the slug of lead from his brother's gun, the watering can.

Danny was thinking about Joey when it happened and this seemed to hold a chilling significance. Would things have turned out differently if he'd been thinking about his girlfriend, Florence Vaughan, who lived down the road? Would their fates have become inextricably entwined?

There was no answer to this question. It was Joey he'd been thinking about, not Florence.

3

The bird was a genius. Joey did all the usual budgie tricks but his vocabulary and ability with syntax was legendary. Besides the standard fare of 'Who's a pretty boy then?' and 'Where's Joey?' Joey could apparently build sentences of his own. The majority of them started out well and ended up garbled and nonsensical, but Joey

Chapter One
Ghosts and Bullets and People On Fire

1

Everything turned sour for five year-old Danny Stafford at two minutes past two on the afternoon of Thursday, 21st of August 1958.

That was when his big brother shot and killed him.

The moments leading up to this event were burned indelibly into his memory, of course, but he wouldn't realise until much later that he had not truly recovered with the healing of the wound.

A part of him did not survive.

2

The rot, as Danny would tirelessly assure himself during the year-long echo of that Bad Day, had probably set in even earlier. Joey the budgie might have been the seed (if you excused the pun and the bad allegory, and Danny did) and the slug of lead from his brother's gun, the watering can.

Danny was thinking about Joey when it happened and this seemed to hold a chilling significance. Would things have turned out differently if he'd been thinking about his playmate, Florence Vaughan, who lived down the road? Would *their* lives have become inextricably entwined?

There was no answer to this question. It was Joey he'd been thinking about, not Florence.

3

The bird was a genius. Joey did all the usual budgie tricks but his vocabulary and ability with syntax was legendary. Besides the standard fare of '*Who's a pretty boy then?*' and '*Where's Daddy?*' Joey could apparently build sentences of his own. The majority of them started out well and ended up garbled and indistinct, but Joey could ask '*Where's that damn' cat from next door?*' and then opine: '*Pooping in our garden again, I s'pose!*' The marvel of this – like his other popular saying: '*That cat'll be the death of me!* – was that no one would admit to having taught him the words. Joey could also recognise and correctly name each member of the Stafford family, would not hesitate to inform you that he was running out of Trill or water, and could hack his way through a cuttlefish in no time at all.

Although Joey could faultlessly recite 'Hickory Dickory Dock', he seemed – in some mysterious birdy way – aware that he could reduce Danny to a giggling jelly simply by becoming stuck on the first line and saying '*Hickory Dickory Dickorydickorydickorydickorydickory*' ad infinitum until, painfully convulsed with mirth, Danny would have to give in and leave the room.

But Joey apparently hadn't been an entirely happy budgie. Like a convict planning a jail-break, he'd kept up his happy banter while underneath he'd been plotting and keeping his eye open for the main chance.

That chance had come two weeks before Danny was shot.

That day, Danny watched his mother open the bird cage door for one of Joey's routine exercise periods. Danny was bored and had requested the release of the budgie, hoping that Joey would, as usual, flutter around the perimeter of the room a few times and then alight on his shoulder and mutter into his ear. Maybe Joey would hang upside down from his finger with those warm thin claws and say the F word again. Joey had said the illegal F word only once before and Danny had been both shocked and thrilled. Although he had yet to hear his father swear, he suspected that this was where Joey had picked up the word.

Danny had watched the bird watching his mother as she walked away and left the room. 'C'mon, Joey!' he encouraged.

The budgie hopped into the open doorway and looked at him disdainfully.

'Good boy!' Danny piped.

Joey's head cocked to one side and then swivelled to face the window.

The window was open. For the first time since they'd had Joey, Danny's mother had neglected to check that the living-room window was closed before letting the bird out.

Danny was rooted to the spot by the sudden knowledge of what was going to happen. The budgie's eyes left the window and turned back to him. Joey knew how to say: '*It's been a long day*' and he may have said that now. To Danny it sounded as though he said, '*Africa's a long way*.' In that moment Danny learned something about captive animals that he would never forget.

'MUM!' Danny yelled, but it was too late. The view of Joey that was pinned in his mind forever after was that of his spread wings and splayed tail feathers as he shot through the window into the sunlight and vanished.

Joey was never seen again.

4

Danny's mother was a tall, thin woman with a misplaced – if not warped – sense of fun which made her want to give her sons the willies whenever possible. On occasion she had feigned death in front of Danny as a kind of scary game. She found this hilarious but Danny did not: the first time she did it she was so convincing that he'd become hysterical and she'd had to spend the whole afternoon trying to calm him down. But even then she hadn't learned her lesson and had repeated the exercise several times since. Danny was used to it now; in a way, at least – it still scared him but not to the same degree as that first time.

Setting aside her penchant for strange games, Marjorie Stafford was a standard 1950s housewife with a housewife's routines. Danny knew them all well and measured his life in washing days and shopping trips.

The regular Thursday afternoon shopping expedition was part of a routine that had been going on for longer than Danny could remember. He was waiting to be taken on one when his life was extinguished.

Lunch had been disposed of and he was in the kitchen with his mother, getting underneath her feet while she washed up and tried to ready herself. The radio was on. It was after a quarter to two because *Listen with Mother* had just started and the compère – a woman whose name Danny had never known – had already asked that well-known question: 'Are you sitting comfortably?' and without allowing time for a reply had declared, 'Then I'll begin.' Now she was singing: Lavender's blue dilly-dilly. . .

That particular day, *Listen with Mother* held no interest for Danny; it was hot and he was a five year old with a lot of things on his mind. Lately there had been parental talk about school, that great and unknown institution he would be compelled to attend starting this September. Brian was already an old hand at going to school, but he could not be relied upon to tell truthfully exactly how bad it was. Danny's parents said it would be fun; Brian assured him it would be horrible – especially the dinners which they set in front of you and forced you to eat. Brian was full of tales about kids who, having refused one of the awful meals, had been forced to sit alone in the dining hall until their plate was cleared. Brian reckoned that some kids had would sit there way into the night rather than fill their stomachs with *that* muck.

But it was still only August and as September was far enough away to be almost unimaginable, Danny had tried to place these worries in his mental 'pending' file. In spite of this he still experienced a constant low-level *ominous* feeling. Besides this, he had to deal with his mother's occasional threat that she would *take him to Redman's and have him fitted for a school uniform* (which so far, hadn't been carried out). Aside from this, Danny's major problem was coming to terms with the loss of Joey which had been weighing heavily on his mind.

The kitchen caught the sun in the afternoons so the windows were flung wide open (which was another poignant reminder of Joey), but Danny still felt hot and uncomfortable.

'What's up, Mogue?' his mother asked.

A Mogue was a bored person looking for something to do. Mogue was Danny's second name just lately. On more than one occasion his mother had offered the opinion that she'd be 'just as glad as buttons' when September finally rolled around and someone else would have to find work for Danny's idle hands to do.

Danny didn't hold this against her. His mother had hunted high and low for Joey and they'd even ridden the bus into Bracknell and then walked two miles to the site of a private aviary in case Joey had been found and taken there.

'Nothing much,' Danny replied.

'Why don't you go outside and play with Brian?'

Danny shook his head. Not only was his brother three years older and quite a lot bigger than him, but he was one of those people who never got hurt – which somehow made him dangerous to be with. Danny avoided playing with him whenever possible; it usually ended in tears when he did – his own. And besides, the mere mention of Brian gave him a feeling in the pit of his stomach that had nothing to do with his fear of school or the loss, of Joey. Danny had no idea what it was and would not become familiar with it until much later in his life.

'Help me with the dishes then?' his mother asked.

'Okay,' Danny said. He couldn't reach the sink to wash them, so his mother handed him a tea-towel and told him to wipe. He pottered about behind her, obediently wiping dishes while he listened to his big brother charging about in the back garden playing war. He was glad he hadn't gone outside: Brian would undoubtedly have nominated him as a German prisoner of war and tied him up.

Danny dried two plates and dropped the third. It bounced and stayed whole, rattled its way to a standstill then fell apart when his mother tried to pick it up. 'Oh, Daniel!' she scolded.

Which was when Brian burst in through the back door like a tiny terrorist. The door crashed into the worktop and Danny's mother gapsed and spun around to face him.

Brian was holding his .22 rifle at his chest like a machine gun. His face was contorted with rage.

The rifle had been bought for him the previous Christmas and upon receipt of it he had been presented with a list of rules that he had sworn to learn by heart and adhere to rigidly. It had been pointed out to him that this was not a pop-gun or a pellet rifle, this was a *weapon* which fired *real* bullets at high velocity and those bullets could *kill*! The second golden rule was that he was forbidden to use the rifle unless his father was there. Brian had broken his own record by managing to stick to the letter of this law for over eight months. But as his mother would have (and had) said, boys would be boys. Brian had recently taken to playing with the rifle in the garden. Not shooting at anything, but pretending; using it like a toy one.

A long time afterwards, Danny would realise that his father could not have known about this recent deviation from the straight and narrow, but his mother most certainly had. In his darkest moments he would mentally lay all the blame at his mother's feet. Why had she allowed it to happen? Like her mistake with the lounge windows and Joey, it was a chink in her adult perfection. Either it had slipped her mind to put a stop to it or she thought no harm could come of it. If the rifle wasn't loaded, it couldn't do any damage, could it?

Either way, what happened was her fault.

Brian pointed the rifle at their mother. 'Okay,' he said in his squeaky voice, 'don't anybody move, I've got you covered. Stick 'em up!'

'But I haven't done anything!' his mother said gaily, glancing back at the broken plate on the floor.

'I know you're a German,' Brian said. His brow furrowed and his face drew into a merciless look. 'And I'm going to have to shoot you.' He put the gun to his shoulder then, pointed it at her and looked down the sight.

Even Danny knew that Brian had completely overstepped the mark. He was now guilty of breaking the first and foremost of the golden rules his father had drummed into him for more than eight months. Had this been done in the presence of his father, it would have lost him the rifle and earned him the biggest beating of his life. Brian wasn't even allowed to try and shoot birds or the occasional rat that crept across the back garden. Pointing a gun at a person was the most terrible and wrong thing you could do with one. Brian wasn't *EVER* allowed to point the rifle at a person. What the consequences would be if Brian *did* this had not been discussed – at least not within Danny's hearing – but it seemed to him that Brian would surely be taken away and locked up for ever in a *bad* place.

Danny was never able to forgive his mother for what she did next. She acted out her part perfectly – as if it had been rehearsed – and knitted together the many loose threads of fate or destiny or mere bad luck that had been gathering around Danny since Joey flew away. Many years later in a letter to his estranged lover, Danny would say: 'You can call it whatever you want, but it amounts to the same thing;

at each key moment in those two weeks I managed to be in exactly the right place at the wrong time. Things stacked against me so precisely that it seems that either myself or the events or both were manipulated by some outside force in order to reach the desired conclusion.'

At the moment his mother spoke, five-year-old Danny Stafford felt a strong sense of this. Marjorie Stafford could easily have acted like a proper parent and shouted at Brian and torn the rifle from his hands, but she did not. She didn't mean any harm, she didn't know the rifle was loaded and she didn't know she was about to blight her son's life forever, but she *did* know the rules. Instead of applying them, she decided to join in the game.

As though the words had been put into her mouth to say, she said,'Don't shoot me, Brian. Shoot Daniel.'

Danny was hovering by the door to the hall, struck as rigid as he'd been when Joey escaped. He saw himself screaming and running for cover, like any cornered German in Brian's fantasies would have; he saw himself slipping quietly through the door; taking two steps forward to hide behind his mother; hitting the floor and covering his head with his arms. Danny did none of these things. He simply stood there and watched with mounting horror as Brian slowly swung the rifle away from his mother and trained it on him.

The heavy feeling in the pit of his stomach vanished, leaving what seemed like a vacuum behind it. Something clicked inside Danny's head and in that brief second he became enlightened. Everything there was to know in the universe suddenly resided inside him. He was, for a split second, a five-year-old Buddha. The rifle loomed before him and he knew where the wood came from that made the stock; he could see the snowy forest and the men with chainsaws cutting trees. Simultaneously he saw the stock being made in the carpenter's shop and smelt the fresh varnish as it was applied from the pot. Behind that – or before it, Danny could not tell which – he watched the hot steel flow from the foundry container into the moulds which would eventually become the trigger firing pin and barrel.

Then it was gone and he was back in the kitchen looking at the dull gleam of the hot afternoon sun glinting off the black barrel. The rifling inside it which made the slugs spin true loomed at him like a tunnel. His mother's laughter rang in his ears. Brian's face, a blank and unfocused pink mass at the other end of the weapon, swam in his vision and looked like a skull.

The rifle wobbled for a second then steadied. Danny's eyes were drawn to Brian's little eight-year-old index finger, its nail full of earth from where he had been playing in the garden, as it tightened on the trigger.

The word *death* resounded in his ears like the crash of a gigantic brass gong. This was now the extent of his enlightenment. He was going to die.

His mind protested vehemently, screaming at him that the rifle wasn't loaded and that the bullets were kept upstairs somewhere in a locked box to which his dad had the only key.

That's why you can't die!

Brian would never actually want to injure him, not in a month of Sundays. Brian was his big brother who looked after him when they went out to play and the big kids scared him. Brian had even slapped Lorna Earhardt when she knocked Danny off his trike, and she was nine.

That's why you can't die!

But in spite of all this, a quiet place in Danny's mind knew he *could die* and that, shortly, he most certainly would.

Brian's knuckle whitened as he squeezed the trigger in exactly the way his dad had taught him. No jerks. A steady pressure.

The rifle barked. White propellant smoke came up the barrel from the empty chamber. Danny saw the black flicker of the bullet as it left the rifle ahead of the smoke.

In the moment between the trigger being pulled and the .22 bullet hitting Danny in the face, two things happened. His muscular control returned and he began to turn away, knowing it was much too late. This knowledge caused his mind to empty itself. Danny reached out mentally for something to cling to. *Joey!* he thought.

The hard point .22 bullet hit him at an angle, entered his cheekbone just below his right eye, passed through and buried itself deep inside his brain.

There was no pain; just the feeling of being struck square in the face with a pillow. Danny was still conscious and felt his head snap back into the door panel as the impact of the slug threw him backwards. He heard the sharp crack of wood as the panel broke and he began to die.

Everything went soft. His sight and hearing were gone, but he was still able to feel in some way. Danny floated downwards as if he were sinking in thick oil. Things blocked his path, dissolving the instant they touched his body. He knew there were surfaces nearby and reached out for them, but each collapsed as he made contact with it. As his senses vanished he became more aware of his body and realised it was shutting-up shop. His lungs were not sucking air, his heart was not beating, his nerves were no longer relaying sensation. What little power of reasoning he still had trickled away from him.

Danny knew he was dead. It was black like it was supposed to be when you were dead, but there were no angels, no gods, and no one was coming to get him.

Being dead was simply a darkness and emptiness that went on forever.

But there was more.

Danny felt the shockwaves of a series of small explosions somewhere in the void and he felt things inside him suddenly start to vibrate with a new kind of life as if his physical death had set them free. Molten metal charged through him in time with the pulsating sensation, but it didn't hurt. Sparks that were not visible showered down on him. Something soft was rocking him back and forth, slowly at first, but then more and more violently, shaking him away from himself.

For a second a huge cool wind rushed at him and Danny felt himself tearing like an old sheet. Then he was in the air, screaming silently as his perceptions returned. New light tore at his eyes in a vivid blast of swirling colour, and sound at incredible volume ravaged his ears. When his senses began to settle, Danny realised he was back in the kitchen. This realisation was followed instantly by a hammer-blow shock as Danny suddenly understood that although he might have been in the kitchen, he was *not* inside his body.

The new Danny seemed to be somehow suspended near the kitchen ceiling, looking down at his mother and Brian and a small bloodied figure in short trousers lying on the floor. Danny understood that he was looking at what his Sunday School teacher had once referred to as 'this vessel of clay'. The body looked more like a bad waxwork of him than the real thing and seemed to bear no relationship to him at all. Worse than that, it scared him to look at it. Neither knowing nor caring how the movement was accomplished, he turned to look at his brother.

Brian's eyes were streaming tears and his clenched fists were over his mouth, stifling his screams and turning them to tiny dog-like whimpers. The .22 rifle was on the floor at his feet, little wisps of smoke still coming from the barrel.

Danny's eyes were drawn back to his lifeless body where his mother crouched, her ear pressed to his chest listening for a heartbeat that was not present. There was blood everywhere; on the door, running from the wound on the face of his waxwork body, on the blue-tiled floor, and all over his mother. Danny could smell it plainly but he no longer felt frightened. The new Danny was totally divorced from the mess down there. It was no longer anything to do with him and he didn't feel associated with it in any way. Danny was only academically interested; there were other things for him to consider now. He thought that God would be coming to get him soon. Or someone.

As he floated and watched, his mother drew her bloody face back from his chest and stared into space, her lips moving in what could only have been a silent prayer. Her hair was awry, eyes bright and glittery and her brow furrowed. Beads of sweat glistened on her forehead. Danny stared at her as she clasped her hands and had an urge to tell her that it was too late for prayers now.

But his mother had not clasped her hands in supplication. She lifted them above her head and brought them down hard on the waxwork effigy's chest.

Although it was impossible, the new Danny felt the pain of the blow in his own non-existent chest. Down on the floor, his mother unclasped her hands and drove the heels of them into his ribcage over his heart. She pumped a couple of times, thrusting down hard.

Bolts of electricity shot through the new Danny and he screamed. His mother put her head to the small, still chest and listened again. Then she balled her fists and hit him again, harder this time. Much harder.

An unseen hand reached out for the new Danny, gripped him so tightly that everything turned black before him, and dragged him away.

Everything stayed black for a very long time.

5

Danny regained consciousness three weeks later in Frimley hospital. The thick blanket of darkness that had lain upon him began to fade and allowed him to experience pain again. Danny hurt badly all over, but his head was worst. It felt as though it had been skinned and used as a football in a particularly hard game. With each pounding beat of his heart, Danny expected it to split in two.

His senses of time and place were badly disjointed; Danny didn't recall the shooting, wasn't sure where he was and didn't know how long he'd been there – or why he was there at all. His consciousness was flicking on and off like a lighthouse lamp. One second he was awake and feeling sorry for himself, the next everything was black for hours or seconds or tenths of a second; there was no way of knowing how long the black lasted.

He lay still for a few moments – or hours – trying to recall where he was and why his head hurt so much. He may have slept in between times because by the time he decided to open his eyes he seemed to recall the comings and goings of a lot of people he didn't know and, for some reason, a long time seemed to have passed.

Danny tried to open his eyes and had to close them again when his head threatened to explode. The light cut into them like knives. More time passed. Each time Danny woke, he practised opening his eyes. After the third or fourth rest period – or perhaps the tenth or twelfth – he was able to open them a tiny amount, but then only for a few seconds. It was enough to verify that he was in hospital; this was a fact that he had somehow already known – probably from the distinctive smell.

Danny was alone in bed in a big white room. There were no other beds there, just machinery which bleeped with every beat of his heart and every thud of his head. There was a window at the end of the room and if he squinted, Danny could see blue sky outside. For a while he cried, wishing he was out there playing and feeling well.

Some time later, he found the wires and traced them with his fingers to the electrode pads which were stuck to his head with adhesive tape. To his horror he found that he was bald and that there was a circular stitched wound around the greater part of his skull. Apparently someone had operated on his head. Danny did not know why. All this was too much for him to bear. He felt the black blanket descending again and was glad.

When he awoke again it was night time. Danny was thirsty and in a great deal of pain. He lay still for a long time, wondering when someone was going to come and see him so he could tell them how much it *hurt*. Eventually he stopped being brave and cried. No one heard his sobbing and came to his rescue and after a time he went back to sleep.

6

Voices from outside woke him up again. He didn't know how long he'd slept, but the curtains were drawn and the lights were on – it might have been the same night or another, there was no way of telling. Danny's head still pounded and his neck was stiff, but he managed to look over to the door, hoping to attract the attention of anyone who might pop their head round to look at him.

Then Danny's mother and father and a doctor were in the room with him. He realised he already knew this was going to happen. It had something to do with the noise of their approach. To Danny, these sounds seemed to have happened months ago. Somewhere in the back of his confused five-year-old mind he realised he'd become unconscious again because he hadn't seen the door open.

The three of them drifted silently towards him. No rubber soles squeaked on the shiny floor, no clothes rustled, no reassuring sound issued forth. Like ghosts, they gathered round his bed and looked down at him. The doctor was a plump, balding man with a small grey moustache. He wore a white lab coat, horn-rimmed glasses, and carried charts in his hand on which he began writing with a black fountain pen.

Danny's mother and father exchanged worried glances. They were both very pale. His father's normally shiny face was flat and dull, his mother's ruddy country-girl cheeks were grey. Their eyes were distant and although they looked down at him they didn't seem to be seeing him at all.

The doctor said something. Or rather his lips moved. Danny didn't hear any sound, but his parents evidently did because they both leaned over and inspected a spot on his face which he suddenly became aware of. It hurt.

His father spoke and his mother replied. But there was no sound.

'My head hurts, Mummy,' Danny moaned. Tears were already welling up in his eyes. No one showed any sign of having heard him. His fear and pain boiled over. He didn't know what had happened, why he was in hospital or why his own mum and dad were acting as if he wasn't even there. Nothing made sense any more. Danny took the only course of action open to him and began to weep bitterly.

No one noticed.

The doctor stood up and walked to the window. Danny's parents looked away from him, following the doctor with their worried eyes. The man turned back and Danny realised that his lips were moving; the doctor was talking and his parents were listening to him carefully. The doctor came back slowly, gesticulating and explaining something. While Danny's parents watched, he laid his hand on the crown of Danny's head where the stitches were.

Danny couldn't feel it.

He screamed.

7

It was a wakemare. When Danny calmed down a little, he realised this. He'd had them before, but none had been as protracted and terrible as this. This was the grandaddy of all the wakemares he'd ever had.

When Danny was very tired his mind would sometimes play little tricks on him and he would see impossible things happen. His father called these hallucinations wakemares and claimed that they only happened when you were almost – but not quite – asleep. On several occasions Danny had seen the lounge door shrink in front of him until it was far too tiny to allow anyone through. He had discovered that if he shut his eyes when things went awry and opened them again a few seconds later, everything would have reverted to its normal shape and size.

Danny bit his lip and closed his eyes.

But things were not restored when he opened them again.

His mother was crying now, but although he could see the thin tears running down her face and her teeth biting the pastel pink of her bottom lip to a pale grey, he heard no sound.

Danny began to sob too.

It was the only sound he could hear.

Brian had once claimed that if you had not said your goodbyes to everyone when you died you would end up as a ghost, doomed to haunt the place of your demise. Danny could now appreciate the wisdom of these words. The sense of desolation and loneliness he felt was almost unbearable. He had become a small, still, unfeeling ghost, trapped and separated from all he knew and loved by his own disremembered death.

In desperation he forced himself up on his elbows and made a grab for his mum's sleeve. Danny's fingers clutched thin air. His hand passed right through her arm and landed back on the bed.

'Noooo!' he wailed.

And then realised that when he'd swiped his hand through the air he had somehow severed the remaining connection with his parents and life. Everything began to fade.

The doctor's hand was still on his pillow and he still appeared to be talking, but the colour in his face was leeching away. Suddenly Danny could see through his white coat to the equipment that towered behind him. Danny's mum and dad were also taking on a washed out look, the colour draining from them like water down a sink. Danny could do nothing but scream as he watched them disappear. To the lonely sound of his voice, they finally became completely transparent and then vanished.

8

A nurse rushed in.

She was alight.

Danny shrieked until he thought he'd torn his throat. He could see the nurse clearly, but she was being consumed by great swathes of brightly coloured flame which flickered and licked around her whole body. Even her features were blazing. Danny hit himself across the face in his frenzy of horror and blood started to pour down his right cheek from the painful area the vanishing doctor had indicated.

The nurse ran across the room, glancing at the monitoring equipment as she passed. 'What's the trouble, child?' she asked in a concerned voice which held a soothing Irish lilt.

Danny was beside himself with terror. 'On fire!' he shouted. 'On fire, on fire! YOU'RE ON FIRE!'

The blazing nurse closed in on him, bringing with her a certain death by burning. Danny pressed himself back against the bed, screaming and trying to draw away from her.

The nurse stopped and looked at him from a distance. She didn't seem aware of the fact that she was burning. 'Shhh!' she urged. 'Nothing's wrong!'

Danny gasped for breath and stared at the flames, transfixed with terror. This was not ordinary fire by any means. The flames were of every different hue imaginable, but mainly cobalt blue and yellow with a lot of green and a tinge of red here and there. They extended about four feet from the nurse's body, seemed to burn with no smoke or heat, and they were astoundingly clear. And yet in spite of the flames Danny could clearly see the red colour of the nurse's hair, the green shade of her eyes and the blue and white striped uniform. Her black-stockinged legs and clumpy shoes were also clearly visible through the swirling conflagration.

But the nurse was not being consumed.

'You're alight,' Danny croaked fearfully.

'No, I'm not,' she assured him. 'You've had an accident, you'll be all right now, the worst is over. No one is going to hurt you. Shhh!'

As the nurse drew closer Danny realised that the flames weren't actually touching her at all. There was a smoky blue capsule around her body which extended for about six inches between her and the fire. This was evidently insulating the nurse and keeping her alive.

Danny found his voice. 'No!' he yelled. 'Go away. I want my mummy! You're on fire! You'll hurt me!'

'It's all right, Daniel. You're going to be all right. You're nearly well again,' the nurse softly assured him.

'Keep away!' he warned, wiping the hot blood from his face with the back of his right hand and smearing it over the white bedsheets. Tears and blood and snot flew as he shouted.

The nurse moved closer and closer, her face full of gentle concern which masked her obvious intention of burning Danny alive.

'*Don't*,' he hissed and his muscles bunched and locked, freezing him into a terrified statue. *It's a long way to Africa*, his mind whispered.

The nurse settled on the edge of the bed, engulfing Danny with her fire.

He gasped and prepared to see his flesh shrivel and run from his body like melted toffee, but this did not happen. There was no sensation of burning or heat at all.

Cool hands pressed him back into the bed and the nurse crooned soft words to allay his fear, but Danny was too far gone by that time. He had finally realised that he'd woken up in hell. The paralysis left him and he began to fight wildly, slapping and scratching and screaming and spattering the nurse's face and uniform with his own blood as he tried to free himself from those strong hands.

Three doctors ran into the room. They were all alight too. 'GET AWAY!' Danny screamed hoarsely. The flames surrounding the three men blazed away ferociously, mixing and mingling as the doctors swept toward him. The riot of pure flickering colour hurt Danny's eyes. Still he fought.

'Hold him still, for Christ's sake!' one of the doctors yelled and Danny finally realised that he could hear again. *This* was not a wake or a nightmare or any other mare. *This* was as real as real could be.

'Pin him down, Daphne, he'll have the top of his fucking head off!' someone shouted.

And while Danny was still wondering, not why the top of his head might come off, but whether he'd actually heard a grown-up using the F word, one of the other men dragged the nurse aside and pinioned Danny's arms to the bed.

He struggled, but the doctor simply slid on to the bed and sat on his legs, yelling, 'Hold still, Danny! For Christ's sake, cut it out! YOU'LL HURT YOURSELF IF YOU DON'T!'

The others grouped around the madly bleeping machinery and there was a lot of heated discussion during which the words delirious, hallucination and sedation were bandied about. Everything that was said sounded ominous and painful and filled Danny with such an overpowering dread that – for the first time since he was three – he lost control over his bladder. And that wasn't all. There was a warm, wet feeling coming from his head too. Danny's vision doubled and the smell of blood filled his nostrils. This reminded him of something that had once happened to him, but he couldn't quite remember what it was.

'His head's bleeding! Get Amis in here, for Christ's sake!' the doctor sitting on top of Danny yelled.

'He's coming!' another replied.

'Blood pressure falling!'

'For fuck's sake!'

Danny's pain had all gone and his head was lying on something soft. He opened his eyes and the doctor he'd seen vanish earlier on was in front of him. This, apparently, was Amis. There was fire raging around him, but Danny could hear him now. He was issuing orders in a soft, authoritative voice and seemed to have taken control. Danny gathered that Amis was worried about loss of blood but it didn't add up because the doctor didn't have a scratch on him.

It's a long, long way, Joey, Danny thought.

'We'll have to do it *now*, not soon,' Amis replied to a distant question.

Dickorydickorydickorydickory! Danny's mind told him. In spite of the dampness at either end of him, he was cool and comfortable.

'Not next week, not tomorrow! Operate *now*! Even in spite of the risk of brain damage!' Amis barked.

'Subcutaneous or intravenous for starters?' another voice asked.

One of the blazing doctors leaned into Danny's field of vision and spoke to him. Through the flames his face was young and fresh. Rainbows danced on the steel rims of his little round glasses, reflections from the fires. 'Can you hear me, Danny?' he asked.

Danny nodded. He felt loose. *Joey was in Africa*.

'My name's Stephen,' he said, and to Danny it sounded like Sven. 'I'm going to give you a little injection. It won't hurt,' he said, and grinned.

Danny could tell by the fire that Stephen meant what he said. He smiled.

'Procedure?' someone asked as the needle sunk painlessly into Danny's vein.

'It's a bit of a black art,' a voice replied. Danny's eyes had grown heavy and closed so he didn't know who it was.
'Signs?'
'Not terribly good, I'm afraid.'
'Intracranial pressure.'
'You were expecting something else?'
That cat'll be the death of me!
'Might not work. . .'
'Slip the lid and take a look.'
'There's going to be damage if we *don't* do it. . .'
'And possibly if we do.'
Joey!
Danny's black blanket descended again, cutting out the voices and even the images of the lost budgie. The emptiness stayed for a long time.

9

Danny was on the operating table for eighteen hours. Afterwards he was kept sedated for two weeks. His consciousness returned to him only twice during that time, and then only vaguely. On both occasions it was the pain of a catheter being inserted or removed that almost woke him.

During these moments it wasn't possible to open his eyes – his eyelids seemed to be bolted down.

Afterwards, Danny remembered only dimly that more terrible things had happened to him; these brief periods of almost surfacing assured him that he hadn't escaped from whatever nightmare he'd been flung into.

10

They let him have his senses back at the end of the fortnight. Waking was like fighting his way up through a massive container of cotton wool.

Danny was alone when he finally broke the surface. He instantly realised that he was still in the same hospital room. He could clearly recall the blazing people, but he was far too drained, both mentally and physically, for any of his previous horror to reassert itself.

For reasons he could not comprehend, Danny no longer suspected that he was either dead, a ghost, or in hell.

Feeling as though he had already done this recently, Danny began to explore his body in search of the reason for his hospitalisation. He seemed to recall an accident and an operation – both before and after the burning nurse and doctors – and could not remember the sequence of events. He was, however, able to piece together the parts. He was in hospital because an accident had happened to him that made him see people on fire. The operation was to mend this damage. It didn't take long for him to rediscover the wires running from his head and the healing wound beneath his right eye – which was painful. Danny seemed to remember pains in his head 'from before'. There were none there now and he was glad about that.

His lips were cracked, his mouth and throat parched, and the tube that went up his nose hurt like hell. He badly needed a drink but found that his vocal cords were dry and seized up. When he tried to call out all he managed was a croak that made him cough. Danny forced himself to lie still and wait, hoping that when someone came in they wouldn't be alight.

11

Daphne Avery, the blazing nurse, waltzed into the room humming a tune to herself. She was no longer on fire.

Danny tensed, studying her carefully, but the nurse did not suddenly burst into flame.

She went out, Danny thought. *They put her out*. But another part of him knew that the operation had been successful.

Nurse Avery glanced at Danny and stopped dead in her tracks, frowning and presumably expecting another tantrum. 'Ah,' she said.

Danny smiled at her. It hurt.

Nurse Avery relaxed. 'So you've returned to the land of the living!' she said.

'Hello,' Danny croaked and began to cough, his vision blacking out with each lung-rending hack.

Then the nurse's strong arms were supporting him and holding a glass of cool water to his lips. Danny sipped it and coughed it back over her, sipped again and swallowed this time. It was like new life being poured into him. Danny began to gulp.

'Easy,' the nurse advised. 'Just sip it or you'll be sick.'

Danny drank some more and looked up at her.

'Good boy,' she said.

'You're not on fire any more,' he said.

'And I never was!' she replied. 'All that was a game your mind was playing with you. It happens sometimes after accidents like yours. You're going to be all right from now on.'

Danny reached for the glass of water but couldn't hold it. His fingers were like sticks.

'It's because you've been asleep so long,' the nurse said gently. 'Here, let me do it.' She put the glass of water to his mouth, feeding it to him a sip at a time, then told him to rest while she went to tell the doctors he'd woken up.

Danny slept. This time, there was no black blanket inside his head to stop him from dreaming.

12

He woke with a start and froze rigid because, in a perfect replay of that time so long ago, his mother and father and the doctor were in the room with him.

But it was different this time; his other senses had been restored to him.

Danny realised he could hear them now. Familiar smells assailed his nostrils – the faint reek of pipe tobacco on his dad and the flowery odour of his mum's perfume brought with them a feeling of safety and Danny relaxed. This time he could feel their hands as they touched him.

'Remember me?' the doctor asked.

Danny nodded.

'My name's Mister Amis, not Doctor Amis. Do you know why that is?'

'No,' Danny said.

'It's because I'm a surgeon. Surgeons don't get called "doctor' they're called mister because they do something that doctors don't. Do you know what that is?'

Danny shook his head.

'They operate on people. We make folks better by opening them up and mending what's gone wrong inside them. Ordinary doctors don't do operations.'

'I had an operation,' Danny said. 'I can remember it.' For a moment, he *did* remember it. They had shaved off his hair and sawed off the top of his skull with a thing that screamed and whined and made his whole being blurred. He could recall the smell of burning bone and the word *trepanning* resounded in his ears. There had been pain but he could not imagine that now.

Mr Amis smiled. 'You may remember the accident, but you certainly don't remember the operation. You were out cold, Danny.'

Not for the first time in his life and certainly not for the last, Danny's mouth ran away with him. 'I got *trepanned*,' he said and wished he hadn't. This was like telling Grandma she had a bogey hanging from her nose. Some things you weren't allowed to say, even if they were true. Judging from the doctor's face, this was one of them.

Mr Amis frowned. 'Do you know what that means?'

Suddenly, Danny *did* know what it meant. He nodded his heavy head. 'It's when you saw off someone's skull.'

'Danny!' his mother reprimanded.

'And that's what you did to me. I remember.' And that was it, out and done with and true. Danny wished he hadn't said it, but he'd *had* to.

Mr Amis nodded. 'That's correct. I don't know how you know that, young man, but you're right. You're a very perceptive fellow. Do you remember the accident?'

Danny did and at the same time he didn't. It was like a film he'd seen and forgotten about. He shook his head.

'You are very lucky to be alive, y'know. You stopped a bullet, young man.' He glanced at Danny's parents and said, 'Your brother shot you by mistake with his rifle. You were shot in the face, here . . .' he touched the sore spot on Danny's right cheek, '. . . and the bullet went right through and ended up deep inside your brain. We had to cut you open – or *trepan* you, as you so rightly point out – in order to remove the bullet. Give me your hand.'

Danny held out his hand. It shook.

'Pins and needles?' Mr Amis asked.

Danny shook his head.

'Can you move your fingers all right?'

Danny wiggled them. They were stiff. The surgeon nodded, took his hand and bent it back and forth. 'Uh hum,' he said, apparently satisfied. He got up and walked to the foot of the bed, pulled the sheet back and asked Danny if his feet felt okay.

'Yes. . .'

'But you do have pins and needles in your left foot.' The surgeon took hold of Danny's foot and squeezed gently. Danny felt a numb electrical tingling like when you put your tongue on the terminals of one of the almost-flat-nine-volt batteries that Brian took out of his radio. 'Feel strange?' the surgeon asked.

'Fizzy,' Danny replied.

'Don't worry, it'll soon be better.'

Mr Amis covered Danny's feet again and came back up the bed. Looking somewhat embarrassed, he took Danny's hand and placed something cold in it, wrapping Danny's stick-like fingers around it. 'A keepsake for you,' he said.

Danny inspected the gift.

It was the .22 bullet that had killed him. The pointed end was flattened where it had smashed into his cheek bone.

Mr Amis said, 'There it is, just to prove that we got it out. Keep it if you like. Luckily it didn't hurt anything in there that will cause you any problem.'

The bullet began to warm in Danny's hand and he frowned. He clutched it tighter and his hand began to sting. Somehow the bullet was expanding and drawing him towards it. He tried to release his grip on it but his fingers wouldn't move. The slug of lead was *sucking* at him.

Then the sensation suddenly stopped. Danny relaxed.

And an invisible hand hit his face with an icy slap.

Words began to pour into his mind; words he knew were the truth. 'I had a cerebral haemorrhage,' he heard himself say. He had no idea what a cerebral haemorrhage might be. A tiny pinprick seemed to have formed in his mind and behind it lay the flattened bullet, glimmering darkly, huge with knowledge.

He tried to clamp his mouth shut but the words *had* to be said and his mouth was working of its own volition. 'I bled a lot. There was tremendous pressure. I died. I was dead when Brian shot me and my mum made me alive again. There was emergency surgery. . .'

'Danny!' his father warned. He sounded frightened.

Danny was scared too, but the words kept roaring in from the bullet and his mouth kept on saying them. 'I died again on the operating table. There were problems afterwards. The bleeding didn't stop! You had to operate again.' Tears filled his eyes. He gasped in a shuddering breath and tore himself away from the image of the bullet.

'True,' the surgeon said. His face flushed and his eyes glittered dangerously but he kept his voice even and soft. 'You did give us a little bit of trouble. When you arrived you were very poorly. The shock of the bullet had caused a haemorrhage – that's a bit of bleeding – in another part of your brain. This was very dangerous so we had to fix that before we worked on getting the bullet out. Unfortunately our fixing wasn't quite healed when you had your little fit and managed to unfix it again. During the first operation your heart stopped for a few moments. This doesn't really count as dying, Danny. It sometimes happens during complicated operations on very sick people.'

The cold hand found Danny's face again; the bullet pulsed. 'I died again the second time too!' he cried. '*Four times!*' Danny's stiff fingers spasmed and straightened and the .22 slug rolled off his hand and fell to the floor.

'It wasn't really dying, Danny,' Mr Amis protested, retrieving the bullet.

The surgeon was offended and Danny's mouth had now run out of words. He was suddenly dreadfully sorry. He snivelled but was unable to apologise.

Mr Amis offered him the bullet but Danny did not take it. He didn't want to touch it again yet.

'I'll leave it here,' the surgeon said and placed it on the stand beside the bed.

Danny's father came across and squeezed his leg through the bedclothes. You're a lucky boy,' he said. 'Especially as you had Mister Amis to look after you. He had to send out for a special kind of blood for you, you know.'

'Yes,' the surgeon said, smiling once more. 'We didn't have any of your kind in our cupboards and we had to send policemen on motorcycles to get some for you.'

'Thank you,' Danny said in a small voice. Saying thank you wasn't enough after his outburst; he knew this and it hurt him. He decided that he was a very bad boy who would most probably go to hell. To make matters worse, he didn't remember either operation and he didn't know what had made him say those things.

'What about these . . . uhh . . . hallucinations?' Danny's father asked.

The surgeon shook his head. 'They were caused simply because of the intracranial pressure. They won't re-occur.'

'What about the other thing? The suspected paralysis?' Marjorie Stafford asked worriedly.

'Well, Mrs Stafford, everything looks to be going according to plan in that department. He may have some trouble with the movement of the left side of his body for some time, but the main problem is cured and the motor centre which took most of the brunt will undoubtedly respond to physiotherapy. There is very little damage, fortunately.'

Marjorie Stafford wrung her hands and looked as if she didn't truly believe him. 'What about the scrap of bone?' she asked. 'Can it be removed?'

Mr Amis shook his head. 'We'd like to avoid further surgery if we can and at this stage it doesn't look as if it will be needed. We don't think the shard of bone we had to leave behind will cause any harm, but it would be advisable to keep an eye on him for a while.'

'You see, Danny,' the surgeon explained, 'when the bullet went in, it drove a piece of bone from your cheek into your brain. It was only a tiny fragment, but we had to leave it where it was rather than endanger your life by keeping you on the operating table for any longer. It's a thin pointed shard and it is stuck into a part of your brain called the pineal gland. This in itself is no problem. This particular gland doesn't do anything, so it doesn't really matter that the bone is stuck in it. What we are a little worried about is that it might move somehow. Become dislodged and prod another, more important part of your brain. Do you understand?'

Danny nodded.

'So, I'm afraid, you will have to stay in hospital for a little while to let us see what is going to happen. If the piece of bone starts to move, or causes you any ill effect, we will have to give you another little operation. But let us worry about that. All *you* have to do is rest and get better, then you can go home. Now, would you like to see where that bullet hit you?'

Danny nodded, still wondering if he had been forgiven.

The surgeon fetched a small mirror and handed it to him, saying, 'It's not quite as bad as you might think, Danny.'

He took the mirror with trembling hands and held it up in front of his face. A terrible stranger looked back at him. A little boy with a pale face and two black eyes. The white of the right one was red with trapped blood. This awful boy had only wires and a dark brown stubble growing on his head where his hair ought to have been; a nose darkened with bruising and one nostril filled with a tube, and swollen, cracked lips. But the worst thing was the hole in his cheekbone just below his right eye. It was not quite scabbed over and the congealed blood had sunk into the hole leaving torn edges showing. The hole's diameter was bigger than the bullet's.

'Oh,' Danny moaned.

'That's where the bullet went in,' Mr Amis said, his voice soft and reassuring. 'You'll soon heal up and look as good as new. Keep the mirror and check on how quickly the bruises fade and the wounds heal. I'll be coming back to ask you soon. Okay?'

Still shocked by what he had seen, Danny set down the mirror and nodded.

'Anything you want to ask me?'

'There won't be anymore alight people, will there?' he asked.

The surgeon shook his head. 'They were just because your brain was upset.'

'Or ghosts? I saw ghosts.'

'No more ghosts,' Mr Amis promised.

'Thank you,' Danny said.

13

Mr Amis was wrong.

During the course of the day, the tube was removed from Danny's nose, the electrodes from his head, and he drank a bowl of soup and talked to several nurses, questioning them about his likely recovery time. He was still sore all over and his head hurt, which tired him rapidly. Danny fell into a deep sleep at about seven that evening.

Something woke him almost instantly. Almost no time seemed to have passed since he had dozed off, but groggily he realised it had because it was now the middle of the day. The sun was shining in through the slightly open window and a gentle breeze toyed with the curtains. Birds were singing outside and this reminded him of Joey.

Danny swallowed and realised his throat was sore again. Then he realised that the tube had been put back up his nose. Wires once more connected him to the bleeping machinery and he wondered if he had become ill again. He reached for his mirror but it was no longer on the beside table.

Then the door opened and Mr Amis and his parents came in.

'Mum!' Danny said, realising that they bore the same greyish look as they had when his upset brain had invented a vision of them. Like the previous hallucination there were no smells and they moved and spoke with no sound.

Danny watched them carefully, telling himself that he was still asleep and dreaming, or if not, that his brain was still a little upset. He tried not to be frightened.

While Danny lay there transfixed, the three grown-ups did a soundless repeat performance of what had really happened earlier in the day, lips moving in the right places, identical gesticulations and facial expressions.

Mr Amis came across and stood in front of him. His lips mimed the words, 'Remember me?' and he paused as another Danny – this afternoon's one probably – nodded in reply.

'My name's Mister Amis, not Doctor Amis. Do you know why that is?' the surgeon soundlessly mouthed.

No, Danny thought, remembering his own responses. As Mr Amis mimed the same speech, word for silent word, Danny thought the words into his mouth, verifying that this was indeed a replay of this afternoon. When the surgeon touched his wound Danny felt no sensation. When Mr Amis took Danny's hand and wiggled the fingers, he appeared to be fiddling with thin air. Danny peered at the surgeon's hand, expecting to catch a glimpse of his own hand there, but there was nothing to see.

The replay ended directly after Danny's father squeezed his leg. As though someone had thrown a switch, the grown-ups suddenly began to lose what little colour they had. Within seconds they were transparent. They vanished before Danny's father had finished mouthing to him that they'd had to send out for a special kind of blood.

14

In an extremely clear and articulate way, Danny realised and noted that this vision or hallucination was different from the first. Unlike his first – which seemed to have borne no relation to reality – this was a repeat of something he had already experienced. Then there were the noises. In the earlier episode everything had been silent. In this one, although the 'ghosts' had been soundless, he had heard noises from outside. Danny heard himself asking searching questions about the nature of the changes and was surprised to hear himself speaking in a mature voice. There was no verbal reply, but to Danny's delight he found he had somehow discovered the answer. He *knew* exactly what had been happening – and why. It all seemed so clear and logical.

That was when Nurse Avery woke him up.

Danny instantly forgot everything. He was surprised to find that he was no longer hooked up to the equipment.

'What's wrong?' the nurse asked him.

'The tube and the wires have gone again,' he said, mystified. 'They were back on me in the night.'

Nurse Avery laughed. 'You're a lad with a vivid imagination, that's for sure. You must have dreamed it, Danny! That's what you did, you dreamed it.'

For a while, he believed that it *was* a dream.

This belief lasted for three weeks – until it happened again.

On that occasion Danny was wide awake.

15

It was the third week since he'd woken up in the hospital and a week and three days since they had allowed him to get up. Things seemed to have settled and a kind of routine had been established. Danny was becoming used to his new 'home' and enjoying the attention of his extended family.

Danny's skull and facial wounds were healing well and after so many x-rays that Nurse Avery assured him he'd soon start to glow in the dark (a prospect he'd looked forward to until he realised she was kidding), Mr Amis had announced that the shard of bone in his brain was not moving and would doubtless be okay.

The main problem was that Danny found it difficult to walk. The day they got him to stand on his own two feet, his left leg had let him down and he'd fallen. This wouldn't have been so bad if Mr Amis hadn't brought a number of his colleagues to witness the event.

Danny was told that he would have to learn to use his left arm and leg properly all over again because the bleeding in his brain had affected his control over them. Intensive periods of physiotherapy had been ordered and had commenced the same day. Even now, Danny expected to die from the physical exertion long before he could hop on his left leg or pick up a jam jar from a high shelf with his left hand.

It was after one of these gruelling sessions that he saw ghosts again.

The day after he'd fallen in front of Mr Amis and half the other doctors in the hospital, he had been moved from the intensive care room into a small ward which already had three inmates. There were a pair of twins called James and John who were recovering from limbs broken in a car crash. They were heavily plastered and confined to bed and their mother had brought in a television set for them to watch. When the television wasn't on, James and John cried almost all the time they were awake. Danny discovered that the twins were the same age as him and that they had a father who was away in the army. Their mother came every day and sat between them and wept too.

The other kid was a six-year-old tough-nut called Robin. He'd had surgery on his back and proudly told everyone that the doctors had inserted a two-foot long steel rod in his backbone and when they took it out again they were going to let him keep it as a souvenir. Danny's .22 bullet with the flattened point seemed paltry by comparison, so he never mentioned it.

When Danny returned from his physio, aching and worn out, the others were watching a programme called 'Rag, Tag and Bobtail' on the twins' television.

Danny lay down on his bed and became engrossed in the escapades of the three furry puppets. He was tired, but he was far from sleep.

It happened so quickly that Danny didn't even have time to cry out.

The hospital faded away and vanished, taking all trace of his room-mates with it. Danny watched in awe as everything dissolved. A spinning dizziness struck him and he shut his eyes and reflexively grabbed at the bedclothes for stability.

There were no bed covers and no bed. Danny's hands grasped at emptiness.

There was a moment when nothing seemed to exist at all, then Danny felt damp grass beneath his bare feet. He opened his eyes and the world tore around in front of him, making him stagger. 'Mum!' he yelled and felt the thump of his mother's clenched fists on his breastbone. For a second he thought he was still at home and lying dead on the kitchen floor.

The world steadied and Danny found himself standing next to a hedge in the corner of a field. He recognised the road that passed the perimeter of the field as the road that passed the hospital, but there was no hospital to be seen. It seemed to be early morning and the sun was trying to break out through the haze. A small gnawing sensation filled his stomach as he wondered what had happened. He felt very small and alone. He did not know where he was, how he had come to be here or what he should do next.

While he was still gathering his wits, a man and a woman appeared before him on the grass. He didn't know where they'd come from – one moment they didn't exist and the next they were there. Their colours were faded like an old film and Danny knew that Mr Amis had been wrong about the operation – his mind was up to its old tricks again.

The faded people were half naked. The man was bad. This information arrived forcefully in Danny's consciousness as if it was a lesson someone was trying to make him learn. The bad man was dressed only in a pair of underpants. There was a knife clutched in his right hand and he was trying to cut off the woman's dress with it.

The woman fought furiously to get away, but the man was faster and stronger. They rolled back and forth across the wet grass, mouths working and limbs thrashing. Like they had been before, the images were silent, so Danny had no idea what the couple were saying – or shouting.

The woman tore herself away from the man and got to her knees. The man scrambled toward her and leapt up, hitting her in the face with a clenched fist.

Please don't! Danny silently implored.

The woman fell backwards and the bad man dragged her legs apart and knelt between them, waving the knife in her face.

The woman supported herself on her elbows. Her front teeth were bloody. The look of helpless terror on her face made Danny want to cry. She shook her head violently and spoke quickly, trying to explain something or perhaps trying to calm the man down.

The bad man seemed very angry. His pale blue eyes were watery and bloodshot, and Danny knew he was drunk. Danny didn't know how he knew this, because he had never seen a drunk person before.

He was badly scared. A part of him knew that it was only his mind playing tricks on him, but although the two people were faded, everything else was so real. He could feel the grass under his feet and the damp early morning chill in the air. There was a stream nearby; Danny could *hear* this. The water was splashing and singing as it passed over stones. At the other end of the field, behind the man and woman, a rabbit sat up on its hind legs, peered around then dashed away in long bounds. Danny thought of Rag, Tag and Bobtail and the hospital. That all seemed like a dream now; it no longer existed. This was surely reality.

Danny began to smell blood. It wasn't the trace on the woman's teeth and lips as she pleaded with the man – what he could smell was a *lot* of blood. Distantly, Danny realised he was smelling the scene a few seconds ahead of the action. He could not understand it, but he knew it to be true.

Danny couldn't stand it any more. Screaming soundlessly, he tried to run away.

Something had paralysed him. He was locked in position and his body refused to respond to his demands. He shouted so hard that his throat hurt, but there was no sound.

The bad man used the knife on the woman's tattered dress, splitting the front wide open.

The woman was crying now and dark bruises were beginning to show on her face. Her bottom lip was swollen and cut and a thin trickle of blood ran down to her quivering chin.

Stop it! Danny cried. *Leave her alone!*

The bad man took hold of the woman's pants, pulled them away from her body and sliced through them with the knife.

When the man cut away his own underpants, Danny clamped his eyes shut. He kept them closed for a long time, praying that when he opened them again he would be back on the hospital bed watching the television.

Listening to the nearby stream, Danny counted to one hundred. When he realised he could still hear the stream he counted again. And again.

Finally, his eyes popped open of their own accord.

As if depending on his visual presence for its completion, the scene had waited for him. Now it continued.

Danny's mind reeled as he watched the brutal rape, but he was also aware that there was worse to come. Much worse.

As the man pounded himself into the woman's body, Danny's head began to hurt and a sharp pain grew behind his eyes. He gasped for breath, now unable to hear or feel himself breathing. His whole body was silently screaming to be let alone. Danny forced his head to turn away, but it was as if the whole field had spun around with him; the naked man and woman were still in front of him wherever he looked.

Danny knew that the man was eventually going to kill the woman. This much was certain. And he knew that he was going to have to watch. He wished he was dead.

The bad man rolled off the woman, got up, grabbed her hair and yanked her up to her knees. The woman began to scream, but Danny could tell from her eyes that she knew there was nothing to be done. She knew the man was going to kill her now.

The man grimaced and held the knife out a foot in front of the woman's throat.

Stop it! Danny commanded, but the Just God he'd learned about in Sunday School wasn't listening today.

Please! Danny implored.

The bad man tilted the woman back by her hair, then pulled her forward on to the knife. The blade went into her throat as if it was butter. He pulled her off it and blood sprayed from the wound in a long pulse. He tilted her forward and again the knife entered her. Blood spewed from her mouth.

The bad man withdrew the knife but the woman was not dead yet. She raised her hands and tried to disengage the man's fingers from her hair.

And Danny's hearing began to turn itself on. The woman was not only still alive, she was trying to talk her assailant out of killing her. Danny's ears were filled with a rush of what sounded like radio static, but he could hear snippets of their conversation, although they were distorted.

'Please . . . Lenny, don't!' the woman choked through her own blood.

'Slut!' the man screamed, dragging her hair upwards.

'You're hurting . . . me!'

The bad man punched the knife into the woman's mouth.

The woman spat teeth. 'Uhh! No mowhhre. Don't hurrr me achhgain!' she moaned.

The knife was red and dripping.

'Lhuhnee! I lhuuv yhou!'

The knife flashed and plunged through her cheek. The woman let go of her hair and took hold of the bad man's wrist, but she couldn't force it away from her. Bubbles of blood formed around her nostrils. 'Lhuvv you!' she gasped.

She didn't die for a long time.

Danny was forced to watch as her eyes glazed over and her body loosened and finally went limp.

But it wasn't over yet.

The bad man had reached a frenzied peak; drenched with her blood he leapt upon her lifeless body and tried to hack her head from her neck.

Danny's mind reeled.

And the scene began to fade.

16

When Danny opened his eyes, he was back in the hospital, lying on the bed. His heart was hammering so hard he thought it would kill him and his breath was coming in great shuddering gasps. His head was ringing with the woman's pleading words, his mind hurt from watching her dreadful death and tears were running freely from his eyes.

In that moment Danny knew he was different from everyone else. The bullet and the brain operation had changed him – permanently. There was no way he could change things back to how they were before. He was unlike other people because he had died, and having done so had become able to see ghosts. They could operate on him as much as they liked, but they couldn't alter the past so that he hadn't died.

That little bullet that lay in the drawer in his bedside table had blighted his life.

Danny knew he wouldn't ever be able to tell the things he'd seen and this knowledge made him feel terribly lonely and burdened.

Everything was strange to him now. The solid and bright world he'd inhabited for five years wasn't as it appeared. It was insubstantial and could all be flushed away in a mere moment. Nothing seemed to be properly real any more.

Danny smelt the faint odour of disinfectant that pervaded the air and knew that it might just as well not exist. There was nothing to hold on to. No safety.

He sobbed and wiped his eyes then looked around the hospital ward.

'Rag, Tag and Bobtail' had ended and James and John's weepy mum had arrived and was fussing over their plaster-casted bodies. Robin was on his bed reading *Just William*.

No one seemed to have noticed that anything had happened to Danny and he realised that his body must have remained in place. It was his mind or his immortal soul that had been swept away. He knew now that he was no longer firmly attached to his body and this made him feel worse.

James and John started to cry softly and after a few moments their mother joined in with them.

Danny cried a little bit too and then went to sleep.

17

During the remainder of his stay in hospital Danny had several more visions but none were of the intensity of those he'd already had.

For a few days after seeing the rape and murder, he toyed with the idea that he'd gone mad and this strengthened his resolve not to tell anyone about the ghosts. After a week or so with no strange occurrences, Danny began to think that it really had been his brain playing tricks on him and that things were going to turn out okay after all. He began to trust Mr Amis and the doctors again and to prove it he worked hard at his physiotherapy.

The other visions he had were few and far between and Danny classed them as nightmares – or wakemares. He taught himself to ignore them and not to think about them afterwards. This was not difficult; there were not that many of them and they were not vivid. Mostly, the things he saw were people dying in this hospital and with the exception of one cardiac arrest (he asked Nurse Avery for a definition of these words and had to nag her until she finally told him), they all died peacefully.

And, as if to confirm his latest – and Mr Amis's only – theory, each episode was weaker than the previous one, until finally the people that inhabited these nightmares were just indistinguishable grey spectres.

Danny never had nightmares about his mother or father again, nor anyone he knew.

By the time he left hospital he had forgotten the term *wakemares* and the very occasional nightmares he had only happened when he was truly asleep.

Chapter Two
Cards of Fate

1

Much later in his life, Danny Stafford would enter a six-month-long dark period during which he would lose everything he loved. Things would fall apart so badly for him that autumn that he would not expect to survive. Danny would mentally christen this period The Tunnel although in its bleakest moments it would seem more like a sewer. During quiet periods inside the tunnel of those tortured months, Danny thought a great deal about the hand of fate and the bad cards its fickle fingers had dealt him. All in all, it came to a hand so shitty that any self-respecting player would have long since folded.

Danny would become obsessed with reviewing his life and charting lines between the 2nd of August 1958 when his big brother shot him and the point he was at on any particular day. There was a twin purpose for this: like a man losing badly in a game of chance, Danny felt that underneath all the randomness, there was logic of some description; he was unable to believe that so many bad things could *just happen* coincidentally – and if he could crack the code, he might be able to alter things, even at this late stage. The second – equally important – purpose was that by plotting the course of his life on a graph and noting down where the cards had been handed to him like Blind Pew's Black Spots, was the only way he might have been able to predict where the end of The Tunnel lay. Or whether there was an end at all.

And like a bad loser in a gaming house, each day Danny would write himself *just one more* marker before he finally quit.

Between the first ace of spades that Lady Luck slipped into his pocket before Brian shot him and the electric shock which gave him a blackout, there would be smaller bad cards for Danny to chart.

2

In the twelve-month period when Danny was recovering, the school he should have been attending sent work home for him to do and charged his mother with force feeding it to him. Marjorie Stafford warmed to the job and did it so relentlessly that by the time Danny finally did walk through the gates, he already had the reading ability of a ten year old.

When he wasn't participating in his mother's crash course in the three Rs, Danny was subjected to intense scrutiny – not only by the medical profession but by a team of jolly psychologists and Mr Reed who, after a lengthy and ominous build-up which scared Danny half to death, turned out to be worse than anticipated.

Mr Reed was a creepy psychiatrist with white hair, a red thread-veined nose and an overbearing military manner. With a five year old's ability for instantaneous character analysis, Danny identified Mr Reed as being much more than scary: he was a *Bad Man* who had taken a job in which his nastiness could be given free rein. Mr Reed wanted to find the bad in Danny too. He made Danny answer some probing questions about the visions of his parents, but there was worse too.

Somehow Mr Reed could tell that Danny was keeping a secret and he badly wanted Danny to say what it was. Mr Reed asked some disturbing and frighteningly accurate questions about the nature of the secret. Over a three-month period Danny spent an hour twice a week in defence of the secret and of what little innocence he had left. He felt guilty about retaining the scenes of sadistic death he'd witnessed – but knew instinctively that it was the right thing to do.

When Mr Reed stopped making him dwell upon death, sex and being shot, Danny's mind dug a deep pit for the memories of the bloody rape and murder, pushed them in and buried them.

Finally it was grandly announced that 'Danny had been found not to be disturbed by his accident'. Shortly afterwards Mr Amis assured his parents that in spite of some minor and insignificant residual brain damage, the shard of bone in his pineal gland was stable and that the bruised (this was the word he chose rather than *dead* which was actually the case, as Danny later discovered) motor centre of Danny's brain was successfully re-orientating itself.

The 're-orientation' was accomplished painfully and slowly through physiotherapy. Danny was told that his brain had to learn how to control his left side all over again and that it could only learn by registering the movement of his limbs. It was hard and tiring and when Danny finally started school he was still limping slightly. The left side of his body would remain slightly weaker than his right for the rest of his life. The doctors did not tell him this. Neither did they see fit to mention that in damp weather the healed-over bullet wound would hurt.

But in some ways, being shot in the head turned out to be useful. Danny was a hero at school before he even started attending. Brian had redeemed himself in Danny's eyes by paving the way for him there. A kind of mystique was attached to him; he was The Boy Who

Had Cheated Death and this not only qualified him as completely socially acceptable amongst his peers, it made him sought after.

3

One playtime a couple of years later, Danny worked up enough courage to ask Brian something that had been bothering him for a long time: what had happened to the rifle?

By the time Danny had got home from hospital the .22 had gone. For a long time he was too frightened to ask and neither Brian nor his parents ever mentioned it again.

'Dad went to pieces when he got back from the hospital that day,' Brian said. 'He was on his own because Mum stayed in hospital. She was so upset she had to be sedated. Florence Vaughan's mum was looking after me and I was so scared about what would happen to me I was sick all afternoon. I thought you were dead and that I'd be hung or something.' Brian's eyes misted over.

'What then?' Danny asked. There seemed to be a huge distance between him and Brian. *Africa's a long way, Joey!* Danny found himself thinking.

'Dad came round Florence's house. He was white and shaky and mad. He grabbed my hand and dragged me all the way home. He kept on saying, "I ought to shoot *you!*" over and over again and I thought he was going to. He dragged me into the kitchen. There was still blood everywhere. He looked at it and moaned like a hurt dog. He cried, Dan. He got down on his knees and mopped all the blood up, crying like a little kid. "Your brother might die because of what you did!" he kept saying.' Brian began to cry too.

Danny felt dizzy. Something was coming and it was going to rank in order of magnitude with the loss of Joey or even that of his own life. Danny *knew* it. 'It doesn't matter,' he heard himself whisper. 'You don't have to say.'

'He got the rifle and made me go outside with him. I thought he was going to kill me. He went to the shed and got a club hammer and made me watch until he'd hammered the barrel flat and the stock and trigger had fallen to pieces. Then he forbade me ever to touch a gun again and then put me across his knee and tanned my backside until I was sick again. Then he sent me to bed. He didn't speak to me afterwards for two weeks. I'm sorry, Danny, I really truly am!' Brian sobbed.

There was more. Danny didn't want to know now. 'It doesn't matter,' he said, wishing he'd never asked, 'I'm all right now.'

Brian shook his head.

Danny shook his head too, meaning, *Okay, that's enough, I quit and I don't want to know any more*, but – maybe because of the brain damage – his tongue ran away with him again. 'What do you mean?' he heard himself ask.

'You were dead too long!' Brian blurted. 'They said your brain is damaged and you're so delicate you'll probably die before you grow up. Oh, Danny, I'm *so sorry!*'

4

Danny never found out where Brian had come by this nugget of information and it wasn't until much later that he was able to understand that the confession had come about because of his brother's unbearable burden of guilt. By that time it didn't matter one way or the other because Brian had been wrong, apparently, and Danny had stopped waiting to die.

5

During the days of The Tunnel Danny would reinterpret this moment in order to fit his scheme of things. He would conjecture that Brian had been almost, but not quite, right. While he was eavesdropping, Brian had misheard: someone had said that Danny was delicate and that his brain would never recover completely and Brian had taken it to mean that death was gleefully rubbing its horny hands and waiting. Whatever had happened, Danny would think that the moment in the playground had somehow sealed his fate because that was when he truly began to believe what he'd fleetingly thought in the hospital: that he was *different* from other people. The information hadn't been held in his mind for long, but had buried itself in his subconscious like a time bomb.

6

Danny waited to die for a time, then forgot about the matter. Birthdays and Christmases came and went and he grew bigger and fitter. Along the way, he learned to ride a bike, got into trouble for playing hooky from school and going fishing instead, played marbles and football, learned to swim at the seaside and once came third in a fifty yard dash on sports day while his mum and dad cheered from the sidelines. Against his wishes he learned things too.

Danny seldom thought about guns, ghosts or death and came to view violence with the same enthusiasm as all schoolboys. By the time he was nine he had learned to use his fists.

Fate didn't deal the next bad card until the school holidays of Danny's twelfth year.

That was when his father came home with what he called 'Big News'.

7

The Big News was not entirely Good News as far as Danny and his brother were concerned. Their father beamed that he had been made sales director of the insurance company he worked for and then instantly defused the good atmosphere by saying that *those who knew best* had decided it would be a good thing to re-locate the company from a dying high-rent area of London to a rapidly expanding 'New Town' called Basingstoke.

Neither Danny nor Brian wanted to go. Danny was developing a secret crush on Florence Vaughan and Brian simply liked where he lived now and had no reason to believe that anywhere else would be better. They argued – somewhat pointlessly since George Stafford's mind was already made up – that Basingstoke was nearer home than London and as their father had always found it easy to commute from Windlesham to London, why couldn't he just get on a train going the other way?

Their father explained that his new position demanded that he live closer to the shop and that his position was not negotiable.

The wheels rolled on and the Staffords moved house between Danny's passing the eleven plus and starting at Grammar School. The big house that George purchased lay a couple of miles outside Basingstoke in the village of Old Basing. It was very similar to the old house, except that the one in Windlesham was smaller and prettier and didn't have a huge city lurking on the horizon.

Both Brian and Danny later found that for all the drawbacks of living somewhere built up, Basingstoke did have something that Windlesham didn't.

Thirwall & Allen, and girls.

8

Brian started raving about the girls after his first visit to Basingstoke's town centre.

'There's *hundreds* of them, Danny!' he said enthusiastically. 'God, you've just *got* to go into town and *see* them!'

Danny wasn't particularly impressed. He only had eyes for Florence Vaughan and just like the old adage, her absence really was making his heart grow fonder. Danny didn't think he could so much as look at another girl, let alone follow them home as his brother seemed intent on doing.

It wasn't until three lonesome months later when he got what his brother charmingly called 'a fuck off letter' from Florence (who had a lot of studying to do, she said, and the distance between them made things *so* difficult) that Danny finally ventured into the town centre on a Saturday.

Just as Brian had said, there *were* girls by the dozen, but Danny had been Spurned & Burned and was unmoved.

He did fall in love though.

With a glass-fronted shop in Winchester Street called Thirwall & Allen.

Propelled purely by Brian's lust for a blonde teenager he had spotted coming out of Greig's Pie Shop, Danny and Brian entered the electrical shop hot on the girl's heels. The girl had noticed she was being tailed some time ago and had turned twice and smiled. According to Brian 'the lights were amber' which meant that picking up the girl was not a surefire thing, but it looked very promising indeed.

Once inside the shop, Danny became mesmerised. It was like Aladdin's cave. Or heaven itself. He was suddenly surrounded by shelves of colour televisions showing football matches; more shelves sporting the latest state of the art radios, hi-fi record players and tape recorders. There were electronic security devices; spying surveillance cameras; burglar alarms; infra red detectors; and a counter selling transistors, diodes, transformers, printed circuit boards. Danny lost sight of Brian and the blonde and staggered to the counter where someone was buying half a dozen rotary potentiometers. He didn't even know what a rotary potentiometer *was*.

I could make things to spy on people! Danny thought.

And fate slapped another bad card on to his green baize table.

9

A year passed during which Danny only had eyes for the mysterious world of electricity. He commandeered the house's spare bedroom and gradually turned it into a laboratory where – courtesy of Thirwall & Allen and all his pocket money (and later his paper-round money too) – he introduced himself to the world of electronics and conducted experiments. He built radios and electric eye burglar alarms which could be relied upon to report 'intruders' when there were none and refuse to acknowledge them when they purposely broke the beam.

10

The year not only broke Danny financially, it broke his voice too. And there were other things that changed – none of them satisfactorily. Danny began to think a lot about girls. He had always privately been proud of what he thought of as his mental superiority over his brother; now he began to realise that intelligence wasn't all there was to life.

Brian reminded him of this every day. Brian was still physically much bigger than Danny and was an early developer. He shaved regularly already. He was even featured and built like an athlete. Brian had an easy, confident manner, and a faultless complexion. Brian naturally found many girls who were eager to hang on his every word.

As far as girls were concerned, how clever you were didn't seem to enter the equation whatsoever. How you looked was *everything*, and Danny didn't fill out like Brian. His body betrayed him and against his wishes grew tall, spindly and gawky. His features – the single aspect of him comparable with Brian – developed a death wish. Spots began to appear on his face in such profusion that even his friends began to refer to him as King Zit. His mouth's ability to say things unprepared vanished and in the presence of girls, Danny became tongue tied and embarrassed, when he needed to be witty and urbane. His brother's girlfriends treated him with disdain and sometimes contempt.

And to add insult to injury, Brian ceased to be his protector and became his chief tormentor.

Danny began to plot his revenge.

11

Danny was not alone in his physical misery; his puberty – and his fascination with electronics – had brought with it a small, but ready-made, circle of kindred spirits, all up and coming outcasts from handsome society. Danny and his three friends christened themselves The Loopies. Fat, thin, tall and almost dwarfed, but full of vitality and crazy schemes, they attempted to give off an aura of intellectualism while remaining aloof from the activities of Brian and his buddies who baited them relentlessly. The Loopies watched their childish antics from a distance and feigned indifference while secretly lusting after their girls.

The other Loopies were only too pleased to join in Danny's plot against his brother.

The Plan of Attack was Kevin Long's suggestion. Kevin was short, fat, bespectacled and horrendously bullied by most of his classmates. In two years of Grammar School Kevin had come to expect to be the subject of his peer group's ill feeling. After all, he was twelve and half years old and still awaiting delivery of his very first pair of long trousers. Kevin said his mother was a harridan who refused to accept that her son was growing up 'after all she'd done for him', and treated his increasing size as a personal insult to her. Kevin was not only long trouserless, but he owned no underpants – a fact which had first been revealed early on in his secondary education when on his very first period of Physical Education he had forgotten his gym kit. The sadistic P.E. master, Mr Smithers, had entered into the annals of The (then seminal) Loopies' 'Ten Most Hated' by forcing Kevin to prance around the gymnasium – for a double period and in front of everyone – stark naked. On the surface, none of this seemed to have affected Kevin who mostly remained cheerful if a little world weary. It wasn't until you got to know about the exquisite tortures he had invented for his tormenters and saw the way his grin turned cruel when he fantasised about putting them into practice that you understood just how badly everything hurt him.

Since Kevin's induction into The Loopies, he had developed plenty of ideas for the use of electrical torture – mainly involving the appliance of live wires to genitalia – and he forwarded a Plan of Attack which would surely have electrocuted Danny's big brother. No one could see a way of making the Plan safe enough to use, so it was shelved until a better suggestion was thought up.

Upon learning that Danny's parents were going away for the weekend and leaving him and Brian alone in the house, Kevin revised his Plan and lobbied the other members of The Loopies to vote in favour of it. The reworked Plan of Attack involved coating two small rubber electrode pads with an electrolyte gel and placing them beneath the bottom sheet of Brian's bed. Concealed wires would be run from his room to Danny's spare room laboratory where, at the critical moment, they would be fed with a high voltage current at an extremely low amperage, thus enabling them to give Brian a hefty zap up the ass without doing him any serious damage.

Lippy Helstead was the tiniest Loopie. He had been christened Humphrey – a name he hated – and dubbed Lippy because of his predilection for making acid-tongued comments to aggressors much larger than himself – which meant almost all of them. He was forgiven this because of his accompanying ability to fight like a maddened terrier. Not only was he The Loopies' martial arts adviser (constantly reiterating the well-known fact that a male human being's weakest points were bollocks, eyes, and throat – in that order), but also their hi-fi specialist and rock music buff. His contribution to the Plan of Attack was to suggest he brought round his four-track Teac tape machine and record Brian's screams as he leapt from his electrical bed.

There were enough drawbacks to this Plan to discourage the most inventive MI5 agent, but The Loopies admitted none of them. No one knew whether or not Brian would find the two damp patches in his bed or if the pads would work through the sheet, and no one cared. It was a Plan of Attack and was therefore viable.

Mil Martin – The Loopies' true electronic genius – set to work on the design of the electronics and by the time the parents Stafford set off on their weekend away, he and Danny had put together a mains-operated pulsing device which actually worked. They had tested it on Lippy Helstead first, using the minimum current, and when Lippy seemed to have survived intact they tested it on themselves. When the electrode pads were held in each hand, the device shot bolts of electricity through you at a rate of four pulses a second. Each Loopie took a turn at the device and all were amazed at how easy it was to make your muscles work independently of your wishes. On its minimum setting, the Pulser simply made your fingernails dig into the palms of your hands with each pulse. As the power level was raised your forearms started to become affected too and your clenched fists would be drawn up towards your inner elbow. After that your shoulders started to twitch too and it became painful.

The Loopies rigged Brian's bedroom the following afternoon and that evening they hid in the laboratory with a flagon of cider and waited for Brian to come home.

At midnight the front door opened. The tense and silent Loopies listened.

Brian muttered something and a girlish giggle echoed up the stairs.

'He's got Sally with him,' Kevin hissed.

Sally was Brian's latest conquest. She was a tall and gorgeous brunette. Every single Loopie was terribly sexually attracted to her and none of them had admitted it to the others.

'He's not going to. . .?' Mil asked.

'I think he is,' Danny replied, giggling nervously.

'Oh, shit,' Lippy groaned. 'We'll have to call it off.'

Danny considered this while the other Loopies grew doubtful about the wisdom of carrying on. With the exception of Kevin, none of them wanted to harm Sally in any way.

'Why not?' Kevin asked.

'She's a girl!' Mil protested.

'And we've got nothing against her anyway,' Lippy added.

'Stuff it, let's do both of them,' Kevin said, totally disregarding the gravity of the situation.

'We *can't*,' Mil said.

'Yes, we can,' Danny replied. Brian had told him some of the remarks Sally had made about him. They were not complimentary. Whether they were actually true was something that didn't enter his head at that moment. He became heartless. 'I just throw this switch and wait to see what happens,' he said.

And pulled a bad ace from the pack.

Brian's bedroom was live. The sounds of him and Sally kissing and whispering to one another were picked up by hidden microphones, relayed to Lippy's speakers and softly broadcast in the lab while they recorded on the Teac. Bedsprings muttered as they laid down. There were giggles and rustling noises as they undressed – or undressed each other – then more bed noises as they got in.

The scar on Danny's cheekbone throbbed once. He pictured himself standing in Thirwall & Allen for the very first time, surrounded by flickering television pictures and thinking: *I could make things to spy on people!* Suddenly Danny didn't want to give his brother an electric shock at all. Worse still, he no longer wanted to have to listen to Brian making it with Sally. The thought sickened him. It was wrong and it was bad. *Just make it stop!* he thought. *Just make it stop and don't ever make me have to spy on people again!*

Danny's heart filled his throat and his ears rang. He felt an urgent need to get up and turn off the tape recorder – rip the wires out if necessary – but he couldn't move.

'Oh, *Briaaan!*' Sally breathed.

I don't want to be like this! Danny thought, and wasn't totally sure of what he meant.

In the next room the bedsprings started to squeak rhythmically. Sally groaned.

'Fuck!' Mil whispered.

'You're right!' Lippy tittered.

Make it stop! Danny thought, and a picture of Joey making a bid for freedom filled his mind.

'Zap 'em!' Kevin said.

Danny shook his head.

'Go on, Dan! Let 'em have it!' Kevin insisted.

There was air out there somewhere. Danny couldn't find it.

'Do it, someone!' Kevin pleaded.

'Yesss, Brian! Ah . . . ah . . . ah . . . yessss!'

'I'll do it,' Mil said. There was a tremor in his voice. He took the Pulser from Danny's clammy hands and threw the switch.

'S-S-Sal!' Brian's tinny voice said from the speakers.

'It ain't working,' Kevin said. 'Turn it up!'

Danny watched as Mil took the control and wound it all the way up to maximum. There was no response from the lovers.

'Bollocks!' Lippy said.

'Wire's off the back,' Danny heard himself say. *Make it stop!*

His hands looked like someone else's as they reached out for the loose wire. He didn't want them to do this, but they intended to do it anyway. In spite of his overriding desire to make things stop, his hands were following through.

I don't want to be a spy! he thought and grasped the wire.

Kevin saw what he thought was the end of their plans and panicked. 'Look out!' he called. 'he's trying to bust it!'

Mil swung around and the fingers of Danny's hand touched the other terminal, received a jolt of full-blast electricity and clamped themselves on tight. In the following second, four high voltage shocks cruised up his arm like a deathly vibration from another dimension, crossed his chest and found an earth through his other arm. Danny's body convulsed with each blast.

Hickory Dickorydickorydickorydickory! Joey sang in his ears.

Then there was lots of screaming and shouting and it sounded and felt as though he were being pounded through the floor.

12

Danny woke up at four-thirty the following afternoon. He was shocked to find himself sitting in the centre of Basing Common with the other Loopies. The sun was shining and he was sweating. There was a half-smoked Players No 6 in his right hand.

'What happened?' he asked, aware that he had not simply woken up. There was more to it than this. He seemed to have suddenly started to exist – as if he had previously been dead. It was as though he had just been switched on. He could not remember where he had been before, but it certainly wasn't here.

'When?' Mil asked.

Danny was confused. 'Now,' he said.

'Nothing,' Kevin assured him. 'Some birds flew by a few minutes ago.'

'And there was that rabbit, over there,' Lippy said, pointing.

A cold dread filled Danny. 'No! *Now!*' he said. 'What happened to me?'

The Loopies looked at him as if he had been struck mad. 'You just started to smoke a cigarette,' Mil said.

'And before that you told that joke about the dead babies,' Kevin reminded him.

None of this recent history existed for Danny. 'I don't remember,' he said, on the edge of panic. He shook his head.

Lippy leaned forward and peered into his eyes. 'It's the electric shock,' he said. 'I told you it'd make you go mad.'

'When?' Danny said.

'Last night,' Lippy told him.

Danny did not recall this either. 'What shock?'

Lippy grinned at him. Danny grabbed his wrist and squeezed it. Hard. 'Tell me!' he insisted.

'There's nothing to tell,' Lippy said, wrestling his wrist away.

'*I don't remember getting a shock!*' Danny shouted.

The Loopies exchanged glances.

'Bullshit,' Mil opined.

'Honestly,' Danny said.

'Okay,' Mil said. 'What *do* you remember?'

'Sitting in the lab waiting to give Brian a jolt. Then being here when I started talking.'

'Nothing in between?' Mil asked.

Danny shook his head. He felt as if someone had winked him out of existence last night and had just winked him back in again.

'You *must!*' Lippy said. 'For Christ's sake, you've been as happy as a pig in shit all day.'

'Yeah, you have,' Mil agreed.

'*But I can't remember! Tell me what happened!*' Danny said.

'I couldn't get you off the Pulser,' Mil said. 'We had to turn it off at the mains. You didn't go unconscious or anything but you got a terrible nosebleed. There was blood everywhere. Still is, in fact. Look.' He showed Danny the sleeve of his shirt. The cuff was brown with dried blood. The rest of the shirt was lightly spattered with tiny brown specks. Mil seemed pleased to have Danny's blood on his shirt – he viewed it as a kind of memento of a battle which hadn't taken place.

Nosebleed, Danny thought. He sniffed and although the airway in his right nostril had been slightly constricted since his brother shot him, he could feel no evidence of the nosebleed. He gently inserted his little finger into his right nostril, but there didn't seem to be any dried-on blood caking it.

'If you can't remember,' Kevin said, 'how do you know that it was only your right nostril that bled?'

Danny didn't know. He had only had one nosebleed since his accident and that had been precipitated by a rash comment to a large skinhead called Paul Homes. Homes had smiled broadly then knocked him to the ground and kicked him in the face. That day both nostrils had bled.

'It stopped just after I turned off the Pulser,' Mil said. 'Afterwards you said it didn't hurt much and you were okay. There were burns on both your hands though. Look.'

Danny looked. The shape of the Pulser's knurled terminal was singed into the finger and thumb of his right hand and there was a hardened yellowish line across the palm of his left hand. Now he'd seen these marks they started to throb.

This happened to someone else, Danny thought.

'You called it all off after you got that shock,' Kevin said sourly. 'You said we weren't to do it.'

'When Brian took Sally home we went into his room and took all our stuff away,' Lippy said. 'We wiped the tape too. Then we went home. Dunno what you did after that. Went to bed, I s'pose. It was gone two.'

'Oh,' Danny said.

'You don't remember trying to pick up those girls then?' Mil asked. 'The ones who giggled at you and told you to piss off?'

This was news to Danny. Bad News. 'When?'

'Just before we came into the common. You scared them, I think.'

'What did I say?'

'Leave it out, Dan. You told them you were going to break their arms. I think they believed you.'

The other Loopies all cackled at the good joke.

13

During the following two days, Danny fastidiously filled in the gaping hole in his reality with second hand details. As far as he could find out, he did nothing unusual – other than (jokingly, he hoped) threatening the girls – which wasn't so terrible for someone with a sixteen and a half hour mental blank. He told no one other than The Loopies about his disrupted continuity and within a couple of months the second hand details slotted in comfortably with his proper memories.

Three years later when fate handed him his next big card – a good one this time – Danny had totally forgotten about his blackout.

14

In an idle moment during the summer holidays of his fifteenth year Danny wandered into the library in Basingstoke. At the time, he thought it was a chance decision, a pure whim, but later he would wonder if the idea had somehow purposely been planted in his mind. He had ridden his bike into Basingstoke with the intention of going to Thirwall & Allen – although he would have admitted that it wasn't an idea that filled him with enthusiasm. His obsession with electricity and spying had waned dramatically since the abortive attack on his brother and if he had been truthful, his visits to the shop were now only made to justify to himself (and his parents) the continuing existence of all the junk that still lived in the spare room. These days Danny spent less time wondering about the mysteries of: *Microprocessors – The Technology of the Future* (as his *Practical Electronics* would have it) and more time wondering about those two much more important (and infinitely more mysterious) subjects: *Girls and Sex*. The inner workings of the new Zilog Z80 chip had become far less interesting than those of the half of the population who didn't stand up to pee.

Danny's new obsession had been brought about not only by his itchy male hormones, but by his big brother's hazy descriptions of what he did with Linda, his latest conquest. None of these things sounded as if they had anything to do with the cold and clinical functions of sperm and ova that had been briefly mapped out in Danny's biology classes and although each Loopie had his own ideas about sex and girls, none of them had any practical experience.

The other Loopies were away on family holidays, Brian was staying in Dorset with Linda (he'd told Danny's parents that he was going with the family, but Danny happened to overhear that Linda's mum and dad had gone to Spain) and Danny was stuck for something to do. So he decided to go to Thirwall & Allen.

Whether it had been mapped out for him or whether it was just his hormones doing the talking was of no consequence at that moment. Halfway to Basingstoke Danny stopped pedalling and thought: *I know, I'll go to the library instead and see if they've got any obscene books.*

This seemed a much better idea and Danny smiled.

Like any spontaneously conceived plan, this had certain drawbacks. Once inside the library, Danny realised he didn't know the names of any authors who wrote filth and was uncertain if libraries stocked this kind of book anyway. He knew they kept literary filth like Joyce and Lawrence, but Danny had already read all the dirty passages they had written and had been unimpressed. Danny wanted straight pornography. He considered asking the assistant if they had any dirty books, felt his face flush at the very thought and ditched the idea. He spent half an hour browsing in the hope of finding something suitable and was disappointed. If there *was* pornography, it was kept extremely well hidden. There wasn't even a *Playboy* or a *Health & Efficiency* on the rack which kept the periodicals. Danny spent a few minutes browsing through *Aeromodeller* and wondering if building a balsa wood plane was an idea worth pursuing, and then he remembered his pineal gland.

He closed the *Aeromodeller* and placed it back on the rack, searching his mind for references to the gland in his biology lessons. He could think of only one reason why this part of one's anatomy was so rarely discussed or alluded to: it must have a sexual function. Questions flooded through his mind and made all sorts of cockeyed connections which may or may not have made sense with regard to his luck with girls.

Danny hurried to the section which dealt with biological and medical books, worried that the pineal gland might have, not only a sexual function, but a *vital* sexual function that no one had bothered to inform him about. He had to know what it did and how impaired a pineal gland pierced by a piece of bone might have become.

Something very close to dread had filled him by the time he pulled the first medical dictionary from the shelf. He hurried over to an empty reading table and sat down.

The dictionary was as vague as everyone else he'd asked had been.

'Pineal gland: Pineal body or gland, a conical gland of unknown function, situated in the brain.'

This may not have been very informative but Danny was relieved to find there was no sexual connection. He wasn't stunted after all. 'Unknown function' may have been vague but it was a whole lot better than: 'Hormone releasing gland controlling development of male sexual organs and drives' – which was what he had half expected. Danny could expect an unrestricted sex life – if he ever got one.

He replaced the dictionary and took down another. He learned from this one that the pineal gland was small, red and oval, situated at the base of the brain and that the author thought it was probably 'a vestigial endocrine gland and despite various theories, e.g. that it is associated with sexual development, it has no proven existing function'.

Danny grew slightly concerned. What the dictionary seemed to be saying was that *some people* thought it *did* have a sexual connection.

The third dictionary said that it lay in the upper part of the mid brain (wherever *that* was) and added mysteriously: 'Thought to be the site of the third eye in certain lizards'.

Danny frowned. *The third eye in lizards?*

Was it a well-known fact that lizards had a third eye? And what did it do? What use was a third eye when it was buried deep in the brain? He wondered if he should do research into the biological makeup of reptiles.

He put the book back on the shelf and stepped back, his eyes scanning back and forth across the rows of books, looking for something that might be entitled: *The Pineal Gland in Humans and its Uses*. Or even something which told you about the brain in detail; they would be bound to mention it in something like that.

Squinting at the titles on the top shelf, Danny walked backwards into a girl.

These things didn't happen outside of romantic forties films. Danny knew the scenario off by heart: you turned suddenly and collided with girl who was carrying a pile of books. The girl would fall and her books would scatter. While helping her to her feet you would apologise profusely and ask her if she was all right. She would be a little shaken but otherwise undamaged. You would glance at her, registering peripherally that she was pretty, then set about collecting her strewn books. The final one would be at her feet. You would retrieve it and while passing it up to her, your eyes would lock with hers.

This did not happen.

The girl *was* carrying a stack of books and he *did* knock them from her arms as he backed into her. That was where the similarities ended.

Danny lost his balance. As both his hands grasped at the empty air, he leaned – much too far – to his left, turning his worst foot. The other one appeared in the air before him.

All this happened in the moment the books left the girl's arms. They seemed suspended in the air around him, open pages rippling like the wing feathers of gliding birds.

Danny went down hard, surrounded by falling books and realising that Newton was way off the mark when he said all objects fell at the same rate. He landed on top of a large format book on Goya and hit the floor ahead of the largest volume, the title of which was: *The Expressionists*. Danny would remember this book for the rest of his life. It was a maroon jacket-less hardcover and its title was gold-blocked down the spine. The author was called A. Hardy. All this information impressed itself on his mind as he watched the volume hammering down toward his face like a meteor.

Danny's eyes were closed when *The Expressionists* hit him. His head was two inches from the floor. This fact probably saved his nose from being broken. *The Expressionists* hit Danny and his head struck the wood block floor with a sound like a cricket ball being swiped for a six. His nose felt as if it had exploded. When he opened his eyes, his vision was blurred and blood was running from his nostrils and pouring into his mouth.

'Oh God, what have I done?' the girl said. 'I'm *so* sorry! I really am!'

She bent down and sat him up. 'Forgive me, please!' she said.

Danny tried to tell her that it was okay. 'S-og,' he said. Her blurred face swam in front of his streaming eyes. He couldn't only *not* tell if she was pretty, he could barely tell if she was even human. At that moment he wouldn't have cared if she'd been an invader from the system X15.

'Here,' she said producing a wad of Kleenex from somewhere outside his restricted field of vision. 'Let me clean you up.'

Cool, soft female hands held the back of his neck and dabbed his eyes and nose. She was very gentle. Danny fell in love before he even knew what she looked like.

She eased him to his feet, led him to a chair and sat him down. 'You'll live, I think,' she said. She handed him a bunch of tissues and told him to hold them to his nose while she went and explained what had happened.

Seconds later three middle-aged female librarians were fussing over him with hot water, towels and more tissues. The smallest woman set about mopping up his flowing blood while the largest pressed an ice cube to the back of his neck. Danny didn't know where she'd got it from. The third woman hovered in the background offering advice to the others and cups of tea and lifts home to Danny. While he thanked them and nasally assured them he'd be able to get home alone, his vision cleared and he peered between their stout bodies, trying to catch a glimpse of his assailant. For a couple of minutes Danny was sure she'd fled.

His nosebleed stopped suddenly as if someone had clamped a patch

over the leaky vessel. It didn't gradually subside, it turned itself off.
'That's it!' the larger librarian said. 'Ice on the back of the neck always works!'
The smaller one gave Danny's nose one last dab and the charge-hand asked him if he would be all right. When he had thanked them, they left him.
'You bleed like a stuck pig,' the girl said. Danny looked around. She had been waiting behind him. She drew up a chair and sat next to him looking concerned.
Danny got his first clear look at her. She literally took his breath away. The girl was tall and slim with wide shoulders which emphasised her tiny waist and made her look like a champion swimmer. Long curly black hair framed her porcelain white face. Her eyes were widely spaced and dark blue. Her lips were of the variety his mother called 'bee sting'. She was wearing a white cheescloth dress beneath which she didn't appear to be wearing a bra.
The girl was a prize.
'It's the right side that bleeds,' Danny heard himself say. 'Something to do with the old war wound and the adjacent blood vessels, I should think.' That was all he could manage. His words dried up again and he simply stared.
'Are you sure you're okay now?' the girl asked, worriedly.
She was gazing at him with an expression he didn't recognise. He saw curiosity which wasn't unusual and that rarer thing – for girls looking at him, anyway – *interest*, but there was something else in her face which was almost, but not quite, shining through. There was some inner turmoil taking place as if a part of her mind was rolling something heavy up a steep hill.
'Yes, yes, I'm fine,' he said, sniffing to prove it. His nose made a horrible blocked noise.
'Oh, good,' the girl said.
The heavy object was about to crest the hill. Danny's stomach filled with butterflies.
He didn't know what he should say. Aware that the colour was draining from his face, he nodded and gave her a tight smile.
The girl took a deep breath and clasped her hands beneath her breasts. Her face cleared and Danny knew the weight was now rolling down the other side of the hill. His heart started to pound and he felt dizzy. *C'mon!* he thought, not even sure if what he thought was happening really *was* happening. *Say something!* he implored her.
The girl smiled. It wasn't the kind of a smile he was used to receiving from girls. This smile spoke volumes.
Got it wrong, Danny, he told himself. It would not be the first time, either.
But there she was, smiling that smile and apparently waiting for him to say something.
Danny was speechless. He wanted to say something witty and there

wasn't a witty word in his head. He knew that if he tried to speak nothing more than a fair imitation of a frog croaking would pass his lips.

Brian would have been chatting her up by now, he knew. That was what the girl seemed to be waiting for. Brian would be in full flow and the girl would be entranced. Very probably she and Brian would be exchanging telephone numbers and addresses by now. But Danny wasn't Brian. They were brothers but they had been struck from entirely different moulds. Danny had been at the rear quarter of the queue when the self-esteem and confidence had been handed out. The girl was not *ordinary*. She was undoubtedly a girl who got chatted up regularly and had come to expect it. Danny knew enough about these things to be able to tell that making anything that even seemed like an advance would bring the girl's scorn pouring down on him. Even if it didn't look as though this would happen he was certain it would. Danny knew he could not deal with the embarrassment of being brushed aside by this girl. His lips were sealed as firmly as if they had been glued together.

He looked at the girl and waited. A rule had somehow been drawn up allowing them to study one another without embarrassment. She smiled. Danny's heart pounded in his ears. Silence hung heavily around them. If he spoke, he knew, he would be confirming his recovery and breaking the spell which was holding them together. Then the girl would simply get up and walk out of his life forever.

He watched her.

She waited.

'What's your name?' she asked suddenly.

Danny's stomach rolled and burned inside him. His heart squeezed painfully against the base of his throat. The lights weren't just flashing amber here, they were blazing green. He could see all of this, but could not allow himself to believe it was true.

Surely she can't be interested in me? he thought. He felt the same way as he had in the swimming pool when he'd made up his mind to duck his head under the water for the very first time. He sucked in one last breath and went for it, not knowing if he would ever see the light of day again.

'My name's Daniel. M-My friends call me D-Danny,' he stammered.

Her eyes were locked on to his, holding them in a firm but gentle gaze. Information seemed to be passing back and forth between them but Danny didn't know what the subtle messages meant.

'Danny,' she repeated softly and grinned as if the word tasted good in her mouth.

'Danneee,' she whispered, tasting it again. 'I like that name. Mine is Susan. *My* friends call me Suzie or Sooze.'

She smiled and waited.

WHAT NEXT? Danny shouted to himself. His heart was threatening to burst right out of his throat. He glanced down and could see it plainly, banging away against his tee shirt. His ears sang. Suddenly it was incredibly hot and he had started to sweat. A stray thought informed him that someone had probably lit a fire beneath his chair. He swallowed.

Suzie began to study him in fine detail, her eyes making tiny movements and reflecting different shades of light as she examined each feature carefully and individually. The library vanished from his consciousness and the small sounds of shuffling and rustling pages faded until there were just the two of them left in the universe.

During this seemingly endless period of close scrutiny a kind of magnetism seemed to develop around them. Danny realised that their faces had begun to drift closer to one another. Close enough for him to feel her warm breath against his chin. There was nothing he could do to stop it but this did not matter – he would have gladly cut off his right arm for it to continue.

For one ecstatic moment he thought she was going to kiss him. Working on reflex or race memory or maybe just his wild imagination, Danny's lips started to pucker.

Then something broke the spell. Suzie drew back and released a long held breath in a satisfied sigh. 'Hello, Danny,' she said, her voice merry and conspiriatorial as though they'd shared an intimate joke.

'Hello, Suzie,' he said, completely out of his depth.

'D'you want to be my friend?'

'Yes,' he replied instantly and found that he was not just smiling, but *beaming*.

Suzie chuckled. 'Okay, you can be my friend but first you have to tell me something.'

'What?'

'Where did you get that little circular scar on your cheekbone?'

Danny later discovered this disquieting personality trait was not affected. Suzie was truly like this and had no control over it. It was in her genes. She turned out to be direct and uncompromising and was the only person he was ever to meet who had enough confidence to disregard totally all the rules of etiquette. Suzie was innocent and unsophisticated in the way she dealt with social relationships; in all the time he knew her she could never understand how anyone might be offended by a direct personal question. Since she didn't mean any offence, how could people *be* offended?

At the time Danny wasn't offended. Surprised, yes, but not offended. People had been asking him that question all his life and he was rather proud of the answer. 'That's the old war wound,' he said. 'My big brother shot me with a .22 calibre rifle,' he explained. 'Not an air gun, but a proper rifle.'

Suzie's face clouded. 'Now tell me the truth,' she said.

Something else Danny found out later was that Suzie did not like to be lied to.

Danny tried to understand the sudden anger flashing in her eyes and couldn't. 'That *is* the truth,' he protested. 'My brother is called Brian and you can ask him any time. I'll give you our phone number if you like.'

Suzie looked at him for a time, her face dark, then got up, turned and waltzed off.

Heart suddenly leaden, Danny stared after her. He watched her until she vanished down the stairs and then looked at the empty space where he'd last seen her. His vital signs settled and the needle of his internal agony meter swept across the dial to the red.

'Blown it,' he muttered. He didn't know how he'd achieved this, but he had.

They're not just a different sex, they're a different species, he told himself bitterly.

Crestfallen and mentally analysing the scene to find whatever wrong word he might have spoken, he went back to the medical book section and half heartedly tried to find a reference to the pineal gland. It may have been true that having a damaged one didn't affect your sexual performance, but there was evidence to show that it might have serious implications concerning your relationships with women.

15

'What are you doing?' a voice demanded from behind him. 'Are you hiding from me?'

Danny looked round.

Suzie was back. She held out a pen and a sheet of paper for him to take. Danny looked dumbly at it.

Suzie tutted. 'Give me your phone number and I'll find out if you're telling me fibs or not,' she said gravely.

Danny was mystified. 'I thought you'd gone. I thought you were upset with me,' he said, taking the paper and pen.

'Write your number. And put your address too. I don't want you supplying false information and if you do I'll find you anyway.'

'Why would I do that?' Danny asked. He glanced at her and wondered if she was still upset. He couldn't work it out.

'You might.'

When big brother Brian was feeling expansive and kindly he would sometimes supply little pieces of man-of-the-world wisdom to his brother on the subject of picking up girls. One of these nuggets was: *When in doubt, fish*. Danny found himself doing this now. 'What difference does it make anyway? You think I'm a liar and you probably don't even like me,' he said.

Suzie's face lit up. 'You must be joking,' she replied. 'I'm not letting you go *now*. Finders keepers, and since I found you, you're my property. So you may as well get used to the idea. Come and buy me a cup of coffee. I can't allow you to hang around in libraries any more, they're too dangerous for the likes of you. You need to be protected. What were you looking for anyway?'

It was that easy. Danny no longer knew which way was up or which was down and he didn't care. What he *did* know was that he was in love. Completely and utterly and brainlessly. All his little, *What would anyone see in ugly old me? I've got a face that even my mother doesn't love*, self depreciating thoughts had been instantly rendered powerless. For all he knew – or cared – they no longer existed.

'I was looking for a reference to the pineal gland. It's a piece of your brain. The bullet that hit me drove a shard of bone into mine. I was trying to find out if it's going to cause me any problems – and I'd like to buy you a cup of coffee but I haven't got any money on me,' he blurted.

Suzie shrugged. 'Don't worry, I'll pay this time. You can make it up to me next time,' she said simply, indicating that their relationship was going to be at least two visits to the café long.

'Thanks,' Danny said. He was awed. And frightened someone would soon be shaking him and telling him it was seven o'clock and time he got up.

Suzie said, 'Think nothing of it. And you won't need to look any further to find out about your pineal gland. *I* can tell you all about it over coffee. Biology is my subject.'

Danny followed her out of the library in a kind of daze, trotting along behind her like a dopey dog. She led him into a cafe called the Gingham Kitchen which was almost next door to the library. She told him to sit and ordered them both coffee and burgers.

While they waited for their order she told him that her full name was Susan Jane Anderson and she was seventeen and had just taken her 'A' levels. She said she intended to take a year off and then go to university to study marine biology. Danny felt a pang of hurt at this time limit being imposed so soon, then told himself it was unlikely to last more than a week anyway – or two at most.

Suzie was funny, talkative, confident and very pretty. Danny tried hard but summoned just about as much sparkle as a soggy cream cracker. Suzie appeared not to mind. She seemed to sense that he was struggling way out of his depth and went easy on him.

After an hour or so of comparing lifestyles – him haltingly and her articulately – Danny knew that she was an only child, her father was a chartered architect, she had a Golden Retriever dog called Thomas and her parents were giving her driving lessons. During a lull in the conversation she went to order them two more coffees and Danny couldn't make himself believe that she was coming back.

But Suzie was as good as her word. 'Your pineal gland,' she said setting his coffee down in front of him, 'is situated deep in your mid-brain. It has no known function, but various silly people have thought that it has something to do with sex. There isn't a scrap of evidence for this.'

Danny nodded. 'I found that much out today,' he said.

'Ah, but there's more!' she said. 'And it's much more exciting! Did you know, for example, that Descartes thought the pineal gland was the seat of the soul?'

'Who's Descartes?' Danny asked.

'A clever dicky with some good ideas.'

'How many?'

'About two-thirds of them,' she said. 'The pineal gland is also reputed to be the source of paranormal abilities. You can't levitate or move objects by your own force of will, can you?'

Danny shook his head.

'That's because yours is split by the piece of bone. You really should be more careful with your body, y'know. Being able to levitate might come in useful for you one day and then you won't be able to do it.'

'Yours is intact, I take it?' he asked then blushed furiously when she looked coy.

'If you mean my pineal gland, yes, it is.'

'Then you can levitate and move objects by mind over matter, can't you?' he challenged, feeling his face and neck burning hot and frantically willing it not to be the colour of beetroot.

'Of course, my dear. Wanna see?'

'I'd love to.' His cheeks were cooling now.

Suzie sank down in her seat until her knees touched Danny's under the table. Danny began to glow again, but she didn't seem to notice.

'Watch and learn,' she said, placing her hands palms down on the table. She drew her face into a parody of immense concentration and closed her eyes.

'I can feel it coming on,' she assured him quietly and began to wobble from side to side, unaware that his attention was fixed solely on the movement of her breasts beneath the cheesecloth dress.

'Grrrr,' she said and pushed herself back up on her seat so that her body appeared to be ascending. She continued until she was standing up, making the transition from sitting to crouching so neatly that he couldn't tell at which precise moment it happened. She stood there, her hands now floating about six inches from the table top, and opened her eyes. 'See?' she asked. 'I told you he could do it.'

'Your feet are on the floor,' he said.

'No they're not. They're six inches above it. Have a look if you don't believe me.'

As he bent under the table, she pressed her hands on the table top, took her weight and lifted her feet from the floor. They dangled in space in her open toed sandals. They were thin feet and perfectly

proportioned. The nails were painted red.
'I'm special,' her voice said from above the table. Not surprisingly it bore the strained quality of great physical exertion. 'And I'm multi-talented. Don't you ever forget that!'
Danny never did.

16

Suzie lived in the village of Oakley, not only three miles outside Basingstoke, but on the opposite side of town to the village of Basing. This precluded any notion of Danny's walking her home.
Instead, he walked her to the bus station, wheeling his bike between them like a steel chaperone. It was crowded in the bus depot and afterwards Danny thought that if it hadn't been for his bike getting in the way of all the passing people, they might have held each other before she got on her bus. As it was she squeezed his hand and pecked him on the lips.
'Will I see you again?' he called after her as she skipped up the aluminium steps of the single decker 103. He felt a strong sense of high melodrama. His so-far-so-boring life seemed to have suddenly turned into something directed, filmed and edited by David Lean. *Doctor Zhivago* maybe; carriages and snow and the feeling of loss as a loved one was transported away to who knew where with little prospect of ever getting back. Except that David Lean films didn't usually use locations like Basingstoke bus station on a hot summer's day. It was dirty, filled with ugly people and smelled of burning diesel oil.
Suzie was the last one on to the bus and she didn't turn round when he called to her. Danny watched as she took a seat on his side and still she didn't look. The doors hissed shut and the driver selected reverse and gunned the engine. The bus backed out in a wide arc, stopped, then started forward.
As it passed Danny, Suzie looked out, held up the scrap of paper with his number on and did a phone calling mime, holding a phantom receiver in one hand and dialling with the index finger of the other. Danny gazed at the bus until it rounded the corner and went out of sight.
He ran over some broken glass on the way home on his bike and both his tyres were punctured.
Danny didn't care.

Chapter Three
Suzie

1

The next major bad card wasn't slapped into Danny's open hand until twenty-three years later when he was rapidly approaching thirty-eight. That was when the incident with the bathroom tiles happened. During the dark months of The Tunnel, Danny would see this time-span as making perfect sense. It would plot nicely on his chart and he would study it with bitter humour.

But fate dealt him many other cards along that seamless ribbon of time and he would tell himself he should be grateful they were all the same mid-pack numbers that everyone else seemed to get: the minor cards of normal life, shuffled and distributed randomly. There were downs to chart, of course, but these were balanced by the ups that gave hope. Some hands were won, some lost, some folded. During those years, which were to be violently terminated by the simple redecoration of a bathroom, as near as he could calculate it, Danny came out evens.

Whilst in The Tunnel, Danny would view these uninterrupted years as an exquisite trick played on him by that Queen of all the Bitches, Lady Luck. She had given him things he loved and cherished in order that she could increase his suffering by wrenching them away from him, one by one.

2

Danny's meeting with Suzie happened on the 14th of July 1968. He began to pine for her by the time he'd mended the punctures in his bike tyres, and by early evening – after staying within earshot of the phone for three hours – he was convinced that she had never intended to call him at all. There was, after all, no good reason why she should. Suzie was lovely and worldly-wise and he was a gangly dumb-cluck lame duck with a bad case of teenage spots. He had misinterpreted that magical moment in the library when their lips almost touched, and she had evidently only taken him to the café for a little light entertainment. All the other stuff about not letting him get away was simply one of those games that girls would play. His brother had related tales of these kind of things. Why *should* she phone him? Danny was hurt, confused, and ached with disappointment. He hadn't eaten, but there was a weight of what seemed to be pig-iron in his stomach and the thought of food made him feel ill. He trudged upstairs and sat in the spare room amongst his dusty electronics equipment wondering if *Practical Electronics* had ever published plans entitled, *Build a Working Suzie Detector*.

At seven-thirty the telephone rang.

Afterwards, Danny didn't recall the trip downstairs. When he replaced the receiver, his feet were hurting so he assumed he'd leapt down most of them. What he did remember were the clouds of butterflies that instantly replaced the pig-iron in his stomach, the rush of adrenaline that turned his face pale and left him with trembling hands, and the intensity of the desolation he felt when he realised it was Mil on the phone rather than Suzie. Mil was phoning from the call box in Belle Vue Road. All the other Loopies were there; '*And guess what*, Danny! There's a bunch of female French students with us! Plenty for everyone!'

Mil was confounded when he learned that Danny 'didn't feel up to it'. Danny could picture his mouth dangling. Mil made a quick recovery, 'Okay, Dan, all the more for us!' he said and rang off.

By the end of what turned out to be a miserable week, Danny accepted the fact that he'd been taken for a mug and now only thought about Suzie for sixty percent of the time. When the following Saturday rolled around, the percentage had dropped to the high teens – although he still felt the familiar warm rolling of his stomach whenever she did trip across his mind. Brian returned from Dorset where he'd been alone with Linda and told packs of lies to Danny and his parents about how well he hit it off with Linda's folks. Fearing endless ridicule, Danny didn't mention Suzie to his brother.

Which was why Brian was so taken aback when a female detective called Julie Riley rang him and informed him that she had been going through some old files of outstanding cases and understood that he had shot his brother. She informed him that she would be sending the relevant paperwork to the Director of Public Prosecutions but thought that the eventual charge would be one of manslaughter rather than murder. Danny, on his way to the kitchen, overheard a very puzzled Brian say that, yes, he had shot his brother but he hadn't killed him, and stopped to watch.

Brian looked as if he suspected a wind-up but wasn't certain. His face was pale. 'Don't be stupid, he's still alive!' he argued. Then, as Danny watched, he started to believe. In exasperation he said, 'I can't help it if you've got him down as murdered, he's still alive and he's standing here next to me!'

Danny's heart was now hammering and pressing up into his throat. He could barely believe it, but he was certain it was Suzie on the other end of the line. What other girl knew enough about Danny and the way his brother tormented him to play such a prank? He suddenly remembered Suzie's promise to verify with Brian, his story about being shot. If he hadn't been physically reduced to something approaching an un-set jelly Danny could have kicked himself all the way down the hall – he'd told Suzie that Brian was away and should have realised she wouldn't bother phoning until he returned.

Brian shook his head violently. 'No,' he protested in a voice a full two tones above normal, 'I am *not* telling lies! He put his hand over the mouthpiece, swore softly, and shook his head. 'It's the police,' he said. 'They think I killed you and they won't believe you aren't dead. Something about an old file on you that's still open. They want to speak to you. Tell them you're still alive, Dan, for fuck's sake!' he said.

He took the phone while Brian looked on anxiously.

'I believe you, Danny,' Suzie whispered in his ear. 'And I'm sorry I doubted you. I've missed you. Meet me for coffee? Gingham Kitchen? Tomorrow at ten?'

Danny took a deep breath and knew absolutely that he wasn't going to be able to speak. 'I'd love to,' his motormouth said on his behalf. 'Wild horses couldn't keep me away!'

'Say sorry to your brother for me. I did it that way to make sure he wouldn't speak with forked tongue. I thought you might have arranged something between you to fool me. White man speak truth! Bye!'

Danny replaced the receiver, smiled at Brian and walked away.

'What happened?' Brian pleaded, following him down the hall. 'What did she say?'

'It was my girlfriend, Bri. You've been had. Sorry!' He went into the kitchen and left Brian staring at him open mouthed.

3

Over the following weeks Danny was amazed at how swiftly things could change and at how good they could become. At first this delight was tempered by his natural insecurity, but this was soon forgotten. Suzie was confident, forthright, funny and a joy to be with. Not only had she chosen him as her partner in what was apparently going to be a long-term relationship (long-term in Brian's book, anyway – his girlfriends didn't usually last more than a fortnight), she was also unimpressed by Brian's advances.

As his time began to be more and more devoted to Suzie, Danny gradually found himself de-Loopyised. It wasn't that any of the other members resented his having a girlfriend it was just that he suddenly didn't have anything much in common with the other members. It rapidly became clear that being a Loopy and having a girlfriend were somehow mutually exclusive. Finally he only ever saw any of them on Thursdays, which was Suzie's night off.

In August 1968, as a late surprise for Danny's fifteenth birthday (and to celebrate her 'A' level results – two A's and a B – a passport to almost any university she decided to grace with her presence), Suzie whisked him off to the Isle of Wight pop festival where he simultaneously heard Jimi Hendrix's last live performance and lost his virginity in a two-man tent. Danny could have stayed in that tent with Suzie until the end of time.

During Suzie's year off, Danny's new sex life took precedence over his schoolwork because Suzie passed her driving test and bought an old Ford Popular with money she saved from doing occasional temporary work. Danny's homework was shunned in favour of being driven away to places where Suzie could 'have him all to herself' during the evenings. Sometimes they went to pubs, sometimes to see bands; more often she would take him out into the country to what she termed 'dark secluded places' where she would have her wicked way with him, often returning him well after midnight in a state his brother would coarsely call 'fanny whipped' or, yet more coarsely, 'cuntstruck'.

And yet Suzie charmed away the many doubts Danny's parents had about her, constantly smoothing over their recurring worries about their poor innocent son.

In spite of complaints from his teachers about his poor work, and his parents' continual carping about 'The Need to Succeed' and how he would never make the grade if he didn't buck up his ideas fairly sharply (whatever *that* meant, he told Suzie), Danny passed seven 'O' levels at good grades.

4

As he had known it would from the very beginning, the shit hit the fan the following autumn just after he had started sixth form to study for his 'A' levels.

Suzie had often spoken sadly about how she would miss him when she went away to university, and although he knew this was meant to prepare him for the final blow when she finally left him, that time always seemed somewhere in the distant future and on each occasion he had filed it away in the back of his mind, refusing to consider it on the grounds that it would be painful enough when it arrived so there was no point in extending the agony. Whenever the subject was broached he would quote Einstein's maxim, 'I never think of the future; it comes soon enough'. Unfortunately, Einstein chose not to illustrate the downside of this – which might have followed, 'And when it arrives, it knocks you down and kicks you with steel toe-capped boots'.

Danny was knocked down and kicked.

One fine Sunday in September, Suzie departed for Exeter where she would take a course in marine biology. This time her departure didn't seem like something culled from a David Lean film at all. It was flat, unromanticised, and it hurt like hell.

Suzie went happily, not a worry in the world, not the tiniest hint of a tear in her eye. Her parting words to Danny were, 'See you at Christmas, kid. Be careful 'cos the Magic Eye will be watching you! And don't forget to practise the levitation!'

After she drove away Danny cried. He was hurt, empty, and felt a terrible desolation.

But it got worse. Suzie never phoned or returned his letters and it gradually dawned on him that he had finally been given the old heave-ho. He began to get angry with her and hot on the heels of his anger came an irrational feeling of jealousy. When consulted, the two remaining unattached Loopies, Mil and Kevin Long, were no consolation and only told him what he thought already. Kevin devised some interesting tortures for the men he thought Suzie was seeing but even these horrendous and comical scenarios didn't help with Danny's despondency. Finally, utterly convinced that she was dragging a different man into bed with her each and every night, Danny became devoutly unfaithful to her. Some of Suzie's confidence and charm had evidently rubbed off on him because he no longer had any trouble picking up girls. There were four between September and December. As the weeks passed, he worked hard at thinking of her less and less. She was a painful barb in his memory and remembering her hurt so much he supposed he was still in love with her, but he vowed to overcome it. He didn't really expect ever to see her again. That part of his life had passed.

5

Suzie turned up at his house on the 13th of December. It was cold and trying to snow outside. Danny went to answer the doorbell and was not only totally stunned to find her standing there but dismayed to find he'd forgotten just how gorgeous she was. For a moment he thought of Joey escaping from the lounge window all those years ago and didn't know why.

It's a very long way to Africa, a birdy voice informed his mind.

Suzie was holding a big box wrapped in Father Christmas paper and she was crying. Tears rolled silently down her cheeks. Snow drifted down around her, speckling her hair and shoulders with tiny flakes. The scene was so still, the silence so complete, that it might have been frozen in time. The only movement was the passage of glittering tears down her cheeks.

'Suzie,' Danny said, but the word didn't escape his lips. The cold steel fist of guilt had taken hold of his insides. He had known her thirteen months and was familiar with every aspect of her except her tears. He knew exactly why she was crying now. As she had promised, the Magic Eye had indeed been watching him. She had found out about his unfaithfulness. *DO SOMETHING!* his mind screamed.

Danny stood there, rigid as a tree, while his insides were crushed. He hated himself. *Don't let her get away!* pleaded a small voice inside him. *Tell her you love her! Tell her you're sorry! Please tell her something! Speak to her, Danny! Oh Joey, don't go to Africa!*

But Danny was wood with a steel fist inside him.

'I love you, Suzie!' he said, but the motormouth which had so often spoken for him had deserted him. There was no movement of the still air, no vibration of his vocal cords.

Suzie held the parcel out to him.

FOR GOD'S SAKE, DO SOMETHING! Danny's mental voice yelled.

'This is for you,' she said quietly.

Danny reached out for the parcel, his warm hands brushing her cold ones as she let go of the box.

Joey!

Suzie blinked two tears from her eyes, smiled unsteadily and said, 'Have a good Christmas,' then turned and walked away.

Screaming internally, Danny watched her walk down the path.

Stop her! he told himself and his desperation broke the paralysing hold of the cold steel fist inside him.

'Suzie!' he called after her.

She did not turn and run back into his arms. She appeared not to have heard him. 'Suzie! Stop! Wait!'

Danny's thoughts speeded up. He placed the parcel on the hall floor, glanced at his slipperless feet, thought, *fuck it*, and ran down the snowy path after her, shouting at the top of his voice.

He got outside the gate just in time to see Suzie drive away.

6

Between then and Christmas, Danny was tortured by his guilt and his need for her throughout every waking hour – and many of his sleeping ones. He rang her every day but she would never come to the phone; he wrote her letters which were returned unopened, and finally he worked up enough courage to cycle to her house – where he was informed by her mother that she was not at home. On Christmas Eve he went into Basingstoke and spent all his remaining money sending her a bouquet of flowers with the message: *I love you. Please forgive me.*

On the morning of the worst Christmas Day of his life, he opened the parcel she had left for him. Inside the box was a pair of Levis 501s, a hand knitted mohair jumper in which the professionally produced maker's label read:

Created by the loving hands of Susan Anderson

and a huge card with a reindeer on the front. Inside were the words:

I LOVE YOU

written in letters three inches high.

Danny could have killed himself.

7

Suzie phoned him on New Year's Eve. She said she thought they had both suffered enough now and would he please meet her in the Gingham Kitchen.

They sat opposite one another drinking coffee, smiling wanly and swapping small talk in tiny, hurt voices. When Suzie began to cry, Danny moved round to her side of the table and comforted her, now tearful himself.

The café staff watched interestedly and openly while Danny swore to be faithful to her forevermore and promised never to hurt her again.

One of these promises he would not be able to keep.

8

Danny was relentlessy faithful to Suzie during the remainder of her time at university. He poured all his energy into his studies and came out the other end with three 'A' levels – two C's and a B. Then he was stuck. *Going to work*, was a phrase he had kept out of his mind in much the same way as he had kept out Suzie's forthcoming departure to university. He didn't *want* to go to work and now he was going to have to, he realised that he had no ambitions. He didn't have a clue what he wanted to do, nor where he wanted to do it. Danny knew that he didn't want to dedicate his life to making money at the expense of doing what he would really enjoy, but he didn't know what he might enjoy. He was happy as he was, thank you very much.

After a couple of months during which he realised the prospect of university thrilled him less than that of working, he chose a job in much the same way as his friends with worse qualifications than himself chose them: he opened the local paper at the Situations Vacant pages and selected something that looked a little less tedious than the others. Since neither Danny, his friends – or the school careers officer seemed to have anything other than a sketchy idea of what various forms of employment entailed, this was largely a matter of taking pot luck.

A few weeks later he found himself working as a computer operator with Macmillan the publishers at their Basingstoke depot. Something else the careers officer had neglected to tell him was that, at an interview, most companies were likely to make jobs sound much more thrilling than, in reality, they actually were. Danny worked shifts and was lonely and often bored. The job was neither complicated nor mentally taxing and Danny wondered why he'd had to have three 'A' levels to get it. In his opinion a half-wit could have run that Honeywell. He once wrote Suzie a letter claiming that an idiot could do his job, to which she replied that an idiot *was* doing it.

But it had its compensations; the money was good and there was always plenty to read.

9

When the fickle finger of fate isn't pointing directly at you, life has a way of slipping by without being marked by any major events and consequently years appear and vanish without you truly noticing them.

For Danny Stafford, life between starting work and arriving in his thirties just flew by. Suzie finished university, came back to Basingstoke and started working for the Automobile Association in junior management. She was intending to get a job somewhere doing what she was qualified to do and she and Danny made great plans for a move to the coast, but the inertia of normal life set in, somehow preventing these plans from ever materialising. Danny changed jobs twice and Suzie rose to middle management and as the unbelievable words *middle age* rolled ever closer, Danny sometimes felt as if he was simply marking time and waiting.

But he and Suzie were happy.

Chapter Four
The Black Mirror

1

In a moment of black humour, Danny christened those endless charts he later plotted the *If Only* papers. When the endlessly refined maps of his life had been drawn with their single long spiked line showing his own personal highs and lows in ever increasing complexity – when you could *see* where you had gone wrong – it was difficult to shake off that feeling of, *If Only*. . .

Seeing those events marked down there near the bottom line of his life chart made him feel the way most people did after a minor car accident that had been their fault: *If only I'd left home a minute earlier or a minute later the circumstances would have been completely differently and the accident wouldn't have happened.*

Of course the converse also applied: there were hundreds of people who had thanked their lucky stars they'd missed that train that might have reduced them to a bloody pulp when it crashed, or that an annoying traffic jam – or even a simple case of the airport lounge shits – had prevented them boarding that plane which had an appointment with disaster, but for Danny these moments didn't seem to exist. There were no lucky escapes.

It was the realisation that things could have been so different that hurt him so much. If he had believed that there was no way he could possibly have avoided those bottom line events, he wouldn't have felt so bad, but knowing – and he *did* know – that they could have been avoided, gave him a sense of having been cheated on a grand scale.

Because it all depended on timing. The bad stuff was all there, coming at you, but if you could read the patterns – as those people who sailed effortlessly through life seemed able to do (even if only at a subconscious level) – those events could be neatly side-stepped. What made it difficult to plan for was the varying delay between those moments of *if only* and their consequences.

Danny saw patterns of time in his life-charts and sometimes, fleetingly, those patterns seemed to make perfect sense. He could see where he'd gone wrong, recall saying yes when he should have shrugged and said no; he could sense the split second timing he had been unlucky enough unwittingly to adhere to and he knew that none of it was written in stone and inescapable. But those moments of realisation, where everything suddenly seemed logical and balanced, were too few and too short for him to *accurately* predict what actions he should take to break the cycle. He tried – in many ways – but failed.

Danny was left with the knowledge that *it need not have happened at all*. And he thought: *if only*. . .

2

The long period of normality didn't end until May 1991, four years and three holidays in the Mediterranean after (despite the dire warnings from his mother) Danny and Suzie had finally bought their house. But the *If Only* point was plotted on his chart on August 1988. That was Danny's thirty-fifth birthday and the same day he and Suzie made the down payment on the terraced house behind Basingstoke railway station.

After five years of living together in rented accommodation, they bought the somewhat run-down (and consequently, cheap) house and were blissfully happy that they finally had a place they could call their own. Later, Danny would wish that he hadn't bought the house at all.

He would not regret this decision as much as he would regret agreeing with Suzie that the bathroom did indeed need redecorating. This *If Only* point on his chart would be ringed in red ink.

Like many things in Danny's life, it started out innocently and with good intentions and then went horribly wrong.

3

That bad Saturday when fate slipped him the next high card, Danny and Suzie were in the kitchen eating breakfast. It was eight-thirty in the morning and Danny had 'bagged' the paper, which meant that he'd laid hands on it first and Suzie would have to wait her turn. She was munching toast and leafing through an old copy of *House and Garden*. Had Danny been alert enough to have realised he would have forgone the Golden 'bagging' Rule and let her read the paper first. Leafing through *House and Garden* often inspired her.

'Danny,' Suzie said, and instantly recognising the imploring tone of her voice, he realised he had made a tactical error.

Danny looked up from the paper. His eyes were no longer correctly focused. Suzie was blurred and seemed to be surrounded by a kind of halo of fuzzy light.

Tired, he thought, *that's all*. He blinked and when that didn't work, screwed his eyes up and gently massaged the lids. When he looked again, the halo – caused by whatever crap had been floating around in his eyes – was gone, but Suzie still seemed to be blurred. *This kid'll have to go see the optician soon*, he thought, and then mentally added: *This kid is a kid no longer*.

This kid had spotted the first grey hair in his sideburns last week and had ripped it out, swearing that if – as Suzie insisted – it would be replaced by ten more, he would tear those out too. But he knew age would get him in the end, just as it got everyone. He had become aware that he was being crept up upon by Old Father Time after Suzie's last foray into the pages of *House and Garden* which had culminated in his rash agreement to undertake the laying of a patio. It had taken him three weekends, pulled every muscle in his body and given him a backache that had only recently been forgotten. A couple of years ago, an ache or twinge would have been history inside forty-eight hours; these days they clung on.

Danny's stomach clenched like a fist – something it hadn't done since his first aeroplane flight three years ago – and almost reminded him of something. He didn't know what. A freezing feeling of *déjà vu* followed so quickly on the tail of the almost-but-not-quite grasped memory that Danny felt as if he had been slapped out of kilter and was no longer properly seated inside his own body. He seemed to be looking at Suzie from two slightly differing points of view. For a moment she looked like a stranger. The comfortable familiarity of the kitchen he had sat in each morning over four years was lost. Danny felt adrift and out of control. He gulped in a breath and closed his eyes again.

It's about time we did something with the bathroom, his mind told him. His eyes blinked open and the fist in his stomach melted. He relaxed.

Suzie grinned at him and said, 'It's about time we did something with the bathroom.'

'I knew you were going to say that,' Danny said. He had turned back the right way inside himself but now he felt empty-headed and shaky.

'It was only a matter of time,' Suzie said, smiling.

Danny shook his head, grasping for words to explain. 'No, I *knew* you would say it. It was a kind of . . . premonition . . . or something. I had your words before you spoke them.'

'Coincidence,' Suzie said. 'Sometimes those things happen.'

'No,' Danny said, 'it wasn't like that. I *heard* your words. They sounded inside my head and they were in your voice. Maybe it was telepathy or something like that.'

Suzie's grin faded. She shuddered, quite visibly. Danny didn't mention it, but he wondered about it afterwards.

She shook her head. 'Those things don't really happen, Danny,' she said gravely. 'They *can't!*' Her eyes flashed in the same way they did when her parents told her that she soon ought to think about having babies and Danny knew – just as well as her parents did – what would follow if he persisted. Suzie didn't want to discuss it. A minefield had been laid.

'Just half asleep,' he said, grinning, and thought, *Hickorydickory-dickory!* and then realised just how long it was since those birdy words had occurred to him. *About twenty years, old Dan*, he thought.

'About the bathroom,' Suzie said, wrenching the conversation back to the original subject.

4

Suzie had good taste, a keen sense of style, *House and Garden* to inspire her, and she knew what she wanted. Danny gave her her head; if there was an artistic lobe in the right hemisphere of his brain that dealt with design (and he doubted it), he was unable to access it. Once or twice during the remodelling process the house had undergone he had ventured the opinion that this particular portion of his brain had been shredded by the .22 bullet that he still carried around in his left hand trouser pocket with his loose change. This was another taboo subject with Suzie, but he could understand this one. The years had not diminished this particular fear of hers. At first she hadn't believed it possible that there was still a shard of bone in his brain and she was just as uncomfortable with the idea now. She had physical evidence of his brain damage – she could see its effect on the left side of his body whenever he was tired – and that worried her enough without considering the fact that there was a piece of bone piercing his pineal gland which might, at any time, see fit to re-site itself somewhere more dangerous.

Like Danny's brother Brian who, like a character from a Colleen McCulloch novel, was now farming sheep in Queensland, Australia, deep down Suzie believed that Danny was going to die before his time.

Just as Suzie had done with all the other rooms in the house, she described how the bathroom would look upon completion, and just as Danny had done with all those rooms, he tried to imagine the finished product and found a black gap where its picture should have bloomed. But – unlike Suzie – Danny could saw a straight line, lay a carpet, hang wallpaper and fix tiles. So Suzie did all the design work and Danny supplied the muscle power. So far he had been delighted whenever he stood back and viewed what they had achieved.

He stood back and looked at the finished bathroom at three in the afternoon on Saturday the 18th of May.

Suzie had told him that on completion the bathroom would be sexy and relaxing. Now Danny nodded, smiling and mentally acknowledging that it had indeed become so – if somewhat more sexy than relaxing. Suzie had a fairly strong streak of narcissism which occasionally bordered on exhibitionism (a fact that had been amply demonstrated the previous Christmas at Danny's works party – to the chagrin of his boss), and had chosen a huge full-length mirror for the back wall of the bathroom, a large one for over the hand basin and black reflective tiles to cover the walls and the panel on the side of the bath. Wherever you stood or sat in the room you could quite plainly see what you were doing reflected from several angles. Danny grinned, wondering when Suzie would want to 'christen' the new bathroom. 'Christening' was traditional and involved having sex as a celebration rather than the performance of a Christian ritual or breaking open bottles of champagne. All the rooms in the house had been christened, as had all the cars either of them had owned.

Danny ran his fingers over the smooth new enamel of the old cast iron bath, picked up several scraps of paper from the thick, off white carpet which had replaced the cold linoleum floor, and called, 'The bathroom's ready!' down the stairs where Suzie was watching sport on the television and waiting.

He went out on to the landing as she hurried up the stairs.

'One bathroom,' he announced. 'And it looks as if it was designed by a pervert.'

'It was,' Suzie replied, glancing in at the finished product and looking at a darkened reflection of herself glancing back out. 'And it was built by another. Ready for testing?'

'Ready as I'll ever be,' Danny replied.

Suzie walked into the bathroom, tore off her clothes, flung them on the floor and turned this way and that admiring herself in the reflections. Standing in the doorway and rapidly growing an erection, Danny admired her too.

'Don't be coy,' she said, pirouetting, 'get your clothes off and let's watch ourselves christen it!'

5

After the christening, Danny lay on the carpet next to Suzie, his buttocks against the cold black mirrors of the bath's side panel (and probably smearing them) while he studied the fractured but still incredibly elegant line of Suzie's body in the black tiles that ran across the wall to the door. He hadn't yet fully understood the doubt he'd felt when Suzie had chosen the black tiles, but there was something about them that bothered him. They had been in Farnham Tiles whose advertising claimed 'Always a Million in Stock' when Suzie had chosen them in preference to ordinary reflective ones. Danny had re-experienced the odd *déjà vu* feeling of being twisted around inside his body the moment he had picked up one of them. Peering at his darkened reflection in the tiles had given him an eerie dizziness as if the tile was expanding and reaching up somehow, as if it intended to swallow him. But the moment had passed and like a compass needle Danny had swung back to magnetic north, unaware until it was too late, that this was another of the key moments in his life.

Now, lying here and gazing into the tiles – which seemed to have an odd kind of *depth* to them – he began to wonder if he hadn't made some kind of mistake.

'What is it?' Suzie asked, stroking his face.

'What's what?' Danny replied, snapping out of his reverie.

'You. What's wrong? Wasn't I any good? I thought we looked great. Very erotic.'

'Yeah,' Danny agreed, brightening. *Like the woman said*, he told himself, *they're very erotic! And you'll get used to 'em too. They only look odd because . . . 'Ow, Suzie!'*

Suzie had nipped his scrotum with her nails. She giggled and began to stroke the pain away with cool fingers. Danny's balls tightened and he grew hard again.

'Bagsy going on top!' Suzie said, dragging him to the centre of the room and pressing him down on his back. 'So I can see how it looks.'

It looked good. Danny forgot his misgivings about the tiles.

6

Danny awoke from the light doze he had fallen into and realised if he didn't act now he would miss his chance. 'I'm getting in the bath first!' he announced, getting up and turning on the water.

'I've already bagged one,' Suzie smiled.

Unlike bagging the newspaper first in which possession counted as the law, bagging a bath depended on who made up their mind first. On days where it was likely that they would both want to bathe within three hours of one another (which amounted to *every* day give or take a Blue Moon), bagging a bath was the accepted practice used to ensure you got the hottest water. After the first tub full the water took hours to return to its original heat. Second baths were to be avoided at all costs; you couldn't soak for hours, topping it up when necessary, and there was seldom enough hot water left to rinse the shampoo from your hair – a fact often not realised until you had worked up a lather.

One of the silliest rules about bagging a bath (recently invented and appended by Suzie and the subject of an ongoing dispute) was that you didn't have to tell the other person.

'Oh no you haven't!' he shouted in the pantomine tradition.
'Oh yes I have!' she replied.
'I fixed the bathroom up, I get first go.'
'I chose the decor, I get first go!' she insisted, standing up and admiring herself in the mirrors.
'Fraid not dear, no emancipation in this house!'
'Okay. You pay my half of the mortgage and keep me at home and I'll let you have first baths. Always. Promise. Cross my heart and cut my throat.'
'Snap!' he said.
'Tell you what, seeing as I *lurve* you so much and seeing as you did all the hard work. . .'
'You'll let me go first!'
'No, course not, silly! What I was going to say was, I'll agree to a compromise. We'll get in together.'
There wasn't much room and Danny drew the short piece of toilet paper and got the tap end, but he had fun. After a mirthful hour of steaming and splashing each other, getting their legs entangled and fighting over who got the sponge, Suzie admitted defeat. She pronounced herself clean and got out of the water. To Danny's dismay the water level decreased so drastically that his body was hardly covered. He turned round the right way, opened the hot tap on and leered at Suzie as she towelled herself dry. 'Gettem off!' he growled.
'I haven't got any on.'
'Then come and kiss me.'
'You've done enough christening for one day, and I don't want to wear you out, so I'm going to get dressed then I'm going to make some tea. If you're a good boy I'll bring you up a cup. I suppose you're intending to stay there until you shrink.'
'I'm not getting out until I'm four feet tall.'
'Good,' she said putting her towelling robe on, 'I've always liked small men. You can knock them about easier.' She went out and closed the door.
Danny turned the tap off, lay back and relaxed, gradually bending his knees so that his upper torso slipped gently into the deep water. While hot water filled his ears and lapped around his chin, he gazed at the freshly painted ceiling and wondered how it would feel to be weightless. The kitchen was directly below the bathroom and he heard the noise of water rushing through the pipes as Suzie filled the kettle. He listened for the sounds of mugs being placed on the draining board, the familiar noises distorted and quieter as the sound travelled through the water. Danny stayed like that for a long time.
Then the mirror over the sink caught his eye and instantly triggered the familiar odd heaviness in his stomach. He sat up frowning, tipping his head back so that the water drained from his

ears. *There isn't anything wrong*, he assured himself, but his stomach, apparently, thought differently.

The mirror wasn't steamed up. This was unusual because the old one always used to be whenever he ran hot water. It even used to steam up when he shaved in the mornings.

It's because it's new, he thought. *It's still clean and that's why it hasn't steamed up. Just relax. Just lie back and forget it and the feeling will pass.*

Danny really did want to lie back and relax because over the past couple of weeks – since, in fact, he had seemingly read Suzie's mind – he had become tense. Not bowstring taut, but tense enough to give him a tiny nagging ache at the base of his skull towards the end of each day. This tension, he knew, had arrived hand in hand with his growing concern about his stability; either mental or physical or both, he didn't know which. At one moment or another during each day that had passed he had found himself dwelling on his brother's ancient prediction that he was to suffer an early demise. A small part of his mind had been not so much nagging him as slipping in the occasional doubtful thought concerning the brain damage and the shard of bone and the electric shock which had lost him almost eighteen hours of consciousness. So far the thoughts – and the *déjà vu* sensations of being set on rails which had been travelled many times before – had passed, but Danny had already asked himself the question: *What if they don't pass? What if they come along one day and decide they like it here and that they're going to stay?*

So instead of lying back and relaxing, he remained sitting bolt upright wondering why that mirror wasn't steamed up.

From his position in the bath he could see the black tiles reflected in it from the rear wall and – arriving at his eyes by God knew what complex route – a section of the mirror on the rear wall. None of them were covered in condensation which struck him as being not only unlikely, but damn near impossible.

You made a good job of those tiles, Dan, he told himself, mentally trying to push away the feeling of strangeness that was creeping up on him. The thought sounded wrong and meaningless as though it had lit up inside his head in a foreign language. It didn't seem to possess any logic or impart any information. The apparent area of the bathroom – increased almost four fold by the reflective surfaces – made Danny feel tiny and lost.

But you put those tiles up die-straight, he told himself. *Not an edge out of kilter on one of them, the edge lines are straight and even and they all lie dead flat.*

The words filtered out of his mind instantly. All except the word *dead* which he wished he hadn't used. *Dead*, Danny thought, staring at the tiles in the mirror, and began to feel dizzy. *A lot of things that aren't alive are dead. Dead is what comes after live. All things must pass. Everything ends up dead.*

He looked away, shaking his head and assuring himself that it was only the hot water in his ears affecting his balance. He clamped his eyes shut and the dizziness began to fade. Down in the kitchen the kettle began to boil and clicked as it turned itself off. The sound was reassuring somehow.

That's all right then! Danny told himself and opened his eyes.

There was a moment while his eyes adjusted their focus and Danny found himself staring at his darkened reflection in the tiles at the tap end of the bath. There were seventy-eight on that section of wall. Six across the width of the bath rising thirteen high to the ceiling. *Six thirteens*, he thought and these two words suddenly seemed very significant indeed.

The tiles glinted darkly before him, looking a lot more reflective than they had done before he'd closed his eyes. Seventy-eight small, black mirrors which, instead of reflecting fractured segments of a whole – as he was certain they'd done before – shone back seventy-eight discrete views of the same scene. In each one he could see a tiny white bath containing a tiny white person, whose chest and knees were above the water; whose arms laid along the rims and whose perspective-distorted fingers were splayed out like a bunches of sausages. This could not have happened.

'*Suzie*,' Danny whispered, breaking out in goosebumps in spite of the warmth of the bathwater. He shuffled his feet in the water, intending to get up and leave the bathroom immediately, but his body was seemingly pinned in place by its own reflections.

As he watched the small, frightened man reflected in the glaze, something behind the tiles moved. The black surface beneath the glaze flickered and seemed to pull back so that the tiles took on an extra dimension of depth that was patently impossible.

Nine inches! No! A foot! A foot deep! Danny thought crazily. *That's right through the cavity wall and outside the house!*

The surface glaze of the tiles stayed where it was but became a transparent membrane sealing the chasm that was forming behind it. The black reflective part of the tiles telescoped smoothly out backwards to a depth of about three feet. Danny shut his eyes, gritted his teeth and swore that it was just a little glitch; that he was tired and it was just a wakemare. Everything would be okay in a moment.

When he looked again the distance was more like six feet. His reflections were now so small they could barely be seen. '*Sooozee!*' he moaned and clung on tight to the sides of the bath. His stomach was a vacuum, his muscles cold iron. *No! DON'T!* he thought and felt the bath buck beneath him as if it was wrenching itself from the floor.

The tiles were still expanding, still smoothly pulling away, and they were transgressing some law of classical, particle, or metaphysics – Danny didn't know which and didn't care – which was apparently trying to rectify itself by drawing him up to fill the gap between the transparent surface and the black chasm behind.

Danny was being *sucked* towards the tiles.

Gasping and moaning, he wedged his feet against the tap end of the bath and pushed himself lower into the water. The bath bucked again as if trying to throw him out.

Stop it! Danny commanded mentally. Something behind him creaked. The bathwater churned and then settled.

And the whole room turned up sideways.

The action was accomplished soundlessly, quickly and smoothly, and the change only seemed to affect Danny. He was now standing in the bath, his weight on his feet, staring down into a black pit which was covered with a transparent, cross-hatched membrane. Impossible though it was, the bathwater did not run out into the chasm but, in defiance of all the rules Danny had ever learned, maintained its position in the bath – now a vertical column, enclosed on three sides and open on the other.

Danny knew he was going to fall out of the bath and into that pit which seemed to have a gravity force of its own directed solely at him. He pushed his arms hard against the side of the bath to wedge himself in, but he was now standing in the same position in which he had been lying – knees bowed, feet too far back, shoulders hunched forward against the top of the bath. He was off balance and his centre of gravity was too far forward to stay where he was for long. The water lapped gently around his body as he tried to maintain his position and shuffle his feet forward for more stability. The craziness of the angle he had suddenly been tilted to and the strong force sucking him towards that black hole made his aeroplane vertigo pop out from its hiding place in his mind. Danny's head spun like a top.

He knew he was falling even before his body had moved an inch and he knew with crystal clarity that if . . . no . . . *when* he let himself fall into that dark place, he would never be able to get back again.

Falling.

The huge depth yawned beneath him.

Falling, Danny! HOLD ON!

All his senses screamed at him that he was already tumbling weightless into the void and yet the warm bathwater still lapped at his sides.

His toes were at the rim of the bath now, but he was still tilted too far forwards to save himself. He was dimly aware that the scar on his right cheekbone was throbbing in time with his racing heart.

Don't fall! Oh, Joey, don't leave me! His arms ached and his left calf muscle knotted in an excruciating cramp. He tried to shout for Suzie and his voice said, 'Sahhh!' in a tiny, hardly audible sigh.

Too late! It's too late and you're falling in! his mind screamed as his bottom pulled away from the warm enamel of the bath. Water ran off him, maintaining its level – *vertical* – position as his hips broke its surface. Danny fought to hold his hips back, but his body was aching terribly and vertigo had hold of the joystick and was flinging it carelessly back and forth so that he was losing his grip on which attitude he was in.

Falling in!

Danny shut his eyes again but his dizziness worsened and his senses assured him that he was now cartwheeling through space. When he looked again, the distance between the transparent surface of the tiles and the black beneath was immeasurable. Everlasting night gaped beneath him, before him and beside him. Everlasting night which would swallow him up and hold him forever.

The worst daymare you ever had! a tiny voice twittered in the back of his mind and for a moment Danny thought it was the voice of Joey himself.

His muscles were screaming. Danny bit his lips until he could taste blood, but if it was a daymare it wasn't going away.

Danny suddenly realised he was going to die. It was death down there at his feet pulling him towards it. He had cheated it once before and it had taken all this time for it to realise. Now it *had* realised and it was coming to claim him. His brother and Suzie had been right to worry about him.

Danny's muscles began to give up the fight and he shimmied an inch forward, his head seemingly engulfed in that pit already. The scar on his face where the bullet had entered throbbed hard and an incredibly loud buzzing filled his ears. Somewhere in the distance huge brass gongs were being sounded.

Danny dragged his eyes away from the tiles, saw more tiles, equally transparent, equally deep. The bathroom was a huge chasm and every way was downwards. This was it. This was the end of good old Danny, the guy who cheated death.

The sound in his ears increased in pitch until it was a high, musical scream. His whole being began to vibrate in sympathy with it, then to be swamped by it. Finally it tore at him, shredding him and reducing him until he no longer seemed to exist. Then it stopped.

Danny stepped limply out of the water and fell. He fell at great speed for a very long time. Everything he knew was gone. The bathroom and his world had vanished. His eyes were open but there was nothing to see but total darkness in every direction; he could not even see his own body. His mouth was open but no sound would come from it although he was screaming in terror. There was no sound; no noise of air whistling past him, no screaming vibration, not even the sound of his own breathing or his blood rushing through his veins. All that existed was the sensation of dropping like a stone and the horrific feeling of impending impact.

The falling seemed to go on forever.

Just when Danny began to think that his own personal hell was to fall perpetually and agonise over the impact that must surely follow, he became aware that the vacuum was not entirely empty. This sensation lasted only for a moment and the information came to him via a different route from the one that knowledge usually took – he didn't know *how* he knew, he just *knew*.

There was something else in the void besides him. It was nothing he could put a name to and it was too distant and confused for him to get anything other than a brief mental glimpse of its presence. He sensed it for an instant, then it vanished; went to where everything else had gone.

Joey! he thought, *Joey, come back!*

Then there was just the death, just the silent falling and waiting for the impact that would finish it and merge him with the universe.

The impact never came.

7

Danny was standing by the roadside as if he had always been there. There was a smell of exhaust fumes in his nostrils as if a car running on full choke had just passed. The sun was shining, although large cumulus clouds drifted in front of it from time to time driving huge lazy shadows across the scene. Danny could hear again. He could see, taste and feel again. He had not bitten the inside of his mouth or his lips. He was dry, dressed in jeans and denim shirt and wearing his old Adidas trainers. He was also shocked and dismayed, and for a moment, uncertain where he was. The last problem was the easiest to resolve.

He was standing at the side of the A30 London road on the edge of The Hatch pub's car park. It was an area he knew well. The A30 ran from Basingstoke to Hook and beyond, passing the southern end of Old Basing at the pub which faced Hatch Lane from the opposite side of the A30. Hatch Lane led directly into the village of Old Basing where he used to live – and where his parents still did.

The big garage and filling station that stood on the corner of Hatch Lane and the A30 was closed. Its three petrol pumps stood guard on the deserted concrete forecourt. A Jaguar and a Daimler shone darkly through the plate glass window of the attached showroom, orange stick-on numbers in their windscreens asking impossible prices. Danny got the distinct impression that it was Sunday – probably because the normally busy road was empty. He turned round and looked at The Hatch behind him. There was a rusty Ford Cortina outside but the pub was closed too. Judging from the long shadows and the position of the sun in the sky, it was sometime during the afternoon.

Danny didn't know what he was doing here, or how he got here.

What the fuck has happened now? he asked himself. He remembered being in the bath and feeling dizzy. . .

And then what happened? he asked himself, feeling an odd variety of numb dread; not in his stomach, but somehow in the palms of his hands. His hands had that aching loose-butterfly feeling.

You blacked out again, he assured himself, flexing his fingers. *Like you did that time you got the electric shock*. But he was certain he hadn't received another shock, certain that he'd been in the bath.

'Nothing is wrong,' he said aloud and his voice sounded flat and scared in the silence.

Then why does everything seem so bright? a discontented part of his mind challenged.

Danny looked around him again and conceded that everything *was* abnormally bright. The colours of the trees seemed have been boosted – the leaves almost *shone* and the trunks were brighter. The tired old paint on the garage looked garish and the grey-black tarmac of the road gleamed darkly. The clouds were whiter, the shadows clearer. Everything seemed bright and fragile as though lit by some invisible internal light source. Danny fleetingly thought of the way the lamps in his house sometimes shone with an extra brilliance for a few moments before they blew, then leapt to the conclusion that *he* might be undergoing a similar period of increased luminescence before finally snapping out forever.

What happened in the bathroom yesterday? Why can't I remember anything after that?

Danny's numb dread was creeping up the insides of his arms now. Something awful had happened in the bathroom. He thought he remembered falling into the mirrored tiles. After that there was a blank. It had to be after two-thirty now and since he'd been in the bath about five in the afternoon it meant a gap of getting on for twenty-two hours. Anything could have happened in that blank space. The question was, what might have happened to have brought him to this particular spot? Had he been walking to Basing to see his parents? This didn't seem likely – it was the long way round from his house. And where was Suzie?

Maybe you murdered her! he thought. It was supposed to have been a jolly quip to himself but, having thought it, he treated it seriously.

'For Christ's sake, Danny, you haven't killed Suzie!' he said in angry admonishment, but he looked for traces of blood on his clothing anyway. There were none.

The numb panic reached out from his shoulders, clasped its cold hands across his heart and began to send down tendrils to his stomach. The bullet scar on his face pulsed once.

'There's nothing wrong,' he assured himself. 'I just had a little blackout–' He paused and swamped the very reasonable voice that informed him twenty-two hours amounted to something much more than a 'little blackout' '– and I've done nothing nasty while I was K.O.ed. The best thing to do is walk home and take it from there. Okay?'

He answered himself that going home was indeed a very good idea because he was frightened, he didn't like this one little bit, and he had the distinct feeling that something nasty was going to happen if he stayed here for very much longer.

Ignoring the urgent ache that was now caressing his guts and testicles, Danny started to walk up the hill towards Basingstoke. He was not delighted to discover he could go no further than the edge of The Hatch car park – a distance of about fifty yards. There was no wall barring his way, no invisible force field – it was simply that when he reached a certain spot the ground under his feet took no further notice of his steps. He could keep walking but he didn't go anywhere.

Danny was still wondering about this dream-like state of things when a lorry rolled down Hatch Lane towards him and the A30 junction. It was a big, dusty petrol tanker that took up two-thirds of the width of Hatch Lane. The windscreen was grimy around the edges where the wipers couldn't reach and the radiator grille was mottled with the blood and crushed bodies of thousands of tiny flies. This tanker had done some high speed cruising since it last saw a steam cleaner. It was being driven by a muscular black man whose bare right arm was resting on the window ledge while his fingers beat the side of the door in time to a tune he was apparently listening to. As the tanker drew closer Danny could see that the man was not only wearing headphones and singing, but that his whole body was movin' to the groovin'. Danny had no idea how the lorry had come to be here on a Sunday, but here it was, large as life and belching blue fumes, its driver in a world of his own.

In spite of the noise from the petrol tanker, Danny was still able to hear a car approaching. He looked up the A30 towards Hook in the direction the noise was coming from. It was hidden from view by a long bend in the dual carriageway which changed to single lane just before the pub, but Danny expected it to arrive very shortly.

Just in time, in fact, to collide with the petrol tanker, his inner voice whispered. *You're here to watch people die!*

The car was a yellow Ford Escort Mexico and its driver had the pedal pressed firmly to the metal. The car was doing eighty, maybe more. It listed badly and shimmied as it took the bend, and Danny suddenly thought it wasn't going to make it. It would surely end up either in the field on the far side of the pub or actually inside the pub itself.

A flash of perfect intuition told Danny everything he needed to know about the occupants of the racing Mexico – and more. There was a nineteen-year-old man driving the car. His name was Dennis Flanders: 'as in the Poppy Fields' he was fond of telling people. Dennis Flanders (who carried the hod and mixed the muck for three bricklayers) was also fond of telling people he worked as a 'construction engineer'. Dennis liked to drink it up – or get seshed – on Friday nights with his mates in the Running Horse in Peckham. Dennis had boxed a bit as a kid but this hadn't prevented his nose being broken in a brawl outside a disco on his stag night six months ago. His right nostril – like Danny's own – remained blocked most of the time and would bleed at the drop of a hat. Dennis, who had done the right thing by his pregnant girl, would sometimes (usually when seshed) tell his drinking buddies that if there was such as thing as love (and he wasn't certain), then he was in it.

Dennis' wife was called Sara (nee Epstein). Sara, who was eighteen, had met her husband during one of his Friday-night sessions and lost her virginity and fallen pregnant that same evening, in the Escort Mexico they were now travelling in. Sara, who worried about some of the comments Dennis' family had made about her distant Jewish origins (and the least of these was that they called her Rachel to her face), had a mole on her chin that she thought was turning malignant. It wasn't, Danny knew, but that was the least of her problems now. Their two-month-old son – James, after Dennis' father – had his mother's blue eyes and his father's generous mouth. James was an excellent sleeper and was currently deeply engaged in the business at which he excelled. He slept in a child chair which was fixed to the car's rear seat. He was not strapped in.

Danny knew all of this instantly. He knew their faces as if he had looked at them each day of his life and he could smell the car's interior; plastic and rubber, damp carpets, extinguished cigarettes and the distinctive odour of baby.

He glanced back at the petrol tanker, could smell the cab, the diesel fumes, the driver's sweat and the harsh odour of recently smoked cannabis. The driver was called Michael White and the tune that was making him groove was James Brown's *Sex Machine*. In Michael White's ears, the Godfather of Soul was asking if he could '*take it to the bridge*'. Michael was nodding his assent and yelling 'Yeah!'

Then Michael's foot hit the brake to slow for the junction. In the next second Danny saw his expression change from bliss to disbelief to terror, and knew why. He could feel the driver's right foot as though it were his own. There was no resistance at the brake pedal. It sailed all the way down to the floor and nothing happened.

Fuckin' brakes failed! Danny and Michael thought in unison.

Neither Danny nor the driver knew how or why this had happened, but unlike Michael, Danny did know what the consequences would be. In his position anyone could have added up the parts and imagined the forthcoming event, but Danny was going to have to view the scene in full-blown colour. This particularly unsavoury snippet of knowledge seemed to come from deep within him, aching its way out through his bones and flesh. He had plenty of time to take it all in as the Ford drew inexorably nearer, its passengers and driver blissfully unaware of their forthcoming demise.

Michael White's right arm shot back into the cab from its relaxed position on the window ledge and took the steering wheel while he fought with the gearbox, trying to slow the vehicle that way. He dropped a gear and the big diesel screamed and belched blue smoke, but hardly slowed at all.

The Escort came on at the same speed, still grounding its nearside suspension as it rounded the bend. Danny intuited the car's bald rear tyre and the areas of rust at several of its critical points and knew that Dennis had been driving it illegally since the M.O.T. certificate expired eighteen months ago. Sara had her right hand on Dennis' knee and was gently touching her suspect mole with her left hand index finger. She was worrying about her grandmother in Southampton who had been hospitalised after a slight stroke and hoped that Gran's first view of baby James would cheer her up.

The lorry driver's terrified face was clearly visible now, and Danny watched in horror as the man desperately selected a lower gear than the tanker wanted to take. The gearbox ground and squealed in protest as its steel insides tried to mesh. Michael White's face twisted into a savage, sweating grimace as he worked frantically at the grating gears. He glanced up, mouthed the words 'Oh, my Christ!' and Danny knew that he'd seen the approaching car. Inside the lorry, Michael White yanked on the handbrake. Wheels bit the ground and screamed, blue smoke flew, but the tanker wasn't going to stop.

In total desperation Danny ran into the road and tried to flag the car down, jumping and screaming and waving his arms high in the air. But, as he already knew, he was a mere witness. He did not exist for the players in this drama. Dennis didn't see him. The car's course didn't alter and it didn't slow down.

Danny got out of the road realising that he had no power to intervene whatsoever. His presence apparently meant nothing. He cursed himself for not being able to do anything, cursed God for letting something like this happen and for making him watch it, and cursed whatever else might be doing this to him if it wasn't God's work.

The tanker's front wheel crossed the white line marking the junction and Michael White hit the air horns. They blasted out a warning bellow as the tanker came out across the road.

Then, just as Danny knew he would, the driver made the fatal mistake. Instead of accelerating across the road and driving the tanker into the pub's side turning, which, while it might have damaged the lorry, would have saved everyone, Michael White swung the wheels hard left, trying to bring the lorry round sharply and stay in his own lane. The cab flew round, but the huge petrol tank had too much weight and momentum to follow. It maintained its original course across the road, jack-knifing the cab so that it angled back against the tank. The cab's screaming tyres were ripped sideways across the tarmac and left six thick black trails of smoking rubber.

Danny saw the faces of the man and his wife as they realised their path was being blocked, there was going to be no way round and that they were not going to be able to stop. Their mouths opened in unison, Dennis shouting and Sara screaming. Sara raised her hands as if to ward off the tanker. The front of the car dipped as Dennis stood on the brakes, but they were too close, moving too fast and the tyres were too bald to avoid collision. Stinking blue rubber smoke rose as the Mexico laid its own black tracks.

The tanker slewed out across their carriageway and came to a halt, the cab bent back on the tanker and directly facing the oncoming car. Michael White, his headphones still clamped around his ears and James Brown still shouting in them, threw the door open and started to get out.

'*JUMP!*' Danny shouted. 'JUMP AND ROLL AWAY!'

There were only two or three seconds for him to do it, but if he moved quickly he would be saved. Perhaps it didn't have to end in four deaths after all.

'QUICK!' Danny screamed. 'GET OUT!' His voice sounded high-pitched and strange in his ears.

But instead of leaping from the cab, Michael White stood there in his overalls and headphones looking at the car hammering towards him.

'JUMP!' Danny screamed wondering how everything was happening so slowly. Time seemed to have decelerated to the point of stalling completely. He seemed to have been watching and screaming for an eternity but only a tiny fraction of a second had passed.

In what seemed to Danny to be achingly slow motion, the tanker driver looked down at the ground, leaned forward and crouched as if to jump. While he was doing this, the door that he had thrown open – in reality probably only a second ago – swung back on him. Michael White caught it, threw it aside and steadied himself, glancing once again at the approaching car.

There was no chance for him now. The Escort Mexico, its bald tyres locked, had skewed around to the right and was sliding towards the huge silver trailer tank. Nothing was going to prevent this – nothing Danny could do or say, anyway.

He watched until the car was only inches away from what must have been thousands of gallons of highly flammable four star, then, able to stand it no more, he shut his eyes.

There was no collision, no sound of impact and wrenching metal, no explosion. The moment he closed his eyes everything ceased. Danny kept his eyes closed for long enough to exhume a memory that had been deeply buried in the unused recesses of his mind. It burst through the soil of his conscious mind like a grand cinema organ rising from the depths of an orchestra pit. The memory had not corroded and rotted away in that dark place as he'd hoped it would when he purposefully back-filled the hole he'd dug for it all those years ago. It arose pristine, sparkling and vivid. The memory was of the hallucination he'd had years ago while he was in hospital. Of the man raping, killing and then trying to decapitate the woman in that quiet dawn field. Danny had closed his eyes then and the scene had simply paused until he opened them again. He resolved to keep his eyes shut forever, if that was the only way he could prevent the accident. As long as he kept them closed, those people would stay frozen in that moment before the collision.

Then he wondered why he was worrying. If this was simply another hallucination, there was no need for concern.

In fact, Danny boy, you may still be at home sitting in the bath. Your last conscious memory may have happened not twenty-two hours ago, but a few minutes ago. You may be still in the bath and hallucinating. When you open your eyes again, you might be back in the bathroom.

But Danny didn't risk it. He hadn't been back in his hospital bed when he opened his eyes during that other episode, and whether the murder, and this crash, were hallucinations or not, he didn't want to see it happen.

He realised then that he'd never truly believed those experiences he'd suffered in hospital *were* just hallucinations. The ghosts and the replays of his mum and dad's visits were real. Deep in his heart he had always known they were scenes from events that had really happened or that would really happen. That was why he'd buried them so deeply and forgotten them so readily. That was why he hadn't mentioned them to anyone, not even his brother or Suzie.

In that moment of realisation Danny came face to face for the first time with his destiny. He suddenly knew what his whole life had been leading up to and he knew what he had become. He was a ghost, a phantom, a recording demon with the tape rolling. A silent observer of the crimes of nature, or the witness of a metaphysical being's displeasure. This was how it was and this was how it would continue from this moment on.

During that moment, Danny wished he was dead.

He knew for sure that the woman really had been raped and murdered in that field and that his unformed suspicions were correct all along.

He wondered if what he was now being privileged to see was something which was happening at this moment, or if he was seeing the shape of things to come. Either way, he hated it.

Danny waited. If he really was still at home in the bath, Suzie would soon be bringing in the cup of tea she'd promised to make. She would shake his motionless body and bring him back to reality and then he wouldn't have to watch the finale of this cine film of death.

I will not open my eyes! he told himself.

He began to sway back and forth slightly on his feet as his balance rebelled against the darkness and tried to make him open his eyes.

I will not!

Waves of dizzieness rolled over him. Danny held firm. He would keep his eyes closed for as long as that scene was frozen out there, waiting for him.

Why me? he asked. *Please God, why me? Why is it* my *scene? Why do I have to see it? What can I do about it if you choose to end four lives in such a violent way? Why are you forcing me to watch? I will not look. I will not!*

He remembered walking into Thirwall & Allen for the first time, remembered how he wanted to make gadgets to spy on people. Was this how you were paid out for your childish sins? What kind of a warped God would play a trick like that? Danny asked Him and received the reply he expected. Silence.

As he fought the waves of giddiness, Danny's time scale changed. He gritted his teeth and kept his eyes firmly closed for what must have been hours, hearing nothing, smelling nothing and feeling nothing. He existed in a total and absolute vacuum. If he was not dead he might as well have been. If the passing time had been real, Suzie should have saved him ages ago.

Help me, Suzie! he thought. *I'm falling over.*

Danny lost his balance, staggered to the left, stumbled – and his eyes opened.

The car smashed into the petrol tanker. Its wheels were locked and still leaving tracks, but in spite of this it was still moving at over fifty miles an hour. The front crumpled against one of the tanker's low cross members. As the bonnet concertinaed, the windscreen exploded into millions of tiny glittering fragments, and Sara flew through it as the back end of the car lifted. Her head was flung against the side of the big silver tank and smashed like a dropped egg. Blood, brown hair and grey-white brains smeared up the side of the trailer and Sara's decapitated body cartwheeled upwards into the mess and hung inverted against the tanker for what seemed like an age. The back end of the ruined car flew up after her, reaching the vertical, passing it and impacting the side of the tanker against her body. Sara's arm came off and flew through the air waving crazily. The car shot up the side of the tanker, in a shower of debris and sparks and flew into the air.

Danny saw a rent in the shell of the tanker where the car had hit Sara's remains. Petrol poured out in freshets, its characteristic acrid smell filling the air.

Michael White the lorry driver was on the ground amongst the flesh and blood and leaking petrol. The force of the impact had knocked him back through the cab and out of the other side. He was bleeding badly from the head, but was still conscious. One of his arms was broken and did strange twists and bends as he struggled to get to his feet. The Escort Mexico had passed its zenith and was falling now, coming back down nose first. Dennis Flanders was half out of the open windscreen, his head flapping loose on his severed neck. Half his face was gone. There was no sign of the baby.

Michael White was on his feet and running and the car was still a second from hitting the ground when the petrol detonated. A long, low roar filled the air and shook the ground. Danny saw Michael burst and vanish in vaporous pieces. There was no battered car anymore, no tanker of petrol. Only the lorry's cab and the chassis remained. The rest of the steelwork was airborne now along with several hundred pounds of minced, charred meat and bone, all powered by thousands of gallons of exploding petrol.

The explosion of searing heat and fire and the shockwave passed through Danny as if he wasn't there. It went on for a long time and gave him ample opportunity to identify various piece of what had been four human beings only seconds before. Danny stood powerless as the explosion ripped up and threw fragments of meat and bone through him. Each time he closed his eyes the scenario waited for him. He was forced to see it all, right to the very end.

When it was over he glanced down and saw a small blackened thing a yard away from him. He wasn't sure what it was, but it looked as if it were a human part. It might have been one of the baby's feet.

Danny screamed.

8

'Danny! *Danny!* What's wrong?' The words cut into him like knives being thrust through from another universe. Danny's whole world spun, as though he had been suddenly lifted off his feet and violently twisted around by some gigantic whirlwind. The reality of the accident shattered into millions of sharp, black fragments as if he had been watching the scene played out on a huge mirror at which someone had flung a brick. That shrill voice heaved him back through the vast black vacuum which was now all that remained of the terrible crash.

'*Danneee!*'

He whirled back through that awful place for what seemed like hours, conscious of movement but not of direction. There *was* no direction there, no up or down or left or right, but still he moved, drawn by the voice calling his name and some irresistible gravity force which seemed to be forcing him back into himself, making him become denser, heavier somehow.

That other presence was in the void again, nearer to him this time and trying to locate him. It reached out slender tendrils towards him, probing the vast darkness for him. Danny knew what it was. *Joey!* he thought crazily. *Joey, come back! Don't go to Africa, Joey!*

'Danny, what's wrong?'

He dimly recognised the voice. It was someone he knew, but she was calling him Danny. *Why not Joey?* he thought. *Why doesn't she call me Joey?*

Then there was a terrible feeling of constriction. The voice and the hands and the gravity were forcing him into a place which was far too small for him.

I'll die if I go in there! he thought, and resisted.

'What's wrong? You're shaking!'

Oh, Christ! Don't make me go in there, I won't fit! Danny thought. The gravity pressed his stomach into the constriction. It was cold and clammy and heavy in there and there wasn't enough room. *Joey!* he called as the clammy thing compressed his chest and sucked it in. *Help me!* His legs were pulled in to that tiny prison, his arms were forced into tubes and his head was drawn down into something tight and fizzling and bright. The light hurt his eyes.

Hands were on him, holding his shoulders. Warm hands. He could feel again.

'Danny, wake up!'

'Joey!' he moaned. 'I'm Joey! Why don't you know that? I've always been Joey. Where's Danny?'

His eyes popped open and for a second he didn't know where he was or who the woman was whose fingers were grinding into his shoulders. Then something slipped away from him like a cold, smooth knife blade being withdrawn from his brain. It didn't hurt and all he felt was relief. *I'm back in my body*, he thought. It felt like a wet blanket – like, in fact, the vessel of clay his Sunday School teacher had spoken of.

Danny was surprised to find that the woman shaking him was Suzie and equally surprised that he was in the bath at home. Almost no time could have passed because the water was still as hot as it was before and there was a mug of steaming tea on the tap end of the bath. Danny's head hurt. There were too many things to think about and none of the questions that were teeming through his head seemed to have answers.

Suzie was pale faced. 'Thank Christ for that,' she said, relieved. 'I thought something horrible had happened to you.'

'What?' he asked, still fighting with his rebelling mind. He was no longer certain that he had seen what he thought he had.

'You were asleep or in a trance or something,' she said. 'When I came in you were transfixed, staring at those tiles. You seemed to be asleep but your eyes were open. You didn't hear me when I spoke to you, and your face kept getting all screwed up as if you were frightened or something. You kept saying you were Joey and asking where Danny was. Are you sure you're all right?'

'Yes,' he said, 'I'm all right now.' He explained about the wakemares he'd had when he was a child and was careful to add that they'd started long before he got shot. He told Suzie that he thought he'd had one of these and that he couldn't remember what happened in it. This thrown together explanation seemed to satisfy her.

'Who is Joey?' She finally asked.

'No one,' he replied. The confusion he had felt about his identity seemed to crumble and dissolve. The vivid vision of the accident swept back and pushed it aside. It was entirely due to his disorientation and was insignificant; it meant nothing. How could anyone imagine they were a budgie?

'It must be someone,' Suzie insisted.

'Joey used to be my budgie when I was a kid. He flew away. My mum let him out of the cage and one of the lounge windows was open. I s'pose I was thinking of him or something.'

Danny stood up and got out of the bath, catching a glimpse of himself in the mirror. He was ashen faced and looked different somehow. His posture seemed to have changed, to have become weighed down. He knew nothing would ever be the same again.

9

Danny didn't confess until later that evening when his motormouth gave into to Suzie's insistent questioning why he was so withdrawn. He had sunk three stiff scotches between tea time and nine-thirty and now he was ready to talk.

It took over an hour to explain gently to Suzie what had happened. He told her his history in hospital and the things that had happened after he was shot. He left nothing out.

Suzie listened carefully and attentively, but somewhere in there her face took on a hardened look and he knew she either didn't believe him or didn't want to.

When Danny fell silent, she thought for a time and then said, 'Look, it just isn't possible for you to have seen a vision, or whatever you want to call it. Things like that don't happen in real life.' She shook her head for emphasis. 'Those things only happen in books or on telly. Everyone knows they don't *really* happen. They don't. Honestly. People just don't have visions.'

'What do you suppose it was then?' he asked, ready to believe anything she told him. Any explanation was better than the one he had for the events. He was as aware as she that things like that didn't happen in real life.

Suzie looked thoughtful, shook her head and sighed. 'Perhaps that splinter of bone in your brain has moved,' she said heavily. 'That's the only explanation *I* can think of. Perhaps you'd better contact your doctor and tell him.'

The longer they talked, the less real the vision seemed and Danny began to think that Suzie was right. He promised her that he would contact the doctor on Monday, just to be sure. She seemed relieved and satisfied with this, tying in today's hallucinations with the earlier ones and saying it proved her theory that the splinter of bone had moved.

They were lying in bed in the dark that evening, having just made love and now listening to the sound of the 23.22 train departing for Waterloo, when he reached out, took Suzie's hand and said to her, 'Since all this stuff is being caused by my war wound playing me up, and not by my suddenly being able to see into the future, you won't mind if we go down to The Hatch tomorrow afternoon and see if anything happens, will you?'

There was a long silence. 'I don't think we ought to,' Suzie said finally.

'Why not?'

'Because I don't.' There was a quality in her voice he'd never heard before. It took him a while to identify it. It was fear.

'But there can't be anything to worry about, can there?'

She withdrew her hand and moved away from him. 'No,' she said, but not in agreement. Her voice was small and petulant and seemed to be coming from a long way away.

'So what about it? It seemed like a Sunday in my hallucination, it's Sunday tomorrow . . . what better way is there of proving me wrong?'

'Going to the doctor would be a better way,' she said sullenly.

Leave it alone, Danny told himself, knowing that he was pressing on a raw nerve. But once again, his mouth spoke his private thoughts.

'I know what it is. You're worried in case I've gone over the edge, and you think that going down there will bolster my fantasies. Crack me up even further.'

Suzie suddenly sat up. 'You're not cracked up!' she said forcefully. 'And there's nothing wrong with you that taking it a little easier wouldn't fix. It's probably just overwork.' She didn't sound very sure of herself now.

Danny lay there in the dark wondering what was going on. During that hallucination, or whatever it was, he was certain that he knew all the reasons for it. He had known without doubt that being shot had changed him in some way so he was no longer a normal person, but now he wasn't so sure. Maybe Suzie was right. Maybe it was just overwork, or paint fumes or something else that had caused the vision. He hoped Suzie was right because he didn't want to be different, didn't want his life to change. He was happy as he was.

After a while he heard her breathing become uneven. He reached over and touched her face. It was wet with tears.

'What's wrong?' he asked gently.

'I d-don't want you to have v-visions,' She sobbed. 'I don't want anything to h-happen to you. I don't wuh-want that bit of bone to have muh-moved in your brain. I just want you to be ordinary and to love me.'

Danny took her in his arms and held her, rocking her gently from side to side. 'I *do* love you,' he promised. 'And you needn't worry, I feel fine now. I'll make an appointment with the doctor on Monday and get checked out just to be sure, but I think you'll find I'm all right. And anyway, you said that it wasn't possible for people to have visions. It doesn't happen. It's against all the laws of physics isn't it?'

'In the d-daytime,' she said sadly, 'it can't be p-possible. There's nuh-no such things as visions of the future in the daytime. But at night the laws of physics duh-don't seem to be so powerful and I can imagine it h-happening. Tell me it isn't true! Tell me you're going to be all right.'

A cold shiver ran down his back. 'People can't have visions, and I'm going to be all right, and I love you to death,' he said.

'Don't go to The huh-Hatch tomorrow. Please,' she said tearfully.

'Why not?'

'Because something will huh-happen to you if you do. I d-don't want anything to happen to you, Danny. I love you and I don't want to l-lose you. You frighten me sometimes. I'm scared when you get tired and start to limp. I'm scared when your nose starts to bleed that it won't ever stop. It hurts me to see you like that. When I found you in the bathroom today, I thought you were going to die and I was terrified. I think something horrible will happen to you if you go to The huh-Hatch and I don't want it to. You're mine and I don't want anybody or anything to take you away from me. I love you, Danny, and I don't want you to duh-duh-die!'

'Shh!' he whispered. 'It's okay. I'm not going to die and I'm not going to leave you. I promise I won't go,' he assured her, slipping his arm beneath her head and pulling her over to him so he could kiss her wet face.

'Nothing would have happened anyway. It was just a wakemare, just a dream.'

10

But in spite of his promise to Suzie, he did go to The Hatch.

Things looked very different the following morning. It was a clear, warm day and thoughts of visions and death were the farthest thing from his mind. They stayed in bed late and then sat in the spring sunshine in the back garden. Suzie seemed to have stopped worrying about him turning into some sort of sideshow freak and in the bright garden with the bees buzzing and flowers beginning to bloom, yesterday's events seemed silly and improbable.

But Danny needed to be sure.

It was easily done. After lunch he told Suzie he was going to the garage to get petrol and pump up the car tyres. One of them had a slow puncture and needed constant blasts from the airline to keep it anywhere near working pressure.

'Okay,' she said. She showed no emotion, but there was a quality in her eyes which showed hurt and betrayal. She knew exactly where he was going and what he was going to do. 'Don't be long, will you?' she called after him as he walked up the garden path, her voice tremulous.

'Back in a jiffy!' he quipped, turning and seeing her white face watching him. He could feel her inward pleading from yards away. The turmoil of mixed emotions she felt shone from her like a beacon. Danny received them almost telepathically and experienced her love and fear, her puzzlement, the aching hurt she was feeling; the anger and her terrible concern.

He wanted to quit his stupid plan then, wanted to run to her and hold her and return her love – but he *had* to know if what he had predicted was going to happen. He was compelled. For the first time since that Christmas, years ago, Danny closed himself off from her. He felt her emotions and let them wash over him, ignoring them, letting them pass and being careful not to return anything. He would not allow himself to be affected by her feelings.

'See you later,' he said, biting his trembling bottom lip.

Danny watched the tears well up in her eyes and felt like the biggest shitheel in the northern hemisphere. Standing there and watching Suzie silently begin to cry, he hated himself more than he had ever hated anyone in his life.

But he turned and walked away.

Chapter Five
Ten-up

1

Danny's insides felt dry and twisted as he drove to the filling station, as if his stomach and intestines were packed with twigs. *I am going to pump the tyres up*, he told himself. *I wasn't lying at all. I'm going to pump up the tyres and put petrol in the tank just like I said I would. And I'm not going to be long either!*

But he knew as well as Suzie that the deception concerned what he intended to do *after* visiting the garage. Danny repeatedly tried to justify this by assuring himself that he hadn't actually *told* a lie, but it just wouldn't wash. He had lied by omission; by being economical with the truth. And he had done this bare-faced, even though he was fully aware that Suzie was able to spot even the whitest lies at a hundred yards. He had hurt her badly and no amount of clever mental juggling of the facts was going to allow him to writhe his way off the hook of guilt he had impaled himself upon.

Danny drove the old Humber Sceptre all the way across town to Davy's Texaco garage on the Worthing Road roundabout, down by the fire station. It had the best car wash and there was always a queue of cars waiting to use it. He would tell Suzie that he'd waited for half an hour and given up hope of ever getting the car clean. If he only filled the tank and pumped the leaky tyre, that would give him twenty minutes to himself during which he could – if he drove fast enough – get to The Hatch by the time the accident was due to take place and. . .

And what, *Danny*? *What are you going to do there?*

. . . see what happened.

He drove into the filling station, realising for the first time exactly why the compulsion to go down to The Hatch had been so strong. Crazy as it sounded – and in Danny's mind it sounded very crazy indeed; almost rubber room and straight-jacket crazy, in fact – he intended to prevent the accident happening.

Although you don't believe that what you saw was a glimpse of the future? Although you think it was just a hallucination? And then there's the fact that even if it wasn't, there's no guarantee that it's due to happen on this particular Sunday and not next week or the week or month or year after?

'Yes,' Danny said, getting out of the car by the air line and noting, with an odd sense of satisfaction, that there was a nine-car queue for the car wash.

The car's pancake-like back tyre had a pressure of nine p.s.i. Danny blew it up to the required twenty-seven and inspected the tread. He knew what trouble you could get into driving on worn tyres. This thought struck him as being both padded cell crazy and hilarious at the same moment and he found himself cackling in an almost hysterical way. He bit off the laughter and raised his head, checking the forecourt in case anyone happened to be looking at him.

He drove the Sceptre to the pumps and filled it with four-star, half hypnotised by the flickering of the price indicator as it rose and rose.

'It wasn't my imagination,' he whispered, nodding to himself. 'And I didn't hallucinate it. I *did* have a vision, and it was a vision of reality. I saw into the future and I know what's going to happen and I can *alter* it.'

Petrol shot back from the full tank and Danny danced aside, getting his trainers away from it. As the pump's nozzle finally clicked out, stopping the flow, the sharp oily petrol smell hit Danny's nose, reminding him of the tanker with its split side. *Almost got on my shoes*, Danny thought, and with a sudden cold shock, realised that he was wearing his *Adidas* trainers – the old ones that he hardly ever wore any more. The ones he had been wearing in his vision. He had not put them on because of the vision – in fact, he'd forgotten until now that he'd been wearing them during it – but simply because they were the first shoes he'd seen this morning when he got up.

Shaking his head, and with a bubble of bright fear growing inside the vacuum of his stomach, Danny replaced the filler cap and went to pay for the petrol.

2

The roads were almost empty and the journey round the ring road and down the A30 to The Hatch took him less than five minutes. Danny turned right at the pub and drove the Sceptre into the parking area behind the hedge which yesterday had marked the limit of his movement. He got out of the car and checked his watch. It was almost three o'clock. Not bothering to lock the car, Danny hurried over to the pub. A glance through the window confirmed that it was closed and empty. The staff were probably upstairs by now, enjoying their Sunday lunch. Danny walked along the parking spaces at the front of the pub, parallel to the A30, passing the Ford Cortina he'd seen in yesterday's vision, and looked in the pub's beer garden in case there was anyone relaxing in the sunshine around there. He wasn't sure how he intended to explain things to them – if they were there – but he'd made up his mind to send them up Hatch Lane to try to flag down the petrol tanker before it reached the road while he ran up the A30 to warn Dennis and Sara in the Escort Mexico which currently had to be speeding through Hartley Wintney about ten miles further up the road. But the problem of what to say turned out to be academic; there were no stragglers in the garden finishing off pints they'd bought just before closing time. Neither was there any hope of enlisting the help of a passing motorist. The A30 was as empty as the pub.

Danny shook his head and glanced up at the clouds scudding by, each one shadowing the brightly lit scene for a few moments. He was barely able to believe the accuracy and detail of his vision. It *had* to have been a vision – no mere hallucination could have so accurately detailed the surroundings or predicted the presence of that Ford outside the pub. Even the atmosphere was identical: oppressive and still. It seemed to Danny that something in the very matter the place was composed of was aware of what was to come and was silently and patiently waiting for the terrible thing to happen.

The bubble of fear in his stomach grew to a gnawing panic and Danny found himself wandering this way and that not knowing what he should do to try to prevent the accident. Suddenly he was overcome by a powerful inertia of the variety he had often experienced in his dreams. He needed to act and act now, but he was getting heavier and more sluggish by the moment. For a few seconds Danny was certain that there was a force resisting him, a force that resented his intrusion. It began to seem impossible even to consider acting, let alone doing something.

'Come *on!*' he yelled, his frustration boiling over. The aching urgency he felt forced one of his feet in front of the other, but he seemed to be moving like a man in a field of increased gravity. 'You've got to stop it!' he hissed, fighting the overpowering feeling of despair that was settling on him. He let his right foot fall to the ground before him and lifted the left. This one was easier to move.

Run down the road and stop the car! he decided and as he moved his legs, trying to work up a trot, his inertia began to dissipate. Gradually it dawned on him that he had not become paralysed and that he could not only jog, but run. A glimmer of hope grew and he felt a rush of adrenaline as he mentally willed himself to run faster. Suddenly he knew the disaster *could* be averted. It was not a fixed event at all and would not become fixed until the last moment.

Danny ran full pelt down the A30 towards Hook, the direction Dennis and Sara would be coming from in their bald-tyred Escort Mexico. There was nothing Danny could do to stop the tanker's brakes failing, but he might just be able to warn Dennis, might be able to make him, if not stop completely, then slow down enough to avoid the collision.

Danny ran until his legs burned and his lungs screamed for mercy, but he did not quit. The earlier he could warn Dennis, the less likely the accident was to happen. *Just a few more yards!* Danny told himself, aware that he couldn't go on much longer. *Just a few. You can stop up there where this field ends! Just get up there. It's far enough.*

When he stopped, gasping for breath, heart pounding and sweat blinding him, he had rounded the bend the Escort would take so crazily and could no longer see the junction. Even at a speed in excess of eighty miles per hour the driver should have enough time to slow down before he got there. But Danny ran some more, just to be sure.

He was barely conscious of what was happening during the following half mile; a big black ribbon of tarmac fluttered and whipped before his blurred eyes and his chest and limbs were being torn apart internally. When his body gave up on him and flung him to the ground, Danny was surprised to find that he'd got as far as Nately Scures crossroads – where he now lay in the middle of the tiny branch road. He lay on the warm tarmac for a few moments trying to force himself to move again. Both knees were out of his jeans and when the feeling returned to his legs he would discover that they were grazed and bleeding. One of his trainers was lying next to his face and the toes of his left foot ached numbly.

The car's coming soon! he told himself. *For fuck's sake, get up!*

He ached all over and the weak left side of his body felt smaller than the right. Danny sat up, forced his trainer back over his torn sock and bloody toes and got to his feet.

The Nately Scures junction intersected the dual carriageway at the bottom of a long, straight hill. Dennis and Sara's Escort Mexico would undoubtedly be coming down the hill at more than eighty, but from here at the bottom Danny would be able to see them from over a quarter of a mile away – and with any luck, they would be able to see him too.

Danny tore off his sweaty tee shirt to wave at the car and hobbled to the middle of the road, still gasping for breath.

Come on then! he urged, mopping his brow with the shirt. *Where are you?*

He stood in the road until his knees and toes began to sing and his heart rate fell to something approaching normal, but the car didn't come.

Danny held his breath and listened. Birdsong. The gentle hissing of the breeze in the leaves. The diesel chatter of a working tractor a very long way off. From somewhere nearby the sound of slow moving water. But no wind hiss of a fast car approaching.

Where is it? Danny asked himself, walking a few paces up the hill. *It should be here by now.* For a terrible moment he was certain the car had been parked up on the roadside between where he stood now and

The Hatch and that he'd run right by it in his unseeing panic. *Could that have happened? Wouldn't you have noticed it?* But he hadn't noticed *anything* since he started to run for the second time. He knew nothing about that second run other than the pain it had caused him.

'Oh God! Help me someone!' he cried, sure that Dennis and Sara were currently starting their deadly journey somewhere behind him.

You would have seen them, he assured himself. *You would have noticed the car if you'd passed it, and if they'd turned on to the A30 much closer than here they wouldn't have enough time to work up the speed you saw them doing yesterday*.

Then the smell of the inside of the Escort slapped Danny's face. Cigarettes and damp carpets and the powerful baby smell. Danny sniffed the air and smelled grass and sweat and murky water but these odours were held at a distance; the car's smell overpowered them. And yet the odour didn't seem to be coming via his nostrils, but rather from deep within the olfactory centre of his brain. His physical sense of smell had been relegated to a position of much less importance.

The vacuum in Danny's stomach boiled up through him in an inverted vee and he thought, *Here it comes!*

And the Escort Mexico crested the hill and shot down the road towards him like a missile. Danny stood tall in the centre of the road and frantically waved his shirt above his head. Deep inside his almost empty mind, Danny thanked the gift of prophecy which was going to allow him to save the lives of four people.

The car smell was stronger now and something in the air around Danny was popping, like light bulbs bursting. Hot glass seemed to be showering across his face. Danny became vaguely aware of his right foot. It was now pressing the accelerator firmly to the floor. The small sponge-padded steering wheel was hot beneath his hands. Sara opened her window and flicked out a cigarette butt and Danny saw this from two entirely different viewpoints. He was inside the car with her, listening to the angry roar of air as she wound the window down, glancing at the butt between her thumb and forefinger as she flicked it out, and from his position in the centre of the A30 he saw the tiny shower of red sparks as the butt whipped into the side of the car and burst.

Sara's hand was placed on his left leg. Danny stopped waving for a moment and glanced down at his own left leg, now uncertain of where he stopped and Dennis began.

Then he was just Danny, and up there on the hill the Escort wasn't slowing down. It was coming onwards like it was jet propelled, picking up speed instead of losing it.

Surely they must be able to see me! Danny screamed to himself. *Surely they must!* He stood his ground and waved the shirt above his head furiously but the car maintained its speed and course.

The car was closing rapidly and Danny could now hear the wind whistling through its radiator grille. He stopped waving and changed his position, making himself into a human barrier in the centre of the road, his legs spread and his arms raised and wide. 'STOP!' he screamed. 'FOR FUCK'S SAKE, DENNIS, SLOW THE CAR DOWN!'

He could see the faces of Dennis and Sara now, but they didn't seem to have seen him. Questions were cascading through the vacuum in Danny's head, flashing and fading so quickly he could not grasp the implications of them. *Can they see me? Am I really present or am I still at home in the bath? Was everything between getting into the bath and now mere hallucination? Have I gone crazy? Why aren't they taking any notice of me? Oh God, what's happening to me?*

The car just kept coming at him, closing the space between him and it very quickly indeed. He realised that if he didn't soon move, Dennis and Sara were going to run right over him. Danny waved and screamed until the car was less than fifty yards away.

Too late! Danny thought, expecting to die and relaxing.

Dennis leaned on the horn and Danny's reflexes took the reins. His leg muscles bunched and pushed and he dived towards the central reservation. The next moment he was rolling in cool, damp grass listening to the Escort's blaring horn and screaming engine as the car shot past him.

Danny was an empty, aching husk. He picked himself up, cursing himself for not being able to divert the flow of time leading up to the forthcoming accident and then cursing whatever unbreakable laws of metaphysics there were that had prevented him from interfering. What was the point of having visions of tragedy if he could do nothing to prevent it?

He pictured some unidentified cosmic being in another dimension who had arbitrarily chosen to torment him. This being would now be laughing at his pointless attempts to stop it snuffing out the lives of four people.

Listing badly to his left, Danny began to trot back towards The Hatch crossroads thinking about the shard of bone in his pineal gland and trying to relate its possible movement to what was happening to him. And while he repeatedly reached the same conclusions of madness, hallucination and coincidence, he listened carefully for the explosion he was certain would soon be coming.

But there was no noise as Danny jogged along, knees throbbing, heart heavy with despair. No explosion ripped through the afternoon quiet. There was no blast; just the singing of the birds in the trees and the sound of the gentle breeze rustling leaves. Then he heard it and froze, his heart standing still in his chest and his mind reeling until he realised it was only the thunder of horses' hooves in the next field as two of them galloped for joy.

By the time he reached the long bend around which the Escort had so crazily careered, Danny was beginning to doubt the validity of his vision. There had still been no explosion. He was relieved and utterly confused, not knowing whether he had somehow prevented it from happening or if he had been badly mistaken in his prediction. Everything seemed to be drifting away from him now; what he'd fondly imagined – *no*, believed *Danny* – was reality now seemed as vaporous as smoke. He no longer knew if *now* was a dream and his *vision* had been reality, if he were asleep or awake, if he was mad or sane.

There was no explosion! he told himself, gritting his teeth against the pain – either real or imagined – and increasing his pace. *There was* no *bang. Nothing happened. Nothing, Joey!*

As he rounded the bend The Hatch pub's car park started to come into view, foot by foot. When Danny had run far enough to be able to see the familiar shape of Dennis and Sara's Escort Mexico parked in one of the spaces, he stopped.

Danny's feeling of unreality increased. The car's boot lid was open and Dennis and Sara were there, calmly pouring themselves cups of tea from a flask.

This didn't happen! Danny complained, and hooked on to the end of this thought: *Why were they going so damned fast if they were intending to stop and drink tea? They were in a hurry. Sara's grandmother is in hospital in Southampton. Why did they stop?*

Danny walked towards them, wondering what had happened to the petrol tanker. He was unsure now if there had even been a petrol tanker.

Dennis and Sara watched him with interest as he approached, Dennis leaning on the back wing of the car and Sara now perched on the lip of the boot. When Danny was within earshot, Sara leaned over to her husband and said something in his ear. Danny thought he heard the word 'Nutter' mentioned, but was as uncertain of this as he was of everything else. They were grinning at him now.

'You the guy who was fuckin' about in the road back there?' Dennis asked angrily as Danny walked up to him.

He nodded.

'What's your fuckin' problem then, pal?' Dennis said. Sara tittered.

'Dennis,' Danny said breathlessly. 'Thank Christ you stopped.'

The man's eyes glinted suspiciously, then surprise registered on his face. He looked almost comical. He took a step away from Danny and closer to his wife. 'How d'you know my name?' he demanded.

'He saw it in the screen!' Sara said, 'Of course he did!'

Dennis shook his head. Eyes fixed on Danny, he said, 'He didn't, Sar. We took the names down the week before last.' He looked frightened, confused, and two seconds away from using his fists. 'How do you know me, you fuckin' weirdo?' he said, setting his cup down on the car and standing up straight.

Sara had become almost translucent in her sudden fear. Her day was no longer shaping up as she had planned. 'He saw it in the screen,' she insisted. 'Must have. It's the only way he *could* have known.'

Danny knew he should have shut up and gone away, but his mouth would not allow it. He *had* to say it. 'Your wife is called Sara,' he told Dennis. 'Your baby's name is James, after Dennis' father. You nearly got killed.'

'SHUT UP!' Dennis shouted. His fists clenched.

'I *know!* I know all about you. You're going to Southampton to see Sara's grandmother. . .'

'How does he know all this?' Sara screeched.

Danny shook his head. 'Doesn't matter, I just *do!* I was trying to warn you!'

'About *what?*' Dennis almost shouted.

'Get rid of him, Den, he's frightening me!' Sara whined.

Danny mentally searched for something solid to hold on to and finding nothing at all said, 'There was a lorry . . . a petrol tanker . . . it jack-knifed, stuck across the road. You were going to run into it . . . you were going too fast . . . Sara's hand was on your leg and you weren't thinking about the road, you were thinking about. . .'

Dennis shook his head, hard. He was almost as white as his wife now. 'Stop it!' he said in a small, horrified voice.

'. . . and you wouldn't have had the time to stop. It would have blown up. You would all have been killed.'

'Where was this going to happen?' Dennis said.

'Here!' Danny swept his arm around the car park and road.

Behind her husband, Sara emptied the cups and screwed the top on the flask. She put it in the boot and slammed the lid. 'C'mon, Den, let's go,' she said tearfully.

'There ain't any tanker!' Dennis said. 'There ain't now and there weren't when we got here. You're fucking mistaken, pal!'

Sara clutched her husband's sleeve. 'Dennis! Let's go! Don't start anything, he's. . .'

He's crazy! Danny's mind finished for her. *He's mad! Gaga! His brain's shot! He's gone to the dogs!*

But Dennis wasn't going to start anything by the look of him. His previously clenched fists were now open, trembling hands. Big bad Den, who liked to get seshed on a Friday night and didn't mind too much if there was a bundle at the end of the evening, was frightened of good old Danny Stafford.

There isn't any tanker! Danny's mind repeated. He stabbed a finger towards Hatch Lane. 'Nothing came out of that turning?' he asked.

Sara slipped behind her husband and got in the car. Danny heard the click of the lock as she made sure he wasn't going to get the chance to drag her out again.

Dennis was slowly – almost imperceptibly – backing away; the way a man with no gun might when confronted by a tiger. 'Not a dicky bird,' he said evenly, then decided that he'd put enough distance between them to relax. 'Anyway,' he said, more forcefully, 'what would a petrol tanker be doing out on a Sunday? For Chrissakes, man, the bleeding garage ain't even open! Look, I dunno who the fuck you think you are, and I dunno what you want or how you know us, and I don't want to know. We're going now. So just you stay there and there won't be any trouble.'

No tanker, Danny! 'You must have seen it cross the road,' he insisted.

Dennis was at his open door now, looking at Danny over the Escort's roof. 'We've been here since about half a minute after we passed you back up there. Not one motor has gone by here since then. Honest. Now, I've answered your questions, I'm going. I think it would be a very fucking good idea if you went home now and lay down. I don't think you're feelin' so well, pal!'

As he spoke, Danny heard the distant sound of a diesel engine and turned toward Hatch Lane.

Dennis was beginning to recover now. 'Hey! Fucker! You listenin' to me, fella?' he called, then he heard the noise too and turned to look.

A huge petrol tanker rumbled up Hatch Lane to the road junction and stopped. The driver was Michael White. His headphones were on and James Brown was undoubtedly urging him to, 'Stay on the scene, like a sex machine!' because inside the cab, Michael was getting on down. The lorry's brakes had not failed and no one was going to get blown to bits. Michael White indicated left and pulled out, slowly and in complete control. Danny watched in astonishment as the tanker drove away up the London road and disappeared round the corner.

'Does that answer your question, you pervert?' Dennis asked. 'You can fuck off home now!'

3

Danny knew that something was wrong at home the moment he opened the front door of his house; something even more wrong than the strange floating confusion that had swamped him. Had he been clear-headed he would have deduced in a matter of seconds that the house was empty. As it was, it took him a five-minute search of the rooms to prove to himself that Suzie was not inside the house or concealed somewhere in the back garden.

But it was worse than this: the house had an odd echoing resonance about it; an atmosphere of people not just having popped down to the corner shop for some milk or eggs to bake a cake, but having left completely.

The letter Suzie had written to him was on the kitchen table. It wasn't until Danny sat down to drink the cup of coffee he'd made in an unthinking, mechanical fashion, that his eyes lit on it.

'She left me a note,' he murmured. 'Wonder where she's popped out to?' But alarm bells were ringing inside his cluttered head – as they had been ringing since he looked in the new bathroom and hadn't noticed things missing. There *were* things missing, but Danny had purposefully not noticed them. He hadn't noticed the way her guaranteed-to-leave-a-ring-around-the-bath scented Body Shop bath oil no longer seemed to be in residence or the way her worn toothbrush hadn't been lying on the sink leaving a hard white stain of paste. In the bedroom, he had been careful not to see the gap on her side of the bed where her beloved pie-jams were no longer carelessly thrown, or the way her make-up bag was absent from the dresser table. He had not looked in any of her drawers or in the wardrobe they shared, because the *terrible* thought had been snuffed out and filed away and the alarm bells – although apparently unstoppable – were already having sandbags piled on top of them.

But there was an ember still glowing in the *terrible* thought that the letter fanned into flame and the alarm bells were ringing.

Suzie's left me, he told himself, setting down his coffee and picking up the letter. Even the envelope felt cold. Danny smiled grimly. *Suzie's best stationery*, he thought, *reserved for letters of the utmost importance*. His name was written on the front of it in Suzie's best handwriting. *What does it say inside, o forecaster of the future? Is it a message of her undying love and devotion? Are you getting the – what do they call 'em – vibes? Are you getting the vibes, o masterful Swami? Can you tell by the touch what is contained within?*

Danny's head spun. He was unable to make sense of anything since finishing the bathroom yesterday. He wasn't even sure that it was yesterday. *A week might be a long time in politics, Dan, but twenty-four hours is a fuck of a sight longer when you're the fucked-up future man.* The letter was cold. Fine white hand-made, deckle-edged paper bordered in red and sealed in a matching envelope. It was cold and serious, not a note from a woman who'd simply crossed the road to visit neighbours – this would have been written on the back of a cornflakes packet or on an old bill.

Danny tapped the envelope on the table, sipped his coffee and decided he needed brandy in it. He took the cold envelope with him to the drinks cabinet in the dining room, holding it away from him while he poured a good slug of Martell into his coffee.

He went back into the kitchen, sat down and wearily opened the letter with a butter knife. Nothing made sense any more. He withdrew the expensive deckle-edged paper, sat back, rubbed his eyes and temples, tried – and failed – to clear his racing thoughts then unfolded it.

Dear Danny,

I didn't sleep very well last night. I kept waking up, terrified and sweating, because each time I fell asleep I dreamed about you telling me things I didn't want to know. You told me a great deal of things I didn't want to know last night and I'm frightened.

I don't want to believe in the paranormal, Danny, not in the Magic Eye or in ghosts, ghouls, or things that go bump in the night. It is easy to push those things aside – except, as I explained already, at night. But it is more difficult, much more difficult, not to believe in the future. The future is far scarier for me than any catalogue of nightmare beasts – whose links with reality are tenuous, even at night. These creatures probably cannot even exist if you do not believe in them, but the future is another matter entirely. The future exists always, by day and by night too. You cannot deny its reality and you cannot stop it crawling towards you, moment by moment, along that passage of time which links it to you. It is impossible to disbelieve the future. The future is real and it is coming. The future is inescapable and it will reach us all in the end.

I've been thinking about it and thinking about it ever since last night, and Danny, I'm afraid I believe you. I do believe it is possible to see into the future and I think you may have unwittingly done this. I did it, equally as unwittingly, when you promised me yesterday that you wouldn't go to the Hatch. I knew you would.

You lied to me when you promised not to go, and again this afternoon when you told me why you were going out. As you are perfectly well aware, I saw the deceit in your eyes. I have always told you that the only condition of our relationship is that you do not lie to me, and today, you blithely broke this rule. That hurts me, Danny. It hurts me badly and I hope you feel bad about it too. You deserve to. This is one of the reasons I have gone away.

Another reason is because of a secret I have kept from you. This secret is to do with the future and with the past, and it may explain some things about me which you have never understood.

The year before I met you, I visited a fortune teller at the seaside while I was on holiday with my parents in Cornwall. I have never told anyone this but I feel I must tell you now. The fortune teller was an old woman who dressed like a gypsy and smelt of gin. She told me a lot of things that I didn't really want to hear, including that I would meet with an nasty accident in my thirties. Here are some other interesting things she told me: that I would meet you; that my mother would break her leg – which, as you know, she did; that I would not end up doing the work I studied for – also true; and most importantly, for both of us, that I would remain childless until my dying day. There was a lot of other stuff which hasn't and won't happen, most of it bad. I don't believe the woman could see the future, or that she thought she could. I think that she lied to me through her teeth and struck lucky a few times. The alternative is that somehow, without knowing she'd done it, she did catch glimpses of my future. That woman told me many lies about the future and some truths. She frightened me terribly and the most scary thing is that I have never known which pieces of information were correct. I am frightened still – most of all that I won't be able to have children. I want children, Danny, and I know you do too and I have a feeling that we won't be getting any – any of our own anyway. I'm confused and worried about everything. I already feel as though I've failed you. Is it any wonder I don't like lies; that I'm scared of what's to come? And there's more.

I'm frightened of our futures, Danny – so scared that it makes my head hurt. I tell myself it isn't possible that the crash could actually happen, but I believe in the future and I'm scared that you won't be coming back from The Hatch today. I'm terrified that it will all come true and that you will be killed in the blast along with the other people you told me about. I couldn't sit here waiting for you to come home in case you didn't turn up. I thought of grave-faced policemen knocking at the door. I couldn't bear that.

But there's more still. There is something very wrong with you, Danny – it's not just that you had a strange spell or saw a vision, it is something much deeper and I'm not even sure you are aware of it. You have changed somehow and the change was quick and terrible. I hope against hope that it's just something minor that has happened inside your brain. I wish to God that all this is due only to a minor movement of the splinter of bone in your pineal gland. I pray that what you saw was a one time only experience and that what's happened to you will only be temporary, because what happened yesterday has changed you somehow. I can't put my finger on it, but you're different since your vision or whatever it was. There is an atmosphere of doom or something following you around. You had a kind of innocence about you until yesterday. Now it seems to have been replaced with a look of hopelessness.

For the first time in my life, I'm scared of you, Danny, and I don't know why or what to do about it. Please get better and prevent me having to make a choice about whether I come back or not, because I don't think I can while you are the way you are now. I don't think I could live with a man who knows what is going to happen in the future. Suppose you could see things about us that were going to happen? I'm too frightened to want to know, Danny.

I am leaving now because I'm very frightened and very confused. I have packed my things and in a few minutes I will have gone away. I don't know if I will ever be coming back.

I will not tell you where I've gone to because I do not want you to try and contact me. I want to be alone so I can have time to consider everything.

Please do not try to contact me.

I love you, Danny.

The letter was tear-stained and the surface was uneven where it had got wet and dried out again. One of the borders had leaked into the plain area. For the first time in his life, Suzie had signed a letter to him and not put kisses beneath her name.

Danny's head swam and the feeling of unreality he'd been wrestling with overpowered him. *She's frightened of me*, he told himself, remembering the pale faces of Dennis and Sara. Suddenly people had become scared of good old Dan. *She hasn't left because I told her a lie at all, that part's bullshit. She's gone because she's suddenly scared shitless of me and as the woman said, she's scared I might tell her things about herself. Which means, old Dan, that she believes, not only in a predetermined future, but that you really can see into it.*

He read the letter over and over again, confused now as to what *any* of it meant. Nothing made sense at all. The words and sentences didn't hang together or convey any information he could understand other than the plain, bare fact that he no longer had Suzie.

Danny folded up the letter, shoved it back into the envelope and put it in his back pocket. He walked wearily up the stairs and went into the bathroom, telling himself that everything would be okay as long as he didn't look into the black tiles. He urinated with his eyes closed and his left hand clamped firmly on to the toilet cistern to hold him steady because when he shut his eyes his head spun as if he was drunk. Afterwards he studied himself in the full-length mirror. If he had changed, he was unable to detect much of a difference. His face was pale, his eyes dark and deep and a little glazed, but he didn't look like a madman. The knees of his jeans were torn and bloodstained and there was a slight graze on his right cheek where he'd fallen but he didn't have the crazy, raging eyes of a prophet or seer. Unless you counted feeling confused, dejected, unreal and badly let down in several different ways, there was no detectable sign of the 'atmosphere of doom' Suzie had mentioned.

He *had* changed, he would concede that point. He'd had something that may or not have been a vision. And he had felt compelled to become a deceitful bastard in order to go to The Hatch. He had suddenly drawn himself away from the person he had shared *everything* with, and for no reason that he could understand. But these things were only temporary and minor aberrations. He could admit them and he was sorry about them. They would not happen again.

'I promise,' he told his reflection, and began to cry.

4

Over the next three hours Danny drank three more heavily laced cups of coffee while he waited for Suzie to return. Then he dispensed with the coffee and drank neat brandy. Then he dispensed with the glass because his mind kept whispering, *That's another biggie, old Dan, there goes another three fingers*! and began to swig from the bottle. The brandy burned his stomach and throat but in some odd way seemed to decrease his dizziness and his feeling of unreality. It did not clear his mental processes. He tried to watch the television but his powers of concentration had been severely diminished. The television just sat there in the corner, burbling away in what seemed like code. The words on the newspaper may as well have been written in a foreign language for all the sense they made. He could read them and pronounce them but they meant nothing. Danny's head ached and the letter felt cold and hard in his back pocket. He did not try to read it again.

Gone away, he thought, trudging up the stairs. *My Suzie's gone away and she ain't coming back*. His weak left leg buckled two stairs from the top and Danny fell on to the brandy bottle that was clasped to his chest. The pain brought fresh tears to his eyes.

Suzie had left a lot of her clothes behind. Danny flicked through the dresses, shirts and skirts that still hung in the wardrobe and tried to deduce if their being here meant Suzie was coming back. Some of the clothes smelled faintly of the *First* perfume she favoured and the smell made him ache for her. At least half her underwear was still in the drawer, but it was the old stuff she only wore to work when everything else was dirty. The fact that her razor had gone meant that she was going to be away long enough to have to shave her legs and this drove a cold spike through Danny's heart.

He went downstairs again, limping badly now. Everything he owned hurt. He could not envisage his survival without her. They had not spent a night apart for the past four years. The house suddenly seemed too big and too empty and unfriendly, somehow as if it disapproved of what had happened.

'I've got to talk to her,' he said, sitting down awkwardly by the phone. 'Got to tell her that I'm sorry and that I was wrong. Got to tell her I need her back.'

He looked at the phone and swigged brandy. *What to say, old Dan? That it wasn't a vision because the accident didn't happen? No need to say the details were nearly all correct. Say you know you were fooling yourself and that you're better now and would she please come back right away?*

'Yeah,' he said, taking the phone off the table and placing it clumsily at his feet. He knew where she would be. Suzie would have gone home to her folks. He dialled the number and while he waited for the ringing tone to be answered tried to tighten himself up internally so that he would sound sober and calm.

Suzie's father Eric answered the phone. 'Lo, Eric?' Danny said thickly. 'Speak Suzie please?'

'I'm sorry, Dan, Suzie isn't here,' Eric said calmly. Then, in a slightly concerned tone, added, 'Isn't she with you?'

Danny thought for a moment, brow furrowed. 'Went off to visit someone,' he said finally. 'Hasn't come back yet. Thought she said she was coming to see you. Must have been mistaken. Sorry. Speak to you later.'

Danny replaced the handset still feeling strangely surprised. *Wasn't there*, he told himself. *You knew she was there, but you were wrong*. He had been wrong about a lot of things in the past day or so. His judgement seemed to be steadily deserting him. He dialled another number.

'Mum? Hi, it's Danny. Listen, you haven't seen Suzie at all, have you?'

Danny wasn't the only member of his family to have made predictions. In her time, his mother had made some of her own. Amongst them was the dead certainty that Danny's relationship with Suzie would come to a sticky end. This wasn't just your average mother's bitterness at having her little baby stolen away by another woman who intended to 'do things' with, and to him; this was for Marjorie a deeply ingrained belief. She had not told him that Suzie was 'no good' in as many (or as few) words, but both Danny and Suzie knew how she felt. They had laughed over this many times. Now it didn't seem quite so funny. This was the moment Marjorie had been waiting for since she first laid eyes on Suzie.

'Of course I haven't seen her,' Marjorie said. 'What would she be doing round here? Why don't you know where she is, Daniel? She's gone off, hasn't she? She's run out on you. Left you. Oh, my gosh, I knew it would come to this. I knew that girl would let you down. I'll tell you this, Daniel, I. . .'

'SHUT UP, MUM!' he shouted. Marjorie fell silent, but he could hear her breathing rapidly. There was a cascade of words waiting to pour forth. 'Danny, I. . .'

'Mum! Listen! We had a bit of a misunderstanding – nothing serious – and she's gone out. I don't know where to.'

'This is the last place she would come to, Danny. She's never liked me. What happened? Why did she go off like that? Is there another man? Oh, you don't know. Well, you wouldn't, would you? The spouse is always the last to know. Oh gosh, Danny, I knew that girl would hurt you. Come home. Come here and. . .'

Danny put the phone down. 'Sorry, Dad,' he said, knowing how his father would suffer for the rest of the evening. 'Bit of a bad move, that.'

The phone rang and Danny pounced on it, knowing it would be Suzie.

'Danny!' his mother said.

'I can't talk now. Go *away!*' he shouted. Marjorie went.

He was becoming frantic. Everything seemed to be drifting away from him, including what little sanity he seemed to have left. *Pull yourself together!* he commanded, and as apt as the words were, they were impossible to put into practice. He stood up and his weak leg dropped him again. Suzie had taken her address book with her, but the telephone numbers of eight of her friends were written in the flip-up directory which sat next to the phone. Danny reached up to the table, swept it off with a crazy wave of his hand and broke the lid in his haste to open it. He took a deep breath which made his head swim and dialled the first number. Eight calls later most of Suzie's friends had gathered that things were not all they should be between the two of them and Danny was cursing himself for having called them at all.

She's at home with her parents, Danny told himself. *You knew she was at the beginning and you know she is now. Your instinct – or whatever you call it – was right. Eric was lying to you*. He began to grow angry. Eric liked him about as much as Marjorie liked Suzie. There was no need for this kind of jealousy, no need at all. *You bastard, Eric!* he thought and yanked the handset from the phone again.

He dialled the number, his head throbbing in time with his heart, his anger simmering. 'Put Suzie on the line!' he commanded as soon as Eric answered.

'As I already told you, Danny, she isn't here,' Eric said patiently.

'She *is* there! I know damn well that she's there, *Now put her on the line!*'

'She *is* here,' Eric admitted, 'but she won't speak with you.'

Eric always said speak *with* you instead of *to* you. It was a simple adoption of the American vernacular and it was understandable – Eric had, after all, spent a lot of time working in the States and probably didn't even realise he was saying it. Although Danny knew all this, it always sounded to him as if Eric had purposely affected it and it always irritated him. Today was the last straw. Danny's anger reached boiling point, vaporised and his motormouth siphoned it off and expelled it as vitriol.

'Don't feed me that stupid shit, you silly, small-minded bastard!' he screamed. 'Just put her on the fucking line and do it now or I'll have to come round there and break the fucking door down and drag her home!'

'I'm sorry to hear that you feel that way,' Eric calmly replied. 'I wouldn't let you talk to Susan while you're in that state even if there was nothing wrong between you. And if you are foolish enough to try to resolve things with violence, I believe you will live to regret it.'

'Now just you listen. . .' Danny said, but the phone was dead. He stared at the receiver for almost a minute, slowly realising what he'd done.

'Oh, Christ, I'm sorry, Suzie!' he muttered, dialling the number again.

'Eric, I'm sorry! Really! I am! Please accept my apologies. I was out of order and I regret it. I'm a little wound up. You see, Suzie's left . . . of course you know that already, but you don't know why. Let me explain. . .'

'Look, Danny, I accept your apology but I'm not interested in the circumstances of your dispute with Suzie,' he said. 'I'd just like you to ring off, get yourself together and wait for Susan to contact you. She's very over-wrought and needs some time alone. To think.' he added ominously. 'Will you promise me you'll do that?'

Even though there was cold stone lying heavy in his stomach, Danny was floating. He promised. Downhearted and defeated, he took the bottle of brandy into the lounge and sat in front of the T.V., alternately picking his fingernails clean and swigging from the bottle while his mind provided him with thousands of explanations for his supposed psychic experience and millions for what had gone wrong with his relationship. Over a period of several hours, his mind slowed down and stopped until his head was thick and empty and heavy with booze. Finally, he fell asleep.

5

A man stalked him through the streets of his dreams, following him carefully at first and taking great pains to keep out of view. Although Danny could not see him, he knew he was there and he knew he was bad.

Danny was lost in a town he didn't know, a town that had a maze of small alleyways, wide streets and the smell of the sea in the air. He didn't remember the transition from being calm to being frightened – it came some time after he knew he was being followed – but he was terrified now. He increased his pace, turning this way and that through the streets and alleys, passing strange shops and houses, but the stalker always seemed to be the same distance behind him.

Danny! the stalker whispered from the shadows, and breaking out in freezing shivers, Danny stopped and turned around.

You know what you did, old Dan, the – somehow familiar – voice whispered.

'No,' Danny replied in a small, hollow voice.

You made it happen!

Danny shook his head hard, the way he used to when his mother accused him of doing something naughty. 'I didn't,' he said, but he was lying. Whatever he was to be charged with, he *knew* he'd done it.

You know what you did to her, don't you? the bad man whispered and stepped out of the shadows.

Danny gasped what felt like cold water into his lungs. The bad man's face was in shadow. He was dressed in an old Gannex raincoat like Harold Wilson used to wear and held a large knife in his hand. Danny could smell the blood that darkened its blade.

You put this on here, the voice whispered, turning the blade over so that it gleamed in the half-light.

'Not me,' Danny said, trying very hard to turn and run away. The Gannex Man had done the murder. It was he who had pushed the steel into the young girl, he who had forced its tip between the joints of her bones, separating them while she screamed for mercy. He who had carved her into fine shreds.

But how do you know all this? the Gannex Man challenged.

Danny didn't know and didn't want to know. He wheeled around and began to run, his suddenly heavy limbs slowing him down. As he ran, the pavement turned to treacle, drawing his feet down, holding him back.

You know what you did, old Dan!

For a fleeting moment Danny remembered the girl. She was a teenager, slender and supple. There was a brown birth mark on the border of her thigh and her pubic hair. She was screaming and there was blood on her. Blood coming from her. He wanted her. Wanted her as she thrashed and moaned, her struggles weakening as her life ebbed away.

'IT WASN'T ME!' he screamed, running faster against the solidifying air.

The Gannex Man's fetid breath was on the back of his neck now; the raincoat was flapping against his legs as he ran.

I want you, Danny! the man breathed. *I want your blood, but I want* all *of you too. You did it to her, old Dan. You know that good and well. You fucked her to death. We belong together, Danny, you and I. We are one and I mean to have you*!

Against his wishes, Danny's head swivelled round until he was looking over his shoulder and directly into the Gannex Man's face. Danny screamed.

He was looking into his own wild eyes, at his own pale, distorted face.

You killed her dead, Dan, his own lips sniggered at him. *You know how she moved under you. You tasted her life. You took her body and you gave her death. How did it feel, old Dan? Ten-up? Bust the barometer? Her blood is still on you.*

The Gannex man was gone, but Danny didn't stop screaming. The girl's blood *was* on him, flowing over his body and clothes in a warm, salty sheet as though it had a motive power all of its own. The blood was a live, seeping thing which soaked through his clothes and slipped across his body, seeking him out, finding every square centimetre of him. It flowed between his buttocks, enveloped and hotly caressed his penis, filled his ears, trickled into his mouth so that he could taste it, ran against gravity into his nostrils. Danny heaved a great scream and sprayed blood into the air.

Then there was simply darkness in which Suzie's satisfied voice asked the old après orgasm question, 'How did it feel Danny? Ten-up?'

It was a trick question. That wasn't Suzie's voice, it was an imitation. 'No!' he moaned.

Then he was hovering – apparently free from the physical constraints of his body – over Athens International airport. Danny had been to Greece, but only to the islands, never through Athens. In spite of this fact, he recognised the airport as though he'd flown in and out of it a thousand times. It was daytime and the sun was high in the cloudless sky. From his position in the air he could see the town of Glyfada nestling on the nearby coast, the tiny fishing boats in the clear sea, the hotels, the minute dots of holidaymakers on the sand, the queues of traffic on the dusty roads.

Below him there was a Lufthansa jet taxiing off the slip and on to the main runway for takeoff. It completed the turn and came to a standstill, the sound of its engines falling while it awaited clearance to leave.

Danny heard the roar of another plane and glanced toward the noise. There was an ancient and noisy B.A.C. 111 approaching for landing. It was throttling down as it descended sharply, flaps and wheels down, its nose pointing up slightly.

There was a click in Danny's ears followed by a sharp hiss of static. A voice which bore a heavy Greek accent said, 'GY 940B. Cleared for take off.'

Another click and hiss and a clipped voice responded, 'Thank you, Athens, commencing run up.'

The Lufthansa jet's engine note rose and it tilted slightly forward against its brakes. The engine reached full working power, the brakes were released and the plane began to roll. A strong smell of burnt aviation fuel filled Danny's nostrils.

His ears clicked. 'Come in EA206!' the Greek controller said, a note of urgency in his voice. 'You are not, I repeat not, cleared for landing. Runway occupied. Turn right climb to two thousand, take holding pattern one, turns to the left please. 206, please respond.'

Danny glanced up the 111 which hadn't either started to turn or climb. *Radio failure*, he thought, and the cold stone hand grasped his insides again. The 111 was intending to land on the same runway the Lufthansa was taking off from.

'206! Please respond!'

It can't hear you! Danny screamed mentally. *Stop the other one!*

'GY 940B. Emergency! Abort take-off and clear runway.'

Danny heard the pause while he watched the Lufthansa gather speed. It was going to be close. The two planes were being drawn towards each other as if they were joined by an invisible and unbreakable thread which was being rapidly reeled in.

Finally, his ears clicked and hissed again. 'GY 940B. Please repeat last instruction. Confirm abort take-off.'

'Confirmed! Clear runway. Disabled aircraft! Emergency landing!'

The 111 pilot finally realised what was happening, because the engines began to scream and the plane's attitude altered as he tried to swing it back into the sky.

This wasn't going to work, Danny was certain of that. The Lufthansa was moving too quickly and the 111 didn't seem to have the power to climb out of danger. *Come on!* Danny urged it.

Down on the ground, the Lufthansa applied full reverse thrust. Its engines screamed and its nose dipped as it braked. It rolled hard from side to side as the pilot fought to keep it straight and for a second Danny thought it was going to turn over.

Two things now became very clear for Danny. The first was that by spotting what he thought was going to be an emergency, the controller had actually created one: if he had not warned the Lufthansa, it would have been away by the time the 111 hit the other end of the tarmac. The second was that the ailing 111, its wheels and flaps down, was now too far into its glide path to abort its landing. It simply wasn't going to be able to turn right, climb to two thousand and adopt holding pattern one. But the pilot was trying and the 111's nose was now up, its engines screaming, its undercarriage slowly being retracted. With a cold horror, Danny realised that the net effect of this manoeuvre would be to keep the plane in the air for long enough, not to land at the far end of the runway – which would have been safe – but just long enough for it to come down very close to the German jet indeed.

Below Danny, the 111 captain throttled down and the plane fell swiftly. Danny realised the pilot was trying to position the plane so that, at the last moment, he would be able to pile the power on, leapfrog over the rapidly slowing Lufthansa and still have enough runway left to stop. This depended on the 111's captain estimating how far the German plane would travel before coming to a standstill. Danny knew, as ground control shouted urgently in his ears, that the 111's pilot was going to get it wrong.

The 111 put the power on and the plane rose, but the Lufthansa didn't stop quickly enough.

Danny fought against the terrible nightmare paralysis and cried out in torment, knowing distantly that he was only dreaming, but unable to deny the reality of what he was seeing. It may have only been a dream but all the emotions he was feeling were genuine. The awful terror and the aching sorrow were real.

The 111 smashed down on top of the Lufthansa, fuselage to fuselage. There was no chance for any of the crew or passengers on either aeroplane; the German plane was carrying a full load of fuel. The silent moment in which the aeroplanes seemed to merge with one another was followed by a huge explosion and a fireball enveloped the wreckage.

Danny felt the heat and the shockwave pass him, watched as explosion followed explosion, throwing debris into the air until the whole runway was strewn. When the first pall of black smoke cleared neither aeroplane was recognisable as a flying machine. The twisted wreckage could easily have been a burned out warehouse blazing away down there. Danny heard sirens and saw fire tenders approaching and knew they were going to find no survivors.

How did it feel, old Dan? Ten-up? a sniggering voice whispered in his ears.

Danny woke up screaming and clutching at thin air.

6

It took quite some time for Danny to calm himself. At first he thought he had died, then was certain he was going to. His throat and lungs were raw and felt burnt, there was the oily smell and taste of burnt aviation fuel in his nose and mouth, he couldn't draw a breath, his heart was pounding so hard and fast that his ribs were under pressure and there was a sharp pain all down his left arm.

Nightmare is all it was! Nightmare is all! he repeated, fighting to breathe deeply and slowly. But the sly, teasing voice that was his, yet *alien* somehow, kept resounding through his mind, asking him if it had felt *Ten-up*.

'I'm okay,' he assured himself, drawing a deep, shuddering breath and holding it in. His heart began to slow and the pain in his chest started to subside. He released the breath and took another. The waving angles and planes of the lounge were now settling; reality seemed to be reasserting itself. Danny looked at his watch. It was two-thirty in the morning. The television was still on but the station had closed down and it was quietly sizzling away to itself in the corner, colour-spotted rain dancing across the screen. The lights were harsh on his eyes and the room seemed too cold and bright; too real somehow.

'Some nightmare,' Danny whispered, wrapping his arms around himself. He was cold and lonely and confused and frightened. His eyes hurt, his head ached and the scar below his right eye throbbed painfully. His left arm and leg were numb, and the images of the two planes colliding wouldn't let him alone.

Danny swigged the dregs from the brandy bottle and walked carefully to the dining room to get another, trying to conjure up good thoughts which would push away those of the crash that kept coming at him. Good thoughts were at a premium tonight though and there weren't enough to keep him supplied until the brandy drove the bad ones away.

Before Danny became anaesthetised he realised that his memory had done him the disservice of becoming – as least temporarily – eidetic and had retained each and every small detail about the crash for him to consider. He was forced to recall the colour of the jet exhaust; the way the sun glinted on the wings of the 111 as it descended; the way in which both planes crumpled on impact, merging with one another until they became one confused mass of aluminium and steel which seemed to be writhing and struggling to separate itself. The dreadful silence between the crash and the first flash of flame had now expanded from its original fraction of a second to a gap of minutes during which he could wonder what the people inside were doing if they had survived.

During this time, Danny became convinced that his nightmare of the Gannex Man had preceded another vision. This part of his dream was not a simple nightmare at all. The crash had really happened – or was going to happen soon – and he had seen it in the same way that he had witnessed the collision of the car and the tanker. The fact that he knew he'd been sleeping in front of the television did not preclude this possibility. People had experienced precognitive dreams of air crashes before. If other people's nightmare visions were anything to go by, there was little he would be able to do to avert the tragedy. Other people seemed to dream crashes either simultaneously with the event or very shortly before. Danny believed that he would soon be able to watch the aftermath of disaster on television, if not on the early morning news, then on the lunchtime edition.

When the details of the crash became hazed by the brandy and the sniggering voice stopped asking him if he'd felt Ten-up, Danny staggered slowly upstairs, dragging his tired left leg behind him. It was worse today than it had been for years. *Falling to bits, Dan*, he told himself. *Suzie's been gone for ten hours and you're already falling apart*.

On the top stair, something in his sinus made an audible *click!* and the pain in his bullet scar vanished. 'Good riddance,' Danny said. The moment afterwards his nose began to gush blood.

Danny tasted the blood as it ran into his mouth, watched it spilling on to his clothes. 'Nosebleed,' he said, smiling bitterly at this final insult. 'Must be the altitude.'

He went into the bathroom and leaned over the sink with the cold tap running and bathed his face until the flow of blood ceased. Afterwards he felt much better. He undressed, threw his clothes in the linen basket and went to bed where he lay on his side, sipping the brandy until sleep came stealing up on him. 'G'night,' he said to Suzie's empty space, placed the bottle on the floor and closed his eyes.

And dreamed the dream again.

7

Danny phoned the doctor's surgery at nine the following morning. His head ached, his mouth tasted sour and there was the smell of alcohol and dried blood on his breath. After a heated discussion with the receptionist, which bordered on, but didn't quite reach, the point of shouting, he was given an emergency appointment with his doctor at midday.

Afterwards he took two of the prescription only Distalgesic painkillers that Suzie had been given when she sprained her ankle playing netball two years ago, and washed them down with brandy. His stomach complained loudly, but didn't chuck them back up as he had expected. When the pain numbed, he forced two slices of toast down after the pills and threw two cups of black coffee down on top of that, trying not to imagine the mess that the guys with the shovels down there were having to deal with. He pulled the newspaper through the letterbox, thinking, *I bagged it first today, Suze*, then fought off the longing for her while he wondered what she was doing today. He doubted she had gone to work. Suzie had probably done what she always did when faced with a dilemma: Gone for a Blow. Like the bagging expression, the Magic Eye and Ten-up, Going for a Blow was Suzie's invention. It meant going for a very long drive in the rusting '67 Sunbeam Tiger she cherished – with the convertible top down and the wind blowing in her hair. Suzie had done this in every kind of weather known to man and claimed it blew away her mental cobwebs.

Danny sat at the kitchen table and leafed through the newspaper looking for details of the disaster at Athens International. There was trouble in the Conservative Party, trouble in the Labour Party where a leading politician had just resigned; there was more starvation in Ethiopia, fresh trouble brewing in the Gulf, the Philippines and Washington. Trade figures were down, unemployment had risen for the third consecutive time and a kid had been reported missing after going to a funfair in Staffordshire. A cat had survived half an hour in a working tumble drier and the *Rainbow Warrior* was out in the Pacific trying to prevent a French nuclear test taking place. There was no mention of anything to do with aeroplanes other than a brief report that pilots had voted Corfu airport number one in their list of the ten most dangerous places to fly into.

Danny went into the lounge and sat on the edge of the sofa watching the television, frequently flipping across the channels for the news. There were no reports of an aeroplane crash.

He dressed at eleven, walked to Rapson's post office and bought more newspapers which he read in the doctors' surgery while waiting for his appointment. There was no report of an air crash in any of these either and Danny concluded, not that it had only been a nightmare, but that it hadn't yet happened. He wondered if he should ring someone at Heathrow or Gatwick – if anything had happened they would be the first to know, and if nothing had happened yet, they were the ones to warn.

And do you suppose they'd listen to you? And if they did listen, what would they be thinking? They'd be thinking that they'd got a madman on the line, wouldn't they? Or worse, that they'd got a terrorist. In these days of hijacks, death squads, Saddam, Qaddaffi, Arafat, and all their good friends, they probably get ten, maybe fifteen, calls a week telling them that one of their aircraft is going to have something nasty happen to it. Even if you could remember the flight numbers of each plane involved – which you've forgotten, old Dan – you have no idea which day the accident is supposed to happen. They could ground both planes for a week and give them a thorough overhaul and the accident could still happen. In fact, the fault that causes the crash might be introduced *while the 111 is grounded! How about that then? You might be able to cause a crash which wasn't going to happen. That would be proper Ten-up, wouldn't it, old Dan?*

Doctor James Rodgers was an elderly man – probably, Danny thought, past the age of retirement – who had a no-nonsense face that didn't fit his gentle, almost diffident, bedside manner. Danny had seen him only three times in the past five years – once to be referred for his yearly skull x-ray and twice for antibiotics for throat infections. He politely asked Danny how he was feeling this morning then listened patiently, nodding occasionally as Danny told him *everything*.

When Danny fell silent, Dr Rodgers looked at him quizzically over his half-framed glasses and asked, 'And is it your view that you are losing your sanity?'

Danny shrugged uncomfortably, a picture of Dennis and Sara's frightened faces as they backed away from him rising in his mind. It was all very well telling yourself you were going insane; another thing altogether when someone else said it to you. He looked at the doctor, gauging his expression for signs that he might feel the same way as the couple in the Escort Mexico. Dr Rodgers' feelings on the matter were neatly and professionally concealed.

'What other explanation is there?' he said.

The doctor smiled. 'The one you gave earlier is most likely. The one your girlfriend favours. I would imagine that something, some blow you received but didn't notice while decorating the bathroom, or a sharp movement you made, has dislodged the sliver of bone still in your brain. I seem to recall from your case-notes that you suffered episodes of hallucination and feelings of unreality after your childhood accident. What you are feeling now is probably a temporary recurrence of those. The problem will doubtless resolve itself without recourse to surgery. However, it may be prudent to get you into hospital as soon as possible for a brain scan. Sit tight while I make a phone call.'

8

By five that afternoon Danny was in a bed in the Neurological Department of Southampton Hospital, which was, Dr Rodgers had assured him, where the state of the art technology and the experts were.

He got his brain scan first thing the following morning – after sleeping a dreamless eight hours. This was followed by more x-rays, blood tests, urine tests, constant monitoring of his blood pressure and temperature – the latter of which was a good two degrees higher than the registrar liked. No one seemed to be able to find an infection lurking within him, but he was treated with antibiotics anyway. His temperature did not fall.

Now Danny had handed over the controls to the experts, he relaxed. Although he was no stranger to hospital routine, it had been a long time since he'd been a patient but to his surprise, he adapted to it with much less trouble than he had anticipated.

By the afternoon of the following day he was beginning to feel like an impostor. The morning had brought a consultation with a surgical neurologist called Brough Lacey who didn't seem old enough to have acquired the reputation of brilliance that seemed to surround him. Brough Lacey enthusiastically told Danny that he had been 'jolly interested' in his case and thought that Mr Amis, the surgeon who had saved his life after he was shot, had done 'some pretty terrific seat of the pants surgery' considering 'the state of things back in what we like to call the dark ages'. Brough Lacey was amazed at the recovery the younger Danny had made 'considering the extent of the damage in parts of the old motor centres'. Lacey smiled broadly. 'Some parts of you are jolly well dead, my friend!' he announced, producing the results of the scan and carefully indicating the damaged areas. Danny was swept along by Brough Lacey's enthusiasm and did not feel offended.

'Here's the sliver of bone!' Brough Lacey said. 'And here it is on both the new and old x-rays! It's only a tiny piece and it's pierced right through the pineal body. Now, if we take this plate which was made at the time of your accident and hold the new one up in front of it, you can see that there has been no movement of the bone at all. It is in *precisely* the same spot! I could probably operate on you to remove it, but since it is in a relatively safe place and since it would be dangerous major surgery to get at it – not to mention the cost to the health service. . .' He wagged his finger and grinned. 'I said, don't mention the cost to the health service. I think it would be advisable to leave the jolly old thing exactly where it is.'

'Mr Lacey?'

'Brough, please, my friend. I don't stand on ceremony.'

Danny nodded. 'Brough. If the bone hasn't moved, why did I have the hallucinations?'

'Ah . . .' Brough said. 'It's a little difficult to say. The cause was evidently not due to anything physical. Everything inside the old cranium looks tickety-boo to me. It was probably a random response to a visual stimulus. These things can happen. For example: in people with a predisposition to epilepsy, visual stimulus can often trigger attacks – fits, if you like. Such innocent things as flashing lights or even the sun flickering through lines of trees as one drives along can precipitate an attack. But don't get me wrong. I don't for a moment think you are suffering either Grand Mal or Petit Mal attacks. I'm just using that as an illustration. Sometimes a damaged brain can report some *very* odd happenings. Reality is a jolly sketchy business, you know. It only takes trauma to certain small parts of our brains to shoot it to shit, if you'll pardon the French. Your brain undoubtedly suffered quite a bit of trauma, as illustrated by your earlier hallucinations, but as nothing has changed in there since, I'd say it was just a kind of visually induced, self-hypnotic flashback. You were tired, you were staring into the mirror – and, *bingo*, the lid on that part of your memory opened and your imagination supplied the rest.'

'But it felt real,' Danny insisted.

'And so it would. As I say, reality is a jolly sketchy business. Unreality is only a hair's breadth away and most times indistinguishable from the real thing. In fact, there are some people who would challenge our definition of what is reality and what is not. Know anything about quantum physics? Those chaps are playing around on the borders of reality.'

For some reason Danny felt a great deal better about things when Brough had gone and didn't think he ought to be in hospital at all. The man's theory of a visually induced flashback was almost certainly right. Danny's head was clear again and he felt very well.

His grave-faced parents visited him after lunch and didn't believe Danny when he told them that everything was going to be okay. They spoke to the registrar and didn't believe him either. Finally Brough Lacey bounded in to ask Danny if he would mind terribly 'doing some physical tests for some of my chaps who are working on re-establishment of limb movement in brain-damaged patients'. Brough Lacey succeeded where everyone else had failed. It was almost impossible not to believe him. Danny's parents went home happy. It wasn't until after they'd gone that he realised they had not mentioned that darkest of dark subjects, Suzie Anderson. Danny considered phoning her and telling her he was in hospital, then decided it would – to some extent at least – be an act of emotional blackmail. He would work on getting better and give her time to start missing him.

During Wednesday and Thursday, Danny slept a lot and slept well, took part in the physical tests, chatted to – and flirted with – the nurses who were still worrying about his temperature and feeding him antibiotics, and saw a psychiatrist. The psychiatric profession had been blighted forever for Danny by the awful Mr Reed who had taught him the meaning of the words 'sexual perversion' while most kids were still seven or eight years away from learning about ordinary sex. He did not attend the session in good heart.

Unfortunately, the shrink, a woman in her forties, was a *Know Better*. The *Know Betters* were another of Danny's least favourite groups of people. *Know Betters* didn't just appear in local government or politics where they would shine, often offering you their wisdom from the other side of the T.V. screen, but in all other walks of life as well. You could instantly identify a *Know Better* simply by the superior expression of self-belief that resided permanently on their faces. And that was all you needed to know. *Know Betters* were closed off from persuasion, logical argument or any of the other devices which could be used to alter or adjust people's opinions. *Know Betters* had already made up their minds and they always knew what was best for you. The psychiatrist undoubtedly belonged to this group.

Danny gave his side of the story, slowly and carefully, knowing that he was wasting his time. *She'll say you dreamed both the episodes*, he told himself.

At the end of the session, as he had known she would, the shrink ventured the opinion that she should refer him to a psychiatrist in Basingstoke. She also ventured the opinion that Danny hadn't had visions at all, but had fallen asleep and dreamed everything. It was just that on the first occasion in the bath he had not realised he had fallen asleep. On the second occasion, she said, as if this was enough to confirm her theory, Danny had actually *admitted* he was asleep. She said that the dreams were a subconscious cry for help. He had known in the back of his mind that his relationship with Suzie was reaching a critical stage and the dreams were no more than reflections of his mental turmoil. He was dimly aware that his relationship was about to explode and fall to bits, etc, etc, and the dreams were allegorical; mere subconscious expressions of his worries.

Danny wondered how many other people Mrs *Know Better* had zapped with this textbook theory. He was about to argue that there was nothing whatsoever wrong with his relationship *before* the episodes, when Mrs *Know Better* told him she thought he might be suffering from a slight depression.

Danny tartly asked her if she thought a slight depression was unusual in someone who had recently been given the elbow by his long-term mate and who had been suffering from terrible hallucinations. Then he got up and left without waiting for a reply.

He was discharged from hospital with an almost clean bill of health at twenty past six on Thursday evening. His temperature remained a constant two full degrees above normal and despite the antibiotics (the remainder of which were rattling in a bottle in his pocket) hadn't budged by a fraction of a degree. It had been concluded that his 'normal' temperature was higher than everyone else's and that as his blood pressure was normal, his brainwave patterns ordinary and there was no evidence to suggest any tumour or disease, there was nothing anyone could do about it.

Danny got on the train to Basingstoke still not knowing what had caused what he had now come to think of as his 'episodes'. The main thing was that they had ceased, his dreams were untroubled, he was fit and healthy and there had been no reports of an air disaster – either in Greece or elsewhere – on any of the newscasts he'd seen or in any of the papers.

He had been wrong and he was glad.

Danny went back to work the following morning which turned out to be a bad mistake.

9

All jobs have their drawbacks and Danny's was his boss. Tom Hicks was a tall, fat man with a crumpled face and an unfortunate habit of pulling his trousers up high when he spoke to you so that you were able to see his prick and balls distinctly outlined against the tight material at his crotch. Danny had this habit drawn to his attention by a young secretary called Georgina who swore that he did it on purpose when he was talking to girls, and although Danny had studied it, he had been unable to decide whether or not it was done consciously. More often than not when talking to Danny, Tom would simply dig away at the pile of loose change that resided permanently in his right hand trouser pocket. The presence of the money made it difficult to tell if he *was* playing what Georgina called 'pocket billiards' or not. But Tom *had* hoisted his trousers in front of Danny on the odd occasion and the habit had become the subject of much speculation.

Dear old Tom Hicks – who liked to be called Mr Hicks – was also one of that elite band of intellectuals, the *Know Betters*. He wasn't a quiet one either. If he happened by when you were talking about any subject, from microbiology to whatever might be happening at the edges of the known universe, Tom Hicks knew about it better than you did and would impart his golden nuggets of information as though in the presence of the severely mentally retarded. If you had a backache, Tom would tell you about his ruptured disc and how he narrowly escaped paralysis; if you'd had a car accident, Tom would have had a worse one; if you had an ingrown toenail, Tom's would have become gangrenous. On one occasion while Danny was sympathising with Sandy – one of his team – who was suffering from flu, she said, 'Look out, here comes Tom. He's bound to have had Black Death.'

Tom's favourite subject was caravanning. He was a leading light of his caravan club and he liked you to know it. Danny dreaded Mondays between April and November because Tom went away every weekend to such exotic spots as Boscombe, West Wittering, Beaulieu and Selsey Bill and came back wanting to tell you every minute detail of the trip. On one occasion Tom had gone home to

Kingsclere on a Friday evening, collected his wife, hitched up their caravan and driven all the way to that weekend's destination – a farmer's field in Hannington – which was less than three miles from his house. If it wasn't for the fact that Danny's relationship with Tom *Know Better* was strained at the best of times, Danny would have found this hilarious.

Tom was due to retire that year and everyone who worked under him was secretly counting the days. From the moment she had found out his date of leaving, Georgina had kept a list of numbers on her desk. They were headed BASTARD and written down in reverse order from 81 to 0, and the first time Danny had seen them, 81 down to 78 had been struck. 'Only seventy-seven more days before we get rid of the bastard,' Georgina had smiled in explanation.

Danny had many theories which explained why Tom Hicks didn't like him. The major one was that, in some unconscious way, Tom had realised Danny knew he was a *Know Better*. There were lots of other reasons; Danny knew that over the years he'd transgressed many of Tom's unwritten laws – and some of the written ones too – and Tom was a man who held grudges and didn't forgive easily. But barring the incident with Suzie at last year's Christmas party, none of these things was huge or terrible; it was just that Danny's relationship with Tom had deteriorated over a period of years. Danny was no longer really conscious of it at all. Since they didn't work in close contact with one another there were no real problems, only advantages as far as Danny was concerned. It saved both of them from having to remember the other's birthday, and unlike some of the staff, Danny didn't feel obliged to listen to Tom's stories for any longer than they interested him (which wasn't long).

But that Friday something or someone had put a hair across Tom Hicks' ass. Danny knew that coming back to work today was a mistake when he found the curt note on his desk requesting that he attend a meeting in Mr Hicks' office at eleven. Danny considered the note for a second or two then balled it and threw it in the bin. He could read between the lines well enough by now to know that Tom *Know Better* was intending to give him a lecture about timekeeping and absenteeism. Danny had phoned in sick and explained about the hospital tests which had kept him away from work all week and personnel would have told Tom, but apparently he didn't believe them. It didn't take any psychic ability at all to work *that one* out. 'If he wants to see me, he can damn well come and get me,' Danny muttered darkly.

And at three minutes past eleven, Tom Hicks did.

After a short time listening to the lecture – which went exactly the way Danny had expected – he began to suspect there was something else at the bottom of it.

'I told you, I was *taken ill!*' Danny said, interrupting Tom's flow. 'Now what's this about?'

But Tom didn't say – didn't seem to have heard in fact. He shook his head and spoke gravely about an offence Danny had committed years ago when he was working a lone nightshift. Once, and once only, he had left the computer running a long program and gone out. That particular Friday night he'd been in possession of a pair of tickets to see The Stranglers at Bracknell Sports Centre but he'd gone to work. The tickets had burnt holes in his pockets while he set up the computer tapes. When the program began to run, Danny went to The Dragon, collected Suzie and drove to the gig. Nothing terrible had happened that night; the computer didn't go off the rails, and he got back before the program had finished – but some creep (and he didn't know who it was to this day) had noticed his absence and reported it. Danny was threatened with the sack, stopped three days' pay, and it had all been forgotten about. Until now.

Anger began to boil beneath Danny's calm exterior. 'That was years ago, Tom,' he said. 'I don't go off sick when I'm well and you damn well know it. I had every right to stay away from work this week and if, for some idiotic reason, you don't believe me, then ring the Neurological Unit at Southampton and ask *them!*'

Know Better Tom glowered. 'Then there's your bad attitude,' he said. 'We've all suffered from it during your time with us. Your application could best be described as indifferent and you have a major problem with your attitude toward your superiors. I imagine your problem stems from your home life, and I don't want it spilling over into your work and. . .'

Danny didn't hear the last part of the sentence; the words: 'your problem stems from your home life', resounded inside his head with a volume that must surely have equalled standing next to Big Ben inside the bell room while it struck. Suddenly Danny knew what Tom was driving at. Suzie. Someone had tipped off Tom that Suzie had gone and he thought it was because of this that Danny hadn't been to work all week. *He can't know,* Danny told himself. *Who would have told him?*

But it sounded as if someone *had* told him. *Know Better* Tom was now talking – in very vague terms, of course – about how he had entertained some doubts about '. . . ah . . . your relationship. . .' and how he hoped things would now improve.

Tom Hicks' doubts about Danny's relationship sprang from the Christmas party, Danny knew. He hadn't spoken about Suzie since and Danny had concluded that old Tom had been so steamed up at the time he didn't remember it, but remember it he obviously did. He had been offended and he was still offended now.

Suzie's exhibitionist tendency had got the better of her at the Christmas party. She had worn a tiny black latex dress which she had bought mail order. The dress plunged to the hips at the back, was very short, and clung in a manner that was almost obscene. Many jaws had hit the ground when she took her coat off and she had been delighted. Halfway through the evening, a slightly drunken Suzie – who had heard all about Tom Hicks – told Danny that Mr*Know Better* had been watching her carefully all evening and that she intended to dance with him. She did not tell him that she intended to wind Tom up. During the dance Suzie had confided to Tom that she was naked beneath the dress; that the rubber made her all sweaty and squishy and sexy, and that she would undoubtedly have Danny in the car on the way home. According to Suzie, she had also listed her favourite sexual positions and practices and the strangest places she'd ever had sex and had then asked Tom to tell her his wildest fantasies. On its own, this would have been bad enough, but in the car park afterwards Suzie had flashed enough buttock at Tom to assure him she'd left her underwear at home that night.

Now, *Know Better* Tom made a tactical error. He said, 'I had grave misgivings about your . . . uh . . . partner before the Christmas party. Afterwards I came to the conclusion that she was a. . .'

A slut! Danny thought. *That's the word you're searching for. Say it and you'll wish you hadn't.*

'. . . uh . . . not entirely suitable.' He shook his head. 'She did not behave in an . . . entirely . . . uh . . . decorous fashion . . . was . . . uh. . .'. *Know Better* Tom wrung his hands and frowned.

Danny boiled.

Tom smiled and his face cleared. He looked up at Danny, completely missed the warning signs and blithely made a second – and worse – tactical error. 'Let's talk about it man to man, Daniel, and cut the crap. As far as I can see, you're better off without her. Face it, Daniel, your problems were all rooted in that . . . uh . . . trollop.'

The word 'trollop' pulsed white across Danny's vision. Blind fury rolled through him. His stomach pressed up against his heart and he wanted to scream that Suzie wasn't a trollop or a slut or anything else, and that he still loved her even if she'd left him. He wanted to get up and walk out, slamming the door behind him so hard that the single pane of glass in it smashed. He wanted to take the big glass paperweight with the sea-horse inside it from Tom's desk and force it down the man's throat. Most of all he wanted to throttle *Know Better* Tom until he died. A picture flickered through his mind of his thumbs pressing so hard on Tom's windpipe he could feel the bones of the spine beneath them.

Ten-up, old Dan? that strange cool voice whispered in the back of his mind. *Is that how it'll feel? Ten-up?*

Danny's legs suddenly stiffened, pushing him to his feet. He reached across Tom's desk, grabbed his tie just below the knot and hoisted him to his feet.

Tom made a single sharp noise like the cry of a hungry baby and his face grew an expression that mirrored the fear Danny had seen in Dennis and Sara down on the A30.

Ten-up? the voice asked, but Tom's expression had shocked some of Danny's rage away. For a moment he was dreadfully confused about everything and thought he knew what the problem was. Then he no longer knew exactly *what* he felt.

Except that Tom had it coming. Danny balled his fist and thumped him on the nose. It was just one simple blow, and he pulled it a little at the last moment, but it was enough. Tom's head snapped back and his eyes rolled up. His neck went limp and his head rolled around in a loose circle. When it had done a full three hundred and sixty degrees and returned to its original position, the lights came back on in Tom's eyes.

Danny had finished. He didn't feel vindicated or avenged or anything at all, other than totally empty and *alien* somehow. He let go of Tom's tie and the man collapsed back into his chair, his face looking somewhat more crumpled than it had done a moment ago. Tears were streaming from his eyes, his nose was pouring blood on to his nice suit and white shirt, and his trembling lips were working soundlessly.

For a short time Danny waited to hear what words of wisdom *Know Better* was trying to impart, then he grew impatient.

'You're fired,' he quietly said on Tom's behalf. 'Well, Tom, old friend, old buddy, old pal, that's eminently fine by me. And just remember, if you can resist calling Suzie a trollop, then we'll never have to see one another again. And that's eminently fine by me too. Goodbye, Tom.'

Feeling giddy and sick, Danny turned and walked out. Five minutes later he was out in the street realising that his job had just gone the same way as Suzie.

Chapter Six
Christine Richard's Last Stand

1

The Friday Danny lost his job would later rate as a Double Critical on the charts he would call the the *If Only* papers. He would tell himself that Lady Luck had woken up in an extremely bad mood with him that day and had excelled herself by handing him not just one simple bad card to be getting on with, but by sneaking a black ace into his open hand beneath it. Because he hit his boss on a Friday and it just so happened that Friday was when the *Basingstoke Gazette* was published.

2

As he had done when he left school, Danny lay on the floor of his lounge that afternoon leafing through the Situations Vacant pages of the *Gazette*. He told himself that he'd found a decent job in it before so there was no reason why he shouldn't do it again. It was impossible to concentrate, though. He was lonely and confused and his thoughts were sluggish and heavy, seemingly moving at the pace of an elderly snail. He felt mentally sick, as if his brain had swallowed something indigestible and couldn't summon the strength to chuck it back up. Danny had tried sleeping to clear his mind, but he'd woken up with an even thicker head. He would, he knew, also try to drown the sick feeling with alcohol, but as good as the idea sounded, he resolved not to try *that* particular analgesic until a little later. Finally, he gave up looking for a new job and leafed through the paper uninterestedly while he tried to piece things together.

There were two major statements inside that woolly thing that passed for a brain and Danny inspected them over and over again. The first was that he had lost Suzie, the second that he had lost his job. He was not only unable to believe either of them, but neither seemed to make any kind of sense at all. He wrote both statements in biro in the space at the top of page twenty-eight of the *Gazette* and found them incomprehensible. He knew what they meant but they wouldn't take their place in his view of things – his World Picture, Brough Lacey the neuro-surgeon had called it. He tried to address both of these items but might as well have tried to imagine what warped space looked like. It was impossible.

'So what can you do about it?' he asked himself, directing the spoken question at his subconscious. If his imagination wouldn't work, maybe the hidden part of his mind would answer through his vocal cords.

'Fuck all, old Dan,' he replied, and smiled grimly as the sickness in his head roiled. He angrily stabbed the pen through the pages of the paper then realised he'd obliterated the name of the woman accused of keeping a 'disorderly house', then realised with a sharp slap of surprise that a distant part of him had been considering looking her up in the telephone directory.

He checked his watch, told himself that he could go to the pub at seven and added that it was only another two and a half hours to wait and that wasn't so bad, was it? Alcoholic obliteration seemed like a very good idea right now. Maybe he would put on his good togs, get a few scotches down his neck in the Dragon and see if anyone wanted to go on what his brother would have called a Cunt Hunt at Martine's nightclub.

Or maybe you won't, old Dan, he thought, knowing that the idea was just as much a fantasy as that of phoning the Brighton Hill Madam. There was only one woman in the universe he wanted and the prospect of a clumsy and fumbling one night stand with a young Suzie look-alike – And *let's face it, Dan, that's what you'll go for* – didn't thrill him one little bit.

Suddenly he realised that what he really wanted was to see a band. Not a sophisticated electronic band, but a noisy hard-hitting rock band, and the louder the better. He wanted to drown in sound at such volume that his ears would ring for hours afterwards; wanted the fuzzy sick-headedness drilled out of him. He got up, thinking, *We'll ring Iain, and find out where the Rod Garfield Blues Band is playing tonight*! Then, halfway to the phone, was shocked at how he could possibly have had the thought. We *should have been* I, *and Iain the guitarist is one of Suzie's friends, not one of yours! Iain's number is in her diary, and her diary is in Oakley with her*.

Danny went back to the lounge and opened the *Gazette* at the entertainments pages to see who was playing at which pubs. There wasn't a great deal to choose from. The Pig and Whistle had a solo guitarist who used tapes to back him up, The White Hart had a reggae band and reggae wasn't what he wanted today, and that was that. Danny's eyes wandered across a review of a local writer's new book, scowled at the picture of the grinning idiot holding a copy up for the camera, and lit on an advertisement on the bottom right hand corner of the page.

Danny was not aware of the bad card that had been passed to him and the moment was marked only by a faint click in his right nostril. He sniffed and thought, *Probably the dodgy blood vessel, Dan*, and entertained the brief and – *almost certainly paranoid!* – notion that the advertisement had been placed purely for his benefit.

The Ancastle Trust Society (for the Furtherance of Spiritual Enlightenment), the advert informed him, were holding a demonstration of clairaudience by the World Famous Mrs Christine Richard, tonight at seven-thirty at Ancastle House, Castle road, Basingstoke. Admission £5 or by donation.

Danny smiled.

DON'T GO!

It was just like his mind to put the dampers on things as soon as something happened that might make things better for him. He liked the idea of going to the demonstration and if there was a cowardly little cry-baby down there in the bottom of his mind who wanted him to stay exactly where he was, in the pit of that little cry-baby's despair, then that little cry-baby could just go and fuck itself. *Someone* had to do something about this. *Someone* had to start making the decisions around here.

Danny ignored the cry-baby. 'That used to be the Family Planning Clinic,' he mused, already feeling the gnawing urge in his stomach which would eventually compel him to go.

Think about it, Danny! the cry-baby implored. *Think about Joey!*

Danny shook his head. '*Joey?*'

Joey!

Danny frowned, wondering if he really was going insane. Somehow, he didn't think so. For once, everything had become clear and logical. The fortuitous advert in the paper was simply that: chance. A stroke of luck. 'It may turn out to be a con run by a bunch of twisters,' he said aloud, 'but what's the harm in going? If there is something in it, I'll know, and perhaps I can talk to someone, ask them how it feels to have premonitions.' The hairs at the nape of his neck stood and a chilly finger traced the length of his spine. Danny ignored it.

'And even if it turns out there isn't anything in it, at least it'll prove to me that I don't have to worry about my visions any more. What's wrong with that?'

Reality is a jolly sketchy business, you know, Brough Lacey's voice said inside his head. *Unreality is only a hair's breadth away and most times indistinguishable from the real thing.*

'Whatever that might mean,' Danny said, and thought about it, long and hard.

3

At a quarter past seven he found himself standing outside the gate of Ancastle House which he had last been inside years ago with Suzie when she went on the pill. It was no longer the home of the Family Planning Clinic and it was no longer the building he remembered. Ancastle House – or whatever it had previously been called – had been half pulled down and rebuilt. The façade remained but the side of the building had been torn off and replaced by an ugly low-roofed timber building that looked like a meeting hall – except that it had no windows whatsoever. This eyesore of a hall extended down into the large garden and Danny wondered what blind man had granted it planning permission.

He stood for a few minutes, looking at the hall and thinking. He was no longer sure of the train of thought which had brought him here, no longer certain that he wanted to be here at all. The cry-baby in him had worked hard over the last two hours, finally resorting to giving him a screaming case of the *What ifs*? Danny had retaliated with a somewhat nihilistic bombardment of *So whats*? but now he was here, he didn't feel so confident. He thought that if there was anything to lose by coming, he was sure to lose it and wasn't certain that the converse would apply. In spite of his dismissal of the cry-baby's argument, he didn't know how much more he *could* lose and still stay sane.

The road was packed with cars, and smiling – mainly elderly – people were hurrying past him and entering the building. None of them looked the least bit frightened – or even mildly concerned. *But that's because they're not the Fucked-Up-Future-Man*, Danny thought. *Those people are expecting messages of undying love and hope from their deceased loved ones, not to be told they're cursed*.

This was the cry-baby's *coup de grâce*. What strategy-planning generals called the Nightmare Scenario. But Danny had some ammunition of his own in this mental battle. He had seen a T.V. program of a clairaudient at work and had believed she was a fake; working by adjusting her responses to fit what she thought her subject wanted to hear. He told the cry-baby that the Nightmare Scenario was not only terribly unlikely, but given that the psychic was going to be a fake, probably impossible.

If she's a fake, then don't bother going in. Go down to The Dragon and have a drink instead.

Something squeezed Danny's arm and he yelped. A tiny old lady smiled up at him. 'Hurry up, if you're coming in,' she said in a quavery voice that was filled with excitement. 'Otherwise it will have started and they don't let you in once it's started. It disturbs the flow, you see.' She went in through the gate, then turned and beckoned him. 'Hurry!' she called.

And Danny thrust aside his doubts and followed.

4

The windowless hall was hot, packed and noisy with whispered conversation. Danny was surprised to see how many people had crammed themselves into it. The congregation was – unsurprisingly – predominantly over fifty, with a sprinkling of the very elderly and one or two younger people. The atmosphere was awed and expectant. Danny walked down the aisle and looked for a seat, peripherally taking in how cheap and tacky everything looked. The seats were rows of dirty wooden pews that looked as if they had been salvaged from a fire-damaged church. There were dull, framed prints hanging on the walls. Tired velveteen curtains draped windows that didn't exist. The hall looked as if it had been here for thirty years or more.

Danny managed to squeeze on to the end of one of the benches, three rows from the front. The old man next to him grunted and shimmied away from him, allowing him a little more room. Danny mopped his sweating brow with a cool, clammy hand and took a deep breath. It was stuffy and hot in there; some thoughtful person had turned up the heating to combat the chilly evening and had neglected to turn it down again when the hall filled up. There didn't seem to be any flow of air through the room and Danny felt as if all the available oxygen had been used up before he arrived.

Told you you should have gone to the pub! Danny told himself as he gulped a deep breath of warm, stale air. That odd feeling of cold grasping fingers was creeping into the pit of his stomach again and Danny didn't care for it very much at all. He'd last had it before his vision and he could remember the consequences of that all too well. He considered simply getting up and leaving, then bit down hard on the thought, telling himself it would be like going to the dentist – not as quite traumatic as you'd feared.

At the front of the hall was a stage with a trestle table set out in the centre. The table was covered with green baize which had been pulled taut and pinned around the edges with drawing pins. On three sides, the covering had been neatly trimmed flush with the side of the table, but on the fourth – the left hand side – it hung in an untamed drape, ragged and fraying. There seemed to be something *wrong* about the table – something more than the fact that it was just as shoddily decorated as the rest of the hall – but Danny couldn't quite grasp what it was. Behind the table were three wooden chairs, their varnish yellowed and cracked with age.

Oh, come on! he thought, checking his watch. *Hurry it up!* But these were forced thoughts; an attempt to restore some of Brough Lacey's fragile reality to a scene which seemed more and more surreal as each moment passed.

The hall was starkly lit with unshaded clear light bulbs, and Danny wondered if they would turn them down when the demonstration started. He hoped they would go down slowly: he thought he might scream if he was suddenly plunged into darkness.

Danny was leaning forward, legs tensed to stand up and leave, when two men and an old woman came in through a side door and walked on to the stage. He sat back and joined in with the audience's warm applause. The men were middle-aged, neatly groomed and dressed in smart suits and the woman wore a white, loose fitting, Grecian style sun dress. The woman was an immense mountain of moving flesh and looked like a Sumo wrestler wearing a pup tent. She must, Danny thought, have weighed eighteen stone or more. Her face was made up and her features were tiny amongst the huge, loose diameter of her face. Her white hair was blue-rinsed and her big bottom lip hung slack. The effort of climbing up the few steps of the stage had sheened her face with sweat and made her gasp for breath.

As the applause died the three took their places at the table, the gasping woman-mountain in the centre and a man each side. The woman's chair was lost beneath her. The lights dimmed slowly – and Danny was thankful for that – and a low spotlight was turned on, illuminating the table at such an angle that the woman now looked like a monster from a cheap horror film.

One of the men stood up and said, 'The Ancastle Trust is delighted to have been able to arrange this evening's visit by the world famous clairaudient Mrs Christine Richard, and would like to extend a warm welcome to her.' He turned to the woman and said. 'It's good to have you here!' The audience applauded. Christine Richard nodded her huge head, her chin coming and going as it rose and fell into her heavy jowls.

The man went on to detail Christine Richard's life, explaining how she had discovered she was a clairaudient psychic at puberty when she first began to hear voices from the other side; how Christine had battled long and hard – and eventually won – against the evil forces that had tried to dominate her and possess her; how she had led a selfless life dedicated to bringing messages of hope and peace to the people from their loved ones who had passed over.

Danny studied the jewellery that hung sparkling from Christine's fat wrists and ringed her chubby fingers and decided that her life hadn't been *that* selfless. *And besides that, she must have a food bill each week as big as the national debt*, he thought.

The first man was applauded as he finished and the other man stood and said a short prayer that Danny didn't recognise.

You could still leave, y'know, Danny's cry-baby told him. *There's still time! If you go now while everyone's praying, no one will notice*.

But Danny wanted to stay. Even though he knew it was a confidence trick; even though the cold iron fingers in his stomach had vanished, leaving a vacuum behind them.

The prayer ended and the two men left the stage and took seats that had been reserved for them in the front row. The angle of the spotlight was adjusted remotely so that only Mrs Richard was illuminated. She stood up.

'There are . . . many spirits here . . . among us . . . tonight,' she announced, looking up towards the darkened ceiling. Between the pauses in which Christine Richard's breath could be heard being harshly drawn in, her voice was surprisingly strong and clear.

'I'd like . . . you all . . . to remain . . . silent for a . . . little while,' she continued, 'until I gather . . . my wits and get . . . in the right frame of mind. It won't . . . take long, and I won't be . . . going into a complete trance, so . . . we'll be able to comm . . . unicate with one another . . . with no problem.'

Followed by the spotlight, Christine Richard walked slowly around to the front of the trestle table and wiggled her way on to it, spreading as she settled. Danny saw the table bow under her weight, heard its legs complain and fully expected it to collapse under her weight. Mrs Richard gasped for breath, folded her arms in her lap and cocked her head up to the side.

'She's got someone,' the old man next to Danny whispered. 'She's listening!' Danny shivered.

The audience was silent and only an occasional cough or the creak of a pew penetrated the quiet.

'Is there someone . . . here called . . . Jack or Jackie?' Mrs Richard asked. The hall lights were raised a little and Danny, steadily feeling more and more strange, joined everyone else in turning round and searching the hall for a Jack or Jackie. There was a few moments' silence and people began to mutter.

'Yes,' a man called out. He was plump man aged about fifty who was standing in the doorway with his hand up like a schoolboy.

He's a plant, Danny thought. *Must be!*

'What is . . . your name, Jack or Jackie?' Mrs Richard demanded.

'Jack, but my wife called me Jackie,' he told her in a small, shaky voice.

'Your wife's name . . . is Yvonne,' Mrs Richard announced. 'She is . . . *here* . . . with us now.'

Danny turned and looked at Jackie again. He was nodding rapidly.

Up on the stage, Christine Richard made a show of listening.

'She tells me she . . . has only recently . . . passed over. She died of cancer . . . Lung cancer. Is that correct?'

'Yes,' Jack said. His voice now contained so much emotion that Danny didn't believe he was a plant at all. Danny no longer knew what he believed.

'She wants you to . . . know that she is . . . perfectly happy and is relieved . . . that the pain is all gone. She says . . . she is with you . . . always. . .' Mrs Richard cocked her ear to the ceiling and said, 'You'll have to . . . speak up my . . . lovely. I can't quite . . . hear you.' Then she nodded and chuckled. 'She says you still . . . have all her clothes and that . . . you should give them . . . to the charity shop because she . . . won't be needing them any more. She says . . . there are lots of needy . . . people who could make . . . good use of them. She says that . . . you know how she feels about you . . . hoarding things. Is that correct, Jackie love?'

If Jackie had entertained any doubts about coming to this meeting, they were now assuaged. If he had disbelieved, he was now a confirmed believer. He looked blissfully happy and tears were streaming down his face. 'Y-Yes, that's her all r-right,' he stammered happily.

'She says to keep . . . the vase . . . the one you broke and spent hours . . . sticking back together because it was her favourite. She says remember . . . her by the vase. Did you . . . buy it for her?'

'I brought it back from a buh-business truh-hip to Rome,' Jackie sobbed, but Christine Richard was busy listening to another spirit voice now and wasn't listening to his reply.

'Carol . . . There is someone here called . . . Liza . . . *wait! No, he can't!*' The woman frowned and her wheezy voice was sharp. A little too sharp for Danny's liking. He thought he detected a note of fear in it. He didn't like the tone of this at all. His head seemed to be full of warm water. *Someone or something is trying to get a message through to you, old Dan,* he thought. *And Christine doesn't want them – or it – to do it. Who do you suppose it'll be? Father Christmas? I think not. I'll tell you who I think it'll be* . . . Danny thrust the thought aside before it could complete itself.

'Do we have a Carol with us?' Christine Richard almost shouted. It was the first time she'd got all the way through a sentence without gasping for breath.

A pretty teenager stood up from a row near the front. Her hair was blonde and straight and hung all the way down to a neat, denimed bosom. 'I'm Carol,' she said, in a matter-of-fact voice which suggested there was nothing odd whatsoever in holding conversations with the dead. 'Liza is – was – my mother's name. She passed over five years ago. Is she here?'

'Yes, she's here . . . darling. She says she . . . loves you and is watching over you and Simon. Is that . . . your brother?'

'He's in Austria,' Carol said, nodding. 'Designing a building.'

Christine Richard frowned again and shook her head. 'She says that . . . the interview was . . . a success. Have you applied for . . . a job, my darling? You've passed the . . . interview and there is a letter . . . on the way. Does that sound likely?'

'Yes, yes!' Carol squeaked. 'It was a job at the B.B.C. I thought they'd forgotten about me!'

'She says you will . . . be happy and you will make . . . a go of it. But to watch out for . . . Mister Miller. Okay, darling?'

The girl chuckled and sat down. Danny wondered who Mr Miller was. Evidently both Mrs Richard and Carol knew.

Many questions and doubts were now popping into Danny's

water-filled head. He had expected lots of bitter tears and disappointment and emotional scenes, but here was the famous Christine Richard apparently acting as a go-between for the dead and the living so they could pass the time of day with one another. She was being a telephone line between this world and the next, and it was of no consequence at all. It meant nothing.

The biggest mystery of life, and no one's wondering about it at all! he thought. *Why doesn't anyone ask what it's like to be dead? Why doesn't someone ask what things look like in the next dimension? Where do the dead live? Ha ha, Danny, good joke. How do they survive? What do they do?*

'Sally Anstey? I have a message . . . for a Sally . . . Anstey . . . She's not here, darling! Oh! . . . No . . . Now go *away*!'

The clairaudient was being harassed again. Danny sank into his seat.

But there was no message coming in for him. Christine shrugged off whatever voice was bothering her auditory centres, got up from the sagging table and glided up and down the stage picking up names and the details of people's lives and giving them comfort. Danny listened carefully and in spite of the vacuum that remained in his stomach, he began to feel more confident.

There wasn't going to be a message coming through for him after all. There now seemed to be a good reason for this. It also explained why no one had asked what it was like in the next world. It wasn't because no one wanted to know; it was because they knew subconsciously that if they did ask, the world famous Mrs Richard wouldn't be able to tell them. The reason why was that the messages were not coming from the dead at all – even if Christine Richard thought they were (and Danny believed she *did* think that). Christine, Danny thought, was not *clairaudient* at all: she was *telepathic*. Unknown to her, she was hearing the contents of people's minds in much the same way as he had heard Suzie's thoughts just before she said, 'It's about time we did something with the bathroom.' It all added up. At no time had Christine told anyone something that they couldn't possibly have known. Even when she had pointed out to Carol that her letter of acceptance from the B.B.C. was on the way she might have been interpreting subliminal signs that Carol had picked up during the interview but wasn't aware of.

Telepathy wasn't so difficult to understand as some of the other psychic phenomena if you imagined that brainwaves – which after all, could easily be measured by machinery – probably radiated out from everyone like T.V. signals only on a much higher frequency and for a much smaller distance. If this really did happen – and Danny couldn't see any reason to doubt it – then it would be a simple matter to receive and decode them with the right machinery. And perhaps Mrs Richard's brain *was* the right machinery, although she was ignorant of it and thought she was conversing with dead people.

Perhaps she was just watching old movies of people's lives and commenting on them.

Danny watched Christine Richard pulling old memories from people's lives for the next half an hour.

She was halfway through telling someone about what their deceased mother was advising about her son-in-law who'd 'been in a bit of bother with the police' when she tailed off and the unthinkable happened.

Christine said, 'And he must . . . darling . . . absolutely *must* seek professional help because . . . there are therapists . . . who understand these . . . unnatural longings and. . .' She winced and clutched her stomach then yelled, '*DANNY!*'

He was taken totally by surprise. He jolted upright in his seat and went rigid, his bullet scar throbbing wildly. Fear poured into the vacuum in his stomach and pulsed through his veins freezing what had been warm blood only a second before. 'Nuuuh,' he heard himself whisper.

Christine Richard stood up straight, an expression of exquisite surprise on her sweaty face. Her jowls wobbled and her bottom lip trembled as she gasped a wheezing breath and raised her hands before her. 'I. . .'. Her hands fluttered like birds, then clawed and pressed her temples as if she had been struck with a sudden pain. She suddenly pitched forward as if someone had given her a full-blooded whack in the stomach with a baseball bat and again she spat out his name as if it was red hot: '*DANNY!*' Her tone was horrified, her face pale and shocked.

Reality is a jolly sketchy business, Brough Lacey's voice repeated in Danny's mind.

Who will it be, old Dan? his mind screamed at him. *Not Father Christmas, oh no, not him! I think I know who it'll be. . .*

Still gasping, Christine Richard straightened herself. It looked as if it hurt her to stand. 'No!' she said angrily, apparently addressing whoever or whatever was standing beside her. 'Daniel is not . . . *NO!* It is not possible. He isn't. He . . . he is not here. We have no . . . NO! *STOP IT!*'

It's a very long way to Africa, a birdy voice informed Danny's rolling mind.

Someone turned the hall lights on. Everything looked as if it had been badly faked. *Crossed that fine line now!* Danny screamed to himself. *We're in the the realms of unreality now and there won't be any getting back! Oh God, oh Joey, help me!*

Up on the stage, still in the extra-bright glare of the follow spot, Christine Richard was either in the throes of some kind of fit or being attacked by the thing she thought she had spoken to. She was being violently thrust back and forth across the stage, staggering and hopping, her huge arms wheeling in circles as she fought to keep her balance. Sweat flew from her as she moved, twinkling in the bright lights. The audience was murmuring in alarm and the two men who had sat beside the psychic on the stage were now on their feet and hurrying up the steps.

Danny was also on his feet. He had managed to get his legs under him, but they had suddenly set as solid as concrete piles and would not bear him away. Other members of the audience were rising. Behind Danny someone screamed and the emergency exit door crashed open admitting a cold wind into the hall.

Christine Richard did a dainty pirouette and sat down hard on the trestle table, the legs of which splayed out dangerously. The huge bulk of her body undulated beneath her dress as if it was being manipulated by unseen hands. Her breasts rose and fell. The wattles of spare flesh at her ankles pulled upwards and and her jowls and neck rippled in fast waves. Her eyelids were fluttering as if trying to clear invisible sand that someone was throwing into them and her hair began to rise, lock by lock, until it was a blue halo around her head.

The two men who had introduced her didn't now look quite so keen on rushing to her aid. They reached the side of the stage and stopped, uncertain of what they should – or could – do. The psychic shook her head and clawed at the air.

'Let me out of here!' a shrill female voice shouted from behind Danny. 'Get out of the fucking way!'

Next to Danny the elderly man wanted to leave too. His face was ashen and he was shaking his head and muttering, 'This can't happen. It just can't happen! 'Scuse me, boy! I said, *GET OUT OF MY WAY!*' He grabbed Danny's arms and pushed him out into the aisle. Danny's row emptied as people fled.

Not quite so much fun now, old Dan, is it? a small, clear voice asked him. *Know who's coming? I do. . .*

People pushed past Danny from the front rows as up on the stage Christine Richard's lips worked soundlessly. Carol brushed past him and Danny felt the softness of her breasts against his chest, smelled her perfume – and *knew* that Carol had never been for an interview at the B.B.C. in her life. Her mother was alive and well and living in Cheltenham and she didn't have a brother at all. He didn't know what this could mean, and he didn't care.

Christine heaved in a breath so ragged that Danny expected it to be her last. 'Danny,' she whispered. Her head juddered back and forth.

'Yes,' he heard his voice say quietly. It wasn't him working it, there was no doubt about that. He was too busy inwardly screaming at his legs to follow those good folks straight out of the fire door. *Guess who's coming, guess who's coming, guess who's coming!* a part of his mind chanted, while another – totally separate – part of it babbled, *Fuck you, legs! Come on and get me out of here! Move, Danny! Run! Quickly!*

He dimly realised that his war wound was pulsing in time with his racing heart and something in his nose was clicking audibly. His balls were drawn up tight to his body and there was a spot inside him between them and his anus that felt as if it were on fire. From the corner of his eye he saw that he was raising his right hand in the air like the old chap with the dead wife had done. He tried to bring it down again but it would not respond.

'Here I am,' he heard his awed voice say and inwardly cursed himself. *Crossed that fine line, Danny! You've crossed that hair's breadth and jumped into the chasm! Now who's coming?*

Christine Richard stood up so fast it looked as if someone had grabbed her head, hauled her up until her body had straightened and then crashed her down on her feet. 'Huhhh!' she groaned, then gasped air and yelled, 'GET AWAY FROM ME!' as she tottered stiff-legged towards the edge of the stage. Her face finally stopped rippling and cleared. 'Are you Daniel Stafford?' she asked in a bewildered voice as her eyes focused on him for the first time.

The hall had suddenly fallen silent. Those who were leaving had gone and those who were doubtful had relaxed now they knew the trouble wasn't coming their way. The two organisers were still frozen on the edge of the stage. All eyes looked at Danny. Everyone held their breath, eager not to miss whatever was going to happen.

Not you, Dan! Don't tell her it's you! Guess who's coming!

'That's me,' his motormouth said. *Hickorydickorydickorydickory! Africa's a long way!*

'Someone wants to . . . h-hurt . . . you D-Dannnnielll!' she boomed. 'Suh-mm-whunn!'

Danny didn't have to guess who was coming. It wasn't Father Christmas and it wasn't any of his relatives who might have died since he last spoke to them. He knew who was coming with a terrible icy clarity. He knew it in his very bones.

That terrible nightmare creation of his own was coming.

The Gannex Man.

Christine Richard yelped like a slapped dog, doubled up and teetered on the very edge of the stage. Something hit her and hit her hard. Danny saw the shockwave ripple through her undulating flesh. The verbal part of his brain ceased operations and shut up shop. His heart squeezed in his chest and cramped, holding the beat. The thing inside his nose clicked, popped and threw a gout of blood down his coat front. Danny went rigid. 'Oh, Christ, look at him! What's *happened* to him?' a girl whispered from nearby.

When Christine Richard spoke again, her voice was no longer her own. It had deepened from a breathless hissing soprano to a tenor, become coarser, and was now slightly accented with a Hampshire brogue. It was a voice Danny knew well.

'*You know what you did, old Danny! You made it happen!*' Christine grated. Her eyes had rolled up and a string of drool ran from her protruding bottom lip. '*You did it to her, Danny! You put the blood on the knife and it was Ten-up!*'

Whose voice? The question bounced around in Danny's empty brain.

And in his vacant mind a picture of the girl's body grew – taut, slender and supple and webbed with rivulets of blood as she scrambled across the floor, not screaming, now, but moaning almost sexually in her terror. He would have her now. Oh God, he wanted her.

'No,' Danny moaned in a small voice.

'*You fucked her, Danny. And fucked her with the steel too!*'

And Danny's memory lit with the way it had felt as the cool knife met solid flesh. The resistance, the squealing, the pushing, the parting flesh, the *wanting*.

Whose voice?

'*How she moved under you! You tasted her life, Danny, and bust your barometer! It was Ten-up, Danny.* TEN-UP!'

Winter filled him. Snow blew through him and crunched under his feet, admitting them easily as they sunk into its coldness. A snow-dappled hedgerow was two hundred yards in front of him and there were pieces of torn material hanging from it, fluttering in the wind. He didn't want to know what was there, but his feet bore him relentlessly toward it.

'*We are one!*'

Suzie lit in his vision, bruised, naked and screaming, arms and legs spread as she backed away across the bed until she could go no further. She made herself small against the wall and gloved hands roughly took her ankles, dragged her back.

Whose voice?

The girl's blood was on him, enveloping him, filling his nostrils and mouth. His feet were in snow. Suzie was screaming. There was something else – something he couldn't see – and it was important.

'*I mean to have you!*' Christine Richard boomed.

Joey cocked his head up sideways, looked disdainfully at Danny, said: '*Africa's a long way!*' and fluttered out of the window, leaving a silhouetted image of spread wings and splayed tail feathers behind him.

Cold filled Danny and flowed through him, chilling him to absolute zero. All motion stopped.

It's your voice, Dan, a hell-like thought pealed in his head. *You are listening to a fat woman you've never seen before speaking in your voice and using your words.*

'*I'M COMING FOR YOU, OLD DAN!*'

Not my words, Danny thought. And the fire between his testes and anus began to rage again, cracking the ice that was in his body. Danny could feel himself splintering. There was sniggering invading his mind. He tried to scream, but his throat was still frozen and no sound came to his lips.

Up on the stage Christine Richard collapsed as though her skeleton had been suddenly removed. She sat down on her haunches and toppled forwards over the edge of the stage, arms in front of her like a swimmer learning to duck-dive. The two organisers ran towards her, not yet realising they would be better employed on the floor where they were going to have to try to pick her up.

Christine Richard's face hit the floor with a terrifying thump and the weight of her massive body drove down on top of her, flicking her chin up and giving Danny one last chance to look into her eyes which were empty and terrified. Her neck cracked audibly and her body flicked back, hit the stage's riser and flowed down it, driving her face five feet closer to Danny. Her eyes were still open, but the light in them had gone. Christine Richard had given her last performance.

The silent hall burst into sound. Men shouted and babbled. A woman in front of Danny began to scream hysterically. The two organisers stopped at the edge of the stage and peered down at their dear departed psychic, and several other people crashed out of the fire door. Danny stood rooted to the spot, blood steadily pulsing from his nose and soaking his coat.

That got rid of her, didn't it? You killed her, old Dan! How did it feel? Ten-up? Danny's alien voice whispered inside his mind.

The fire inside him cruised up his spine and filled his head. Danny's bladder squeezed then evacuated itself.

'Don't get near that one!' someone shrieked shrilly. 'Keep away from him!'

Danny's head turned and saw more of the expressions of fear he was becoming used to. There was no one within five feet of him.

'He's pissed himself!' a disgusted voice called out. 'And look at the *blood*!'

'What did you *do* to her, you *bastard*?' another voice demanded.

The ground parted beneath Danny's feet. It crumbled and yawned under him and Danny dropped into extreme darkness. Parts of him began to move. There was motion out there somewhere.

Something hard hit him, and Danny bounced off it, listening to the distant sniggering, knowing and terrible. Cold air washed over him. Gravel crunched under his unseen feet and then they began to pound a non-existent wet pavement.

You can run, but you can't hide from me, old Dan! The taunting evil voice filled his head and Danny knew the alien voice was his own.

Somewhere out there a mouth was filling with a warm, salty liquid while a fire raged up and down a lightning conductor which may or may not have been his spine. Urine, now cold, stuck cloth to the running legs and a young girl's blood was enveloping and caressing a distant penis.

You can run. . .!

Balance was lost. The uninhabited body sprawled on the ground, sliding on damp tarmac. A cheekbone juddered and bounced on hard ground and cloth tore around knees which were instantly grazed. A car horn sounded. An unintelligible voice shouted.

. . . but you can't. . .!

Now the body was up again, zig-zagging this way and that through an obstacle course of what felt like parked cars whenever the body slammed against them. Then the ground liquefied and there was only fizzling and popping and the voice.

. . . hide from me, old Dan!

Then even the voice faded. Its echoes resounded growing steadily fainter, more distant until there was nothing at all.

Nothing.

5

Danny was cold and wet and he hurt all over. They had caught him and made him pay. Tortured him until he'd blacked out. Still semi conscious, he shifted his position on the cold, hard ground, feeling the hands on the back of his neck again, pressing his face down so that he breathed in water.

They're drowning you! his mind shrieked. *Fight back!* Choking and coughing out dank water, he forced himself to his knees, fully expecting another blow to the back of his head. The last blows had taken away his consciousness. If they hit him again, he was certain he would die.

But there was no resistance to his movements. No blow came and no strong hand forced his face back into the water. Danny's eyes opened and he blearily saw a vast, black empty plain extending out in front of him. The hard surface was studded with pools of water which rippled and reflected orange light. He blinked hard and felt as if his mind was pouring back into his brain from wherever it had been hiding; jetting in at high pressure through a tiny aperture.

When his senses settled – although he didn't think they would remain stable for very long because they no longer seemed fixed in place – Danny realised that he was not in a torture chamber, or lost in a black desert, but on his hands and knees on the wet tarmac of the top storey of Basingstoke town centre's multi-storey car park. It was raining hard. There were no torturers and the tub of water his head had been forced into was nothing more than a puddle in which he had evidently been lying. The car park was desolate, empty of cars and people, and it was lit with sodium lamps which reflected orange in the wet and gave the place a nightmarish quality.

Danny had no idea how he had come to be here and no memory whatsoever of where he'd been. The last thing he remembered was wanting to hear music and leafing through the *Basingstoke Gazette* to see who was playing where.

Which means that it's Friday, he told himself. Then added, *unless you've been out of it for quite a bit longer than it seems.* This was possible. He had lost sixteen and a half hours that time he'd almost electrocuted himself. *So it could be anywhen*, he admitted. He searched his mind for the missing details, but as on the other occasion there was an empty section in his memory. It had turned itself off at the point where he was looking in the *Gazette* and turned itself on again now. *Either that or it erased itself*, he thought.

Danny tried to stand up and found it harder going than he had anticipated. His head felt as delicate as a cracked egg and when he moved it, shot pain into him from several directions simultaneously. His left cheek was badly grazed and all his joints ached. He stood up slowly, crouching first and letting his balance settle, then slowly raising himself. At each point in this marathon feat he discovered a new injury. His knuckles were cut and bleeding slightly from beneath the loose caps of ripped skin, both the knees of his trousers were ripped out and his knees themselves were grazed. His nose had been bleeding – badly, judging by the amount of blood around his sore chin and the stains on his coat. There was an egg-like lump on his forehead. Danny looked at his watch to see what time and what day it was and there was a space where it should have been. Now he was on his feet, nausea began to rise.

I got mugged, he thought in dazed surprise, *that's what's happened. I must have gone to see a band and been attacked on the way home.*

But he didn't remember the fight – and there *must* have been one – or any of the other details of the ordeal. Even the word sounded wrong. Danny shook his head – which was a mistake. His stomach contracted in a violent spasm and he threw up, long and hard, gradually folding again, so that by the time the biliousness had ceased he was back on his hands and knees.

He observed the ancient and respected getting-up ceremony once more and staggered over to the wall at the edge of the car park. The town centre was empty too. No muggers or torture teams lurked down there in the orange-tinted shadows, waiting to attack him again. Marks & Sparks' lights were on, but there was no one in there either. A lonely wire shopping trolley waited outside for the following morning's rush.

Danny's penis hurt and he thought someone might have aimed a kick at his balls and been slightly off target. He undid the waistband of his trousers and gently slid his sore hand into his underpants.

She's dead now, he thought, and didn't know where the thought had come from.

In seconds he had a fairly good idea.

His balls were tight – so tight in fact that the left one seemed to have slid back into his body and was drawn up snugly against his pubic bone. The right one wasn't far behind it. His penis had become small and stiff – not engorged with blood and erect, but as if all the blood had been removed from it. He was sore but now he didn't think he had been kicked at all. It was worse than that. His underwear was soaked and sticky with recently ejaculated semen. This, combined with the odd thought, pointed to the mind-numbing possibility that during his fugue he had sexually attacked and probably killed a woman.

'That isn't *possible!*' he gasped, remembering many bold headlines in countless woman's magazines asking: *Could your Partner be a Rapist?* He and Suzie had discussed the possibility and found the contention that there was a rapist lurking inside every man wanting, if not laughable. There was no rapist inside Danny Stafford. *But there's come in his pants and signs of a violent struggle on his body, isn't there? And there's a missing watch for evidence, too. What'll you do in the morning if there's a reported rape attempt that ended in murder? What'll you do then, poor thing? Hide your head under your wing, poor thing?*

But there was a chance – however slim – that the ejaculation had been caused by a blow or shock of some kind. He'd seen films in which vets had collected semen for artificial insemination by sliding probes up the anuses of anaesthetised animals and electrically stimulating their prostate glands until they had orgasms. It *could* happen.

But no one stuck anything up your *ass, did they?* he asked himself, vaguely remembering something that felt like a fire burning deep in his crotch.

'I was robbed. Someone landed a blow on me that made me come,' he said, fighting off the dread that was slowly building in him. 'That's what it was.'

And his hand went to his inside jacket pocket to confirm that he had, indeed been robbed. His wallet was missing.

Except that his wallet was still there. Danny's fingers touched the old leather and he distantly imagined the wallet grinning at him and then doing a wheezing laugh like Dick Dastardly's dog Muttley used to do in Whacky Races.

Then his fingers found something else in that pocket, backed up behind the grinning wallet. It was a piece of cardboard and Danny had not put it there.

Unless you did it during your blank period, he reminded himself.

Frowning, he pulled the piece of cardboard from his pocket, a picture of an immense blue-rinsed woman falling on to her head forming in his mind. Was that the woman who was dead? Did he kill her? He thought not.

The cardboard was an oblong which had been carefully cut from the front panel of a packet of Frosties so that Tony the Tiger was neatly framed.

Why would I put a picture of Tony the fucking Tiger in my pocket? Danny asked himself in bemusement staring at the picture.

The Gannex Man did it, he suddenly thought. And the memory of being stalked through his nightmares came back to him. That alien part of him seemed very close to him now. He thought he might have *become* the Gannex Man during his blank spell.

Christine Richard, he thought. *That's who the woman was. She died, Dan. You didn't kill her. She died.* But he didn't know who she was or how he knew of her death.

He threw away the picture of Tony the Tiger, spinning it like a frisbee. As soon as he threw it, he realised that he'd made a mistake. There was writing on the grey side of the cardboard. He saw the scrawled words the moment the picture left his hand.

The Gannex Man had left him a message.

And the message sailed over the parapet and fluttered down on to the wet pavement of the town centre.

Good riddance, Danny thought. *Leave it where it fell. I don't want to know, thank you very much.*

Then he realised that there was a possibility – if he *had* done something wrong – that he might have written something on it that would incriminate or identify him, or both.

Danny's insulted mind was now detaching itself from him again – he could feel it trying to force itself back through that tiny hole into nowhere land. There wasn't much time before the emptiness that would surely follow admitted the Gannex Man again, and trying – and failing – to ignore his pains and injuries, Danny hurried to the nearest staircase, pausing halfway to throw up again.

By the time he retrieved the message from the wet pavement and took it over to Marks & Spencer's lit window to read it, his mind was almost all gone again. His wallet was still sniggering in his jacket pocket and voices were rolling around in his head like thunder. Some were accusing him of having committed some unspecified crime, others pointed out that he had pissed himself. Women screamed and men shouted and the Gannex Man was whispering that he meant to have Danny and that Danny could run but he couldn't hide.

The message written on the grey, unprinted side of the Frosties packet had been clumsily inscribed in pencil. Danny's eyes wouldn't immediately focus on the words – they were too faint, and the steady rain was already darkening the cardboard. He blinked his eyes and squinted at the message. It was not written in his handwriting. The words were too spiky and cramped, the descenders had no loops and were too long, and there was no punctuation.

Neither was it a message from the Gannex Man. It read:

Daniel

You already know no doubt that you are in trouble It is just starting for you and now things will only get worse I'm sorry to say You are going to need help and there are people who can provide it When you do realise you need help telephone this number 93 0234770 and you will be helped with your difficulty Do not throw this number away I must warn you of this This problem of yours is only just starting and will get much worse perhaps even to the extent of killing you Remember you can be helped

The light was fading before Danny's eyes. It was a Reading telephone number; he recognised the code. He had not been mugged. Something had made him lose consciousness, just as something was making him lose consciousness now, and someone else knew about it. That person who, surprise surprise, had neglected to leave his name, had been following Danny while he either moved on automatic pilot or was being driven by his old friend the Gannex Man, and that person had watched him collapse and instead of helping him, had stolen his watch from his wrist and put the message in his pocket. The question was, *why?*

But too much of Danny had fled down that pin-hole into the elsewhere for him to address the question, let alone answer it.

As the last vestiges of his sanity turned sour, Danny thrust the cryptic message back into his pocket, pointed himself in the direction he hoped would eventually lead to his home and started to shuffle across the steadily softening concrete. The buildings gradually altered, turning into structures he no longer recognised or understood. Within minutes he was travelling through a blasted alien landscape.

But no longer knowing or caring, Danny walked.

He walked for a very long time.

Chapter Seven
The Week at Nine Twenty-one

1

Everything was black-rimmed and ugly. Furniture which had once been comfortable and cosy was now quietly threatening, silently challenging him to: *Just try to use me!* while it hunched there wishing him bad thoughts. Danny thought he could see the dark and convoluted strings of hatred sluggishly extending out from the furniture towards him in fat, knobbled ropes. The carpet seethed angrily beneath his feet, wishing to swallow him, to draw him down and overcome him, swamping him and making him a part of its too-garish design. The oily air tasted of diesel fumes and pressed on him hatefully, restricting his movements. James Brown rang distantly in his ears, urging him to 'stay on the scene, like a sex machine!'

Things flickered in and out of existence at the periphery of his vision and Danny recognised none of them except the huge figure of Christine Richard who constantly repeated her death-dive from a stage which wasn't there, landing with her neck broken and her empty eyes staring at him. Danny screamed each time, swinging his head around to rail against her dead body, but she simply winked out of existence the moment he moved.

Bird wings beat the air around his head, fluttering madly, and somewhere down below the rasping voice of the Godfather of Soul, Danny could hear Joey's bell taking a beating, the way it always did when the bird wanted to come out for a fly-by.

Danny thought he could hear another voice below that, muttering dark accusations, but he wasn't certain. He was no longer certain of anything at all other than the dimly realised fact that he had been transported to one of hell's many chambers of torture.

Time had ceased. Danny searched the house for a clock that still worked and couldn't find one. Every single clock and watch in the house had stopped. Blank digital faces stared up at him, taunting him. The analogue clocks on the cooker and the kitchen wall had frozen at nine twenty-one, the lounge and dining-room clocks at the same time. It was vitally important to know the time. Danny didn't know why, but the overriding urge to know forced him to search the house again. Then, curled up in a ball on the lounge carpet, he remembered that he needed to know the time and conducted the frantic search all over again. He looked at his wrist a thousand times and thought, *Someone stole my wrist watch and I'll never be able to tell the time again!* Then instantly forgot it and thought, *My watch has vanished from my wrist! Someone stole my wrist watch!*

At nine twenty-one by the kitchen clock, Danny found himself standing in front of the only item in the house that didn't seem threatening. It was the drinks cabinet. This too was edged in black, but there didn't seem to be any fearsome emanations coming from it. The door slid down easily to make the dispensing shelf and Danny watched a hand – it might have been his or it might have belonged to a stranger – rise before him and select a bottle of dark rum. Its glass was cool and smooth under the hand, the ridged glass neck welcomed his lips. The rum trickled into his mouth and down his throat, scalding like molten metal.

Is it too early to drink before half-past nine? a distant part of Danny's mind asked as Christine Richard death dived into the carpet to his right. *It's okay if it's nine twenty-one in the evening*, he told himself, *but is it evening or morning?* He looked at the white strip of skin on his wrist – the only evidence of last summer's tan – and thought, with a fresh shock, *My watch has vanished. . .*

Looking out of the window didn't work. It was grey outside, neither night nor day. Everything out there was fogged and insubstantial somehow. Jimmy Reed's Volvo may have been a cardboard representation of the real thing; the houses at either side of his terrace could not be seen and may well have slipped away to another dimension – or stayed where they were when Danny's house tripped through that hole in reality. The flat car park on the other side of the road was, barring the odd faked vehicle, almost empty, and beyond that – where The Great Western pub and the back of the railway station lay – nothing could be seen at all. At the bottom of the car park everything faded to a bleary greyness.

Danny poured liquid fire into himself. Joey twittered in his ears.

2

At nine twenty-one, Danny found his lips closing round the welcoming coolness of a different bottle, felt the fiery liquid scalding his throat and stomach. Later, the greyness brightened and then grew dull again, but nothing made sense anymore. The television was on but he recognised none of the programmes and the presenters spoke in a language so unlike English that Danny only understood a few words of each sentence – not enough to comprehend what was being said. Someone had turned on the teletext clock and up in the right hand corner of the screen, it flickered through hours, minutes and seconds. But each time Danny read the figures – and he *knew* they weren't stuck because he could see the numbers changing – they were magically translated by his mind to match the time stated by the clocks elsewhere in the house and always seemed to read nine twenty-one.

At nine twenty-one, Danny's legs folded under him. He fell down softly on the carpet and immediately began to leach into it. For a few moments he struggled against the vampiric pattern then he lost consciousness.

This was the first of many periods of unconsciousness that would follow, but it was neither true unconsciousness nor true sleep. Those seemingly brief periods of rest which always began and ended at nine twenty-one were simply moments when his senses refused to take any more external input. During them, Danny was plunged into a tortured darkness in which nothing existed but the sound of his own voice, echoing across the vast plain of his mind as it whispered terrible things to him. In the seconds before his eyes flipped open again, he dearly wanted to respond to the foul suggestions and commands because he dimly knew that he was nothing and would remain nothing until the wishes of his subconscious had been complied with. In those seconds, the fire behind his bladder would light again and pulse molten messages up his spine. His penis would become erect – not just hard, but as rigid as steel tubing – and Danny would see steel flashing, experience the good power as it drove solidly home into flesh.

But when he woke, the images and the voice vanished and his memory of them faded almost instantly, leaving him with the dying embers of the fire and a quickly subsiding erection.

Danny woke up in the hall with the telephone handset clutched in his right hand and the bitter aftertaste of the words *Help me!* on his lips. A small flicker of hope lit in him. *Broken out of it! Got help!* he thought groggily, bringing the receiver up to his ear to see who was coming for him.

Please replace the handset and try again . . . please replace the handset and try again . . . please replace the handset . . . the recorded announcement suggested.

Danny slammed the receiver back into its cradle and sat back staring blankly at the phone as the knowledge of what it was and how you used it trickled out of his head. Tears of despair grew in his eyes, brimmed and trickled down his cheeks, reminding him faintly of a girl he once knew. He knew nothing about her other than the fact that he had loved her. A huge, aching emptiness grew inside him and he sobbed.

Her tears, Dan! Her tears!

Christine Richard appeared from the wall, fell like a massive blancmange on to the telephone table and broke her neck. Her blank eyes looked up at him, accusing. Danny lost consciousness.

He woke with an empty bottle in one hand and a picture of Tony the Tiger in the other. There was a message scrawled on the reverse of the piece of cardboard and the message read: *Nine twenty-one nine twenty-one nine nine twenty-nine one nine twenty-one twenty-one.*

Danny tore the cardboard into small pieces, put them in the dry, fuming pit that had once been his mouth, chewed them and swallowed them, fighting off the gag reflex until he was certain the message would stay where it belonged.

Light grey followed dark grey, and at nine twenty-one Danny found himself finishing another bottle. This one didn't burn as much. Nothing burned as much now – there was very little of him left to burn. He was physically empty and mentally vacant. At nine twenty-one there was nothing left to drink. No cool glass bottles of fiery relief. Only clear, empty ones. Danny took one from the kitchen table and hefted it at the kitchen window. The window burst and the bottle smashed on the garden path with a noise like fairy bells. Greyness washed in from outside and smelled of blood and steel and diesel fumes.

Danny drank water. The stream of water that ran from the black-bordered cold tap in the kitchen was also framed with black. Danny found himself upstairs again, standing on the threshold of the bathroom with his trousers and pants down round his ankles. *The water!* he thought, but the water in there was just as tainted as that from the kitchen and it was more dangerous to obtain. Danny didn't remember going into the bathroom at all, but he must have visited it before because he *did* recall the gravity situation in there. The gravity situation in there was zero. No gees at all. One step inside that bathroom with those tiles that telescoped out and Newton's favourite force was no longer. You went in there, you fell. For ever and ever amen. Even Danny, with no thoughts in his head and very little left in the way of memory, knew that.

Not knowing whether he'd learned this by attempting to take a crap – and not caring whether or not it had been accomplished – Danny pulled up his clothes and went downstairs for a drink.

Where he was surprised to find there was only black-outlined water available.

Somewhen during the everlasting nine twenty-one, Danny opened the fridge door. There were things in there, but like the programmes on the television, these were things he no longer understood. The word *food* rose in his mind and Danny did not recognise it. He closed the door, stood up, leaned into the sink and threw up a great deal of a liquid which was hot and bitter. He did not know why.

At nine twenty-one, Danny woke up in the lounge. The television was on and showing a coloured storm which hissed like a monsoon. He lurched to one side, almost losing his balance, then glanced at his feet which hadn't moved. He no longer *had* anything below the ankles. His feet had been completely consumed by the vampire carpet. Danny gazed in astonishment at the way they had become flat, two-dimensional representations, incorporated in the carpet's weave. The representations were almost perfect, except that they were bare where he had been wearing socks and shoes.

He glanced up at the television and was shocked to see his missing shoes and socks on the floor in front of its stand. They were, even now, in the process of being consumed by the carpet.

An ache grew deep inside him as the carpet ran threads through his veins tracing his shape. Danny closed his eyes.

And when he opened them, panting and drenched with sweat, the carpet was dead and his feet were released. There was a kitchen knife in his aching right hand. Not a square foot of the carpet remained unviolated. The carpet was killed, but his clothes were still alive and the furniture was still beaming out the ropes of hate at him. Danny sat down, grinning vacantly.

At nine twenty-one he woke up sitting cross-legged on the cold floor. He was naked and covered in stinging cuts. A memory lingered of the way the good, sharp steel had hacked through his clothes and caressed his flesh. The clothes were now no more than a dead, black-outlined mess of material. Danny spread his legs and laid the sharp edge of the knife against the tendon in his crotch, pressing slightly and thrilling at the bite. Tiny teeth rasped against his skin, bringing minute beads of bright red blood to the surface.

Arteries, a small, clear voice whispered in Danny's head. It was a calm and sensible voice and the only logical one he had heard since his mind had been put into solitary confinement what seemed like months ago. It was Danny's own, sane, voice and it offered the one and only way out of this mess.

There are big arteries in there, old Dan, it said, You don't need to know what they do just at the moment, but they're important, you can take that from me. There's a good one in there, Dan. One of the best ones you have. It's called your femoral artery, if my memory serves me well. The best thing you could do right now, old Dan, is to push a little harder with that knife, maybe saw a bit through that old tendon, and open that femoral artery. The tendon'll hurt when you cut it and the artery might sting a little too, but believe me, it's the best way – not to say the only *way – out. It'll be a bit of pain now, then you'll start to feel chilly, then everything will stop. You'll be in peace, old Dan. If you don't do it, you won't have that little while of pain. But pain remembers its debts and calls them in, old Dan, as well you know. And the interest rates make loan-sharks look like toothless minnows. If you don't do it, that pain will get you, but it'll get you a thousandfold and it won't just be physical pain. It'll be mental and emotional pain too.*

Danny nodded sagely. 'I've got that now,' he agreed in a voice that was rusty with abuse and disuse.

So go on, the voice encouraged.

Danny pulled the knife lightly across his groin and drew a line of blood. It did sting, but it was not unpleasant.

Over by the fireplace, Christine Richard dived out of nowhere and thumped to the ground, snapping her neck. Danny thought of snow in a windy field. A hedgerow with something beneath it. His legs, relentlessly taking him toward that something.

Joey was in Africa.

His brother was pointing the gun at him.

He's cheated death this time! someone yelled across the years from an echoing operating theatre.

The voice was the voice of Danny's cry-baby.

But it was right.

Too long a time and too much pain, Danny's cry-baby added.

Joey was flapping around his head.

Danny lay down, his knees apart, and brought the knife lightly back. It hurt, but it was good. His muscles tensed.

Out in the hall, the phone rang.

And as Danny went rigid at the sudden shock of reality, his bladder evacuated itself. The stream of hot urine rose high, spraying off his belly and trickling back down to his crotch.

He stared down at himself, more shocked and disgusted than he'd ever been before. The phone's ringing drilled into him and Danny hated himself. A black rage built in him and the fire lit again inside him. Still dribbling urine, he got up, staggered to the hall, knocked the telephone from its table and fell to his knees sobbing.

'Danny? Is that you?' a worried tinny voice asked. It was a woman's voice. A woman he knew.

'NO, IT IS NOT ME! NOW FOR GOD'S SAKE FUCK OFF AND LEAVE ME ALONE!' he screamed and yanked the cord away from of the wall. When this didn't cut off the voice, he picked up the handset and sawed through its connecting wire.

The woman's voice rattled through his head for a long time afterwards. *It's me, Danny, it's me! Are you okay, Danny?*

Danny woke up at nine twenty-one, hacking away at one of the three-piece suite's armchairs with the bread knife. He couldn't make himself stop for a long time and when he finally did stop, he instantly forgot what he had been doing. But the evidence remained. The armchair was the last piece to be destroyed – the other chair and the sofa had already been attended to. The room was full of ruined foam rubber and torn material. There was other evidence that Danny couldn't understand either. The smell of shit and piss which now followed him everywhere; the vomit coating the television screen, the blood smeared on the wallpaper.

After the lucid thoughts preceding the phone call, Danny thought nothing at all and now, his last relief, the periods of unconsciousness deserted him. Danny became a raging mass of bright pain which crawled on its belly, screaming, ranting and raving at the nothingness which surrounded it. The light grey followed the dark grey but the mass of pain no longer knew even this. It had turned inwards, feeding from itself and distilling itself into still more exquisite agony. The grey made no impression on him any more and as the days and nights passed he became more and more divorced from reality.

And when the pain stopped at twenty-one minutes past nine, Danny thought he was dead. He lay on his back, exhausted and gasping for breath, his heart pounding against his throat. *It's all over*, he thought.

He lay there gradually realising that as his heart was still beating and his lungs still sucking air, something other than death had happened to him. That misty thing up there in the distance before his eyes was not the Pearly Gates but the lounge ceiling, smeared with something that might have been excrement.

He drew a deep breath and relaxed slightly, lying still. He was alive, but, he thought, only just. There didn't seem to be any energy left in him at all. He felt like a dried, pressed flower, an empty shell. Someone could have carved away his insides for all he knew.

What happened? he asked himself, but didn't even force this question when no answers came to him. Later would be good enough. Now he would just relax until he felt he could get up, which probably wouldn't be very long. *When this last ache goes away, in fact*, he told himself, finally recognising that a part of him *did* still ache. The ache was in his penis, but it took him another few minutes to realise that. Thinking he'd injured himself somehow, Danny pushed himself up on his elbows and was greeted by the sight of scabbing knife cuts which ran down his chest and belly to a large, nasty-looking scab in his groin, Beside this large wound his penis towered in the hugest, angriest erection he had ever had. His foreskin was pulled back and his whole penis was the same purple colour as its head.

What's happened to me? Danny thought, his heart starting to race again. He leaned on one elbow and put out the other hand to touch it. It didn't hurt to the touch – the pain seemed rooted deeper than this – but it was rock hard and the skin over it was stretched tight. His scrotum was drawn up and this time, both his balls were so high they were snug under the skin at the sides of his penis. Danny ran a finger through his pubic hair and felt them there, surely too high to be possible. He waited but the erection didn't subside. He grasped his penis again and squeezed, testing its resistance. It remained hard. Then he made the mistake of touching the bulging head.

His muscles instantly began to pulse in the most violent orgasm he'd ever experienced. Semen splattered up his chest, hit him in the face, flew over his shoulder – and the muscles kept pumping. It began to hurt after he'd run dry but the orgasm continued and cramping muscles kept on contracting and pumping until Danny clutched at himself, screaming in agony. His balls were exploding now and the pain was immense, but nothing – no matter where he grabbed, squeezed, probed or slapped – could stop the relentless muscular throbs. Danny doubled up, writhing and moaning as the muscles inside him locked solid released, locked solid and released. Something was tearing in him now. Danny shot three gouts of blood on to the floor and fainted with the pain.

3

When he woke up at nine twenty-one, time had come back. He was in bed and the sun was shining in through the open curtains. The room was clean and neat. Danny ached all over but the pain in his crotch was a hot wire. He turned over – very slowly and with the utmost care – and was surprised to see Suzie sleeping quietly beside him.

I just woke up from a nightmare, Danny told himself. There was no other alternative. Discounting the pains which still lingered, it wasn't possible to have lived through the hell he'd been in and to feel so mentally fit. His mind felt good and clean; totally renewed and working smoothly.

What happened? he asked himself again, and this time he *could* remember – some of it at least. Like the way he'd hacked his way through the furniture and carpet in the lounge. Like the unprovoked orgasm he had thought would kill him. Like the lack of time. He could recall some of these events and was disturbed by them but the recollection of the mental and physical anguish he'd suffered was missing. He remembered being frightened and feeling a terrible burning rage, but now, lying here in his bed next to Suzie, it all seemed as though it had happened to someone else. Like waking from a nightmare, the reality soon vaporised. Danny rolled back to his side of the bed and slowly sat up, pushing the covers away from him. The fact that the nightmare had indeed been real and had starred him in its leading role quickly became undeniable. The evidence was there, staring him in the face. He inspected the scabbed knife cut in his groin with mounting horror as he started to recall how it had got there. *You were going to slice through the femoral artery, Dan*, he told himself. *You couldn't stand it any more and you decided to finish yourself.* This knowledge was simply impossible to take in. But its truth chilled him, especially in the light of the knowing voice inside him which had assured him that pain remembered its debts and he would be forced to pay a thousandfold.

'Christ,' Danny muttered, shaking his head. His brain felt as if it had become loose in there and was bouncing from side to side. Moving very slowly, and with joints that popped and muscles that creaked like those of the world's oldest man, he got up and went to the bathroom.

He didn't much care for the naked man who looked back at him from the mirrors in there. This man was not Danny Stafford, tall, trim and fit. This man had sunken bloodshot eyes under which lay dark hollows. This man's complexion was grey. There were grey hairs in the week's growth of beard. This stranger was stooped and emaciated – not skeletal, but close. There were shallow knife cuts across this man's arms, legs and chest, some of them still weeping.

Danny went to the toilet, lifted the seat and stood there, wanting to piss but not being able to. The stranger – a man holding a penis which bore a distinct bruise – glared back at him.

Christine Richard was a psychic, Danny suddenly remembered, and the door to that memory cracked open: the fat woman apparently being attacked. The way her folds of flab had rippled. Christine Richard calling out his name and the dread he had felt. Then the voice of the Gannex Man – his voice – booming out of her, accusing.

A trick, Danny told himself. *She read my mind, that's all.* But the trick had been good, Danny was forced to admit that. It may have been the voice of Danny's subconscious dream memory and not that of an angry spirit, but it had worked magically on him. Danny had believed there *was* a Gannex Man. He had pissed himself in terror, blacked out and gone completely mad over what seemed like a long period. And Christine Richard had fallen and died. *Which wasn't a bad result for a simple mind reading trick, old Dan, was it now?*

There were further thoughts on the matter now trying to bloom in Danny's mind. These thoughts – which he quickly squashed and refused to consider – would fit together nicely, not only with his telepathy theory, but with his nightmares and his own private worries. And, he realised, if he allowed himself to think them, they would make his cry-baby's solution of suicide seem a very good option indeed.

Danny still couldn't piss. To keep his mind from the matter of Christine Richard, he examined his prick and balls and wondered – somewhat forcefully – what was wrong with them. The answer was, nothing very much. His balls were slightly tender but now hanging normally again; his prick was bruised and swollen but not unduly painful, and the flesh between them and his anus seemed okay. The trouble – if it wasn't simply tension stopping him pissing – might be rooted up inside him somewhere; maybe at the prostate. There had been something that felt quite like a fire burning around that area not so long ago and there had been that orgasm which had made him come blood. There was probably a torn muscle or perforated tube in there causing the trouble. It would get better, he assured himself.

It stung when he finally began to urinate and the liquid was tinged brown with old blood. Afterwards it didn't feel so bad. Danny needed a bath but he didn't think he could face those treacherous tiles so soon and he was already feeling an urge of guilt about the damage he thought he had done downstairs. He flannelled his face and went down hoping that his memory had magnified the damage. It couldn't possibly have been that bad. He glanced at the sawn-through telephone wire, held his breath and opened the lounge door. A dull ache grew in his heavy heart. It was not only as bad as he remembered, it was worse.

Suzie had evidently done her best at cleaning up all the mess, but the state of the room still brought tears to Danny's eyes. The carpet – or what was left of the carpet – was rolled up against the wall. There were more holes in it than a mesh fence. Three plastic dustbin liners full of what had once been in the holes stood beside it. The suite looked as if it had been nearby when an anti-personnel mine had gone off. It was slashed, tattered, and great gouges had been torn from the foam lining. There was another dustbin bag in one of the seats, but Suzie had evidently tired before finishing clearing this up because a lot of tiny bits of mangled foam still surrounded the sofa. All the porcelain ornaments were gone from the shelves. Wallpaper was torn and spattered with blood. The lounge window was broken. The lampshades were badly misshapen and the bulbs were smashed.

You did this, you bastard! Danny told himself. He sat down on the sofa and cried for a while.

When he went back upstairs Suzie was awake and sitting up with the bedclothes drawn tightly around her. Danny felt a powerful flash of love and longing for her which was swamped by guilt when he realised she was tense and frightened. Suzie was looking at him in a way he was becoming very familiar with now. Wherever he went just lately, people looked at him that way: faces taut, lips compressed or mouths agape, eyes wide and glittering with fear. But this was worse still. Suzie's face was also strangely wan and still puffy with last night's tears. Her bottom lip was split and one of her eyes was blacked.

You did that to her, you bastard! he thought, wishing that he'd kept on sawing away at his groin with the bread knife. *Suzie came back to you. She came back to help you and look what you did to her, you complete cunt!*

No memory of last night – or whenever it was – existed for him. So there was a chance, however slim. . .

'Suze,' he said, raising his eyebrows in question.

She looked at him, her glittering eyes answering him.

'Did I do that?' he asked, grasping at a straw which was no longer there and thinking, *Shithead, Danny! You utter, contemptible bastard!*

'Yes,' she said.

Danny clamped his eyes shut and began to cry, silently at first, only his shoulders and chest conveying the soul-wrenching sobs. Tears forced themselves from his eyelids and trickled hotly down his cheeks. 'I'm s-sorry, S-huh-oosie,' he gasped. 'I d-didn't m-hean it. I didn't know I w-hos d-huh-ooing it.' He wished he was dead.

When he opened his eyes, she was looking at him gravely, still

examining him to gauge how much of a threat he was.
'I'm all right n-now,' he said, starting towards her, then stopping when she drew back from him. 'I'm buh-better. Honestly. I didn't mean it. Puh-leese forgive me. I'm better.'
'Are you?' Suzie asked. There were tears in her eyes now. 'Are you really?'
Danny nodded, wishing he was dead. He badly wanted Suzie to hold him, to comfort him. To *forgive* him. He loved her and he hated himself for hurting her and he wanted to promise her that he would never make her cry again.
'I'm better,' he swore.
Suzie's eyes bored into him for a time, searching his face for more of the treachery and violence she had so evidently suffered. Then her face softened. 'I believe you,' she said finally. 'And I'm sorry too. Now come over here and hold me.'
Danny was a tiny boy, lonely, sorrowful and filled with fear of the world. He went to her, lay against her, his head on her breast and her cool arms enfolding him as she murmured words of hope and comfort to him.

4

Danny sat in the bath at the tap end, facing Suzie. The black tiles were safe while she was there. They had bathed one another's hurts and begun to talk. Danny told her about the loss of his job and a little about the clairaudience demonstration and how he'd woken up in the rain in the car park and finally wandered for hours looking for home. He told her that after that time had stopped for him and everything had become hazy. He was surprised to learn that a week had been contained within that period of 'no time'. Today was Saturday. There were more surprises in store for him.
The first was that Suzie had telephoned on the Sunday following his trip to Ancastle House. She had gone for many blows in her Sunbeam Tiger and had finished with thinking about things. Suzie had been ready to come back.
'Did I answer the phone?' Danny asked.
Suzie smiled grimly and nodded. 'Yes, you did.'
'What did I say?'
'It doesn't matter.'
'It *does*,' he insisted. suddenly realising that it *didn't* matter and that he didn't want to know what he'd said.
Suzie considered it for a few moments and Danny watched his chance of telling her not to say it slipping silently away. 'You said I was speaking to the Hoodoo Man.'
Danny frowned. 'Are you sure I said hoodoo?' *Hoodoo doesn't sound like Gannex*, he thought.

Suzie nodded. 'Hoodoo. Definitely. I thought you were joking at first, but you kept on saying "I am the Hoodoo Man. You are speaking to the Hoodoo Man", and that was all. You didn't respond to any of my questions, just kept on saying the same thing over and over again.'

Danny shook his head.

Suzie nodded. 'You did. I didn't know what "Hoodoo" meant so I looked it up when you rang off. D'you know what it means?'

'Like voodoo?'

Suzie shook her head. 'You *must* know. You said it,' she insisted.

Danny smiled wanly. 'I wasn't myself,' he countered, thinking, *The Hoodoo Man*. Even if he wasn't sure of the meaning, the title he'd apparently chosen for himself sounded strangely apt.

'According to my dictionary, a hoodoo is a thing or person thought to cause bad luck.'

That's me, Danny thought bitterly. His subconscious apparently had a strong sense of irony. 'I don't remember saying it,' he said.

'It gets worse,' Suzie told him. 'Want to know more?'

Danny didn't. 'Okay,' his mouth said on his behalf.

'When I rang back again you asked after Joey who'd gone to Africa. Then you said you couldn't read Jamie. What's wrong?'

What was wrong was that Danny was visibly shuddering. Something wearing very large shoes had just walked over his grave. *Couldn't read Jamie. Those words should have been spelled out in capital letters*, Danny thought. This meant everything. This was the key to . . . to what?

He shook his head, watching the gooseflesh prickle across his arms and chest. 'Nothing,' he said. 'Just the shivers.' *Couldn't read Jamie*. The words possessed a great – and unfathomable – significance.

'Who is he?' Suzie asked.

'He was a genius budgie,' Danny said, trying to put the thought of not being able to read Jamie out of his mind. It didn't fit comfortably.

'I know who *Joey* was. I meant *Jamie*.'

Danny shrugged. The Hoodoo Man couldn't read Jamie. *Why couldn't you read him, old Dan?* he asked himself, and didn't even have a vague theory. 'No one,' he said.

'It must be *someone*,' Suzie persisted.

Danny's eyes felt hot and bleary from. . . . *trying to see, Dan?* He thrust the thought from his mind, rubbed his bleary eyes and said, 'It's no one I know, or have ever known. There *are* no Jamies in my life. Must have been another trick of my imagination.'

Suzie searched for lies on his face and found none. Danny smiled mirthlessly at her. She said, 'You wouldn't hurt me Danny, would you? Not intentionally?'

Danny looked at her black eye and split lip and his loathing for himself grew. He wanted to say 'Have I ever?' but he couldn't. Some deep inner part of him obviously could and would hurt her intentionally, given half a chance. He had already proven that, hadn't he? He shook his head instead.

'Do you promise?' Suzie appealed.

Danny nodded, remembering how *cheap* promises came to him these days and how glibly they liked to trip off his tongue. 'I promise,' he said, trying not to remember sneaking off to The Hatch that Sunday.

Suzie watched him carefully when she spoke. 'When I phoned up the third time – on Monday, it was – you said you were going to cut off my clitoris and then fuck me with a carving knife.'

She had tried to keep the tone of the statement light, but there was an accusation lying just below the surface.

'Before I went to the seance or whatever you call it, I had this nightmare,' Danny explained quickly, 'in which a man accused me of murdering a girl with a knife. I must have been reliving the dream or something.' *Or maybe you were making a statement of intent*, he told himself.

'Oh,' Suzie said, nodding.

'Look, you can leave again if you don't feel safe yet,' Danny said, thinking that it might be the best course of action. He didn't remember saying any of those things to her and there was a good chance that he could slip back into that state again. 'I could, I s'pose, have another attack of the heebie jeebies and you don't really want to be around if I do, do you?'

'You said you were better.'

'And I think I am, but I don't know. I don't even know what happened. I was thoroughly checked out at the hospital and there's nothing wrong with my brain and I'm not psychopathic or anything according to the shrink. I think it was just a glitch brought on by all the stress, and I don't think it'll happen again. But I can't guarantee it. If you want to stay away for a few more weeks, I'll understand. I won't be offended.'

Suzie smiled and squeezed his leg. 'That sounds more like the old Danny,' she said. 'I'll think about it, but I may well stay now that I'm here.'

'When did you arrive?' He asked, more to take his mind off the threat that he might now be than because he wanted to know.

'I came yesterday evening, at about twenty past nine,' she told him. 'I'd tried to phone you again, but the line wouldn't work and I guessed you'd cut the cord. You were writhing about on the floor in the lounge when I got here. You were delirious still and there was blood and dried come all over you, and piss and shit and sick on the floor. I was going to call an ambulance. . .'

'But you didn't?'

Suzie shook her head. 'I thought that if they took you away, you'd never come back. I couldn't face having to visit you in a mental ward and see you all flat and drugged or after ECT. I thought I'd wait until today. Anyway, I tried to pick you up. You were babbling about how all the clocks had stopped and how you'd crossed some fine line or other. I stood you up but your eyes were empty and you looked at me with such hatred that I nearly ran out. And then. . .'

'I hit you,' Danny said. 'I'm sorry.'

Suzie nodded and smiled sadly. 'You called me a cunt and hit me twice and I got mad and kneed you in the nuts in return.' She shook her head. 'I'm sorry, Danny, but I was livid and hurt. I grabbed your arms and pushed them down and all the fight went out of you, but it didn't go out of me. I threw you back against the wall and kneed you again, twice. You blacked out then, and when you came round a little I led you upstairs, cleaned you up a bit and put you to bed. I'm sorry too.'

'Don't be,' Danny said, 'it must have been just what the doctor ordered.'

'Are you sure you're okay? Your dick bled a bit after I kneed you. I thought I'd done something nasty to you. Shouldn't you go to the doctor or something?'

Danny shook his head. 'Don't worry about it, I'll heal,' he said. He moved closer to her, spilling water over the side of the bath, and pulled her to him hugging her and kissing her neck. 'I don't need a doctor, all I need is you,' he said.

'What about the vision?' Suzie suddenly asked, pushing him away from her so that she could look into his eyes. 'It didn't come true did it? It *wasn't* a glimpse of the future at all. Was it?' Her voice bore a hint of desperation.

Danny remembered her letter that had felt so cold in his pocket. How Suzie felt about the future crawling towards her, moment by moment. The predictions the fake fortune teller had made about her inability to conceive and the nasty accident she would have during her thirties. Suzie evidently thought that Danny might predict her 'accident', or be the cause of it, or both. He thought about the way he had lied and betrayed her and how she'd left him for it.

'No, it wasn't a glimpse of the future,' he assured her, not knowing now *what* it was. He didn't tell her about the dream of the air disaster that hadn't happened, or what Christine Richard had said to him in his own voice (he had claimed, in fact that it was merely being witness to the psychic's death-dive that had made him flip).

'We're back to normality again then,' Suzie said hopefully.

Danny nodded and summoned up enthusiasm. 'You betcha,' he said, wondering at the conviction in his voice. Too much had happened now for things to ever be the same again. He had a strong sense that there were too many things hanging in the air awaiting development for it to be all over. Like the fact that a part of him thought he was the Hoodoo Man, or the appearances of Joey in his mind (no longer in Africa – if he'd ever made it – but by now safe in that great bird sanctuary in the sky), or the worrying thought that he *couldn't read Jamie*. Danny somehow didn't think things would ever return to 'normality' again.

He summoned up a grin and another lie tripped glibly from his tongue. 'Yep, I think we're back to normality,' he said, kissing her quickly so she couldn't read the doubt that surely filled his face.

5

'Promise me something else,' Suzie said later, suddenly opening the bathroom door.

Danny jumped and spun around feeling dizzy and guilty. He had returned to the bathroom alone in order to shave the week's growth of beard from his face. He was lathered up, but he wasn't in front of the mirror with the razor in his hand – he was staring, half hypnotised, at the mysterious space which had just formed behind the black tiles at the tap end of the bath. The hold that magical nothingness had been putting on him was instantly broken.

Back to normality, eh, Dan? his mind asked.

'You frightened me,' he said truthfully, stealing a glance back at the mirror tiles which were now no more than black mirror tiles.

'Sorry,' Suzie said, 'but you'll have to get used to me just barging in from now on. I'm intending to keep a close eye on you.'

Which was why, presumably, She had removed the sliding bolt from the bathroom door. They hadn't spoken about it and Danny supposed Suzie wanted him to think he'd done it during his spell of craziness, but he'd studied the door and the bolt hadn't been torn off, but carefully unscrewed. This was fair enough – they had never felt the need for privacy and had always come and gone while the other was using the bathroom. Danny nodded. 'Good idea,' he said.

'Will you promise?'

Danny managed a grin. Humour came harder than lies these days. 'Depends what it is,' he said, attempting banter but sounding sour.

'Promise me that if you ever have another vision, you'll tell me. Don't keep anything from me ever again. Never lie to me, and let me know if you so much as get a tickle at the back of your throat. Will you do that?'

'I promise,' he said.

But this was another promise that was far easier to make than to keep.

Chapter Eight
Another Danny, Knocking

1

After the double critical on Danny's chart and the bottom line week that followed it, that Queen of all the Bitches, Lady Luck took a five-week time out. Looking back, at first Danny would think – and plot on his charts – a good spell, a period of relief during which things healed over and got better. The quality of his life was improved. Then he realised that the bitch hadn't forgotten him at all. She was letting him build himself up for two reasons. The first was that there was no pleasure to be gained by applying torture to a numb mind and body – she couldn't knock him down any further than rock bottom. And the second was that she was spending time shuffling her cards of fate; stacking the pack against him so when she slapped the next card down in front of him on that green baize card table called life, it would be a real stinger. And after *that*, she intended to give him the whipping of his life.

The card that Danny picked up at the end of those five free weeks was a black Jack, and much later, in his imagination, it would have its forfeit written across the bottom for him to see: *Receive one electric shock*.

2

On Suzie's instructions Danny stayed in bed and rested for most of the week following her return. Suzie went back to work and Danny, obeying her orders to the letter, spent a large amount of the week in bed, sleeping – heavily and dreamlessly. Towards the end of this rigidly enforced recovery period, he had to admit that Suzie had been right. He felt very much better, mentally as well as physically.

But while he extolled the virtues of getting plenty of sleep and swore to Suzie that he felt 'as good as new', doubt about his apparent recovery gnawed away at him. Danny dug a hole in his mind for it and relentlessly shovelled normality on top of it to keep it in place. He purposely thought as little as possible about what had happened to him and when he did think about it, he tried hard to convince himself that it was simply a temporary aberration which was over and done with. While the level of success was not total, it crept higher up the scale with each attempt. Danny refused to ask himself the question, *You don't suppose you're only fooling yourself, old Dan, do you?* not on the grounds that it might incriminate him, but because he chose not to.

The feeling of guilt he still felt about the damage he'd done to the house was also slow to fade. To help assuage it, he talked Suzie into going out on a spending spree with him and (studiously ignoring his steadily diminishing bank balance) wrote cheques for a new lounge carpet, another suite, and fixtures and fittings to replace the damaged ones.

That evening, on the ruined sofa in the echoing, carpet-less lounge, they made love for the first time since Suzie's return. Danny experienced a moment of pain during orgasm, and that place inside him where the fire had previously raged grew very hot and smouldered on after his orgasm had ceased. Suzie was dewy-eyed and held him very close for a long time, whispering how good it was to have him back and how much she loved him. Danny didn't want to break the warm spell that bound them together so he didn't mention the pain or the heat inside him. It didn't matter; it would pass. And as he lay there, the heat died away. *See*, he told himself, smiling as Suzie's body relaxed and her breathing became even and deep, *it's gone. It went away just like I told you it would.*

Danny didn't try very hard to get a job. For the first time in his life he discovered the dubious delights of signing on the dole and filling in forms for the grim-faced people at Social Security. He gazed at the adverts on the wall in the Job Centre in much the same way as he gazed at the advertisements in the *Gazette* – without enthusiasm. The new experience of not going to work was far more enjoyable than he'd imagined. His money was running out and he knew he would have to get a job soon, but nothing in those ads seemed very enticing and Danny told himself that he deserved a good rest after what he'd been through.

Suzie's money was still coming in though, and although he felt vaguely guilty that she now seemed to be paying for everything, she didn't seem to mind. She certainly didn't pressure him or hurry him along. Danny thought she rather liked having what she called a 'house husband', and he enjoyed being one. He threw himself into doing solo all the household chores that Suzie and he used to share. He shopped, cooked all the food, washed up with a ruthless efficiency, and scolded Suzie if she dirtied the sparkling kitchen he had now proudly taken over. The mysteries of the washing machine were revealed to him and all the flat surfaces in the house now gleamed.

The weeks flew by and Danny found it harder and harder to imagine that he'd seen visions or had 'prophetic' dreams. All that weird stuff seemed to have happened to someone else; some other Danny Stafford.

He still had the copy of the *Gazette* with the banner: *FAMOUS PSYCHIC DIES IN HORROR FALL*. He'd intended to throw it out because it distressed Suzie to think that he'd witnessed the woman's death and she didn't think he should be reminded of it. But for some reason he hadn't been able to part with it. He'd slipped it beneath a pile of old magazines, and from time to time – when Suzie was at work – he got it out and re-read the article. But although he could remember being there and hearing Christine Richard speaking in his own voice, he could make no mental connection with it at all. Like all those other strange happenings, it held no significance for him now.

Even the visual problem he had with the black tiles in the bathroom went away. After the time Suzie had surprised him when he was supposed to be shaving, Danny had been careful not to look too closely at the tiles whenever he went in there. Then, last week, he'd found himself alone in the bath, staring into the tiles while his mind wandered. The slap of realisation shocked him and brought him back to himself instantly. He'd thrashed about in the water for a few seconds before he realised that the tiles hadn't been sucking him in at all. There was no black distance telescoping out behind them and drawing him in. They were simply black mirror tiles which gleamed his somewhat dull reflection back at him.

That was when Danny truly began to believe it was all over.

3

The electric shock, when it came at the end of those five good weeks, was remarkable only because it broke his routine and gave him another humorous underpants story to relate to Suzie when she came home. It didn't hurt and afterwards Danny gave it no further thought.

It was a Friday morning and Danny was being Mrs Mop, sweating as he ran the upright vacuum cleaner over the new lounge carpet. The weather was warming now, the windows were open, and because cooking and cleaning made him so hot, Danny was dressed in those most fashionable of housework clothes, his most ancient underpants and a pair of basketball boots. The pants were extremely thin and small and Suzie swore that his reasons for wearing them were not entirely innocent. She knew that Danny was proud of the weight he had lost during his bad week and was impressed by the way the exercises he'd been doing had firmed his stomach and re-shaped his shoulders and arms. Danny would never be a muscle-man but his slender body was now harder and more finely defined than ever before. Suzie opined that he constantly posed in the tiny pants, hoping to impress passing housewives or schoolgirls and lure them into the house where he could have his wicked way with them. The tiny pants had impressed Suzie on several occasions – the first time she'd come home from work and seen him in them, she'd whipped them down and had him in the hallway while the dinner turned crisp in the oven – and now they seemed to have become an almost irresistible signal to her. On one occasion he had ventured out into the back garden in them to hang washing and spotted Claire Briggs watching him from her garden – somewhat lasciviously, he thought. When he called out hello, Claire had unconsciously licked her lips. Danny hurried back inside before she had time to ask him over for coffee.

Halfway across the carpet, the Electrolux died. *Pulled the bloody plug out again, I s'pose*, Danny thought, glaring at the socket. Electrical extension leads were never quite long enough. He went to the socket and slapped the plug, realising it hadn't been pulled out. The vacuum cleaner did not roar into life. Danny sighed, got a screwdriver, and inspected the fuse which was okay. He told himself the trouble was either in the lead or the cleaner itself, put the plug back together and committed the Electrical Repairman's Number One Sin by absently pushing the plug back into the socket.

He upended the vacuum cleaner, propped it against the wall and removed screws. This end of the lead seemed okay too. Nothing moved when he wobbled it. *It's the foot switch then*, Danny thought, and instantly spotted the loose connector. He wiped sweat from his brow, plunged his hands into the machine and plugged in the connector. The machine roared into life, Danny jumped and his right hand hit the live side of the switch. The shock was only momentary but it cruised through him, lighting his vision blue. standing his hair on end and snapping the tight elastic in his pants. The circuit breaker in the kitchen cupboard clicked out as the pants fell down. The Electrolux slid down the wall and Danny staggered backwards, the pants hobbling and tripping him.

As he would later tell Suzie, he lay on the floor with his pants round his ankles for five minutes while he giggled helplessly at his stupidity.

4

A few days after the incident was forgotten, Danny found himself in the public library where he had met Suzie all those years ago. Things had changed somewhat. Everything was now computerised and admission was easy, but to get out again you had to pass through electronically operated gates which presumably would shriek if you were stealing a book. Danny joined again, recalling old tales about the library police and how they would come to get you if you were in possession of overdue books. It might not have been Suzie's Magic Eye watching everything you did now, but Big Brother certainly seemed to be in evidence.

Once he had his card and was inside the book area Danny realised why he had come. It was because it was now safe to do some research on what had happened to that 'other' Danny who'd had strange things happen to him. Now, he told himself, that he was certain he wasn't psychic after all it would be safe to ask some searching questions about those experiences. Danny made a bee-line for the P section and picked out books on psychology, parapsychology and psychiatry.

He spent the next few hours learning about Freud, then Jung and Synchronicity, then about mechanical and electronic means of testing for psychokinesis and telepathy, and then he became bored. None of the countless case histories of psychic phenomena seemed to have anything in common with his experiences at all. Each book seemed to be a confused mish-mash of differing ideas.

But Danny didn't give up easily. He returned the following day and struck lucky with two badly written books whose subjects were *Out of the Body Experiences* and *Near Death Experiences*. Some of these sounded just like what had happened to him when his brother shot him. The person who had written the first book firmly believed that your soul was detachable from your body in some way, and the second – a doctor – argued that oxygen starvation of various parts of the brain caused these experiences, which were, in fact, merely false memories distorted and stored by a brain close to dying.

Both of the opposing theories sounded good to Danny and he was unable to decide which one, if either, was right. Both seemed to list some of the things that had happened to him – although not all of them – and both had things that clearly hadn't ever happened to him. Danny hadn't walked down dark corridors towards beautiful golden lights or seen people he knew beckoning him or telling him to: 'Go back, it's not time yet!' In spite of his experience with the mirror tiles, he favoured the oxygen starvation theory. Parts of his brain *were* dead – had died after his brother shot him – and he had been forced to re-route some of his neural pathways. But there might still be some live wires lying dormant in those mangled parts. Not many, but just enough so that sometimes one could light up briefly and flash him garbled messages. The odd experiences that felt like precognition were simply bad messages.

This theory would have been okay if it wasn't for the fact that those bad messages had been so accurate – in detail, if not in the sequence of events.

But later that day Danny forgot all about the problem when he noticed that his perception of time had begun to act in a peculiar fashion. It was nothing mind-blowing; just enough to give him a good cold shock. Danny had been sitting at a reading table with the books in front of him, reading and thinking. When he looked at his watch he was surprised to discover that two hours had passed without his noticing. They had, in fact, vanished. Danny shook off the cold feeling, mentally arguing that it was easy not to notice time passing when you were engrossed in interesting work. He closed the books and put them away, and marvelling at his increasing powers of concentration, hurried home to make the dinner.

But on the following visit to the library, a few days later, he was forced to admit that things were not quite as simple as he'd thought. On this occasion, the vanishing time wasn't so easy to explain away. The hours and minutes between two o'clock and three-thirty simply vanished. Which would have been all well and good if he hadn't found himself finishing the same sentence he'd started when he sat down. Danny quickly scanned through the book in case he'd read on and forgotten, but none of the text rang any bells for him. He felt the cold iron fist reaching out for his stomach again and rationalised it away by assuring himself he'd fallen asleep.

He did not go back to the library again.

But like a stray dog once patted, the problem followed him home. Time for Danny Stafford had now decided to work to different rules than it did for everyone else . . . or to no rules at all. Sometimes it held steady and sometimes it didn't, but there was no way of telling the difference until he looked at a clock – or the old wind up watch that now resided upon his wrist to replace the stolen one. While Danny remained conscious – and as far as he knew – aware, time played tricks, speeding up and slowing down in an arbitrary and erratic fashion.

Danny broke his faithful promise to Suzie by not telling her about it. He justified this on the grounds that it would worry her needlessly if she knew and in any case no one would be able to fix it for him. It was not a physical disease, but a mental problem which doctors and shrinks would not be able to cure. But a part of him knew that he was ignoring the problem in the same manner you might ignore a Jehovah's Witness knocking at the door; if it remained unacknowledged for long enough, it would go away. He also knew this approach never worked, not with God's fishers of men and not with strange new lumps in the testes. They always stayed there, waiting. . .

Danny did his best not to address this part of him. *It'll pass*, he assured himself each time he looked at his watch and was hit by the nasty feeling of unreality. *It'll go away and the watch is old and probably cranky anyway. The driver's probably dead in there*. But deep down he knew the watch's driver wasn't dead at all, nor even severely injured. It was the part of his mind that marked passing moments that was in trouble.

It'll pass, Danny told himself whenever the shock of seemingly losing two hours, or of walking the mile home from town in less than five minutes, slapped him hard.

It did not pass, but as Danny well knew by that time, his mind was an extremely resourceful thing which would assimilate almost anything, given the time and the opportunity. Danny gradually got used to losing or gaining time, realised it didn't happen often (and never at all while he was in company) and since it seemed to cause no harm, he finally accepted it as an everyday part of his existence.

This lasted precisely two weeks and four days.

Which was when Suzie started to scream.

5

Suzie had gone to work and he was gathering up dirty clothes and carting them to the linen basket in the bathroom where he would dump them, ready to take it downstairs to the washing machine when it was full. It was a simple routine he'd fallen into and it was Monday. Like several million other people who stuck to tradition in spite of having modern equipment, Monday was Danny's washing day. He was feeling good and he was back in his tiny pants and basketball boots – although he didn't remember when the pants had been fixed. A sluggish thought somewhere in the distance informed him that the pants had been thrown away, but Danny ignored it. He had them on and that was proof enough.

He gathered up some of Suzie's underwear, picking it up from where she had left it on the bedroom floor. Suzie had never been very tidy but since Danny had been at home to clear up after her she had become a regular slattern, dumping things wherever she was and leaving them there. In spite of nagging her about it, Danny didn't mind this at all. Wild horses wouldn't have dragged it from him, but he *liked* clearing up after her.

He went into the bathroom with these last few pieces, and as he crossed it, something in the tiles twinkled on the periphery of his vision. Danny automatically turned to look and the black tiles captured him, immediately telescoping out into a black hole. The room jolted and rearranged so the field of high gravity was now under his feet instead of in front of him. For a second Danny hovered in space over the chasm, clutching Suzie's undies tightly to him. His head spun and he dropped the garments and groped desperately behind him for the towel rail. His hands found it and closed around it, and Danny knew the small screws which held it in place wouldn't support his weight. He screamed as he began to fall and the towel rail dissolved and passed through his hands. Its cool metal, now no more substantial than mist, flowed through his palms. Danny dropped like a stone through the perfect darkness, his sense of balance reeling so he couldn't tell if he was falling up or down.

Then he was in the bedroom, standing at the foot of the bed by the dressing table. There was no coverlet on the bed, no eiderdown, just a white sheet and a single pillow. Suzie was on the bed doing her 'sex show' party piece. She was naked and writhing about, inflamed with passion. Her eyes were closed and her hands were caressing herself; running back and forth between her belly and breasts. She was groaning quietly.

You're not here, a clear voice said inside his head. *You're imagining this. You're having a vision.* Everything seemed wrong. It wasn't like the other visions he'd had. In spite of the fact that he remembered the black tiles dragging him in, he was certain this wasn't a vision. It was surely happening here and now.

'Suzie,' he said, and his voice didn't sound flat and wrong, just sounded like his own voice.

Suzie opened her eyes and looked at him, grinning. She fondled an erect nipple with her left hand and her right trailed down her body. She raised her knees and began to pleasure herself with those slender fingers, hips thrusting, breath coming in short gasps. 'C'mon, darling,' she moaned. 'Come over here and give it to me.'

Danny was naked and erect. He got on the bed, crawled between her legs and Suzie grabbed his prick and pulled him into her. Danny's mind flickered and rolled as she bucked beneath him, taking him deep inside her. Suzie shuddered as she ground her clitoris against his pubic bone, moaned and urged him to make her come. He took her wrists and pinned them to the pillows above her, stretching her taut as he pounded into her, the blood raging in his ears, the fire raging inside him and shooting white bolts of power up into his brain.

Then he was being invaded, dissolving in agony as sharp things that tore like fish hooks began to probe the skin around his spine, forcing their way into him in the gaps between each of his vertebrae. Danny screamed and drove deeper into Suzie who screamed back at him. The hooks wound down through him, tearing his internal organs, and Danny thrashed wildly, arching his back and thrusting forward. Suzie fought to get out from under him now and she was bleeding the way she wanted to bleed, the way she *had* to bleed. The way he *wanted* her to bleed.

'STOP IT, DANNY! YOU'RE HURTING ME!' she squealed, and Danny wondered who she meant. It didn't matter. Didn't matter one tiny little piece. He was home. Safe. Complete.

'DANNY! *STOP!*'

And the agonising hooks were instantaneously withdrawn.

What the fuck are you doing? Danny asked himself and heard his old friend the Gannex Man asking him if it had been Ten-up.

His eyes opened and a star-shell burst in Danny's mind.

Suzie thrust him away and sat up, saying, 'Christ, Danny, that *hurt!*'

Danny clutched his head, not even knowing what he'd done. 'Sorry, Suzie. I'm sorry!' he heard himself saying as his mind railed against the sheer *impossibility* of everything. None of what he had just experienced had been right. None of it had actually happened. Not only was it most definitely not Monday morning, it was not Monday at all. He knew that now. The day was Thursday and it was late in the evening. Eleven-thirty according to his watch. Both he and Suzie were naked and they had been making love, but they were not in the bedroom as he had thought – or even in the bathroom – they were on the lounge floor. Danny felt like a man teetering on the edge of a precipice.

'I'm sorry,' he said again.

'I should bloody well think so,' Suzie snapped. 'I don't mind playing it a little bit rough, but that was beyond belief. That *really* hurt and I'm bleeding a bit. You'll have to take it a bit easier!'

'Got carried away,' Danny said miserably, and thought, *Literally in fact*. His mind was currently doing a slow swoon and he was losing his balance. He hadn't been picking up clothes and intending to do the washing at all. As real as it might have seemed – and it had seemed undeniably real – none of that had happened. What *had* happened was something that would need careful piecing together.

'I've never known anything like it,' Suzie said, taking her hand away from her shoulder and inspecting the bleeding mark she'd had it clamped over. It was clearly a bite; Danny could see his teeth marks there. 'You looked mad,' she said. 'You came your brains out but just wouldn't stop pumping away. I think something tore inside me.' She glanced over at him. The anger was leaving her face now and rapidly being replaced by something that looked like admiration. The expression chilled Danny, as did her next words.

'You were like a man po-zest!' Suzie said getting up.

Possessed, Danny thought wildly, *there's a word to conjure with*. 'Are you sure you're okay?' he asked.

She nodded. 'I think so. I'm just going to the bathroom to check. If there's any serious damage done, your nuts are history!'

As Suzie left the room, Danny noticed the cross-hatched lines of bleeding scratches across her back and buttocks and thought, *You did those*, but deep down inside him, he knew he hadn't.

Another person entirely had done them.

Chapter Nine
A Know Better Calls

1

Danny heard sounds over the following few days. Not the sounds of Christine Richard speaking in his voice, or her neck cracking as she hit the floor, and not the sounds of that would-be invader, the Gannex Man, knocking on his psyche; since that slip in reality when the real Danny was elsewhere and the other part of him had control, these things had fallen silent. Danny thought that the shock of finding himself somewhere other than where he thought he was had slammed the door on the invader – hopefully for ever. These new, less frightening, sounds were fluttering noises. They came and went in no particular pattern and they might merely have been spasms of his eardrums – or the works behind them – twitching the way they did the day after listening to a very loud band. At the time, Danny thought he was hearing the ghostly beating of Joey's wings as the bird broke for Africa. Later that year, looking back, he would think he had been listening to Lady Luck riffling her deck of cards into final order.

2

Danny did a lot of thinking in the days that followed his attack of spurious reality and he drew many conclusions, none of which he liked and all of which he tried very hard to forget. In his mental file of Suzie's sayings, there was a bitter entry under E which now seemed particularly apt. It was a saying reserved for the bleakest moments and it didn't get used very often. Now, looking back at what she'd said in her letter about the fortune teller's predictions for her, Danny could see its origins – date them to the month, in fact. The saying went:

EVERYTHING TURNS OUT FOR THE BAD IN THE END

Previously, Danny had always countered this with optimistic sayings of his own; now, none of these words of wisdom would spring to mind. In spite of Suzie's claims that she hadn't really been hurt and was completely healed now, she hadn't wanted to go to the doctor to get herself checked over. Danny knew exactly why. Suzie had believed the fortune teller and she believed in the inherent wisdom of her glib saying. If she went to the doctor she would be told she had become infertile, just like the nice lady said she would. What was worse than this was that Danny believed it too – which was why he hadn't insisted she go. Everything *really did* turn out for the bad in the end, even if you were the world's number one optimist. That was the top and bottom of it and there was no way around it.

Although everything was falling to pieces around him these days, Danny was developing an expertise for marking the precise moments at which things happened. If Suzie had become infertile, Danny knew exactly when it happened: when the hooks drove into his spine and Suzie screamed, 'STOP IT, DANNY! YOU'RE HURTING ME!' If the prophecy had been fulfilled and Suzie *was* barren, the man who stared back at him from the mirror every day was the man responsible, and there was no way around *that* either.

3

Danny was trying not to think these things the following Monday morning as he gathered washing from the bedroom floor. He reached the bathroom and suddenly realised he was clutching Suzie's cast-off underwear as he had been in the false reality. He smiled grimly; the similarities ended there. The day was cool and rainy and he was dressed in jeans and sweatshirt. His posing pants had long since been taken by the dustmen. Even the underwear was different. Danny entertained a passing thought that there might be almost identical parallel worlds populated by almost identical parallel people and that it might be possible – due to a glitch in the metaphysical plan – for the people unexpectedly and briefly to exchange places, when the fluttering noise started again. Danny suddenly felt very dizzy and the *déjà vu* feeling he'd expected to experience earlier but hadn't, fell on him like a ton of crushed ice. He dropped the underwear, reached behind him and his hands closed around the cool steel of the towel rail. *Ha ha! This is funny, Danny, isn't it? Who thought this one up? What a good joke!* he thought stupidly as he was drawn forward by the mirror or the parallel world or whatever it was that wanted him. In front of him the black tiles stayed perfectly still. There was no yawning chasm making him an offer he couldn't refuse, no crack in the fabric of reality drawing him through. None of this mattered. In a moment, the room would tilt and his hands would pass through the towel rail and he would be flung in the void again.

The sickening fluttering which could have been either inside or outside his head, suddenly vanished, leaving a nasty electrical buzz behind it. Behind him, screws crunched, loosening themselves from the wall as he pulled on the rail.

Danny finally let go of the rail and fell face down on to the carpet, his rebelling sense of balance assuring him he was falling even after he had landed.

The electrical buzz began to sound familiar. *Like what happens when the solenoid in the front door bell jams, in fact*, a distant matter-of-fact part of his mind said.

These were undoubtedly magic words. It most certainly *was* the front door bell making that noise. There was somebody down there waiting for the door to be opened. Danny's feeling of *déjà vu* vanished, but the buzzing and the swooning dizziness clung on.

He got to his feet, the room still spinning crazily. Nausea took a firm hold on him and he staggered sideways to the toilet bowl, hugged it, threw up, hard and noisily.

The door bell was still buzzing when the room settled around him. He got up, spat, rinsed his mouth with water straight from the cold tap, spat again, drank some, then wiped his face. Whoever had pressed the bell and jammed it, would be long gone by now, believing that no one was home.

Danny walked carefully down the stairs, already targeting the errant bell which was high on the wall behind the door. He reached it and leapt up, whacking it angrily. The buzzing stopped and the bell grudgingly gave the second half of its two-tone ring.

Danny didn't spot the man outside the door until he rapped sharply on the frosted glass. His heart stalled for a second. *Jesus Christ!* Danny thought.

He reached for the catch, missed it, fumbled with it and finally got the door open.

A tall, thin man carrying a briefcase stood there in the rain. He was grey-haired and probably, Danny guessed, at the tail end of his sixties. The expression on his gaunt face and in his blue, red-rimmed eyes gave him away. He was one of that elite band of intellectuals, the *Know Betters*.

Danny was speechless. His heart was hammering, there was still a distinct taste of vomit in his mouth, and here was an ageing insurance salesman just *dying* to make his pitch. Danny's motormouth saw free reins and quickly grabbed them. 'What the fuck d'you want? *You scared me half to death!*' he heard himself complain. The man's expression did not alter. He was evidently used to this sort of behaviour – which didn't exactly rule out his being an insurance salesman, but made it less likely. He looked at Danny impassively. Officially.

'Mr Stafford, Mr*Daniel* Stafford?' the *Know Better* enquired, his tone implying that he knew exactly to whom he was speaking.

Not a policeman, Dan, he can't be a policeman, he's too old! Danny quickly assured himself, but his mind laid out a random example of a page from the kind of *Today's Schedule* leaves you find in any Filofax. The entries read *10 am* library, *11am* left library, then they were blank until 5pm. Arrived home, this one said. The blanks between 11 and 5 glared up at him balefully. *Perhaps*, Danny's mind suggested as he glanced down at the *Know Better's* briefcase, *you could fill those in with something like this: Had schizophrenic episode during which I killed a girl.*

The *Know Better's* briefcase didn't look like a police issue one, though. It was more the kind of thing you would expect to see a doctor carrying. Battered black leather with brass reinforced edges and clasp. There were two letters engraved on the clasp: A.L.

'You *are* Mr Daniel Stafford?' the man repeated.

Game's up, old Dan, you've been catched – and so early in your career! 'Yes,' he said wearily. 'What do you want?'

'I want to talk to you.'

The insurance man theory was still favourite. Old A.L. wasn't going to snap the wrist irons on him by the look of it and he didn't have the rapt expression of a Jehovah's Witness or the squeaky-clean look of a Mormon. Suddenly Danny didn't want to know *who* he was. His bullet wound had begun to pulse like a healed fracture sensing rain in the air and that meant trouble, even if it was only a forthcoming nosebleed.

'I don't feel like talking at the moment, thank you very much,' he said.

The *Know Better* smiled genially, letting Danny know he'd anticipated this resistance. Danny wanted to hit him.

'Then would you just listen for a few minutes? I think you'll find what I have to say is very interesting. And pertinent.'

'I think I may be about to have a nosebleed,' Danny said, 'and when it goes, it goes, as they say, like Elsie.'

'It won't take a moment.'

'Then just say what you want and leave me alone,' Danny told him.

'May I come in?' the man asked.

The age old vampire/salesman question. Once you'd invited them in, you were sunk. Both species were very difficult to rid yourself of once they had crossed your threshold. The *Know Better* evidently had something to sell after all.

Danny shook his head. His nose hurt when he moved. It felt like there was a balloon full of blood up there waiting to fall.

'I'm getting wet,' the man appealed.

Danny grinned coldly. 'That's because it's raining,' he said.

This time, Mr A.L.'s smile was more rueful than genial. 'I can talk out here,' he said 'but it really would be better if you allowed me to talk to you inside. You need to talk too. You need help, Daniel,' he said.

Danny frowned. 'Help? Are you from the hospital? Do you know something I don't?' He'd thought the briefcase looked like a doctor's bag. It looked as though he'd been right. But why would the hospital have sent someone? Wouldn't they have simply sent him a follow-up appointment card?

The *Know Better* shook his head. 'I think you know what kind of help I mean, Daniel,' he said slyly and all sorts of strange and guilty thoughts flickered through Danny's mind. He took a pace back.

'My name is Mr Alistair Lerner,' the man said. 'I'm not selling anything and I don't want anything from you. I just want to help you.'

Danny knew with a sudden clarity that Alistair Lerner was trying to deceive him. Only a part of what he said was true and Danny didn't know which part.

'I was expecting you to call me,' the man continued. 'When you didn't, I thought I'd better visit you.'

'Call you? I don't *know* you, for Christ's sake!' Danny said. He was feeling a heady cocktail of emotions. There was anger there, and guilt, and plenty of both, but there was more riding just below the surface. There was exhilaration, hope, sadness, suspicion – but the emotion that encapsulated them all was fear. Sirens warning of incoming missiles wailed away in his ears and a part of Danny – a very large part – was screaming at him to slam the door in the face of the man, preferably after having lashed out at him in the same way he'd lashed out at his boss. That part of him badly wanted to see Mr Alistair Lerner's eyes blank as his head did a slow roll around his shoulders. *Shut the door before it's too late*! his mind warned. *This man's bringing more trouble than you can deal with. You can almost see it surrounding him and weighing him down. This is a man wants you to take his burden from him. He doesn't want to help you, he wants you to help him*!

The *Know Better's* hand stole into his jacket pocket and Danny's mind yelled: *Shut the door now! Time's running out and you'd better get rid of him before you see what's coming out of his pocket. You don't want to know. Once you know what he's got there, you'll be hooked! Once you've seen it, it'll be too late!*

But Danny had turned leaden. The guy was going to hand him the Black Spot and Danny was going to stand there and take it – and probably thank him politely for it too. His scar pulsed and the bag of blood in his nose stretched.

'Go away,' he murmured in a helpless voice and thought, *Well, that was forceful, wasn't it?*

Mr Alistair Lerner's clenched hand came out of his pocket and swept towards Danny, stopping just in front of his face and so close that Danny could smell the cigarette tar coming from the man's yellowed index and second fingers.

Fifty a day, Danny knew. The information crept into his mind as if he'd known it all along. The *Know Better* obviously didn't know better as far as smoking was concerned. Danny also suddenly knew that Alistair Lerner had smoked his fifty a day for the past thirty-three years; that he smoked only untipped, favouring Woodbines but sometimes buying packets of Nelsons; that he found it hard to breathe sometimes and had a bubbling cough of the variety that Danny's mother would have called 'Graveyard'; and that Mr Lerner knew it was not the smoking that would kill him.

While Danny was trying, not to understand the sudden and instantaneous transfer of information direct to his mind, but simply to deal with it, the *Know Better's* fingers unfolded like a conjurer's and the magic prize was revealed.

Hooked, Danny thought. *You should have closed the door, old Dan, and you should have done it when you had the chance, because that option has just vanished. You're hooked, just like he intended.*

The hook was the watch that had been stolen from Danny's wrist some time between Christine Richard's demise and his waking up in the multi-storey car park. Lerner's fingers did a little more prestidigitation and the watch was now hanging from his fingers by the strap, swaying in front of Danny's face as though manipulated by a hypnotist.

'My watch,' Danny said in a small voice, while he noticed that it was running and that the time was a quarter past twelve.

'Your watch,' Lerner repeated.

The bubble in Danny's nostril burst and blood coursed down, running into his mouth and spraying his shirt. Anger and confusion suddenly filled him, thrusting aside the wide-eyed little boy. He wanted to go inside and fix the nose bleed before it made too much mess, but there was a thief standing in front of him, taunting him. He stood there bleeding and looking from the watch to Lerner's self-satisfied face and back to the watch again.

Danny's hand floated up and snatched the watch away from Lerner and he heard himself say, 'Are you the bastard that mugged me?' knowing that his fist was clenching around the watch. *If it breaks when you hit him, it's too bad*, a part of his mind thought.

Lerner shuffled backwards two paces and did his rueful smile again, unconsciously making himself harder to hit. 'No one mugged you, Daniel. Your watch was just borrowed. I intended that you should have it back and I expected to be able to return it to you much earlier. I'm sorry.'

Danny thought about it. He suddenly didn't want to punch the *Know Better* any more, just wanted him gone. 'Well, you can stick *sorry* up your ass!' Danny shouted, swallowing warm blood and turning away.

'Some strange things have been happening to you recently, Daniel, haven't they?' Lerner called after him as he strode up the hallway.

'All I want is to help you to understand them.'

Danny spun round. Blood dotted the wallpaper. 'Well, you can just fuck right off before I deck you!' he shouted. 'I don't want to know!' He marched down the hall to the kitchen, turned on the cold tap, put his head under it, closed his eyes and waited. The pain of the cold water cleared his head and eventually the nosebleed stopped. When Danny took his head out of the sink and turned round, Mr Alistair Lerner was in the kitchen watching and dripping rain water on to the floor, just as Danny had known he would be. These days, problems just wouldn't go away.

'Get out,' he said coldly.

Lerner nodded his head. 'A bleeder,' he said mildly.

'What?'

'You're a bleeder. We all have our problems, y'know. I'm a bleeder too.'

Danny shook his head. 'I don't care what you are or what you think I am – just go.'

'I expected you to telephone me,' the *Know Better* said mildly. 'Perhaps you lost my number?'

'I never *had* it,' Danny protested.

'It was left in your inside jacket pocket on a piece of cardboard. If what I'm told is accurate, the cardboard was taken from a Frosties packet and bore a picture of Tony the Tiger on one side.'

The piece of cardboard lit in Danny's imagination. He remembered the picture of Tony the Tiger and he *thought* he remembered *eating* that picture (*You ate it? Ate a picture of Tony the Tiger? Surely not?*), but he didn't recall the telephone number on it at all.

Lerner mopped the rain from his face with a large handkerchief. 'I know all about you, Daniel. I know what's happening to you. I can help you if you'll listen to me. And you *should* listen to me.'

'An offer I can't refuse?' Again Danny felt the sensation that Lerner wanted to trick him. He didn't want to listen to the man, but short of removing him by force – which didn't look quite so attractive now he'd had a chance to cool down – there seemed to be no other way of making him leave.

Lerner was nodding his head again, indicating that it was indeed an offer which couldn't be refused. And to Danny's annoyance there was a strong urge inside him to find out what the man had to say.

'Sit down,' he said, pointing at the kitchen table. 'Take off your coat and sit down and talk.' He towelled the moisture from his hair, took a seat opposite Lerner and said, 'Go.'

'You haven't been very well, have you?' Lerner said.

'Haven't I?'

'I don't think so. We usually start out that way. Confused and frightened, like you are now.'

Danny shrugged. 'Is this the royal "we"?'

Lerner shook his head then pulled his cigarettes from his pocket.

Danny wasn't remotely surprised to find they were Woodbines. 'Yes you can smoke,' he said and got an ashtray. Lerner lit up, sucked hard on the cigarette and Danny got to hear the wheezing graveyard cough. *And he doesn't think it's going to kill him*, he thought.

Lerner's cough subsided after his second inhalation, but when he spoke his voice was breathless and occasionally the demons that lived in his lungs sang high-pitched tunes to accompany his voice. 'What did you feel about the death of Christine Richard?' he asked.

'Were you there?' Danny asked suspiciously.

Lerner shook his head. 'No, but I heard all about it. Relax, it wasn't your fault.'

Danny's motormouth grabbed at the reins, but he caught it and slapped it away, stopped himself telling Lerner that it had felt as it if was *entirely* due to him. 'It was weird,' Danny said. 'Scary.'

Lerner nodded. 'And what happened to you afterwards?'

'I don't know,' he said wearily. 'But you do, I suppose. You mugged me.'

'No one mugged you, Daniel. A friend of mine was present at Christine's unfortunate demonstration and he saw everything that happened. When you ran from Ancastle House in a state of distress he followed you, intending to help you. It was he who borrowed your wrist watch. He did it for me, he meant no harm and he did not beat you up, I can assure you of that. He is seventy-three years old and suffers badly from emphysema. He could not keep pace with you, let alone beat you up. He only found you by . . . uh . . . luck and he was not well when he did. As I said, we all have our problems – they come with the territory.'

'And what territory is that?'

'You know really, Daniel, don't you?'

Danny thought he might but refused to admit it, even to himself. He did not want to find himself a member of an exclusive club whose patrons 'all had their problems' because they 'came with the territory' so he pretended he didn't have a clue as to what the *Know Better* meant.

'When my friend Mr Mills found you lying unconscious in the car park, he thought that it would be a good idea to borrow your watch, and as it turned out, it was. I'll tell you why eventually. You might like to know that you blacked the old man's eye while he was borrowing your watch. But Mr Mills in distress is as thorough as most people at the peak of their form. He got the watch, he wrote you a note and he also went through your wallet, found your driving licence and wrote down your address.'

'Oh,' Danny said, searching his memory and finding no recollection of any old man. Those hours after Christine Richard's death were blank.

'What do you think happened to Christine Richard?' Lerner asked.

'I think she fell off the stage and broke her neck,' Danny said.

Lerner smiled grimly. 'Leading up to that.'

Danny didn't know what he ought to say. Pictures of the cross-hatched scratch marks on Suzie's back leapt into his mind. He thought the psychic had linked with his mind and found a killer lurking there in his subconscious. He thought his subconscious had somehow possessed Christine Richard and had used her to speak to his conscious self, then caused her to fall. He thought that other Danny was doing the driving during his blank periods and he thought the blank periods would get longer and longer until the real Danny Stafford was swamped forever. But he wasn't about to tell *that* to someone he didn't know from Adam. 'I don't think she talks . . . talked to the dead at all. I think she was some kind of a mind reader,' he said.

Lerner grinned a *Know Better's* superior grin and Danny hated him for it. The man butted his cigarette and said, 'As it happens, you're not far wrong. Christine did operate in a fashion very close to this. She didn't realise she was not talking with the dead, of course. She firmly believed that *was* what she did. Our Christine tapped in on your brainwaves without realising what she was letting herself in for. Your thoughts were incredibly unstable and powerful. Once she found your mind, all your terror, anguish and confusion filled her, and like a person grabbing a live wire, her mental muscles locked and she couldn't get off. She couldn't let go of you. She dredged your unconscious and spoke the things she found there, while she fought desperately to be released. When she broke the link, she simply lost her balance and fell.'

'And now she's dead,' Danny added.

Lerner shook his head. 'An accident, that's all. Not your fault.' He leaned back, lit another Woodbine and suffered the mandatory coughing fit. When he could speak again, he asked, 'What do you know about psychics?'

Welcome to the club, old Dan! Danny thought. 'Nothing,' he said.

'Well, I can tell you what you need to know, but perhaps you could tell me about the scar on your face first.'

'What d'you mean, *what I need to know*?' Danny demanded.

'You're coming out,' Lerner said. 'You know that, surely? You didn't kill Christine Richard and you're not possessed. All that's happening is that you are coming out. You're psychic and your talent is blooming. Believe me, I *know*. I'm psychic too.'

Danny shook his head. *Not psychic, Dan. Not that. You don't wanna be the Fucked-up Future-Man. None of those visions came true, Dan. None of them! Nightmares and wakemares were all they were!*

But Danny realised that sometimes *Know Betters* really did know better. Lerner was just confirming what Danny had refused to admit to himself. Like it or not, he had joined that elite band of men and women who belonged to The Paranormal Club, where everyone had their problems, because those problems came with the territory.

Danny had known this all along, if he was truthful with himself. But *these days being truthful is getting much harder, isn't it? Not just with yourself, but with everyone, old Dan*. Being made to face up to it in this way made his heart heavy with dread.

'How do I stop it?' he asked.

Alistair Lerner gave him another of those rueful smiles. 'I think you already know that you can't stop it. You have to learn how to use it, train yourself to control it. Your talent can be a dangerous thing if it's allowed to run out of control. Remember what happened after you went to see Christine Richard?'

'I blacked out and woke up on top of the car park, that's all,' Danny said guardedly.

Lerner inhaled his Woodbine and exhaled the next word in a puff of smoke. 'Afterwards,' he said.

The word hung in the air with the smoke, heavy and blue.

Danny shook his head.

'I know what happened,' Lerner said. 'Your uncontrolled talent suddenly reached maturity, probably because of the probing of your mind by our Christine and due to the stress of what happened next. Your spine seemed to catch fire and your unprepared mind was swamped.' He paused, looked at Danny's expression and nodded, satisfied. 'The sudden emergence of your full-blown talent attacked your logical mind, pushing you over the edge into madness. You felt as if your very being had been terribly burned. You suffered excruciating mental and physical agonies from which you thought there would be no release. You were unable to think or act; you saw awful visions and entirely lost touch with reality. You became starved, dehydrated and filled with the violence of madness. You tried to kill yourself to make it all stop. . .' Lerner tailed off and smoked silently for a moment. 'How do I know all this? You might well ask,' he said after a moment. 'I know because I was unprepared when I came out and it all happened to me. I know you have convinced yourself that it is all over, but it is not. Unless you train yourself, channel your talent, it will drive you permanently insane at the least and probably to your death.'

'And you can help me?'

Alistair Lerner looked at him through watery blue eyes and again Danny got the distinct impression that he was concealing something. 'That's what I'm here for,' Lerner said, 'Now perhaps you would tell me about that scar?'

4

Danny handed over control to his motormouth and let it do the talking for him while he listened – from what seemed like a mile or more away – to the *Know Better* who had something to conceal.

'My brother shot me when I was a kid,' he heard himself confessing, and thought *Confession is good for the soul*. He distantly wondered what the man would say if his mouth decided to tell him that Danny Stafford thought he was becoming a murderer.

Over there in the muddy world of Dannyland, a psychic was asking him, 'Did it cause brain damage?' and his voice was answering that parts of him were dead, hence the limp when he got tired; that his nose bled at the drop of hat; that there was a piece of bone still in his pineal gland – while that voice's tone intimated that when you were a member of The Paranormal Club you could expect to have your cross to bear.

Lerner's watery eyes twinkled and concealed as he asked about the after effects of the shooting and Danny told him about the Out of Body Experience, the hallucinations and the people surrounded by fire. Out there in Dannyland, his voice was recounting experiences that he'd totally forgotten. Danny listened and learned and it all sounded old and frayed around the edges and too boring to be of any consequence, but the *Know Better* was fascinated and excited.

'Listen!' he commanded and Danny listened.

'No one in the medical world knows what the pineal gland is for. If you've tried to discover its purpose, you've almost surely failed. It has no known function. . .'

'Thought to be the site of the third eye in certain lizards,' Danny heard himself say. Lerner nodded. Danny listened across that huge distance while Lerner told him that, 'The pineal gland is the part of the brain which deals with the other senses. The ones that are usually known as psychic abilities.' It was a defunct part according to Lerner, a part that had become unnecessary over the ages and diminished in size until it was vestigial – like that other useless organ, the appendix. But unlike the appendix, it remained connected to the channels of energy – undetectable *psychic* channels – that ran through the body and that touched and connected *all things*, past, present and future, and living or not living. Danny had once heard Robbie Robertson reading a speech by a Red Indian called Chief Seattle who had made similar claims and he felt myself smile as he recalled it. *Man did not weave the web of life*, Chief Seattle had claimed, he is *merely a strand in it*. Danny knew exactly what he'd meant. He listened to Robbie Robertson saying: '*This we know*' while Lerner explained that the pineal gland had to be stimulated before it would work and told him tales of Tibetan monks who had holes drilled in their skulls so that splinters of wood could be inserted and driven through their brains into their pineal glands, thus awakening their psychic abilities. It was Lerner's opinion that the piece of bone driven through Danny's pineal gland had served the same purpose and since it was stuck there, Danny was stuck with his talent.

Danny felt himself nodding, heard Joey chirruping in the distance and thought of Brough Lacey who would, no doubt, be proud of him. He had certainly crossed Brough's fine line between reality and fantasy now.

Like *Know Betters* the world over, Lerner loved the sound of his own voice and rambled on about the coloured auras that surrounded every living thing like fires – if only one could see them – the difference between all the branches of the paranormal, ghosts and spirits, and everything else he could think of.

Danny learned that psychics were usually only blessed with one of a multitude of talents. They could either (and most commonly) pick up thoughts as Christine Richard had done; less commonly, perceive things with the auditory senses (and Lerner doubted these were the voices of the dead, but believed they were the sounds of things yet to come or of things past); or much less commonly see the the past or future – sometimes both. People who were pyrotic – able to generate heat or start fires with their minds – or psychokinetic – able to move objects in the same way – were, according to Lerner, not making use of their full capabilities since these were minor off-shoots of more important ones and not usually very powerful. Then there were healers of various types. And then there was the higher echelon to which Lerner himself belonged to, the clairvoyants. True clairvoyants, he claimed, could see into the future.

Danny felt as if his brain was being battered with a stick and the violence to his sensibilities went on and on, his mind closing down but always remaining as sensitive to the blows as it had been when they started.

5

Somewhen during that time, Danny's motormouth threw down the reins in disgust and retreated, leaving him speechless. When the pain ceased and Danny's head cleared he found himself standing at the top of the stairs with Lerner behind him on the landing. He was mildly surprised to discover that the cold iron fist had reached out and grabbed his stomach and was squeezing gently; more surprised that he was shaking with fear. He had a dim recollection of his voice telling Lerner about the bathroom tiles some time before it packed up and left him. When Lerner had finished listening to himself holding court he'd asked Danny if he could see the bathroom and Danny had simply got up, motioned him to follow and taken him up there. Now he was standing on the threshold, too frightened to go inside.

Lerner pushed gently past him, went to the middle of the room and gazed around, tut-tutting and shaking his head. 'Amazing,' he said. 'I can hardly believe you installed these merely coincidentally and without prior knowledge. Everything is lined up and ready for use.'

'Suzie designed it,' Danny said, closing his eyes and holding on to the door jamb. The iron fist around his stomach had vanished now, leaving a vacuum, and Danny knew what happened when he got that vacuum sensation. It started to reach out for the vacuum that hid behind the mirror tiles, wanting to link with it. If he closed his eyes, the dizziness faded slightly.

'Is Suzie your wife?'

'My girlfriend. Live in lover. Common law wife. I dunno what to call her any more,' he said, keeping his eyes firmly closed. Talking to Lerner had kicked everything into play again. Precipitated another *weird* attack. Or clairvoyant experience, if Lerner was to be believed. He was certain it wouldn't have happened if he hadn't let the *Know Better* into the house and dearly wished he could go back to that moment when he'd turned and stormed off down the hall, so that this time he could slam the door in the man's face first.

'Yes,' Lerner agreed, apparently having read his thoughts. 'But it would have been only a temporary measure. Nothing would have prevented another clairvoyant episode. Eventually you would have had one. Perhaps not today, but soon. Nothing would have stopped it; the configuration of the tiles is too powerful. Is your girlfriend psychic too?'

'No,' Danny said from behind his closed eyes and suddenly thought she might be, in some faint and unrecognised way. It would explain a lot. *Maybe the things the fortune teller told her were her own precognitions, plucked from her head by telepathy*, he thought, then thrust it from his mind when it made his head spin. It was like holding a mirror up to a mirror and seeing endless diminishing reflections. Madness lay at the end of that path.

'Come into the room,' Lerner said.

As Van Morrison would have said, it was *too late to stop now!* Danny opened his eyes and tottered into the room, fighting his vertigo and taking huge steps as the floor buckled beneath his feet. Each time he glanced at the black mirror tiles they expanded and reached out for him, threatening to suck him in.

'I'm going,' he said, closing his eyes and staggering sideways.

Lerner caught him and held on to his arms. 'It's okay,' he said, steadying him, 'we'll have you out of here in a jiffy.'

Danny didn't open his eyes again until Lerner had led him downstairs and sat him down on the new lounge sofa.

6

Alistair Lerner looked at Danny for a long time before he spoke again and Danny knew that he was considering how much or how little he should conceal. Lerner was evidently wondering how to pass the burden he carried to him without Danny realising it was happening.

'You *are* clairvoyant,' Lerner finally said, frowning. 'Naturally and very powerfully clairvoyant.'

'Great,' Danny said sourly. 'Just what I wanted for Christmas.'

Lerner simply smiled.

'And it can't be stopped?'

Lerner shook his head. 'But you can learn to control it. However, to learn to control it, you have to learn to use it. Are you willing?'

'No,' Danny said heavily, 'but it looks like there's no other option.' He sighed. 'Go ahead. Do your worst.'

Lerner clicked into lecture mode again, but this time Danny paid close attention. He expected to be duped and thought that the seams would show in Lerner's argument. He would see the gaps where Lerner had concealed or excised the truth and he would be alert when Lerner tried to pass him the Black Spot. Whatever it was Lerner wanted to get rid of, Danny was going to do his utmost not to take it. He was a little more confident now; sure he could deal with it. Danny had done enough lying himself lately to have learned the tricks of the trade and he was certain he could detect those that Lerner was bound to tell.

Lerner lit up a Woodbine and coughed heartily. 'Let me explain a little about what is known as the Akashic Record. Some background information will make things easier to understand – if not believe.

'Time, as any physicist will tell you, is not what it seems. Everything that has ever existed, everything that has ever happened, is linked within this web of time. Linked in ways that, as yet, no one fully understands. All things that have ever existed have radiated waves of energy of various frequencies, including what we would call, for want of a better word, psychic energy. This energy, this *essence*, is not corruptible – it exists forever; both in the place it was created, or originated from, and radiating out through the universe. All the things that happen in this world, every conversation, every motion, every rock, stone and blade of grass that was ever here, are recorded in a steady flow as time progresses from and vanishes into its own web. We see only a single strand of that spiral web as it passes by us and we call it "Now'. The part of the strand that has passed us, we call the past, and the parts yet to come, we call the future. The centre of the web exists in what we can call another dimension. Were you able to detect that strand of time and follow it to where its centre lay – in that other dimension – you would be able to experience things that had happened in every detail; sight, sound, smell and hearing. A clairvoyant is a person who can send his or her mind across the time web and penetrate one of the centre's many entry points. The entry point we can access is known as the Akashic Record. There are ways to gain entrance into other parts of the centre and the core around which *everything* revolves but since it takes a wild talent and is almost never successfully accomplished, these are beyond our scope of interest.'

The core around which everything revolves, Danny thought, his mind refusing to believe it, but building on it anyway. *He's talking about the core of everything – not just us and good old planet earth. He's talking about the centre of all universes, of all time and all dimensions.*

'You're telling me the future already exists,' he heard himself say. 'Everything is pre-determined, according to what you said. Yet the visions I saw of the future didn't come true.'

Lerner lit another Woodbine from the butt of the last one. 'The Akashic Record also shows the probability of things to come. On both personal and world levels. The likely events of the future are contained within it, along with the record of the past.'

'But I had a vision of a car crashing into a petrol tanker. I went to try and stop it and it didn't even happen. The car was parked up when the tanker went by.'

Lerner shook his head. 'I said *probabilities*, Daniel. At any given moment there are many things that can happen. The most likely of them are held in the Akashic Record. Not every possibility, but the most likely ones. And the most likely possibilities are *probabilities*, aren't they?'

Danny shrugged, then nodded. At the moment he wouldn't have been able to deny that two plus two equalled seven.

Lerner smiled. 'Imagine our sitting here now. If we were to consult the Akashic Record, we could predict with a reasonable amount of accuracy what the outcome of this situation will be. Neither of us knows at this point. You may have left the gas oven on for all we know and the next time I light a cigarette we might be blown sky high. That's a possibility. The major *probability* is that you will sit here and listen to me. However, there are bound to be other probabilities; for instance, you may soon call me a crank and throw me out. That is a probability of a more minor order and would not be the first you would experience when consulting the record. There are usually more probabilities held in the record. This explains your vision of the tanker crash, and since the original cause of your vision was the black tiles in your bathroom, and knowing how inexperienced you are, I'm not surprised you came up with the wrong result. What you saw was probably the fourth or fifth most likely event. Clear?'

'As clear as mud,' Danny said.

'You'll soon get the hang of it,' Lerner assured him, putting out his Woodbine and lighting another.

7

By the time Alistair Lerner asked Danny to darken the room and went upstairs with his briefcase, Danny knew a great many new and unbelievable things and was certain that he hadn't just crossed Brough Lacey's fine line, but gone so far beyond it, it was back there somewhere over the horizon. A part of him wondered if this was another example of the split reality he'd previously suffered and forwarded the theory that he was probably, at this precise moment, sitting in the library reading a book.

And that idea, Danny thought, *is a damn' sight more appealing than what's going on here*. Things were steadily getting worse. After spending the greater part of his life wondering about the purpose of his pineal gland, he had been presented with a theory which – in the light of his recent experiences – seemed unassailable; he had been pronounced a member of that elite band of individuals, The Paranormal Club (where everyone had their problems); he had tripped Lerner up and then failed to get the truth while cross-examining him, and he was now sitting here in semi-darkness waiting for Lerner to come back downstairs and show him . . . God knew what . . . after which Lerner would undoubtedly try to unload his burden on him.

If he hasn't already passed it to you without you noticing, that is, he told himself.

There was a distinct possibility that Lerner wasn't just a *Know Better* and a miser with the truth but also a master tactician. What had happened earlier when Danny thought he'd tripped Lerner up, may well have been intentional. Although Danny thought he'd scored a good point against the man, he now began to think he may simply have been out-manoeuvred.

Lerner had been trying very hard to come across as being totally free from doubt. Trying too hard, in fact.

Lerner had – apparently – slipped when he told Danny why his watch had been stolen. Slipped badly, but not fallen. Wild horses wouldn't have dragged the information Danny wanted from him and Danny had been forced to concede this point. Now it looked as if it was another piece of bait which he had taken.

Lerner had been busy telling him how clairvoyants usually needed something to focus on, which would help them access the record, when Danny remembered his watch.

'Real psychics almost invariably use fine crystal to aid their visions,' Lerner was saying. 'You focused on the black mirrors in your bathroom and it just so happened that black mirrors are the most powerful clairvoyant aid available, but they are dangerous and should not be used. Don't use them again. Once you have control, you'll be able to prevent it.'

'Why did you want my watch?' Danny asked suddenly.

Lerner looked momentarily flustered. 'Watch?' he asked.

Danny waved his wrist in front of Lerner's face. The watch was back on it now. 'This. The one your friend stole. If you use a crystal, why did you need the watch?'

Lerner was silent for a second and when he started to speak, looked as if he wished he'd kept his mouth shut. 'You don't use personal items to access the record. You access that with a crystal.'

At which point, Danny thought, *he'd have changed the subject if he didn't want to put questions in your mouth.*

But Lerner had carried on. 'Personal items are used to target a subject when you do a clairvoyant reading. If you wish to see into another person's future, you hold something that belongs to them and has traces of them on it. Everyone – every living thing and most inanimate things too as a matter of fact – has a separate and distinct wavelength which they transmit throughout their centre existence. . .'

'You looked into my future,' Danny had said.

Just like he wanted you to, he thought, remembering the feeling of satisfaction at having caught the man out.

Lerner's watery eyes had glanced up at him then looked back at the ashtray where the latest smouldering Woodbine lay. He ignored the question – purposely, Danny now thought – and said, 'These vibrations affect everything the person comes in contact with in some way. The more the person in question is in contact with something, the more its vibrations are changed. If you can get hold of an item that a person has been in close contact with for a very long time – a gold ring, for example – then its own vibrations are swamped by those of the owner. With an old gold ring you might detect the frequency of the gold, but not enough to have a vision of the gold's past or future. The overpowering vibration would be of the owner, and if you were to hold this ring you would either see the past or future of its owner. If you had a brand new gold ring you would probably have a vision of the gold's past, or of the miners that took it from the ground, or more likely, the jeweller and packer and the shop assistant. . .'

And Danny, thinking he was in control, had taken each sucker punch as it was delivered and hadn't even realised it.

'You looked into my future, didn't you?' he'd cut in.

Lerner shook his head. 'Mr Mills is clairvoyant. He took your watch so that he could have a look at what seemed likely for you in the future. That's why I'm here. He saw that you were going to need help.'

'But you did a reading, too, didn't you?' Danny insisted.

'No,' Lerner replied.

Danny smiled grimly. 'What did you see?'

Lerner looked at him for a long time with those red-rimmed eyes. 'I didn't do a reading,' he said, and they both knew it was a lie.

'I'll throw you out if you don't admit it,' Danny said. 'What did you see about me?'

Lerner had made a steeple with his hands and sighed. His fingers were long and spindly and the veins on the backs of his hands stood out like electrical cables buried just beneath the ground. His hands trembled slightly.

And then he turned the sympathy screw, didn't he, old Dan? He manipulated you relentlessly and you didn't even know he was doing it. Some lie detector you turned out to be!

Lerner said, 'I'm not a natural psychic and I don't often practise clairvoyance any more. It is too painful for me; it siphons off my energy and gives me terrible headaches. If I do a reading it takes me a fortnight to recover. It used to be my trade, y'know. I was well known when I was younger. The headaches were a mere inconvenience then; they didn't matter so long as I could access the record, and I thought they were something I would grow out of. I didn't, of course. As I grew older they became more and more severe until they were the only thing worthy of consideration. The future or the past didn't matter; the pain did. Nowadays, I would rather walk over hot coals than put my mind into that place. Too painful, far too painful.' He shook his head and pressed his lips together, sighing through his nose.

'But you did a reading on me,' Danny said, thinking, *Why am I that important to him*?

'Yes, I did a reading. I saw you at the clairaudient demonstration, and then I saw you rolling around in mental agony on your lounge floor. Nothing more.'

'Yes, there is,' Danny said, nodding. 'Now what is it?'

Lerner shook his head. 'Nothing,' he said.

And seeing the hurt in the man's face, Danny had dropped the subject.

But Lerner's skilled management of the situation hadn't even ended there. Now, while he waited for Lerner to return to the lounge, Danny realised that and told himself that they were going to have to re-write that old saw, 'There's no fool like an old fool', because now there was somebody younger who disproved it. There was, in fact, no fool like a Danny Stafford.

Lerner had smoked his next cigarette in silence, then asked Danny if he was ready to learn to control his gift. Lerner looked pained and against his better judgement, Danny felt sorry for him. Lerner promised that, afterwards, Danny would be able to live a normal life if he chose and use his talent if and when he wanted to. Danny had ignored the fact that the part about living a normal life was obviously a lie and said nothing, telling himself that if Lerner *could* teach him how to turn off his *weird* attacks, then it was worth trying to learn. That, at least, would be a step in the right direction.

Lerner had put out his cigarette, got up, picked up his case and said, 'I'm going upstairs to the bathroom. I'll be five minutes. During that time I would like you to darken the room as much as possible. There is to be no direct lighting at all. We need gloom. Can you arrange that?'

Danny had nodded. 'But what are you intending to do?'

'I'm going to hurt myself again, I'm afraid,' Lerner said. He flashed his rueful smile once more and left the room.

8

You've gone mad, old Dan, he told himself as he drew the curtains. *You've gone stark staring mad. There's a man up there in the bathroom – currently running the cold tap on full blast – who's carrying something so heavy it bows his shoulders and so black you can almost see it, and you're sitting down here in the gloom waiting for him to come back down and pass it to you.*

Danny sat on the sofa for a full five minutes listening to the water hammering though the pipes while he reviewed how Lerner had guided him to what was about to happen and told himself that the best thing he could do was open the curtains again and then vacate the house until he was sure Lerner had given up and gone home.

But it wasn't that simple. Nothing was simple any more. The danger of inadvertently taking Lerner's load was outweighed – or, at least, balanced – by the dangers of what might happen if Danny didn't address the problems that were currently weighing him down. They were obviously not going to go away of their own accord. That last straw had been grasped and found wanting. If there was even a slim possibility that Lerner could help him gain control of himself – *And that, dear Danny is exactly what it's all about, controlling yourself* – then the risk had to be taken. There was no other way.

On a scale of one to ten, Danny's scare rating was bubbling just below six, but he also felt a new excitement. Maybe some good could come of all this after all. It might have only been a fresh straw to grab at, but any straw was better than no straw at all.

Up in the bathroom the tap was turned off and the pipes fell silent. *Are you sure you want to go through with this, whatever it is, old Dan*? he asked himself, and answered that he was.

He heard the bathroom door snap back. Butterflies flittered around his stomach and vanished. He fought off the urge to run as he heard Lerner's measured tread on the stairs and whispered, 'Here goes nothing!'

Lerner came into the room and stopped, silhouetted in the doorway by the brightness out in the hall. Both his hands were close to his chest, cradling something wrapped in what seemed to be black velvet. His lung demons sighed though his nostrils and he seemed very old and terribly tired.

'Here we are,' he said, closing the door behind him. He sounded more terrified than Danny felt. He sat down on the sofa beside Danny and placed the bundle gently on the coffee table. 'Would you please go around the other side of the table and sit on the floor facing me?' he asked. 'It's better if we're face to face.'

Danny moved and sat cross legged on the carpet directly opposite Lerner so that the bundle of cloth was in the centre of the table between them.

'What is it?' he said, knowing very well what it was and feeling much more comfortable about it than he thought he had any right to.

Lerner's expression was hidden from view by the gloom, but his breathing was uneven and ragged. 'It's the way in,' he replied.

Danny watched entranced as Lerner's hands carefully drew back the velvet cloth from the object it covered and revealed a perfectly round hole in the fabric of reality.

Danny gasped and checked his fleeing senses as Lerner tucked the black cloth in around the bottom of the hole, as if to keep it from rolling away.

'My crystal,' Lerner said in a pained voice. 'Is it hurting you?'

Danny gazed at the crystal, shaking his head. The sphere was made of the clearest glass he had ever seen. It seemed to be both there and not there at the same time, as though it hardly existed. It was brighter than it could possibly have been, considering the darkness in the room and the fact that no light was falling on it or being reflected from its surface. The crystal seemed to have its own faint light, coming perhaps from the source of *everything* in Lerner's alternate universe.

Lerner removed his hands from the cloth and Danny instantly forgot them. He forgot everything except that there was a hole into another dimension just in front of him. The sphere lay – or floated – there, fixing his attention more powerfully than a hypnotist's watch. He could not draw his eyes away from that hole which was so open and inviting and surely not solid at all, in spite of the fact that it should have been cold, hard glass. Danny was certain that he could put out his hand and reach right inside that welcoming globe of nothingness if he wished. Then it seemed to pulse and Danny saw a faint iridescence as the sphere glowed dully. Now it seemed to be not a hard, dead thing, but a soft and warm object with a life of its own.

You can't see through it! Danny marvelled as the pulse faded. He could see in one side, but not out of the other. There *was* no other side, just a warm depth which promised to blossom and swallow you up in an endless heaven. The emptiness – or maybe the crystal itself – seemed to radiate a kind of silence. Danny was enveloped with deep feelings of peace and tranquillity and rightness and felt like he was home amongst friends after a long term of solitary confinement. He distantly thought that he'd forgotten feelings like this had ever existed for him.

'I want it,' he heard himself saying and realised he was giggling, not with madness this time or with bad humour but with a perfect childish delight. The globe pulsed again and this time Danny saw a speck of brilliance right down deep in the emptiness.

'Touch it,' Lerner coughed from a billion miles away.

From a billion miles away, Danny raised his hands and placed them near the sphere, no longer caring if he was drawn in and never seen again. Warmth radiated from the crystal and numbed his fingers. His mind began to clear.

'Feel the surface,' Lerner said.

And to Danny's surprise, there *was* a surface, thinner and more delicate than egg shell and more pliable than a party balloon. He only knew he was touching it at all because the warmth suddenly became entwined with the crystal's own coolness. It was frail in his hands and the gentle sensation of warmth and cold together slipped up his arms, found his body and caressed him, sparkling through his nervous system and revitalising him, finding the disused centres of him, re-kindling their fires.

'How does it feel?' Lerner wanted to know.

'It feels better,' Danny replied.

'Better?'

'Better than anything.'

Lerner coughed. 'Make it stop,' he said.

'I don't want to. I can't.'

'Yes, you can. Just will it away.'

'No,' Danny complained.

And felt the most intense pain of his life. It sounded like a long strip of velcro being parted and it felt as if someone had hit him in the cheek with a chainsaw then curved it round and brought it right down through the centre of his body, cleaving him in two.

He screamed and the carpet rose and thumped him in the back. He rolled on the floor in agony as fires lit where he'd been cut apart and the smell of burning flesh filled his nose. 'Help me!' he screamed into the darkness. 'FOR GOD'S SAKE, HELP ME!'

But no help came.

Chapter Ten
Passing the Parcel

1

When Danny's consciousness finally came back it felt as if it had just returned from a long and arduous journey, the details of which he did not wish to recall. After the tearing sensation and the terrible heat, everything was vague.

'What did you do? For Christ's sake, *what did you do*?' he demanded in a hurt voice. The left side of his face stung and he felt as if he had been taken apart and reassembled in the wrong order. He didn't know how much time had passed and looking at his watch just told him that it was now two-twenty. He was lying on the lounge floor supporting himself with his elbows. The curtains were still closed but Lerner had put the lights on. On the coffee table the crystal was once again covered with the black velvet cloth.

Lerner was sitting on the sofa massaging his temples with his fingers. 'I slapped you,' he said, looking up. 'Sorry about that.'

'What else?' Danny demanded. He still had the smell of singeing flesh in his nose.

'Nothing at all. You wouldn't respond when I asked you to and the only way to break the connection you had was a sharp shock, I'm afraid. I merely slapped your face once.'

Danny got up. He ached all through the centre of his body. 'I felt as if I was being torn apart and set alight.'

'That tends to happen when your link with the crystal is terminated forcibly,' Lerner said. 'And that's what happened.' He smiled, tight-lipped, thought for a time then added, 'Doing that is quite dangerous actually, but it was the only way. You wouldn't have wanted to become stuck in that mode, would you?'

'What do you mean?' Danny asked him suspiciously.

'I mean, I could have packed up and left you exactly how you were. You may have snapped out of it, but I doubt it. Most likely the men in white coats would have eventually turned up and taken you away.'

'And I would have *stayed* like it? For ever?'

Lerner shrugged.
'Christ,' Danny said.
'You must try to apply some self-discipline if you're going to get through this,' Lerner said, massaging his temples again.
'Get through what, exactly?' Danny asked, going straight for the chink in Lerner's armour. As usual, the chink was too small.
'This period of uncertainty. This time of learning. Nothing more. Had I known you were quite so talented, I would have warned you before showing you the crystal, but it takes most people quite some time to make the connection and I didn't think it necessary.'
Danny sat down next to him. 'Great,' he said dryly. 'I need help and I get a crap instructor who doesn't tell me anything until it's too late.'
Lerner looked at him, long and hard, saying nothing.
Danny seemed finally to have communicated his mistrust. Lerner surely realised now that Danny knew about the secret present the man wanted to pass him. Danny held Lerner's gaze, glowering at him and trying to crush the feeling of guilt that was stealing into him. Although he still had the odd *cracked* feeling that ran through his chest and abdomen, and in spite of the short period of agony he'd suffered, Danny felt a great deal better than he had before Lerner arrived. Using the crystal had undoubtedly been good and right. The greater part of him was revitalised and strong, ready and eager to take another crack at using it. Danny wanted to play some more.
Which was more than could be said of Lerner. He seemed dried up and empty and he was certainly suffering. An odd kind of transference seemed to have taken place in which Danny's condition had improved while Lerner's had worsened markedly. His burden was rapidly becoming untenable and he looked as if he would soon snap under its weight.
Danny felt vaguely sorry for him again and quickly crushed the emotion, reminding himself that Lerner was here because he wanted Danny to take that load, not because he hoped to save him from having to take it. Danny didn't want it and wouldn't have it – if he could help it.
'I apologise for my mistake,' Lerner said. 'Look, it's terribly simple. All you have to remember is that when you want things to stop, you have to imagine them stopping. Assure yourself that they're not happening or that they *won't* happen. It'll work with the black tiles in the bathroom just as easily as with the crystal. Are you ready to try again? I'll have to leave soon so we don't have much time.'
Danny nodded, the guilt rising in him again. Lerner plainly couldn't take much more of this. Danny didn't now expect to bleed after the experience, but it looked as if Lerner might soon start. The man might have been a *Know Better*, but he was a *Know Better* in pain, he was holding a crushing load that Danny wouldn't take from

him, and he was going to spend the next two weeks – at least – laid up because of this.

And it might well kill him, Danny's cry-baby voice chipped in. *That would feel pretty good, wouldn't it, old Dan? You've already killed one psychic and now you're going to do for another. Maybe you should leave The Paranormal Club and join that other famous one along with Lee Harvey Oswald, Jack Ruby, Charles Manson, the guy who shot Lennon, and all the others: Assassins Incorporated.*

2

'Put the lights out and sit opposite me.'

Lerner unwrapped the crystal again and asked Danny to tell him what he saw.

Danny looked back down at the crystal, feeling a kind of relief at not having to look at Lerner any more. There were too many bad things lurking just below the flesh of his pain-creased face; too much knowledge. Gazing at the crystal, Danny suddenly knew that Lerner would not pass his burden lightly. He would do it because it was necessary but he would pay by feeling as if he had betrayed Danny and would suffer for it on top of what he already had coming to him.

Maybe the only weight he has is you, old Dan. What if he's only here because he wants to help you after all? Maybe he just wants to discharge his duty, go home, forget all about you and never gaze into his crystal again. He said it hurts him to look into the future, and judging from the state of him he's looked into yours a good few times just recently. And he's here now doing it all over again.

'You don't have to do this,' he heard himself say, 'if you don't want to'.

'No one *has* to do anything they don't want to,' Lerner replied. 'But everyone does, just the same. What do you see?'

What does he know about you, o Danny boy, o mystic of the West? What drives him? What are his secrets? You'll never know because he'll never tell. You'll just have to wait and see what things lie in store for you.

'Well?'

Unless you can look into your own future, o master mystic!

Danny gazed into the crystal, his muscles relaxing and the *cracked* feeling beating a hasty retreat. He let the calm the sphere seemed to radiate wash over him.

Lerner was growing impatient. 'Well?' he asked sharply.

'I feel good,' Danny told him.

Lerner sighed a whistling sigh. 'I don't want to know how you *feel*, I want to know what you *see*.'

'I see the crystal. It seems to be only half there. It's clear and faultless and sometimes it seems to be a bubble of smoke, like a deep opal, only the texture of it moves and swirls about. Now it's clear again and sparkling the purest rainbow colours in sharp points of light. I've never seen so many different hues. They don't clash. . . . they seem to belong with one another. It makes my eyes feel . . . new. Wait . . . it's clearing again. There's a huge emptiness in there but it's . . . not frightening . . . it's . . . beautiful somehow. It's smoky again now; blue, like cigarette smoke that hasn't been inhaled.

'Okay,' Lerner's harsh voice rang in his ears. 'Now make it stop.'

Danny felt intense irritation at being asked to stop and fought a brief battle with himself as the crystal's effervescent display drew him to it and away from Lerner's voice.

'You shouldn't have any trouble getting out this early in the proceedings. Self-discipline, Daniel! You must be able to control it. Now, make it stop!'

Danny forced himself to think it stopped, now believing he would suffer some kind of withdrawal pains after all – a bad nosebleed at the very least. *After all*, a disjointed part of him thought, *when you're a member of The Paranormal Club, the subscription fee is pain and disability. Ask our leading light, Alistair Lerner.*

Danny tried to look away from the crystal and found his vision was locked on to it. *It's nothing but a glass ball*, he thought, ignoring the small pang of panic that was worming its way around his intestines. *Everything is going to be all right and you're most definitely not frightened!* Danny was too far away from himself to know if he was smiling or not, but he thought he might be. The panic worm had been vanquished. *I'm just sitting here in the lounge looking at an empty glass ball*, he told himself, mentally picturing the scene. *It's just a simple exercise, that's all! Nothing unusual is happening inside that glass ball. Believe me, Danny, I speak without the use of forked tongue!*

And it worked. The crystal's luminosity began to fade instantly. Within seconds it was a dead thing, a null area in the centre of the coffee table. An empty glass ball that could barely be seen in the gloom.

And it didn't even hurt.

He looked over at Lerner who drew his lips up in a pained smile and all his self-satisfaction vanished. It might not have hurt him, but it hadn't done Lerner any good at all. 'Are you okay?' he asked as Lerner's smile became a grimace.

Lerner shrugged. 'I've felt better,' he said.

'I think we ought to stop now. . .' Danny said, and carefully edited out the words . . . *before it's too late*, as they prepared to trip off his tongue.

'But I've felt worse, too,' Lerner said, clasping his hands tightly in his lap. 'I'm able to continue. Anyway, how I feel is not important. How do *you feel*?'

'Okay,' Danny said. *And a little like a vet with a badly maimed dog in front of him and the hypodermic full of the Big Sleep in his right hand*, he added mentally. *I don't want to be responsible for killing you, but I think it's going to be me who deals the final blow.*

'Good,' Lerner said. 'You can control the black mirrors in the bathroom in much the same way as you broke contact with the crystal. You simply think in a totally negative fashion. Can you do that?'

Oh, I can think in a negative fashion all right, Danny thought. *Negative thinking is my forte in fact*. He nodded.

Lerner plugged in another Woodbine and wheezed like a leaky air line. 'It becomes easier with practice. I use a simple visualisation technique to assert control. I think the words: ABSOLUTELY NOT, enlarge them until they fill my mind's eye from side to side and make them impenetrable. It's a good trick if you begin to get into difficulty.'

Lerner sniffed, coughed, then pulled his handkerchief from his pocket and blew his nose noisily. Afterwards he inspected what he'd collected and Danny knew he was looking for blood. Lerner frowned, folded the handkerchief and pushed it back into his pocket.

'Okay?' Danny asked.

'Fine,' Lerner lied. 'As I was saying, the key is iron discipline and a flexible imagination. And your worst adversary is fear. To panic is to relinquish control. Remember that, because we're going to use the crystal again now and it's going to be quite different this time. We're going to practise making your talent do what you want it to. This time, we're going into the future. My future. But not too far into it. You have to learn to walk before you can run so we'll only be going to tomorrow. Does that sound all right?'

Danny thought about it. 'Yes,' he said, but didn't sound all right at all. Judging from Lerner's current state, there was the distinct possibility that his future was going to be severely curtailed before tomorrow and Danny didn't particularly want to see a corpse.

Lerner butted his cigarette. 'I'll try to guide you, but I want you to will yourself into my future at three-thirty tomorrow afternoon. I have planned for this, and I know exactly where I'll be and what I'll be doing at that time.'

'Then it won't be looking at the future, will it?' Danny said. 'It could just as easily be thought transference, the way Christine Richard did it.'

'No,' Lerner said. 'I have planned what I'm going to be doing at this time tomorrow, and it's likely to be very high in the order of probabilities – either future one, where we will look first, or future two. With your innate ability, you should also be able to access futures three and four – even without training. However, futures one and two may not be what I expect. We might both be surprised at what we see.'

That's exactly what I'm worried about, Danny thought. 'You've already looked at these futures, I assume?' he said.

'Of course, but if you're still not convinced that it isn't thought transference, we can look elsewhere. Perhaps go to a time that I haven't planned or consulted.'

Danny shook his head. 'That's okay,' he said, relieved. If Lerner had seen tomorrow at three-thirty there was a good chance he would live at least that long – even if the future was constantly swapping tracks. Lerner must have checked the four or five most likely futures and found them all identical. 'Tomorrow will do,' Danny said.

'I'm afraid we'll have to link hands around the crystal,' Lerner apologised. 'Ordinarily I would give you one of my personal items to fix you on my future, but it's more powerful if hands are held, and as I'm coming with you anyway, I need to touch the crystal.'

3

Danny was very calm and relaxed. He might have finished up on the wrong side of Brough Lacey's fine line, but it felt like home after all the doubt and dread and anguish. He felt a strong sense of having been waiting for this moment ever since the sliver of bone had been driven through his brain by the flat-ended .22 slug that was in his right hand trouser pocket.

He parted his fingers naturally, and as if he had been doing it all his life, reached across the table and took Lerner's fingers in the gaps between his own. Lerner's fingers were bigger than Danny had anticipated and pushed his own apart slightly. These fingers were warm and leathery and hard. Danny distantly realised he hadn't held hands that felt like these since his father had last helped him cross the road when he was a small boy. In fact he hadn't held *anyone's* hands but Suzie's since his teens.

Danny guided the four linked hands to the crystal so that it was cupped between them and welcomed the feeling of smooth glass and the peculiar sensation of heat and cold that wound up his arms. The crystal instantly began to pulse faintly, sending out tiny tingling shocks of clear energy which chased the cool heat up his arms, spread across his shoulders and diffused through his body.

Danny grinned and glanced over at Lerner who no longer seemed aware of him. Lerner was concentrating on the crystal, his brow furrowed and his watery eyes distant. They flickered back and forth as if he could see something in there but it wasn't what he wanted.

Danny glanced at the cool hole between universes and his eyes suddenly locked on to it, instantly becoming fixed in position. It had filled with the swirling smoky substance he'd seen earlier, but this time something golden glittered amongst the haze.

I can't blink! Danny realised. *My eyes are stuck open*!

In the crystal – or the alternate universe, or whatever it was he was looking into – the tiny pinpricks of golden light sparkled in glowing and dying waves, rolling like Hawiian surf.

Danny tried to blink again and tensed, realising that all the muscles working his eyes were paralysed. Then he realised he didn't even feel the *need* to blink. For some reason his eyes were not stinging or drying.

Across the table, Lerner's breathing became forced and harsh, his lungs sighing with the effort. Danny could not look up. 'You okay?' he asked and was surprised to find that his voice was now coming from somewhere above and behind him.

Lerner did not reply, just wheezed in and out.

Danny's palms began to itch and he realised the crystal had become very warm. More disconcerting was the fact that he was no longer able to tell whether he was sensing this through Lerner's hands or his own. They seemed to have become linked, to have run together and merged. There were two hands only on the crystal now, four wrists probably, but only two hands and no fingers at all.

Lerner gasped and his breathing stopped. Danny didn't even know where he was now. *Miles away, on the other end of two of these wrists*, he thought, staring into the waves of twinkling golden lights and feeling their pull on him. *Too far away for you to help, even if he's dying. Unless. . .*

Danny tore back his mind's eye and erected huge granite lintels in the shape of those magic words, ABSOLUTELY NOT, enlarging them until there was no spare space on that white projection screen inside his head. The granite words were heavy and scored, weatherbeaten but immovable. . .

He blinked.

Christ, it works! he thought, and as the glittering lights in the sphere dimmed, Lerner breathed out through his nose with a small sigh.

Danny waited until he was certain Lerner was going to breathe in again and dismantled the magic words. The waves of light grew bright instantly.

Lerner drew a sharp breath. 'Is it high yet?' he whispered and his voice seemed to be coming from above and behind Danny, just as Danny's own voice had done.

Between the merged hands, the crystal became thinner and softer, pulsing ever more gently as it faded to nothingness and the haze inside it expanded, sweeping over Danny and enveloping him. Danny's body had gone. He could no longer see, feel or sense anything with it. He free-floated in this vast, sparkling haze, not moving, but able to see in every direction at once.

'Is it high yet?' Lerner asked again.

And the haze fell away, dropping rapidly so Danny was looking down on it from an immense height. He was now floating in a vacuum above an endless layer of sparkling cloud, ten miles below him. A part of Danny expected his aeroplane vertigo to pop out of its hiding place, but the bad sensation didn't arrive. Danny only felt freedom and an intense exhilaration. 'Yes,' he replied, hearing his voice but not feeling the words being made in his throat and mouth, '*It's high!*'

'Fall in,' Lerner called. 'Let yourself go.'

Danny thought himself falling and fell at a rate that was not in keeping with accepted laws of gravity. The estimated ten miles down to the sparkling haze was covered almost instantaneously. The distance through the haze was covered in a second or two. The glittering golden lights passed through him and Danny felt the same odd sensation of heat and cold coursing though a nervous system that didn't seem to be present.

'Where are you?' Lerner's voice was harsh and stretched; elongated to such a degree that Danny hardly recognised it.

The fall finished suddenly. Not with a landing from above, but with a kind of sideways jerk as if something had taken hold of Danny and yanked him to the right. There was no feeling of deceleration, just a quick wrench and it had been accomplished.

Danny was suddenly standing on a tarmac path in a sunlit park, late in the afternoon. There were lots of trees around the perimeter and to his right a hundred yards or so away, children splashed and played in a paddling pool while their mothers sat nearby in small knots. The children's yells and shrieks, carried on the still air, could be heard plainly. But there was more than this, much more. Danny quickly discovered he could pick out the individual shouts of the children from the confused mêlée, target and hear the conversations of any of the parents and *know* what they were talking about, how old they were, and, he thought, if he tried harder, could probably learn anything about them he wished to know. But there were too many other things to consider to hope to concentrate for long enough. He could hear birds' wings beating, insects buzzing, the distant roar of a jet that had passed some time ago, the steady hiss of unseen traffic on a nearby road. And the colours here were brighter, equal to his vision of the car crash at The Hatch. Flashing reds seemed to shout at him from people's clothing; the clear green of the grass and leaves was soothing; browns seemed old and comfortable; blacks and greys empty and null. He could smell the differing odours of the flowers and trees that bordered the park, the perfume on the two bikini-clad girls way over on the rise and the ever-present underlying taint of exhaust fumes.

'Where are you?' Lerner's stretched voice asked again.

'I'm in a park,' Danny replied, realising that his own voice was as distorted as Lerner's. 'I've no idea where it is. I don't recognise it.'

Danny turned around – or at least his ability to see turned around; in spite of the fact that he was looking at things from his normal height, his body didn't seem to exist. If he looked down at the ground, there was nothing below him holding him up or controlling his ability to move. It all seemed to be being accomplished remotely.

At the other end of the park was a bandstand. There was a clock on top, white-faced with gilt hands and Roman numerals. It read three twenty-five. There was no sign of Lerner anywhere.

'Where are you?' Danny asked, watching a young couple holding hands coming towards him along the path.

Lerner's voice came to him on a ribbon of stretched elastic and sounded very far away. 'I'm here. I'm with you,' he said.

'I can't see you,' Danny shouted, dimly realising that, as expected, the approaching people could neither see nor hear him.

'And I can't see you either,' Lerner told him. 'I don't know why. When two people go together they can both experience the same things, but they can't see one another or themselves. We're probably occupying the same space because we're locked together.'

The teenagers reached Danny and passed through him. He felt their warmth; two distinct and different signatures. The girl, he knew, was called Louise. She was eighteen and looking forward to getting married in July. It would be a good wedding and a long and happy marriage. Danny wished he could tell them both that, then realised he was starting to sound like a side show fortune teller already. How long would it be before he told someone like Suzie that she would never have children?

'Where *is* this?' he asked, trying to put Louise out of his mind. What did it matter? He would never see her – or her fiancé – again. *It matters a great deal, old Dan, because at this point in time they've got a long and happy future laid out ahead of them, unlike some people you could touch with a very short stick. They're proof that there's still some good stuff kicking around, even if there isn't much of it.*

'This is one of my favourite parks,' Lerner said. If he had picked up Danny's thoughts, he wasn't letting on.

'Where?' Danny said.

'I won't tell you.'

'Why not?'

'You'll see.'

The springy elastic words were hard to pick up and each seemed to take an age to arrive. 'Is this the main probability then?' Danny asked. 'What you called future one?'

There was a long pause before Lerner's voice came winging down to him again. During that time Danny realised that Lerner was going to muddy the truth right to the very end and wondered why he didn't just spill the beans.

Just as Danny had anticipated, Lerner said, 'Ah . . . no, it isn't. It's the fifth alternative.' Then added, 'But it is the one I wanted you to see.'

'What happened in the other four?' Danny asked pointlessly. Lerner certainly wasn't going to tell him and, besides, it didn't take a fortune teller to work it out.

'Nothing very interesting,' Lerner replied.

'Are you okay?' Danny asked, telling himself it was another pointless question. Lerner was not only not okay, he was living his last hours – or minutes.

'I'm fine,' Lerner grunted. 'Watch.'

There was a man with a dog approaching along the path. He was tall and thin and in spite of the sunshine he was wearing a heavy red sweater. The dog was an elderly white mongrel that looked as if at least one of its parents was a Jack Russell. It trotted along in front of the man, occasionally putting on bursts of speed then stopping to peer round at him, shuffling its feet and wagging its tail as if to hurry him along. When the pair drew closer Danny realised that the man was Alistair Lerner.

'Here I am,' Lerner said.

But Danny was busily homing in on that fifth most likely Lerner of tomorrow and desperately trying pull information from him as he'd done with the paddling-pool mums and the teenage couple. But Lerner had evidently thought of this one too and erected defences. There was nothing to be had from tomorrow's Lerner. Nothing at all.

A cloud passed over the sun then, and a shiver ran the length of a back Danny no longer seemed to possess. Lerner was closed off because. . .

Because there is *no Lerner tomorrow*, Danny thought.

'See me?' Lerner's stretched voice asked.

'Yes,' Danny said quietly and thought, *But I could stand in this park all day tomorrow and you wouldn't turn up, would you, you old trickster? You're making me watch a man that at best only has a one in five chance of doing what I'm watching you doing. Much less than that actually: the odds are probably much higher if this is the fifth most likely probability. Maybe as much as a thousand to one, in fact.*

'Can you see me?' Danny asked, looking at the blank figure approaching.

'Neither of me can see you,' Lerner replied. 'Not me as I am now, and not me as I might be tomorrow. However, the future me you can see knows where you and I are standing. Tomorrow's me has today's memory to work with. He knows where you and he stood today, so he can go to that spot tomorrow, can't he?'

The dog stopped about a foot away from Danny's non-existent body and looked him up and down, its nose twitching.

'The dog can see me,' Danny said.

'It may be able to, but personally I don't think so,' Lerner replied as the dog sniffed the air where Danny's leg should have been. 'Her name's Judy. Try calling her.'

'Judy!' Danny shouted from somewhere above and behind him. *What you can hear is your voice coming from back in your lounge in Basingstoke*, Danny told himself. *A voice that's shouting yesterday and travelling fifteen or sixteen miles to where you are now – not to mention the fact that it's probably following you through the other four alternate futures before it arrives here. The dog cannot possibly hear it. None of this has happened yet and it's very unlikely that it will happen. It can't hear you.*

And while Danny wrestled with the mind-numbing craziness of the metaphysical logic, Judy grinned up at him, her tongue lolling from the side of her mouth . . . and cocked an ear.

'Sit!' Danny commanded.

Judy sat.

The impossibility of the situation suddenly hit Danny full force. Had he been able to faint dead away, he would have done it there and then, but that ability had been removed along with his physical body.

'*It can't happen!*' he heard himself screech, and in whatever now passed for his ears he sounded like a man grasping desperately for Brough Lacey's fine line and missing it by a mile.

'Coincidence,' Lerner claimed.

The fifth most likely Judy of tomorrow wagged her tail and looked round at the fifth most likely Lerner as he approached.

The future Lerner stopped just in front of Danny, grinned his rueful grin, pulled out his Woodbines, inserted one between his tight lips and lit up. Danny felt the heat of the match on his face, smelled the smoke, and as Lerner withdrew the untipped cigarette so he didn't choke during the following coughing fit, Danny saw the tiny strands of yellow tobacco which had stuck to his lips and was aware that somewhere else, in some other time, his own tongue was trying to lick them away.

The future Lerner spat into his handkerchief and examined it, frowning. He folded the handkerchief carefully, put it back in his pocket and advised his past self – who was apparently occupying the same space as Danny – that he ought to give up.

'Hello, Daniel,' the future Lerner said, plugging in the Woodbine again and talking round it. 'How's this for a demonstration of being able to see into the future? I can't see you, of course, but I know you're there watching me. I imagine this proves that what I told you yesterday is the truth.'

'Can you hear me?' Danny asked in his stretched voice.

'I know you're going to ask if I can hear you in a moment,' Lerner announced, 'because I was there when you did. I can assure you that even though I'm clairvoyant I can neither see nor hear you. I must go now or people will hear me talking to myself and think I'm crazy. Goodbye.'

The fifth most likely Lerner smiled and walked through Danny. There was a moment of warmth during which Danny felt Lerner's pain and the darkness in him. Danny reacted quickly and had almost grabbed some of the tightly held information he so badly wanted when Judy followed her master through him and blasted it all away. Danny was shocked by the dog's internal heat and rolled under its alien and primal thought mode. In an unsophisticated way the dog was aware of much more than its master had claimed. Judy knew

Danny and Lerner were there, but such occurrences were matter-of-fact for her. Judy saw and heard such ghosts all the time and since they had no odour, she paid them no heed. This was the only information Danny was able to pull from Judy. There were many other garbled messages coming from her, but the shock was so sharp and the dog passed through him so quickly he only caught them fleetingly.

'Did you get that?' Danny asked the part of Lerner which shared the same space as him. If he'd got it, Lerner must have done too. The question droned on for an age, during which Danny somehow turned and watched Lerner and Judy walking slowly away from him. Neither turned back.

Lerner's voice looped down to him: 'Geeeeettttt whhhhaaaatttt?'

There you go, old Dan, he told himself. *You've only just started with this madness and you're already better at it than The Paranormal Club's leading light. Lerner didn't get it. He doesn't know his dog saw us.*

Of course it could have been a lie, but this time Lerner's response didn't carry that metaphorical black bar-code that had given him away so many times already.

No sooner had Lerner's voice finished swooping down on him than it started again. 'Geeeeettttt whhhhaaaatttt?' he asked.

'Doesn't matter,' Danny said, and listened to his words moving slowly away from him, expanding as they went. This time they sounded different somehow – as if they were being forced through a small hole under pressure, perhaps. It took a long time for their echoes to diminish.

'Whhhhere arrrre yooou, Danielllll?' Lerner asked. 'Whhhat's haaaapened tooo youuuu, Dahnee. . .?'

Lerner's voice was chopped cleanly off in mid-sentence. There was a moment of absolute silence and the next sound that came careering down to Danny came from a *huge* distance – across years and continents.

JOEY! JOEY JOEYJOEY! HICKORY DICKORYDICKORYDICKORY DICKORY!

The sound spiralled round as it fell, and increased in intensity as it drew nearer, destroying Danny's capacity to hear anything else, slicing through and banishing his vision of Lerner's favourite park and leaving him in total, paralysing darkness. Dread rose in Danny as he identified the calling voice. The words changed to laughter; the gleeful sound of a capering madman.

That's you! Danny's mind told him needlessly and repeated it over and over again. *That's you, that's you, that's your voice, that's you!*

Then the laughter abruptly stopped. Total silence roared in Danny's ears. Absent parts of him began to hurt. He didn't know *which* parts, but he suspected that hooks were once again being driven into his spine.

Pained moaning rained down on him and ceased instantly.

Lerner, Danny thought. *What have you done to him?*

'What's happening?' Danny screamed into the silence. 'Lerner! What is it?'

But he was certain what it was. The psychic experience had opened the door to the cage deep within him and let out the lurking part of him he called the Gannex Man.

'Ohhh!' Lerner moaned. 'Nuhhh!' Then there were three sharp yelps which might have been Lerner's dog being punished with a cane, but which were more likely Lerner himself being punched with a knife.

'Stop it! STOP IT!' Danny screamed.

And the Gannex Man began to laugh again. 'Ten-up, old Dan! I'm coming for you and I mean to have you and you didn't read Jamie! *Oh, no, you didn't!*'

Lerner again: 'DON'T!'

'You fucked him like you fucked the rest!' Danny's voice rang in his ears. 'His blood's on your hands! *Our* hands, old Dan! You know what you did to them all! They liked to be hurt, old Dan, and you liked to please them! You fucked 'em till they screamed. Until the barometer bust! And I'm coming your way to fuck you too! I'm fucking you now, old Dan!'

What, or who, is Jamie? a distant part of Danny's mind asked, while he screamed back at his disconnected voice.

'It's hurting!' Lerner moaned.

Danny was free floating now, in a humid and dank limbo. Lerner's laboured breathing and harsh moaning beat against his eardrums, the sound punctuated by those dog-like yelps of agony. 'STOP IT!' he screamed again and searched his mind for those stone lintels, painfully erecting them into the magic words.

By the time he'd raised ABSOLUTELY the Gannex Man voice had ceased. Before he'd completed NOT, he'd lost Lerner and been jolted back into the lounge feeling as if he'd been given a thorough going over by the All Blacks after they'd lost an important match by twenty odd points and decided he was the cause. His battle scar was pulsing crazily and there was a fresh bag of blood gathering in his right nostril, swelling the way a droplet of water will build on the spout of a leaky tap.

Danny realised all this only peripherally. There were two much more important things for him to consider. The first was that he had not punched a steak-knife – or any other weapon – into Lerner while he'd been away (and in his relief his mouth had begun to chant 'Thank God!' over and over) and the second was that Lerner had not yet followed him back.

In fact Lerner is never going to follow you back, his cry-baby told him. *He can't: Lerner isn't breathing. He's dead.*

Danny's voice was instantly short-circuited. He stared, open-mouthed, at Lerner while his cry-baby insisted that he *had* managed to kill Lerner after all, maybe not with a real steak-knife, but there was no reason why a metaphysical one wouldn't have worked just as well, was there?

Alistair Lerner sat erect on the sofa, his cold hands still locked in Danny's, his head tipped back as far as it would go. He was not breathing and there was no tell-tale throb of the arteries in his stretched neck.

'Come on, wake up!' Danny heard himself call while his mind asked, *How are you going to get rid of the body, old Dan?*

He tried to pull his hands free of Lerner's cold ones, but they wouldn't come loose and Danny's mind started to scream that he was holding the hands of a corpse. He yanked his hands back and Lerner's arms straightened, his shoulders moved and he started to topple forward. Knowing that his forehead would impact the crystal and that if it did, it was going to look even more like murder than ever, Danny pushed back, trying to catch Lerner's weight and steady him.

Lerner's elbows simply folded.

In what seemed like slow motion, Danny fought to uncross his numb legs and stand, picturing the hollow indentation the crystal would make in Lerner's forehead. One of his legs – *the weak left one, surprise, surprise, old Dan!* – was completely dead, but although the other fizzled like a damp firework it was movable. It hurt when Danny pushed himself up on it and as he rose, Lerner's weight teetered on the brink for a second. 'Come *on*!' Danny hissed and shoved forwards. Lerner started to tilt back again and inwardly Danny rejoiced. Which was when the damp squib leg dropped him.

Danny fell on to the coffee table. The crystal hit him in the vee of his ribs just below his sternum, robbing him of breath. Lerner limply completed the act gravity had been encouraging and toppled forward on to Danny, driving the crystal into his stomach even further.

And at the exact moment Danny's muscles let his oxygen-starved lungs gasp in air, Lerner also gasped.

Thank God! Danny began to chant again, but only mentally this time; there was too much pain for him to speak yet.

He lay under Lerner, the crystal against him while he gathered his strength. Every second or so Lerner twitched violently as if he was being electrocuted. When Danny finally pushed him back into the sofa, he was able to see the man's stomach pulling in as though someone was steadily punching it. But he was alive.

At the moment, Danny warned himself as he snapped on the lights and looked at the psychic's grey face.

And as he watched, the unconscious or absent Alistair Lerner proved that each member of The Paranormal Club did indeed have his cross to bear and that as he had promised, he was a bleeder. Lerner's nose started to pour blood down his shirt front as if a dam up his nose had suddenly burst.

'Lerner!' Danny shouted. Then, listing badly to the left, ran to the kitchen and grabbed a damp cloth and a kitchen roll to mop up the blood. But Lerner was not just a bleeder, he was a bleeder and a half. *Should have brought a bowl*, Danny thought and hobbled back for one.

Danny tilted Lerner forward and caught what looked like at least a pint and a half in the washing up bowl while he listened to Lerner's laboured and wheezy breathing, watched the steady flow of his blood and the rise and fall of his chest, and hoped he wasn't going to die.

Then the lights blinked back on in Lerner's eyes and Danny felt a cool relief that temporarily quelled his own hurts. Lerner's face was grey and as his consciousness returned, it became contorted with agony. He pushed Danny away and bent over the bowl, pressing on his temples with the thumb of each hand while his fingers massaged his eyes.

'Are you all right?' Danny asked. 'Should I get a doctor or an ambulance or something?'

Lerner glared up at him balefully and Danny had enough time to realise that Lerner had not accomplished his task. He still had his weight. 'No,' he gasped. 'Get ice.'

'Ice?' Danny said in surprise. *Two pints in that bowl now, old Dan. Maybe a blood bank would be a better bet.*

'ICE! QUICKLY!' Lerner began to rock back and forth now, cradling his head as the blood fell into the bowl.

He'll faint soon. And then he'll die if you don't get a doctor!

Danny looked at the telephone in the hall as he passed it, but he didn't stop; his rubbery legs took him straight on to the kitchen.

The ice tray had been over-filled with water and was stuck fast to the bottom of the icebox. Danny stared at it stupidly for a few seconds then got the steak-knife he'd so fondly imagined he'd used on Lerner and hacked at it until it came free. There was a bright wire of pain between his own temples now and it was getting worse. And on top of that, his own nose badly wanted to bleed.

Comes with the territory, he told himself, taking the ice tray to the draining board. He would save a few cubes for himself. They would feel very good when applied to his temples and his throbbing nose and bullet-scar. He inverted the tray and whacked it down on the drainer, wincing at the sharp sound and the proportional increase of the pain in his head. *Not to mention the ones in your arms legs and spine, old Dan*. Nothing happened. When he hit it again, eighteen cloudy ice-cubes shot out and cascaded across the worktop, rattling into the sink and clattering to the floor. He willed his bag of blood not to stretch too far when he bent over, and frantically gathered them up in a breakfast bowl, while a callous but practical part of his mind tried to think up plausible excuses for having a dead psychic in his lounge. He was sure Lerner would be just as dead as the proverbial doornail by the time he got back in there.

That practical part of his mind turned out to have very little imagination and came up with not one good excuse. When Danny cursed it, it told him he would simply have to cross that bridge when he came to it, which was not encouraging. He got a fresh kitchen roll and hurried back down the hall, his eyes lighting on the phone once more and the practical part of him resolving to call an ambulance if Lerner's nose didn't stop bleeding in five minutes – and fuck the questions he would be asked; it wasn't *his* fault and no one could say it was! He elbowed the door handle down, hurried back into the lounge, and stopped dead in his tracks.

Alistair Lerner had gone.

4

Danny gazed at the settee in dumb astonishment. There was no blood on it whatsoever and no sign that Lerner had ever sat there. If it hadn't been for the strong smell of smoke, the pile of bent-over Woodbine butts in the ashtray and the bowl containing at least two pints of thick red blood – which now resided on the coffee table where the crystal had been – Danny would have doubted the whole episode had taken place.

He may have been on his last legs, but he packed the crystal and took it with him, Danny thought. He wouldn't have estimated that Lerner was able to stand, let alone wrap the crystal and put it back in his briefcase then sneak out of the house without being heard. Danny couldn't believe it – Lerner had even taken the blood-stained tissues and what remained of the kitchen roll. He put down the ice cubes and the new kitchen roll next to the bowl of Lerner's blood and went to the front door. It was latched – which meant Lerner had somehow closed it without his hearing it. A picture lit in Danny's mind of what Lerner must have looked like, staggering from the house. What he looked like even now: tottering down the road in the rain, his briefcase in one hand while the other held a wad of bloodstained tissue to his face. The front of his shirt and his trousers would be red with his blood, and his face would be distorted with agony.

He'll look very much like I've attacked him, Danny thought, imagining neighbours' itchy trigger fingers even now punching their phones' nine buttons three times in quick succession. *Worse than that, old Dan, he might even have got outside and collapsed and died in front of the house!*

'Oh fuck!' Danny said, reaching for the latch on the front door as panic rose in him. He had to do something . . . and quickly. He glanced at the phone not knowing if he should call an ambulance first then go out after Lerner, or if he should bring him back first then get help. For a few seconds, Danny's feet wouldn't work and he wobbled on the spot doing neither while he thought, *There's a man out there not too far away, dying. And he might be a* Know Better *who intended to stitch you up, but he also came to help you, so you'd better do something fast*!

Then he regained control over his feet, took the door latch, opened the door and stepped outside.

And the tight bag of blood in his right nostril chose this moment to split a seam.

Cupping his hand under his nose, Danny got the new kitchen roll, soaked up warm blood, wadded a fresh strip and packed it under his nose, holding it in place while he threw the roll across the lounge, unwinding a further six feet or so. He tore this off, gathered it up one-handed, and leaving the front door open, hurried outside.

Lerner was not dead on the path or the postage stamp-sized lawn Suzie and Danny called their front garden, neither was he collapsed in a bleeding heap out in the road. *Can't have gone far, Dan. Not in that state, he can't*! he told himself and hurried down the road to its junction with Vyne Road, where Lerner surely still had to be. Halfway along the hundred-yard stretch of un-metalled road known as Phoenix Park Terrace, Danny began to think that Lerner might be able to outpace him after all. The whole left side of his body hurt, someone was plunging hot knives into his temples, and all his weak left leg would allow him was a painful – and not very fast – shuffle.

And to top it all, here was Claire Briggs coming towards him – the neighbour who liked to do a little man watching – specially if the man was him and if he was dressed only in a tiny pair of underpants. Claire, weighed down under two heavy Sainsbury's carriers of shopping, didn't look one little bit lascivious today though. At first she just looked tired and careworn and bowed under the weight of the food. Then, as Danny had known she would, she looked up from the ground and spotted him and her expression instantly changed to one of concern.

'Danny! What's happened?' Claire put down her bags and gazed up at him.

He halted in front of her, badly wanting to push past and hurry down to Vyne Road. 'Nosebleed,' he replied, realising his friendly it's-no-problem grin was hidden behind the blood-soaked tissue.

'Where are you going?' Claire almost screeched. 'You ought to be *lying down*! Really, Danny, you don't look very well at all. Go back indoors. . .'

He shook his head. 'Can't. Got to find someone. Hurry.' He realised that he wasn't even standing up straight; his weak left side was giving him a distinct list and he could do nothing about it. He knew he must look like a bleeding Leaning Tower of Pisa.

All of this would have been bad enough if Claire's concern hadn't started to change to the shuffling-away combination of horror and fear that Danny seemed to inspire in people these days. She didn't inquire if his phone was broken and he was trying to find someone who could take him to the hospital or doctor and she didn't invite him into her house or offer to take him back to his. Suddenly she looked as if she wished she hadn't seen him at all. Claire shook her head and moved to her left a little, unconsciously clearing the way so he could pass. 'Oh,' she said, biting her bottom lip.

'You didn't see him, did you?' Danny asked.

Claire shook her head, then said, 'Who?' Her face was steadily losing its colour.

'The guy with the nosebleed,' Danny said.

'*You've* got the nosebleed,' Claire said carefully, glancing past him to her garden gate.

She's wondering if she can make a run for it, Danny thought. He didn't blame her.

Danny shook his head, staggered to his left and caught himself before he fell. 'The *other* guy,' he said. 'You must have just passed him.'

Claire badly wanted to tell him what he wanted to hear. If she did that, perhaps he would go away. But Claire wasn't a confident liar. 'Yes . . . no . . . I mean . . . I don't know . . . I . . . Look, Danny, I think you ought to lie down. You're losing a lot of blood. There *was* no other man, Danny. Call a doctor. You've got the nosebleed, no one else.' She looked at him carefully, inching backwards and tensed to spring aside if he struck out.

'Sorry, Claire,' Danny said thickly, 'but there is another guy and I've got to look for him. I'm sorry. Excuse me.'

He shrugged, grinned his hidden apologetic smile again and hobbled past her thinking, *That's the last time she clocks you up in the garden and wonders what you'd be like in bed! She thinks you're crazy now, just like everyone else seems to.*

But by the time he reached Vyne Road and was halfway down the hill to the back of the railway station, Danny was suffering an attack of the What-Ifs. What if Claire had been right? Lerner, who would have been heading for the railway station if he intended to go back to Reading, would have walked straight by her and there was no way she couldn't have seen him. He would have stuck out like a fish in a filling station, as Suzie would have said. You simply didn't see badly bleeding old men staggering down Vyne Road. *What if*, Danny thought, *Claire didn't see Lerner because Lerner didn't exist except as a product of your crazy mind? What if that blood in the washing up bowl came from the nose of Danny Stafford while his alter ego, the Gannex Man, was doing the driving?*

But he could not let himself believe this.

Danny passed The Great Western pub, crossed the road and limped down the steps of the pedestrian tunnel which ran underneath the railway lines, linking the front and back of the station. The tunnel was long and Lerner was not in it. *He couldn't have got this far*, Danny told himself, *even if I did stop to talk to Claire*. And another part of him chipped in, *Unless he really doesn't exist, of course; unless you're chasing a ghost*.

Danny tried to run and managed a curved, lolloping shuffle which bounced him off the brickwork every few paces. But it was quicker than walking. At the end of the tunnel he made the turn towards the station entrance and collided with an elderly woman coming the other way. Danny fell backwards, reached out for support and his fingers found the woman's coat and dragged her down on top of him. She began to scream and didn't calm down until two teenagers had picked up both her and Danny.

Danny's blood was on the front of her coat and he felt very light-headed. 'I'm sorry,' he said, wadding a fresh piece of tissue.

'You *drunk*!' the woman accused. She turned to the teenagers – two trendy fifteen-year-old boys in chunky Nikes, shiny hooded track suits and peaked baseball caps worn back to front – and said, 'He *attacked* me!'

'I fell over!' Danny said.

'Yeah, he didn't attack you at all, lady,' the shorter boy said. 'We saw what happened.'

'I want the police!' she insisted.

Danny thought his head would explode. 'I'm sorry,' he said again. Was there such a person as Alistair Lerner?

'He said he's sorry, now leave him alone,' the boy said. 'You okay, man?'

Danny nodded.

'Think you'd better fuck off out of it before the old girl screams for the filth,' he said. 'We'll try and calm her down.'

The station foyer was empty. Danny went to the ticket collector and said, 'Did an old man just come through? Tall and thin. His nose was bleeding.'

The ticket collector looked at Danny for a time, his head tilted back while he thought about it.

'Nope,' he said, 'the only person I've seen with a nosebleed, is you.'

'*He must have done*!' Danny insisted.

'You calling me a liar or what?'

What if Lerner doesn't exist? What then, old Dan? What if you've lost a good two pints of blood – probably three by now; you're feeling pretty light-headed, aren't you? What if you don't get help? What if you're found dead on Vyne Road?

Danny shook his head. 'No, I'm not saying you're a liar. But are you *sure*?'

'Sure I'm sure. Now, are you getting a train? Because if you're not, I strongly recommend that you piss off and pester someone else, somewhere else.'

What if he fell into Claire's front garden? What if he found his way into the ruins of the old Holy Ghost churchyard?

Danny was suddenly sure that Lerner had somehow found his way into what was left of the ruins – which lay behind the tall wall on the opposite side of Vyne Road to Phoenix Park Terrace.

Danny glared at the ticket collector, left the station foyer and headed back towards home, going round the long way this time, following the road instead of going through the pedestrian tunnel. There was a chance that Lerner hadn't known about the tunnel and might still be on his way here – and Danny didn't particularly want to meet up again with the old lady he'd pulled over.

The traffic was heavy but, as always outside knocking-off time, the pedestrians were few and far between. There was no sign of a tall thin man, either standing or collapsed in a pool of blood.

His vision now blurring, Danny made his way back to Vyne Road and stupidly attempted to vault the wall which enclosed the Holy Ghost ruins and cemetery. He only tried once; it hurt, and this time there was no one to pick him up. Cursing silently, he staggered to the allotments behind Burgess Road where the gate was and let himself in.

The place was abandoned and unkempt, the gravestones cracked and falling apart, the grass growing wild and high. The ruins contained a few raised, casket-style tombstones which had apparently been popular in the early-nineteenth century. They had once been ornate granite or marble structures, standing three or four foot high, three foot across and six or seven foot long. Now, they were crumbling and weatherbeaten and holes had developed in the sides of many of them. In his pain, Lerner might have crawled into any one of half a dozen. Leaving trails of blood-soaked kitchen tissue behind him, Danny painstakingly checked them all.

Lerner was not present.

If there really was a Lerner, Danny thought as he made his way out of the ruins, *he may not have been as ill as you thought he was. You don't really know if he was seriously ill or not. For all you know, he might well look like that after every psychic jaunt. He might be okay after all.*

'With two pints or more of his blood missing?' Danny said aloud. 'I don't think so.'

How about this then: what if Lerner went upstairs while you were in the kitchen getting his ice? You didn't hear the front door open or close, did you? What if he's currently lying on your bathroom floor, dying in agony, while you look for him out here?

Danny limped back along Burgess Road and as he turned the corner into Vyne Road, found himself face to face with the old woman he'd dragged down.

She stopped in her tracks and started to scream.

Danny hobbled by her, crossed the road and hurried home

Claire Briggs was watching from her front room window. As he passed her house, Danny waved gaily at her, threw himself off balance, collapsed, got up, nodded and grinned – remembering to remove the tissue this time – and bled all down his shirt.

He pushed the already open front door so hard that it crashed against the telephone table and sent the phone clattering and tinging across the carpet.

LERNER!' he bellowed. 'LERNER, I KNOW YOU'RE HERE!' *You're out of control again, old Dan. Where's that iron will*? 'Gone,' he told himself. 'LERNER! COME OUT, COME OUT, WHEREVER YOU ARE!

He stumbled and fell up the stairs and burst into the bathroom, feeling a numb kind of relief when he found it empty. He glanced at his reflection in the mirror, dimly realising he looked like something from a Slash & Hack horror movie. He dismissed the thought and shambled into the bedrooms. Lerner wasn't in either of them.

Danny didn't recall the journey downstairs. He found himself peering into the coat cupboard under the stairs and announcing, '*He's not in here reading the fucking gas meter either*!' and this scared a little of the madness from him.

He took a deep breath, rolled into the kitchen where he found melting ice cubes everywhere, but no Lerner, and went back down the hall to the lounge.

The lounge door was closed and Danny couldn't recall if he had closed it or not. He pulled the handle down and pushed the door open.

'IT DIDN'T HAPPEN!' he heard himself yelling. 'NONE OF IT HAPPENED!'

The bowl of blood was not in the centre of the table – or in the room at all. The ashtray full of Woodbine butts was not there either.

'Please God, help me!' Danny pleaded.

And fainted.

5

The tantalising smell began to wake him up again. It was a smell he recognised but couldn't place. It was an unpleasant smell, but it was also a smell which bore distinct undertones. One of them was the smell of drying blood and the other was the essence of hope.

Hope? an almost aware part of him asked. *The smell of hope*?

But the unconscious part of Danny, the part now steadily emanating beta waves while it skipped around untethered, understood.

The knowledge, however, vanished the moment his eyes flicked open, and lay just out of reach, waiting to be learnt all over again.

If you could bottle that, you could get Mike Tyson or Robin Givens or maybe both of them to advertise it, he thought and didn't know why.

Danny first realised that his nose was no longer bleeding. The inside of his right nostril felt sore and was crusted with drying blood, but the sharp pain between his temples had gone and the left side of his body no longer ached.

Some of our crosses are a tad lighter than others, Danny thought, and felt the fear rise in him again as he began to remember.

He pushed himself up and gently prised away the tissue that had dried to his face just to the right of his nose. The tissue was dark with blood but there didn't seem to be any on the new carpet, which struck Danny as being an almost impossible stroke of luck.

It stinks of cigarettes in here, he thought, and caught the essence of hope again.

'Which means that it did *happen!*' he said aloud. 'It wasn't another reality fracture. Lerner *does* exist and he *was* here.'

Danny got up and sat on the the sofa, frowning. 'He came back,' he said slowly, shaking his head in disbelief. 'He came back and cleaned up while I was out looking for him.' *And quite possibly came back again and put the tissue under you so you didn't bleed on the new carpet*, his mind added.

'Are you still here?' he called, realising that Lerner wasn't here and that he would not be able to find him. If Lerner didn't want to be found he wouldn't be – Danny had already proved that to himself.

He was considering this when he noticed the package on top of the television. It was a brown cardboard box of about nine inches square. *I didn't put that there, and it certainly wasn't there when I came back just now*, he told himself as he got up.

The box was heavy and sealed with Sellotape. Danny shook it but whatever was inside was firmly packed – nothing moved. He placed it on the coffee table and went to get the steak knife – which provided more evidence: it was now slightly bent where he'd used it to force the ice tray from the fridge.

Danny sat down on the settee again, the steak knife in his hand and the box on his lap. He didn't know what was in it, but he knew exactly what the package represented. It was the Black Spot. The weight Lerner had been trying to relieve himself of. Danny knew that if he opened the box that weight would be his and Lerner's mission would be accomplished. And in spite of that knowledge, he *wanted* to open it.

If you don't like what you find, you can just put it back in the box, seal it up and dump it somewhere, he told himself. But he knew that was not true. Once accepted, weights like this were not easy to rid yourself of. Ask Lerner. Ask Pandora, come to that. And opening the box would constitute an acceptance.

But the longer Danny sat there with the thing in his lap, the greater the need to see what was inside became. After five minutes the desire to know became almost palpable. After ten minutes it was eating into him like a live thing.

Danny grinned. 'Things can't get any worse,' he said, and slipped the knife through the tape. Nothing happened when he lifted the lid.

There was no sensation of doom; no bad spirits flew out, never to be recaptured; no weight settled on his shoulders.

'It's going to be all right,' Danny said and peered into the box

There were several sheets of foolscap paper in there, lying on top of something packed in newspaper; the sheets were folded in half and Danny's name was written on the blank side which faced him. He picked them up and unfolded them.

The letter was from Lerner. Danny wasn't terribly surprised by this discovery, but he was a little relieved. A part of him had been busily suggesting that *he'd* packed the box and put it there to complete his deception of himself. But the handwritten letter was convincing. Had it been typed, Danny's doubting part might still have insisted he'd done it on the old Underwood in the wardrobe, but he didn't think he was capable of writing like this. The hand was a fine copperplate, written in Royal Blue with a fountain pen. And unless he'd been out, bought a pen and ink and somehow managed to change his own untidy scrawl, it was safe to assume that Lerner had written it.

The letter bore no return address, but Danny hadn't really expected to find one. Now Lerner had passed his weight, he didn't want it coming winging back to him, special delivery, did he?

The letter confirmed a great many things for Danny, including the fact that Lerner had recently been doing plenty of crystal gazing – which had made him ill. Reading between the lines, Danny thought that the gazing Lerner had been doing had been undertaken with the sole intention of working towards this outcome. Lerner had looked at the probabilities and somehow guided them together. He said he'd known he would be ill if he used the crystal with Danny, and that Danny was not to worry about him because his days of being a practising psychic were now over.

And not only those days, Danny mentally added.

Lerner's letter apologised for what he called 'any inconvenience' he had caused and promised that they would not meet again. He said his job had been completed now and he hoped to retire and take things easy.

Danny wondered who he thought he was fooling.

The letter went on to congratulate Danny on what Lerner called 'his talent' and said that the following pages would give hints on developing it. There was no mention of what had been in it for Lerner – if anything, no clue as to why he'd gone to so much trouble – probably, in fact, to the brink of his own death, to 'help' Danny; no indication of what might be in store. Lerner had kept his secrets right to the end.

Danny flicked through the other pages which might as well have been titled *Do It Yourself Clairvoyance*. It seemed to be a complete instruction manual on using a crystal to look into the future. The last few pages were a treatise on the manipulation of the future by close study of the events leading up to a crisis point and physical interference at key points.

There were also notes on sub-probabilities and possibilities, which – Lerner claimed – were of a much finer type of energy and would need a great deal of practice to be able to detect and change from possibilities to future ones or future twos.

Danny no longer knew if he believed that the future was malleable and manipulable but – as Lerner had surely known – he found the concept delightful. It meant that everything didn't have to turn out for the bad in the end, after all. If it was true, there *was* hope. It if was true, it gave a solid purpose to being for being able to see into the future. If it was true. . .

Danny put the pages aside and pulled the newspaper packing out of the box. He already knew what the heavy thing was in there. It was Lerner's gift; the Black Spot he had so ably passed.

It was Danny's very own crystal.

As he pulled the newspaper from the black velvet cloth surrounding his gift, a Yale door key fell on to the table. There was a crumpled tag tied to it. An address in Brighton was written on the tag, and underneath, in Lerner's copperplate, were the words: 'You will need this key. Use it when it becomes necessary. The place is yours now, use it and keep it; there is no charge.'

'You've got it all worked out, you bastard, haven't you?' Danny said, feeling a sudden urge to take the key outside and dump it in the dustbin. No wonder Lerner was so ill – he hadn't just manipulated the circumstances up to now, he had apparently mapped out Danny's life for some time to come.

Well into the future, in fact, Danny thought bitterly. *If not for ever*.

'We'll see about *that*,' he said, and with a dull shock noticed that his right hand was placing the key deep in his pocket, beneath the wad of tissue that was always in there. The one that stopped the flattened .22 bullet from falling out and getting lost. Danny thought about it for a few moments, then he thought about it again.

He left the key there.

6

Danny carefully took the crystal from the box and placed it on the table – still wrapped in its black velvet cloth. Lerner's instructions had said to keep it away from bright lights so Danny drew the curtains again, then sat down and unwrapped it. Again he had the feeling that he'd been doing this all his life and that it was the most natural thing in the world. An idea lit in his mind and Danny smiled, imagining a cartoon lightbulb winking on above his head.

The crystal was identical to Lerner's – could, in fact, actually have *been* Lerner's for all Danny knew. Lerner's copperplate instruction manual stated that the crystal must be run under cold water for ten to fifteen minutes between readings as the water would remove the residual traces of the last person who'd handled it, but Danny did not intend to do that. The crystal must last have been handled by Lerner and Danny liked it just that way. Two could play at Lerner's game and Danny had decided to pry into *his* future as Lerner had snooped on his own.

Danny did not touch the crystal but he started to see the milky white haze in it almost immediately. *Futures one to four, old Dan*, he told himself. *That's where we'll go. To the ones Lerner didn't want you to see*!

The haze sparkled in golden crested waves and Danny nodded. *Easy-peasy, lemon squeezy! Future one, please, driver*!

The crystal seemed to expand.

We'll soon find out the truth of the matter, Mr Know Better Lerner.

The mist fell rapidly away.

It's getting high, all right, Mr Lerner, Danny thought as the crystal completed its magical expanding trick. Once again he made the transition from being outside the crystal looking in, to being inside the crystal with no outside to look out at, without being able to spot the precise moment at which it was accomplished.

I'm inside, Mr Lerner, and I'm coming into your future, he thought, and let himself fall.

Within seconds he was swooping down through the glittering mist, letting its peculiar hot and cold sparkling into his nerves. The sideways jerk as he landed – or arrived or whatever they called it – was barely perceptible this time and Danny fell lightly on his feet.

He was surprised to find that he did have feet this time – and legs, a body and arms to keep them company. Unlike the tandem experience with Lerner, he felt solid and real.

Danny was in a dimly lit bedroom he didn't recognise. He knew many things about the small room instantaneously. It was in Lerner's bedroom, and had been, off and on, for twenty-nine years (Lerner had another bedroom miles away from here but he never went there any more.) The window in the eight by ten foot room faced south, which was the way Lerner liked to point his head while sleeping and the reason why he chose this room rather than one of the other two the house had. The room stank of ages of heavy smoking and even in the gloom caused by the closed curtains, Danny could see layers of yellow tar and nicotine on every flat surface. There was an ancient dressing table with a chair across one wall. This was strewn with empty and sour milk cartons, overflowing ashtrays, hundreds of sheets of typed paper and a portable typewriter. Across all this, various items of clothing had been flung. They flowed off the table on to the chair and off the chair to the floor like a dirty snowdrift.

Alistair Lerner lay outside the single bed's sheets, face up, eyes open, staring blankly at the yellowed ceiling. He was wearing a maroon-striped pyjama top and was naked from the waist down. His arms lay at his sides, his big gnarled hands open as if he was waiting to catch something. *A brown cardboard package containing a crystal and a key, perhaps*, Danny thought grimly.

Even in death, Lerner looked pained. Danny had expected him to look relaxed and peaceful now that the weight had gone, but the lines of age and the expression of pain that had been engraved on his gaunt face still remained. The man looked as if he expected someone to resurrect him any minute and force him to go through the whole thing again.

Danny heard a faint scratching at the door, and realised that Lerner's dog was trying to get in. 'It's okay, Judy,' he said in his elongated voice. 'Your dad's gone, but someone will soon find you. You'll be all right.'

The dog began to whimper quietly and Danny suddenly felt a terrible desolation and an aching pity for the man he hadn't even liked and for the dog who no longer had a master. Somehow, the keening dog made it terribly real and painful.

It won't happen until tomorrow, Danny told himself. *I can find her. I can get the address and go there, or alert someone to the fact.*

Lerner might have been in pain before his death, but he'd been just as thorough and sly to the bitter end. He had evidently expected just this and worked some more of his magic tricks to keep Danny out of things. Danny could not leave the room and when he tried to pick up the house's location from the room itself, he only perceived a swirling grey fog.

Blocked! Danny thought as the dog's whining filled his ears. *Why didn't you want me around, Lerner? Why did you try so hard to keep me away? Were you frightened of what I might discover?*

He realised that in his own home – where his body of yesterday sat before the crystal on the coffee table – he was crying. Crying for Lerner and his little dog and crying for himself – but most of all, crying for the hopelessness of it all. It was a strange sensation. The Danny that he now was remained dry-eyed – bleak, but dry-eyed.

Danny willed himself to go to future two, the second most likely event. It was ridiculously easy to do; no sooner had Danny thought about it than it had happened. The room flickered before his eyes like a video picture on pause and began to fade. There was a brief high-pitched screech in his ears which mellowed to a tuneless kind of trumpet fanfare, and as the picture blanked, a jolt sideways. The jolt was bigger this time but Danny compensated for it and landed standing – in the same bedroom at the same moment he'd arrived in it before. The scene flickered before his eyes, blinked and settled.

Danny pictured the flow of time as a set of many parallel rails, the biggest and clearest one in the centre and those that spread away from it becoming fainter and thinner until they were thread-like in the distance. He didn't think he'd gone into what Lerner had called 'the Centre of all things' but had rather leapt from one track to another. The Centre – if there was such a thing – was way up ahead.

In future two, Lerner's room was exactly the same. The only difference in this one was that the door was open and Judy was on the bed with her master, snuggled up tight to his side. She looked up at Danny with doleful eyes.

'Sorry, dog,' he said to her. 'Sorry, Judy. I'm so sorry!'

Danny flicked himself into future three and found more of the same. In this one, Lerner was still alive, but in the process of dying. It was peaceful and Lerner lay there, Judy clasped to his bosom and his eyes closed as the gaps between his intakes of breath became longer and longer. When they ceased altogether, Danny waited to see Lerner's spirit rise. And was disappointed.

Danny's chest and stomach started to jerk and quiver and a moment later the sound of his sobbing came to his ears from far away. *Good deal, old Dan*, he thought bitterly. *Ten-up at least.*

The fourth most likely future gave him the biggest jolt and Danny had to pick himself up off the floor while the scene settled. This future was also the most harrowing. Danny watched helplessly as Lerner writhed in agony, alternately choking on blood which ran down his throat from the back of his nose, and screaming it out in a spray while he tore at his temples and cheeks with his fingernails.

While Danny tried – and failed – to will himself away, something downstairs made from glass smashed, then something else banged and Danny heard voices.

Somebody heard him! Danny thought. *Someone's coming to help.*

The bedroom door burst open and Judy charged through it, leaping on to the bed, turning and baring her teeth at the two ambulance men who followed her through.

The first man stopped in his tracks, glancing from the writhing Lerner to the dog and back again. 'Jesus,' he breathed, 'look at him!' Then hissed, 'Get away, dog, for fuck's sake!'

'Okay, Bri,' the other ambulance man said. 'I got her.' He pushed past his partner and approached the bed. 'Okay, hound,' he said gently, his voice almost drowned under Lerner's incessant moaning. 'We've come to help the boss, not to hurt him. Lemme move you.' He reached for Judy – who snapped at his hand – and quickly withdrew it again.

Somewhere miles away, Danny drew a shuddering breath and spoke. '*Get down, Judy!*' he commanded and the dog looked directly at him.

'What?' the ambulance man called Brian said.

'I didn't say anything,' the other replied.

Judy stopped growling, leapt off the bed and curled up in a tight ball on the floor.

'How'd you do that, Dave?' Brian asked, still glancing from Judy to Lerner and back again.

Dave shrugged, then went for Lerner and began his business. 'He's in a bad way,' he announced after a few seconds. 'Faint fast pulse. Fever. Collapsed lung, too, judging from the racket. Let's get him out of here.'

But Lerner was dead before they'd transferred him to the stretcher.

7

Danny had made up his mind long before the crystal grew small and expelled him back into that cold, clammy body which was still being racked with uncontrollable sobbing.

It took a long time to calm himself down and again he experienced that odd duality which now seemed to exist between what he thought of as the *real* him and the body in which he lived. The *real* Danny Stafford was empty and desolate, but as steely and cold as a gunfighter – it was the *body* that was doing the sobbing. Danny drove the body upstairs and stood under the shower, trying to wash away the feeling that everything to do with life was dirty and terrible and jaded, while he wondered why he hadn't seen Lerner's spirit taking flight and assured himself that he could do nothing to alter the man's tomorrow. It was too late to act now – the critical moments had passed long ago.

By the time he stepped shivering from the steaming spray of water, Danny had become whole again, but even this minor miracle hadn't changed his mind.

Danny had had enough.

He didn't want the gift and he wouldn't have it. He didn't want to know the future or to look into it ever again. The future was cruel and unrelenting and too complicated to comprehend, let alone manipulate.

I didn't ask to be shot in the head, he thought bitterly. *I didn't ask for my pineal gland to be activated and I don't want to have to be different. It's too dangerous and too heartbreaking.*

Others could have the gift if they wanted it, but like Greta Garbo, Danny Stafford wanted to be left alone. He dried himself, dressed, took the crystal to the kitchen and put it in the sink where he let cold water run over it for fifteen minutes. He opened the curtains and windows in the lounge, hoovered the carpet, cleared away the pieces of bloodstained tissue and remembered the washing up bowl. Lerner had washed it and placed it in the cupboard under the sink but there were still traces of blood in it. Danny rinsed it again. The Woodbine butts were in the kitchen waste bin – along with a lot more bloodied tissue. Danny pulled the carrier bag liner and dumped the lot in the dustbin outside. Then he piled old newspapers on top so that Suzie wouldn't see what was in there.

Suzie doesn't need to know any of this, he told himself, realising it would mean many more lies and not really caring. It would be excusable. He would be protecting her.

He put on rubber gloves to take the crystal out of the sink. It was clean now and he didn't intend to touch it again with his bare hands. He dried it with what was left of the kitchen roll then took it back into the lounge and packed it carefully into its box with the key and the pages of notes. He sealed the box with sellotape, took it back upstairs, pulled down the loft ladder and stored it away behind a box of old blankets, laying several ancient *Dandy* and *Beano* albums on top of it.

'There,' he said defiantly when he got back downstairs. 'Make what you like of *that!* Old Danny boy is, henceforth and officially, out of the game. He's passed the parcel one more step down the row and has now retired hurt. He tried it once, didn't like it, and he will not play again!'

Chapter Eleven
Lies, Damned Lies

1

The box in the attic wasn't the only gift Lerner had left behind when he walked out of Danny's life. He'd also left his glib economy with the truth, and in this area – like that other which Danny had finished with – the pupil outclassed the master. Without realising it, Danny had sailed through his Master's course in Falsehood and gained an honours degree.

An insurance man had called, he told Suzie in reply to her question about the smell of cigarettes (which still lingered in spite of the open windows and liberal applications of Haze). He glanced at her as he started to lie and seeing her innocent, interested face, started to ache. For a few moments he felt a shitheel, a cheap trickster, but this passed as he continued.

He was turned away from her, facing the cooker – where plaice and chips were undergoing the patented Stafford flash fry – but Danny doubted this would matter. He could face her and lie just as easily, he knew. He had been bored, he told her, so he'd invited the insurance man in and sat there while the man had made his pitch, starting with high pressure techniques and finishing with soft sell.

'What kind of a policy did you take out?' Suzie asked, coming up behind him and kissing his neck as he stirred chips.

'Me? Buy insurance? You're joking!'

'So what happened?'

Danny didn't know where it all came from and marvelled at his new capacity for invention. He told her that the insurance man was a forty-five-year-old heavy smoker called Clarence Whitby. He winced as the unlikely name tripped off his lips, but Suzie didn't question it. The Clarence Whitby in Danny's suddenly fertile imagination had a younger wife who, Danny opined, reading between the lines of his own story, was more likely than not, cheating on poor old Clarence. His kids were twins, like as peas in a pod, and both had made identical 'A' level grades and both had been accepted at Cambridge.

'Reading what?' Suzie asked.

'History and politics,' Danny said, having no idea if the two things went together. 'I think. Something like that anyway.'

'Oh,' Suzie replied, soaking it all up, and warming to the web of lies he was spinning so convincingly.

The strange rush of power Danny felt when the initial feeling of guilt and the hot flushes (which made him wonder if he was blushing) had subsided told him he could embroider the story even more without Suzie doubting him. And now he knew he could do it, he *did* do it.

'He kept telling me about his friend Bobby – except that I think Bobby is probably his *wife's* friend – who's thirty odd and director of a computer company. Bobby has a red Ferrari and Gucci loafers and Rolex watches. He lives in the country in a huge bungalow with a heated pool. He collects vintage cars.'

'What brought this up then?'

Danny shrugged and turned the fish. 'He was using Bobby as an example of how much money you could take out at the end of your fifteen years or whatever it is. Bobby's got hundreds of thousands coming. He buys his insurance from Clarence Whitby and they're both interested in home video, which is how they got pally.'

Danny served the fish and chips, still lying through his teeth. He had given up expecting his face to give the game away, as it had when he'd told Suzie he was going for petrol and went to wait for the tanker crash instead. If there was something about the eyes and the body language that showed amateur liars in their true colours then Danny had become a professional with almost no practice. His transparency was gone; he was unreadable.

He told her another elaborate tale about the nosebleed and his meeting with Claire and the little trick he'd played on her and Suzie scolded him and made him promise to apologise.

She didn't suspect a thing.

Feeling good about everything now, Danny opened a bottle of wine, poured Suzie a glass, laughed and joked over anecdotes Clarence Whitby had supplied, then went to phone Claire. Danny was charm personified and within three minutes she was eating out of his hand.

'I overheard some of that,' Suzie said when he returned to the kitchen. 'She'll definitely invite you over for coffee now.'

'And I'll go,' he said.

'She'll want to see inside your posing pants.'

'And I'll show her. She'll be impressed.'

'I doubt it.'

Danny smiled. 'You don't complain.'

'Not to your face.'

'Or behind my back.'

Suzie filled her glass again, sipped the wine. 'I'm complaining now.'

Danny took her hand and tugged gently. 'Come with me and I'll give you something to complain about.'

Suzie giggled and got up. 'What is it?'

'You'll see,' Danny said and led her upstairs.

He didn't think about Lerner again until three the following morning, when he woke shivering from a dream where skeletons stood smouldering in a rain of glass globes. Somewhere in Reading, Lerner was living his last hours.

Nothing you can do, old Dan, he told himself. He moved over to Suzie's side of the bed and cuddled up against her warm, naked back, but neither Lerner nor the smouldering skeletons left him for a very long time.

2

Things started to improve a few days after Lerner died. Towards the end of the following week, Danny had re-established his routine of job-hunting and housework and gentle exercise.

When you were busy keeping busy you could also keep those nagging thoughts at bay, Danny knew.

The best times were when he was with Suzie. Then, all his troubles seemed so far away, as Lennon and McCartney had so rightly said. While Suzie was there, Danny was as happy as he'd ever been. Which was good. There were other good things: the mirror tiles in the bathroom no longer worried him and there were no further episodes of split reality – but there were bad things too.

Like the busy-busy daytimes. Danny kept his mind carefully empty most of the time, but if he let his guard down, even for a moment, the doubts would creep back in, seeping through him like thin oil. He became so desperate on one occasion that he phoned Claire and invited himself over for coffee. She didn't exactly dive on him, but the feeling that she *might* at any moment ruled out any possibility of a return booking, so Danny found other things to do.

But there were still times when Danny's cry-baby voice threw in comments on the pack of lies he'd told Suzie about the insurance man. This particular incident – however inconsequential Danny told himself it was – seemed to have become stuck on an audio/visual tape loop in his memory and popped up to say hello whenever there was a gap in his thoughts. Danny was unable to file that day away neatly and each time the tape began to play he would feel a terrible aching guilt as all his lies were paraded before him. The guilt would pass the terrible stage and become sublime when it occurred to him – as it always did – that a part of him had not simply enjoyed the deceit, but *revelled* in it.

Danny complained that the alternative to this particular lie would probably have resulted in a curtailed relationship, but the cry-baby and its tape loop didn't care.

There were other worries about that day too. He was certain about what had become of Lerner, but he still didn't know Lerner's purpose and wasn't likely to find out until that ribbon of time had passed far enough under his feet. Then there was the book he hadn't read. Who had written a book called Jamie? And what was its importance? Danny searched his childhood memories for the book he hadn't read (or had been unable to read) but there was nothing there.

He fought back by keeping himself occupied, and one day, when the housework had been completed, and the nag had started, it occurred to him that the doubts never came to him during his bouts of physical exercise. He dropped to the floor and did his ten sit-ups. The nag ceased operations at the third and didn't return until quite a while after the faint discomfort in his stomach had gone.

Over the following days, Danny's fitness fad became a major pursuit. Whenever his mind asked a question about Lerner or the crystal or the key to the mysterious place in Brighton, he started to work out and the thought went away. His daily jog became a fast mile run, then the mile became a mile and a half. His sit-up count quickly grew until he was doing eighty, then a hundred. He had already been doing press-ups, and he increased these too – until his shoulders screamed and his left arm buckled under him. But his appetite improved and he started to put on weight again. But this time the weight was muscle.

Then one day the worries about Lerner and the lies and the crystal went away and did not return.

3

'Why don't you wear your watch any more?' Suzie asked one Saturday afternoon while they were soaking up the sunshine in the back garden.

'Because of my tan,' Danny instantly replied, knowing how thin it sounded. 'I don't want the little white strip you get.' *Complete change in character there, old Dan*, he told himself. *Once upon a time you wouldn't have left the watch off for the world. Suzie used to complain how it scratched her in bed.*

'What about the big white strip where your trunks have been?' Suzie said. She was desperately trying to catch him up in the tan department – flinging her clothes off and lying down in the back garden each time the sun crept out from behind the clouds – but she knew she never would and it irked her. *Some of us have to go to work*, she'd said when Danny had last compared the colour of his body to the colour of hers. *Some of us have to bring home the bacon!* So far this was as close as she'd come to commenting about his lack of a job, but Danny expected more of those barbed remarks soon. *In July*, he'd told himself. *Not yet, I'm not ready yet. July . . . or maybe August*.

'I can't do anything about *those* white bits, can I?' he replied and his mind asked, *Just why* did *you leave your watch off?*

'You could take your trunks off,' Suzie said, thumbing the waistband of her bikini down slightly and looking for a sharply drawn line that didn't yet exist. 'I'm sure Claire would approve.'

'You take yours off and I'll take mine off,' he challenged, grinning hard as he ignored the question his mind was repeating. He didn't know why he'd left his watch off. He just didn't fancy wearing it any more.

'Anyway, these days I can tell the time without a watch,' he said.

Suzie looked up from the bow at the side of her bikini bottoms, where her fingers were toying with the string. She was already topless and the *I dare you* expression on her face told Danny that she was taking his lightly made challenge seriously. She had already forgotten about the missing watch. 'What?' she said.

'The watch. I don't need it any more. I can tell the time without it.'

'Okay, clever clogs, what time is it?'

'Twenty past two,' Danny said. They'd been here ten minutes or so and it had been just after two when they came out. It would be close enough.

Suzie picked up her own watch. 'Right,' she said.

Danny spread his arms and smiled. 'See!' he said.

Very good, Dan, but that isn't the reason you don't wear the watch any more, is it? his mind asked. *I don't know what you mean*, he replied.

Danny had become very good at not admitting things and covering up with lies. He had told lies to himself too, including the one that since he no longer had a strict timetable to adhere to, he no longer needed a watch. And he had told it so well, he believed it.

The real reason – the one he had successfully masked – was that he was again losing hours of his life somewhere. The physical exercise as a doubt-quelling device had worked well. Sometimes – now that he was fitter – he would do long distance runs, heading across town to the nearby villages of Cliddesden, or Oakley where Suzie's folks lived, and returning via circuitous routes – round trips of eight or nine miles or more. During these runs he didn't simply stop worrying about things, he stopped thinking completely. After the first time he'd gone out then found himself back home again three hours later, drenched in sweat and muscles screaming, but with no memory of the run, he thought the blackouts had returned. After the second incident, he told himself he had simply cleared his mind as anticipated and that there was nothing to worry about.

And the same day he had removed his watch and placed the subject of time on the back burner.

'That was a lucky guess,' Suzie said. 'I'll try again later.'

'And I'll get it right,' Danny promised, trying – and failing – to squash the recurring thought about the real reason he didn't wear the watch. *I think its because. . .*

'Remember what you said?' Suzie asked.

Danny looked over at her and the voice inside him fell to a whisper. 'About what?'

'Taking your trunks off.'

Danny nodded and forgot about the reasons he didn't wear his watch. *Stupid thing to say*, he told himself. *How could Suzie resist a dare like that?*

'The neighbours will see,' he protested, becoming aroused at the thought of Suzie taking off her briefs and knowing that she would drag his trunks off him if he refused to remove them, hard-on or not.

'No they won't,' she said, toying with the bow.

'Yes they will,' Danny said, desperately nodding his head.

'I've got nothing to be ashamed of,' Suzie said, pulling the bow.

'Don't!'

'Too late,' she smiled, pulling the other bow and removing the briefs. She flung them at Danny then lay on her side, stretching and posing and smiling at him. 'Your turn!' she said.

4

Almost a week later Danny found himself lying again. His watch was back on his arm and it was two-thirty in the morning. He and Suzie were lying entangled on their bed in the glowing and relaxed quiet that followed the longest period of solid sexual activity Danny had ever experienced. Two hours and fifteen minutes if you started counting from the moment Suzie climbed on top of him and guided him into her. Three hours if you added the forty-five minutes oral foreplay, and longer still if you started counting from when Suzie first unzipped his flies and slipped her hand inside his trousers (outside Sainsbury's in the town centre) and included the mutual manual stimulation that had turned the ten-minute walk home from the restaurant into thirty.

Susie had claimed eleven orgasms.

And all you did was ask her to marry you, Danny thought, staring at *that* spot on the ceiling.

That Friday afternoon, Suzie had phoned and told him she'd booked a table at Palmer's restaurant for seven-thirty because – and she sang the rest: 'she's too hungry, for dinner at eight!'

'What are we celebrating?' Danny had asked.

'Us,' Suzie said. 'Us persons what loves each other. That's all. So get yourself clean, shaven and dressed in your best duds.'

'Done! Is Colin cooking?'

'The mad chef will be there. I asked.'

'Thanks, Suze,'

'Don't mention it.'

In spite of the fact that Colin – who Danny knew from school – sent out each course bearing a rude note claiming he hoped Danny choked, and that Danny returned each set of empty plates with ruder notes criticising Colin's ability as a chef and refusing to pay whatever extortionate bill was eventually presented, the candle-lit meal turned out to be a romantic one. Suzie bought champagne and shrugged and smiled when Danny again asked her what they were supposed to be celebrating.

Eventually – and claiming he was overcome by the atmosphere and the booze – Danny had popped the question. But it was not the drink talking and there was no doubt in his mind whatsoever. It was the clearest and strongest desire he'd ever had. It was *right*, Danny was certain of that.

Suzie smiled. 'Marry you?' she asked in a tone of false disgust. 'Whatever gave you the idea I might want to marry you?'

'Do you accept?'

'What are your prospects?' she asked coquettishly. 'Will you be able to keep me in the manner to which I am accustomed? Provide for me and protect me, forsaking all others?'

Danny grinned. 'I doubt that very much,' he replied.

Suzie reached over and took his hand, pulled it to her lips and kissed it gently. 'I love you Danny,' she said, and he saw tears glisten in her eyes. 'I love you very, very much and I knew you would ask me to marry you today if I took you out. Don't ask me how, but I knew.'

'And you still took me out?'

She nodded.

'Then what's your answer?'

Suzie blinked back the tears. 'Wait a minute,' she said.

She took a deep breath and stood up, coughing loudly. 'This gentleman,' she announced to the other diners, 'has just proposed marriage. Should I accept?'

'Yes,' someone shouted instantly and began to clap. Within three seconds almost everyone in the crowded restaurant had laid down their knives, forks and spoons and were giving Danny and Suzie a round of applause.

'Stand up!' she urged.

Blushing to the roots of his hair, Danny stood.

When the applause had died down, Suzie said, 'Then I accept,' and dragged Danny from his place and kissed him, long and hard to the sound of wolf whistles, cheers and more applause.

Colin came out of the kitchen and presented them with a free bottle of champagne, kissed Suzie and slapped Danny on the back while pumping his hand, and asked if they needed someone to do the catering at the wedding.

It was as easy as that.

Now they were lying on the bed on the edge of exhaustion and Suzie was asking, 'What is it?'

'What's what?' Danny replied, still staring at the ceiling.

'What is it you're looking at so intently?'

Danny looked for an answer and found only a blank. He hadn't been looking at anything in particular, just staring at the ceiling and letting his mind wander. He was fit and happy and in love and he was going to get married. He wasn't *looking* at anything. *Just staring into space*, he thought dreamily, intending to make the thought into words. He was very surprised to hear a sentence come out of his mouth, not just altered, but totally changed.

'That's where it is,' he said, and had no idea why he'd said it. The panic worm found his guts and a frantic part of him screamed: *Don't fuck this evening up, Danny! Fuck up any other evening, but FOR CHRIST'S SAKE NOT THIS ONE!*

He turned to Suzie and realised she was searching his face with suspicion glinting in her eyes. The terrible knowledge of what he *had* been doing trickled into his mind like iced water. He'd been staring at a patch of white ceiling; a spot directly above his feet. Now he knew its significance.

'Where what is?' Suzie asked, frowning.

Don't fuck it up now! Danny forced a grin. 'And what's it got to do with you, wifey?'

'A bit less of the wifey, please,' she said, her face clearing. She started to tickle his ribs. Danny squealed and wearily fought her off. The only way he could prevent a further attack was to sit astride her and pin her arms to her sides. It wasn't easy to achieve, but when he had her held down he took advantage of the moment and kissed her.

'Where what is?' Suzie insisted, when she'd pulled her face from his.

What can you tell her, old Dan? That patch of ceiling you were looking at, totally unaware of its significance, is the spot directly below where you put the crystal in the attic? That although there's maybe six inches between that spot and the crystal – the ceiling board, the plaster, and the loft insulation – and another nine feet or so between there and you, you've been lying here picking up its vibrations? Listening to it calling you to use it? Are you going to tell her you think it might be glowing up there?

I won't use it! he swore to himself, knowing that its calling would eventually draw him up the loft ladder when Suzie was out. *I don't want to and I wont!*

'That's where the damp patch is,' he lied, craning round to look again. 'It's gone now, but it was there the other day. You can just see the outline if you look closely. There's one in the back bedroom too. I'll have to go into the attic and check the pipes, I suppose. One of them's probably leaking.'

Suzie realised he was off balance and pulled his arm, rolling him off her. She straddled his chest and knelt on his biceps. 'Don't be a dummy!' she said. 'There's no damp patch up there. What did you see? What were you imagining?'

She grabbed his hair, tilted his head back and threatened to torture him if he didn't tell her what he'd seen. Danny told her his name, rank and serial number and closed his mouth firmly.

The torture was painful but delightful. Danny forgot all about the crystal and his lies.

5

First thing on Monday morning, when Danny heard the roar of Suzie's Sunbeam Tiger fade into the distance as she headed along Queen Mary Avenue towards work, he went upstairs, got the attic pole, opened the hatch and drew down the steps.

You won't get me, you little glass bastard, he thought as he climbed the rickety ladder, but he wasn't sure. Saturday night hadn't been so bad but the crystal had called him from the moment he entered the bedroom on Sunday night until he got up early this morning and got the only good two hours' sleep of the night on the settee in the lounge.

Suzie had found him there, sound asleep, when she got up and Danny had blearily concocted a story about his insomnia being caused by a headache that had only gone away after four painkillers and a good slug of brandy. Suzie had instantly become worried about the headache and Danny regretted this lie – not because it was a lie, he discovered with some discomfort, but because it made things more complicated. He told Suzie it was a different kind of headache to the ones he usually had and she had become even more concerned. Danny didn't get back on to the right track until he told her he thought it was a muscle stress ache rather than his usual kind and blamed it on the torture two nights ago. This, apparently, satisfied her. She'd warned him not to drive if he'd drunk too much and had gone to work happy.

There were no floorboards in the attic and there wasn't much headroom. Bent over almost double, Danny had to hop from rafter to rafter, being careful not to put his foot through the ceiling while he skirted all the junk that had accumulated there over the years. With each rafter he came eighteen inches closer to the hidden box and the feeling that he wouldn't be able to put it down again once he picked it up increased.

But the little glass bastard wasn't going to get him!

Danny knelt on the box of blankets, bent over and moved the old *Dandy* and *Beano* albums and picked up the box.

It was glowing faintly.

This isn't possible, he told himself. *This glass ball has no power source and, according to Lerner, only acts as a focusing device for your mind. It cannot be glowing, therefore you must be imagining it.*

The light Danny was imagining was misty and white and radiated from the sealed box in a sphere of about two feet in diameter.

'Doesn't matter a jot,' he said aloud. 'I'm not opening the box to find out what's going on.'

The odd sensation of cold warmth began to make his hands tingle.

It feels good, a part of Danny thought. *You forgot, didn't you? You forgot exactly how good it does feel.*

He got up and whacked his head on one of the roof beams, wobbled but didn't fall off the two rafters his feet were firmly planted on. The tingling was running up his arms now, crossing his chest and meeting in the vacuum that had formed in his stomach.

ABSOLUTELY NOT! Danny thought, but the tingling wouldn't stop.

He carried the box to the far end of the attic, ducking lower and lower into the angle the roofing timbers made at the eaves. He had to crawl the last few rafters, the wood biting into his knees, and he still hadn't made it to the very edge of the attic. He pushed the box along the last two feet and felt a sharp shock, like static, as his hand left the cardboard. The crystal didn't *want* to be put over here.

'Too far away from me for you?' Danny said as the tingling ceased and his stomach came back to re-inhabit the vacuum behind his ribs. The box was now at the far corner of the spare bedroom – as far away from where Danny and Suzie slept as was possible without taking it outside the house.

And why didn't *you take it outside? Why didn't you put it in the dustbin? The lorry will be along later to take the garbage. It could have been out of your life forever.*

'Dunno,' Danny answered himself. But he *did* know, he was merely practising what he had become good at and lying to himself.

He went back to the trap door feeling a distinct yearning in his guts to go and retrieve the box. He turned off the loft light and stared over at the box. It was not only still glowing faintly, it illuminated part of the attic with its soft, somehow welcoming light.

Danny went down the steps, wondering.

6

'There *is* a damp patch,' Suzie said, inspecting the bedroom ceiling. Danny had lied that he'd been in the attic all day working on the leaky pipe and she had gone to take another look at the patch she didn't believe existed.

'Of course there is,' he said evenly. 'I told you so.' But inside he was fighting to retain his composure. There wasn't a patch on the ceiling two evenings ago but there was certainly one there now. *And it wasn't made by water from a leaky pipe, either*, he told himself. For one thing the patch wasn't the right shape. Water would have made a ragged, uneven mark as it seeped into the plasterboard by capillary action. This mark was the circular shape you would find if you truncated a perfect sphere.

'Is it wet up there?' Suzie asked.

No, but there's a strange light shining, he wanted to say. *The kind of light that leaves marks on the ceiling*. 'Just a little damp. Nothing to worry about.'

'What about the damp patch in the other room?'

Damp patch? For a moment, Danny didn't remember telling her about the one in the spare bedroom. 'I haven't looked,' he said, 'but it was no wetter than the other one. The pipe runs all the way along the attic up there.' The errant pipe of Danny's fabrication had now been replaced by a new length he'd fitted, the builder's merchant's bill for which had mysteriously gone missing.

'Let's have a look then,' Suzie said, leading him to the other bedroom.

She stopped just inside the door. 'Oh, yeah, I see it,' she said while Danny's heart sank. 'It's a bit worse than the other one. And it looks fresh. Still, I expect it'll dry out now the pipe's fixed.'

'Yeah, I 'spect,' Danny replied, looking up the mark – which was the same shape and size as the one in the other room – and imagining he could see it darkening as he watched.

'Let's eat,' she said, and Danny followed her downstairs while he dimly wondered if lead would insulate the box and prevent the rays leaking out.

Chapter Twelve
The Bad Future

1

The summer reached its blazing peak and Danny's flexible mind began to shuffle memories – mimicking, he would later think, the way that Queen of all the Bitches Lady Luck had shuffled her cards of fate. Everything became stacked *just so* and he didn't think of Lerner any more, or of the things that had happened to him during that dark period, or of the crystal which had apparently given up on him as a bad job and ceased its calling. Hours would still vanish, but Danny had developed a knack of not following them too closely and not considering where they might have gone. This was a simple after effect, he rationalised, and like the continuing ache where a bone had broken and healed, would eventually fade into insignificance.

Things were looking good. Suzie had started talking about a holiday in Barbados in September and, maybe, a small register office wedding in May the following year followed by three weeks in the Seychelles – if Danny would be good enough to get a job to help finance it, that was.

He worked on his physical fitness, cooked, cleaned and soaked up the sun, occasionally scanning the Situations Vacant pages of the paper. Some of the jobs there began to look a little more interesting and Danny thought he would soon be able to return to work. But not *too* soon – perhaps after the Barbados trip. Meanwhile he was happy to rest and recuperate and maybe do a little re-decorating.

The ceilings in the the two bedrooms proved exceptionally hard to fix. It took three coats of paint to cover the 'light stain' in the master bedroom and the mark in the other room could still be detected after four coats. For several weeks, Danny thought the mark would seep back through the new paint in the spare room and considered painting it again. But by the time July began to run out of days he was sure that the little glass bastard in the attic had ceased operations for good.

If anything, the faint mark faded.

2

Lady Luck, Danny would later reflect, seemed to have a distinct predilection for snapping her cards down on, or very near, the weekend. His charts would bear this out and Danny would wonder why the bad cards never came mid-week.

The next bad ace was, true to form, dealt on a Saturday morning.

And it put paid to all Danny's plans.

3

As was traditional at the weekends, the getting-up roles were reversed and Suzie rose first. Danny got downstairs about ten minutes after her, knowing that by now she would have had enough time to make the tea and toast and put the Sugar Puffs (their current favourite) into the bowls. All he had to do was roll out of bed, stagger downstairs and start eating and drinking in much the same zombiefied way as Suzie did during the week.

But this morning, Danny became instantly alert the moment he entered the kitchen.

Suzie was standing in the kitchen intently reading the front page of the paper, her mouth open and an unbitten slice of toast in her hand. Hot butter was dripping from the toast and falling to the floor.

'What?' Danny asked, feeling the atmosphere and not liking it one little bit. Suzie was close to tears.

She didn't look up. 'This is terrible,' she replied in a quavery voice. She took a bite from the toast, chewed mechanically, swallowed and quoted from the paper. 'The worst air disaster ever. Four hundred and fifteen people killed. No survivors.'

Danny felt the ground shift sideways under his feet. His senses did a brief pirouette and settled leaving him light headed.

'Burnt to death. All of them,' Suzie said.

Danny sat down quickly, remembering his dream of smouldering skeletons. How long ago had *that* been?

Not as long ago as dreaming the actual crash, old Dan, he told himself. *The one that didn't happen. The one Lerner told you was just a glitch as your talent asserted itself. The one you searched the papers for news of before dismissing its possibility. This is that crash.*

'Where?' he asked, grasping for the final straw again and knowing very well what he was doing. He already knew all the details. Had seen them first hand, as they had happened, and in glorious technicolour and Vistavision.

'Athens. Yesterday afternoon. A charter plane came in to land at Athens . . . its communications stuff was out of service for some reason and it was in some kind of trouble. The captain put it down on the runway he'd been directed to earlier, but there was a German plane on it taxiing for takeoff. The charter hit the German plane.'

It can't *have happened!* Danny screamed inwardly, while he shook his head hard enough to make himself dizzy. 'We didn't see it on the telly last night! It would have been on T.V.,' he protested, suddenly remembering that neither of them had watched the television the previous evening. Danny had collected Suzie from work, they'd eaten out and gone to see Iain playing in the Rod Garfield Blues Band, hadn't they? The gig was in Hungerford and had gone on until late and they'd gone straight to bed when they got home.

Suzie explained all this to him while Danny's inner voice whispered, *It's easy to join The Paranormal Club, old Dan, but once you're in, getting out again isn't that simple. These things don't just go away, y'know. They lie fallow for a time, and while you're forgetting they ever existed, they're doing the old fitness regime too, building up power so that when they come back, you won't be able to ignore them ever again.*

'. . . but it's eleven now so it'll probably be on the news. Let's turn it on,' Suzie finished and went into the lounge.

Suzie was right. It was on the television.

Danny settled down beside her on the settee and got to look at the tangled and smoking wreckage which countless firemen, ambulancemen and military personnel were trying to untangle in order to remove the charred bodies. The picture cut to grim-faced Greeks loading body bags into an ambulance while a voice-over announced the emergency telephone numbers you could contact. *If you had relatives on that flight*, Danny thought bleakly, *you wouldn't need to phone up to find out what happened to them. There weren't any lucky escapes this time.*

Suzie began to cry. 'Think of all those poor people going on holiday and dying as they touched down in Greece. How could it have happened? How?'

Danny would normally have swept her into his arms and comforted her, but he sat frozen in place, staring at the carnage on the T.V. and wondering. It was a horrendous accident but Suzie wasn't usually this emotional. She'd watched the aftermath of Michael Ryan's killing spree and the Waterloo train crash and the Gulf War with the same kind of horrified awe as Danny had, but she had not cried during any of them. Suzie simply wasn't a woman who wept over this kind of impersonal tragedy. Tearjerker films and documentary character studies of folks with fatal diseases, yes, but those were different somehow.

Is your girlfriend psychic too? he heard Alistair Lerner asking him and began to wonder if Suzie had also had dreams. . .

'Did you know?' Danny's motormouth had jumped into the driving seat again. He was surprised to hear himself asking her the question.

Suzie looked up at him then, and he saw her tear-stained face harden. 'Know?' she said. 'Know what?'

'Nothing,' he said, yanking the controls back from his mouth.

Suzie looked at him long and hard. 'About this?' she said, her voice spiralling upward and cracking. 'About the crash? Beforehand? What do you mean?'

Danny shrugged. 'Nothing,' he repeated, but it was too late; he couldn't withdraw it, couldn't take it back.

Suzie shook her head and her face fell as the realisation of what he'd asked sank in and bit deep. '*Like me*, you meant, Danny, didn't you? You meant, did I know like you did! No. I didn't!'

Suzie's eyes flashed. 'But you did, didn't you, Danny?' Her bottom lip began to tremble. 'DIDN'T YOU?'

He watched Suzie's expression change back and forth from sadness to horror to anger and knew it was too late to brazen it out now. She waited for him to speak but his glib tongue had deserted him. He had no words. He shook his head again.

'TELL ME THE TRUTH!' she shouted. 'YOU KNEW THIS WAS GOING TO HAPPEN, DIDN'T YOU?'

The cat was well and truly out of the bag and the game was up. There were no apparent escape routes. *You knew it would come to this, didn't you?* he asked himself and replied that, yes, he did. He began to nod his head, slowly and deliberately. 'Yes,' he said.

Angry tears brimmed in Suzie's eyes. 'And you didn't tell me? You promised faithfully that you'd tell me if anything else happened to you, and when it did, you broke your promise. Why do you keep lying to me, Danny?'

'It was a dream,' he said, his own voice cracking now. 'Just a dream, a long time ago when I was fucked up and you'd gone. I didn't think it would happen. I thought I was going to be wrong!' he sobbed.

'But you could have *done* something. You could have *warned* someone. *You could have stopped it happening!*'

'I couldn't!' he insisted, shaking his head for emphasis. Tears flew.

Suzie's eyes blazed away behind her own tears and Danny wasn't sure if she was simply going to fall apart or if she had decided to murder him first. There was a confused blend of emotions writ large on her face, and hatred or contempt or something close seemed to be coming out on top. Her expression was not one Danny cared to gaze on for long. He looked away, knowing he wouldn't be able to make her understand.

'Don't do it, Danny! Don't do it any more. Make it stop!' Suzie pleaded, finally falling apart.

'It has stopped,' he said miserably. 'It's never happened since you came back to me. I *didn't* lie to you about it. It's stopped.'

He glanced up at her in time to see the anger and hurt leaving her face and being replaced by sorrow. She reached out for him and held him to her, rocking him from side to side. 'I'm sorry, Danny, I'm so sorry,' she whispered. 'It's just that it scares me so. I don't want you to be different. I don't want you to know what's going to happen. I'm scared that you'll see something about me. I'm frightened of dying, Danny. I don't want to die. Don't ever see anything about me, Danny, promise!'

Danny promised.

And didn't break it until a fortnight later – when the itching of his palms grew too strong to resist any longer.

4

During that fortnight, his relationship with Suzie underwent a slow and insidious change. Her attitude towards him cooled; subtly at first so that he hardly noticed it, then as the days passed, he was able to detect the chill in her body language, and in the way her once regular touches, hugs and quick pecks on the cheek became infrequent. During the first few days, Suzie became quiet and withdrawn. Her only response to his questions about what was wrong were a simple wan smile and the reply, 'Nothing'.

Suzie didn't want to discuss anything any more, including the trip to Barbados she'd booked, and the wedding seemed to have become a taboo subject that was never pondered about – or even alluded to – verbally.

It'll blow over, Danny assured himself as he watched her staring dully at the television. But it didn't blow over. By the time Danny realised he was looking at a relationship which was staggering on the edge of a chasm, it seemed too late to rectify the situation.

Setting aside the fact that he still believed Suzie was, in some way, a member of the Paranormal Club too and had shared his air crash dream, Danny knew what was going on inside her head and knew he could tell her nothing that would make things better again. Suzie had suddenly begun to believe she was living with a man who was a Jonah, a harbinger of doom, a teller of forthcoming disaster. As far as she was concerned the future held only bad news and she didn't want to have to think about it. The bad news may have been the accident the fortune teller had predicted or her inability to conceive, but these things weren't the Truly Bad News. The Truly Bad News was the kind of news she thought Danny was best at predicting. The Truly Bad News was death and she thought Danny was the one who was going to receive that particular news first. Suzie believed that if she stuck around long enough she would see the bad news – or the Truly Bad News – in his eyes and know what it was; even if he didn't tell her.

So she was retreating.

And Danny didn't really blame her.

It was a desperately unhappy fortnight. In the evenings he watched helplessly as Suzie pulled away from him and in the daytimes spent much of his time running; keeping his mind empty and trying to ignore the itching that had started as a light tingling in the palms of his hands. In the gaps when Suzie wasn't reading philosophy or intently watching television, they held polite conversations on unimportant matters. At night times they lay in bed, carefully not touching one another.

And as things slid, the itching in Danny's palms increased. At the beginning of the second week, his bullet scar began to itch too. By the middle of that week Danny had ceased to consider courses of action that might – or might not – save his relationship and had begun to believe that the little glass bastard in the attic had gained a new lease of life. By the end of the week he was certain it was calling him on a line connected directly to a secret place in his brain. This place popped and fizzed as it received the power, directing his thoughts towards it and drawing him to use it.

5

By the time he eventually crept up to the attic to retrieve the crystal, he had countless good and proper reasons for doing it. There was the itching and mental fizzling, of course, but there was also the knowledge that it wouldn't do much more damage to his relationship than he'd already done unaided, and the belief that the future couldn't be all bad. There might well be something good to see; something that would show him a way out of the mess his life was in, show him that it was possible to live happily ever after, after all.

Or it could just be your morbid curiosity at work, he told himself as he climbed the loft ladder.

Danny knew it was right before he'd even got the package back downstairs. The crystal's lights were on again and the refreshing – and somehow *welcoming* – sensation of cold and warmth filled his body as soon as he picked up the box.

He drew the lounge curtains, slit the tape on the box, pulled out Lerner's instructions and set them aside, then unpacked the (warm) velvet cloth containing the crystal and set it on the table, wadding the cloth beneath the globe to hold it steady. A thin, high, trumpet-like note started to resound inside his head before he'd even finished putting the crystal in place, and the phosphorescent glow turned to a sparkling milky mist before he'd placed his hands on the cool, reassuring crystal. The odd heat and cold now tingled its electrical charge through his body unimpeded and it felt very good indeed. Danny didn't just feel better than he'd done in weeks, he felt *complete* for the first time in that period.

He'd waited a long time and the crystal wanted him badly – or he wanted *it*, it was difficult to tell which was which – and before he'd even had time to think about where he wanted to go, he was inside and falling through the glittering mist and revelling in the exhilarating sensation.

This time, the sideways step into the future was roughly curtailed. For a few moments, Danny thought he'd run into a column of cold, hard mud and struggled to be released as it closed around him. It didn't work. The cold stuff squeezed him hard, compressing him until he was certain he was shrinking. This was followed by a violent twist, after which he realised he was standing in the lounge on another day.

And he was inhabiting his future's body.

As a passenger.

This was a new experience entirely; there was none of the ghostly lightness he'd felt in his dreams when he had been there but not there, or the insubstantial quality he'd felt during his visions of Lerner's bedroom, just a nasty feeling of constriction and the knowledge that he had no control over himself. He could feel his body breathing and the movements it was making, but they were nothing to do with him. The future Danny had control over that cold column of flesh while the time-traveller was somehow squeezed in there too – as an observer who could now watch what the real Danny would see in the future. His mind and his future mind were independent of one another, but there seemed to be a one way hook-up between the two of them: the future Danny was not aware of or affected by the thoughts of his passenger, but the time-travelling one could receive all the sensations and emotions he would eventually have on that day.

Then the link was completed and Danny forgot all about the feeling of constriction and the other unpleasant sensations because the information started to come in thick and fast.

And the information was not good.

The lounge was wrecked again. But Danny, who had this moment discovered it, had not done it. He was horrified to find it in that condition. Danny squirmed inside his future head: experiencing his emotions second hand seemed to make them more powerful than they were first hand. A distant part of him realised they were magnified because all the other mental clutter that normally muffled the feelings was absent. None of this ever-present background material was coming across.

The coffee table – which had escaped his earlier violent spree – was now no more than sticks of firewood. The sofa was upside down, its stuffing spewing out where someone had slashed it. There was a strong smell of burned plastic in the air and both Dannys realised – independently and at the same moment – that someone had tried to set light to the new carpet. It was covered in large black patches where it had burned and gone out.

Danny felt his future's few moments of confusion which were immediately followed by disbelief and then panic which rose so quickly and strongly that the watching Danny felt nauseous. The future Danny wasn't now feeling anything other than a numb dread.

'Suzie!' he heard his voice scream as, on leaden legs, the future Danny staggered clumsily around to face the door. There was a moment in which the watching Danny reflected on how much he sounded like the Gannex Man, then he was swamped by the knowledge that the future Danny had known this would happen – had expected it – but still couldn't believe it was actually taking place.

The body ran upstairs, bleating to itself that it was sorry. Danny knew why. His future self had discovered all this much earlier in real time – had discovered it *now* in fact as the observer Danny was discovering it. But he had somehow been unable to prevent it happening anyway.

The travelling Danny had the unpleasant sensation of picking up, second hand from his future memory, what he was going to find out today. It was like looking into a series of mirrors and it hurt. By the time his future body burst through the bedroom door, he already knew what it would find. It found just what it thought it would find. Everything was instantly confirmed and gelled into one solid irrevocable fact.

They had got Suzie.

The bastards had found his address, and to prove it, they'd been here and smashed the place up. And having found Danny wasn't home, they'd exacted their revenge on Suzie.

The time-travelling Danny knew that his future self had been out that evening and knew that it was going to be important to find out where to and for how long but the future Danny had no inkling of that; the memory of this evening was completely missing from his mind.

This is all your fault! both versions of Danny thought. *This is why she didn't want you to see into the future. This is what she expected the consequence to be and she was right. Suzie's had the accident her fortune teller predicted and you caused it to happen!*

Both Dannys knew *why* they'd caused it to happen and both knew it was the lesser of two evils, but neither would ever forgive themselves. That much was certain.

The bed was cut to ribbons. The room was awash with mattress stuffing, feathers from the pillows, and the sheets were slashed rags. Suzie was huddled up in a ragged ball in the centre of the wrecked bed. She was naked and clutched the remaining tatters of her beloved pie-jam top tightly to her in an effort to cover herself. She rocked endlessly back and forth, looking up at Danny with hurt and confusion in her eyes. One of them was swollen almost shut. Her hair was wild and her face was badly bruised and crusted with drying blood. Her nose had been bleeding and her nostrils were rimmed. Both her lips were fat and split and there were red weals on her neck that clearly showed the weave of the rope which had been fastened there. Her limbs were so badly scratched she looked as if she had walked into a room full of rabid cats.

'*Oh my God!*' Danny heard himself say.

Suzie looked slowly up at him. 'They raped me,' she said in a distant, beaten voice that was so quiet it could barely be heard. She shook her head as if she still couldn't believe what had happened. 'I . . . I opened the door and they . . . just burst in. They . . . they wanted to know where you wuh-were,' she sobbed. 'They said they wuh-were going to castrate you. Oh God Duh-hanny, where wuh-her you? I wanted to tuh-tell them but I didn't know. They beat me up duh-Danny, to make me tell. They huh-hit me until I *wet* myself. Then they ruh-raped me. Fuh-four of them. They raped me and made me suh-suck them and buh-buh-*buggered* me. And they kept on and on and on.' Her fingers went to her neck. 'Then they chu-choked me with a rope until I bluh-blacked out. Whu-when I came round one of them was buh-buggering me again *with an empty Coke bottle*. He suh . . . he suh-said he wanted to see how far in it would guh-go.'

'Oh Suze,' the future Danny said and went towards her, stopping as she shrank back from him.

'Don't come near me,' she said. A sob caught in her thoat and her chest heaved. 'I d-don't want you near me,' she sobbed. 'Not now, nuh-n-not ever again.'

The future Danny went to her, wanting to hold her and comfort her in spite of knowing what would happen next.

Suzie pulled back from him, then slapped him, hard.

The future Danny moved away, tears of hurt and dismay in his eyes.

'You knew, duh-didn't you?' Suzie whispered.

The future Danny said nothing.

'Answer me. You already knew, Danny, didn't you?'

'No Suzie,' the future Danny lied, shaking his head in emphasis. Both Dannys knew she'd seen straight through the untruth.

'You saw it Danny, didn't you? You saw this future!' Suzie said, in a small, shocked voice. 'You already knew, you buh-bastard.'

'Suzie I. . .!'

Tears ran from her eyes. 'You betrayed me!' she sobbed. 'You *already knew*. You knew this would happen and you knew when.' Her voice rose slightly and its tone was as cold as the Arctic. 'You betrayed me Danny. You knew they were coming and you went out, you coward, so you wouldn't get hurt. So they'd get me while I was alone. I can't believe you did that, you bastard!'

'I didn't know when . . . I mean . . . I . . . thought it wouldn't happen!' Danny insisted, his voice rising a note.

'Tell the truth Mister Psychic Seer!' Suzie hissed. 'Oh Danny, you knew it would happen! You fucking well *knew*!'

Frantically dredging his future self's memories for information about things which were yet to happen to him, as his future self stood there knowing it was impossible to explain, the watching Danny realised Suzie was partially right; his future self had known *what* would happen, but he hadn't known *when* it would. It was the knowing *when* that was important. Knowing *when* might give him a chance to avert all this.

Suzie dropped the rags that had once been her pie-jams. Both her breasts had been badly bitten. 'Look,' she said. 'Look at what you've done to me. You knew they'd be coming and you let it happen. Why didn't you stop it? Why? Because you're a coward, that's why! How could you do this to me? *How could you know and still let it happen?*'

The compressed Danny looking out of his future body tried to make himself ask Suzie what day it was, but the future body simply stood there making little horrified moans. If he could find out what day this was now he would be able to make plans to prevent it happening later. If it wasn't already too late to change the future that was.

Again his shocked future self stumbled towards Suzie, reaching for her.

'DON'T YOU TOUCH ME!' she shouted with such vehemence that the future Danny stopped in his tracks. *It's over*, his future self thought with an aching finality. The words boomed in the travelling Danny's mind and hurt to the nth power.

But it doesn't have to be! the travelling Danny thought. *Future One or not, I can prevent it happening. All I need to know is what day it is!*

'Where was I?' his body asked her stupidly. 'Where did I go?'

WHAT DAY IS IT? the watching Danny shouted. But the link was only one way.

Suzie's face darkened. She winced and when she spoke there was fresh blood staining her teeth. 'Out! OUT! *You were hiding because you knew they were coming!*'

Even with the memory of having seen this before and surely knowing what he needed to ask in order for this never to have to happen, the future Danny just couldn't make the logical switch of track. He was confused about where he'd been when this happened and that seemed to hold the most importance. 'Where to? Where did I go?' he pleaded.

Suzie wiped tears and blood from her face. 'I don't *know*,' she moaned. 'Christ, I'm *hurt*. I can't think. Just get out and nuh-nuh-never come back.'

WHAT DAY IS IT? Danny screamed.

'What day is it, Suze?' his future body finally asked.

Beneath all the turmoil in that Danny's mind, a faint light had begun to glow. There was a dim knowledge in there now, but that Danny also wondered why he was asking, because he knew exactly what day it was.

Suzie drew herself up wincing as she moved. With as much venom as she could muster she said, 'It's the day the psychic seer gets out of my life and never returns. It's Danny's last day. Get out. Get out Danny and let me get help. GET OUT!'

The future Danny was numb with shock. 'I'll get the police,' he told her, and both of him knew he was grasping at that absent last straw again. 'And an ambulance,' he added.

'Stop right there,' Suzie said, her voice now low and controlled. 'I don't want the police. I'm injured and I think I'm bleeding internally and I want an ambulance, but I'll get it myself. What I want most of all is you out of here. For ever. Get out Danny and don't ever come back. Go and join a circus or something, you bastard. Get yourself a tent in a fairground sideshow. Then you can sit there and tell the future to your heart's content. Just get out of my life. *I hate you for what you've done!*' She drew herself up on her knees then, so he could see the full extent of her injuries. 'You did this to me Danny,' she said. 'It's all your fault. Get out of the house, Danny. Run away in case they come back for you. And take your dirty stinking talent with you. GET OUT!'

A sharp tearing noise filled Danny's ears and he felt himself split through the centre of his body in the same way as he had when Lerner had forcibly brought him back from his first crystal gazing experience. The scene was snatched violently away from him as he tore from his future body and Danny whirled through space, filled with the sickening *disconnected* sensation he'd had when the black mirrors sucked him in. Coloured lights flickered before his eyes, then he saw his own body, way out in front of him, realised that he was heading towards it at an impossible speed. As the static body rushed over to meet him Danny thought this was surely going to kill him. This was surely the end. Nothing could survive such a collision.

He hit his body hard and his world exploded in bright light. When his consciousness came back to him he was being forcefully fed back into that cold vessel of clay through a minute fault just above his navel. The body was too small and horribly cramped, but there was nothing he could do to avoid being thrust into it.

Then he was back where he started, on the settee in his lounge, his hands touching the crystal. His head ached terribly and his body felt as if it were destroying itself. He seemed to have become the human equivalent of a glass of Eno's, his flesh and bone fizzing and bubbling madly. For ten minutes Danny could not move and was convinced that he was going to die. It was the longest ten minutes of his life.

When the feeling came back to Danny's legs, it returned at the same moment as the nausea hit his stomach. He got them under him and ran down the hall to the kitchen where he threw up, long and hard, over the breakfast bowls still in the sink.

After that he slept.

6

And dreamed of skeletons. Endless ranks of them. They marched towards him, those at the front blackened and still smouldering from the fire after the plane crash. Danny ran, but the running did no good: each time he looked back the skeleton army had gained ground and was closer to him although their steady clacking pace had not increased. As the legion drew closer still, the rattle of moving bones grew to a crescendo and Danny knew he was listening to the sound of millions of years of human destruction and decay.

He sensed someone at his side and turned, knowing what he would see, yet unable to stop himself looking. Another Danny gazed back at him. A Danny from the extreme future. A Danny to whom the Truly Bad News had come and gone long ago. Danny looked upon its tattered face, felt its deep black eye sockets boring into his soul and he knew it hated what it saw. The flesh of his dead face was shredded and crawling with tiny white maggots. The hair was gone except for a few strands which were slicked down over the forehead with something slimy. The top lip was in tatters and the bottom one was gone altogether along with the skin of the chin and neck. The jawbone gleamed dully through, and the base of the rotting tongue nestled in there, blackened and disgusting.

'Save yourself the pain,' the dead Danny Stafford said in a rush of fetid breath.

Behind Danny the skeletons drew closer, their huge clashing racket vibrating through him as they marched in step. Then there was one louder crash and Danny knew they'd halted, stamping their right feet down hard as they came to a stop.

Then there was silence in which he knew what they wanted.

'I'm you, Danny. Save yourself the pain,' the corpse said. 'Come with me. Accept your fate. You let this happen so march with me in the wretched army of the unfulfilled.'

'Noooo!' Danny shouted. His voice was slowed down to a deep blur.

'It's your fault, o Great and Wondrous Psychic. You are the cause. What didn't you do?'

'I didn't read it,' Danny replied in a horrendous bass tone. 'I couldn't.'

'What didn't you read?'

Don't say! he thought. 'Nothing,' he replied.

'What?'

Danny began to shrink. The monster Danny towered over him now. 'You cannot win. Tell me what you didn't read.'

'I don't know.' He knew he was lying and so did the other Danny but it was important not to say. He didn't know why, but the other Danny did and this terrified him.

'You are me, Danny. And I am death. I'm coming for you because you too are death. We are one. I will know you as you knew the girl.'

And the girl's blood appeared on him again, flooding over him and enveloping him with its own peculiar welcoming life. Danny became erect.

'Now you have what you desire, give me my desire, o Master Mystic. Tell me what you didn't read!'

'Nothing,' Danny coughed.

'No more lies,'

'There was nothing I didn't read.' Danny choked out the lie which seemed to take an hour to rise from his throat. It flowed out and became solid, forming a huge dark mass in front of him, grey and veined and corrupt. The lie pulsed with each beat of his heart. The dead Danny took it between his skeletal hands, heaved it from the ground and tore a chunk from it with his teeth. Stinking yellow pus oozed from it as the lie deflated.

'Now I will have you!' the dead Danny said reaching out for him.

When cold fingers burned into Danny's arm, he woke up.

'I didn't read Jamie!' he sobbed, still not knowing what it meant.

7

You can find out, Danny thought, when his head had cleared, but he was no longer wondering about the significance of the nightmare or of the missing book either written by, or starring, the mystery celebrity Jamie – he was wondering about the details of the attack on Suzie that was going to take place soon. There was very little to work with. The future Danny had known all about the reasons for it, but the present Danny had been unable to access the memories properly and none of them had sprung to the forefront of the future Danny's mind for him to look at. The whole bad future revolved around a payroll robbery which hadn't yet happened. But Danny wasn't sure what the robbery was or what part he had played in it.

But he could find out and when he knew, he could get himself to those important turning points Lerner had written of and divert that particular future so far down the list of possibilities that it would become impossible for it to happen.

He washed the crystal, dried it and set it back on the coffee table then drank three fingers of whisky to calm himself and settle his stomach. Somewhere in the not too distant future there was a trip-wire set for him and he was going to find it and snip it neatly. Of this, there was no doubt.

His body tense and with an expression of grim determination on his face, he reached for the little glass bastard again.

And found himself standing on the pavement in Kingsclere Road before his fingers touched the crystal. He was standing on the corner where Sherbourne Road joined it. Behind him was the wall of the Holy Ghost ruins where he'd looked for Lerner all that time ago and opposite were the offices of Eli Lilly, the drug manufacturer. A hundred yards down the hill was the railway bridge under which Kingsclere Road ran. It was raining, but he wasn't getting wet. This time, Danny knew the date and time: he didn't have to ask or grope for this information, it was just there, inside his head. It was September the 9th and it was Thursday, quarter past ten in the morning. Pay day.

Danny watched the procession of cars swish along the road spraying water into the air. The rain that passed through him felt cool and fresh but he realised this only subliminally. Danny now knew exactly what was going to happen and he was searching the road for the first car.

It was a blue Ford Sierra. It drove slowly past him and turned right into Sherbourne Road, where it swung round and parked close to the junction. Danny knew that its position gave it a good view both up and down Kingsclere Road.

But after the sudden momentary flickering in which Danny linked with the minds of both men, jumping from one to the other in a crazy lightning zig-zag, he knew a great deal more.

The two men in the car were called Geoff Ridge and Phil McFarlane. Geoff was forty-two and Phil thirty-eight. Both were five eleven and Geoff, at thirteen stone, weighed a stone and a half more than Phil. Both men were pumped full of adrenaline and Phil had eaten his breakfast this morning knowing full well that he would throw it up again before leaving for this job. This always happened to him on the day of a job but he always ate his fried egg and bacon just the same.

Phil had an eagle tattooed on his left shoulder that had gone septic after he'd had it done. A subsequent blood disorder had put him in hospital for a month soon after. He had sworn his revenge on the tattooist, but it had never been exacted and never would be. The tattooist had been forgiven because Phil liked the tattoo very much.

Geoff had been in hospital too, but he had arrived almost dead and he had not forgiven the man who put him there fifteen years ago before he left Hackney. That man was called Dave Tate and he had opened Geoff up from his belly right down to his testicles with a broken Watney's Pale Ale bottle. Dave Tate had done this not to kill Geoff, but as a warning: to make him understand that he must leave the district of Hackney. It had taken three men to strip Geoff and hold him down and in the excitement Dave had had got carried away and instead of simply cutting Geoff, he'd jammed the broken bottle into Geoff's belly, twisting it as it sank it and then, screaming, he'd raked it downwards, suddenly intending to cut off Geoff's cock and balls too. The other men had made him stop, but by the time Geoff got to hospital there was very little blood left inside him.

Sometimes Geoff's scar throbbed when it rained and it was throbbing now, but he didn't know whether the wet weather was causing it, or if it was the tension he was currently feeling.

Phil had a woman called Jackie and he often hit her. Jackie seemed to like it.

Geoff had a younger boyfriend who liked to suck him off.

Phil didn't mind Geoff being queer as long as Geoff didn't touch him. Geoff didn't mind Phil calling him a queer and didn't fancy him one iota.

Phil and Geoff had been a team for twenty years this Christmas and had pulled thirty-seven armed robberies. Today would be the thirty-eighth.

Both were carrying guns. Phil's was a Browning .22 pistol and Geoff's was a Smith and Wesson .38.

There were six more men in the team. Four were in two stolen cars, one of which was parked opposite the Lansing Linde fork truck factory about two hundred yards away, and the other a little further up Sherbourne Road. The remaining two were in transit box vans which were parked nose to tail in Kingsclere Road about fifty feet away. Danny knew all their names, their histories and what kind of weapons they were carrying.

Shortly a Securicor Transit van would be approaching from town, coming under the railway bridge and heading for the trading estate at the top of Kingsclere Road. It would be carrying almost one hundred thousand pounds in wages and there would be no police escort. It had been checked out over a long period and there never was an escort.

The van didn't have far to go, it left at differing times and took a fresh route every Thursday. It hadn't come this way for two months, but all the other routes were exhausted and it would soon. The thieves had waited here for it to take this course for the last three Thursdays and were prepared to wait for as long as it took.

Phil McFarlane would be getting out of the car in a moment. He would pass Danny and cross the road, giving him a better view, and wait there until he saw the Securicor van approaching from the other side of the railway bridge. He would give a signal and the cars would start to move.

The first van's body had been heightened specifically to exceed the railway bridge's headroom. On the signal it would rush down to the bridge, arriving as the Securicor van exited. The driver would take the van to the centre of the road and wedge it beneath the bridge, preventing any further vehicular access from that direction. The other van would seal the top end of Kingsclere Road by skidding and rolling over just the other side of the junction where Danny stood.

If necessary, Geoff would put his own car across the Eli Lilly office driveway and the car behind him would block Sherbourne Road, leaving the Securicor van in a blind alley. But Geoff didn't think it would be necessary – he intended to ram the Securicor van head on as it approached.

Meanwhile, the occupants of the third car would seal off the top end of Sherbourne Road and re-direct traffic, saying there'd been a bad accident down at Kingsclere Road.

The car blocking Sherbourne Road would then drive down to the crippled Securicor van to perform the can-opening exercise.

The thieves had differing views about how this part of the operation would go. Some believed its occupants would, under threat, open up and hand over the cash; others thought it might well get a little messier. None of them minded if there had to be shooting. All of them – bar the kids in the vans – had previously been involved in gunplay of one kind or another, and if the worst came to the worst, there was plenty of plastique in the can-opener car. All of them were of the opinion that the plan was just about as sweet as a nut and that it would run like a brand new Rolls-Royce.

But, as Danny already knew, the best laid plans of mice and men could easily go awry.

Phil McFarlane got out of the car and passed Danny, leaving a reek of sour sweat behind him. He stood on the other side of the road, his hand clutching the gun in his pocket as he gazed down toward the bridge.

Danny glanced up the road towards the box vans and learned that the men behind their wheels were identical twins called Paul and Robert but known either as 'the Twinnies' or 'The Bob' which saved people from the almost impossible task of distinguishing between them. The twinnies were good-looking twenty-two year olds who made a living from driving – stock cars, bangers and the getaway varieties. They had many girlfriends and like the twins in the Jeremy Irons film (which they'd seen and been unimpressed by) they liked to indulge in secret swaps.

Danny found it scary getting information from them because they didn't seem to be two people at all, just a double version of the same person. They thought, imagined and concluded in identical ways; saw exactly the same things; missed the same things; and sometimes – although it was their best kept secret ever – they could silently converse with one another.

McFarlane saw the Securicor van and gave the signal. Paul and Robert gunned their engines and Paul, in the lead van, rocketed down the road, passing the target as it came through the bridge.

Robert felt the crunch as his twin's van forced itself under the too-low bridge, and in perfect unison with his brother, he ducked.

Geoff Ridge was already squealing down towards the target and the second car was sealing the Sherbourne Road junction as Robert dropped the clutch of his own van.

Grinning, as his brother was grinning as he got out of his trapped van, Robert roared down towards the junction and spun the steering wheel to the right. It was an easy manoeuvre and one he'd done many times before. Nothing bad had ever happened. The van would teeter on its left hand wheels, then fall gracefully over. As soon as Robert felt the van begin to tip, he killed the engine.

The van toppled on to its side, skidded into the kerb in a shower of sparks and, just as Danny had known it would, burst into flame.

Down near the bridge, there was a huge crash as Ridge drove into the Securicor van.

But Danny was still with the twinnies. Inside the overturned van, Robert was trapped by his seat belt and fighting with the catch and screaming as fire licked towards him.

Down on the far side of the bridge where, prior to making his escape, Paul had been sheepishly explaining to a growing number of drivers that he'd forgotten how high the van was, he suddenly stopped talking and started screaming.

The band of angry motorists broke into instant confusion.

'What's wrong?' someone asked, but Danny and Paul knew exactly what was wrong. Robert was burning to death and Paul was feeling the pain. Surrounded by a suddenly very frightened ring of people, Paul fell to his knees and began to blister.

'What were you carrying, mate?' a man demanded. 'What have you got in that van?'

Robert and Paul ceased to exist for Danny at the same moment as the first gunshot was fired. The scene blanked and he was wrenched off his feet. For a moment he thought he'd stopped another bullet. Out there in the void there was another tight bark and Danny's head flew back so hard he thought his neck had broken.

Then the lights came back on and he was standing beside the Securicor van realising he'd felt the blasts the driver and his mate had taken. The two men in the cab were very dead. The metal bars across the windscreen were still intact but the glass was gone. There were two bloody circles dented into the steel back of the cab where their heads had been driven back by the shots. The driver's mate was either on the floor or slumped low on the seat, but Danny could not see him. What was left of the driver's face was pressed against the side window. His crash helmet was split at the crown of his head and his brains were leaking out through the rent.

McFarlane was at the back of the van with Ridge and the occupants of the second car which was now parked behind the van with its engine running and its boot lid up.

'OPEN IT UP!' McFarlane shouted and the guard in the rear of the van insisted in a muffled voice that it couldn't be opened.

'Blow the fucking back off!' Ridge shouted, but Neil and Trevor – the can openers – were already at work. Neil was drilling frantically and Trevor was filling the holes.

It took almost four minutes during which time the police didn't arrive and no one ventured out from the Eli Lilly offices to see what all the noise was about. Danny could not believe the police would take so long. Surely someone had alerted them?

'GET BACK!' Trevor shouted and the men ran to the front of the van while the charges didn't just open the doors, but blew the rear panel off entirely.

The guard staggered out with his hands up and McFarlane took hold of his jacket front and poked the .22 into his right eye.

'Don't!' Danny shouted, knowing that he wouldn't be heard, but trying anyway.

'Why'd you have to make it so hard?' McFarlane asked. 'Why didn't you just open up?' And without waiting for a reply, he pulled the trigger. The guard cannoned back against the van, his eye spouted a single pulse of blood and brain and he slid to the ground.

No one else took any notice; they had already formed a chain and were quickly loading bags from the van to the car.

And that was when the impossible happened and the woman appeared.

Danny had no idea where she had come from or *why*. She had surely heard the gunshots, and ever since she'd come under the bridge where the wedged van was she must have been able to see what was going on. No one could possibly have been that preoccupied with a pushchair and a toddler they hadn't noticed.

But in spite of all this, there she was, walking slowly up the road towards the robbery on Danny's side of the pavement, bent forwards against the weight of the pushchair and being hampered by a small boy and a heavy bag of shopping. Her eyes were fixed on the pavement ahead of her and she looked sweaty and harassed.

And she's just gone past a guy who died of burning when there wasn't any fire and a big van crushed under the bridge, Danny thought in disbelief.

Both the children were tiny and blonde. The girl was strapped tightly into pushchair and the boy was walking, holding on to one of the pushchair's handles as he had evidently been instructed. The mother didn't look up until the boy stopped in his tracks and in a very loud and clear voice demanded to know what those men were doing.

Until then the only sound had been the creaking of cooling metal and quiet grunts and dull thuds as the money bags were thrown along the chain from man to man. Now, work stopped and silence fell. As one man, the criminals turned in the direction the question had come from.

The woman finally looked up.

And Danny linked. He didn't want to because he thought he knew what was going to happen – but he did it just the same.

Julie Walker was twenty-four years old. Her twenty-fifth birthday would be on Boxing Day. Julie's thoughts were fleeting and layered. On one level, she was very tired; aware that the pushchair was making her back ache and her shoulders stiffen up. The pushchair had a buckled wheel which made it harder to push and this wheel squeaked constantly, adding to her annoyance. Beneath that, there were thoughts in her mind in which she wished she was already at home, sitting in the kitchen with a steaming cup of coffee. Danny knew there was a Battenberg cake in her shopping bag and she had intended to treat herself to a slice or two with the coffee she had been so looking forward to.

Beneath that business-as-usual Julie, there was another, happier Julie – one that was dewy-eyed, romantic and dreamy.

Danny hit this vein and understood how she had come to be here. Julie had not come under the bridge where the van was wedged, she had walked up Vyne Road and cut through the Holy Ghost ruins, coming out of the main entrance a few yards down the hill. She'd gone that way – the long way round from the town – because of the romantic thoughts.

Julie's eldest child was the boy whose name was Nathan. Today was Nathan's fourth birthday. Four and three-quarter years ago, Julie and her boyfriend Mike – now her husband – had tumbled into the ruins after Martine's nightclub had closed at two and had made love on the frosty grass there. Nathan had been conceived that night and on each of his birthdays Julie had re-visited the spot where he'd been created. It was a kind of tradition now and Julie thought that one day, when he was old enough, she might actually tell Nathan this.

Danny caught all this and more in the two seconds or so that it took Julie to realise that her day-dreaming of the warmth she'd felt that cold night four and three-quarter years ago had somehow put her in mortal danger. As Julie protested that something that good surely couldn't lead to something this bad, and tried to deny what her eyes were showing her, terror rapidly filled her.

This can't be! she thought and Danny's link with her was terminated.

Ten feet away from him, Julie Walker's mouth dropped open and her aching body went rigid.

Like a loose hosepipe spraying high pressure water, Danny's psychic link serpentined across the scene and whipped through the air. It passed through Julie's children and he knew that the girl in the pushchair was sleeping. She was two and her name was Judith and she was dreaming of a cat named Bagpuss. In her dream Bagpuss was telling her secret things. Four-year-old Nathan who had opened many presents and cards this morning and who was looking forward to opening some more when Grandma came round later on, wasn't scared at all. He was confused and getting impatient. This was a new and interesting experience for him. In his short life he'd seen nothing like it before and he badly wanted to know what those men were doing. But, as usual, his mummy wasn't telling him. If there was a major fault with his mummy, it was that she often took a very long time to respond to the questions that teemed non-stop through his mind for most of his waking hours. Nathan did not mentally verbalise this thought, but he did feel the familiar frustration and he reverted to the only method he knew which might alleviate the feeling. Sometimes it worked, sometimes it didn't, but it was the only way he knew.

Nathan asked the question again, louder this time.

Out of control, Danny's link snaked over to one of the can-opening team. He was currently overdosing on adrenaline and reaching for the sawn-off pump action shotgun which lay in the boot of the car. This man's name was Trevor Watts and he was again burning on the short fuse which had caused him to needlessly terminate the lives of the Securicor driver and his mate. Watts pumped the shotgun and raised it at Julie Walker, because she was a problem and a problem shot was a problem that would often go away.

Danny was thrown violently out of Watts and back into himself, knowing that Julie Walker's plans for a romantic evening with Mike when the kids were asleep was not going to happen. Mike would doubtless spend the night telling himself the same three words his wife had thought: *This can't be!*

In front of Danny, great minds were thinking alike and Phil McFarlane and Geoff Ridge were raising their weapons too. He understood that, kids in tow or not, no one was going to make Julie an offer. These men had caught Watts' madness and life had suddenly become very cheap.

'DON'T!' Danny shouted.

Julie Walker stood frozen in place, her mouth dangling.

'Get down!' Danny shouted, mentally commanding her to hit the deck at the same time.

Phil McFarlane's finger tightened on the trigger.

The gun cracked.

Julie Walker caught the .22 slug in her midriff. Blood appeared on the front of her blue dress. Her mouth snapped shut and she looked down at the wound in surprise.

Nathan began to wail.

Judith woke up and looked blearily about her, frowning slightly.

Trevor Watts screamed and the shotgun blasted. Judith took the cloud of twelve-gauge shot in the side of her pretty head. As she swung away with the force of the blast, her pushchair toppled over and her mother was sprayed with her blood. Watts pumped and fired again. Nathan was driven violently backwards over the toppled pushchair, his chest open and gouting blood. His head whipped back and hit the wall behind the pavement with a horrendous force. It sounded like someone hitting a golf ball for a long distance with a wood.

Julie Walker's paralysis left her and she shook her head in small movements. *This can't be!* she would be thinking, Danny knew. Her face was a picture of dull realisation. She started to walk woodenly towards the thieves, her lips working soundlessly as the patch of blood on her dress spread.

'Stop it!' Danny screamed.

'My kids,' Julie said in a flat, horrified voice. 'You killed my kids. My children are. . .'

Ridge squeezed the trigger of his .38. The gun boomed and a fair-sized portion of Julie Walker's right shoulder blew away. Julie twisted from the waist, steadied herself and kept on coming, her right arm dangling limply at her side. 'My kids,' she said again.

McFarlane shot her again with the .22, putting a gouge across her left cheek and removing her earlobe. Julie flicked her head as if removing a bothersome fly and kept right on coming.

'FALL DOWN! WHY DON'T YOU FALL DOWN!' Ridge shouted and fired again. A chunk flew out of Julie's ribs, but her legs kept her up and kept her walking.

The next shot from the .22 took Julie's left eye, knocking it in pieces from her face. Julie staggered, no longer sure which direction she was facing.

'My children,' she said, presenting her profile, and her teeth exploded from her mouth as the next .38 slug hit her.

Still she didn't go down, just stood there swaying from side to side, her left arm held up as if reaching for a lifeline and tottering slightly as each fresh chunk of her body was blasted away. Julie took an uncertain step forward, her broken mouth still accusing. A .38 slug passed through her neck and severed her carotid artery. Blood jetted from the hole in great gouts, but Julie didn't go down. The next shot removed three of the fingers from her outstretched hand, then there was silence as Watts walked towards her.

Danny could hear the hiss of the blood jetting from Julie's neck and Julie was sagging badly now, her body was crumpling down on her pelvis and her legs were splayed and there surely couldn't have been any blood left in her, but she would not go down.

Danny heard Watts pump the gun and he mentally screamed, *Why don't you just leave her alone! She's dead now. LEAVE HER ALONE!*

Watts stood in front of Julie for a second, staring into her remaining eye and apparently not liking what he saw. He raised the shotgun, held it about six inches in front of Julie's face and pulled the trigger.

Julie's face vaporised, her head snapped back and she crashed to the ground.

'Bitch!' Watts grunted and abruptly turned away from her.

8

And now you know, old Dan, old Magical Mystic of the West, don't you? Danny asked himself. *Do you feel better for knowing?*

Danny didn't. The only thing he could think of that might possibly make him feel better was a little do-it-yourself brain surgery with his Black & Decker drill.

The crystal was washed, packed away and hidden in the attic under the ancient annuals once more. The puking and the crying had been done, the level of liquid in the whisky bottle had fallen and now there was only the thinking to be done. And Danny did not want to do it now the appalling nature of the dilemma which faced him had been discovered.

He thought that if God was up there watching him, he must have an extremely perverse and vicious sense of humour. Either that or his subject, Little Danny Stafford, had displeased him most severely.

The Bad Future held an exquisite irony which could be summed up roughly like this: Curiosity Killed the Cat.

The painful fact was that Danny had drawn himself into the Bad Future by giving in to his itching palms and using the little glass bastard. If he'd left the thing in the attic where it belonged he wouldn't have had the *après* rape vision of Suzie and he wouldn't have looked again to see how it had happened and seen the robbery. Which meant that, like the rest of the population (with the exclusion of the criminals themselves), he wouldn't have known when the robbery was going to happen or what was going to happen during it.

But he *had* looked. And now he knew, he couldn't *un-know* it again. And because he couldn't un-know it, he had drawn himself into the picture. He was now going to be forced to stop the robbery taking place and although the consequences of *that* action would save the lives of the three Securicor men, The Twinnies and three-quarters of the family Walker – eight people in all – it would also lead to Suzie's torture and rape by the members of the gang that would get away, and the end of his relationship with her.

A prime case of curiosity killing the cat if ever there was one, Danny thought bitterly.

'You could just forget all about it,' he told himself as he began to prepare the evening meal. He had no appetite whatsoever, but Suzie would be home soon and she would be ravenous as usual. Things were bad enough between them already without his making them worse.

Ha ha, Danny, good joke, he thought. *Old Dan doesn't want to make things worse. You already did that this afternoon. You made things worse all right. You've just got Suzie an appointment for a gang rape. And that's a dead cert because there is no way you can just forget all about what you've seen.*

'What's worse?' he asked aloud. 'Knowing that Suzie's going to get tortured and raped and then throw you out, or knowing that eight strangers are going to die?'

And for a few minutes he thought that what would happen to him and Suzie would be worse. That, he would have to live with; the death of the Walker family would only have to be lived with by husband Mike and whatever relatives were still alive. The Securicor people and the van-driving twins should all have known what dangerous jobs they were in when they signed up for them.

Then a picture of Julie Walker lit up in his mind. Julie Walker's tiny horrified voice accusing the robbers of shooting her kids while those same robbers stood there and blasted chunks of her away. Danny knew he would never be able to live with the guilt of having known it was going to happen and having done nothing to prevent it.

But can you live with the guilt of knowing what will happen to Suzie?

He didn't know. All he knew was this was his problem and it wasn't going to go away. Danny Stafford was going to have to make this particularly nasty decision. Not God who got paid for the job, and not Satan who did it for fun, but little old Danny Stafford, The Man With The Power. The power of life and death.

Not for the first time in his life, Danny cursed his mother for gaily telling his brother to shoot him instead of her. He raged at God and his unwanted girlfriend Lady Luck, he cursed his brother for doing the dirty deed and he swore at Lerner, wherever he was. None of this changed the situation.

'Let me swap!' he pleaded, looking out of the kitchen window at the clear blue sky where God might be lurking. 'Just take it all off my shoulders and I'll change places with Julie Walker and her kids. I'll walk up Kingsclere Road on September the 9th instead of them. Just take it off me and I'll do it!'

9

When it came, two days later, the final decision was based on common sense.

If you can call that common sense, Danny told himself, and found that he couldn't. He preferred the phrase 'the lesser of two evils'. Whatever you called it, it was agonising and he still wished he didn't have to do it.

He had reached his decision by removing pain, fear, guilt and any lasting psychological effects from the equation and simply counting lives. If he did nothing, eight lives would be lost. If he stopped the robbery, the maximum amount of lives that could possibly be lost were two: his and Suzie's. He didn't feel good about making himself responsible for Suzie's life, but he didn't care about his own and he didn't believe Suzie would be killed anyway.

But the Nightmare Scenario was two lives against eight.

And one choice would have left him eight lives in the red.

When you looked at it like that, there *was* no choice.

Danny would tip off the police.

Chapter Thirteen
Brutality, Rape and Broken Hearts

1

The number of days between the moment Danny made his mind up and time he would have to phone the police and spill the beans seemed endless, and now he'd made his decision Danny felt some measure of relief.

This was not merely because he had decided on a course of action, but also because that same evening, while he was pushing his food around his plate, not wanting to put any in his mouth because he knew it would make him gag, Suzie had asked him what was wrong. Danny had looked up and was surprised to see concern on her face. It was not the fright of a woman who had just looked into his eyes and seen Bad News lurking there, but the concern of a woman who cared about him and cared deeply. And in that moment Danny realised two things. The first was that their relationship had drifted as far as Suzie was prepared to let it go and therefore it was salvageable, and the second was a bright kind of revelation.

It doesn't have to happen to her! he thought. *There might just be a way out!*

And that was all there was. Danny did not know what the way out might have been. He was certain this information existed somewhere inside his head, but it wasn't coming out to play just yet.

But like the concern on Suzie's face, it was another slender ray of hopeful sunshine breaking through a vast grey covering of cloud.

'I'm okay,' he said, shrugging and breaking eye-contact quickly enough to ensure Suzie knew he wasn't okay at all.

'You haven't eaten anything,' she said awkwardly. The tone of her voice carried the message: *Please don't cut me dead, I'm doing the best I can to re-establish contact and I'm worried about you.*

'I'm not hungry,' Danny said, and shrugged again, smiling wanly.

Suzie looked at him, her eyes checking the signals. 'Oh,' she said. 'What kind of a day did you have?'

Danny nodded. *I saw eight people die and I saw what you will look like after you've been gang raped and tortured*, he thought and said,

'Okay, I s'pose. Nothing much happened.'

There might just be a way out.

'I've been busy,' Suzie volunteered. The message in her voice said: *Please talk to me, Danny. I need help.*

What is that way, Dan? 'Oh, yeah? What happened?'

'The mainframe hung up, Jolie Sanderson fell down most of the stairs from the tenth floor to the ninth and broke her pelvis, and Oliver Wase had a row with the big noises and quit. A busy day.'

Oliver Wase was Suzie's boss. 'Why did old Olly pack it in?' he asked, grabbing the line she threw. He knew Olly and liked him. *Everyone* liked Olly. *Come on!* he commanded his secretive brain, *What's the way out?*

'No one knows,' Suzie said, and for a moment Danny thought she was referring to what he was thinking. 'But they've been demanding too much and slashing the budget – and you know Oliver, he's just a guy who can't say no. I suppose he couldn't stand it any longer. If he'd just put his foot down at the beginning he could have got what he wanted and everyone would have been happy.'

Danny nodded, still searching his mind for the elusive answer to his dilemma while another part of him was clinging desperately to the life line Suzie was struggling to draw in.

'They've offered me his job,' she said.

'They didn't try to get Olly to come back?'

Suzie nodded. 'But he wouldn't listen.'

'Will you take it?'

'Of course. Under certain conditions I've made clear. They buck up their ideas, I do Olly's job. They've agreed.'

'Great,' Danny said.

'And I think it calls for a little celebration,' Suzie said, watching him carefully. 'Will you come out with me?'

That night, in bed in the dark, Suzie reached over and held Danny's hand. It was the first time she had touched him in weeks. Danny cried silently, so that she wouldn't know.

2

Over the next few days Danny learned how Judas must have felt. In the evenings and at the weekend he slowly re-built his relationship with Suzie, cooking her exotic meals, bringing her flowers every other day, joking with her across the rapidly narrowing gap between them, and trying hard to be the Danny she'd fallen in love with all those years ago. It was awkward and hesitant at first but as the chasm closed to a crack, both of them started to thaw.

And during the daytimes Danny snuck the crystal down from the attic and looked at Suzie's raped and battered body as he tried to discover what the *way out* might just have been.

Whatever the magical answer was, it couldn't be found by flinging himself into the little glass bastard. In order to prevent the attack on Suzie, he needed to know its date – and if possible, how the thieves had found his address – but he could discover neither of these facts. Each time Danny used the crystal, he found himself at the same event – the day of Suzie's rape – and each time he was unable to discover the date. He tried to send himself to different days, hoping to find out the date by a process of elimination, but regardless of where he made up his mind to go, he always found himself at the same scene and the date was never revealed. And the same scene extended all the way through from futures one to five. The ones beyond future five were hazy; nothing more than blank canvases, each showing only a few preliminary daubs of fate's paint.

And Danny knew that these futures were waiting. They were, in fact, *his* futures, waiting for *him*. These were the blanks that could be beautifully painted by his own hand and turned into future one. Any of these could be carefully shaped into a *good* future . . . if only he could remember what the way out might have been for Suzie.

But Danny couldn't remember, and since he couldn't (and had decided not to tell the police until he could) there were no alternate futures to look into. He finally realised that there was a major turning point here and it depended entirely on his own actions. As the days ticked by, the alternate futures remained static, waiting for him to act. This was the reason he could not see beyond the attack on Suzie.

Danny was now responsible, not just for Suzie's future, but for his own.

Finally, he packed the crystal away, shoved the whole situation forcefully to one side and relaxed for a few days while he let his arid mind lie fallow. Hopefully it would become fertile again. There was still plenty of time.

3

Two days before the robbery he'd predicted, and the day before he would either tip off the police or allow eight deaths to happen, Danny found himself sitting across a desk from an elderly, white-haired, bespectacled woman with a friendly face. There was a microfiche machine set on the table to one side and there were glowing amber words on the screen which swum before Danny's eyes.

'. . . happened back in nineteen oh three?' Danny had just heard himself ask. His mind had suddenly turned itself on in mid-sentence as though someone had just snapped its switch. He felt a dull, aching panic and for a few seconds his head spun sickeningly. He did not know where he was, who he was talking to (or what about) and had no recollection whatsoever of getting here or why he had come.

'That's right,' the woman said, now studying his face and frowning. 'Are you okay?

You don't have to tell them! Danny thought dizzily and didn't understand. He followed this by thinking, *There's only one of her, and what don't you have to tell her?*

Danny looked at his watch. It was twenty past two. What did *that* mean? *Nothing, except you can't remember the time before you were turned off. Have you been conscious at all today? I don't think so. You might have been out for days, Dan.*

'What day is it now?' he asked anxiously, glancing quickly around him and realising he was in a large, quiet building filled with book shelves. *Library*! It was not Basingstoke library though and Danny had to fight off a strong urge to follow his last question by demanding to know where the fuck he was.

'Still Tuesday,' the woman – *the librarian* – replied. 'And it was, in fact, a Tuesday when it happened. Today's date. Ninety years ago to the day. I thought you knew. I thought that's why you'd come all the way to Camberley today.'

Camberley! Danny realised, his mind instantly filling with questions. 'It's not far,' he said, trying not to look frightened or sound confused. The librarian was already frowning and if he wasn't careful she would soon be backing away with that familiar look of fear in her eyes. After which the police might be phoned and Danny would not be able to account for his movements today. 'It's only twenty minutes or so,' he smiled.

'Longer on foot though,' the librarian said, still frowning.

Danny's hand stole into his jacket pocket, feeling for his car keys. They were not present. *You walked*, he told himself. *Or hitched. You've certainly told this woman one of those two things*. He began to wonder what he might have done during the journey. He had no idea how long it had taken and no memory of today at all. The last thing he remembered was dropping off to sleep last night after having made love to Suzie for the first time since their relationship began to crumble. *That was last night, wasn't it? If this is Tuesday, yes, it was.*

Danny shrugged. 'No problem,' he replied, smiling. 'I got a lift the moment I stuck out my thumb. Brought me almost to the door. Lucky, I s'pose.'

The librarian's face lightened somewhat. She seemed satisfied with this response and Danny supposed he'd already told her he'd hitched.

'So why did you want to know?' she asked, looking at him over the top of her glasses.

You don't have to tell them! Danny thought, and again wondered who he didn't have to tell what to. Worse than that, he had no idea to what the librarian was referring. Whatever it was, it had happened in nineteen hundred and three and apparently he'd hitched here this morning to find out about it. 'Just curiosity,' he said evasively.

'Is it research for a book?' the librarian asked coyly. *You can tell me in confidence*, her expression said. *I won't pass it on so that someone else can beat you to the press with the idea, and maybe I'll get a credit in the preface*.

Danny glanced back at the glowing screen and remembered the snap of the switch and the flicker of light as the librarian had turned the machine on. That was the moment he had become conscious and she'd just outlined the story for him after coming back with the microfiche plate. *It happened in nineteen oh three!* Danny told himself and suddenly realised why he'd come to Camberley.

He was here to find out about the murder he'd had the vision of when he was in Frimley hospital all those years ago.

The memory of that vision suddenly broke out of the vault Danny's mind had constructed around it all those years ago and everything came rushing back to him. The sensation of the wet grass under his feet, the sound of the stream splashing and singing as it passed over stones. The rabbit dashing across the field. The smell of blood as the man – Leonard Elroy, it said on the microfiche screen, but the woman had called him Lenny – cut off the woman's clothes and pounded into her. The knife being punched into the girl's throat. *Twenty-one-year old Amy Carless' throat*, he corrected himself. The way the blood had spewed from the wound; the way Amy's teeth had smashed when Lenny plunged the knife into her mouth.

Why did you want to know this, old Dan? he asked himself, as horror chased away his disorientation. *Why did you want to remember?*

'Lhuhnee! I lhuuv yhou!' the badly damaged Amy Carless screamed in his mind, and suddenly the word Lenny sounded a little too much like Danny.

What plans do you have, old Dan? he asked himself.

'Is it?' the librarian asked again.

You don't have to tell them!

'What?' he asked.

'For a book. About murders.'

Danny nodded. 'Yes.'

The librarian seemed satisfied and got up. 'I'll leave you to read the report now. Any further help I can be to you, I'll be only too glad. . .'

'Thanks,' Danny said, relieved that she wasn't going to ask more questions about his intentions. He didn't *have* any intentions. Those belonged to the part of him that had woken up this morning in the driving seat.

Danny fought off the urge to run from the library and forced himself to read the remainder of the ninety-year-old newspaper report from the microfiche screen.

Lenny Elroy had murdered Amy Carless on the site of the hospital where Danny had been taken after his brother shot him. This was no surprise. The details of the crime, however, *were* surprising. Lenny was a sailor and Amy was his fiancee. They had intended to marry when Lenny came back from a trip to Haiti – the trip after which he murdered, rather than married her. The newspaper report gave an account of Lenny's trial and added hearsay evidence from some of the sailor's friends and acquaintances. Everyone said Lenny came back from Haiti a changed man. Something had happened to him there but, according to the paper, 'Mr Elroy said he did not have to tell them what it was'.

The similarity to the large and important thought that had been echoing in Danny's mind when he regained control over himself and became sentient again, struck an icy chill through him.

Some of Lenny's shipmates who had given evidence said that during the spell in Haiti Lenny had begun to act furtively, often disappearing from the ship during rest periods and staying out all night. Everyone thought he'd got himself a woman but some suggested the woman might have been involved in some sort of voodoo practice to which she had introduced him. Lenny had vanished two days before the ship was due to leave and shortly before it set sail was found wandering aimlessly round the harbour. He had become violent when picked up and had spent most of the return trip under lock and key. Various accounts followed, detailing Lenny's bouts of wild-eyed fear and rage in which he claimed 'he had been somewhere else' and now 'he could *see* right through people to what lay underneath'. Then, a week out of Portsmouth, Lenny had suddenly recovered. The ship's medical officer had reported a bout of hysteria due to possible infection and had pronounced him fit.

Amy's sister, who gave evidence during the trial, said that her sister had found Lenny to be 'changed somehow, as if haunted' and had constantly asked Lenny what was wrong, to which he had given the standard reply – the one he'd also used during the prosecution's cross-examination of him. He didn't have to tell them. Amy had refused Lenny's sexual advances 'because of the perverted things he seemed to intend' and had subsequently been dragged to the field, raped and murdered.

When asked why he had murdered Amy, Lenny had replied, 'Amy knew things'. When asked what it was Amy had known, his response was, 'I don't have to tell them'. Lenny had been found guilty of murder and hanged.

You don't have to tell them, Danny thought, telling himself he'd picked up those words from the screen. *But didn't the librarian say, 'I'll leave you to read the report?'*, he asked himself. *I think she did, old Dan. Which means you hadn't read it already and didn't pick them up that way.*

But he wasn't sure of this. His alter-ego – or whatever it was – might have glanced at the screen while the real Danny was still locked away in his blank mental prison. This didn't diminish the huge importance of Leonard Elroy's words though.

Danny read the report again, shut off the machine and crept out of the building when his friendly librarian was otherwise engaged.

He searched the nearby car parks for his car, almost certain he hadn't walked or hitched a lift here. His Gannex Man half probably wasn't used to driving and would simply have left the keys in the Humber's ignition.

Danny searched for a long time before he admitted to himself that his other part probably couldn't drive. The Humber was not in Camberley.

Danny walked the mile and a half to the A30 and stuck out his thumb.

4

Lenny Elroy's words came back to him as Jason Brown rocketed him through Hartley Wintney in excess of the thirty miles an hour speed limit to the tune of twenty-five. Jason Brown was a tall, electrical wholesaler's rep who wore a sharp suit and a spiv's moustache and drove like a maniac. He also talked endlessly in a peculiarly fractured manner.

'Ole Jase getted pulled by the law. Once. Going through here,' he confided.

You don't have to tell them, Danny thought. 'Yeah?' he replied.

'Right. Didn't do me, though. Fifty-three. Clocked me at,' Jason shook his head and turned to stare at Danny, grinning. 'Nah. Warning. S'all right!' he said.

'Good,' Danny said.

And Jason began to relate a long tale of how he'd gone through an amber traffic light and been hit in the side by a car jumping the lights the other way, but Danny was no longer listening because he suddenly understood the meaning of Lenny's words and his own thoughts and he was wondering how he could possibly have been so stupid as not to have realised it before. He thought he'd probably overlooked it because it was so ridiculously simple, but he still couldn't believe he was *that* stupid.

There was a way he could shape the future so that the robbery wouldn't happen and Suzie wouldn't have to pay by being raped and molested.

YOU DON'T HAVE TO TELL THEM!

'What say?' Jason asked, looking at him quizzically.

'I don't think I spoke,' Danny said.

Jason kicked the car down a gear and overtook the car in front, seemingly oblivious of the lorry approaching on the other side of the road. 'Oops!' he said as he swung viciously back into his own lane. 'Jasey boy didn't see that one. Oh no he didn't! Going blind, he is. What were you saying?'

'Nothing,'

He turned to Danny and nodded hard. 'Yeah. About not telling 'em. You were pleased about it or something.'

'I didn't speak,' Danny said, and kept his mind perfectly empty for the remainder of the journey.

It's going to be easy, Danny thought as he walked home from the bus station where Jason had dropped him. He was certain of that now. Everything was fixed and it was going to be okay because he didn't have to tell them. Meaning the police. He did have to tell them about the robbery, but he didn't have to tell them who or where he was. He could still make the tip-off but he would do it anonymously. And if no one knew Danny Stafford had foiled the attempt, no one was going to find out where he lived and come looking for him. Easy-peasy. Future changed in one fell swoop.

A nagging doubt remained, and that doubt insisted that Danny had never intended to supply the police with his name and address anyway and surely the future couldn't be *that* easy to alter? But he quickly squashed this one. Anonymity meant safety.

5

Danny phoned the police at midnight as Wednesday became Thursday. It was later than he had anticipated but he'd had to work hard on getting Suzie in bed and asleep before he did the deed, and that particular evening, she hadn't been at all tired. Danny had anticipated this and had bought a bottle of champagne, certain it would put her out for the count. Suzie could not be romanced with champagne. Whisky or brandy, yes, but bubbly sent her straight to sleep.

Except this particular evening it didn't; it put her in the mood for love. Love was duly made – without a huge amount of enthusiasm on Danny's part – but Suzie still wasn't sleepy. Danny mixed her next glass of champagne with a good measure of brandy and Suzie finally gave in.

She fell asleep at twenty past eleven and by half-past Danny was heading for the telephone kiosk in Oakridge shopping centre with a pocket full of ten pence pieces.

The sight of the empty row of shops made his heart sink and as he turned the corner to where the phones were, his adrenaline began to pump. The light-headedness his share of the champagne had given him wore off instantly, leaving a slight ache in its place. The phones were covered by a walkway formed where the upper storey flats bridged a gap in the row of shops and instead of being in boxes they were simply mounted at chest height on poles and cowled with aluminium surrounds. The three phones struck fear into Danny and he found he could not approach them, let alone pick one up and make the call.

They can't find out who you are! he told himself. *It's going to be all right. Nothing bad will happen!* he insisted, but a large part of him did not seem to believe this was true.

At ten to twelve he picked up one of the handsets, laid five ten pence pieces on the top of its cowl, watched as the message panel instructed him to insert his money, then replaced the handset. It felt wrong. Very wrong indeed.

'Wrong phone,' Danny said, and moved to another, feeling just as bad about it. There was dread building in him, his hands were trembling and his voice just wasn't going to carry the impact and urgency it should have.

He picked up the phone, fed the machine with thirty pence and punched out the number for the police station, wishing he could just go home and forget all about it. When the connection was made and he heard the ringing tone, he pictured the telephone at the other end of the line and saw the policeman's hand reaching out for it.

Danny replaced the receiver, a feeling of anxiety now mingling with his dread. 'Come on, you bastard, you can do it! You can!' he muttered and repeated the procedure.

It took three more attempts before he made himself go through with it.

The phone was answered on the third ring. The call box's display altered and informed him he had twenty pence left to play with.

'Basingstoke police station,' a bored professional voice said. 'How can I be of assistance?'

For a moment Danny's voice wouldn't work.

'Hello?' the policeman said.

'Uhh . . . hello,' Danny managed. 'I . . . uh . . . want to talk to someone about a robbery that is going to take place tomorrow morning,' he said, his voice shot through with what sounded like terror – *and probably is, old Dan.*

'Hold on,' the voice said, now not quite as bored. 'I'm putting you through to one of our detectives.'

The line clicked and the next voice spoke almost instantly. There was just enough time for Danny to wonder whether some kind of recording apparatus had been switched on before the detective said, 'D.S. Murphy, C.I.D. What's the problem?' Detective Sergeant Murphy managed to sound sharply intelligent, brisk, businesslike and very suspicious all at the same time.

Danny took a deep shuddering breath. 'I'm phoning to warn you there is going to be a robbery tomorrow. A number of thieves are going to raid a Securicor van in Kingsclere Road.' *There it goes*, he thought. *There's no turning back! It's too late to stop now!*

'Uh huh,' D.S. Murphy said, and Danny pictured him nodding. 'You're in a call booth, aren't you?' the detective asked suddenly. 'What's your phone number? I may need to call you back.'

Gotcha! Danny thought and smiled grimly, his heartbeat speeding up. Old D.S. would have to work harder than that to catch him out.

'Sorry, I can't tell you,' he said primly. 'And if I hear any clicks or strange noises which sound to me as if you're starting to trace this call, I'll ring off immediately.'

'Okay, calm down, we won't try and trace you,' the detective said, sounding faintly amused, 'it wouldn't be possible anyway.' Then he slipped in another. 'What did you say your name was?'

No names, no pack drill, now don't fuck it up! Danny thought. *This guy is thin ice to skate on, he wants to trip you up and have you plunge into the freezing water and he's good at his job. He's done this before and you haven't. Be careful!*

'I didn't,' Danny said, 'and I won't, but you can call me Murphy after yourself. If you like.'

Ten pence left now, the machine stated.

'Tell me about the crime you think is going to be committed,' Murphy said.

Danny took a piece of paper from his pocket. On it he had written down the names and descriptions of the thieves, the types of weapons they would be carrying, the car and van registration numbers, the time of the planned robbery and the method. He read all this information to D.S. Murphy in a flat voice.

Three ten pence pieces later, the detective knew everything Danny did except what would happen if the robbery was allowed to proceed.

The insert-more-money sign came up and Danny fed the telephone.

'Do you have any more change or would you like me to ring you back?' Murphy enquired.

'I can manage,' Danny said.

'I'm sure you can. Might I ask how you came by this information?'

Danny was ready for this one, too. 'I overheard it in a pub,' he lied. It was a good lie. Danny knew which pub it had happened in, how hard he'd had to strain to bear the men's voices, who else had been there, what time it was. He intended to tell the detective none of this though. It was simply there for his own confidence.

'You were very close to them then, weren't you?' Murphy asked in a disbelieving – almost incredulous – tone. 'How come they didn't notice you eavesdropping?'

'I have very good hearing,' Danny replied. 'I didn't have to get that close.'

'Oh, yeah?' Murphy replied, his voice now wearily cynical. 'Are you sure you're not feeding me a lorry-load of bullshit?'

For the first time in the conversation Danny was shaken. For the first time in an age someone had not fallen for one of his lies. 'How do you mean?' he heard himself ask in a surprised voice.

'Look, son, I know a crock of shit when someone pours it into my ear. And someone has done just that. That someone is you, in case you were wondering. It's gob-shite, son.'

In that moment Danny saw it all drifting away from him and panicked. The question, 'What if they don't believe me?' had somehow – magically, perhaps – not occurred to him until now. 'No!' he yelled. 'It's the truth!'

And, amazingly, D.S. Murphy did not argue. He said, very quietly, 'Are you a member of this gang, shitting out at the last moment?'

Danny was lost now, his head spinning. This wasn't turning out the way he had anticipated at all. 'I'm nothing to do with it,' he said.

'It has been known,' Murphy replied. 'Level with me, son, you didn't overhear all this detail in a pub conversation – I caught that fib as it left your lips – and I have a distinct feeling you're telling the truth when you say you're not a gang member, so where does that leave me? It leaves me wondering about all the other shite. It doesn't hang together, you see. If you're telling the truth, where, oh where, did you come by so much detail?'

Danny drew a ragged breath and spoke the words of Leonard Elroy. 'I don't have to tell you.'

Murphy thought about it for a long time. 'No, I suppose you don't,' he said thoughtfully. 'But why should I believe one part when the other part is obviously a lie?'

'*Because it's the truth!*' Danny yelled.

Then there was silence. According to the payphone's display it lasted for eight pence – however long that was. It was long enough for Danny to realise that no attempt was being made to trace the call and that was because no one thought it was worth it. Apparently D.S. Murphy didn't believe any of the story at all.

'Well, thank you for your information,' he finally said. 'These men are known to us. We'll look into it.'

Danny's mind rolled and his motormouth took charge. 'No!' it shouted on his behalf. '*Don't look into it. DO SOMETHING! STOP IT FROM HAPPENING!*'

'Calm down, Mister, uhh. . .'

A part of Danny saw the trap, looming like a tunnel. This part knew what was coming next, but this part didn't currently have control over his speech. This part of him screamed inwardly and instantly grabbed for the reins. But it was too late – even to fudge the sound.

'Stafford,' his motormouth said.

The word tripped off his tongue and toppled down the mouthpiece. Danny staggered, thinking he would faint, while the alert part of him mentally tried to reverse the direction of time in order to grab the word back or make it incomprehensible. Nothing happened. The word was gone. Right down the wire and into Murphy's ear from where it could never be retrieved or extracted.

For a swooning moment Danny goggled in horror at the distorted reflection gazing darkly back at him from the Oakridge chippie's plate glass window. That staggering goon with the dangling lower jaw and the look of total horror on his face was the grade-A fucking idiot called Danny Stafford who had just done the very thing he'd sworn to himself he would not do. There was a guy who had just written the future for himself and his innocent girlfriend. A future in which the forthcoming attractions were brutality, rape and broken hearts.

Danny watched his reflection's mouth snap shut and his body straighten. 'Stafford McKenzie,' he heard himself say in a last ditch attempt to rectify the situation. It did not sound remotely convincing.

'Well, thanks, Mister Stafford . . . uh . . . McKenzie,' the detective said. 'I'll get on to this straight away. I don't know *why* I will and I'm mystified by how you know so much, but I'm inclined to take you seriously. So thanks for the information. No doubt we'll be in touch.'

'I don't think so,' Danny said, hoping to muddy the situation a little further, 'I just gave you a false name.'

Murphy chuckled. 'I know *exactly* what you did, believe me,' he said. 'But I won't tell if you don't.'

'Thanks,' Danny said, suddenly wanting to vomit.

'Goodbye, Mister McKenzie.'

Wishing many things, the foremost of which was that he was dead, Danny replaced the handset, ran to the gutter and threw up.

6

Danny spent the following morning fighting an aching need to make the two hundred-yard walk across the Holy Ghost ruins and peer down into Kingsclere Road from the bank where he would be able to see the robbery either taking place or being foiled. To be present might endanger him – either from a random shot or by identification by the police or the criminals – so he sat in the house with all the windows open, listening for the sound of gunshots.

There was a single bang just before the correct time and Danny tensed, waiting for more. There were none and he began to believe it was nothing more sinister than a car backfiring. There was no other noise – no distant shouting, no squealing of tyres or revving engines – not in the morning or in the early afternoon. When Danny's will finally broke at two-thirty, he put on a coat and went to the junction of Kingsclere Road and Sherbourne Road to look for evidence. He walked up and down the length of road where the robbery was supposed to happen but there was nothing to see – no tyre marks, no spent cartridges, no scrapes under the bridge where a high-sided van might have become stuck. *Maybe*, Danny thought as he walked slowly home, *I got the day wrong. Maybe it's next Thursday or the Thursday after*.

But he had not been wrong. The three o'clock news on Radio 210 confirmed that a robbery attempt had been foiled in Basingstoke, and on both the local and national news that evening Danny watched Detective Sergeant Peter Murphy telling news teams how 'acting on information supplied by a worried member of the public' they had foiled the robbery but had only managed to capture two of the thieves. Murphy was a lot older than he'd sounded on the phone; around fifty, stocky and balding. He sported a black eye where one of the crooks had hit him but he looked happy. There was, he explained, a constable in hospital with shotgun wounds to the leg, but the injuries were merely superficial. The picture cut to photographs of the six men still at large, while Murphy named then and warned that they should not be approached because they were armed and extremely dangerous.

'What are you grinning at?' Suzie wanted to know.

'Nothing,' Danny said, thinking of Julie Walker and her kids, not now lying in some morgue but probably celebrating Nathan's birthday while Julie plotted her romantic evening with Mike. It was a moment of triumph Danny could not share and on its own it would have been enough, but there was more: Detective Sergeant Peter Murphy – soon to become Detective Inspector, or whatever the next rung up the ladder was, Danny was certain – had an air of integrity about him. He looked totally trustworthy. Murphy had seen through Danny's lies and undoubtedly knew his surname was Stafford, but Danny believed the man when he'd promised not to tell. And if Murphy didn't tell, there was no way the escaped criminals could trace Danny.

His feeling of confidence got another boost the following morning when he picked up the *Gazette* and read the front page. The newspaper report assumed that another underworld figure had learned of the robbery and grassed on his enemies.

You did it, old Dan! he congratulated himself.

And this good feeling lasted until precisely nine-thirty-two on the following Monday.

That was when Tim Gould came knocking at the door.

7

'Mr Stafford?'

Danny didn't like the look of the man. He was in his very early twenties, had cropped blond hair and large, wire-framed glasses behind which cold blue eyes glinted.

'Who wants to know?'

The man took his hand from his right hand jacket pocket and held it out in front of Danny. There was something bulky in that pocket where the hand had been and Danny got the distinct impression it was a dictation tape recorder.

'Tim Gould, from *The Comet*, Southampton,' he said. 'I've come to ask you how you knew about the robbery. You tipped off the police, I believe.'

Danny felt the blood rush away from his face and hoped – but doubted – that Tim Gould hadn't noticed it. He drew his face into a puzzled frown, took the man's hand, held it tightly and closed his eyes whilst pumping it. 'Robbery?' he asked as he learned about Gould. *The Comet*, he learned, was a small, but rapidly expanding local paper which specialised in exposing frauds, liars, cheats and underhand councillors. Tim Gould was its star reporter and a man who strongly believed he deserved better. Tim Gould wanted to work for the national press and was marking time and honing his talent for the great day when he got that proper job. Tim Gould was intent on making a name for himself and didn't much care how he went about it. His motto 'Publish and Fuck 'Em' had brought the paper three writs for libel in the last three months. It had also increased circulation by a factor of fifteen.

Gould thought he was on to a very big one indeed this time. He had spent a great many hours on the phone over the weekend speaking to his extensive network of underworld contacts and he had come up trumps. On his behalf, a friend was currently negotiating with the escaped robbers for an exclusive Tim Gould interview. Gould had also learned during the weekend from a contact in the Basingstoke police force, who had overheard that the informant who had pulled the plug on the robbers may or may not have been named Stafford McKenzie. There were twelve S. McKenzies in the Guildford area phone book, six M. Staffords and Gould had visited them all during the weekend. Gould was currently working his way down the list of Basingstoke Staffords and McKenzies and was doorstepping them all with the same accusation. Now he thought he'd struck lucky.

'Last Thursday,' Gould explained when Danny dropped his hand. 'The foiled one. The police got their information from you.'

Danny grinned tightly. 'I think you're mistaken,' he said.

Gould shook his head. 'Nope. Don't think so. It was you. Come clean, guy. My paper pays good for exclusives.'

'You're wrong, *guy!*' Danny said.

Gould shrugged. 'Probably ten grand in it.'

'If I knew anything, I'd sell it to you,' Danny said.

'Then please do!'

'It wasn't me.'

Gould grinned. 'It's you all right, guy. D. Stafford, that's you, that's the one! What is that guy, Derek? Dave? Duncan?'

'What does it matter?'

'I like to get the names straight in my pieces.'

'Get this straight,' Danny said, starting to boil, 'I have no idea how you got my address – but I suspect you chose it at random from a phone book – I've got no idea why you think I had something to do with a foiled robbery rather than any of the other people you've undoubtedly accused of the same thing, and I'm getting a little weeny bit pissed off with you. If you don't go away quickly, I'm likely to become violent.'

'Black belt, sixth dan. Karate,' Gould said. 'Don't fuck with me and I won't fuck with you. They said the guy's name was Stafford, *your* name is Stafford, and I'll get my story whether you like it or not.'

'Mr Gould, I'm about to fuck with you. I am the wrong Stafford. Go away.'

But Tim Gould didn't give up that easily.

He knows it's me, Danny thought desperately. I don't know how he does, but he's certain now if he wasn't a moment ago. Which means that you really did write your own future. This man standing in front of you will relay your name – and probably your address – to those six criminals still at large as a part payment for his interview with them. That's how it's going to work. D.S. Murphy might have been as good as his word but someone else either overheard his conversation with you or looked at his notepad afterwards. And this is what follows. And short of killing him, there isn't a damn' thing you can do.

Danny balled his fist and snapped it square into black-belt-sixth-dan Tim Gould's grinning mouth. Gould's teeth buckled just like any normal person's would have done and he fell over in a rigid fashion – rather like a felled tree – which surely wasn't how they taught you to fall in karate classes.

Gould looked up at Danny dopily. Both his lips were split and bleeding badly and one of his top teeth was missing – presumably swallowed. For the moment, at least, Danny felt better. A lot better.

'I fucked with you,' Danny said, glancing down at the tooth-shaped marks on his knuckles. 'If you get up before I've closed the door, I intend to fuck with you again. If you knock on my door ever again, I'm quite prepared to fuck with you some more. If you ring me or publish allegations that I was involved with your robbery, I will not resort to litigation – I will come looking for you with the express intention of giving you the biggest fucking of your life, black-belt-sixth-dan or not. Do I make myself clear?'

'Very,' Gould said, except the word came out 'wewwy'.

Danny went back inside and slammed the door.

8

Tim Gould was as good as his word. Danny took out a subscription to *The Comet* and throughout September and October, there was no mention of the robbery and no advertisement that the paper's drooling readers would shortly be able to peer into the minds of men who made a living from armed robbery.

There was a time as the nights grew longer and October turned to November when Danny thought it was all over and done with. He hadn't had a blank spell since that time in Camberley's library, the crystal hadn't called for him, and he was back on an even keel with Suzie.

Then, on November the 4th, Danny's dreams of a permanent return to normality were shattered.

That was when he found himself staring at his front door from the outside.

This was wrong for very many reasons. The first and most important was that it was dark and Danny didn't leave Suzie on her own at night any more; hadn't, in fact, since the day he'd slugged Tim Gould in the mouth. The next reason was that he had no recollection of having gone out and he had no idea where he might have been. He tried to remember what day it was and found he couldn't do that either. The blank spells had come back.

Danny thought he knew what this unexpected fugue might have coincided with and his heart began to batter his ribs as he got the door key from his pocket.

They got her! his mind began to yammer. *They got her they got her they got her!*

His suddenly trembling hand couldn't make the key fit in the lock. *Don't let anything have happened to Suzie!* he thought as the other part of him screamed that they'd got her. *Oh please God, don't let them have come!*

But Gould had bargained for his interview and they *had* come. A glance into the lounge confirmed that. It was the lounge of his vision, wrecked and charred. Danny knew there was a time-travelling Danny from the past now squirming inside his head but he couldn't think about it now. He could barely *think*.

He needs to know the date! a distant part of him thought, but Danny didn't know what date it was. And it didn't even matter now. None of this could be changed retrospectively, could it? If it was happening now, it couldn't suddenly *unhappen*. He glanced at the sticks which had once been the coffee table; the stuffing spewing sofa and the charred carpet, and his mind rolled in confusion while panic built in him and distilled into a cold, numb dread.

'SUZIE!' he heard his voice scream just as it had in his vision. He turned to face the door on leaden legs he remembered well.

Moaning over and over that he was sorry, Danny ran upstairs to where he knew Suzie was huddled on the bed. He already knew – to the last terrible detail – what he would find. Already knew the words that would be spoken, the emotions he would feel. It was like suddenly having to live out a film you'd seen twenty or thirty times. He felt drained and numb but there was still room in him for the cutting edge of his guilt and he knew there would be room for plenty more.

Danny burst through the bedroom door, glanced at the mess of torn bedclothes feathers, blood and stuffing and thought, *This is all your fault! This is the consequence of all your good work!*

Suzie was huddled on the bed, naked, battered bleeding and defiled as she rocked back and forth clutching the remains of her pie-jam top to her. Danny distantly realised you didn't get the full effect in the visions. In real life it was worse. Much worse.

Suzie looked up at him with a terrible expression of hurt in her bruised eyes and again, Danny could barely believe the beating they'd given her.

'Oh my God!' he heard himself say.

Suzie looked slowly up at him. 'They raped me,' she said in a distant, beaten voice that was so quiet it could barely be heard. She shook her head as if she still couldn't believe what had happened. 'I . . . I opened the door and they . . . just burst in. They . . . they wanted to know where you wuh-were,' she sobbed. 'They said they wuh-were going to castrate you. Oh God Duh-hanny, where wuh-her you? I wanted to tuh-tell them but I didn't know. They beat me up duh-Danny, to make me tell. They huh-hit me until I *wet* myself. Then they ruh-raped me. Fuh-four of them. They raped me and made me suh-suck them and buh-buh-*buggered* me. And they kept on and on and on.' Her fingers went to her neck. 'Then they chu-choked me with a rope until I bluh-blacked out. Whu-when I came round one of them was buh-buggering me again *with an empty Coke bottle*. He suh . . . he suh-said he wanted to see how far in it would guh-go.'

'Oh Suze,' Danny said and went towards her, stopping as she shrank back from him.

'Don't come near me,' Suzie said. A sob caught in her throat and her chest hitched. 'I d-don't want you near me,' she sobbed. 'Not now, nuh-n-not ever again.'

Danny went to her, wanting to hold her and comfort her in spite of knowing what would happen next.

Suzie pulled back from him, then slapped him, hard.

Danny moved away, tears of hurt and dismay in his eyes.

'You knew, duh-didn't you?' Suzie whispered.

Danny said nothing.

'Answer me. You already knew, Danny, didn't you?'

'No Suzie,' he lied, shaking his head in emphasis and knowing she'd seen straight through the untruth.

'You saw it Danny, didn't you? You saw this future!' Suzie said, in a small, shocked voice. 'You already knew, you buh-bastard!'

'Suzie I. . .!'

Tears ran from Suzie's eyes. 'You betrayed me!' she sobbed. 'You *already knew*. You knew this would happen and you knew when.' Her voice rose slightly and its tone was as cold as the Arctic. 'You betrayed me Danny. You knew they were coming and you went out, you coward, so you wouldn't get hurt. So they'd get me while I was alone. I can't believe you did that, you bastard!'

'I didn't know . . . when . . . I mean . . . I . . . thought it wouldn't happen!' Danny insisted, his voice rising a note.

'Tell the truth Mister Psychic Seer!' Suzie hissed. 'Oh Danny, you knew it would happen! You fucking well *knew*!'

'I didn't know . . . when . . . I mean . . . I . . . thought it wouldn't happen!' Danny insisted, his voice rising a note, just as it had done in his vision.

She dropped the rags that had once been her pie-jams and showed him her bitten breasts. One of them had deep teeth marks and a distant part of Danny informed him that the guy who did that would be easy to identify from dental records.

'Look,' she said quietly, 'Look at what you've done to me,' and her words bit into him like whips. 'You knew they'd be coming and you let it happen. Why didn't you stop it? Why? Because you're a coward, that's why! How could you do this to me? *How could you know and still let it happen?*' Danny stumbled towards Suzie again, reaching for her.

'DON'T YOU TOUCH ME!' she shouted and he stopped in his tracks.

It's over, he realised with an aching finality. *It's all over*.

'Where was I?' Danny heard himself asking and was suddenly surprised because he hadn't intended to ask the question. This particular question – or one like it – came from a Danny Stafford of the past. The one who was currently sharing the inside of his head. The one that didn't yet know his motormouth was going to be the cause of all this. Danny wished his passenger from the past would just shut up and fuck off. There was no point in all this. It had already happened and the stupid bastard inside his head wasn't going to be able to change it.

'Where did I go?' his mouth said, and Danny knew this wasn't the important question for the past Danny, knew he should have been asking what day it was.

Suzie's face darkened. She winced and when she spoke there was fresh blood staining her teeth. 'Out! OUT! *You were hiding because you knew they were coming*!'

There was a foul up in the communication between them. Danny tried to ask what date it was and heard himself say, 'But where to? Where did I go?'

Suzie wiped tears and blood from her face. 'I don't know,' she moaned. 'Christ, I'm hurt. I can't think. Just get out and nuh-nuh-never come back.'

Danny heard the distant screaming inside his head and – for what little good it would eventually do – this time the question came out right. 'What day is it Suze?' he finally asked, knowing the reply off by heart.

Suzie drew herself up, wincing as she moved. 'It's the day the psychic seer gets out of my life and never returns. It's Danny's last day. Get out. Get out Danny and let me get help. GET OUT!'

Danny wished the floor would open up and swallow him. 'I'll get the police,' he said lamely, knowing he was grasping at that absent last straw again. 'And an ambulance,' he added.

'Stop right there,' Suzie said, her voice now low and controlled. 'I don't want the police. I'm injured and I think I'm bleeding internally and I want an ambulance, but I'll get it myself. What I want most of all is you out of here. For ever. Get out Danny and don't ever come back. Go and join a circus or something, you bastard. Get yourself a tent in a fairground sideshow. Then you can sit there and tell the future to your heart's content. Just get out of my life. *I hate you for what you've done*!' She drew herself up on her knees then, so he could see the full extent of her injuries. 'You did this to me, Danny,' she said. 'It's all your fault. Get out of the house, Danny. Run away in case they come back for you. And take your dirty stinking talent with you. GET OUT!'

Danny felt a brief tearing sensation and knew that the time-travelling Danny had left him.

'I thought I told you to leave,' Suzie moaned. The split in her lip had opened up again. Blood ran down her chin and dripped on to her chest, a tiny rivulet that made a line between her breasts down to her navel.

'Please, Suze, don't make me go,' Danny pleaded. In spite of the tears blurring his eyes, something inside him had retreated into a hard, cold shell and again he felt as if he was acting out a screenplay drama. He hated himself for retreating from that pain. He deserved every ounce of it, every last twist of its screw.

'GET OUT! GET OUT GET OUT GET OUT!' Suzie screamed, spraying blood across the bed. Her voice was so high and ragged Danny thought her throat might rupture.

You'd sound like that if you'd been betrayed and had to go through what she's just experienced, his cry-baby voice accused.

Suzie grabbed the bedside lamp and flung it at him. Danny ducked, but the lamp was still plugged in and fell short.

'I love you Suze,' he said, 'and I'm sorry.'

The fight had gone out of her now. 'Go,' she sobbed. 'J-just go!'

'Okay,' Danny said.

While Suzie lay back on the bed, clutching her pie-jam top to her like a child's familiar, Danny got his suitcase and threw in a few of his clothes, cursing the king of the *Know Betters*, Alistair Lerner.

Lerner had known this would happen. The bastard had looked this far into Danny's future and had correctly predicted this. It had been a part of his game plan. *He knew you'd have nowhere else to go, Dan. Why do you think he left you the key to the place in Brighton*?

Danny packed, aching for Suzie to change her mind and tell him she didn't want him to leave after all.

But Suzie wasn't going to change her mind. It didn't take a psychic to work that one out. She lay there face down on the wrecked bed, her back shuddering as she cried silently. There was an angry red bite mark amongst the wide weals on her left buttock, and looking at it broke Danny's shell and made him cry again.

He put his cheque book and credit cards into his jacket, put the two ten pound notes he'd saved from the housekeeping money into his wallet, then went up to the attic and got the box containing the little glass bastard. He opened the box on the landing and read the address on the tag, wondering if he should write it down on the telephone pad so that Suzie could contact him later if she wanted to. Not knowing quite why, he decided against it, telling himself he could call her later, when things had calmed a little. Perhaps there was a still a chance she would change her mind. *But that's a question for the future, isn't it old Dan?* he asked himself.

He wondered if he should take the crystal with him or simply dump it in the dustbin. Lerner's little glass bastard was the root cause of all this, after all. It might feel very good indeed to crack that thing into slivers with a hammer.

Take it. It may come in handy.

Danny did not think these words. They simply appeared inside his mind and he didn't know their origin. The word Joey also occurred to him and the implication followed that he might well have a dead budgerigar as a spiritual guide. Danny smiled grimly, took the box back to the bedroom and made room for it inside his suitcase.

Suzie was still face down, sobbing quietly.

Danny looked at her for a time, biting his bottom lip. 'Goodbye Suzie,' he finally said in a thick voice.

She did not reply.

Danny ached terribly for her. He badly needed to touch her, to hold her to tell her how sorry he was. 'I'd like to kiss you one last time before I leave,' he said as again his vision suddenly blurred with hot tears. 'A kind of good riddance kiss, if you like.'

'No,' Suzie replied.

A sob escaped from Danny before he could catch it. 'Ok-ay,' he said fighting his shuddering chest. 'But I'm s-sorry. I luh-love you. I'll love yuh-you for ever. Remem-ber that.'

Suzie didn't look up, her face full of compassion and open her arms for him, but Danny didn't really expect her to. It was just a last fantasy. The realistic side of him expected her to lie there making no sign of having heard at all, and it wasn't disappointed.

Danny picked up his suitcase, went downstairs and let himself out of the front door. His heart like dull lead in his chest, he closed it behind him for what looked like the last time ever. Just as he had known they would be, the Humber's tyres were all slashed. He looked at the car for a time then walked down the street to Vyne Road.

He didn't let himself look back.

Chapter Fourteen
The Fortune Shop

1

Danny walked down Vyne Road and took the tunnel that ran beneath the railway station. There would be taxis on the station forecourt and he would use one, but not for the whole trip. Halfway through the tunnel, the truth about why he hadn't written the Brighton address down on the pad beside the phone hit him like a freezing avalanche. Danny put his case down, sat on it and sobbed bitterly. The real reason he had not left his forwarding address was that part of him thought the thieves would return and that if Suzie knew where he was she would tell them. He was, in effect, running away and leaving her to deal with everything.*They might come back*, he told himself. *And what will they do to her the next time?* But he already knew what was likely to happen if they came back. They would kill her.*And you, old Dan, famous Mystic of the West, are so fucking cowardly you've put her life at risk to protect your own. That feels real good, doesn't it? That certainly feels Ten-up. When in doubt, run away, you spineless little shit! So much for being the protector and the provider. You've done neither of those things lately, have you?*

But he knew that if he went back, Suzie would not let him into the house. She didn't *want* his protection. And after tonight that wasn't terribly surprising. Danny currently had very little to offer in the way of protection. (or anything else come to that), even if he *was* there. Danny knew as well as she did that the Famous Psychic Seer would simply have a blank period and leave the house the moment before the trouble arrived.*She's better off without you, old Dan. You have nothing left to offer but more trouble*, he told himself, and the simple truth of this hurt him even more.*So you can either fuck off to Brighton, or just buy a platform ticket and wait for the next express train to hammer past. A second and it would be all over.*

Except that others would have to live with the mess. Suzie, for one good example. What would *that* do to Suzie, to whom he'd never wished any harm in his life?

Danny sat on top of his suitcase sobbing openly as people walked by, going about their business and studiously ignoring him. *But the more people who see you here, his cry-baby voice whispered, the greater the chance that someone will remember you when Tim Gould comes looking for you – on behalf of his newspaper and probably his criminal friends too. And he will come looking for you, there's no doubt about that at all. So I suggest you get your act together and get out of here, because the milk has been well and truly spilt, and as we say in that ancient and revered institution, The Paranormal Club: Milk, once spilt, can never be un-spilt, no matter how long one cries over it.*

And Suzie would not be alone. There would be an ambulance or doctor with her now and she would undoubtedly be taken to hospital for treatment and she would be there for a couple of days at least. The police would be informed whether Suzie liked it or not, and afterwards she would be safer.

Danny blew his nose, dabbed his eyes dry and got up. By the time he got to the taxi rank he was as composed as was possible under the circumstances. There was a Mercedes cab waiting and Danny got inside it, the palms of his hands instantly starting to itch.

'Where to?' the driver asked.

'Guildford?'

The driver looked at his watch. 'Where in Guildford, exactly?'

'The station?'

The driver thought about it.

Danny's itching hands began to tingle. *Alan Harman*, he thought wearily, wishing this didn't have to keep happening to him. He hadn't even touched this driver, just sat *in his cab. Aged thirty-eight. Married, two kids. Fat mortgage and heavy payments due on the Merc. Struggling. Now slowly computing if a trip to Guildford would make more than the six or seven local trips he would do in the same time. Alan Harman doubted it.*

'Forget it,' Danny said, saving him the mental struggle, and got out of the cab.

He went and sat on the steel bench seat outside the station intending to wait for the next cab to join the queue. Almost immediately a tall, unshaven man cradling a Canon video camera sat down beside him. Danny groaned inwardly.

'Going away?' the man asked, smiling.

Danny nodded, wishing the man would go away too. Now. His hands were still itchy and the proximity of the man was starting to make them tingle again. Danny clasped his hands together and scratched each palm with his fingernails.

The man pointed the camera towards the station entrance and said, 'I was going to film my girlfriend coming out of the station when her train arrives but I've got an awful interference pattern here. It's weird.'

Danny tried hard not to know what was going on inside the man's head. He hoisted and erected those ancient granite words ABSOLUTELY

NOT, but not before he'd glimpsed the roiling mess of plots, plans and jumbled ideas and words that lived in there.*Like a kind of cobweb*, Danny thought, in spite of himself.

'It's like a kind of cobweb,' the tall man said from behind his camera. He brought the machine down and switched it off. 'Y' know what I reckon?' he asked.

'You reckon this is an area of high static electricity,' Danny told him wearily.

The guy looked at him, his head cocked to one side and a grin dangling on his open mouth. 'How'd you know?' he asked in a delighted voice.

'I read your mind,' Danny said.

'You know what else?'

Danny did. 'Yes,' he said, getting up.

As he rose, his right hand brushed the back of the seat where the plastic finish had been chipped off, and just as both he and the guy with the Canon camcorder and all the bright ideas already knew he would, he earthed himself and electricity jumped from him to the metal with a small blue spark and an audible *crack*! Both his hands immediately stopped tingling.

Danny walked away before the guy with the boiling mind could point out that, A. Danny had seemed to be the centre of the cobweb of electrical interference and B. that, surprise, surprise, it had gone now.

The next cab arrived and Danny got straight into it, leaving Mr Camcorder goggling after him. This driver didn't mind a trip to Guildford and since he'd discharged his psychic battery – or whatever he'd done – Danny didn't have to learn all about his private life.

By the time he reached Guildford railway station, Danny's palms were starting to itch again. He hurriedly paid the cabbie, got out, discharged himself on a chain-link fence and took another taxi from there to Dorking, then another to Horsham.

After which he hitch-hiked. Or intended to. It was now nearly two in the morning and there were very few cars about – and most drivers these days were well aware that picking up a hitcher in the dark in the middle of nowhere was something akin to signing, if not their own death warrant, then a warrant to be battered, terrorised and robbed.

The guy driving the milk lorry which stopped for him about three miles out of Horsham, evidently did not expect to be robbed, terrorised or battered. He had muscles that might have doubled for Arnie Schwarzenegger's had this man been in the movie industry. The lorry driver leaned over and peered down at Danny, asking him where he was going and why was he going there in the middle of the night.

'My sister lives alone in Burgess Hill,' Danny said selecting the name from a road sign he'd seen back in Horsham. He didn't know exactly where Burgess Hill was other than that it was fairly near to

Brighton. 'She had a bust up with her husband, he walked out and she wanted me there pronto. I couldn't get a through train connection to Brighton until the morning, and to tell you the truth, she sounded suicidal. Old George is pretty highly strung at the best of times.'

'George?'

'Georgina,' Danny said, and mentally apologised to his ex-colleague whose face he had stolen to fit on the head of his fictitious sister.

'I can take you as far as the 273 just before Hayward's Heath, but that's all,' the Arnie lookalike said. 'I've got to go right into Hayward's Heath or I'd take you to the door. The 273 will take you right down to Burgess Hill.' He reached down and grabbed Danny's hand to help him up and yanked him off his feet. Danny shorted himself on one of the steps, scrambled into the cab and thanked the driver, telling himself that any diversion would only make him harder to trace.

Arnie – whose name turned out to be just that (but Arnold Gregory, which didn't quite have the same ring to it, he confided) – was a witty out-of-the-closet homosexual who turned out to be the most open and uncomplicated person Danny had met for ages. Arnie spoke well, had an overwhelming urge to have the best body in the country (if you liked muscle-men that was, and he would be the first to admit that many people found them revolting), never went out without a packet of Jiffies, these days, and one day hoped to become famous. He was charmed by the coincidence that he too had a highly strung sister whose husband had left her and told Danny he knew what he was in for and felt sorry for him. 'Just don't make the same mistake I did and end up living with her,' he advised.

Danny, who doubted very much that he would make a similar mistake, was not so enamoured by the coincidence. He had unknowingly pulled the sister story from Arnie's head and as far as he was concerned, it was only luck which had prevented him choosing Arnie's sister's name, Gillian, as the name of his own sister. The name had flickered through his mind back there as Arnie reached down for him.

2

The night, however, was still alive with bad magic after Arnie dropped him on the A273 to Burgess Hill. Danny had trudged almost all the way to Hayward's Heath with the heavy suitcase before the first car passed him and a dirty grey dawn was forming in the east; empty and dull like the life that stretched out before him. His arms ached, his legs were beginning to seize up and his left hand limp had made itself well known almost an hour ago.

Before he heard the sound of the approaching car, Danny's feet lit up and he grew a long shadow. He stopped, put down his suitcase, stuck out his thumb and turned to face the silently oncoming car, letting them see he had a kind face. *Ha ha, Dan, if that isn't a joke, I don't know what is!* he told himself bitterly.

Then his scar pulsed and Danny decided there was something wrong about this car – and it wasn't just its soundless approach or the way the driver hadn't bothered to switch to dipped beam to avoid blinding him. There was something about the way it had turned up that bore a hint of finality.

Danny dropped his thumb and stepped well back on to the verge, suddenly thinking this car might try to run him down. Stranger things had happened.

Thought you wanted to die, his cry-baby voice accused. *Why didn't you just stay where you were?*

Danny shook his head. 'I don't want to die,' he said. 'I'm frightened of dying. And I'm frightened of what's inside that car.'

He turned away from the headlights, picked up his case and limped wearily along the verge, knowing now that the car would stop for him and also realising what was inside it.

One of the passengers in that car was death. Danny didn't know if it was his death or someone else's, and he didn't want to find out.

The car swished silently by him, its slipstream tousling his hair. It was a white Bentley.

You were wrong, o Mystical Master, Danny told himself as the car grew small in the distance and he was glad of this. The car had seemed to *fit*. As if it was one of the pieces of the complex jigsaw that Lerner made out of Danny's future. A key piece, without which the rest of the jigsaw couldn't be completed.

But Danny had been wrong.

Except that the Bentley's brake lights had come on, right up there in the distance.

Slowing for a junction, Danny hoped.

The red brake lights went out and were replaced by white reversing lights. Danny's heart sank as the car serpentined backwards towards him, making far more noise in reverse than it had going forward.

Danny's war wound began to throb again and the blood bag in his nostril started its swelling trick.

The car stopped in the road beside him, straddling the white line. A peak-capped chauffeur, his face lit by the panel lights, sat in the driving seat staring rigidly in front of him. There was a glass partition between him and the passenger section of the car. The rear windows were all darkened.

Danny glanced at the car then stepped down on to the road and limped past it.

The Bentley rolled silently forward, its driver still staring ahead. Danny increased his pace and the Bentley matched it, drawing forwards so that he was hobbling along level with the rear window.

You can't keep this up, old Dan, he told himself with certainty. *You're going to fall down in a moment.*

To his right, one of the darkened windows rolled silently down. Danny didn't look, just kept hobbling along.

'Excuse me,' a well-spoken female voice called.

Danny fought an urge to rub his scar and kept tottering along. He felt very dizzy now.

'Hello!'

Danny's legs stopped walking. He staggered around to face the open window.

'May I offer you a lift?'

The woman's face was very pretty and looked familiar somehow. *You don't know her*, Danny assured himself, but a distant part argued this was not the case and that, in fact, he *did* know her.

The woman's familiar oval face was impeccably made up. Her long blonde hair was pulled up showing off the flawless white skin of her neck and shoulders. Her eyes were blue and friendly.

'No,' Danny said distantly, 'I don't think you may.'

And blackness flooded his vision. Danny felt his sense of balance deserting him and a flicker of pain as his knees thudded down on to the tarmac, then he knew nothing.

He woke up with a feeling of having been trapped. He was inside the car and the car was moving. He was sitting on a leather seat with his back to the driver and his head resting on the glass panel that separated the front of the car from the passengers. His hand was propped under his nose, pressing a wad of scented tissue paper against it. Danny removed the tissue and realised his nosebleed had stopped.

The familiar woman sitting opposite him with her make-up on and her hair up although it was dawn was wearing a sparkling silver evening dress. She was evidently one of those fabled young and rich people who danced most of the night away in exclusive London discotheques.

'What happened?' Danny asked. His vision was flickering – pulsing in time with the throb at his scar as if someone was flashing a bright light.

'You collapsed. I thought you would and you did. Arthur and I picked you up and your nose started to bleed badly. You could probably get those vessels cauterised, you know.'

Danny shrugged and closed his eyes. The pulsing continued.

'Well, we put you in the car, propped you up with the tissues under your bleeding nose, and that's that.'

'How long?'

'Were you unconscious? Five minutes or so. We thought you had to be headed for Burgess Hill or Brighton so we drove slowly away. Where are you going?'

'I want to get out of the car,' Danny said.

The woman was startled. 'Do you feel sick?' she asked.

'I just want to get out,' he said. Being in here was too *right*, and someone in here was doomed, and Danny thought he might turn out to be the trigger.

'It's okay,' the woman soothed. 'Nothing's going to happen to you now. You're safe. Relax. We'll take you to Brighton.'

Static, Danny thought. *That's what Mr Camcorder thought*. He reached for the door handle.

'Oh no! *Don't!*' the woman squealed, then saw the spark as Danny's fingers closed on the metal.

'Oh God, I thought you were going to leap out!' she said as Danny withdrew his hand.

'Static,' Danny said. 'I always get it in cars. Makes me feel car-sick if I don't discharge it.' The flickering and pulsing had stopped now but the feeling of having been trapped didn't go away. Danny sighed, realising it was probably too late now anyway – he'd met the woman just as he was supposed to and meeting her was probably the key event. If he got out now it wouldn't make any difference at all.

'Yes, I am going to Brighton,' he said, defeated. He was too tired and groggy to make up any more stories.

'Good. So are we. We can take you all the way there.'

'Why did you stop?' Danny asked.

'You were hitching,' the woman replied. For the first time, Danny realised she was holding a half-full Martini glass.

Danny shook his head. 'No I wasn't,' he said wearily.

'Oh. My name's Stephanie Osmond,' she said, deftly changing the subject and extending a delicate hand with perfectly manicured fingernails. Its attitude suggested that Danny should kiss it rather than shake it. He did neither. His palms were itching again and he had no intention of touching her while they were like that. There was death riding in this car and it could be Arthur's or it could be hers and Danny didn't want to know which it was. He had a feeling it was going to turn out to be hers.

'My friends call me Steffy,' she said.

'Can't shake. Sorry,' Danny said thickly.

Stephanie Osmond nodded and said, 'Uh huh,' sounding rather like a doctor making an examination. She withdrew her hand, not looking offended at all. Danny thought he might have just confirmed a suspicion she'd had.

'Can you tell me your name?' she asked, a friendly smile wavering at the corners of her mouth.

'Can you tell me why you stopped for me?' Danny countered.

Stephanie Osmond sighed and shrugged. 'It might sound silly,' she said.

I doubt it'll sound silly to me, Danny thought. 'Try me,' he said. 'I won't laugh.'

'When I woke up this morning – yesterday morning, actually – I had one of my funny feelings. . .'

Danny nodded. He had guessed as much. He had guessed, but Lerner had known. Lerner had made him into a magnet for people with gifts and odd ideas and they wouldn't stop being attracted to him. He wished he was back in the milk lorry with Arnie the gay bodybuilder. He had felt safe and secure in Arnie's uncomplicated little world.

'A foreshadowing,' Danny said. 'A premonition.'

Stephanie grinned knowingly. 'Yes, that's it. I get these feelings from time to time and this morning I woke up knowing I would meet somebody in deep trouble. Someone I should help. I didn't know who, where or when, but I did know. Sounds stupid, doesn't it?'

'Sounds fine to me,' Danny said.

'And it turned out to be right after all. I think that person is you.'

Danny nodded. It was surely a joke. All of this surely had to be very bad joke played out on a grand scale. 'I'm not in trouble,' he said.

Steffy ignored the remark. 'You remind me of someone, y'know,' she said, looking at him with a new intensity. Things seemed to be slotting into place for her, if they weren't for him.

'Who might that be?'

Stephanie shrugged and shook her head. 'No, I'm wrong. Just a wild thought.'

'Oh,' Danny said. He felt terribly tired. The gentle motion of the Bentley was making his eyes grow heavy. *One of us is going to die*, he thought, and for a moment imagined he'd said it.

'You can tell me, y'know.'

Danny's head had been drifting down towards his chest. He snapped awake again, thinking he really had spoken those words.

'You're not a terribly good liar,' Stephanie said. 'You *are* in trouble and you can talk to me about it if you wish. It'll make it easier for you. A trouble shared and all that. I promise I won't breathe a word to anyone else.'

'Nothing to tell,' Danny lied, then added, 'I'm just going to stay at a friend's place. I'm going away to do some thinking.' In the silence that followed his eyes grew heavy again. Something soft touched him inside. It was an odd feeling, but not unpleasant.

'Danny,' she said.

He snapped awake instantly, his heart hammering. 'You looked!' he said in a wounded voice, not quite certain of what he meant. 'I didn't tell you my name!'

Steffy shook her head. 'Oh God, I'm sorry! I didn't mean to. It's a gift I have and I can't control it. I can tell people's names. I don't know how I do it, it just happens. Like my funny feelings. Like the way I could sense the atmosphere over you as the car passed. I knew it was you I'd had the feeling about. It was like there was a little black cloud following you.'

Welcome to The Paranormal Club, Danny thought, and wondered what cross good-intentioned old Steffy had to bear. He realised he now didn't have to shake her hand or fall into the little glass bastard in order to find out which person in this car had the death monkey riding on their back. Steffy was psychic and the last two of that particular breed Danny had met had ended up well and truly dead.

'Do you think you are psychic?' Danny asked.

Steffy shook her head. 'No, not really. I think I may have a hint of something unusual but compared to some of the people I've met, it's not worth mentioning.'

'You called it a gift,' Danny said, wondering who the other people were that she'd met. Did she make a career out of being magnetically drawn to psychics in trouble and trying to help them out? A kind of paranormal counselling service?

'I didn't really mean that,' she said. 'Ability would have been a better word. Like the ability to tell when people are lying or concealing something from me. Lots of people can do that. Being able to guess people's names is a bit different, but not much. And the funny feelings don't really amount to much. Sometimes I just wake up with a stomach full of butterflies and know something is going to happen. The rest is just my imagination building on it. Sometimes I get the butterflies and nothing happens, but I don't count those times. I tell myself I missed it, whatever it was. Like yesterday morning's butterflies. I thought I'd missed that happening. Until I saw you, that was.'

'A guy needing a lift.'

'There's more to it than that and you know it!' Steffy said, her eyes flashing. 'I can't help it if you choose not to tell me truth.' She drained her Martini and put the glass back into the bar between the rear seats.

'I'm sorry,' Danny said, 'and I appreciate the lift. I lied to you because I didn't think you ought to know the truth.'

'Why?'

Danny shrugged. He could hardly say he thought it might get her killed. 'I didn't want to involve you.'

'I don't mind being involved.'

If only you knew! Danny thought. *The part of me you see now kills psychics shortly after meeting them, but there's more. There's another part of psychic slayer Danny Stafford. A worse part. A person called the Gannex Man whom our Dan has no control over. A dangerous person who leaps out of his cage in the dark part of Danny's mind and takes the controls, leaving no memory of his actions. This is the part I think I'm going to Brighton to address and this is the part which might do you harm if it has a chance. You're a very attractive girl and this part dreams of violent, bloody sex. It came close with Suzie a while back and it might go further with you if it can.*

'Look,' Danny said, 'I don't want to know anything about you. I do not wish to know where you live or any of your history. I am in trouble and I'm not sure what kind and I don't want to involve you. My trouble got my girlfriend very badly hurt last night and she threw me out because of it. I don't blame her. At the moment I'm very bad news for anyone who gets involved with me and I have no desire to fuck anyone else's life up. Can we leave it at that?'

Steffy nodded. 'I'm sorry,' she said in small voice.

'So am I,' Danny said.

They drove the rest of the way in silence.

3

Danny climbed wearily out of the car on the seafront by Brighton's east pier at five to seven on the cold, damp morning of November the 5th. There was a stiff breeze blowing in from the sea and Danny immediately began to shiver.

'Where will you go now?' Steffy asked from inside the car.

'My friend's place,' Danny told her.

'You don't know where that is, do you?' she said.

Danny nodded. 'Yes,' he lied. He had visited the town once before – his parents had taken him there for a day out the year before Brian shot him – but he had no recollection of the place at all.

'I can take you there if you tell me where it is,' she offered.

'I'll find it,' Danny muttered. 'Thanks for the lift.'

'No problem,' Steffy said and closed the door.

The darkened window rolled down as the car pulled away.

'Be seeing you,' she called, waving gaily.

'That's what I'm afraid of,' Danny said to himself.

4

Fifteen minutes later, having obtained directions from a milkman (along with the promise of fresh dairy produce delivered to his doorstep every morning – just leave a note out to say what he wanted), Danny limped up a side street just a few yards from the promenade and found his new home.

He looked at it, grinning grimly and shaking his head. There wasn't a doubt about how Lerner expected him to make a living from now on.

Lerner's place was a small, ancient, glass-fronted shop. The big, cream-painted (but badly peeling) painted over windows were bowed, curving gracefully in to the recessed front door – the upper floor of the building forming a small porch between the pavement and the door. The curved glass looked as if it would be difficult and expensive to replace. The ravaged wooden window frames and the peeling door were painted green. There was a clear oblong area in the centre of each window which bore what had once been (in the sixties, Danny imagined) elegant gold sign-writing. Now the lettering was dull and the paint cracked.

The Fortune Shop

the words said, and underneath in small letters:

Your Future Predicted By Alistair Lerner, The Well-known Psychic
No Appointment Required

.Below this was the telephone number.

If you think this boy's going to play that *game, Mr Lerner, you're very much mistaken!* Danny thought.

He took the key from his pocket, walked into the chequered-tiled porch and looked at the front door, still shaking his head.

The door was half-glazed and handwritten testimonials to Lerner's talents were posted there, stuck to the glass with tiny squares of yellowed sellotape.

Everything he told me came true! proclaimed the spidery handwriting of a man from Coventry.

Mr Lerner is truly gifted, I have never know him to be wrong, claimed a badly typed message from MrsAvery of Dundee.

There were several dusty thank-you notes from people who'd received the good luck he'd predicted for them.

Apparently, Danny thought bitterly, *Lerner didn't ever tell people that home truth that, in the end, Everything Turns Out For The Bad.*

Danny put the key in the lock, wondering with a moment of black humour if he should replace one of those notes with his own testimonial: *Thank you, Mr Lerner, for predicting that my life would fall apart, and that I would be faced with problems far greater than I imagined possible. It all came true!*

The front door opened on to a dark, musty hallway. The walls were whitewashed and also peeling.

This is going to take a great deal of cleaning up, Danny thought tiredly.

There were two doors just inside the hall, one on each side. He assumed they led into either side of the shop front. An ancient and threadbare red carpet led down the hall to a bare wooden staircase at the far end. Danny knew without doubt that the carpet would be sticky to walk on. There was no mail on the mat inside the front door which meant that up until his death Lerner had paid the bills for the place from Reading.

'He could have sold it,' Danny said, stepping on to the sticky carpet and putting down his suitcase. 'He hasn't been here for years and he needed the money. He could have sold it, but he didn't. And you know exactly why that was, old Danny boy, don't you? He kept it because he'd looked into his own crystal ball and seen you entering the place. He kept it for the future. For you.'

Which meant that Lerner had lied when he'd intimated that he had done only one reading on Danny from his stolen wristwatch. Lerner had been saving this place for five, maybe ten years – or even longer. Which meant that he'd known all about the grown-up Danny while the boy Danny was still at school.

Before he had opened the door to his left – before he'd even touched its handle, in fact – Danny already knew that this was the room where Lerner had worked. A part of his mind whispered that it was his own work-room now, but Danny studiously ignored it. There would be none of that kind of funny business taking place here.

The work-room – *or the* Reading Room, *Dan, that'd be better, ha bloody ha!* – was in better condition than the outside of the building or the hall. Someone had recently been in here and made an attempt at cleaning this room, Danny thought. It had the same musty smell of disuse, but the brown carpet – which still had a little spring left in it – bore the marks of a recent hoovering and and the cream paint on the walls and the inside of the window had been washed.

One of Lerner's little buddies, Danny thought. *Being dead is of no consequence when you're a leading light of The Paranormal Club. You can carry on your manipulation of someone from beyond the grave simply by checking the future while you were alive and handing out your instructions well in advance.*

It was gloomy in the Reading Room and it didn't lighten much when Danny pressed the light switch. The electricity was still on – Danny expected Lerner's helping gnome had taken care of this – but the globe that hung over the round oak table in the centre of the room did not light. The gnome had evidently thought this unsuitable and had removed the bulb and installed a single uplighter column in the corner of the room. The lamp in this could have been no stronger than sixty watts – if that. A vague puddle of light pooled on the ceiling, looking rather like the stain the crystal had made in Danny's bedrooms. This light would give no reflection at all in the crystal, Danny realised, and would provide exactly the right sort of illumination to use it.

On either side of the oak table – recently polished, Danny noted, and looking suspiciously like a drop-winged dining room table – stood a padded straight-backed wooden chair. On the wall behind the better of the two chairs – Lerner's presumably – was a low shelf, holding several leatherbound books purportedly dealing with the paranormal, a supply of headed paper and two ball point pens. The books were to impress the clients, Danny supposed, and the paper and pens so they could take notes while Lerner gazed into his crystal and spoke, or so that Lerner could write what he'd seen afterwards.

Apart from the electric radiator – placed on the wall so that Lerner's body would shield its reflection from the crystal – there was nothing else in the room. Danny turned on the radiator then went to look in the other shop-front room.

This had evidently been Lerner's office-cum-library. It was cluttered and might have looked welcoming if it had been cleaned and if Danny hadn't been able to see his breath each time he exhaled.

There was a fireplace here, containing a gas-log fire. The mantelpiece shelf was strewn with cheap ornaments and overflowing ashtrays filled with bent over Woodbine butts. There were two armchairs in the room, a desk on which stood an old Olivetti manual typewriter – the ribbon of which was missing – and a Grundig battery radio with a circular dial. Danny turned on the radio and caught a brief hiss of static before the batteries died. The room was full of books. On psychology, psychiatry, and parapsychology; not only on the two four-row book shelves, but stacked on the floor and the window sill. Paperbacks stood in two piles on either side of the hearth; one pile contained what must have been everything Dick Francis had ever written and the other was a selection of adventure and spy novels, some of which Danny had read.

There were two Delft chamber pots filled with earth and dead geraniums, one each side of the fire. Danny knelt and turned on the fire. All the services had apparently been restored; the fire lit first time. He crouched in front of it, warming himself and wondering what he was doing here. He felt as if he'd suddenly been shot into another universe. In some strange way, Basingstoke and Suzie and the Securicor robbery no longer seemed to exist.

It'll all need cleaning, Danny thought again and his cry-baby asked, *Before what? Before you start doing the work Lerner intended?*

'If I'm going to stay,' he answered aloud. He wanted to cry then, cry for the thing he'd lost, the things that no longer seemed to exist because they were now gone, probably for ever. He *was* going to stay, he realised, simply because he had nowhere else to go.

But no tears would come to accompany the pain. Danny was empty.

He got up, limped down the hall and plodded up the stairs to where the living area must have been. There was a kitchen so tiny you couldn't possibly have fallen over in it without receiving head injuries on the way down. The fridge was empty but there were five cans of food in the cupboard: four of which were baked beans, the other corned beef.

The bathroom was equipped with a cast iron bath, its enamel crazed and stained; a wooden-seated toilet with a chain flush and a hand basin with no plug. Lerner's gnome had thoughtfully left a roll of Izal toilet paper for him – stuff more suited to tracing pictures than applying to delicate parts of your anatomy. The ashtrays in here had been emptied though.

Danny found the immersion heater switch in the airing cupboard and turned it on. He needed a long hot bath and intended to follow it with an even longer sleep.

There was no lounge, just a big bedroom with a single bed, an ancient (and undoubtedly black and white only) television which stood in the corner on rickety looking legs and an easy chair.

The gnome had fitted fresh sheets, pillow cases and clean blankets, and he or she had left the bedclothes turned back. The bed looked very inviting and like Goldilocks, Danny thought he might just climb in right now and have a long comfortable sleep. The fact that there might well be bears around when he woke up was neither here nor there.

Danny found the bear before he went to sleep and after he'd noticed the dog hairs still on the carpet, in spite of the fact that it had recently been vacuumed. The bottom of the bedroom door was scratched where Lerner's dog Judy had tried to open it countless times. Danny remembered Judy snuggled up to Lerner's dead body again and wondered what had become of her.

Still thinking about the dog, he undressed and climbed into the bed. The bath could wait. The bear waited for him on the bedside table next to a Westclox wind up alarm he didn't intend to wind up and a bible he didn't intend to read.

It was a paper bear, similar to the one Suzie had once presented him with but written on cheaper paper.

Danny saw the envelope and ignored it. He pulled up the sheets around him and closed his eyes.

It was addressed to you, a suddenly alert part of him said.

I doubt that most sincerely, Danny argued back. *And if it is, I'll see it later.*

But the nagging didn't stop until Danny sat up and reached for the letter.

It was addressed to him – in Lerner's neat copperplate handwriting.

'Oh, fuck off!' Danny moaned. 'Not now!'

Like the last handwritten bear, this one was cold; not just from the room's slowly escalating background temperature, but cold in the way Suzie's letter had been. It was cold bad news in there and once opened Danny expected it to slash its claws through him as Suzie's had done. Danny did not want to read it. Ever. But especially not now.

But the bear will be there when you wake up, and it might just have its Mummy and Daddy with it by then. Wouldn't it be better to read it now – get it all over and done with?

They're all in there already, Danny told himself. *Mummy, Daddy, baby, and probably the whole damn' family right down to second cousins. They can wait until I can deal with them.*

He flicked the letter across the room, pulled the sheets up around his head and within thirty seconds he was asleep.

5

Danny dreamed of Stephanie Osmond. It was an extraordinarily erotic dream in which he visited Stephanie's large and lonely house, danced with her, drank wine from her lips and traced the contours of her face and neck with his fingertips.

The scene changed often and each time Stephanie's hair was up and her long, slender neck swam before him, swan-like and inviting. Then they were outside in the spot-lit garden, naked and making love in the golden-tinged twinkling snow. Stephanie was all fours and Danny had entered her from behind, but her back was somehow not visible, just that long glistening neck and her tightly-tied golden hair.

'I want to be right inside you,' Danny told her as he shuddered into her. 'I want to take the core of your being, tear it open and wrap it around me!'

'Oh, yesss! Yes, Danny, do that to me!'

'I want to wear you like a glove!'

'Do it!'

Danny touched Steffy's neck and orgasmed.

He woke up in a dark strange room and wasn't sure this hadn't really happened. He looked at the Westclox which was stopped at three twenty-five then he looked at his wristwatch which informed him it was five-thirty. Danny didn't know if that meant evening or morning and he didn't want to think about the bear waiting for him or the significance of the first wet dream he'd ever had in his life. He rolled away from the damp patch and slept again.

6

Danny finally read the cold letter on Sunday morning. He woke at seven, shivering, with the bedclothes tied around him in a tangled rope. He did not know where he was, how long he had tossed and turned in this creaking bed, what day it was or why his bladder ached so powerfully. The letter was clutched in his hand and pressed against his right cheek and it was from this point of contact that the terrible chill seemed to be seeping into him.

Danny took it away from his numb face and frowned, dimly remembering throwing the letter across the room before he'd fallen asleep. Some time during his sleep he had not only retrieved it, but inserted a finger under the envelope flap and torn it open. The ragged split gaped at him, showing him the paper bear inside. Danny wondered if he (or that other part of him) had already read the letter, already knew what bad news was contained in its three or four pages.

Brighton, he reminded himself. *Lerner's Fortune Shop. Your new place of residence. Your new career.*

'I don't think so,' he said, disentangling himself from the sheets. He put the letter back on the bedside table, went to the bathroom and pissed for a very long time – which was when he began to suspect that he'd slept through Friday and Saturday.

While he sat steaming in what still seemed like someone else's bath, Danny's stomach started to rumble. It was the first time he could remember feeling hungry for weeks. An odd feeling accompanied the new sensation in his stomach and it took him a while to work out that it was the kind of excitement he'd last felt on waking up for the first time in a foreign country.

You've woken up in a new country, all right, he told himself bitterly. *You've woken up in a realm of existence previously un-dreamt of – except by Lerner*. But the excitement would not go away. *A part of you is enjoying this*, Danny scolded himself. And then he wondered *which* part exactly.

The cold spot on his right cheek would not go away, not even after he'd shaved and pressed a warm face cloth on it for a long time. Danny got out of the bath, dried himself, dressed and went out into Brighton's chilly streets to look for a corner shop where he could buy things to feed his hunger.

The flat felt warmer after Danny had eaten, but the letter was still as cold as ever. He picked it up, sat down on the bed and withdrew the three paper bears, his excitement fading now and the food he'd recently wolfed down suddenly growing heavy in his stomach.

All this wasn't done just to help a new member of The Paranormal Club out of a hole, that's for sure, Danny thought, suddenly not wanting to read the letter at all. He didn't think that Lerner had prepared this place for him simply because he'd known about the robbery and what would happen afterwards. That had just been the beginning. There was worse to come. Much worse. To all intents and purposes, Lerner had sacrificed himself by looking into Danny's future. What cause might he have considered more important than his own life?

There was no date on the letter, but Danny hadn't really expected to find one – what did dates matter when you were writing for a reader of the future? The paper didn't look old, but when Danny picked it up, it *felt* old. Maybe as many as three years old. Maybe more.

Dear Daniel,

First of all let me apologise for having perused your future without your permission – this is not my way. Circumstances, however, are such that I have been forced to.

I would like to point out here that although I knew of you long before your experience at the clairaudience demonstration (I first became aware of you at the time you were reaching puberty), I did not address myself to the schoolboy Daniel Stafford, nor attempt to manipulate his life.

However, as you are doubtless aware (and I know how you will curse me for it) I am guilty of a little manipulation of your later life. This manipulation is on a very tiny scale and I can assure you it is much less than you currently imagine.

My visions of your future were grouped around the period commencing with Christine Richard's death and going a little way forwards from that moment. They were originally apprehended second-hand; gleaned from the future of someone else. They were very hazy indeed and despite my early attempts to identify you I was unable so discover who you were or your whereabouts.

This problem was resolved recently – still several years before you will attend Christine Richard's demonstration of clairaudience. By the time you read this I will have told you face to face that I only did one reading on you using your watch. This, in a way, is the truth. But it is also a lie.

I do not like to look into my own future but I have spent many hours searching it for the point in time at which our paths will cross. I have located and experienced a moment from my future when my friend Mr Mills calls at my house bearing your wrist watch. At the time I'm writing this letter, Mr Mills knows nothing of you whatsoever and I intend to tell him nothing. By the time you read this, Mr Mills will know only that at a clairaudience demonstration during which Christine Richard died, he witnessed a powerful psychic called Daniel Stafford in the midst of what we call 'Coming Out'. As you now know, Mr Mills followed you, left my telephone number in your pocket and borrowed your wrist watch.

From that point I located, it was a simple matter for me to slip still a little further into my own future and put myself into my own body at the point where I will use your watch to do a reading on you. In this way I have been able to discover – well in advance – some of the things that are likely to happen to you. As I claimed, I did only one reading on you using your watch – but I have addressed this point in my own future many times.

I know this may look complex when written down, but I also know you will understand it because by the time you read this note you will have ridden in your own future body and formulated plans from that experience.

I too have formulated plans.

I have already said that I am guilty of having manipulated your future in a small way. This was achieved simply by turning up at your door at the correct moment and handing you the gifts of the crystal and the key to the Fortune Shop where you now sit. Your future one has been averted. You may not believe this (and in a while you may not thank me for it) but if I had not interfered, you would now be dead. Without the focus provided by the crystal I left you, your gift would have run out of control and led to your suicide. I have changed your future one to future six and saved your life. I'm sorry if this sounds a little melodramatic, but it is true. Believe me, Daniel, the future CAN be changed.

I know you must be wondering about the reasons behind the machinations I have undertaken, but there are a limited number of things I may tell you. I have already stated that I will not discuss you with Mr Mills and there is good reason for this. If I alert him beforehand he may inadvertently change his own future, the consequences of which will alter mine and yours too. As I have said, all things are linked by the web of time. There is a strong case currently held in my own future two for not telling Mr Mills about you. It follows that if I were to alert you of your own future from this point onwards, things might change again.

I am terribly sorry that all the things you have suffered had to happen to you. When I met you I already knew about them and told you nothing of them for fear that forewarned you might have acted differently. I could not allow that to happen.

I refer, of course, to the Securicor robbery you managed to avert – and its grim consequences which have led to your presence in my Fortune Shop. In your heart, Daniel, you know you have done the right thing. I wish I could have acted to alter things so that you might have saved the lives of those innocent people and not had to pay such a terrible price. I know your thoughts in the next weeks will be mainly of the love you have lost, and I know you will feel bitter. However you feel about what happened to your Susan, you did the right thing. You saved eight people by taking the right course of action. You must realise that the price you had to pay was not too high. In time you will come to terms with it. And the criminals will be caught, Daniel, I can assure you of that. I am afraid I cannot tell you that your Susan will come to terms with what has happened since I have been unable to address this part of your future as I so dearly wished to.

From this point onwards, Daniel, you are a mystery to me. I do not know your whole story and I don't expect ever to learn it. Your future, Daniel, is blurred with variables and occluded. Perhaps it is best that some things remain withheld.

I had hoped to be able to leave you on a note of hope, but I am afraid I am unable to. There is a storm approaching you, Daniel – you know this already. All I can do is wish you the best in weathering it.

What is to come is your responsibility alone, Daniel. I know you will shoulder the burden admirably. I would like to end with some words of advice:

DO NOT BE EASILY DECEIVED

You know yourself better than anyone else. You know what is right.

HAVE FAITH AND DO NOT DOUBT YOURSELF. EVEN FOR A MOMENT.

Once again, I offer my apologies and best wishes for your future.

HAVE FAITH!

Alistair

P.S. The building and everything in it now belongs to you. The deeds and details of the legal proceedings etc are in a drawer in the office downstairs. My solicitors have been instructed. Their telephone number and address is also in the drawer. I had no money to leave you, and I doubt you have much of your own. However, you have the means to make a living and I suggest you use them. Sharpen your talent. You will need it.

Danny read the letter then re-read it. *This letter from beyond the grave was written three years ago – or more, he told himself. Long before any of this happened and long before I knew of Lerner's existence.*

Alone, this fact was mind-boggling. The frightening predictions of what was going to happen next were impossible to take in. *There's a storm approaching!* Danny told himself, and couldn't decide whether the storm was of Lerner's making or if the psychic had simply manipulated him so he was here when the storm arrived. Lerner's letter seemed to have quite lightly dismissed the consequences of the Securicor robbery, so God only knew what the next little lot was going to add up to.

But you're going to find out, old Dan, he told himself. *There's no doubt about that at all.*

Not knowing was like being in a long, dark tunnel. There wasn't the faintest glimmer of light at the other end.

7

That evening the *If Only* papers were born. Danny sat – as he would sit each evening over the following three weeks – in the gloom of in what he'd christened the Reading Room with a sheet of A4 before him, noting down dates and joining them with lines while he toyed with the flattened .22 slug that had started it all. On the right hand side of the sheet he'd written the words DO NOT BE EASILY DECEIVED and HAVE FAITH AND DO NOT DOUBT YOURSELF. EVEN FOR A MOMENT. He did not know what they meant. Yet. But mathematics would tell. He would go out tomorrow and buy himself a supply of graph paper and plot all the points he could remember. All those key-point moments that had led him to this. All those times that bitch Lady Luck had slipped him bad cards. He would chart it all and then he would be able to tell, not by using the crystal but by mathematics, where the exit from this tunnel would be. Or if there would be an exit at all.

Danny's eyes grew tired as he gazed at the words DO NOT BE EASILY DECEIVED and for the thousandth time he asked himself, *What did he mean?*

8

And he woke up in a café thinking, *Joey says you'll burn yourself out if you don't take it easy. Just keep your mind blank, lie low and recharge your batteries.*

For a few moments Danny thought he was still dreaming. Then his heart started to hammer and he wished he was. *Another blank spell, Dan*, his cry-baby voice told him as he took in his surroundings. He did not recognise the place or have any memory of it. His clothes were soaked – presumably with rain – and there was a half empty cup of tea suspended in his hand between the table and his mouth. The tea taste was in his mouth – along with a greasy aftertaste which meant he'd eaten something. *Whatever used to be on that empty plate in front of you, in fact*, he told himself.

He set the cup down and concentrated on breathing deeply until his racing pulse settled and the feeling of unreality left him. It was raining outside, the wind driving the water on to the misted plate glass window in sheets.

That was how you got wet, he told himself. *You went out shopping in the rain.*

Shopping?

There were three damp carrier bags full of food on the floor beside him. *I don't remember!* he mentally raged, forcing his mind back as panic filled him. There were some vague and misty pictures in the back of his mind, but many of them didn't make sense. Steffy Osmond was there, showing off her neck with a sparkling diamond necklace. There was a smiling man in a grey suit, congratulating him on something. Young girls behind what seemed to be bank-teller windows.

Danny checked his inside pocket and found many things stuffed inside. There were solicitors' papers concerning the ownership of the Fortune Shop – now apparently his – the deeds of the building and insurance documents. There was a Switch slip for the groceries; paperwork from the bank he had apparently transferred his account to (and Danny didn't have the faintest idea where it was), and two hundred pounds in cash in his wallet.

You've been very busy this morning, he told himself.

A young waitress dressed in a black skirt, white shirt and frilly apron came over and gathered up the crockery, then mopped the table with a dishcloth.

'Everything all right, Mr Stafford?' she enquired. She was about nineteen, a thin, oval-faced bottle blonde with extremely attractive liquid brown eyes.

The kind of girl you'd like to. . .

Like to what? Danny demanded.

A picture of Joey fluttering away to Africa filled his mind and the remainder of the sentence vanished.

'Yes . . . Yes, it was fine,' he said, summoning up a smile.

'The steak was okay then? You said you wanted it very rare. Chef just showed it to the pan.'

Danny's stomach rolled. He hated steak and the mere thought of a bloody one turned his stomach.

'Lovely,' he said, thinking of the Gannex Man who evidently didn't share his taste in food. *Or women*.

Danny paid the bill and left, his stomach now feeling decidedly queasy.

His queasiness turned to sickness when he got home and unpacked the shopping his alter-ego had done for him. There were things in those bags he didn't want to have to think about. Like the length of thick cord that might have been just right for tying up someone. Like the brand new steak-knife. The *Why Have Your Sleep Disturbed?* eye-shade '*for that day-time snooze*' looked very much like a blindfold and Danny didn't even think about the way the sturdy pair of side-cutters he'd bought might crop off a child's finger.

He laid the items out on the table in the lounge office, looked at them for a time then ran for the toilet. When he'd jettisoned the undercooked steak he gathered the new things together and dumped them in the dustbin.

9

That evening, prior to his stint in the Reading Room working on the *If Only* papers, Danny watched *Coronation Street* on the little black and white television and thought of Suzie who was probably watching it in what might as well have been another universe. While the actors argued, Danny reviewed the endless procession of happy memories that tripped across his mind. Meeting Suzie in the library that first time and her demonstration of levitation in the Gingham Kitchen afterwards. Suzie taking him away to the Isle of Wight and taking away his virginity. Holidays. Christmases. Making up after fights. The way she had stood in the restaurant and asked the other diners if she should accept Danny's hand in marriage. All those things were gone and they all seemed to have happened to someone else. By the time the *Coronation Street* closing credits began to roll Danny could no longer see the television through his bitter tears.

Suzie was gone, just as all those moments had gone.

Danny worked on his charts until twelve and then sat up until three-thirty writing a long tearful letter to her. Tomorrow he would hitch hike to Bognor and post it so that no one would know where he was from the postmark.

10

When Danny turned on the television the following evening, TVS was reporting that that the six 'Basingstoke Bandits' who had been at large since an attempted payroll robbery and who had viciously attacked and raped the wife of a man they thought had tipped off the police, had been run to ground and were currently holed up in a third-floor flat in Ealing. There had been gunplay and a policeman had been taken to hospital with superficial injuries. The block of flats was now surrounded by armed policemen. The broadcaster announced they were now going to Carol Levonosky who was live at the scene and a second later the outside broadcast picture came on.

The reporter stood beside the road. Behind her was a wide stretch of grass containing the block of flats. The grass was a hive of activity. Police vehicles were still arriving, their flashing lights slicing chunks from the night. Flak-jacketed and helmeted policemen carrying rifles scurried back and forth and over at the block's stairways residents could be seen being led along the safest route away from the building.

Twice, as Carol Levonosky recited the names of the wanted men, uniformed policemen crossed the line between her and the camera. Danny ticked off the names on his fingers, a sudden bright hatred burning through him. The greater part of him hoped the police killed them all, even if they came out with their hands up.

The reporter gave details of what had happened in the foiled robbery, adding that the unnamed woman who had been attacked and raped was making a good recovery and that she had told police that the attack was a case of mistaken identity.

'The twenty-eight-year-old woman,' the reporter said, 'said the man she lived with, whose whereabouts is at present unknown, knew nothing whatsoever about the robbery and was not the man who gave police detectives the tip off. Police, however, would like the man to come forward in order that he might be eliminated from their enquiries.'

A policeman walked quickly up to the reporter, took her arm and said, 'You'll have to move away from here. You're right in the line of fire. I've already told you. . .'

The picture flickered back to the studio where the announcer said, 'We'll bring you more on the Ealing siege when we have it.'

Half an hour later Danny took a taxi to the police station and went forward in order to eliminate himself from the enquiry. He was arrested and put in a cell.

An hour later he was taken to an interview room and grilled by two detectives named Ray Johnson and Jon Vinge – in tandem at first, then one after the other. Neither Johnson nor Vinge believed a word Danny tiredly told them and both seemed to hate him with a vehemence that was totally beyond his ability to understand.

Danny repeated the same old story a different Danny in another universe had told to Detective Sergeant Murphy but either the story was dead or it hadn't stood the translation into this new world's tongue. In Danny's ears the tale of the overheard pub conversation rang about as true as a cracked bell. But as Joey had evidently warned him, his batteries were low and Danny just couldn't be bothered to embroider it, just told it over and over again when each detective demanded a fresh telling.

After two hours, Danny's palms began to itch and he shorted himself twice on the steel legs of his chair because he knew that if he didn't he would begin to find out all about the disgruntled Vinge who was sitting before him firing accusations. On the first occasion the tape recorder shut off which did nothing for Vinge's temperament and on the second, the man somehow received a jolt of static himself. Vinge's mouth snapped shut and he frowned. The fact that his protruding bottom lip lay over the top one and that his face crumpled into such deep ridges of surprise made Danny smile. Vinge looked like a puzzled bulldog.

'I don't know how you did that, sunshine,' he told Danny, 'but I strongly recommend you don't repeat it.'

Towards midnight – while Johnson was taking his turn as inquisitor – Vinge returned to the room to inform Danny that his mate Trevor the Jelly Man had come out of the Ealing flat fighting and had taken a sniper's hit. Trevor was now hanging leaning over the balcony balustrade rail with his guts unwinding and slowly descending the three stories towards the ground.

'Good,' Danny said.

'You cold son of a bitch!' Vinge said. 'That's your chum we're talking about!'

'Did you contact the Basingstoke police?' Danny asked through gritted teeth. 'Those guys gang-raped my girlfriend. One of them stuck a Coke bottle up her arse to see how far it would go!'

'You disgust me!' Johnson said.

Danny's palms started to itch again. This time he didn't earth them. He sighed. 'They can tell you all that. Her name is Susan Anderson. For Christ's sake, why don't you make the phone call?'

'We did,' Vinge said. 'Basingstoke think you're a gang member. You're the only local connection, see. The others are all from the Smoke. Basingstoke think your bit of fluff was attacked because you shat out and turned informant. The attack was an act of retribution.'

'Bollocks!' Danny shouted angrily and thought, *Now you know exactly why they hate you.*

Ray Johnson smiled grimly. 'What kind of a man fucks off and lets his tart take his rap for him? What kind of a coward *are you?*'

Danny's anger turned to a violent blind fury. His palms grew hot and he began to shudder. 'The same kind of coward. . .' he hissed. 'The same. . .' Danny did not know what kind of coward he was the same as, but he was soon going to. His mouth snapped shut, his feet did a quick spastic tap-dance on the floor and suddenly his legs stood him up. 'Oh, good lord, they've got guns! Don't let them shoot me!' his motormouth cried in a high voice. 'Helen's out in front. Christ Almighty, I can't go after her! I've wet myself. I can't do it. No one saw me . . . I wet myself . . . I'm thirty-nine and I wet myself . . . Christ, they've shot her . . . they didn't see me . . . Helen's down . . . help . . . where's help? Run, Ray. For fuck's sake, run!'

The pictures started to form in Danny's mind and Vinge was asking, 'Ray?' but Ray Johnson was already on his feet and his fist was flashing towards Danny's chest.

The blow knocked him backwards over his chair. He hit the ground hard and Johnson leapt across the table after him, yelling at the top of his voice.

'RAY!' Vinge shouted but he got two more good punches in before his partner pulled him off. Danny's nose started to bleed.

'Shut the fucking tape machine off!' Ray Johnson shouted.

'What kind of a coward,' Danny yelled, 'pisses himself and runs away while his unarmed colleague – a twenty-two-year old policewoman – faces armed robbers?'

'Shut the fucking thing off!' Johnson screamed as Vinge bundled him away from Danny.

'Halifax Building Society nineteen eighty-nine!' Danny screamed at the tape recorder.

Vinge shouted, 'Two minutes past midnight. Suspect became violent. Restrained by Detective Sergeant Johnson.'

Johnson had gone limp now. When Vinge let go of him he doubled over as if someone had given him a stiff kick in the balls.

'Interview ended three minutes past midnight,' Vinge announced and turned off the tape recorder. 'Just you stay there!' he warned, pointing at Danny. 'C'mon, Ray, let's get you out of here,' he said, pulling his partner up. Danny thought he heard a distinct note of contempt in Vinge's voice.

Jon Vinge came back alone. He threw a box of Kleenex at Danny. 'How did you know that stuff?' he said, settling into the seat opposite.

'You haven't turned on the recorder,' Danny replied. His lip was split and his nose was still bleeding. He pulled tissues from the box and dabbed his nose.

'I think you've done enough damage with it tonight,' Vinge said. 'And this is unofficial. Just tell me how you knew.'

'Will you wipe the tape?'

'I don't know yet. I'll play it back and see how it sounds. It'll ruin Ray if anyone else hears it. Maybe I can clip the end off. I don't think we'll be charging you with anything.'

Danny shook his head. 'Why not?'

Vinge smiled. 'Defence would want the tape for one thing. Just tell me how you knew.'

'Same way as I found out about the Basingstoke robbery,' Danny said. 'Sometimes things just come to me.'

'And those things about Ray just *came* to you?'

Danny nodded.

'I didn't know them,' Vinge said. 'But judging from Ray's reaction it sounded like the truth.'

'I didn't mean to say it. It just came to me,' Danny said. 'He was being a hypocrite. Accusing me of something *he'd done*.'

'I ought to ask you how you know so much about the Halifax robbery in eighty-nine,' Vinge said, 'but I have a feeling I'd be wasting my time. I saw you apprehend that stuff from Ray. I also think you've been telling the truth about the Basingstoke job.'

'Jon,' Danny said softly.

'What?'

'You hit your wife last Tuesday.'

Danny saw the familiar retreating look steal into the policeman's eyes. 'That's enough,' Vinge said firmly.

By twelve-thirty the police in London had stormed the flat, captured The Twinnies and Neil, and shot Phil McFarlane and Geoff Ridge dead. On the balcony Trevor the Jelly man had died from his wounds.

By one-thirty Danny had been released without charge.

Chapter Fifteen
Steffy's Fate

1

The money officially ran out on November the 3rd when Danny received two letters in the early morning mail. The first was from his new bank, informing him that during the period since transferring his account to the Brighton branch he had exceeded his two hundred pound standard overdraft facility to the tune of three hundred and forty-two pounds and twenty-five pence. The letter went on to state that further credit had been disallowed and that interest on the overdraft was being applied at a premium rate. The second letter was an astonishingly large gas bill.

The party – if you could call the dark, empty tunnel Danny had been living in since his arrival 'a party' (and Danny only did so bitterly) – was well and truly over. The party, in fact, had been on its last legs the moment it started, and over the past fortnight Danny had become aware of its ragged breathing rapidly turning into a death rattle. And this wasn't simply because of the money. There were many other good and plain reasons pointing fingers at him. Danny had ignored them to the best of his ability while he took Joey's birdy advice and laid low trying to recharge himself during the day from the effect of working late each night on the time-maps of his life.

But the party was over now; because the money had run out and because the other reasons could no longer be ignored.

The itching palms for instance. Danny knew exactly why his palms were itching: it was because he was forcibly subduing his talent and denying his membership of that infamous institution to which he had been inducted. Lerner had said that he could learn to control his talent, but as usual. Lerner hadn't told him the whole truth – that there really was no such thing as a free lunch. Like Joey the genius budgie, the talent seemingly had to be let out for exercise at regular periods. The price that had to be paid for keeping it locked up in its cage was the terrible itching and the build up of static. If the static wasn't regularly earthed – and Danny had found many ways to earth himself over the past few weeks – the itching would turn to heat and shortly after this you might very well be treated to an unwanted character study of a passing person and your mouth might just tell that person what you'd seen. Since the episode in the police station he had developed a habit of constantly earthing himself and an almost physical aversion to other people.

But the battery inside Danny which was discharged with the earthing had recently developed a fast charge capacity and was now almost recovered before the snap of the shock had left his hand.

But this doesn't have to happen, Danny's cry-baby had begun to whisper each time he cursed.

Then there were the charts which straight-lined from the moment Danny had entered what he thought of as The Tunnel and had not predicted the light at the other end. Judging from the lengthy hiatus between his first electric shock and the incident with the black tiles, it was possible that The Tunnel was endless.

And the vocal part of him would say: You could easily rectify that situation, old Dan!

And there was the recurring thought that came knocking late at night when Danny was softly toppling over the brink into sleep. Almost every night the words appeared, shocking Danny instantly awake and chasing any notion of sleep away for at least another hour.

You didn't read Jamie.

Danny didn't know whether the accusation was being transmitted to him by an extinct budgie, or his own subconscious and although each time it stole into his mind it seemed to possess a huge significance, the waking Danny had no idea what it meant.

Only one way to find out, his inner voice had been assuring him over the past fortnight.

And the little glass bastard lay at the centre of everything. It stood, still packed in its cardboard box, where Danny had placed it on the circular table in the Reading Room and each time he entered it drew his gaze, calling to him like a small packet of pure heroin would call to an addict undergoing cold turkey.

You don't have to hurt anymore! the crystal's soothing yet somehow *taunting* voice seemed to say. *Just hold me and I'll make all your pain go away. Think how good it will feel, Danny. Think of that cool heat tingling up your arms and flowing into your body. You can feel so good! You don't need the pain Danny, you need me!*

And although the box gave Danny a yearning ache deep in the pit of his stomach each evening as he settled down with his charts, he had not removed it and stored it away.

Because you knew this day was coming, Danny told himself as he read the bills again. *You've known all along that there was only going to be one way out of this tunnel and you've known all along that the crystal was that way. In spite of what you've promised yourself, you have intended to use it again right from square one.*

Danny put the bills back in their envelopes and feeling oddly relieved now he'd given in, reached for the telephone.

2

The box advertisement in the *Brighton Evening Argus* (paid for with a credit card stretched well beyond its capacity, but surprisingly accepted) ran from Tuesday to Saturday and read:

YOUR FUTURE REVEALED
With the blessing of Alistair Lerner
The Fortune Shop will re-open from next Monday
Under the management of the renowned psychic
DANIEL STAFFORD
Full consultations £15
Open 10am till 10pm
No appointment necessary
The Future Shop
31 Western Ride
Tel: 799265

Danny bought the papers all week and groaned inwardly each time he saw the advertisement. It was the kind of thing you could see in any local paper and the kind of thing he doubted very much if anyone at all replied to. By Saturday no one had phoned to book an appointment – or even phoned to ask after the famous Alistair Lerner. *But then again, you put no appointment necessary,* he told himself. *Why should anyone phone to book? You're the psychic; you should know when they're coming!*

And on Sunday morning, Danny found himself sitting at the round table in front of the – still unpacked – crystal and wondering if he could still do it.

Try me! the crystal challenged.

But what if it doesn't work? he asked himself. 'It doesn't really matter, old Dan,' he said aloud. 'If it doesn't work you can do what the majority of these so-called psychics do. Make it all up.'

But he didn't know if he had the verbal skills to do that either. For all he knew, his truth-bending talent had deserted him too. The best lie he'd come up with in the past few weeks was the one he had written on Lerner's old Olivetti and posted to the bank manager claiming that the deficit would be made good in short order.

Get the little glass bastard out of the box and try it! he told himself.

But he remained where he was, weighing up the probabilities. He was frightened by the possibility that he might no longer be able to use the crystal, more frightened that it might work very well indeed.

'Fuck it!' he said, not making up his mind at all, but dismissing any further thoughts on the matter. He switched off the Anglepoise lamp he'd been using as a desk light while working on his charts, turned on the uplighter in the corner and carefully unpacked the crystal, laying it in the centre of the table on its velvet cloth.

As soon as he felt the weight of the glass inside the velvet cloth, Danny knew that he hadn't lost it. This was going to work. The empty feeling in the pit of his stomach ceased as he laid out the crystal and a distant part of him informed him that the little glass bastard was even more beautiful than he remembered. The itching in his palms turned to a warm and gentle sensation and the only word Danny could bring into his mind to describe the feeling was *frothy*. He grinned, realising he had also forgotten just how good the crystal could make him feel. This was the best – the most *complete* – he'd felt for a very long time. Danny ached to feel the familiar cold heat cruising up his arms, but he also wanted to extend this moment for as long as possible. He pulled his reaching hands away from the table, smiling again when he noticed they were already cupped to accept the curved surface of the crystal, and went to the far side of the room to look back at it.

The dimly lit room seemed to have increased in size, and against what seemed to be a circular opal door into another universe, the shadows seemed thicker and blacker. But not at all threatening. Again Danny thought the crystal must surely be something more than an inert glass globe. It was possessed of its own strange life and it was somehow altering the room; interfering with its reality. The ever-present background street noises had ceased but instead of the silence being threatening a strong atmosphere of peace and tranquillity had formed. Even the shadowed planes and angles of the room seemed softer somehow – more welcoming.

The crystal gleamed dully, seemingly insubstantial, as though its mass had vanished leaving only a vaguely pulsing emptiness. There was a slight *click!* like a cooling oven or radiator and Danny wasn't sure if he'd heard it or perceived it as a feeling deep inside his mid-brain.

And the crystal suddenly lit.

A tiny golden spark formed deep inside the empty hole and points of rainbow light leapt from it, extending outwards in razor sharp beams that widened from strands to ribbons as they entered the room.

A shiver of excitement ran the length of Danny's back as the coloured ribbons danced crazily around the room, crossing and passing through one another like patterns of searchlights; splitting into dazzling prisms as they found reflective surfaces and broke into fresh paths.

Danny experienced the differing frequencies and temperatures of colour as the perfectly clear iridescent beams flickered back and forth across him.

This can't be happening! a part of his mind complained, but its voice was delighted rather than frightened.

The golden speck suddenly increased in brilliance and the rainbow light it threw off became stronger. The room was filled with thousands of shafts of multi-coloured light, each beam hitting a surface and shattering into a variation of the rainbow. Danny stepped back before the sudden surge of brilliance and felt the wall behind him. His mind emptied before what must have been a million shades of complimentary colour.

A red beam found his eyes then, shattering his vision, washing along his optic nerve and enveloping his brain in the purest clearest warmth he had ever experienced.

Then it was gone and by the time Danny's eyes had re-adjusted to the dim room the display was over.

A blue-grey smoke swirled in the space where the crystal had once been, calling to him; drawing him to it in what suddenly seemed to be not just the line of least resistance but the line of maximum irresistibility. Danny stepped towards the crystal and felt his other foot come forward a little more quickly as though a steep down-hill channel had been carved between him and the crystal. His other foot flew out in front of him, taking him down that channel at whose lowest point the crystal glittered invitingly.

Danny swept down the hill, fell into the seat that waited there and reached out his hands for the crystal.

It did not exist at all. His hands closed around a firm nothingness, but the familiar tingling cold heat flooded up his arms and into his body. The sensation was no longer a single step short of orgasmic but ten steps beyond.

Junkie! Danny distantly accused himself, but he was already gone; already falling through that sparkling mist.

There was no landing, no sideways step into the future, just a cessation of the falling after which there was pink and red and the birdy kind of chattering Joey had made when he badly wanted something.

Pink and red!

'Joey?' Danny asked into the pink and red, and the noise ceased. Danny's fingers closed around something hard and wooden but there was information to be had from it; it was just short, hard and round and the fingers of both his hands were locking themselves on to it.

There was a weight on his lap.

Pink and red?

The weight felt good. Very good.

A bombshell containing what might have been molten steel exploded in his mind and Danny screamed. The pink and red had gone, leaving a universe of unbearable white-hot pain behind it.

'ABSOLUTELY NOT!' Danny shouted, and his magic words tumbled down to him, stretched and distorted but apparently powerless.

The future – or whatever it was – did not let go of him.

The bombshell pain faded and once again Danny felt the good weight on his lap and the wooden

Pole – is it a pole?

thing clenched between his rock-hard fingers.

The pink and red started to fill his vision once more but before Danny could see what it was, another shell exploded, ripping through his mind and searing sound, vision and thought out of him.

Is it a pole or the . . . handle?

Molten steel spattered through his mind.

Pink and red. Weight. Big. Handle?

A bombshell exploded but this time Danny felt the movement of the handle. His hands shot downwards towards the weight on his lap.

Oh, Christ, it's. . .

Another moment of agony.

Pink and red.

Something wet hit him in the face.

The next explosion ripped though him.

. . . a knife!

Pink and red.

And the bombshells stopped, but Danny could not. In his pink and red universe he screamed and his hands powered up and down, thudding the knife deep into the thing that lay across his lap, relishing the feeling as the knife met resistance then buried itself up to the hilt. Loving the wetness that hit his face each time his hands rose again.

'Oh, Christ, I'M KILLING SOMEONE!' Danny screamed and his vision returned, rising slowly from the dim pink and red through to full, sharp colour.

He was naked and sitting cross-legged on wet grass. The red was blood. The pink was the naked and torn body of Steffy Osmond which lay across his lap, and despite the damage he had already inflicted upon her, Steffy was still conscious and struggling feebly. Her hands were bound together behind her achingly long, swan-like neck and anchored there with the kind of cord Danny had bought on his shopping expedition. Her eyes were covered with a *Why have your sleep disturbed?* eyeshade.

'ABSOLUTELY NOT!' Danny screamed but the vision didn't cease and his hands didn't release the wooden-handled knife. His muscles bunched and he brought it down hard into her belly. Steffy jerked with the force and bright frothy blood shot up from the punctures in her ribcage and hit Danny's face.

'NOOOO!' Danny screamed but he was hard and he wanted not just to fuck her, but to take her inner core, spread it apart and wear her like an overcoat

Then hysterical laughter filled his ears, expanding until it grew solid and became the whole universe, blotting out every sensation but Steffy's weight on his lap and the relentless movement of his arms.

Danny writhed in agony, grasping for the magic words he'd now forgotten, and somewhere out there in emptiness, his arms kept on striking out at Steffy; slashing now and hacking. Opening her up.

Then Danny realised where the laughter was coming from. It was not the taunting laughter of the Gannex Man, but his very own voice coming from his very own throat.

IT'S ME! he screamed and the shock slapped him hard in the face. His arms stopped punching and his vision cleared once more.

It was no bad mental joke, no passing fantasy or nightmare, and there was no one else to blame. Danny had done this. Steffy lay across his legs, not just dead but hacked open from her pubic bone all the way up to her neck. Danny was wearing most her blood. It sheeted his face, chest and legs, dripping from his hands and arms to the grass in thick droplets. Stephanie Osmond's hot blood was in his nostrils, trickling down the back of his throat. It ran from his lips. It was under his tongue. It was in his eyes, stinging and blearing his vision red.

Danny roared in anguish but his hands had dropped the knife and were reaching for the gaping rent in the woman's body.

NO! Danny commanded. *ABSOLUTELY NOT!* But his hands knew exactly what they wanted and were now beyond his control.

'NOOOOO!' Danny screamed as his fingers touched Steffy's flesh. His voice wheeled down from above and battered hard on his eardrums.

Inside Steffy it was hot and wet and soft.

Ten-up? Danny's mind asked him.

Then there was nothing.

3

Danny crashed back into the incredible density of his small, cold body with such force that he screamed aloud in agony, certain that this time he'd smashed himself into a million sharp pieces. The force of being reunited at such speed knocked him backwards off his chair and he writhed across the floor like a broken snake, his guts surely torn apart and his spine alight with bright fire, from pelvis to skull.

The fire slipped down his spine, gathered in that internal area deep inside him between his anus and his scrotum, pulsed three times and vanished.

Danny's senses slowly returned and his first thought was that something dreadful had happened to his alignment inside his body. He no longer fitted squarely into it and everything hurt. His penis was shrunken and his scrotum had drawn agonisingly tight, compressing his balls against him like a vice and sending dull pain up into his abdomen. He was twisted inside himself and seemed to have three arms and three legs, none of which were separate from the others. He was drenched and it took a while for him to realise that he was no longer soaked in Steffy's blood but his own sweat and urine. Like that brave detective Ray Johnson, Danny had wet himself.

He curled himself into a sobbing, hurting ball, found one of those alien arms, brought it towards him and, like a frightened child, inserted his thumb into his mouth and sucked hard on it, while his fingers curled around his nose.

When his mind began to work again, it started with a sudden click – like an errant piece of machinery having been suddenly and forcefully kicked – and Danny's first thoughts were: *You didn't do it! You didn't kill her! Everything is all right!*

He heaved a further sob and exhaustion hit him like a warm, comforting blanket. As he drifted off to sleep the cry-baby part of his mind corrected those three sentences his rationality clung to so tightly.

You didn't do it yet, *you mean, old Dan,* the voice whispered. *Everything* might *be all right. You haven't killed her . . .* yet!

4

Danny dreamed of a vast, snow-covered field, rising gently up before him in a rolling hill. The sky was covered with icy grey cloud which dropped a few fluffy flakes now and promised a further heavy fall very soon. A soundless gentle breeze cast flurries across the ankle-deep virgin snow in which Danny stood. The silence was dreadful.

He was halfway up the hill and although his shoes and ankles were beneath the snow and his breath hung in the air before him, there was no sensation of cold, just an aching emptiness. There was a hedge at the side of the field about two hundred yards to Danny's left and he turned to face it, knowing he did not want to go that way and knowing he had to. His legs started to move him towards the hedge, his feet sinking into the snow with a slight crunch at each step. A scrap of red cloth hung from a branch in the hedge, fluttering gently in the breeze, its colour vivid against the grey-white monotone of the surroundings.

That's where it is, Danny thought as his legs took him relentlessly towards that awful marker and the knowledge lay heavily in his mind. *That's where it is.*

And Danny trudged endlessly towards it through the snow.

Chapter Sixteen
Playing God

1

Lady Luck in her own, sadistic but somehow *elegant*, way was a master torturer. She could – and would, Danny believed – push you all the way to the red line which marked the boundaries of agony and keep you there until you were almost, but not quite, burned out. Like all professional torturers, she knew the value of keeping her subjects alive and kicking. A dead or overloaded nerve could supply no more pain. And a numb brain would not respond to those other exquisite bringers of pain, which were two of every torturer's favourite party-pieces, *The Waiting and The Hope*.

Ordinary torturers would simply cease to cause pain and allow their victim's hope to generate itself – the simple hope that the beatings had finished for good – but Lady Luck was no ordinary torturer. *The Hope* would be allowed to grow, but not in its own ragged haphazard way. Lady Luck would fertilise and tend it, prune it and shape it, allowing glimpses of *what-might-be* and occasionally presenting you with a gift you would gratefully receive and perhaps fall on your knees to thank her for. And when you finally told yourself that life, perhaps, wasn't so bad after all, doubts would creep into your mind and you would enter the next phase, *The Waiting*.

And sometimes the wait didn't last very long.

Danny knew all this from the moment he woke shivering on the floor of the Reading Room feeling purged and clean; better, in fact, than he had done in weeks. And if he hadn't known it, he might have proved it to himself by looking at the symmetries in the spikes and troughs of his own life-charts, The If Only Papers. What he did not know and could not tell from the life-charts, was the nature of the gift that would keep him heading resolutely forwards toward his destiny like a donkey following a carrot while the whip was raised behind him – or at which moment the whip might fall

The gift turned out to be the friendship of a small boy on whom Lady Luck had already done her worst and the whip-crack followed when Steffy came back.

But before either of these things, there was business to be attended to.

2

The business lasted three weeks and was so ridiculously easy that, at first, Danny felt guilty about taking the money.

He opened for business at 10am the day after his vision of Steffy and was surprised to discover that not only was he not the least bit concerned about suffering another nasty episode, but that he truly believed it was an aberration caused by his refusal to practise his talent. *As Lerner so truly said*, he sardonically told himself as he unlocked the front door, *belief in yourself is a wonderful thing*. But Danny *did* believe in himself – to the extent that he'd slept like a baby the previous night and woken up feeling refreshed and confident this morning. He had even eaten his first cooked breakfast since his arrival – and had fallen on it with relish.

He had cleared all Lerner's old letters of recommendation from the clear pane of glass above the front door and had bought a small sign that now hung there, suspended by a length of chain and a sucker. The word OPEN was written on one side and the words SORRY WE'RE CLOSED on the other. Danny flipped the sign over from closed to open and went back inside to wait.

And as if by magic, customers began to turn up.

Danny's first paying customer came in at twenty past ten, bursting into the room just as Danny had become absorbed in the Dick Francis thriller he had picked at random from the pile in Lerner's office and lounge. The paperwork all said that it was Danny's own office and lounge now but he still didn't feel as if it belonged to him, still expected Alistair Lerner to walk back in at any moment, a smouldering Woodbine plugged firmly into his gaunt face.

Danny jumped as the door banged open and told himself that if he intended to keep his heart going through this particular part of his life, it might be a very good idea if he considered purchasing some kind of a door bell. *And a vacant and engaged sign for the Reading Room door wouldn't go amiss*, he suddenly thought and wondered how Lerner had prevented people barging in while he was doing a reading.

'Where is he?' the woman demanded. She was large, well dressed, blue rinsed and in her mid sixties. She looked extremely angry.

Where is who?' Danny asked mildly as his heartbeat began to settle.

'Alistair. The psychic. I came to see a psychic. I was informed he was back in business. Who are you? What are you doing here? Where is Alistair?'

The woman's manner was overbearing and her face was flushed

with resentment, but behind her gold-rimmed glasses her eyes were large and scared.

'What are you frightened of?' Danny asked, but he didn't really need to. He suddenly became vividly aware of the size and weight of the responsibility he had taken on by opening the shop. He had not given it a great deal of consideration until now. *You've been too tied up with other things*, he told himself, then added that this was no excuse. *What kind of people did you expect would come?* his cry-baby asked. If Danny was honest with himself he had expected to meet non-believers; happy tourists on late holidays who turned up out of curiosity 'to have their palms read'. He hadn't envisaged meeting real people with real fears and worries.

'What do you mean, frightened?' the woman asked, still standing in the doorway.

Danny groped in his mind for her name, hoping to prove something to her. Nothing came. He did not have Stephanie Osmond's talent and his own ability to pick up information from other people seemed to have ceased yesterday when he laid his hands on the crystal again. 'You are frightened,' he said gently. 'You needn't be. Nothing bad is going to happen. Come in and sit down.'

The woman didn't move. 'I expected to see Alistair. Where is he?' She was quickly running out of anger, her face falling as its bright prop faded away.

'I'm afraid Alistair is gone,' Danny said.

The woman's face paled visibly. 'Gone?' she said.

'Passed over.'

'Dead?' the woman said in a small disbelieving voice.

As sometimes happened in a grave situation, Danny felt a sudden violent surge of hilarity. *As a Dodo!* he wanted to say. *One small death for mankind, one giant leap for Alistair!* After which he wanted to cackle hysterically. He bit the insides of his cheeks and nodded, giving her an undertaker's sad, understanding smile while his cry-baby (currently in the ascendant, it seemed) reminded him that Jon Vinge had thought – with good reason – that he was a callous bastard.

'Oh dear,' the woman said. 'I didn't know.'

'It was peaceful,' Danny told her. He realised he was still holding the Dick Francis. He closed it and placed it on the floor beneath the table. 'I have taken over from Alistair with his blessing. If it's possible, I'd like to help you with your problem.'

Danny's mind suddenly switched tracks and his hilarity and false humility left him. He frowned as information began to trickle towards him from the woman then he found he didn't want to laugh at all. *Her husband is sick*! He knew this without a shadow of a doubt and also understood just how terrified the woman was. 'Is it your husband?' he asked, his mind quickening in a way that was barely under his control. A good feeling stole across him and made him smile inwardly. Distantly he realised he had finally gone to work.

His name is Tom, Danny thought.

'Yes,' the woman said.

'Tom,' Danny said.

Still in the doorway, the woman – *Margaret* – nodded. She was now wearing the frightened backing-away face Danny had first seen on Dennis and Sara – what now seemed like years ago – and had last seen on Jon Vinge the detective, but she didn't look as if she was about to flee. A part of her looked very impressed.

'If you'd like to sit down, I'll see what I can do,' Danny said. 'There's no guarantee though. If nothing happens this time I'll refund your money and let you try again tomorrow or whenever it suits you. For free.'

'Okay,' Margaret said and finally came into the room. She sat on the far side of the table, fiddling with her handbag while Danny switched on the up lighter, turned out the Anglepoise and placed it below the table.

'We have to link hands,' Danny said, unwrapping the crystal. 'I don't know if Alistair worked that way, but I do.'

Margaret didn't look as if she wanted to hold Danny's hand. 'He used to hold my gloves,' she announced. 'I've brought them,' she added hopefully.

'Sorry,' Danny said. 'I have to take your hands.'

'What about the notes?' Margaret said, doubtfully. 'How will I take notes?'

'You won't have to,' Danny said. 'I'll tell you what I see as I go along and you can write notes afterwards if you wish. I don't think you'll need to though.'

'Okay,' she said uncertainly

Danny unveiled the crystal which immediately began to grow a similar gold speck to the one he'd seen yesterday. 'Give me your hands,' he said.

Margaret's hands were small and soft, frail and trembling slightly. Danny linked his fingers with hers and guided them to the cool surface of the flickering sphere. Rainbow points of light danced inside the almost invisible crystal but they were softer and smaller than yesterday's. None of them found their way out into the room.

Danny gently placed their hands on the crystal and felt the tingling energy flow into him from a surface which was neither cold nor hard.

Margaret gasped. 'Oh dear!' she cried in a distant voice.

'What do you see?' Danny asked. Wafer-thin rays of vermilion and blue twinkled inside the emptiness, their light tickling Danny's retinas.

'Hardly anything,' the woman replied in a small, shaky voice. 'It's just that. . .'

'What?'

'Alistair said I wasn't to speak once he'd started. . .'

'I'm not Alistair.'

'It's . . . *different*,' she said hesitantly. 'I felt a kind of electric shock when I touched the ball. My arms are still tingling. And it's all happening so fast. Alistair used to take ages to make it start and when it did it wasn't like this. The ball seems to be almost . . . gone. It's like . . . holding empty air . . . but it's . . . warm.'

'Don't be frightened,' Danny said realising that if the woman couldn't see anything inside the crystal she almost certainly would not accompany him when he fell into it. And he was going to fall into it very soon. It was getting high now and the crystal was expanding.

'What do you want to know?' Danny asked and did not need to be told. His stretched voice followed him as he fell through sparkling mist and Danny already knew precisely where he was going. Hospital.

He jolted sideways and was amazed to find himself inhabiting the sixty-seven-year old body of Margaret Miller. Margaret was sitting beside a bed in an intensive care ward that smelled strongly of disinfectant. She had piles which were hurting her, and many aching joints, some of which were arthritic. The ones in her right thumb and right big toe were the worst and constantly grated on her nerves. But these minor pains were of little consequence to her today; she was totally absorbed in the man who lay unconscious in the bed beside which she sat. Margaret Miller was currently a very happy woman. The psychic had been correct now she believed what he'd said because Tom was alive after all.

But there had been a time when she had not believed. A fortnight after her consultation with the psychic – whose name she could never quite remember and whom she had mentally christened Little Alistair – her belief in his assurances had begun to wear off. She had begun to doubt and that doubt had changed into a suspicion – God forgive her – that Little Alistair had been a charlatan who had made it all up. Her doubt had reached its peak last night when she was alone in her house trying to become tired and failing because poor Tom was alone in hospital – alone for the first time in what was very nearly fifty years of marriage – and the last hours had been ticking away before he underwent the triple by-pass heart operation the surgeons had been so enthusiastic about (and so careful to point out that the chances of a full recovery from were fifty-fifty or sixty-forty in his favour for a man of Tom's advancing years). After hearing these words of wisdom, she hadn't wanted Tom to have the operation at all, but the doctors, the surgeons and finally Tom himself had all pointed out that it might just give him a new lease of life, and the alternative – lurking just around the corner – was certain death. So she had finally given in.

But last night Margaret had come to believe that the psychic was wrong and Tom was wrong and that all the surgeons in the world – and all the king's horses and all the king's men, come to that – just wouldn't be able to take Tom apart and put him together again. Last night she had almost worn a groove in the lounge carpet with all the pacing she had done while she had assured herself over and over again, God forgive her, that Tom would not survive. Her muscles and joints and her head had ached but she had found it impossible to relax or to sit down.

She had paced all night and then, at six this morning, she had walked all the way to the hospital, arriving just after Tom had been taken to the operating theatre. They had told her everything would be fine and dandy and that she *really ought to go home and try to get some rest*, but she had refused and had spent eight tortuous hours pacing the tiny waiting area, thinking of nothing but the expression that would be on the face of the doctor who would finally come to see her. He would be grim and concerned. 'Mrs Miller? We've had a few problems, I'm afraid. Would you mind coming into my office for a few moments.' And then she would be told.

But it hadn't happened, thank God and all his angels. The sweet-faced nurse who had finally come to see her had been bearing good news. Great News with capital letters. Tom had come through. Margaret had wept with joy and relief and again she had refused to go home and rest until she had been allowed to visit her husband.

Now she sat staring happily at the old fool, who at seventy-eight was a sight tougher than she'd thought and who still had a few years left in him yet.

'Maggie?' Danny said softly. He didn't hear his voice for what seemed an age. *Mggghееe!* it came back to him.

'Yes?' the reply swept down to him.

'You mustn't doubt me.'

'No,' she said.

'Tom's had a by-pass.'

'He's booked in for one.' She gave a single grunted chuckle. 'Sounds like a car going to the garage, doesn't it?'

'He's had it,' Danny said silently. *Hsss hatitttt.*

Silence.

'He's had it,' he repeated, waiting to hear his stretched words. They came but the reply didn't.

Margaret finally wailed, 'Oh no, *please!*'

'The *operation!*' Danny said, cursing his choice of words. 'Tom's had the operation. It's okay. It was successful and he's well. He's going to be all right!'

'Thank God!'

And all his angels!

'And all his angels,' Margaret said.

I wonder, Danny thought as he looked at Tom from Margaret's future eyes, *if it's possible to switch from here to there*.

And then he wished he had not entertained that notion at all because he instantly found himself inside Tom and discovered that when you had open heart surgery they sawed through your sternum and pulled your ribcage apart in order to get at your heart. Danny could feel the pain – crushing, even though it was picked up second hand and sent back in time – in his own distant chest.

Danny would have flicked himself back to Margaret instantaneously but for the strangely interesting fact that Tom was still unconscious from the anaesthetic. Tom was dreaming – for some reason – about earth moving machinery digging a deep pit he didn't want in his back garden and Danny found he was able to watch the dream as if it were his own. The interesting thing was that Tom himself – his personality – could not be accessed. He was either locked up in a very small part of his brain that Danny could not address, or not present at all.

Danny looked for him, couldn't find him, then began to wonder if he was going to pull through this at all. He tried to shunt himself into Tom's future and could not.

'You *are sure*?' Maggie's stretched question was distant – almost inaudible. Danny flicked himself out of Tom and back into the woman, surprised again at how easy it was and relieved that the weight on his distant chest had suddenly vanished.

'Just a moment,' he replied, thinking of the flicker he'd just experienced. *There's another interesting thing, old Dan. A very interesting thing. What do you suppose* that *was?*

Margaret's hand came up and wiped a tear of joy from the corner of her eye. 'Are you sure?' she asked again from back there in the present.

'Hold on,' Danny replied. *Hulll huuun.*

When he had transferred himself from Margaret's future body to that of her husband, he had thought the transfer was instantaneous but during the return journey – if it *was* a journey – Danny had perceived a kind of flicker of light. Except that now he thought about it, it hadn't just been light. It had been a huge dark space with a kind of cat's-cradle of something bright in it. Danny thought he might well have just caught a glimpse of a tiny part of something very much bigger and thought he knew what it was.

You may have just seen the hidden machinery which makes things run, he told himself. *You've just seen your entrance to the web.*

And Danny knew he had to see it again. There was no question about it; no argument against it. The need was imperative.

He flicked himself out of Margaret's body and found himself, not at one of Lerner's time gates at the edge of the web, but hanging in nothingness close to the very centre of it. The hub. The hub itself was not visible and the plain on which Danny stood and the vast open pit where the hub surely lay was defined only by the curved nature of the searing light which flowed in and out of it in a billion thick and ragged columns, each turning gracefully through ninety degrees at the edge of the pit. The movement of the massive trunks of light was perceptible only by watching the furious crackling and sparking of raw energy that played around their circumferences. Somewhere in the vast distance behind and above Danny the columns were suddenly truncated as they fed out of this place into their own universes.

Danny's body was not present here and his senses screamed out at the stunning view of creation from outside it: he was suspended in nothingness, completely outside time, place or existence itself. Two huge cables of white energy passed beneath his null place, one entering the pit and one leaving it. Each contained a billion more strands of innumerable colours and shades. And each of those, Danny suddenly knew, would contain a billion more. These were undoubtedly the strands of creation of his own universe.

And Danny gazed at the pit – the source not just of the very universe itself but of all possible universes past present and future. All life. All time. All creation. All dimensions.

The mouth of God! Danny's mind screamed. *You're gazing into the mouth of God himself.*

Danny flickered, hit the raw energy at the edge of the white column and crackled into nothingness.

When he became aware again he was falling like a stone, except that he was falling sideways, flickering and jolting through complex connections of strands of space, time and place, none of which he recognised. Somewhere behind him, Joey the departed budgie, was twittering and chirruping noisily, and somewhere beyond *that* something very dark and cold was reaching for him.

Danny was very suddenly and violently snapped back into the strand of time that was connected to (or along which ran) the future of Margaret Miller and he was thrust through it at great speed, her days and nights falling before him like a deck of collapsing playing cards.

'Are you sure?' Margaret asked and her voice was time-lapsed. Rushing towards her end, Danny realised that he was now hearing her previous question at the moment he had previously perceived it but he was also hearing it a fraction of a second later. The time that had passed since he flicked himself into the mouth of God and the time that was now passing so rapidly meant nothing whatsoever in the world where his body sat linking hands with the woman.

Danny soared to the end of Margaret's life, hit a hard junction where it merged with the life of her husband, and burst through that into a dimension in which there was no room for him. Danny's mind was scalded as the place he could not inhabit stretched like elastic and then violently expelled him, flinging him backwards through time.

He came to rest back in the hospital but entirely out of phase with Margaret and Tom and able not to *see* their futures and pasts but to *know* each event intimately as if it had all been suddenly poured into his memory. Joey's chirruping was absent and the reaching thing that had wanted him so badly had lost the scent of him way back there somewhere.

Danny was stunned by the different facets of character of the two people and the richness and symmetry of their intricately interwoven lives. He started to talk, not knowing if Margaret could hear him, and not caring. Danny felt as if the scales had suddenly fallen from his eyes. There were many ordinary things in those lives that suddenly seemed astonishingly significant and *beautiful* somehow. Each mundane detail of those lives had suddenly become imbued with a shining new reason. Everything mattered and everything counted; all those tiny pieces were a part of a great new mystery. And the compulsion to tell those details was too great to resist. 'Tom's got a lot of wires on him and tubes in his arm and nose and he's unconscious, but the operation went well and the machinery is all bleeping in the right order. Everyone's happy. Tom used to be a bank manager. He did thirty-nine years at Barclay's. He loves his garden. He's dreaming about earth-movers digging it up. You were childhood sweethearts and you were married on your eighteenth birthday and both. . .'

Danny caught his tongue . . . of you were starry-eyed virgins, he had been going to say as he recalled their first clumsy giggling night together, but he caught himself in time. The Margaret out there might not want to hear some of this.

'. . . of you were starry-eyed with love,' he said. 'And you both still get starry-eyed when you're alone.'

Margaret and Tom had ten more happy years together, Danny suddenly remembered, and felt a momentary pang of what might have been jealousy. The symmetrical pattern their lives wove would be completed when they died together in a coach crash on a tour of Scotland. They would die holding hands and smiling at a joke they had just shared and their deaths would be instantaneous. They would suffer no fear and no pain. Here were some of the people Lady Luck had not drawn kicking into a high-stakes game. She had smiled on them and a part of Danny was happy for them. The envious part was temporarily subdued, but Danny thought it would make itself known later.

'You have many more years of happiness together,' he said. 'There's plenty of life left for you both.'

Danny flicked himself easily back into Margaret's body and from there back into his own.

He entered himself smoothly and without pain this time and was surprised to learn that his bullet scar was throbbing deeply, that he was drenched in sweat, that he was terribly tired, and that Margaret Miller's small, soft hands were crushing his own.

'How did I do?' he asked shakily and his mind said, *You did very well, old Dan, you just came very close to seeing creation itself in action.* There were many questions piled up behind this comment but Danny refused to contemplate those until later. Much later, probably. The sort of questions he had to ask had no easy answers and possibly no answers at all. Some of those questions, if directly addressed, might drive a person over the edge.

Margaret Miller nodded. She was crying silently.

'Okay?' Danny asked, trying to extricate his fingers from hers and failing.

'I was frightened,' she said.

'Why?' Danny said. 'Everything's going to be all right. Tom is going to have the operation and he's going to be okay. You've got loads more years together. Didn't you hear me?'

'Yes,' Margaret said.

'And you know I told you the truth, don't you?'

Margaret nodded. She sniffed and finally released his hands.

Danny flexed his fingers. They felt bent and stiff but the relaxed euphoria of having done good work allowed the smile to remain on his face. 'Then what's wrong?' he asked.

Margaret placed her handbag on the table, opened it and took out a tissue into which she blew her nose, long and hard. She snapped the bag shut and put it on the floor, but kept the tissue. 'I didn't like the noise,' she confessed.

Danny frowned. 'Noise?'

'Didn't you hear it?'

'What noise was this?'

'I thought you were making it at first,' she sniffed, lifting her spectacles and dabbing the corners of her eyes with the tissue. 'Then it seemed to be coming out of thin air just above the right side of your head and I got scared. I don't know what it was and I didn't like it. It frightened me.'

Danny was mystified. 'What did it sound like?'

Margaret Miller clasped her hands together tightly, turned her head away from him, leaned as far back into her seat as she could and looked at him from the corners of her eyes. 'You're scaring me again now,' she said shakily. 'I thought you would know. I thought it was just a kind of trick you did to impress me. A hidden speaker or something. It was that, wasn't it?'

Danny shook his head and waited.

'It sounded like a dicky bird whistling at first,' Margaret said. 'A canary or something. I thought I could hear a bell being pecked. Then that went away and it changed to a scary noise. . .'

'What did it sound like?' Danny asked.

'I don't know,' Margaret said, and thought about it. 'I can't explain it, but it sounded like something coming. Like something big and nasty was coming.'

3

During the next twelve days Danny turned himself with remarkable ease into a production line psychic and did successful readings on eighty-six customers – with no mishaps at all.

Margaret Miller's words, *Like something big and nasty was coming*, haunted him for the first three of those days – in fact he had put the closed sign up in the window after she had left and had seriously considered quitting while he was ahead and fuck Joey and the Gannex Man and the now recurring dream of the snow-filled field. If there was the remotest chance that he might either materialise that 'something nasty' during a reading (and he still knew so little about the process that this had to be taken very seriously indeed), or create some kind of a split in reality or a short-out in the web of time that might cause injury or death (or worse) to him or his clients, then he could not continue.

That afternoon he had asked himself some very serious questions, all of which seemed incredibly juvenile and gauche to the pragmatic part of his mind, and that part of him had provided a great many earnest and down-to-earth explanations while being careful not to tell him how silly he was. For the first thing, to the best of his knowledge, there were no detailed accounts of anyone ever having 'introduced' a metaphysical being into the real world – other than the events the film *The Entity* was based on, and Danny suspected that the real woman (the one who was now supposed to be in a mental asylum) who believed she was being raped by demons was a victim of some kind of psychosis. This possibility, therefore, was extremely doubtful. The worry that he might inadvertently cause a short-out in time sounded so ludicrous – even less than an hour after the reading – that he suspected even down-market science fiction writers would reject it. There were even fewer recorded instances of this – none at all, in fact.

By the end of the afternoon Danny had convinced himself that he had somehow made and projected the sound of Joey into the room – perhaps telepathically; that the sound of 'something big and nasty coming' had been him tearing backwards through Margaret Miller's own future and that there had been no danger at all.

This was accomplished by a great deal of clever mental juggling during which Danny sorted things into two piles: those he had to believe and those he chose not to. The fact that the things he had to believe were just as unbelievable as the things he chose not to, highlighted a flaw in his logic that Danny simply chose to ignore. He may or may not have gazed into God's mouth and seen the hidden source of all things; he may or may not have felt something pursuing him across time, and there may or may not have been another Danny Stafford hidden beneath this one and fighting its way out. He *could* see into the future – as crazy as it sounded (and he reminded himself that Brough Lacey's fine line had been left behind a very long time ago) – but for practical purposes and reasons concerning mental health, the rest of it, for the moment at least, would have to be stacked in pile B.

At the beginning of the first reading of the following day – ten minutes to the dot from the moment he'd swung the sign round from SORRY WE'RE CLOSED to OPEN – the phrase, *There's a first time for everything*, had stolen into his mind and Danny had imagined a crack opening up in the air just to the right of his head and 'something nasty' on the other side, clawing and breaking brittle pieces from the air with black teeth and talons like a huge mutant chick pecking its way out of its egg shell. Danny did not believe, but he was subsequently very careful where he put himself in that other metaphysical world. He could not risk further exploration while with clients and addressed himself solely to the task in hand.

And there were many tasks, some of which were achingly sad, some of which were fun and some of which presented him with tricky moral dilemmas.

A young man called Clive had lost a dog called Betty and wanted to know where she could be found. He had brought her lead to give Danny her scent. Danny had expected to fail but had got her scent straight away. The experience of inhabiting the body of a dog was disconcerting to say the least. The dog's body was very hot, the olfactory sensation was mind-blowing, and the dog knew Danny was there and wanted to talk. Betty's thought patterns were simple and friendly – welcoming even – but Danny was swamped by their bright ferocity and they were too alien for communication. Betty became frustrated very quickly and howled mournfully until Danny left her. Betty – who had spent three days and nights being hopelessly lost and very hungry – had been picked up and was now living happily in Hove with a twenty-three-year-old divorcee called Ruthie Turner.

Danny checked Clive's future one and found that he was presently on what Lerner had called a 'key moment' and what Danny had come to call 'a moment of if only'. Clive's future was in Danny's hands. If he simply said that Betty was alive and well, Clive would be a little disappointed he would not get Betty back but pleased to know the dog was alive. A long way up the road – a very long way – Clive would get another dog and also call it Betty. He would be thirty-seven by then, unhappily married and in a job he didn't much like. His future three, which Danny now blithely switched to future one simply by telling him where Betty could be found, was a great deal more satisfactory. Meeting Ruthie Turner would be the biggest single stroke of luck in Clive's life. A great deal of love and happiness would follow.

'Fuck it,' Danny said after Clive had gone and the seemingly ever present cry-baby had started bemoaning the fact that Danny didn't ought to be playing God with people's lives, 'there's enough bad stuff about already. If I can improve someone's chances of having a good and satisfying life, I'm damn' well going to, and no one's going to stop me! So shut up and sod off!'

And in that fortnight Danny relentlessly played God whenever the opportunity arose, frantically trying to sort out the grade A mess God or fate or Lady Luck herself had got innocent and undeserving people into.

About half his clients did not have anything nasty waiting down the road for them – in the near future, anyway – but there was a vast and varied selection of ills stalking the rest. Some – like the woman whose husband's brain stem was rapidly becoming a very large tumour, or the old man whose manic depressive wife had a high probability of throwing herself beneath the wheels of an express train – could not be helped. Danny tried to help all these people, checking main futures, sub-futures and possibilities (all of which he rapidly became expert at accessing) but sometimes all the *If Only* turning points had been passed and at these odds there was no such thing as a damage-limitation exercise. For these people, Danny could do nothing but make things a little easier with lies or half-truths. Some he told that he had been unable to see their futures and refunded their money; some who knew what he'd seen without being told, he sympathised with; some he cried with. But those who seemed to have a good – or even a *slim* – chance of cheating their most probable bad future, he instructed, gravely and in great detail, never telling them what might be in store for them, but strongly advising them of things they should do on certain days and in certain places in order to avoid what he euphemistically termed 'possible problems'. Danny quickly developed a bedside manner worthy of a doctor, watched his language and struck the word 'probable' from his vocabulary completely. Possible sounded easier to change.

In this way he prevented two men and a woman from dying of heart attacks during the following month, got a teenage girl early treatment for a breast tumour that would otherwise have killed her before her twentieth birthday, and saved the lives of a chubby and jolly lesbian couple whose 1959 Morris Minor had appointments with death at 2.15 the following day in futures one to five.

Each time Danny sat alone sweating profusely and vibrating like a tuning fork after having saved a life or averted a disaster he would ball his fist, extend his middle finger and pass on the defiant message 'Up yours!' to Lady Luck, wherever she might be.

Just be very careful, his cry-baby whispered to him in the quiet moments, *because playing God could turn out to be addictive and very dangerous. And it'll have its price. You know what happened to Suzie when you tried to change the future, and you don't want* that *happening again, do you?*

But Danny didn't think it would happen again or that there would be a price to pay. Before, he had been an amateur; now he was an expert. He could take on time, Lady Luck and God Himself, and still come out on top.

And as if by magic, the customers kept on coming. Danny most enjoyed the ones who didn't have any real problems: younger ones mainly – those who were simply curious – but these were outnumbered by that sad body of people, the lonely and unloved. Like Danny himself these poor souls ached to know if there was any chance of, not love particularly, but a good emotional relationship a little further up the road. Danny felt for every single one of them, and wondering why Lady Luck needed so much pain to keep her happy, tried hard to change things for them where he could.

But there were lighter moments, too, mostly provided by suspicious schoolgirls who wanted to know who else their boyfriends were seeing, what their chances were with the form heart-throb (and Danny found there was a lucky sixth-former called Ricky Pierce who currently had three girls on the go and another five in waiting) and, most of all, what their 'A' level results would turn out to be.

A pretty schoolgirl called Adele Fletcher visited him three times, her questions gradually changing from vague generalisations to specifics as she gained confidence in Danny's predictions. Like others before her Adele had started out asking if she would be happy, then asked about her career prospects, then got down to the nitty gritty as far as exam results went. Adele pushed Danny hard, wanting to know not just whether she would pass the three 'A' levels but demanding grades and enquiring after just how much effort she would have to expend in order to attain A, B, or C grades, because she said, she had a busy social life and didn't want to have to work herself into an early grave. Danny simply told her not to worry.

By her third visit, Adele had done some serious thinking and come up with a good solution to the problem she was having with physics. She asked Danny if he would supply her with the answers to next summer's 'A' level exam. Danny told her he doubted he could even find out the answers and then amazed himself by doing just that. But he refused to tell Adele what they were, because he knew that, having cheated, she would feel a fraud for the rest of her life.

And Danny knew Adele would sail through all her 'A' levels – the physics one included – without cheating, but this was something else he could not tell her.

Telling her she would pass would make Danny a liar since Adele would simply cease to make the required effort which would lead her to fail. Sometimes, it seemed, there was no easy option. Danny told her he couldn't reveal the answers to her but that if she worked as hard as she was doing now there was nothing to worry about.

But Adele didn't like working that hard. Half seriously she offered Danny her body on condition he cribbed the answers for her. When Danny smiled and turned her down, her offer became totally serious. Adele said she found Danny – and the idea of an extended physical relationship with him – extremely attractive. Danny told her he was flattered but not available. When Adele had gone Danny began to feel the familiar aching loneliness that plagued him and part of him wished he had accepted. And had Adele returned he might have done.

As Danny knew very well, keeping busy would fend off thoughts you didn't want to have, but there were times – crawling into a cold, empty bed last thing at night, for instance – when those thoughts came creeping back. And the most painful thoughts were always at the front of the queue. In those quiet moments Danny would remember Suzie's warm love, and dull, aching despair would accompany the dull ache of longing in his guts. In these moments Danny would feel the full weight of his guilt and he would entertain fantasies in which Suzie picked up the letter he'd sent her and read it, her eyes filling with tears of sorrow when she realised how badly she'd misjudged him, realised how deep her longing for him was. Suzie would read the letter over and over, crying and forgiving him and wishing that he was back with her. In these fantasies it would be raining and Danny would watch as Suzie came out of the front door of the house, glancing up at the sky then lowering the convertible top of her Sunbeam Tiger, nodding gravely and thinking: *Going for a Blow.* But Danny knew exactly where she was going. She was going to drive all the way to Bognor in rain where she would cruise the wet streets, looking for her missing lover. And her missing lover would be *there!* On the promenade in the rain, walking quickly towards the post box with a fresh letter to her in his hand.

And Danny would turn slowly as before him an ancient Sunbeam Tiger skidded to a stand-still, its tyres hissing on the road. And Suzie would be getting out – not fighting with the cranky driver's door, but climbing right over it in her frantic hurry to get to him before he vanished. And she would run to him, her clothes soaked, her hair in wet rat's tails, her eye-liner blurred in black smudges around her eyes by the wind and the rain and her sudden hot tears. And Danny would drag her to him, sweep her from her feet and spin her joyously around, relishing her damp warmth, the taste of her lips and the feel of her slender body.

And in the mornings when he woke, reality would return with all its solid iciness and Danny would remember the fantasy, and the words: *Mills and Boon* would light in his mind, and he would feel stupid and empty. In the daytime, the fantasies were laughable. The probability of Suzie even having read the letter was so slim that Danny thought he wouldn't have been able to detect it psychically. Suzie would simply have thrown the unread letter straight into the bin.

But Danny was so desperate that a part of the Mills and Boon fantasy extended a nagging root deep inside him. During the twelve days of his sudden success as a psychic this root drove him to write two more letters to her.

These letters were not sad letters proclaiming unrequited love, but considered accounts of what had happened, what Danny expected to happen now and what he hoped for as soon as he had knocked his life into shape, his major ambition being a reconciliation.

He posted both these from Brighton, but after a great deal of consideration had not enclosed his address. He no longer chose to believe that – in Margaret Miller's words – 'something big and nasty was coming' but had decided to play it safe in case what he chose to believe was wrong. If there *was* some dark thing lurking in his future, he did not want Suzie to be exposed to it.

Danny played God and worked on his charts and waited.

4

After the twelfth day of playing God, and just as magically as it had started, the stream of customers into the Fortune Shop dried up.

Danny spent the morning and part of the afternoon of the thirteenth day sitting in the Reading Room with the Anglepoise on and another Dick Francis book before him while he waited for the first customer of the day to come through the front door. The book wasn't one of Dick's best but it kept kept his mind busy and while his mind was busy his cry-baby could not keep telling him that there might be a certain significance in the fact that this was the *thirteenth* day.

Just after two-thirty someone burst in through the the front door. The shop bell Danny had installed tinkled crazily and was silenced as the door crashed into the wall. Danny jumped, automatically closing the Dick Francis and hiding it beneath the table while he thought, *That didn't sound very much like the normal run of the mill customer, did it, Dan?* His heart squeezed hard and Danny tensed and listened while he tried not to think, *That sounded just like something nasty coming*. If it was a customer out there – and he couldn't hear any movement at all – that customer should be reading the sign that said: ENTER ONLY IF THE LIGHT ABOVE THE DOOR IS GREEN. IF THE RED LIGHT IS ON PLEASE WAIT IN THE HALL. Danny glanced at the switch on the wall. He had not left the red light on by mistake so there was no need for the customer to sit down on one of the four chairs he'd set in the hallway . . . *Which means that it's not a customer out there at all.*

Then what is it?

No idea, but perhaps it would be a good idea to get up very slowly, take the chair you're sitting on over to the door and wedge the back of it underneath the handle so whatever it is out there can't come in.

But Danny did not move. It might just be a short-sighted pensioner out there groping in his pocket – or her handbag – for an elusive pair of glasses, but Danny doubted this. He had a strong sensation that Lady Luck might have just given him a present and he wasn't sure he wanted it, whatever it was. He held his breath and listened.

And when he grew used to the sound of his heart hammering in his ears, he hear faint sounds of something that sounded like sobbing.

A kid?

A *trick*!

There was a child out there. A child in distress.

You didn't read Jamie! his mind accused him, and Danny didn't have the faintest idea why.

He got up, went to the door and placed his ear against it while he held the handle in case there was a sudden onslaught. It was a child out there and the child was now crying quite loudly.

Do you need this? Danny asked himself, and a part of him answered, *Yes, you do, because you couldn't, or didn't, read Jamie.*

Danny slowly opened the door and was flooded with relief. It wasn't some kind of black demon bird that had cracked its way through into this reality and had called him with human sounds, it was a real small boy.

The boy was aged perhaps eight or nine judging from his height, but it was difficult to tell because he was backed up against the door to the study opposite Danny and he was hunched up as if expecting a blow. His head was ducked low, his elbows were tucked into his waist and his face was hidden in his hands. The boy stood there and sobbed hard, his shoulders hitching as he breathed.

The boy was dressed in grubby jeans, big cheap trainers and a stained nylon bomber jacket. He looked as if someone had very recently rolled him in the gutter – and judging by the muddy footprint on his back, kicked him while he was down.

There was something else about the boy that caught Danny's eye, but he couldn't put his finger on what it was. *The proportions, Dan*, he finally decided. *He looks like he was assembled by someone who was a little weeny bit pissed.*

'What's wrong?' Danny asked gently.

The boy looked up at him with an exquisite expression of surprise, gave a single gasp of horror and went rigid. His cheek was bruised and a very thin trickle of blood ran from his left nostril.

'It's okay,' Danny said quietly, knowing now why the boy had looked a little strange. Lady Luck, in her infinite nastiness, had seen fit to blight this kid with an extra chromosome. The boy had Down's-Syndrome – he was what Danny's mother had always called a mongol. And that wasn't the end of his troubles, by the look of it. Lady Luck had evidently seen to it that others would beat him up because of it. And the appearance of Danny had apparently terrified him almost to the point of death.

The boy's eyes were wide with terror beyond comprehension. Just when Danny thought the boy would faint from suffocation, he drew a violently shuddering breath and his mouth began to work. 'The huh the huh the hoo the hoo. . .!' he moaned.

Danny held his hands up, palms out. 'It's okay,' he insisted, 'I'm not going to hurt you.'

'The huh-the-huh-the-HOODOO MUH-MAN!' the boy finally wailed.

Now where have you heard that one before, old Dan? a part of his mind asked him.

'Don't hurt me! KEEP AWAY!' the boy sobbed, clutching his hands to his cheeks. 'YOU MUSTN'T HURT ME!'

'I won't hurt you. I promise!' Danny said, not knowing what to do. The boy looked as if he was on the verge of collapse. 'Honestly, I won't!' he added.

The boy looked at Danny with those huge, terrified eyes and fought for words. 'They say you . . . *hurt* me. They say you . . . Hoodoo Man. Huh-hoodoo Man magic me! Duh-don't.

'It's okay,' Danny said, holding up his palms again. 'I won't magic you. I couldn't magic you even if I wanted to. And I don't want to. I want to make you feel better. I want to help you. Honestly.' Not knowing why he was doing it, Danny placed his right hand on his heart to emphasise the word honestly. It was a gesture he had never made before in his life but it felt like a good one and the boy seemed to recognise it in some distant way.

He took two shuddering breaths and spoke very slowly, visibly relaxing with the concentration. 'They said you would magic me bad,' he said.

Danny shook his head hard. 'Not me. They told you lies. Who said it?'

'The others,' the boy said, glancing at the open door as though 'the others' might burst in at any moment to finish off the job.

'Some other kids? They hit you?'

The boy started to sob again, then caught it. He nodded gravely, took a deep breath and composed his reply. 'They made me come inside here. I did not wish to come. They hurt me. Hit me. I falled down. They kick me until I get up and they make me come in here. They say you would magic me.' He glanced at the door again.

'I won't hurt you,' Danny promised, his hand literally on his heart. 'And neither will the other kids. You're safe now. Wait here and I'll go outside. If they're there I'll chase them away.' Danny went outside to look for the boy's tormentors with more than a chasing away on his mind. A cold rage swept through him at the injustice of what had happened to the boy. If the children were still there the Hoodoo Man would work some very bad magic on them indeed.

But the kids were long gone.

Inside the Fortune Shop the boy had started to sob again. 'They've gone,' Danny said. 'You're okay.'

'Close the door,' the boy replied.

Danny had left the door open so the boy wouldn't feel as if he'd been trapped. Obviously the feeling of being trapped with the

Hoodoo Man was preferable to the chance that the other kids might come back.

Some bogey-man you turned out to be, Danny told himself as he closed – and locked – the door.

'What's your name?' he asked, already knowing the answer had to be Jamie.

'Mark,' the boy said, wiping his eyes.

Wrong there then, old Dan. 'Okay, Mark, how about you coming up to the kitchen with me and I'll clean you up a bit. Then I'll give you a glass of lemonade or a Coke or something and then I'll ring your folks.'

Mark's brow furrowed. 'What's *folks*?'

'Your mum and dad.'

'Can't find my dad.' Then Mark had what looked to Danny like an excellent idea. His face brightened like the sun sliding out from behind a dark rain cloud. 'You help me?' he asked, suddenly grinning.

Danny knew that Lady Luck had sucker-punched him once more, but for the moment he didn't care. He felt his own face brightening in a direct and somehow primal response to Mark's own. 'Help you? Help you what?' he asked, smiling. *Looks like you've found a friend, old Dan*, he told himself.

'Find my dad!'

'We'll see,' Danny said. 'Let's get you cleaned up first.' He pointed the way and said, 'Upstairs with you!' and when Mark chuckled and offered him a hot grimy hand to hold, Danny took it gladly.

Chapter Seventeen
Steffy's Book

1

Three days and a single customer later Danny heard the distant riffling of cards and almost felt the whip-crack as the next black ace was forcefully delivered. This was one he had been expecting. Since meeting his new friend, Danny had started making connections. These, as yet, were tenuous but they had allowed him to predict this particular event on his life-charts. At ten past eleven, just as he'd known she would, Stephanie Osmond walked back into his life.

Danny heard the bell rattle as the front door of the Fortune Shop opened and he thought, *What am I going to do?*

But as yet there was no answer to that question.

2

Danny had made the first link three days earlier after taking Mark home, but earlier than that – while he and Mark were in the bathroom, in fact – he had rediscovered something he'd totally forgotten. That the sound of laughter could give you a fresh perspective on life, however bad things were. And little Mark, whose life had been so cruelly blighted, liked to laugh a lot. Mark was not remotely concerned about Down's Syndrome, his reduced life expectancy, his inability to read or his problems with speech. Neither did he weigh himself down with the burden of other people's attitudes towards him. Within ten minutes of deciding Danny wasn't going to hurt him, he had forgiven and forgotten his tormentors, simply shrugging them off. Life for Mark, Danny thought, was literally going to be too short for bad feeling. Mark, with his strange face and his huge grin, radiated fun and warmth and a kind of bright uncomplicated love which drew you to him almost magnetically, lifted your spirits and formed an odd kind of bond between you.

Danny cleaned him up – a process that had rapidly degenerated into a hilarious no-holds-barred tickling contest which Danny lost –

gave him Coke and biscuits, chattered to him, joked with him, and when Mark could neither remember his address nor his telephone number, began to panic.

Mark claimed he knew his way home but Danny didn't like to let him prove it on his own and went with him. Outside, Mark took his hand again and skipped up the street dragging Danny along behind him. Danny realised how absurdly paternal and protective he felt towards the boy and the hook bit deeper.

Will you be someone's dad one day, old Dan? he asked himself, then remembered Suzie's fears about not being able to have children. There was a good chance now that this was true, even if it hadn't been before. *If only. . .*

Mark sensed his mood change instantly. He pulled Danny to a standstill and looked at him gravely. 'Cheer up you, Danny,' he said and warned, 'or I have to tickle!'

Danny's mouth pulled up into a grin of amazement which magically widened into a smile of pleasure. 'Okay,' he said. 'Done!'

Mark lived about three-quarters of a mile away from Danny's shop in an elderly council terrace. During the walk there he claimed he lived with his mother and elder sisters. There was some doubt in Mark's mind about the number of sisters; sometimes there were three, sometimes there were just two. Danny thought he would just have to wait and see.

But when Danny and Mark arrived at the house, Danny forgot all about the number of sisters because what Mark's mother said when she opened the front door slapped him hard in the face.

'Hello, Jamie,' she said resignedly. 'What have you been up to now?'

JAMIE!

You couldn't read Jamie! You couldn't read Jamie! YOU COULDN'T READ JAMIE!

Danny was invited in and ushered into the lounge and – out there somewhere – a part of him was explaining to the boy's mother, Carol, what had happened, but inside the real Danny was reeling while his mind snapped links together and made confusing connections.

While Danny's mind tirelessly repeated the phrase, *You couldn't read Jamie*, he learned peripherally that Mark's name was Mark James and that he was known by his friends at the school – and now by his family – as Jamie. Carol James made tea, then shooed Jamie and the sister who was fussing over him from the room because she wanted to talk to the Hoodoo Man. Carol James spoke like a woman who didn't often get to exercise her talking muscle. She had a great deal to say. Danny was thanked endlessly for looking after Jamie because there weren't many people who took an interest in him; he was told the history of the James family – warts and all – and learned that Jimmy James had a done a runner shortly after his son's fifth birthday and that Jamie still went out to look for him, certain he would return. Carol told Danny she knew the reason why Jamie was sometimes confused about the number of sisters he had and that it was something of a mystery. There were two sisters, but there had been another. The third sister, Claire, had been stillborn. Jamie had followed and Carol thought there was a kind of psychic contact point between Jamie and the sister that never was, and wanted Danny's expert opinion on the matter.

Danny's mind was still making connections and things were almost fitting into place and he was not capable of considering the matter, let alone offering his expert opinion. He said he thought that it was possible, but he couldn't be sure. He assured Carol that he could only look into the future and had no knowledge of, or contact with, those who had passed over.

When Danny eventually excused himself, Jamie escorted him to the gate and whispered into his ear that Danny was his friend.

Danny had walked home smiling.

3

And by the time Stephanie Osmond came into the Fortune Shop, Danny knew there were three parts to the key that would unlock the mystery of his destiny. The first was Jamie, and Danny thought that a part of him had known this all along. Hadn't he told Suzie, even before he'd met Lerner, that he couldn't read Jamie? The second – and the most scary – part was Stephanie who had stopped him from using the crystal to look into his own future. After that first experience when he'd found himself stabbing her to death with a wooden-handled knife, Danny had not tried to see into his own future again. His vision predicted that he was going to murder her – and that worry had been sorted and dumped in the B pile along with all the other things he chose not to believe because surely that experience of the future had been very wrong. Danny chose to believe it was wrong but he didn't know the cause of the experience and did not want to relive it, so he had adopted Lerner's maxim: *I never look into my own future if I can help it.* The result of ignoring this vision was the recurring snowy field dream, but this was much easier to live with.

The third part of the key was Joey the genius budgie who had gone to Africa. Danny didn't have a clue how this might fit with the other two pieces or what they might unlock, but the sinking of his heart when Stephanie walked in told him that he was surely going to find out.

You tasted her life, Dan! the voice of Danny's dreams resounded in his head.

'Hi!' Stephanie said as the accusations flew around inside his head.

She looked stunning; her blonde hair was pulled back into a tight pony tail and her face was so radiant it seemed unreal.

'Stephanie,' Danny murmured. 'You came back.'

'Steffy, please. We're friends.' She took off her coat and placed it on the back of the spare chair. She was wearing a white knee-length skirt and an almost transparent white blouse which revealed a lacy teddy beneath.

Danny tried hard to summon a smile but his head was swimming and a powerful image leapt into his mind's eye and crushed it.

Her long neck, Dan!

Inside his mind, Danny was on the other side of the table, pulling hard on that pony tail and arching Steffy's back against the chair. Her breasts strained against the thin material of her underwear and shirt, her nipples making peaks in the material. Steffy's head was tipped right back exposing that long, perfect neck and Danny's right hand was in the air, locked tightly around the familiar wooden knife handle.

Her long neck!

'What's wrong, Daniel Stafford, famous mystic and crystal gazer?' Steffy asked lightly. 'Aren't you happy to see the person who helped you when you were down and out?'

Danny forced the image away. *You will not kill this woman!* he told himself.

'Yes! Yes, of course I am. I'm sorry, I was thinking of something else.'

'Something unpleasant, judging by your expression.' Steffy smiled. She looked him up and down. 'You've lost weight and you're tired. How about that for a psychic reading?'

'Very good,' Danny said heavily.

'And I see you haven't lost that ready humour you displayed when I picked you up. Anyway, I've been hearing all about you. Good things. You're now the South Coast's leading psychic, I gather. I knew it. I *knew* there was something special about you when I picked you up! Anyway, I was wondering if you would consider returning the favour.'

It might be a good idea if you refused here and now. Before it's too late, the cry-baby warned, but Danny's mouth had already said, 'How?'

'I told you about my book, didn't I?'

As Danny shook his head another tenuous link was formed in his mind and his cry-baby voice fell silent. *Steffy's book*, Danny thought. *Yeah, that sounds about right. Why didn't you think of it before?*

'As you know, I'm interested in psychic phenomena. I suppose that interest was seeded by my ability to just *know* people's names. Now I think about it, the book was probably an attempt to explain that mystery to myself on paper. But there have been other questions raised along the way. Other mysteries, both grand and minor.'

Danny nodded. That odd out-of-phase *déjà-vu* feeling had descended on him again as Steffy continued. *You knew all of this already, didn't you?* he asked himself. *From the moment you saw the car coming toward's you on the way to Brighton – and possibly before that too.* New parts of Danny's mind were awakening now, blasting into life and throwing out grappling hooks to other parts.

'Anyway, I've been researching and writing a book on the subject for the last three years. It's going well but there's a shortage of really good source material. . .'

Everything now seemed to be unrolling before him like a long red carpet woven with an intricate white design. In the last few days important parts of that design – parts he'd always known were there – were being revealed. The dizzy *déjà-vu* feeling was so strong that Danny began to believe that a distant and hidden part of him had been able to look into the future ever since the moment his brother shot him – and had been doing so. This was the nature of his childhood belief that he was *different* from others. That Hoodoo Man part, which was now reaching the zenith of its ascendancy, had been trying to tell him these things all along and the normal, sensible Danny had been studiously ignoring it.

Steffy was gradually winding up to the sixty-four thousand dollar question now. 'I've tracked down one or two genuine psychics but finding them amongst the loonies and confidence tricksters is akin to trying to catch the fairies at the bottom of one's garden, and most of them aren't very good when you do find them. . .'

Steffy's book, Danny realised, *is the shape beneath the hedge in the snowy field of your dreams. It's not Steffy's body under there, it's her book. Her book is the fulcrum on which your own future balances, but there's going to be a price to pay. A heavy price. For both of us.*

'. . . then I hear that Mr Daniel Stafford, a man who has ridden in my own car, is quite simply the best psychic in the country. Amazingly perceptive, they say, and able to see into the future with deadly accuracy. Serendipity! I *knew* there was something special about you. So here I am wanting to test you and talk to you. For my book.'

Danny sighed. 'Look, Steffy, you think you might be a little weeny bit psychic yourself, don't you?'

She thought about it, then nodded. 'A little.'

'So do I. I knew, I think from the moment your car headlights lit on me, back there on the way to Brighton. You confirmed it when you told me my name. I felt you inside my mind, looking for my name. Well, when you said "deadly accuracy' just now, you were a little closer to the truth than you thought. I'm not just a fortune teller – where other psychics are concerned, I'm the Hoodoo Man. A bringer of bad luck. I've only met two psychics in my whole life and I think I killed them both.'

Steffy's face clouded with a look that Danny could not identify. It might have been doubt, or perhaps realisation, or Steffy may have just made a mental link of her own. It passed so quickly that Danny didn't have time to think about it further. 'But you wouldn't kill me, would you?' She asked.

Danny didn't tell Steffy the whole story – just the parts about Lerner and Christine Richard. This would, he hoped, be enough to change her mind about testing him. It had exactly the opposite effect. Steffy believed that Danny was mistakenly blaming himself for the deaths. By the time he'd finished she was bubbling with excitement. Whatever doubtful thought or unpleasant notion she'd had a few minutes ago was long since forgotten.

'This is really hot material for me, Danny,' she said. 'I'd love you to do a reading for me, I really would. I don't think there's any danger at all. Would you?'

Danny shook his head. 'I don't think so,' he said, knowing that this was just a warning label, like: KEEP AWAY FROM CHILDREN or NOT TO BE TAKEN INTERNALLY. In spite of his doubts and fears, a large part of him knew that doing a reading for Steffy would be a turning point for him and was urging him to get on with it. *And anyway*, he justified to himself, *if there's anything to know about Stephanie Osmond, anything terrible in her future that might involve you, you ought to know. If you know, you can act to try and change it.*

'Just to find out something small and specific. What harm could there be in that?' she said.

Plenty, Danny thought, and shrugged.

Steffy smiled. 'Pretty please,' she said.

'Okay,' Danny said, ignoring the voice that whispered, *You fool*! He felt better now he'd made the decision. In spite of his doubts it felt like the right thing to do.

So did a trip on the maiden voyage of the Titanic *for a lot of people*, his cry-baby chipped in.

'What do you want me to do?' he asked.

'What I always do with fortune tellers. I need to ask a specific question. Generalisations are fine for side-show psychics, but the real ones ought to be able to be more specific. Then, if what you say is accurate, we can talk about material for the book. I'd pay you. That sound okay?'

Danny nodded. 'Ask the question,' he said. 'I'll answer it.'

Steffy smiled. 'Tell me, if you can, what my boyfriend is going to get me for Christmas. That's simple enough, isn't it? It's far enough in the future for neither me, you nor my boyfriend to know yet, so you won't get it telepathically. I can verify it on Christmas Day and get in contact with you in the New Year if you're right. Even if you make an error, I'll get in contact with you. Then we can discuss what went wrong.'

'It won't be a surprise present then,' Danny said.

'I've had three birthdays and three Christmases since I started doing this,' she said, 'and all my presents were surprises. The surprise this year, I hope, will be your prediction having been right.'

Danny turned out the Anglepoise, switched on the uplighter and took the velvet cloth off the crystal. Butterflies swarmed in his stomach.

'What do I have to do?' Steffy asked.

'Just relax,' Danny said, speaking to himself as much as to her. He took her hands and linked their fingers, suddenly knowing that Steffy was wearing false fingernails. He told her so and she nodded, smiling. Danny guided their hands towards the crystal.

'It's pretty,' Steffy said.

Danny moved their hands away from the crystal. 'Sorry?' he asked.

'The colours dancing about in there. They're pretty. How do you do it?'

Don't take her with you, Dan!

'It's a trade secret,' he told her, and was about to suggest that it might be a better idea if they didn't hold hands when Steffy suddenly placed their hands on the crystal.

Danny felt the familiar sensation cruise up his arms and Stephanie made a small sound of surprise. Then it was too late – he was inside the crystal and falling. 'Are you inside?' he asked.

'No,' Steffy replied from above and behind him and Danny relaxed.

He jolted sideways and found himself standing in the snow-covered field of his dreams. He was closer to the hedge this time. Too close. The red scrap of material fluttered in the breeze. The date was December the 5th and the field was somewhere on the nearby downs. A few fat flakes of snow were falling but the skies were still heavy with it and Danny knew that by the next morning the six inches on the ground would have increased to eighteen.

*THE RED MARKER. . .*Danny tried to force himself to Christmas Day.

. . . IS WHERE. . .

Nothing happened. The chill breeze picked up little flurries of snow and threw them through Danny. He was rooted to the spot.

. . . YOU. . .

There was a small movement deep inside the hedge. Something settling. He could only just make out its snow-dappled form behind the leaves and branches. It was an odd shape. A *wrong* shape. It was not the shape of Steffy's book at all.

. . . PUT. . .

Danny felt something warm and very familiar begin to flow over him.

. . . HER BODY. . .

His scream of denial died in his throat when he realised the warm feeling was Steffy's blood.

Ten-up, old Dan? his mind asked him. *Bust the barometer*?

Then he was flung violently back into his body in the Fortune Shop.

'It didn't work, did it?' Stephanie said miserably as though she'd known all along that it wouldn't. 'What went wrong?'

Danny shook his head. There were hot wires in there and it felt as if it were coming apart. A feeling of nausea gripped him and he couldn't make himself look into Steffy's eyes.

'You couldn't get past December the 5th, could you?' she said tiredly. 'I knew you wouldn't be able to.'

Danny looked up at her. Steffy's face was ashen and her eyes were bright and very close to tears. *She didn't come here to see if you would help her with her book*, Danny told himself. *She came here to have you exorcise her doubts. Somehow she already knew about that particular date and she wanted you to tell her that everything would be okay.*

'Tell me what happened,' Steffy said.

'Nothing,' he replied, looking away from her burning gaze.

'Tell me the truth, Danny,' she demanded. 'I died, didn't I? That's why you couldn't get past that date. I *have* no future after December the 5th, do I?'

'Don't be silly,' he said, 'It was just a block. I've had them before. It doesn't mean anything. You are not going to die on that date.'

'You don't have to lie to me,' she said. 'I got it from you. I got the information from you while you were entranced. I don't know how I did it, but the message was loud and clear.'

'The message was wrong,' Danny said. 'And I'll disprove it. I can't try again now, but if you leave me a ring or your watch or something you've worn a lot, I'll have another go later. Leave me your phone number and I'll ring you when I have a result. But believe me, you're not going to die.'

Steffy took off her watch and handed it to him. It was by Cartier. Her hand trembled as she passed it to him. 'Look,' she said gravely, 'you *must* promise to tell me if I'm going to die. You won't be the first person who's told me that and I *can* handle it. Promise?'

Danny's mind found another connection and slotted it into place but his head hurt very badly and he could not make sense of the demand the new knowledge was making.

'I promise I won't have to tell you you're going to die,' Danny said, adding one more glib promise to his long list. 'You won't die. It was just a glitch. It sometimes happens. I'll do it again. Give me your phone number or address, and I'll call you soon.'

'What did you see on that date?' Steffy demanded. 'Where was I and what was I doing?'

Fresh pain lit behind Danny's eyes. 'You were on the downs in the snow. Your boyfriend was there. You were building a snowman. That's all.'

During the next fifteen agonising minutes Danny tried every trick he knew to assure Steffy that nothing bad was going to happen to her. If he was going to avert her death he needed to keep her calm, get her out of his way in case he really *did* become dangerous, and use her watch to get more information on what was going to happen.

When Steffy finally gave in and left, she still was not convinced that he was telling her the truth. Danny couldn't think about it any more; he climbed the stairs, fell into his bed and slept for a very long time.

4

That night, using Steffy's watch as a focus point, Danny sent himself into her future sixteen times.

Danny had decided that if he really was the killer Christine Richard and the other Danny Stafford of his nightmares thought he was, then he would be able to prove it to himself using Stephanie's watch. All he had to do was look at the time preceding the event he had seen. If that shape in the hedge really was her body – and that belonged in pile A amongst the things he believed to be true – he would surely see who killed her. And if the killer was him, then he would act to prevent himself from killing. And if his attempts at altering Steffy's future failed, he would take the ultimate solution and kill himself.

It was going to be as simple as that.

Except that fate, Lady Luck or God Himself had seen to it that it wasn't going to be that easy. Danny addressed Steffy's future sixteen times and each time he was thrown straight back to the shape in the hedge on December the 5th. And on each occasion he saw the bundle under the marker with increasing clarity and learned new and horrifying details by a strange kind of osmosis. The knowledge was all there, contained in that wrapped bundle; everything he needed to know, except who had killed her. By the eighth time, Danny knew that the shape was indeed Steffy's body. By the twelfth it had become evident that Steffy had either been confused about the identity of her murderer or that she had not known who it was.

But worse followed, emerging slowly over the subsequent four attempts.

By four o'clock the following morning, when Danny finally blacked out and slid gently to the floor under the table, he knew that Steffy's murder was merely the first in a forthcoming series. There would be forty-two in all: thirty-four girls, all around Steffy's age, height and build; two middle-aged men, and six children, all female. All of them would be horrendously tortured and violently sexually abused.

When he woke and started all over again, Danny was driven by a fresh hope because during his four hours of sleep he had developed a very bright idea.

The information about the series of murders was not seeping into him from Steffy's corpse as it settled in the snow, it was coming to him from her watch. And since Steffy's watch couldn't have told him anything about a future that didn't involve Steffy (and the future *wasn't* going to involve Steffy, there was no doubt about *that*), it could only mean one thing.

The killer had handled it.

And added his own vibrations to those of its owner.

Danny chose to place the obvious inference into pile B and gave it no consideration whatsoever.

But the inference chose not to stay where he had placed it and by midday he was certain that the only killer who had handled Steffy's watch and left traces of himself behind was a man named Daniel Stafford.

Chapter Eighteen
Not Reading Jamie

1

Danny slammed the phone back into its cradle and swore. A week had passed since the Fortune Shop's business had ceased with Steffy's last visit. A week which had contained forty-eight unanswered telephone calls to the number she had given him while, moment by moment, December the 5th drew nearer. A week of visions of a snow-dappled shape beneath a hedge; a week of endless plotting on charts, running, sit-ups; a week of trying to assemble information which was all there but difficult to access and impossible to slot into place.

On the third day, Danny had broken the Golden Rule and looked into his own future again and bomb-shells had gone off in his mind while he plunged the knife again and again into the shape he couldn't see but knew was Steffy. No alternate future was available to him and it was impossible to direct himself elsewhere in the flow of time.

It was a week of clutching for missing straws, a week during which the non-stop panic Danny felt had gradually turned to black despair as he came to realise he wasn't going to be able to change the future at all. And in those seven days, Danny's piles of facts marked A and B shuffled themselves into a new and confused order.

There *was* a killer and it was him. There was a killer and it was *not* him. There was no killer and Danny Stafford the Fucked-Up Future Man had finally lost his bearings on the vast plain of Brough Lacey's unreality. Lerner had enticed him here to trap a mass murderer. Lerner had enticed him here so Danny would discover *he* was the mass murderer before he actually started doing the killing.

And in that week there was a burning need to contact Steffy and tell her to forget the book. Burn the book and forget all about it because the book was going to kill her. Burn the book and get the fuck out of Brighton long before December the 5th so he couldn't find her. But most of all he needed to ask her about two things she had said: one in the car the first time they had met, and the second after he'd done her reading.

These two sentences had meshed into what had become his last desperate hope.

His mind had lit on the second sentence when Steffy had said, 'You won't be the first person to have told me that,' but he had been frightened and confused and in pain and had let it pass. It was not until the other sentence swam back into his head in the evening of the following day that he realised their combined significance.

And Danny had phoned Steffy's number forty-eight times because of these two sentences. In the Bentley, shortly after she'd kidnapped him, Steffy had said, 'You remind me of someone, y'know.' She had said this as if something had suddenly fallen into place for her.

You remind me of someone, y'know.

You won't be the first person to have told me that.

Danny desperately hoped – and since he had resolved to kill himself if he was wrong, it was truly his last hope – that Steffy would tell him that the person Danny Stafford reminded her of was the very same person who had also predicted her death on December the 5th.

So he had phoned her, imagining as he waited endlessly for her to pick up the receiver, that she would say, 'Oh yes, *him*. His name's Joey.'

But after forty-eight tries, this little fantasy had shifted itself from the stack of things that Danny chose to believe to the stack he chose not to.

But still he tried again.

And still there was no reply.

She's gone away, he told himself. *She's taken off for a safe place until the deadline has safely passed*. But he did not believe this either. Wherever Steffy was, she would return in time for her appointment.

Like the two piles of facts and fallacies in his mind, Danny also entertained two plans of action marked A and B. Plan A was to obtain enough drugs to do away with himself painlessly, and plan B was so stupid it hardly bore thinking about.

Plan B was to look up Steffy Osmond's address in the telephone book and present himself at her house before December the 5th to warn her – or if that couldn't be done (and if it couldn't be done by telephone, it couldn't be done at all, he told himself), to arrive at her home on December the 4th and wait for her, hoping to protect her from the killer.

Which, if he believed he was potentially the killer, would be an act of supreme idiocy.

2

Danny went back to the Reading Room and propped up the two

pieces of paper on which – what now seemed like a lifetime ago – he had written the words of wisdom from Alistair Lerner's letter:

DO NOT BE EASILY DECEIVED

and

HAVE FAITH AND DO NOT DOUBT YOURSELF. EVEN FOR A MOMENT

Why, you despicable old bastard, Danny thought bitterly, *didn't you just write YOU ARE NOT THE KILLER if that's what you meant? Why did you have to make things so fucking complicated for me?*

'You sad, Mister Danny?'

Danny looked up into Jamie's round face, saw that heartbreaking half-baked smile and suddenly wanted to cry.

'Hiya, Jamie,' he said heavily. 'I didn't hear you come in.'

'I was quiet,' Jamie said, grinning. 'I would surprise you. Go BOO! But you look too sad.' His face fell. 'Don't be sad,' he said tenderly. He took hold of Danny's neck, hugged him and gave him a sloppy kiss on his unshaven cheek. 'Prickle!' he announced, trying it again. 'You be happy now!' he commanded, pulling away then holding Danny out by his shoulders and examining his face to see if he was going to obey. Danny blinked back tears, swallowed the lump in his throat and asked him what he was doing here.

'I come to see my friend Danny,' he said, placing his right hand on his heart as Danny had once done to assure him he was telling the truth. 'I like Danny! Like Popeye the sailor man!'

'Popeye?'

Jamie shrieked with laughter. 'Danny the Hoodoo Man!' he chortled. 'I might cheer you up! I think!' He threw himself at Danny again and found the exact spot on Danny's ribs that was the most sensitive to being tickled. Danny's head magically emptied itself of everything except the fact that some kind of a defence was going to have to be made if Jamie was going to be stopped from tickling him to death.

Danny tickled him back, realising through the sound of hysterical laughter that his face felt funny because he was smiling.

When Danny had finally cried 'Uncle!' and declared that not only had Jamie won game, set and match but that Danny the Hoodoo Man had cheered up a great deal, he realised that he did, indeed, feel as fresh as if he'd been washed, tumble-dried and ironed. Somehow, Jamie had that effect on you. 'Want to come upstairs for a Coke? I've still got some Swiss roll if you're peckish. It's been there a while and the rats have been nibbling it, but it's edible.'

'Edible?'

'You can still eat it. Coming?'

Jamie thought about it. 'Can I edible it here?'

Danny shrugged. 'If that's what you want. Sit down and I'll bring it down, but don't touch the thing under the cloth on the table. Promise?'

Jamie nodded solemnly, making a show of placing his hand on his heart again.

When the Coke and cake had gone, Danny discovered why Jamie had wanted to stay in the Reading Room.

Jamie took something from his trousers pocket, came over to Danny and pressed it into his hand, closing his fingers around it. Danny looked at the gift, not yet realising that his palm had been crossed with silver. Jamie had given him two ten pence pieces.

'You tell me?' the boy asked.

'Tell you what? What's the money for?'

Jamie grinned sheepishly. 'So you tell me.'

Danny's mind was still empty, still coasting along in neutral. 'Tell you what? What do you want to know?'

'What happen?'

You couldn't read Jamie, Danny thought, realising at last what the boy meant. Again the thought seemed huge and overpoweringly important. More connections reached for one another in Danny's mind and he felt again as if someone was orchestrating all this. He had forgotten about not being able to read Jamie – dismissed it in favour of what had seemed to be the bigger problems – and now, with amazing coincidence (or synchronicity if you preferred Carl Jung's word), he was being reminded of it. Danny suddenly decided that Steffy's book was not the fulcum or the pivot – or whatever he'd called it – around which everything revolved, but just one of several. Not being able to read Jamie was of equal and possibly of *greater* importance.

Danny grinned, suddenly determined that the statement about not being able to read Jamie should not be allowed to be proven true. The statement implied that Jamie's future could not be read because of his Down's Syndrome, but to prove this wrong would prove to Danny that everything was flexible. And that there was still a little hope left.

'You want your future read, is that it?' he asked. 'You want to know what lies in store for you?'

Jamie nodded. 'Mum say you will tell me.'

'Does she indeed!' Danny said. 'Come here.' He pressed the two coins back into Jamie's hand and the boy's face fell. 'Keep your money,' Danny said.

Jamie looked distraught. 'You won't tell me?' he asked.

'You be happy now!' Danny commanded. 'I'll tell you what'll happen, but I'll tell you for free. Do you know why?'

Jamie's face brightened and his grin started to return. 'Why?'

Danny thumped his heart with his right fist. 'Because you're my friend!'

It might have looked like something Red Indians would do in a Hollywood Western but it spoke directly to Jamie, it felt good to do it and it emphasised the truth of the words.

Jamie beamed at him.

Here we go then, old Dan, he told himself as he dimmed the lights, undressed the crystal and linked his cool hands with Jamie's hot and sticky ones. *See what you can make out of this.*

Danny placed their hands on the surface of the hole in reality and gazed into the twinkling smoky mist that had already gathered there. 'What do you see?' he asked.

'Nothing!' Jamie announced proudly.

'What do you feel?'

'Tickly.'

'Does it hurt?'

'Nice!'

'Okay, just sit still and hold my hands and don't worry about anything that happens. If I look as if I've gone away or anything like that, you're not to worry. It's just because I'm looking at what's going to happen to you later. Okay?'

'Okey dokey,' Jamie said happily. 'Hurry back.'

The crystal did its expanding act and Danny fell. And fell. And fell. Just when he thought that he wasn't going to be able to do it after all, he was was hitched violently sideways out of the grey mist which sparkled gold and into another which was blue and flickered with many colours.

I think we might be on to something here, he thought and skipped sideways again, hitting a hard surface and stopping.

'You gone?' Jamie asked. *Yhooo ghhhhnnn?*

'Yes,' Danny replied and his voice wasn't stretched, but shattered like glass.

At first Danny didn't seem to be anywhere, then he began to see a grey, insubstantial place where nothing seemed to fit properly. The fabric of this new world didn't mesh and knit together solidly, but was vague and ever changing. Angles fluctuated, planes changed, flickering stroboscopically; holes opened, filled and closed and substantial parts of other worlds appeared and vanished. Then the world exploded with white light and Danny was shaken savagely. He staggered giddily across nothingness, holding out his hands as huge bands of brilliant coloured light sped by, scorching his face with their intensity. Danny jolted sideways again and was plunged into a tiny place from which the view of the phantom grey world was too large and too misty. The misty shapes hardened into visible forms and Danny was surprised to find that he was in the Reading Room of the Fortune Shop, and that he was looking at it through the eyes of Jamie's future body. And then he knew why Jamie could not be read. He and Danny were not compatible. The currency of Jamie's mental language was entirely different to that of his own and as Jamie's future world became more solid, Danny's own senses were correspondingly more fogged.

And Jamie's skewed manner of thinking hit him like a hail of machine-gun bullets. This foreign mode of thinking was powerful and simple and completely beyond Danny's ability to comprehend. Jamie seemed to think emotionally and in a reactive way rather than rationally. There was no abstract for Jamie, and no words, just big direct pictures and the feeling that went with them. There was no doubt, no logic, just good feelings and bad feelings.

And as Danny stood in the doorway with Jamie's vision blinding his own eyes, the incoming mental information suddenly all became Bad News. Jamie had just realised something that simultaneously frightened and angered him to an astonishing degree and this had a massive effect on the inner working of his mind. The big powerful images of Jamie's inner eye didn't just become more confusing to Danny, they suddenly ceased altogether. Danny could still sense his movements and the strength of his emotions but he could not apprehend what had caused them. He had been plunged into the boy's terrified inner darkness.

'NO DON'T YOU!' Jamie roared, and distantly Danny realised that English was not a mother tongue for those with Down's Syndrome – it was an alien language.

Danny felt Jamie's small body tense, gasped as the boy gasped, then tensed as the boy began to wail. Suddenly Jamie charged across the room, every nerve in his body a burning bright wire of hatred and fear.

Christ, what's happen–?

The sound and pain of the blow Jamie received around the head from an assailant Danny could not see slapped the thought out of his mind, replacing it with a shining blue flash that dimmed to purple as the boy reeled away. Danny's ears rang, matching the boy's own.

Jamie took another blow which lit stars in Danny's head. Then another.

The boy fell, rolled, hit something hard and scrambled to his feet, screaming words which were jumbled by his rage and hurt.

I'm beating him up! Danny thought. *God help me, I'm hitting Jamie!* He strained to see, fighting for dominance over Jamie's huge thought patterns. A part of him found the visual centre of Jamie's brain and the grey room began to swim before him, just out of focus. *Come on!* Danny thought, grasping something in Jamie's mind and holding on hard.

Jamie's hand flew to his temple, then fell, bunched into a fist.

'GIVE HIM BACK TO ME!' he screamed, running once more towards a formless grey shape that Danny knew must be himself.

And Danny heard the strangely familiar fluttering of Joey's wings as the bird headed for Africa. And with a flash of something that may have been intuition – or a glimpse into his own future – he suddenly understood that Jamie was going to run right on to the knife blade that was now being levelled at him.

He clamped himself down on the thread of Jamie's mind he'd caught but the boy's determination was massive. Jamie gasped but didn't stop running.

For a moment Danny squeezed so hard that he felt himself flood into the boy's body. He threw it to one side, but it was too late. The knife hit Jamie in the stomach and was punched home with tremendous force. The blade was as cold and cruel as ice. Jamie and Danny's lungs coughed out air and locked as the terrible ache in their stomach grew, radiating pain through their body like lightning. Finally they gasped in a breath and screamed, long and hard, in pain and frustration as their legs buckled beneath them.

Then Jamie was gone and the fog cleared as there was only Danny looking out through his eyes as his small body fell.

And there was another Danny on the floor, a Danny from the future. A Danny whose face and chest was awash with blood while a jetting artery in his right arm steadily added to the mess. A Danny who was curling up in agony. A Danny who was close to death.

Jamie's body hit the floor and Jamie had suddenly returned and was tearing back control of his damaged body and forcing Danny's vision to fade. Then Danny's vision and balance vanished completely as Jamie kicked and hissed and rolled crazily around, searching for his feet. Danny tumbled in nothingness, aware that Jamie was rising, finding his own balance.

There was darkness now and pain and the sound of Jamie hissing and spitting then more pain as he reached out. . .

3

'Hello,' said Jamie as Danny flooded back into his own body. 'Where did you go to?'

The sign Danny had made from Lerner's words of wisdom was still on the desk:

HAVE FAITH AND DO NOT DOUBT YOURSELF. EVEN FOR A MOMENT.

Danny glanced at it and told himself the words while in his mind the memory of the vision did a strange diminishing trick, drying up and growing steadily smaller as though it could not exist in his own mental landscape. Danny's mind seemed to hold the wrong kind of soil to nurture the clippings from Jamie's future. *You killed him*, Danny told himself and found he did not believe this to be true. For some reason, as that memory shrank, Danny found that he *did* have faith and *did not* doubt himself. He did not know how long this feeling would last.

'I went to see what you are going to be doing one day soon,' he told the boy and thought: *The Danny Stafford you saw lying there and pumping blood on to the floor could not have been the same person who punched the knife into Jamie's stomach. That Danny Stafford would not have been physically capable of that action. That Danny Stafford was badly damaged and near death.*

Jamie grinned. 'What I do?' he asked, squeezing Danny's hands so hard it hurt.

Danny's fertile mind blanked. 'Uh, much the same as you're doing now,' he said vaguely while his cry-baby argued: *But there was no one else in the room except you and Jamie. If that was a true vision, you killed him, old Dan.*

'But what did I *do*?' Jamie insisted, frowning.

Jamie was trying to save *you, not kill you, and he certainly couldn't have made that mess of you.* But the memory was fading fast and Danny no longer knew what the mess was, that part had gone. The rest now felt like nothing more than a fading nightmare and Danny didn't think he would be able to remember any of it in another hour.

'What I *do*?' Jamie asked.

Danny finally found his lying muscle and flexed it. 'You lived to a ripe old age,' he said. 'You won't die until you are at least ninety.'

Jamie looked at him suspiciously. 'When is ninety?'

Give him back to me, Jamie had said. *But there was no one else there*!

'A very long time away,' Danny said. 'Lots of birthdays and Christmases. You'll be older than me by then, older than your mum. You'll have grey hair and a long white beard.'

Jamie's eyes had widened with each sentence. The thought of having a beard had astonished him. 'Will I?' he asked, dragging his hands free of Danny's and feeling his smooth chin for signs of it starting already. 'What else?' he demanded.

'Lots more!' Danny said, as the vision withered in his mind. 'You're going to be a good boy, then a good grown up. You'll have lots of friends who'll love you and look after you just as much as you love them and look after them. You're going to make a lot of people very happy, Jamie.'

He nodded sagely and smiled.

Give him back to me! What did it mean?

Danny smiled back at the boy. 'And I think I saw a girlfriend too,' he added confidentially.

Jamie blushed hard and clapped his hands to his face. 'Yuk!' he said, grimacing. 'Girls!'

'That enough?' Danny asked.

'What about the birdy?' Jamie said.

'Birdy?' Danny asked, suddenly feeling very cold.

'The birdy in the room. I saw him. He said his name was Joey.'

'Which room? Here?'

Jamie looked confused. He thought about it then shrugged. 'A room,' he finally said.

'You don't need to worry about the budgie. Sometimes you just see them when you have your future told.'

Jamie nodded, satisfied.

4

The days fell away rapidly as December approached and Danny still could not contact Stephanie Osmond. His days were filled with a strange blend of hope and despair – according to whether Danny was in Jamie's presence or alone. During the hours he was alone he tried desperately to contact Steffy by phone then he tried to pass the snowy field of her future using the crystal and her watch. Then he tried to find an alternate future for himself other than the one in which he plunged the knife into Steffy's body. During the hours when Jamie was there, Danny was restored and his belief in himself returned. Jamie had a certain kind of spontaneous magic about him that gave Danny a new resolve. However bad things seemed to get, Jamie could slice through them with his half-baked grin and a well aimed tickling finger.

But there was more to it than that. A strong bond had developed between them and Danny thought it was made up partly of love and partly of responsibility. Somehow they were linked in what was going to happen and both of them were aware of it. And Jamie's innocent helplessness awoke Danny's protective paternal instincts. The boy was going to have to be looked after and this gave Danny a new will to survive and a burning desire to make things work out. He knew now that he would see this thing through, whatever was going to happen. In some way he owed it to Jamie.

And when they were playing on the windy beach, or walking through The Lanes window shopping, or eating sandwiches outside the Pavilion, Danny would think the words: *GIVE HIM BACK TO ME* which, other than the knowledge that Jamie would probably be badly hurt – if not killed – in the Reading Room, were all that remained of the failed vision. And those five words spoke volumes to Danny. There *was* someone else involved and therefore Danny was not the killer. That someone else who could not be detected was a psychic named Joey; a man who had predicted Steffy's murder on December the 5th. The prediction had been easy for him to make because Joey was going to make sure it was fulfilled. And after this, if Danny could not stop Joey, there would be a long series of slayings.

5

On December the 2nd when the temperature fell suddenly and the skies began to promise a pre-Christmas fall of snow, Danny became so certain that the killer named Joey was not his alter-ego the Gannex Man, but another person entirely, he allowed himself to look for Steffy's address. It took all of three minutes. Stephanie was the second S. Osmond in the phone book. *Now you know*, Danny told himself, *and you can't un-know it again so be careful!*

On December the 3rd when the first few flakes of snow fell and the council began to grit the roads, Danny's desire to warn Steffy became so desperate that he travelled to her house near Peacehaven by taxi. He crunched his way up the long gravel drive, his heart hammering in his ears. He didn't think Steffy would want to talk to him and had decided that – if it became necessary – he would abduct her and take her to a safe place. He leaned on the door bell for a very long time and although there was no answer he was certain she was at home.

He stood in the porch trying to stamp warmth back into his freezing feet and blow feeling into his numb fingers while he wondered what to do. He rang the bell again, then went over to the garage and tried the door, which, surprise, surprise, was locked. There was a gate beside the garage which opened on to a path to the back garden. The gate was bolted. Danny stood back from the house studying the curtains for movements which would confirm that Steffy was at home and wondering who was outside. There was no movement.

She could be dead already, his cry-baby voice told him, but Danny did not believe this.

There was no way from the front of the house to the back other than the locked gate. After a few minutes' deliberation, Danny flung himself up at the gate, hooked his arms over the top of it and reached down for the bolt. His weight on the top of the gate drove it downwards, tightening the bolt, and Danny's hands were numb. It took four attempts to slide it back. Finally, he opened the gate and walked down the concrete path towards the back of the house, expecting to hear the sound of police sirens at any moment.

Halfway down the path there was a locked door to the garage and beside this was a window. Steffy's Bentley was inside standing next to what must have been her second car – a convertible Morgan.

She's got to be home! Danny told himself.

The back garden brought a fresh shock of *déjà-vu* to him. It was identical in every respect to the spot-lit snow-covered garden of his dream in which he'd made love to Steffy under the spotlight in the golden snow. The snow was not yet deep enough in the garden to match exactly, but the layout was identical. The trees stood in the same places as those he'd dreamed; the pool lapped quietly at the bottom of the garden a hundred yards away; the spotlights were not illuminated but they were in exactly the right places and their light would shine in the same way as the dream. Danny walked to the very spot where he'd knelt behind Steffy and thrust into her, watching her tightly tied hair and her long glistening neck as he told her he wanted to wear her like a glove.

This happened! he told himself. *Or it's going to. Except that it won't be you doing it, it'll be Joey. The other guy.*

There was a patio over by the French windows and Danny went over to it and peered through the net curtains at the empty lounge, thinking, *You could get in through here at a push.*

But he did not break in. The place would be alarmed and he was beginning to think that in spite of the presence of the cars in the garage, Steffy was not home after all. He could quite easily imagine being arrested for house-breaking and knew that the two detectives, Jon Vinge and Ray Johnson, would not be so easily handled the next time they came in contact with him.

Danny went back to the front of the house, rang the door bell again and gave up.

For a time.

He went back in the afternoon and waited until five in the evening when the cold finally drove him away. He returned again at eleven and at two in the morning – certain that Steffy had been inside all along but was neither answering her phone nor the door bell – and finally pushed the Jiffy bag he had brought with him through the letter box. The bag contained Steffy's Cartier watch and a message imploring her to contact him the moment she read it.

The door had glass panes – more easy entry points, Danny knew – and he could see the envelope from the outside. He rang the bell again then went away for an hour, pacing the roads and wondering if he ought to break in now or leave it until tomorrow. When he got back again, the envelope was gone.

Which meant that Steffy was inside and that she'd picked it up.

Danny leaned on the bell and wasn't remotely surprised to find that it was no longer working. He wondered why she hadn't thought of disconnecting it before. He hammered on the door so hard that one of the panes of glass cracked, then he dropped to his knees and shouted through the letter box that he badly needed to talk to her.

Then, just as he was about to shout the warning about the man he thought was called Joey, it struck him that it might not be Steffy in there at all. It might actually be *Joey*. And Danny was not prepared.

He stopped in mid-sentence, let the flap of the letter box fall shut and walked quickly away down the drive, not feeling very brave at all.

It was two miles to the nearest phone box. By the time Danny arrived and called a cab, he had thrust aside his notion about the killer already being inside Steffy's house and stacked it in pile B. While he waited for his taxi, he dialled Steffy's number again and again.

But there was no reply.

When he finally arrived back at the Fortune Shop, the snow was falling steadily and Danny had developed a plan. He would not let Steffy be killed. Tomorrow night he would go to Steffy's house, break in, remove her if she was there, then he would lie in wait for the killer.

That night, after Danny had selected the largest knife from the small supply that Lerner had bequeathed him (a rather sorry old bread knife with, thank God, a plastic handle rather than the wooden one of his visions), he lay in his bed wondering, his mind far too alert for sleep. . .

And found himself in Steffy's back garden again, taking her from behind while he gazed down at her long white neck and told her that he wanted to take the core of her being, tear it open and wrap it around him.

When he awoke, sweating and speaking the end of a sentence to which he didn't know the beginning, it was almost lunch time of December the 4th. Danny got up, looked outside at the covering of snow in the Fortune Shop's tiny back yard and nodded grimly.

'Today,' he said aloud, 'I'm going to finish this for good!'

6

Danny's belief in Joey the psychic as a separate entity lasted until precisely nine twenty-one on the morning of December the fifth – when it was violently shattered.

Because some time in the afternoon of December the 4th – after he'd taken the visiting Jamie home and tried again to contact Steffy by phone – he suffered another lengthy lapse of consciousness.

But this blank period wasn't like any of the others he'd had where his body had taken care of itself while his mind was away. This time, it was far, far worse.

Because at nine twenty-one the following morning Danny was vividly able to recall every detail of what had happened during the seventeen hours his mind was out of the driving seat.

He had killed Steffy.

Chapter Nineteen
Taking Her Time

1

In the early evening of December 4th, some time after he'd given up trying to contact Steffy, something clicked inside Danny's head. He got up and turned off the television, and as the screen dimmed he was suddenly unable to answer the somehow important question: *What was I just watching?*

He ached. Everything he owned ached because the time had come. He sat down on something soft – a chair maybe, or a bed – while the fucking fluttering noise resounded in his head. The noise that had haunted him for so long would soon be gone and nothing could stop it now because the other guy – the one he needed so badly – could not read Jamie. Whatever *that* meant.

Danny's brain seemed to be rippling from back to front, undulating under the force of incoming waves that hit him like the great rolling breakers he and the boy had played in front of. His eyes tingled and his body sizzled like a Bonfire Night sparkler. The bullet scar below his right eye pulsed in time with his heart and the blood bag in his nostril started to swell.

The last time, Danny thought. *This will be the last time ever. And the first time ever, too. The whole time, in fact.*

His scrotum started to itch and prickle as the fire lit deep inside his body between his balls and his anus. Tiny bolts of molten energy started to blast up his spine from that hot fire as his testicles clamped up tight in his body and his erection began to grow and pulse. Now, at long last, the time was right. The fire that had burned in him for so long would be fed and the agony of *not knowing* would be quashed, never to return.

Danny undressed and folded his clothes neatly, laying them on the pillows of his bed while he distantly realised that this was something he never did. A part of him watched in disbelief as he pulled back the bedclothes, placed the neat stack of clothes inside and then pulled back the sheets.

As Danny went into the bathroom, he thought: *This is all wrong.*

Everything is different here! This isn't the bathroom in the Fortune Shop, or the one at home! Then wondered *what* he'd been thinking, then wondered nothing at all. He suddenly knew exactly where he was, what he was doing and why.

He filled the bath with cold water, got in and gasped as the shock of cold stirred the fire inside him which responded by blasting two slugs of molten heat into his brain. When his vision came back, there was a sponge in his hand which had a rough nylon skin-sloughing surface on one side. There was no need for soap. Danny scrubbed every square centimetre of himself with it, working methodically and slowly, making sure no part was missed. It hurt, but the pain stoked the fires in his groin and spine, making him ache for release.

But no matter how hard he rubbed or how much it hurt or how the fires made him ache, the flapping sound of the bird would not go away.

But it would soon. Soon, everything would be resolved.

The cold water bit into his flesh, chilling him past the point of pain and into numbness. Danny began to remember things that hadn't yet happened, misty things that could and *would* be. Good things. The fire in his groin began to rage as his excitement increased and Danny scrubbed at himself even harder. He had been preparing for this since. . .

Dead skin must have been falling and much of it should already have gone. But there were places that needed special attention if the old Danny was going to peel away to present the new one. The links had to be broken.

Danny stopped scrubbing his upper body when the thin skin of his sternum began to bleed. He stood up and worked at his buttocks until they were raw, then worked at his feet and legs, leaving his aching penis and balls until last.

The pain was exquisite. The heat blinding.

Finally, Danny sat back down in the freezing water, lay back and submerged his head, letting the icy cold water invade his ears and destroy his sense of balance; letting it run up his nose and down into his throat.

He sat up quickly, his head spinning as he coughed out water. When his balance returned, he laughed. Danny submerged his head again, not bothering to close his mouth this time. The water flooded in, filled him with power that fed the fires inside him. He came up choking, but aware of the new power he had drawn from the water when it had flowed into his body.

Danny got out of the bath, dried himself carefully, and went back to the bedroom where the equipment was. The equipment he had so carefully assembled over the past few weeks consisted of a length of cord, a *Why have your sleep disturbed*? eyeshade, two trouser legs (which had been cut from a pair of jumble sale Chinos), a roll of industrial strength sticky tape, scissors, a pair of shoes, the knife and the coat.

Danny had bought these items from a variety of shops in a variety of towns over a period of more than a month. Should any of them be mistakenly left at the scene (and he didn't intend to allow *that* to happen), they would not be easy to trace to him. Almost impossible, in fact. Everything had been planned to the last detail: even the rest of the trousers had been properly disposed of. He had burnt them after removing the legs, then picked out the zipper and the waistband clips from the ashes and had disposed of them in the sea.

Danny picked up the tape and the scissors from the bedside table (which for a moment he did not recognise), pulled on the legs and taped them in place low on his thighs.

The old three-quarter length Gannex raincoat was in a cardboard box beneath the bed. This was another jumble sale item and Danny had decided that he would always use this coat: it held good memories for him. Memories of *coming* to be. All the buttons were missing, but it had a belt to hold it together. Danny was no seamstress or tailor, but he had managed to alter the coat's right hand pocket, adding to the lining so that it was a foot deep. He had completely removed the lining from the left side pocket.

Danny put the coat on and pulled it tightly around him. His penis tented the front, and this was the reason for removing the lining from the left hand pocket. If it became necessary, he could slip his left hand through the empty pocket and use it to hold his erection back against his body. He had done this before, several times, and it worked well.

He slipped his feet into the plain, leather-soled slip-on shoes and nodded. They would be slippery on the snow, but they would leave no tread marks.

Danny picked up the eyeshade and the cord and slipped them into the coat's deep right hand pocket. He considered taking the industrial sticky tape and decided against it. Steffy wasn't going to make much noise if he could help it, and anyway, her nearest neighbours were over two hundred yards away. Danny picked up the wooden-handled carving knife with the nine-inch blade, tested the sharp edge with his thumb, nodded again – smiling this time – and placed it carefully inside the deep pocket. This knife was sacred. It was the key to his release from the fluttering sound inside his head, but it was much more than that. It was the key to *becoming* and the key to the future. The key to many futures; many of those threads of flowing time which he would tap into and divert, collecting them and making them his own.

2

It took an hour and a quarter to walk to Stephanie Osmond's house. It would have taken less but on this important occasion (and even though his body and mind were jolting with power and lust), Danny was being very careful. Each time a car or pedestrian approached, he would conceal himself in the shadows or dodge into a driveway. When he arrived at Steffy's house he was sure he hadn't been seen by a soul.

Danny already knew what would happen because he had seen it before, in exactly the same way as he'd seen everything else: reflected in the long glittering blade of the knife. Steffy would be alone in bed asleep. She would be naked. She would not wake up when he entered because she had taken the sleeping tablets her doctor had prescribed for her. Steffy had been taking a great deal of these sleeping tablets since he had predicted that there was no life for her after December the 5th. Steffy had, in some way, sensed her own death and been unable to admit that it was the truth. Steffy wished she had never decided to investigate the reasons for her ability to tell people's names; wished she had never met him; wished she could simply sleep until December the 5th had passed. She would wake up and see him standing there and her sleepy confusion would turn to a sedated kind of terror. She would not be paralysed with fear. She would comply with his suggestions, hoping that she would come out of this alive. She would kneel naked on the lawn under the golden spotlights because she would be clinging to the words he had told her, those six innocent little words of promise that made up a big bad lie: 'I'm not going to hurt you!' Steffy would believe this lie and hope she was going to get away with just being raped – because there was simply nothing else she was able to believe. Right until the end, Steffy would believe those words because she could not allow herself to believe in her own death.

Her suffering would be magnificent.

Standing in her porch, Danny shrugged the coat off, slipped out of the shoes, released the trouser legs.

He punched out one of the panes of glass in the door with the wooden handle of the carving knife. The sound was small, insignificant. Steffy would not even stir in her drugged sleep. He put his hand through the broken pane, undid the catch and silently opened the door.

Blasts of molten metal exploded in his head like bomb-shells as he went inside and started up the stairs.

Danny opened Steffy's bedroom door, went inside, closed the door again and turned on the lights. Steffy was sleeping face down and her blonde hair was held back in a pony tail. She stirred, but did not wake. Danny stood for a few seconds, aching for her and watching that swan-like neck which seemed to offer him so much. He wanted her badly – not just to be inside her sexually, but literally. He wanted – no, *needed* – to take everything she had; her sensation; her emotions; her whole existence. Steffy's life had to be his. Steffy's life was the way forward, the way to perfection. The way to release.

Danny went over to her and pulled back the covers. His scrotum clamped hard over his balls feeding a dull ache into his guts. The fire surged frenziedly up his spine and burst a white-hot shell in his brain.

Steffy's unblemished skin looked soft and silky and warm. Perfect. Danny ached for her. He needed her, needed to *become* her in every way. He wanted to burrow into the damp warmth of that perfect body, sinew by sinew and nerve by nerve, taking each one and making them his. Steffy's organs would be his own organs, her heart, *his* heart. And when he reached the very centre of her being he would take it away from her and make it exclusively his, wrapping it around him like a cloak.

And he would. He'd seen it all already. He would force himself into her like a man into a child's clothing; he would crowd her out, take her blood for his blood, pushing and squeezing until there was no place left for her essence to go, no deeper form of retreat. And when that moment arrived, Steffy's life would come moaning from its hiding place and give itself to him.

Steffy rolled over when he touched her, bleary-eyed and confused. Her nipples were erect and he interpreted this as a sign.

'I'm not going to hurt you,' Danny promised as her expression changed to a numb kind of terror. 'I just want to have you. I want you on all fours in the snow in the back garden. That's all. I won't hurt you. I promise. I'm not going to hurt you.'

Steffy did not resist when Danny put the *Why Have Your Sleep Disturbed?* eyeshade on her face and she was only trembling very slightly as he took her hand and led her downstairs, carrying the cord and knife. Steffy got down on her hands and knees in the snow and obediently repeated the words Danny had told her to say as he entered her. Steffy moaned as he gazed at her long neck and pulsed fire into her. She did not protest afterwards when he tied her hands to her neck with the cord and laid her across his lap. She didn't begin to scream until he used the knife on her and by then the molten steel bomb-shells in his mind wouldn't have let him stop even if he'd wanted to. Which he did not. Danny's universe turned pink and red.

But now Steffy had found her voice, she wasn't going to let go of it again. The bucking and writhing as the knife probed her was good but the screaming rapidly became tiresome. Danny grabbed her hair and yanked her head back, exposing that gorgeous throat. 'Going to have to de-bark you now,' he said and then promised, 'It won't hurt you.' With an undreamed of expertise, he jabbed the carving knife a little way into Steffy's adam's apple, not pushing hard enough to kill, but hard enough to pierce her windpipe and vocal cords. Bright blood sprayed out on a hiss that was now all that was left of Steffy's screams.

Danny pounded Steffy with the knife, chasing her life force from hideaway to hideaway in her body, sometimes catching parts of it in the bright jets of blood that flew up at him, sometimes glimpsing its power as it changed places in Steffy's jerking body.

When he laid the knife aside, his body was sheeted with Steffy's hot, somehow *live* blood. It was in his nose and under his tongue; it trickled down his throat, thick and coppery; it stung his eyes and blurred his vision red.

But Steffy's inner core of time – her life-force – was still present. Danny plunged himself into her slippery warmth and through her to her life's hiding place. It had retreated to the brink of that other dimension he had become so familiar with and now only touched her physical body in a sizzling pin-prick. Now, half in the physical world and half that other place, Danny's fingers encircled it and he carefully drew it back into the physical world and out through her body. It was a single hot wire of energy; a sparkling and hissing pink strand of light both ends of which looped back down into Steffy's body. Danny stretched it and took it into his mouth, ripping it from Steffy and making it his own. When her connection with it was finally broken, Steffy's gorgeous strand of time fizzed into him with an orgasmic intensity, expanding him, increasing his own power.

And in that moment – and in the ones that followed as his passion was slaked – he loved Stephanie Osmond. She was his and his alone. He had absorbed her, completely and utterly and for all time. There was no Steffy any more, present or future, this life or the next, just a hot junction where they truly merged.

And when it was over, Danny and Steffy stood in one another's arms in the shower until they ran clean.

The disposal presented no unanticipated or unforeseen problems. Danny dressed Steffy in red silk and sacking, loaded her into the boot of her car, drove carefully up to the Downs and dumped her body in the hedge, leaving a single strip of red silk on the branches as a marker for the other part of him to find.

His whole body singing with Steffy's energy, he drove the Bentley back to town, parked it in a car park near the sea front and went home where he showered again.

He was brimming over with power and a new vibrancy, and there were still things to do, but he thought they could wait until daylight. Danny lay down on his bed and smiling serenely, fell asleep.

3

And woke up at nine twenty-one, screaming.

And when the memory of what had happened during his blank period crashed into place like the the huge steel door of a bank vault, Danny went rigid.

You killed her. Steffy's dead and you killed her! You killed her you killed her you killed her! his mind screamed as it rolled the images slowly across the screen in his mind.

The curtains in the room were thick and heavy and admitted no light, and while he tried to deny the sickening memory, Danny stared into the darkness, too frightened to move because of the evidence he would surely find if he did.

'I didn't do it!' he croaked over the yammering of his mind, but in his ears this sounded like a feeble lie. This nightmare was one that it was going to prove impossible to wake up from. This one wasn't going to go away. The smell that clung to his nostrils bore testimony to that. It was the strong, earthy odour of Steffy's intestines.

You killed her you killed her you killed her!

Danny did not want ever to have to get up and face what he'd surely done. Because if he were to turn on the light or pull the curtains open he would be presented with more evidence. His whole body felt sticky and he knew *exactly* why this was. If he were to reach out and pull the cord for the light he would be able to see Steffy's dried blood streaking his arms and chest. The bed sheets and pillows would be – were – stiff with it. There would be dried blood and, perhaps, flesh beneath his fingernails. And worse, parts of Steffy could still be attached to his body – stuck there by their own drying fluids.

On the Vistavision screen in Danny's mind, he saw his hands plunge deep into Steffy's body and his stomach squeezed hard.

Gonna be sick! his cry-baby voice announced, but Danny fought off the queasiness. There was a lot more he was going to have to look at after this and if he made himself steely and cold he might be able to get through these memories. Turning the light on and actually seeing the mess his room was in here and now would not just make him throw up, but might very well push him over the edge into the babbling insanity that was currently waiting in the wings for its cue to enter stage right.

Danny's sticky arms lay like two rigid poles outside the sheets. The muscles inside them ached sharply and it wasn't just because they were now tensed – it was because of all the hacking and slashing and tearing he'd done last night.

And now he had become aware of the ache in his arms, he became conscious of the other pains that filled him. His stomach muscles were pulled; his legs hurt; dull fire pulsed deep in his groin and shot flickers of pain into his tightly cramped penis and balls.

You killed her!

Danny moaned and finally managed to thrust the pictures away from him.

In the momentary blank space caused by his astonishment at having stopped the memories, his cry-baby voice announced that besides killing Steffy, it thought he might well have eaten some of her.

Danny flew out of bed, ran for the toilet and thrust his head deep into the bowl. Eyes clamped shut and mind empty, he threw up until his sore stomach muscles cramped and bitter bile filled his mouth. For the following five minutes, he knelt before the toilet, his head deep in the pan, his hands clutching the cool porcelain rim, and the veins bulging in his forehead while he was racked with a painful bout of dry-heaving.

When this finally ceased Danny discovered that he was too frightened to open his eyes because there might be bloody evidence in the water at the bottom of the pan. Keeping his eyes tightly closed he got up, and holding tightly to the cistern in case he lost his balance or fainted (either of which seemed quite likely), he pulled the flush, waited for the cistern to fill, and flushed again.

Then, keeping his eyes closed for fear of what he might see in the mirror, he felt his way to the sink and turned on both taps. He swilled his mouth out with cold water, then swallowed some, wondering if it would start him heaving again. The next time his guts might come up.

But the water tasted good and clean and as long as he disallowed the thought about having eaten some of Steffy, he felt he would be all right.

What now? he wondered, knowing he still could not look at himself in the mirror. He found the soap on the side of the sink and washed his hands, face and chest, realising there was little point to this. There was only one option open to him now and that was to bring everything to a quick end. He could not give himself up to the police because that way he would be punished but he would not die – and he didn't think he could stand to live with the knowledge of what he had done. There was a packet of Wilkinson Sword razor blades in the cabinet and he would take one of these, lie down in the bath and draw the sharp edge lightly over both his wrists. It would not be painful. You just grew cold and sleepy as the bathwater turned red.

Dan? a part of his mind asked as he swilled suds from his face.

'What?' he asked sourly, distantly aware that he had now descended to the level of carrying on spoken conversation with his mind. It didn't matter.

Where's the tape then?

'Tape?'

And all the other stuff. The trouser legs. The wooden-handled knife. The blindfold. The cord. The shoes. The Gannex mac. The knife the shoes the trousers the cord the knife the knife . . .!

A small golden ray of hope shone out through the dark clouds of despair in Danny's mind as his eyes began to sting with soap. He stood up from the sink, wiped the corners of them and they fluttered open. The naked Danny Stafford that stared back at him from the mirror didn't bear so much as a single streak of blood or a solitary bruise.

'You washed it off,' he said. 'And anyway, you showered last night at Steffy's and again when you got home.'

YOU WEREN'T AT STEFFY'S! *The shoes the cord the knife!*

Danny remembered that first shopping expedition when he'd come home and found the length of cord and the *Why Have Your Sleep Disturbed?* eye-shade in his bags. He had thrown them away, but there was a possibility he might have collected them again during a blank period he hadn't even noticed. But he doubted it. Too much work had been done and he'd only had two fugues since he'd been here which surely hadn't been enough time. And if he had gone out and bought those things – and a Gannex raincoat so he could build himself into the Gannex Man of his dreams – he ought to have seen them around the house.

And he hadn't.

But they should be here, he realised. He distinctly remembered taking them out from beneath his bed last night and he remembered laying them in the bath when he arrived home.

And those things were not in the bath.

You might have moved them, Danny thought, but relief was steadily pumping into him. He went back to his bedroom and opened the curtains, relaxing when he found the bed clothes were not blood-stained either, then tensing again when he found his clothes.

They were not strewn across the floor in the usual fashion, but had been neatly folded and placed beneath the pillows at the head of the bed.

You didn't do that, Danny told himself. *He did!*

There was no long wooden-handled knife anywhere in the house, or in the dustbin, or in any of the other likely and unlikely hidey-holes he checked. There was no Gannex raincoat, no leather-soled shoes or blindfold, and not even so much as a roll of Sellotape, let alone the industrial strength ducting tape the Gannex Man had used last night.

4

The search took two hours, during which Danny again beoame convinced that the Gannex Man was a separate physical entity and not the product of his own skewed mind. Questions rained down on him; questions to which there were no easy answers. Apart from guessing that the Gannex Man's name was Joey – which would seem peculiarly apt and ironic – Danny had little to go on. The man was a killer, that much was certain, but the reasons that lay behind his slaughter of Steffy were unclear, as was the reason Danny had experienced it so fully he had believed he'd actually committed it himself. There was a close link between him and the Gannex Man and Danny suspected it was a psychic one. Which meant that the entity, or person, or whatever it was he had become entwined with, was powerfully psychic. The moments immediately before Steffy's death, when he had plucked her life-force from her and made it his own, now seemed of a vast significance. Danny could recall the feeling of her power flooding into him, adding to his strength, but had felt no evidence of it since. The reason why was now glaringly obvious. The Gannex Man had committed the murder and it was he who was now using the energy of Steffy's time-stream for himself. Danny still had no idea about what happened to people after death (except that they entered that junction in God's mouth from which he had been violently expelled when he reached the end of Margaret Miller's life), but he doubted that whatever it was had happened to Steffy. Her essence was now a part of Joey the Gannex Man.

And if it were possible for the Gannex Man to reach psychically through the here-and-now to the web and to corrupt parts of it so that it added to his own power, it seemed likely that he would continue to do so, perhaps eventually making himself strong enough to escape the bonds of mortality.

And after that? Danny did not know. Neither did he know the answers to the more important questions that presented themselves: how did the killer know about him, how were they linked, and what was he going to do about it?

Danny suddenly felt too weary, too emotionally drained to face all this. *You'll find out soon enough*, he told himself as he gazed at his bed. *He's been telling you he's coming for you for months. You've got something he wants and he'll soon be coming for it. Steffy was the first step for him and now he'll be strong enough to take what he wants from you.*

He climbed back into bed, weary with the knowledge of what his whole life had been building up to since the moment his brother shot him. A confrontation with a real, honest to God, psychic murderer. A confrontation from which – like in all the best Westerns – only one of them would walk away. As he pulled the sheets up around him, he remembered that single moment of clarity during the hazy reading he'd done on Jamie. 'GIVE HIM BACK TO ME!' Jamie would scream, but it would be too late because he would take the full length of the knife and Danny would already be lying on the floor pumping blood from a severed artery. Unlike all the best Westerns, it didn't look as if the guy in the white hat would be walking away from *that* particular confrontation.

O Dan, Mystic of the West and Proven Psychic Slayer, where are you now I need you? he asked himself as he drifted off to sleep.

5

And there the bastard was in his Gannex raincoat, down below Danny as he hovered high in the corner of a dingy room. The bastard's name *was* Joey, just like the budgie, but Steffy had known this Joey as Joe. Joseph Aston. The frightened little girl on the bed whom Joey was towering over and hiding the knife from was Kim Santos. She was five. Joey was promising her he wouldn't hurt her.

A black rage shot through Danny like lightning. He felt himself shorting out. 'JOEY!' he screamed.

And the Gannex Man turned and looked directly up at him. This time, the face the man wore did not belong to Danny. When he spoke, his lips did not move. 'Ten-up old Dan!' he whispered.

'STOP IT, YOU BASTARD!' Danny screamed.

'You'll feel it too,' Joey promised. 'When I do it to her, you'll feel her life caressing you. And when I'm done here, I'll be coming for you. I want you, Danny, and you want me. We need one another. We *are* one. We are two parts of the same thing; two chips off the same old psychic block.'

Even through his sleep Danny could feel his teeth grinding. 'I'll kill you!' he promised. *'I'll kill you for what you've done!'*

'I'm doing it for us, old Dan. You and me. The twins. You'll thank me for it. I'm making us strong. I'll take you, old Dan, and then we'll be complete. You'll be me.'

'I'LL KILL YOU, YOU FUCKER!' Danny roared.

Joey grinned – an act which made him look absurdly handsome. 'Which part do you think you can kill, old Danny? A part of me is dead already, just as a part of you is. We're brothers, Dan, a pair of walking dead men both with links into the Great Beyond. We're the only two. Did you know that? The only two people in the world who are alive and dead at the same time. The only two living Hoodoo Men currently walking the face of the planet. We're like Jesus, you and me; we can work miracles.'

'It won't work! I won't let you do it!'

Joey nodded. 'It'll work. It's been working all along. It worked last night when we took sexy Steffy's time, didn't it?'

'*You killed her and I'll see you suffer for it!*'

Joey grinned again. 'I don't think so. Have you looked into your own future lately, o Danny boy?' he said softly, shaking his head. 'No, I didn't think so. Too . . . *frightened*? I've been looking into it for you, my brother, just as I have looked into it all along. I got a part of you, Dan. I hooked it years ago. Remember that day when Brian shot you? You died, Dan. You died and I hooked some of you, out there in the void. I was dead too. Car crash. I was lying on an operating table in a Johannesburg hospital and my brain was damaged and my heart had stopped and they didn't think I'd come back. I was in that void when you arrived. I saw you twinkling like a little star and I knew what was going to happen to us both.'

On the bed, little Kim Santos began to weep. Joe turned to her. 'It's okay, sweetie,' he said. 'I'm not going to hurt you and your mummy and daddy will be along to collect you soon. It'll soon be home time.'

Danny fought for information about the location and the time and date, but there was nothing to be had. Joey had evidently seen to this. 'Let her go!' Danny cried as Joey tenderly wiped away Kim's tears.

Joey turned back. 'I've been reaching for you ever since, old Dan. I nearly had the rest of you a couple of times. I chose the black mirrors for you, old Dan. I put the thought in Suzie's mind!'

'You won't get me,' Danny snarled.

'Don't you worry your little head,' he said, smiling. 'There are great things in store for you when I take you. There *is* no separate future for you, old Dan, only *my* future. We don't have to live like this, Dan. We can be greater. We can buck time and space. We can take control.'

'No!' Danny said helplessly.

'Yes!' Joey smiled and spun around, slashing the knife across the girl's belly.

Kim's breath left her in a small 'Ooohh!' and she doubled up, her hands flying to her belly.

Joey looked back up at Danny, a slight frown creasing his forehead. 'One thing I've been meaning to ask you. . .'

Kim found blood on her fingers and gasped in a breath. Her moan started low and rose to an ear-shattering scream: 'nnnnnNNNN-NOOOOOO!'

Joey ignored the noise and completed his question in a puzzled tone. '. . .why did you send that motherfucking *budgerigar* to haunt me old Dan?'

'MUMMEEE!' Kim screamed.

'I hate you for that, brother,' Joey said in a hurt voice. '*Why did you have to do it?*'

He turned back to the girl. 'Okay, sweetie,' he said, 'I think it's time we debarked you.'

The insistent hammering on the front door back in Danny's house finally woke him up.

Chapter Twenty
A Visit From Vinge

1

'Did she?' Vinge asked the moment Danny opened the door. The detective was holding out his identity card but this was a totally unnecessary action; Danny would never forget the look of shocked surprise on his bulldog-like features when he'd told him he'd hit his wife.

Danny felt the blood rush away from his face. For a moment he thought he might faint. This was something he had not expected. He had expected to have to make another tense phone call to the police to tip them off about the murder and the location of the body under the hedge in that snowy field. Now it looked as if someone had already found what was left of Steffy.

'Did who do what?' Danny asked, trying to collect his thoughts. He already knew what the policeman was alluding to: the message he'd left with Steffy's watch imploring her to contact him. The thought that he'd failed abysmally in his protection of her crossed his mind and Danny had no answer to it but the words: *I tried*. To which the answer, of course, was that he hadn't tried hard enough.

Vinge grimaced 'Phone you.'

'Who?' Danny asked.

Vinge smiled grimly. 'Cut the crap. The girl is dead and you're number one on my lengthy list of possible perpetrators.'

'She didn't,' Danny said, 'but I think you'd better come in and talk. Unless you're arresting me, in which case my lips are sealed till there's a solicitor present.'

Vinge sighed and shook his head. He folded his I.D. wallet and put it back in his jacket. 'You didn't do it, did you?' he asked.

Danny shook his head. 'Would you expect me to say yes if I had?'

Vinge shrugged. 'It's been known. I could also be wrong in my snap assessment of you – that's been known too. But on first look, your reaction wasn't right for a guy who's recently killed. It's all down to body language. I can usually tell in a moment.' He nodded to himself and said, 'I should have known it wouldn't be that easy where you're concerned, Mr Stafford. But let me tell you this: if you did it, I'll have you for it. Eventually.'

'Call me Danny, and come in,' he said wearily.

Danny led him into the cluttered lounge-cum-office, sat him down in one of the armchairs and offered him tea.

'You don't leave my sight until I'm done, Mr . . . uhh . . . Danny,' Vinge said uncertainly.

Danny's original feelings of fear and guilt were suddenly swamped by a kind of righteous indignation that might soon turn to anger. *That's what you think!* he thought, realising his palms were growing that itchy tingle again. He thought it might be something to do with the proximity of policemen. 'In that case you'd better follow me upstairs because you just woke me up, I'm dry as a stick and I badly need a piss. You can stand outside and guard the door while I'm in the toilet, if the sound of piss on porcelain turns you on,' he said tartly. 'But you can't come in there with me. You're not my type.'

Vinge waited where he was.

When Danny returned with the tea he was calm and ready. 'How's your wife?' he enquired sweetly.

Vinge glared at him. 'You tell me,' he said, shifting uncomfortably in his seat.

Here, for a change, is a man who is more frightened of you than you are of him, Danny told himself and then he smiled.

'I'd say things were pretty good,' he said. Then politely, 'How can I help you?'

Vinge scowled. 'You already know what happened. I don't know *how* you know or how you're involved but I intend to find out. A woman called Stephanie Osmond has been murdered. I want to know who did it, what part you played in it and why you're looking so fucking pleased with yourself.'

'You already know what I can do,' Danny said, sipping his tea. 'So you already know how I know about Steffy. I tried to stop it happening. That's the extent of my involvement. And I'm looking so fucking pleased with myself, as you put it, because for the first time in months I think I may be able to save myself some trouble.'

'You predicted her murder? She came to you for a . . . what d'you call 'em . . . reading?'

Danny nodded. 'She did. I saw the result in the hedge on the downs. That was all. The date in my vision was today's date.'

'Why didn't you call us?' Vinge demanded.

'Be sensible!' Danny snapped. 'What was I going to say? Please protect this woman because I've had a vision of a bundle beneath a hedge on December the 5th and I think it might be her and I think someone is going to kill her? They would have liked that just fine down the station, wouldn't they? They would have said, "thanks, Mr Stafford, we'll be right up to her house with marksmen in less than five minutes."

Vinge's crumpled face broke into a smile. He put his mug down and held up his hands. 'Okay, okay! I take it you didn't find out the name of the murderer?'

'What I told you was all I could get. I thought I could get more so I borrowed her watch. . .'

Vinge nodded. 'We have that with your letter.'

'. . . to try and get more information. And during the past few weeks I did get more information. More than I wanted.'

Danny could see Vinge's face hardening. 'You knew what was going to happen?' the detective said.

'Yeah. And last night I saw the murder happening and found out the name of the killer.'

'Look,' Vinge said, sounding like a man who had listened long enough to the most stupid alibi he'd ever heard in his life. 'You saw the murder happening, you knew the name of the man and you didn't even bother to dial three nines? It isn't remotely convincing. Give me one good reason why I shouldn't run you in this minute.'

Danny nodded. 'I couldn't phone for help. You won't like this, but I was asleep. I dreamed it.'

The detective sighed through his nose. 'You *dreamed* it,' he repeated, nodding. 'I might have known.'

'They won't like that back at the Nerve Centre, will they?'

Vinge didn't answer the question. Instead, he asked another. 'What did you dream?'

'The guy who killed Steffy is called Joseph Aston. Steffy was writing a book on psychic phenomena and he was one of her sources. I was going to be another. When I predicted her death she told me that someone else had also seen it, but I didn't think to ask his name then. To put it simply I was certain this guy would kill her, but didn't know any of the details. I tried to contact her endlessly over the past few days, but got no response. I went to her house and had a feeling she was inside and I hammered so hard on the door that I cracked a pane of glass in it.'

'You didn't actually break it?'

Danny shook his head. 'Aston did that last night. Anyway, I put the bag with the watch and the letter through the box and when I went back it had gone, but she didn't contact me. Last night I dreamed what happened to her. I could tell it to you in great detail, but I imagine you're starting to believe I'm your perpetrator by now and I'm frightened that if I do, you'll become convinced it was me.'

'Why should I?' Vinge asked.

'I would if I were you,' Danny said. 'And, anyway, you don't need to be psychic to spot it: like you said, you can tell by the body language. It sounds to you like a double bluff.'

Vinge nodded. 'Okay,' he said, 'but bear with me and tell me everything.'

'On one condition.'

'What's that?'

'That you don't arrest me. It'll be the wrong track and it'll waste time. This guy is still out there and he's warped and he's going to do more damage. And while you're wasting time getting me genetically fingerprinted – which will prove I didn't do it – the guy will kill a five-year-old girl called Kim Santos. Please believe me when I tell you this. It's very important that you find this girl and give her some kind of protection.'

Vinge shook his great head. 'I can't promise that kind of thing.'

'I'll give a blood sample you can have analysed. It won't match the stuff at the scene. And, anyway, by the time the results come in, we can have all this settled.'

'We?'

'You'll like this part even less, I'm afraid. The guy knows I'm on to him and after the little girl, he's going to come after me.'

Vinge thought about it. 'If it was anyone else but you, I'd arrest them on the spot and let them cool their heels in the cells, then I'd have them questioned for as long as it took to get a confession. But I keep remembering how you took that stuff from Ray Johnson and said it out loud, and now I'm. . .' He shook his head.

'How's he coping?' Danny asked.

'He's gone,' Vinge said. 'Gone from work, gone from home. No one knows where he is.'

'I'm sorry.'

Vinge nodded. 'So am I. Ray was the best guy I've ever worked with. . .'

'Let me tell you about Joey,' Danny said quickly.

'Joey?'

'The killer.'

Looking doubtful, Vinge took out a note pad and pencil.

'You're looking for a man named Joseph Aston,' Danny said. 'He's white, aged about thirty-five or -six and has very dark brown eyes – almost black, in fact. He's about six one or two and has an athletic build, weighing twelve six to thirteen stone. He's either South African born, or he lived there when he was young. Johannesburg. Around the age of ten or eleven. But he doesn't speak with a South African accent.'

Vinge looked at him in something close to disbelief. 'He *spoke* to you? He *spoke* to you *in your dream?*'

Danny nodded. 'He was in a nasty car crash there and there's going to be accident and surgical scars on him, probably somewhere around his head. He wears a Gannex raincoat, leather-soled shoes and carries a knife with a round wooden handle and a blade about nine inches long. . .'

Danny told him everything he knew about the killer, leaving out the more complex elements – on its own it sounded crazy enough.

Vinge looked up when he'd finished scratching at his notepad.

'Listen,' he said, 'is there any chance, d'you think, that you might be having blackouts and assuming the identity of this Joseph Aston? That would explain a lot.'

'Would I have told you all this?' Danny asked.

'You suggested the double bluff,' Vinge said.

'Believe me, I'm telling the truth,' Danny said. 'And if you look through the preparation for Steffy's book, you'll undoubtedly find some mention of him.'

'It's a mess,' Vinge said. 'There's loads of jumbled stuff about Tantric magic and sex. I think she was probably a bit. . .' His protruding bottom lip snapped up over his top one as he bit the words off.

'Touched,' Danny said. 'It's okay, I'm used to people thinking that about me too. Sometimes *I* think I'm a bit touched.'

Vinge looked at him suspiciously.

'But if you check her research material you'll undoubtedly find references to two genuine and impressive psychics. I'm the later one and Joseph Aston is the earlier one. She'll have named both of us, I'm sure.'

'And you say that in your vision, this guy promised to come after you?'

Danny nodded.

'It wasn't a dream then, like you said?'

'It was a prophetic dream if you like. It was like a vision.'

'But it was two way. The guy could communicate with you.'

'That's right.'

'I can hardly force myself to believe any of this, Daniel,' Vinge said. 'It's like that fucking crazy film *Nightmare on Elm Street*. Did you ever see it?'

Danny shook his head. The tickling in the palms of his hands abruptly went away. 'No, but you did,' he heard himself say. 'Your daughter . . . Emma . . . was sixteen then and still two years too young to go. You told her so but she kept on and you caved in. You took her to London to see it – your wife wouldn't go – and all the way you complained that you'd rather go to see Andrew Lloyd Webber's *Cats*. Emma promised she'd take you to see *Cats* another time, but you're still waiting.'

Vinge shuddered. 'I wish you wouldn't fucking well *do* that,' he said. 'I don't much care for the look on your face when you do it.'

'Was I right?'

'You know you were,' Vinge nodded.

And Danny knew he'd bought himself some time. At last, Vinge had begun to believe.

2

Vinge's parting words were still ringing in Danny's ears when his next visitor called. *We'll get the bastard*, he'd said. *Don't worry, we'll get the bastard*. But Danny doubted this. Vinge was going to have a hard time finding the man in the Gannex raincoat and an even harder time making up a story about Danny that would convince his colleagues. Vinge had made it clear that he was going to stick his neck out on Danny's behalf but warned that if the axe that was suspended above happened to fall, then Danny would be charged with, tried for, and undoubtedly found guilty of, Stephanie Osmond's murder. Danny had asked what Vinge would tell his colleagues about him and Vinge had replied that he would think of something.

Danny opened the door to answer the slow, rhythmic thud, already knowing it was Jamie standing outside. Jamie came in, announced that he didn't have to go to the school all week because the doctor said he had a bad cold, and did a wheezing Alistair Lerner-like cough to prove it.

Danny took him up to the kitchen, fed him and played a half-hearted game of I-Spy with him while, his mind was elsewhere.

Jamie chose peanut as his word – a fact that wasn't revealed until Danny had exhausted the supply of things in the room which began with the letter W.

'Peanut doesn't begin with a W,' he complained as Jamie cackled snottily.

Danny got him a tissue and made him blow his nose. 'It can if I want it to,' Jamie said thoughtfully. Then dissolved into a fit of giggling which rapidly turned into a harsh, hacking cough.

'There aren't any peanuts in here and you ought to be at home in bed,' Danny told him.

When Jamie looked up his face was sheened with sweat and there was an odd expression on it Danny had not seen before. Jamie chose his words carefully and spoke slowly as if his grip on them was tenuous and he didn't want them to slip away. 'I came to see Danny the Hoodoo Man because I'm worried,' he said solemnly.

'Worried? What about?'

Jamie's face drew up in a grimace of intense concentration. 'Vinge has came and now I'm worried about the birdy. About the . . . future birdy. About how we can bring it back.'

Joey? Danny thought. 'I don't understand,' he said.

'I'm trying,' Jamie said, his face distorted and his eyes gleaming. 'I'm trying very hard but I don't understand neither. Vinge has came and now we got to bring back the birdy. Time is short.'

'Who says?'

'I says,' Jamie rasped. 'Just don't forget . . . or I'll . . . lose you.'

Danny put his arm around the boy. 'Don't worry,' he said, aware that he was telling another lie, 'nothing is going to happen to me. Or you.'

'The birdy!' Jamie said, coughing hard.

'Okay,' Danny soothed, stroking his hair. Jamie was damp and sticky with sweat and there was a good possibility he had become delirious. 'I won't forget the birdy,' Danny said.

3

Early that evening, after the seventh try with the crystal, Danny was sure that it was all over. Joey would come for him tonight, even though he couldn't yet have killed the little girl called Kim Santos (and if Vinge was as good as his word, wouldn't be able to). The time seemed right: Danny was at a low ebb – mentally exhausted from fighting with the crystal; emotionally drained from the experience of Steffy's slaying, and physically tired from carrying Jamie most of the way back to his home.

And the crystal said that everything was hopeless: after tonight Danny had no future.

But during the return journey from Jamie's house it hadn't seemed that way. Danny had limped badly and his war-wound had begun to throb. *Vinge has came*, he'd thought as he walked home and the message seemed terribly important. *Vinge has came and now we got to bring back the birdy*.

Doreen James had been apologetic when Danny arrived carrying her semi-conscious son. Jamie had kept her up all night with his illness and his nightmares and when he'd finally settled down, she sat down on the sofa for a rest, then decided to have forty winks, and when she'd woken up an hour and a half later Jamie had been missing. She had been about to go out to look for him when Danny arrived. Jamie was fed antibiotics, put back to bed and warned to stay there on pain of death. Doreen had explained that Jamie sometimes had nightmares when he was ill and that the thing no one told you about Down's Syndrome kids was that they got ill *a lot* – mainly with chest infections. Jamie had previously had bad nightmares during which he thought he received important messages that he was supposed to pass on, Doreen said, but the one about Vinge and the birdy was a new one to her. Doreen claimed Jamie's usual sleep messages were, 'The chicken angel is green', and 'We must make blinds build fish triangles in the desert', and said that he often woke with a burning urge to impart these messages.

Sitting in gloom in the Reading Room while he was gathering the courage to use the crystal, Jamie's last nightmare message seemed to contain a strong warning. He had said he didn't want to lose Danny, and in a way *that* was simple to explain. Jamie had either dreamed Danny was in danger or had somehow picked it up telepathically from him. The pieces of his message about Vinge having been and time being short could also be explained this way, but Danny was stumped as to how to interpret the piece about bringing back the birdy. This was evidently a reference to Joey the budgie, who had apparently appeared to Jamie when Danny had tried to look into his future. Jamie wanted Joey the genius budgie to be brought back, and the fact that he had surely been dead for the past twenty years or so was neither here nor there.

So once again Danny had tried to use the crystal to see into his own future.

And the results told him that he was wasting his energy wondering about the message about Joey the budgie or the visions of Joey the Gannex Man or anything else. Tonight would be his last night alive and Danny was apparently going to give in without a struggle.

According to futures one to seven, Danny would give up trying to gain information from the crystal at six-thirty when he would wash it, dry it and cover it up in the Reading Room. After this – and in spite of the fact that he wasn't the least bit hungry – he would go to the kitchen where he would peel, chip and fry potatoes along with the piece of plaice he had in the fridge. He would try to eat it, fail dismally and throw the lot into the dustbin.

At seven he would lie down on the bed in front of the television and fall asleep for forty minutes. After this he would wake up feeling an urgent need to have people around him. He would wash and shave, change his clothes and walk to the nearest pub where he would drink four shots of brandy which would have no effect on him whatsoever. He would watch all the other normal, everyday people and jealousy would cut him like a knife. Over the following two brandies he would think long and hard about Suzie, and at nine thirty-three he would suddenly realise he had seen her for the last time. There was going to be no reconciliation. As Suzie – a far better psychic than any of them – had so confidently predicted, everything was going to turn out for the bad in the end.

Danny would leave the pub at ten trying hard not to cry and failing. At the door Lady Luck in her infinite nastiness would have placed a woman for him to meet – a gorgeous woman who looked and sounded very much like Suzie. The woman's name would be Sophie and she would take his arm and ask him if he was okay and could she help him? Danny would instantly realise the intentional irony and shake her hand away from him, brusquely telling her that no, he was not okay and no, she could not help him. He would hurry home, dial Suzie's number (and what used to be his own number) intending to tell her that he didn't expect to see her again but that he loved her and would always love her no matter what happened. But Lady Luck would have fixed this one too and Suzie would not be home. The phone would ring and ring but no one would answer it.

Danny would cry for a while then he would walk down to the sea and wander along the windy beach, the snow and pebbles crunching under his feet while he cried again. And then he would grow angry and swear and rage at God and Lady Luck and all their demons – and then he would walk down to the tide line where the sea had cleared the snow and would sit at the water's edge with the waves crashing before him, flooding up to him and filling his shoes.

At midnight, damp and utterly defeated and knowing now that bringing back Joey – and all those other important things – didn't matter one tiny little piece, he would limp home where he would try one last futile time to contact Suzie.

At one-fifteen the expanding blood-bag in his nostril would burst and Danny would lean over the sink for twenty minutes hoping he would bleed to death while some unseen demon inserted an invisible drill into the site of his bullet wound and screwed it slowly down into his brain. At a quarter to two Danny would fall into his bed simply because there was no other option open to him.

And at three-seventeen then next morning Danny's future, and therefore his life, would fizzle out like a damp firework and fade away.

4

Already feeling the overpowering sense of *déjà-vu* because he'd just done all this – literally, this time – Danny took the crystal upstairs and ran it under the tap to clear it. Even this act seemed futile and pointless – he didn't intend to use it again today and tomorrow there would be no Danny Stafford on the planet *to* use it.

Wondering how it was going to finish, and working on a kind of auto-pilot that seemed to have taken over his controls, Danny peeled and chipped potatoes he knew he wasn't going to eat. He was either going to pass away peacefully in his sleep due to a heart failure or a brain defect (*And that would be a fine irony to end with, wouldn't it, old Dan?*) or Joey Aston was going to come calling and take him while he slept. Danny fried the fish, thinking, *fuck it! Fuck it all! I'm not going to play this game any more. I know what's coming and I can bloody well change it. I don't have to run down this track like a train. I'm going to buck the fucking system.*

But when he tried not to carry on frying the fish, Danny discovered that he was not running along a track at all, but gathering speed in a deep, icy downhill channel which he did not have the energy or the will-power to climb out of. Death suddenly seemed like the perfect release from all the shit that had been – and that was *still* being – thrown at him.

5

After the nosebleed and before Danny finally stopped fighting and gave himself up, he did find the energy to buck the system, if only in a tiny way.

The idea came into his head and he grasped hold of it with a ferocity he didn't think he was capable of. *I'm going to do it!* he defiantly told himself – and whatever other force for good or evil (but most likely evil) might be listening in. He took his face out of the sink, dried it, went out on to the landing and looked down the stairs. It looked like a very long way to the bottom and his whole left side was so weak now that he didn't think he could walk down there.

But you can make it, he told himself, and if you can't get back upstairs again, it's just tough fucking shit: it won't make one damn' bit of difference to the outcome anyway. In fact, there's no good and proper reason why you should even try *to get back up again. Why put yourself out to fulfil a lousy stinking vision of end of your life? Just get down there and do the biz and let the fucking future sort out the rest if it wants to.*

Just as he had done in the house in Windlesham when he was a child, Danny sat down on the top stair, his legs out in front of him. He leaned forward slightly and let the alteration of his centre of gravity slide his bottom forwards and bump down on to the next stair, leaning back as it made contact and bringing himself to a halt. The stairs in Windlesham had been carpeted and these were bare and Danny was a lot heavier – which presumably explained why it hurt so much more than he remembered. It was a good solid jolt that made his left arm tingle and shot a bolt of pain down his left leg.

He bumped down the next step and began to wonder about the wisdom of his idea. There were another fifteen to go to the hallway and by the time he arrived he was going to be in no fit state to get to the Reading Room.

You can crawl, he told himself, bumping down the next stair. *You can just fucking well. . .*

But Danny didn't get time to finish the thought because he hadn't leaned back far enough to halt himself on the following stair and momentum had suddenly taken control. And Danny now remembered another forgotten lesson from his childhood: momentum didn't care two hoots about how much you got hurt. He straightened out and slid painfully down to the hall, his mind flashing blue as his head bumped and bounced on each passing stair.

For a few moments he didn't remember how he had suddenly come to be lying in a tangled ball on the sticky hallway carpet, then he didn't think he was going to be able to move. Then he grew angry about all the injustice that had been meted out to him and straightened himself out and began to crawl.

The tiny plan took almost an hour to achieve, which meant that he now had between forty and fifty minutes left to live. Danny realised this when he found himself back on the stairs, going up backwards in a sitting position, lifting himself up them one at a time and powering himself with his right arm and leg. He didn't care about the remaining time, but a while ago it had suddenly started to seem important to get back upstairs because of what Jamie had said. It didn't make sense, but Jamie had said, *Just don't forget, or I'll lose you*, and being upstairs when he died was the best he could manage; the furthest he could go in satisfying this request.

So he worked his way upstairs to die, knowing that he had bucked at least a little of his fate. The evidence was scrawled over the life-charts that were now laid out on the table in the reading room.

Danny had taken a thick black felt-tip marker and over the neatly plotted lines of his life had written his full name, his home address in Basingstoke and his telephone number. Beneath this he had left the message:

PLEASE CONTACT SUSAN ANDERSON AT THE ABOVE ADDRESS AND TELL HER THIS:

DANNY LOVED HER BEFORE
DANNY LOVES HER NOW
DANNY WILL LOVE HER FOREVER

Chapter Twenty-One
The Floating Danny

Danny's life did not simply fizzle out and fade away at three seventeen.

At three twenty-one he realised that he'd woken up and was now sitting bolt upright in his bed staring at the chink of light that shone in from the street through the almost closed curtains.

What happened? he asked himself groggily – and his calm cry-baby voice replied, *You're expanding*!

The soft yellow light was hurting his eyes and his whole body was tingling violently as if a powerful electric current was being applied to him. It was an extremely unpleasant sensation and he felt as though the atoms and molecules his body was composed of were coming unstuck and separating from one another, drawing him out and filling him with nothingness as the odd electrical force sought him out, broke the links in him and vibrated him apart.

Danny tried to move and could not. He could feel muscles sliding about as he moved his arms and legs, but they no longer seemed to be attached and moved without resistance.

You've come unhooked, he thought stupidly. *That's what's happened; you're free-floating inside your own body*.

His bullet scar throbbed once and Danny felt it open like a rapidly blossoming flower bud leaving a hard core in the centre. Something jabbed the centre of it like a white-hot knife blade. The pain was not just immense, it was total. For a second nothing existed except a universe of agonising pain.

Danny drew a non-existent breath and screamed a non-existent scream.

HE'S COMING IN! his mind shouted. *He's found you and unhooked you from your body and now he's coming in after you!*

The white hot pain hit the hard core in the centre of his scar again and reaching out through the thick sheet of agony, Danny tried desperately to find his limbs. Joey Aston had found him in his sleep and had somehow targeted and paralysed him, holding him in position while the white-hot knife blade he'd sent probed Danny's weak point, opening a way in for him. If he could move himself away from the beam the killer had sent, Aston would lose his grip.

He found his left arm and slapped it up across his face, feeling, with fat and almost numb fingers, the trickle of blood that was running from the old wound. The hot point drilled into the back of his hand and Danny thought he could smell its flesh burning.

A laser beam! he thought stupidly as he clamped his hand around his face and tried to turn it away. *He's sending out a fucking laser beam*! *He* can't *be; it's impossible*! But whatever Aston was doing *was* possible and how he was doing it didn't matter. What mattered was that Danny could not turn his head away from it. The loose muscles of his locked neck and spine could not be re-connected and his arm was getting too heavy to hold in position. The fierce pain drilling into the back of his hand was too much to bear.

Danny lost his grip on it and it fell to the bedclothes, vanishing from his internal perception of it before it stopped moving.

The pain stopped and Danny wrenched himself violently sideways before it could return. He was not terribly surprised to find that his fizzling body had not moved: he had simply twisted himself around inside it. He could still see out of his eyes but everything was now at a new angle and slightly skewed.

Come on! Hurry it up! You're still in your body and it's still yours so just get it back and get it out of the way before he does it again! he told himself, but the locked body still felt vaporous and still seemed to be expanding. It was difficult to tell which parts were which, let alone fit himself to them internally.

The next time the white hot pain hit his bullet scar, Danny's twisted vision allowed him to watch it arrive. It was not a laser beam at all, but something very close to one. The slender tube of fire entered the room through the wall over by the door. It was pink and gently curved and it constantly adjusted its trajectory, seeking him as it touched the bedside table, moved up the wall and veered right, inching its way towards him. The pain, when it locked on to the hard core of his bleeding scar, was immense.

And the tough core twitched then opened like a relaxing sphincter.

Molten metal flooded into Danny through the slender conduit Joey Aston had sent out for him. It hit Danny's spinal cord and rushed down it, lighting fires deep in his groin which quickly expanded, crushing him and pushing him away from his body; forcing him upwards through a savage flood of corrupted thoughts and emotions. Danny screamed silently as he was infinitely and agonisingly compressed into a null and dead spot inside his own brain.

He beat you! Danny thought into the total blackness that surrounded him. *He's killed you just as surely as Brian killed you when he shot you. You're dead, o Danny boy o Master Mystic. You're dead!*

Something soft was rocking him back and forth, rapidly becoming more violent as it shook him out of the dead part of his brain. Showers of invisible sparks rained down on him and Danny felt himself tear away from his body.

Then he was floating high in the room looking down on that strange vessel of clay which was not dead but now hooked up to and possessed with the life of Joey Aston.

Without a shadow of a doubt Danny knew what Aston intended for that body. Joey was not going to use it to kill the little girl, Kim Santos – at least not yet. Not until after he'd drawn Danny back to his home and. . .

But he's lost me! Danny thought. *He wanted me but he's driven me away. He's only got my empty body!*

But when the body started to move and Danny started to move with it, he realised he was not dead at all. *You're still attached!* he thought, and felt a terrible knowing dread rise in him. Lerner's books would have called this an *Out of Body Experience* and Lerner's books would have been right. They'd said that during these episodes, the *spirit* remained attached to the body by a *silver cord* which was connected through the stomach to an internal centre of energy. That silver cord existed all right, but the one Danny could faintly see, pulsing in and out of existence and looking more like a slender chain with very thin links, wound out from the bullet scar on his physical body's face wound, passed around the tube of fire that Joey had driven into him and drifted slackly up to him.

According to these very same books in Lerner's collection, all you had to do to re-inhabit your body was to think yourself back inside it. Danny knew it wouldn't work but he tried it just the same.

His body now only answered to the commands that came down that tube of fire from Aston. Danny was locked out.

He hung in the top corner of the room and looked down as his body pushed the bedclothes back and tried clumsily to sit up. Danny willed himself to lie down again, but it might have just as well been a stranger down there; there was no connection with the body at all. Danny no longer had any of its sensations, none of its thoughts or emotions. There was no traffic at all between him and his body.

Down there on the bed, the body managed to sit up. It was grinning inanely and Danny thought the grin might belong to Aston. The first obstacles had been overcome – Danny had been driven away and Aston had discovered he could make another person's limbs move for him.

The Danny body turned on the light and his head swept the room like a radar scanner, turning in a great arc from shoulder to shoulder.

The floating Danny suspected that Aston had somehow not managed to tap into the body's memory and this gave him a faint hope. Down there, Aston was searching for the clothes Danny had scattered not fifteen minutes ago. The floating Danny knew exactly where they were.

The Danny body got up clumsily and stood wavering on the spot, looking down at its erect penis and nodding in jerking movements.

It found Danny's trousers and spent five full minutes putting them on. Danny was filled with a dark delight as he realised Aston could not make the fingers work properly. The body drew on a sweatshirt, thrust its feet into shoes and made two clumsy knots with the laces while the floating Danny tried everything he knew to get back inside the body. This was impossible and when he tried to swoop down to interfere with Aston's tube of fire, he found he could not move from his current position.

But when the Danny body began to stagger like a drunk towards the door, Danny realised two things he was very thankful for. The first was that since Aston was looking out of Danny's physical eyes, he was unable to see his own fiery tube of force, and the second was that Aston was going to have to keep that tube connected at all times and, as Danny well knew, the tube *hurt*. Aston was going to have to follow it all the way back to his place like a blind man following a strand of an electric fence. The second thing was that Danny's deep internal Hoodoo Man part – the part he mostly kept locked away in his subconscious for fear of what it might do – had known this all along. Which was why it had insisted so strongly that he make the painful and slow return journey upstairs after bucking the future and writing the message of eternal love to Suzie.

Joey Aston could not see his own navigational beam, but he could feel it.

And he thought he knew where he'd placed it.

Which was why when he closed the eyes of the Danny body and strode it unsteadily across the room to the door, the body passed the door and walked smack into the wall where the pink tube of fire came through.

Yes! Danny thought as his body's face hit the wall hard and bounced off it again, throwing the body back on its heels to a point from which balance could not possibly be regained.

The floating Danny smiled grimly as the physical one fell heavily. There was no pain, but it had surely hurt and he hoped it had hurt Aston badly.

When the physical Danny got up again, its nose was bleeding badly.

He's not going to get me out of the room, let alone down the stairs! Danny realised, knowing that if he'd let himself sleep on the sticky hall floor where he'd so badly wanted to lie down and rest it would have been a simple matter for Aston to get him out of the front door.

But Aston was not defeated yet. The physical Danny stood before the wall and leaned forward into the strand of energy until its head touched the wallpaper. Then it reached out its right hand and found the door. Then it moved slowly to the right, leaving a smear of blood on the wallpaper as, using its senses, Aston adjusted the direction of his beam.

Its eyes now open, the physical Danny moved back from the door as the floating Danny looked on helplessly. It opened the door, stepping awkwardly backwards and managing to hit its face once more on the door's edge as it moved away.

Here we go! Danny thought and began to wonder what it would really be like to be dead. That was how this little escapade was shortly going to end up – that much was obvious. The prospect didn't chill him as much as he'd thought it would. He was no longer frightened of dying – there were worse things than that which could befall you. Much worse. *If I could just reach down and get my legs back* . . . Danny thought.

But he didn't have to. The Hoodoo Man in him had known *that* all along too.

The weak left side of its body and the pronounced limp made the journey across the landing all the more difficult for the physical Danny, and the floating Danny wondered if good old Joey Aston was beginning to doubt the wisdom of his actions yet. It was unlikely that this poor bleeding thing would make it back to Aston's hiding place – however close it was. *But that doesn't matter*, the floating Danny thought tiredly as he was tugged along after the physical one by the thin silver chain. *That doesn't matter a jot or an iota or any other little thing. Aston may not know it yet but I do. This poor worn-out body isn't even going to be alive by the time it gets to the bottom of the stairs.*

Then it was proven to Danny that Joseph Aston had not been able to access his memory, because if he *had* he would have known better than to try and walk down that huge gaping distance the stairs had surely become for him. Had he looked into Danny's memory of less than twenty-five minutes ago he would have known that the thing to do was to sit on the top stair, lean back and let gravity do the rest. Harnessing gravity rather than taking it on face to face was the key to a successful descent, but good old Joey was too arrogant to realise this – or to take notice of it if he did.

Instead of sitting down, the physical Danny stepped out with its right leg and bent the weak left one to take the weight.

He should have known not to do that! At least he should have known that! Danny thought.

Down there on the top stair, the physical Danny's left leg gave way and the body fell forwards into the yawning gap. The floating Danny felt a shock of pain as the body's contact with the burning tube was broken and as the tube vanished he realised that although it was all over for *him*, Joey wasn't going to be killed or injured in the fall at all. Joey, the bastard, had gone.

Danny watched the bleeding body fly, its arms spread, its legs bent and its head tilted back as it swan-dived into oblivion, paying out the slender silver chain as it fell. Danny was glad that his death would be painless and strangely sorry for the body that would have no occupant to feel its few moments of pain when it hit.

The body hit the stairs about halfway down. Its back bent and its head hit the next stair down and it jack-knifed, its pelvis and limp legs flying through the air, crashing down on to the stairs and dragging the top half of its body over to repeat the whole process again.

It took a further two and half turns before the body hit the sticky hallway carpet and the head was whipped violently round into the bottom banister post. The wood splintered with the force. The body tensed and twitched twice then settled into a crumpled heap. The silver chain it had paid out began to fade.

There I go! Danny told himself.

And darkness seized him.

Chapter Twenty-Two
The Hoodoo Man, Coming

1

If it hadn't been for the damned telephone keeping on ringing I could have been out of here hours ago, Danny thought distantly. *These days you don't even get to go to meet your maker in peace.*

Something hurt. Something hurt but it was miles away. Light years away, maybe. Perhaps at the other end of a different universe. Something hurt and the telephone was making it hurt a great deal more.

QUIET! Danny thought and the incessant drilling of the telephone miraculously ceased to be.

Okay, sweetie, I think it's time we de-barked you. . .

Okay, Danny thought, *go ahead; it won't hurt me now, not out here in the Phantom Zone where I'm busy being dead. You do what you like to me, Mr Mortician. You can stuff me and mount me if you like. It doesn't matter, it won't hurt me now.*

But something *did* hurt. Every time the telephone rang it started hurting and the telephone was ringing again now.

And little Kim Santos with the huge dark eyes was screaming. It was back there where the telephone was and the sound was reaching his ears (ears that he no longer possessed because dead men didn't have ears) by the same route. If it would all just shut up, he could simply drift away from the pain and float in perfect peace.

DON'T PUT THAT IN ME! PLEASE! PLEASE GOD! I WANT MY MUMMMEEEE!

Why don't you take mine? I've got one I don't need any longer. I know I didn't like her much but maybe she won't pretend she's dead so much with you as she did with me. She used to frighten me once, y'know, and when she stopped scaring me she started nagging me. Maybe she won't do that to you.

The phone stopped ringing again – perhaps five minutes later or maybe five hours. It didn't matter and it was impossible to tell because there was no longer any time to have to deal with. No past, no future – just *now*.

One final step for a man to make that giant leap, Danny thought, and a part of him knew it wasn't an ordinary step. It was going to have to be the same kind of sideways *click* as when you went time-travelling; or the slippery and gentle jolt you were sometimes aware of when you went from being awake to being asleep – except this jolt was infinitely more gentle and consequently infinitely more difficult to find.

Impossible if that phone doesn't leave me alone! he thought. *I should have been out of here hours ago! Come on, where's my bus? Where's that last slippery step?*

The phone began to ring again. The little girl began to wail pitifully.

'For fuck's *sake!*' Danny heard a strangely exasperated voice croak.

That was you, his cry-baby voice told him. *That was your voice. You're not dead at all!*

Bollocks! Danny answered but the pain and drilling ring and the little girl's voice were ganging up on him, making him want to cry.

'No peace for the wicked,' the strange voice said in his ears.

And Danny's eyes flicked open.

In the moment of confusion that followed he thought: *There are cobwebs on the ceiling!*

Then the full weight of his pain crashed down on him along with the knowledge he had been trying to deny. In spite of what Vinge had promised, good old Joey Aston was forging ahead with his plans.

He had Kim Santos. Now.

And Vinge was trying to get through on the telephone.

Danny pushed himself up on to all fours. All fours ached intensely but none of them seemed to be broken. Twisted, bruised and badly wrenched, yes, but broken, no. That Queen of all the Bitches had evidently not finished with her tortures yet. The pain in his head hurt worst of all but it was the *raped* feeling of having been totally physically invaded that made him want to throw up. The scar where he'd been shot was throbbing and sore and Danny was frightened to touch it in case Aston had left a gaping hole there – a gaping hole which might still contain a broken-off part of him.

The phone fell silent and instantly began to ring again. 'Coming,' Danny croaked and dry-heaved violently the moment he began to crawl.

It took another four failed calls for him to get to the phone.

2

When Vinge rang again, Danny was slumped in an armchair, the telephone receiver in his lap with the cut-off buttons held down with his fingers while he held the handset to his ear.

'Vinge. It's me,' he said. 'He's got her.'

Vinge sounded surprised. 'Who's got *who?*' he wanted to know.

'Joey Aston has got Kim Santos. He's got her now and he's torturing her, just as I predicted. Why didn't you protect her?'

'What are you talking about? She *is* being protected. She's *in school*, for fuck's sake. I'm ringing to ask you to come down and give us some blood for testing.'

'He's got her now.'

There was a short silence during which Danny became wearily aware that Vinge's surprise was turning into annoyance. He thought he knew what would follow but there was no way around this if the girl was to be given a chance. 'Impossible,' Vinge finally said. 'We found the Santos family and they're under twenty-four hour surveillance. There are two detectives who are protecting the girl at this very moment. She was escorted to school this morning and they're waiting there right now for her to come out.'

'Inside the school?'

'*Outside*, of course. They're waiting outside and keeping watch on the comings and goings. What good would they do in her classroom?'

'Better than they've done outside,' Danny said. 'What time is it?' he asked quickly.

'What are you fucking talking about?' Vinge snapped. 'It's a quarter to three. She comes out at half-past and there are guys waiting for her. No one's got her.'

'Lunch time,' Danny said. 'He got her then. Your guys were eating. They went to the shop.'

'They *didn't go to the shop!*' Vinge yelled. 'They wouldn't! And anyway, *she doesn't come out for lunch!* She stays. . .'

Vinge's voice tailed off on a note of shocked realisation. The annoyance had gone out him now and had been replaced by grim certainty. Danny knew why: Vinge's brittle mind could not easily accept many of the things Danny had told him. The stuff about Ray Johnson was difficult to deny and at times Vinge had felt his mind creaking as he tried to wrap it around that undeniable truth. And since it hurt Vinge had set that one aside, out of harm's way, and had been looking for ways around some of the other stuff ever since. And now his mind had suddenly begun to provide him with those ways.

Vinge was no longer impressed that Danny had supplied him with the name and description of the little girl; in fact, he was at this very moment telling himself that Danny could have quite easily come across this information by other means than psychic ones. Vinge rapidly (almost simultaneously, Danny realised) thought several different things following this. The first was that he'd been *had*: even though he'd been certain Danny was his man, he'd stupidly put his arse in a man-trap to buy Danny some time. And now the trap had been sprung. The second was that Danny had somehow taken the girl from under the noses of her protection and already killed her – probably while Vinge had been trying to get through on the phone –

and the most important thought was: how quickly could he arrest Danny?

Danny perceived all this but there was nothing he could do about it now. His head was clearing and the memory of his dream – or vision or whatever it had been – was coming back to him one last time, reeling past his inner eye and fading again. The details were vanishing but one passing part became branded into his mind forever. He held it still while it sizzled into him and now he had it, he thought he would remember it until his dying day.

He had the *address!*

'Listen. Don't bother checking this – you'll find it's true. She's gone. He got her in the playground at lunch time. He told her he was a policeman. She went with him. If you want to save her. . .'

Vinge didn't want to believe what his mind was telling him; he clung desperately to his last hope – that all this was a lie. It *had* to be: things *couldn't* fall apart like this. The watchers *couldn't possibly* have gone to lunch! '*She's in school, for fuck's sake!*' he shouted.

'Get someone round to 425 Wicklow Road. NOW! That's where he's taken her. She's hurt but she's still alive. You don't have much time.' Danny knew without a doubt that Vinge didn't believe him but also knew that Vinge would have to check it out.

'How do you know?' the policeman asked, now not knowing what to believe.

'Listen to me!' Danny half screamed. 'Just do it. Don't think about it, just send a car and then check the school. She's gone. I've told you where it is, now do it!'

'How *do you know?*' he insisted.

'I fell down the stairs last night. Just after three. I've been lying there unconscious and I just woke up. I dreamed it or saw it while I was asleep! *I've just been hearing her scream, for Christ's sake!*'

And Danny heard Jon Vinge's next thoughts as clearly as if the man had spoken them aloud. *What if he's right and you're wrong? Dear God, what if he's right and those stupid fucks* did *go to lunch and he really did get the girl? What if he's right?*

Vinge suddenly sounded very frightened. 'Wait there,' he said, and rang off.

3

By the time Vinge turned up, Danny knew all about it. As Danny had replaced the handset after his conversation with Vinge, he'd *felt* a tiny switch in his mind tripping and linking his dream-vision memory of the murder with the present.

But the memory was time-lapsed because it began to roll too late – out of synchronisation with what was actually happening. And the echoing pictures of what was happening *now* mingled with what had already happened, splicing themselves clumsily together like scenes from a film, cut up and stuck back together in the wrong sequence.

'You'll feel it too,' Joey promised. 'When I do it to her, you'll feel her life caressing you.'

But Joey was already doing it – had already been doing it for some time. There was blood on the knife, on Joey and over the walls.

'Ten-up, old Dan!' Joey whispered.

'IT WON'T WORK!' Danny heard himself shout.

Joey tenderly wiped away Kim's tears. 'It's okay, sweetie,' he said, 'I'm not gong to hurt you and your mummy and daddy will be along to collect you soon. It'll soon be home time.'

'IT WON'T WORK! I WON'T LET YOU DO IT!' Danny shouted, but it was already too late: the scene was overlaid with another, later one – the one that was happening in *real-time*.

An earlier moment occurred. Joey turned and looked up at him and said, 'And when I'm done here, I'll be coming for you.'

'And when I'm done here, I'll be coming for you.'

The connection faded and broke into white-noise interference like a T.V. with a bad aerial, but Danny received enough of the echoing fragmented words and hazy pictures to see what Joey did long after he said: '*We're like Jesus, you and me; we can work miracles! . . . I saw you in that void, twinkling like a little star . . . There is no separate future for you Dan, only* my *future . . . We can be greater . . . Why did you have to send that fucking budgerigar to haunt me. . .?*

Back in the Fortune Shop, Danny's mind was shorting out under the onslaught. He fell from the armchair and the telephone rattled and tinkled across the floor.

Got to make it stop! he thought and this thought was swamped and submerged by Aston saying, 'We're brothers, Dan, a pair of walking dead men both with links into the Great Beyond. We're the only two. Did you know that? The only two people in the world who are alive and dead at the same time. The only two living Hoodoo Men currently walking the face of the planet. We're like Jesus, you and me; we can work miracles.'

Danny fought off the overlaid pictures of what was happening in real-time, and began to crawl. If he could just run his head under the tap, the same way you ran the crystal under it to remove the old pictures, everything would be all right.

The stairs loomed before him like a mountain and Danny started up them, trying not to see the hazy fragments of Joey using the knife like a surgeon; working carefully and prolonging things.

Police will be there soon. It's not too late! he assured himself, knowing that he was lying.

When he finally put his head in the sink turned on the tap and broke the connection, it *was* too late. Joey Aston had literally stolen the girl's life.

And by the time Vinge arrived and began to thump the door, Danny knew that Joey had strengthened himself by a factor of two and needed to reach the magical number of three.

Joey was coming.

4

A black hatred for Joey Aston built in Danny over the following twenty-four hours. It started when Vinge and two other detectives arrived and arrested him on suspicion of the murders of Stephanie Osmond and Kim Santos and it continued to grow through the pointless and incessant questioning. Danny was dog-tired, hurt badly from the fall he'd taken and in total mental anguish at having been unable to save the girl. He refused to speak during the first three hours of questioning, submitted to a blood test without protest and after that, while a detective named Adams baited and cajoled him, he fell asleep, elbows on the table and his chin cupped in his hands.

Vinge woke him immediately.

'Got the blood results?' Danny asked. His hands were starting to tingle now but he resolved to keep his motormouth locked away. Another demonstration of his wonderful ability to read minds wasn't going to cut any more ice.

Vinge shook his head. 'No, but soon.'

'So how did you do it?' Adams asked for what must have been the thousandth time. Danny knew exactly how both Adams and Vinge (*Who you thought was on your side, you silly boy*!) thought he'd done it. They, along with the other detective – whose name Danny thought was Haines – had found him badly bruised, in pain and covered in blood. Adams had believed Danny was the guilty party from that very moment, but Vinge had had to do some clever mental juggling to arrive at the same conclusion. Danny admired him for this – he'd done some of this difficult mental sorting and stacking himself over the past few weeks. The two men (Haines who was playing the good guy had a strong gut feeling that Danny didn't do it) believed that Danny had stood outside the school at lunch time watching the two men in the unmarked car until they went away to buy a sandwich. They thought he had then gone into the playground and abducted Kim, telling her he was a detective. He had taken her to the flat in Wicklow Road where he'd tortured and slain her in such a perverted way that it left them sick to their stomachs – and had actually made two out of the three of them throw up – and then he had gone home, arriving shortly before Vinge had phoned.

Only Haines of the three of them did not believe there would have been time for this to happen. Only Haines did not believe there was enough blood on Danny for him to have been the killer – an opinion he had voiced and had seemingly discarded when it fell on stony ground. Haines was now keeping his opinions to himself.

'I didn't do it and you know it,' Danny said, the black rage increasing with the tingling of his palms. 'The blood test will bear it out.' For quite a long time now he had badly wanted to tell Adams about the Zulu. He forced himself not to.

'You already told us how you did it,' Vinge said. 'What we want to know is *why* you did it and *where* you put the knife.'

'How about asking why there isn't enough blood on me? How about asking why the blood on my clothes is *my* blood and not the girl's?' Danny countered. *Joey's coming*! he thought. *Joey's coming for you and we gotta get the birdy back*!

'We don't know that it isn't your blood,' Vinge said. 'What we *do* know is that you were standing in the bath fully dressed when we arrived, trying to shower it off yourself with a hair-washing attachment.'

'It's about time you started talking turkey,' Adams the Zulu-hater said.

'Okay,' Danny said angrily, 'how about *this* for turkey. . .?'

'*Don't*!' Vinge said suddenly. Danny glanced over at him and saw that scared expression flickering on Vinge's face. *Fear*, he thought. *What did he say? He didn't much care for the look on my face when I did this? Fuck him!*

Suddenly a sadistic part in him woke up and was as delighted as a child on Christmas morning. Danny felt very cold and hard and wanted to hurt Vinge and Adams; wanted to damage them badly. *Joey's got you now!* his cry-baby sang. *It's Joey coming through!* but Danny didn't think it was – it was merely a part of the process he had been undergoing over the past six months. It was the steely hatred of a man who knew there was only one way out for him and that the way was to kill.

Danny grinned hatefully. 'Carnegie Brown, Zulu. Drugs bust 86. Fitted up. Mariette Franklin, Zulu. Prostitution 87. Case dismissed; insufficient evidence. Mariette Franklin. Cocaine 88. Planted. James "Boy" LeFevre, Zulu. Car theft and breaking and entering 89. Case dismissed; insufficient evidence. Winston Smith, Zulu. Murder: 91. Confessed under considerable duress during interview. Case pending.'

'STOP IT!' Vinge yelled.

Adams' face was ashen. Unlike Ray Johnson he did not leap at Danny, but just sat there, stony-faced. Vinge was moving across the room, but going away from Danny and towards the tape recorder.

'You don't like black people much, do you?' Danny asked Adams. 'Sorry, I mean *Zulus*.'

'Shut the fuck up!' Vinge yelled, coming back.

But Danny did not want to shut up; Adams was beginning to cringe but he wanted to make him squirm. 'Here comes the punchline!' he said. 'Are you ready? No? Shame. Your wife's called Jane Mary Adams and she's twenty-eight and brunette and pretty and her birthday's on September the 9th. Am I right? Yes, I am, of course I am. Well, here's a surprise for you, old detective Adams: since she was twenty-six, Jane Mary Adams has regularly been fucking a Zulu called Desmond Graham. And whaddya know? She last fucked that old Zulu only yesterday evening in the back of his Mercedes when he picked her up from the squash club. You wondered why she was a little late home and she said she'd gone for drinks with the girls. Well, now you know the truth!'

Danny's head sang and his heart hammered hard. For a moment he thought Vinge would hit him, but Vinge had apparently thought better of it and returned to his seat. Maybe the man still had some secrets left then.

Adams was shaking his head. 'No,' he said in a quiet, reasonable voice. 'That's not it. No. Not a Zulu.'

The door opened and Haines came in. 'Can I see you outside, Jon?' he asked Vinge.

'Stay there and keep your mouth shut!' Vinge said, getting up.

Adams looked at Danny. 'Liar,' he said in an unsteady voice.

Danny grinned. 'In a moment Vinge is going to come through that door and tell me the blood on my clothes and in my flat is B rhesus negative. An uncommon type. He's also going to tell me that my own blood group is B rhesus negative. It won't match the group taken from the semen at either scene. He'll have to let me go. If that happens, you can rest assured that your wife is seeing Desmond Graham. If you know what's good for your marriage, you'll let it continue until it ends naturally.'

The door opened. Vinge came in with a face like thunder. 'Get out!' he said.

Danny got up and limped to the door. 'It was A positive at the scenes, wasn't it?' he said, turning back.

Vinge nodded.

'He's coming for me next. You know that, don't you?'

Vinge grinned and thought, quite distinctly, *I hope he cuts your balls off!* While he said, 'We'll get him first.'

Danny grinned back humourlessly, showing his teeth. 'He'll have to try very hard,' he replied and walked out.

5

Joey was coming.

Danny spent the remainder of that night slumped in the scalding water of his bath, with a hot flannel pressed to the aching bullet-scar where the only other living Hoodoo Man currently walking the face of the planet had forced his way in. There were many other bad pains, but the scar was not only sore and throbbing but the source of the disgusting *soiled* feeling which filled Danny. The idea that his body had been permanently tainted by that invasion would not go away, no matter how hard he rubbed nor how long he soaked.

And Joey was coming. This information was true and undeniable. The time was almost right. Danny could feel the information coming in through that sore and dirty scar; it pervaded the atmosphere, hanging heavily in the air. Out there in the void he could feel the other Hoodoo Man reaching out for him again, the way he had that first time when he saw Danny's life twinkling like a little star in the blackness; the way he had on the day Danny fell through the black mirror tiles; the way he had *always* done.

Fear glowed inside Danny in a bright point, but he had solidified around it, growing cold and hard. He *could* kill. He knew that now and he clung to it. The Hoodoo Man was coming and Danny would kill him if he could.

And while he waited for the killing time to arrive, Danny walked alone along the sea front in the wind and watched the huge breakers roll in from the grey sea and fought against the bleak loneliness and the aching fatigue that tried to swamp him.

That evening he picked up his life-charts with his message of love to Suzie scrawled across them, folded them neatly and placed them in a drawer. He wouldn't be needing them any more because he was going to phone her and tell her himself.

He tried his home number, and when there was no reply, phoned Suzie's parents. Suzie's father Eric answered the phone and told Danny that she was well and taking a late holiday in the Canaries. He thought Suzie would be glad to know that Danny was still alive and kicking but wasn't sure if she wanted to hear from him yet. Danny told Eric that he thought something nasty might soon happen to him and asked him if he would promise to tell Suzie that Danny loved her always. Eric wanted to know what Danny thought might happen to him and became faintly annoyed when he was denied this knowledge. His tone suggested that he thought now, as he had thought all along, that Danny ought to see a psychiatrist.

There was a bottle of brandy in the kitchen. Danny remembered how alcohol had tipped him into the week at nine twenty–one and had so far refused to open it; it was simply there for emergencies. Now seemed about as good an emergency as was likely to present itself. *Unless you save it until the only other living Hoodoo Man walking the face of the earth arrives*, he told himself, *and I doubt very much that he'll want to stop for a drink*.

He opened the bottle and swallowed a good long draught that burnt his throat and made his stomach contract violently. When he stopped wanting to vomit and started to feel warm, he did it again. Then he phoned Jamie's mother and told her not to let the boy come round again until he called to say it was okay. He told her that things were getting a little hectic. It wouldn't be any problem, Carol James told him while he swigged brandy, Jamie's flu and chest infection had worsened and he didn't feel up to much at all. She asked Danny about the budgie that Jamie was so looking forward to seeing and, his speech now getting just a little bit slurred, Danny told her that it wasn't here yet but would soon be coming. The lie tasted bitter as it passed his lips but a part of him felt good about doing a little lie-telling again.

Joey is coming, he thought afterwards as he listened to the recorded voice saying: *Please replace the handset. Please replace the handset. . .*

Time was running out for him. He would prevail or he would die or he would meld eternally with Joey Aston, the other chip off the same old psychic block, and in his slightly tipsy state none of the options seemed to be particularly worse than any other. Whatever happened he would have soon done his bit and things would have drawn to an end. *Joey will come and then it will be all over*, he thought. *Easy-peasy*!

Danny took the bottle of brandy to the Reading Room, set the Anglepoise up on the table and wrote Suzie one last letter. There were no tears to stain it and crumple the paper this time. The time for tears had gone, as had the chances of making up and healing rifts. Danny set down what he knew in plain facts, wrote his *Danny loves you now . . .* piece at the bottom, folded the letter, sealed it in the envelope, stamped it and took it down to the letter box.

When he came home he swigged down more brandy, laid down on his bed to wait and slept.

And Joey Aston's voice whispered through his dreams: *Here I come, old Dan*! *I'm coming for you. Soon! Very soon!*

6

Something remarkable happened during the night. When he woke the following morning – smiling and *sans* hangover headache – Danny did not know what the remarkable thing was, but he could feel its effects. He suddenly felt fresh and strong and *prepared*.

You went somewhere, be told himself as he got up, marvelling at the fact that the endless list of aches and pains he'd been suffering had fled along with the dreadful fatigue. *You went somewhere and someone told you something. Something good*, he thought. But there was no proof of this, no memory of the magical dream that had apparently healed and strengthened him. The limp was still there when he walked, his left arm had a faint feeling of pins and needles and his scar was throbbing gently, but this represented a huge improvement over the previous evening.

Joey's coming, he thought, and knew that he still had a little time.

The big day would be tomorrow – either someone in his dream had told him this, or he was picking it up via the atmosphere like a radio receiver; he didn't know which. And when he thought about the big day, he was surprised to realise that there was now only one acceptable outcome. He *must* win.

They got at you! he thought as he washed. *Some bastard got at you and wound you up while you were asleep. Gave you a pep talk or something*.

Suddenly he felt very hungry. He cooked himself a huge fried breakfast – something all Lerner's books on psychic ability warned against – and wolfed it down, imagining his insides extracting pure energy from it. By the time he'd washed the pan and plate the tingling in his left arm had ceased.

Joey was coming but there was still a little time.

Danny pulled on his trainers, went downstairs, passed the Reading Room wondering about trying to use the crystal again to view the final outcome and realised that this was one thing he didn't want to know. *I never worry about the future*, he told himself with a sudden dark humour, *it comes soon enough*.

Outside the snow had gone. The streets were wet and the wind cold, but the air felt good and fresh in his lungs. *C'mon, legs, let's see what you can do*! Danny thought and began to trot.

It felt good to run again. After the first few hesitant steps his weak left leg came on song and matched the power of the right. The blood started to pound in his ears and the throbbing of the sore bullet scar lessened considerably.

The promenade was empty. The tide was up, the grey sea was rough and a salt spray flew off it, stinging his eyes and making his face sticky. But it felt good. Very good. *Good to be alive*? Danny asked himself as he forced his pace and picked up speed. *Is life sweet after all*? When he thought of the alternatives, life did indeed seem sweet. Danny's mind tried to make him think of Steffy and Kim Santos and Jamie who wanted get the birdy back, but Danny crushed these thoughts and kept them at bay. He didn't know if the glimpse he'd had of the future through Jamie's eyes was going to happen and he refused to think about it. In a way, Suzie had been right. Sometimes it was better not to know.

Danny's legs settled into an easy rhythm under him and began to feel as if they could go on forever. His head cleared and he began to feel invigorated and strong. Danny leapt over an old newspaper that blew across his path, hit the ground and suddenly realised it would be good to run barefoot. He stopped and tore off his shoes and socks, thinking, *Either I've gone completely bananas, Brough, and I'm fooling myself, or I've discovered how to pick up the earth's random energy like a backwards lightning conductor*. He threw the shoes and socks into the next bin and began to run again, suddenly feeling whole and more in tune with the world than he had ever been before. The cold air was good in his lungs, the hard ground solid under his feet. Everything seemed sharp and bright and new. The end of The Tunnel was at last in sight. Danny pounded the ground and thought, *you're ready*!

7

At seven the following morning, Joey Aston woke.

Danny felt this happen. From the moment he'd woken this morning at five he'd been strongly aware of the link that now connected the two of them. At first Danny thought it was Joey's link, formed when Aston had stolen the little girl's life, but later, when his palms began to itch, he realised the truth.

The link was his. When he hadn't been using the crystal his own psychic abilities looked for an outlet and the outlet they'd found this time was Joey Aston. At first the link had been vague and tenuous but late last night it had grown solid and strong.

And this morning it had begun to deliver information: Danny had woken thinking, *Joey's coming today.*

Danny did not know how the link worked, how it had been formed or even if it permitted one or two way information. If Aston could perceive him as well, he wasn't going to learn much. Danny kept his mind perfectly empty.

Since Danny had risen, he had been waiting in the Reading Room, sitting behind his table and facing the door, the shrouded crystal before him, and his largest, sharpest steak-knife on his lap.

Joey would come today.

And Danny would make him pay.

He felt Joey wake, still stupid with sleep but knowing that something had changed.

It's because I can feel *you*, Danny thought. *You don't know that yet, but you soon will. This isn't going to be as easy as you think, my old chip off the same psychic block. Little Danny Stafford is going to fight back.*

Cold water hit Joey's face. There was only sensation; no sound, no pictures, and none of Joey's thoughts.

Can you hear me, Joey? he asked and there was no reply. Danny nodded.

And waited.

The nervousness had gone now. The fear had vanished. Danny was steely and cold and brimming with a bright hatred.

The time slowed until it was almost at a standstill, but Danny could wait.

Joey Aston dressed. Danny could feel the clothes on his own skin; soft track-suit trousers, a thin tee shirt, running shoes. He felt Aston pull out the Gannex raincoat from beneath the bed, felt the cool lining on his own arms.

Joey went outside into the cold, reached high, forced his hand into a tight place – probably behind a low gutter, Danny thought – and his fingers closed over the knife. Danny knew the feel of that wooden handle very well indeed. His own hand closed over the steak-knife in his lap.

Joey went back inside the house and came out through the front door.

Danny's link flickered and hot pain lit in his scar.

I'm coming, old Dan! Joey thought. His voice was distorted and distant and echoed as if it was coming over a bad satellite telephone connection, but the words were clear enough. *Can you see me yet?* Joey asked. *Are you watching me coming for you? I don't know, but I think you can! Are you there?*

I can hear you, Danny said, but again there was no reply.

I'm saving my energy, old Dan, Joey thought, *but I'll bet you're watching me coming for you. I don't need to see you, Danny boy, because I already know where you are and what's going to happen. You're sitting there in your little shop waiting for me to come. There's a big steak-knife in your lap which you intend to kill me with. Well, I'm sorry, brother, you won't get to touch me with it. You don't know how it all turns out old Dan, but I do. This is a movie I've watched many times before and one that you didn't get to see. I know it word by word, action by action, and I know how it ends. It's a shame, old Dan, and it's going to hurt, but you'll thank me for it in the end. You'll be me, old Dan, and you'll be with Steffy and Kim. It'll be Ten-up, old Dan. We'll be like Jesus!*

And Danny's link broke with an audible *snap*! He closed his eyes, searched for Joey with his mind. This time he *saw* Joey.

He was on the seafront, strolling along in the breeze and grinning, his raincoat filling with wind and billowing out around him.

Here comes the Hoodoo Man! Joey thought and broke the connection again.

Danny stayed frozen in place, thinking nothing, feeling nothing, while he searched for the link.

Time reeled past in an infinitely slow stream.

Now Aston was inside a newsagent's buying cigarettes.

Now he was sitting on a bench smoking and watching passers-by while his right hand held on to the knife.

Now he was sitting in a café drinking tea. Sitting in the café Danny had once woken up in. Talking to his waitress with the bottle blonde hair and liquid brown eyes.

Isn't she lovely? he asked. *Shall we take her next, old Dan, old Psychic Slayer?*

Now he was back on the street, his footsteps light and athletic as he approached the turning to Danny's street.

Phone the police! Danny's cry-baby suddenly urged.

'No!' he said aloud.

No? Aston asked. *Did you speak, old Dan? No, what? WHAT ARE YOU DOING, DANNY?*

He doesn't know, Danny suddenly realised. *He doesn't know how it'll all turn out any more than you do. He's playing it just as blind as you are*! He fought for contact.

And watched Joey come slowly up the street, frowning pensively, his right hand holding the knife steady in his deep pocket. *Here I come, old Dan!* he thought and turned into the doorway.

'You won't win,' Danny promised aloud and the words vanished because Joey Aston had suddenly turned on everything he had.

There was a brief smell of something like burning paint and Danny heard a dull rumbling like a massive piece of machinery approaching at a million miles an hour. The sound grew to an unbelievable volume, swept over him at full force and Danny's mind exploded into uncontrollable series of overlaid and out of sequence bright pictures which had a jumbled and deafening sound-track.

Danny was on the floor, naked and glistening with blood and entrails, while Joey knelt before him, forcing his head deep into the cavity he'd made. Joey as a child paddling in the sea while he held his mother's hand. Kim Santos screaming for her own mummy. A vast and empty blackness that roared. Bands of brilliant light that cut like razors. Danny slashing out the steak-knife and missing by a mile. The mouth of God, gaping and spewing power. Joey taking Steffy from behind then drawing out her life-light in a shining ribbon. Joey failing his driving test and screaming into the examiner's face. Black confusion. Pain. Brilliant starbursts. Joey trying to bring the smouldering dog back to life and screaming when it didn't work. Danny screaming in agony as the knife opened a deep diagonal across his chest. Jamie running hard and falling with a small surprised sound and Danny's own steak-knife quivering in his stomach. The taste of warm blood in his mouth. The car crash. Blackness and crying. A deep far away future, mixed and mingled into senselessness.

Here I come, old Dan! Joey promised through the swirling images that battered Danny's mind. *I've got you already!*

Danny was on the floor, struggling and losing; gasping as the knife entered his flesh, tearing at his life. Futures, pasts and presents whirled chaotically: some real, some alternate, some alien, some imagined.

I let you in, Joey chuckled somewhere off in the distance. *How do you like it inside my head*?

Danny screamed as Joey came in through the front door. There was something way out in the distance in front of him that had to be done but his head was packed to bursting with Joey's personality and it was pushing his own mind away from his grasp.

'*What do I have to do?* he wailed in the violently spinning maelstrom.

Danny could hear footsteps out there in that other world. Slow and measured footsteps as Joey came down the hall to the Reading Room.

'You have to give yourself up to me!' Joey's voice said, cutting through the wall of deafening noise. 'Here comes the Hoodoo Man!'

Chapter Twenty-Three
Bringing Back the Birdy

What do I have to do? Danny screamed inwardly as out there in that other world, the door handle moved, turning slowly.

I'd break the link, if I were you, his cry-baby voice calmly told him from somewhere off in the distance. *Break the link. Break the link!*

Danny closed his eyes as the door slowly opened.

'I'm here,' Joey said.

Danny focused what was left of his own mind on to the aching scar. Joey could break the link so he could do it too. If he could figure out how to.

'What a pretty picture,' Joey said.

Out there in the other world a killer was standing in the doorway, smiling and handsome, his left hand held out in a gesture of welcome and his right hand buried deep into the pocket of his Gannex raincoat.

He tried to make the dog alive again! Danny thought. *No more! Stop this! Stop it!* Then the words – the magic words he had been searching for – slowly rose from the stony ground of his mind: massive slow-moving granite lintels, pushing back earth and rocks into piles as they emerged. Danny watched them rise, watched them blot out the spinning hell of Joey's mind as they powered up between him and the alternating pictures of Joey killing Steffy and Joey furiously beating the smouldering dead dog with a stick.

ABSOLUTELY NOT! Danny thought.

And the link broke with a painful *snap!* Danny felt as if someone had let him have it in his bullet-scar with an elastic band, but the sensation which followed was worse. The scar was bleeding now – just a hot trickle – but it felt as if it was opening up, dilating slowly like the iris of an eye might as the lights dimmed. A tube was surely being formed there; an open canal right into the centre of his brain.

'We can be like Jesus, you and me!' Joey said.

Danny's hands knew what they were supposed to do long before his stunned mind had the thought. They were out there in front of him, not waving the steak-knife, but grasping the velvet cloth and taking it away from the little glass bastard.

'DON'T' Joey yelled.

And the crystal lit with a blinding white flash.

The room was suddenly filled with a dazzling lattice-work of searing light. Thousands of brilliantly coloured ribbons extended from the crystal and swept the room like searchlight beams, reflecting and refracting; bouncing from walls at all angles, breaking into needle-sharp prisms where they shone through glass. Danny's retinas screamed and heat built inside his head.

The noise which battered the aural part of Danny's brain had started as a low hum when he had revealed the crystal – now it was quickly growing to a painful grinding throb which seemed to be making him flicker and fade in and out of existence.

Someone here has just made a very bad mistake!

Danny heard the words and didn't know who had thought or said them. There now seemed to be very little left to choose between the two Hoodoo Men. The distinction was becoming blurred.

'You shouldn't have done that!' Aston shouted, and Danny's lips moved with the words.

Joey was coming towards him now, flickering around the edges as if he had become an electronically reproduced image of himself. The man was still smiling but Danny could see the rage and hatred in his eyes as he pulled his right hand slowly from his pocket.

We gotta bring back the birdy.

Jamie's plaintive plea echoed inside Danny's mind as his own right hand closed around the handle of the steak-knife. What did you mean? Danny thought. *How do you bring back the birdy? Joey the budgie? He's gone! Long gone. And you can't bring things back from the dead. It can't be done! Ask Joey the Hoodoo Man! Ask him about the dog!*

'I'll hurt you now, old Dan,' Joey's flickering image said. 'You've made a mistake and you've hurt me and now I'm going to hurt you right back. But you'll thank me for it. We can put all this right. We'll work *miracles!*'

Hickorydickorydickory! Danny thought. *It's a long way to Africa!*

'Depends which way you go, old Dan,' Aston said. And the shining blade of his knife slipped into view. Bands of light found it and flickered from it in searing hues. 'You shouldn't have done it, old Dan!' Aston said in a wounded voice. 'Something's happening now and I don't know what it is.'

'You know the end!' Danny shouted, not knowing if the words were coming from him or from the flickering image of Joey Aston. There was rage in the voice and a sudden realisation. 'You said you knew how it all turns out. You couldn't see, could you? Could you?'

Then their two voices merged and they shouted, 'YOU DON'T KNOW!' and Danny broke the link again.

And Joey was coming slowly towards him, a strange expression on his face and his knife held out before him like a glittering lance. 'Why'd you send that fucking *budgerigar* to haunt me, old Dan?' Joey asked angrily. 'Why d'you have to make things so *complicated?* You've shorted every-fucking-thing out now. Look what you've done!' He stabbed the knife into the air towards the far corner of the room. A scorched circular hole was appearing in the wallpaper over there on the side wall, but it wasn't just a hole in the wallpaper which showed crumbling plaster underneath, or a hole through to the bricks, or even a hole through to the outside of the building: it was a hole through reality itself.

A black nothingness grew there, opening up like the scar on Danny's face. As he watched, it widened from the size of a small marble to the size of an orange and settled. Danny realised it wasn't merely happening in two dimensions, but three. so that it bulged out into the room.

'Why'd you have to make things so *fucking* complicated?' Joey asked angrily.

The hole flickered and instantaneously expanded to the size of the crystal, then smoothly grew to the size of football. Danny felt its gravity exert itself and it pulled him towards it, the way the black mirrors in his bathroom had drawn him. He fought for control over his balance while the lattice-work of light coming from the crystal wound itself into a thick knotted rope and flew directly into the yawning nothingness.

'We can put it right!' Joey screamed, 'BUT YOU CAN'T BRING BACK THE DEAD!'

Danny tore his eyes away from the hole, dizzily got up on to his leaden legs and pushed the table aside. There was something happening in the air above the right side of Joey's head and a picture lit in Danny's mind: Margaret Miller, his first customer, dabbing her eyes with a tissue and saying, 'I didn't like the noise . . . it sounded like a dicky bird whistling at first . . . then like something big and nasty was coming. . .'. Margaret vanished and Jamie said, 'The birdy was in the room . . . he said his name was Joey. . .' Then: '*Vinge has come now we got to bring back the birdy*'. And then Joey himself: 'BUT YOU CAN'T BRING BACK THE DEAD!'

And there was something happening in the air over the right side of Aston's head *over the dead part of his brain!* It was rippling like a heat-haze. Why did you send that fucking *budgerigar to haunt me, old Dan?* Aston had asked.

You haunted him! Danny thought. *Somehow you sent Joey the budgie to him across the void when you were shot – when he linked with you that first time. And he's frightened of him! Joey's dead but his memory or his ghost is trapped in the web where it links with the dead parts of our brains!*

But Joey's like the dog! Danny thought. You can't bring him back! Joey gone to Africa and you can't bring him back. Come on Joey! Come back to me. Joey, COME BACK!

'It can't be done!' Aston said, shaking his head. 'Not yet!'

He was almost within striking range now. Danny's hand tensed on the handle of his steak-knife. 'COME BACK, JOEY!' he yelled and heard the fluttering of wings making for Africa. Hickorydickorydickory! Joey trilled in his right ear and Danny was so certain he was there, he looked up for him.

And Aston struck, slashing the knife out in a sweeping arc.

In his mind's eye, Danny saw the immediate future and reacted in time to draw back. The tip of the knife licked across his left cheek leaving a stinging cut.

Come back! Danny thought and instantly punched out his steak-knife at Joey Aston's stomach in a clumsy uppercut. Joey was still turning and the knife blade slipped under the lapel of his coat, caught, tore material and ground through to his collar bone, sawing across flesh and nicking the bone beneath.

Agonising pain blasted through Danny's own shoulder as Joey screamed. The pain ran down Danny's arm in a great numbing wave and he knew that he had to keep his fingers locked around the knife because Joey was going to drop his own.

The knife clattered to the table and fell to the floor. Danny could hear wings beating deep inside the thundering noise in his head. He slashed out the knife at the man in front of him and Joey dodged, thinking, *Saw that one!* as the blade whickered through thin air.

And Danny also saw him step into the passing arc of the knife and grab the still-moving arm a moment before it happened. There was absolutely no chance of protecting himself this time – the time-lapse was too short, the future too close. Aston leapt forward and caught his arm at the wrist with his left hand while the point of the knife was facing away from him. He pushed Danny back off balance and turned him away while he ground his fingers into Danny's wrist with incredible force.

Danny clawed clumsily at Aston's dark eyes with his left hand and Aston reached up and caught it with his right hand a full foot before it got to him. He crushed Danny's clawed fingers into a knot and a wave of hot nausea filled Danny as his stressed bones began to give.

Joey! he thought. *Come back!*

'You can't do it!' Aston hissed, pulling Danny's crossed arms tight against his body and drawing him closer. 'Not yet and not ever! I'm going to have you now, Danny, *then* we'll work miracles!'

Danny linked again with Joey's mind and the connection broke instantly. 'Not like that!' Joey hissed.

He's going to tear your throat out with his teeth, Danny's cry-baby suddenly warned.

Danny dragged up the granite words, emptied his mind, and as Joey's head dipped he brought his right knee up into the man's groin with all the force he could muster.

Joey gasped and stepped backwards, doubling up. And in what seemed like motion so slow it was almost stopped, Danny leaned towards him and slashed out wildly at his face, no longer knowing whether or not the knife was still grasped in his screaming hand.

But the knife was there, still locked solidly in place, and it swept out in a slow and graceful arc. Aston saw it coming and turned his head away but he was a moment too late. The tip of the knife hit him just in front of his left ear, pierced his cheek and sank in, opening flesh. Then it met the solid resistance of teeth and ground against them as Joey pulled back.

When the knife swept away from him, the right side of his mouth extended to the back of his jawbone. Joey inserted his fingers between the bleeding flaps, pulled out a bloody tooth and dropped it as Danny brought the knife back in another arc.

This time he was ready. He caught Danny's wrist with one hand and the other closed around the fingers locked on to the knife. He twisted and bent Danny's hand so the protruding part of the steak-knife handle lay close to the tendons in his wrist then bent it forward violently, forcing the handle deep between the bones of Danny's wrist. Danny heard bone crack and molten metal poured up his arm. The knife fell from his fingers as the agony sheeted his vision. Holding Danny's wrist in both hands, Aston's fingers probed the broken bones while he forced Danny to his knees, then down to the floor on his back.

'I know where you live, old Dan,' Joey said, crouching over him. He jabbed his finger into Danny's scar. The finger ground into his cheekbone but Danny also felt Joey pouring down into him through the tunnel that had opened up there. Searing white light lit in Danny's brain. 'That's the way in! That's the entrance, and I'm coming in. Soon!' He withdrew the finger and the burning light vanished, leaving a vacuum which screamed to be united with the vacuum in the corner of the room.

Danny hardly felt the blow when Aston slapped him hard across the face with his open hand but the blood which instantly poured down the back of his throat from his suddenly bleeding nose brought him back to himself, choking.

'You're open for me, Danny!' Aston shouted, 'And I'm coming in! But I'm going to *hurt you first*, old Dan, old Hoodoo Man.'

The hole in reality was steadily drawing the air from the room and as Aston shucked off his Gannex raincoat his hair fluttered in the breeze. The wind coming under the door began to sing. Aston glanced around at the hole. 'We'll work a miracle, old Dan,' he said. 'We'll be like Jesus!'

Locked on to the floor in the iron grip of his pain, Danny looked up at him. The air around the right side of Aston's head was still rippling but Danny didn't know how to bring back the birdy or what it could do if he did. It was too late now. He'd lost. I tried, he thought. *At least I tried.*

Aston sat down on Danny's hips, leaned over him and picked up the steak knife. Blood fell from his face into Danny's eyes as he moved and it stung and bleared his vision. 'Come back, Joey!' Danny pleaded.

'It can't be done!' Aston said angrily. 'It's too soon!' Then his face cleared. He looked at Danny as if he'd just had a nice idea. He set the knife down, grabbed Danny by the shirt, yanked his shoulders and neck from the floor and ducked his head as Danny's swung up. Danny's vision flashed blue as Aston's head connected squarely with his nose and teeth. There was a moment of unconsciousness as his head floated back down to the floor then the bump woke him up again. Blood filled his mouth and ran steadily down from the back of his – now surely broken – nose. His two upper front teeth slopped about in their sockets when he touched them with his tongue.

Be like Jesus, he thought. *Come back, Joey! Come back from Africa!*

'A tooth for a tooth,' Aston said, and smiled a wide, bloody grin.

I'm trying, Jamie said in Danny's mind. *I'm trying very hard and I don't understand neither. Vinge has came and now we got to bring back the birdy. Time is short. Just don't forget or I'll . . . lose you!*

I'm trying, Jamie! Danny thought as Aston ran the knife through his shirt and down both legs of his trousers. *I didn't forget and I'm trying but I can't bring him back!*

Aston drew back the remnants of Danny's shirt and showed him the knife. Danny batted up at him with the bright mass of pain that had once been his hand and Aston knocked it away. 'This'll hurt you, old Dan,' he said.

He laid the sharp edge of the knife on Danny's left collar bone and put weight on it. The blade broke the flesh and bit bone. Danny screamed, his muscles bunching and tensing as he coughed out blood. And Aston carefully drew the knife diagonally down across his body, nicking ribs, biting stomach and belly muscle and finally grating across Danny's pelvic bone.

And over by the door the air-flow increased with a *whoosh* as the door was opened.

Let it be Vinge. Please God, let it be Vinge! Danny thought.

And Jamie stood there, a numb and horrified expression on his face while the wind rippled his clothes and fluttered his hair.

Joey, come back! Danny thought.

'DON'T!' Aston screamed, turning to look at Jamie, and Danny felt his sudden confusion. Jamie couldn't be read or predicted for and he was a variable that hadn't existed in whatever version of this event Aston had seen.

Jamie's hands flew up to his face in horror.

Let me be like Jesus! Danny thought.

Aston looked away from the boy and angrily thought: *Don't do that*! and as if to prove his point, picked up Danny's left arm and hacked across it with the knife, not carefully this time but like a butcher with a tough hunk of meat.

Got the artery! Danny thought as the first bright pulse of blood jetted up.

'NO DON'T YOU!' Jamie roared angrily, and as Aston turned to face him, Danny brought the arm into the air with the intention of clamping his broken right hand over the wound. The gash gaped at him as he moved the arm and Danny's mind reeled. *Lots of blood*! he thought stupidly as the arm hung in the air before him, steadily spraying him with his own warm life.

Jamie gasped and charged across the room wailing. Aston swung a fist through the air in a lazy, perfectly timed punch. Jamie ran into the blow and stopped dead in his tracks, but he didn't go down. Aston hit him twice more and Jamie tottered backwards and fell heavily. *Stay down, Jamie!* Danny implored. *He'll stab you next time. It doesn't have to be like this! Just stay down!*

Bird wings fluttered nearby.

Jamie got up. 'GIVE HIM BACK TO ME!' he roared. 'HE'S MINE!' His fist clenched and went to his temple and Danny knew that a Danny from the past was inside him, trying to prevent the run. That past Danny was going to fail.

Come on, God, give me the birdy! Danny thought as his arm sprayed blood on to him. He was soaked in it now and starting to feel weak and faint and a little cold. He decided to hit Aston one last time and flung his open hand towards the man's face. The hand simply fluttered in the air and then fell to the floor.

Jamie charged at Aston once more, screaming at the top of his voice, and as Danny saw the knife blade flash up he thought, *Please, Joey, come back! Please! Let me be like Jesus! Come on, God, it's only one lousy budgie!*

Aston plunged the knife into Jamie's belly. 'Hooo!' Jamie said, doubling over. Aston yanked the knife free and Jamie went down, writhing on the floor in pain, his heels kicking out a broken rhythm as his legs tried to get beneath him again. 'Danny!' Jamie called, his voice shrill and pained. 'We gotta bring back the birdy! Come here!'

Come here? Danny thought. *How does he know about that?* but his mind was already reaching out for the boy. Danny jerked as he made the link. His mind twisted sharply as he met Jamie.

'DON'T!' Aston raged, looking from the boy to Danny and back again. He pressed his finger against Danny's gaping bullet-scar, but this time there was no flash of light, no invasion. The link with Jamie's skewed and powerful mind had somehow erected a defence. Aston could not tap into Jamie's mind or his future. A part of Danny felt him trying and failing and this part of him rejoiced. Aston was confused and suddenly truly frightened.

It hurt inside Jamie and it was very confused but it was warmer; more alive. Danny thought: *Help me be like Jesus, Jamie! Help me call him back!*

And the link broke.

Danny crashed back into his cool body.

'DON'T DO IT!' Aston yelled into his face.

'Come back, Joey!' Danny croaked. He was a long way away now. A lot of blood had gone and more was going. He was closer to Joey now – almost as close as when his brother shot him.

Africa's a long way! the budgie's voice said clearly. The air above Aston's head flickered and crackled.

Aston screamed and clapped his hands to his ears.

Wings beat the air.

Jamie had found his feet and was dragging himself up. 'Come back, birdy!' he piped. Come back!'

'SEND IT AWAY!' Aston shouted.

'Come to Danny, Joey! Joey come back from Africa!' Danny murmured.

Hickorydickorydickory Dock!

Aston drove a fist into Danny's jaw. It did not hurt. Or matter.

Joey's fluttering blue feathers appeared above Aston's head, circling inside the shimmering volume of air. A wing passed and Danny felt an urge to laugh triumphantly – an urge he was too weak to obey.

'TAKE IT AWAY!' Aston screamed.

And Joey burst in from the past.

'NO!' Aston screamed.

Crackling with some kind of electrical force, the budgie swooped out of the shimmering volume of air, tail and wing feathers spread as it turned tightly, wheeling around between Danny and Aston.

Over by the side wall, the hole in reality increased its gravity and air began to scream into it.

'SIC 'IM!' Jamie cried as the bird spiralled above Aston's head, fighting the sudden wind.

Aston ducked and screamed and slashed the knife through the air at the budgie, and Joey turned tighter. The knife missed by a foot.

Tiny fluffy feathers dropped from Joey as he circled and bumped through the turbulence from which he had emerged. Danny could see him in both places now: the *here and now* and the *there and then*. There was hardly any difference.

The feathers fell on Aston and Danny suddenly knew why he had been so frightened, knew why the dead dog had been smouldering. Neither of the two Hoodoo Men had been enough like Jesus. Joey was back from the dead but he had been brought back clumsily and temporarily. And some metaphysical law had been horribly broken in the process. The tiny fluffy feathers sizzled as the wind caught them and ignited as they were drawn across the room to the vacuum. And they didn't simply burn and extinguish themselves. The minute fires raged with a blistering ferocity as if the energy contained in their matter was forcibly extracted.

Joey chattered and swooped as the web exerted its gravity through the hole in the back wall of the room.

'SIC 'IM!' Jamie roared.

I CAN DO IT! Aston thought, rocking back and forth on Danny's bleeding body as he chased the bird through the air with the knife.

Feathers flew.

That cat'll be the death of me! Joey chirruped inside Danny's head.

If it touches Aston, he'll die! Danny thought. *He'll die, just like I'm dying*.

There was a series of white-hot explosions as feathers touched parts of the room. The table was suddenly peppered with holes through which air screamed.

Sic him, Joey! Danny thought, and the bird turned suddenly and flickered past Aston's face, touching him with a wing. Aston screamed and drew back as the bird passed. There was a deep, smouldering zig-zag line burnt into the flesh of his good cheek.

Danny gazed up at him dazedly and thought, *You can't see where he's going to go next, can you? You're fucked now, old Joey, old pal!*

'TAKE IT AWAY!' Aston screamed as he slashed through the air after the budgie which wheeled, turned and swooped back at him, chirruping angrily. 'MAKE IT GO AWAY! SEND IT BACK!'

But Danny couldn't send it back, even if he'd wanted to.

Get him! he thought.

'NO!' Aston screamed.

Jamie's measured voice spoke in Danny's distant mind. *I'm . . . getting it!* he said haltingly. *It hurts . . . but I can . . . get it. I'm getting it . . . now!*

Joey the budgie swooped, sparks dancing on the tips of his wings and his black eyes glittering with the reflections of the streams of light that were being drawn from the crystal into the void.

Danny felt the boy's movement as Joey the budgie flashed past Aston's ear, his wings crackling with white lightning. Part of Aston's ear vanished. Hot specks of fiercely burning matter scattered across Danny's chest, but he didn't feel this. What he felt was the grinding ache in Jamie's stomach as the boy moved towards the table, and his cast-iron determination. Each step hurt terribly but Jamie was *getting it now*, whatever *that* meant.

Aston yelled and slashed out the knife towards Danny as Joey passed low over Danny's chest. The blade sung and flashed. Above his chest the air parted with a shattering *crack!* and the budgie screamed. Danny saw its smouldering clawed foot spin towards his face and rolled his head away from it. The claw hit the floor, blew a hole an inch in diameter in it and vanished. The air shrieked past Danny's ear as it was drawn into the nothingness that had appeared there.

'Got you!' Aston screamed.

And Danny knew what was going to happen next.

Joey swooped away and turned back towards Aston, wings beating frantically against the steadily increasing wind. Showers of feathers flew from him in bright sparks as he came in for the kill.

But this time, his namesake was ready. Joey the Hoodoo Man turned to meet him, raising the steak-knife and taking aim.

NO! Danny thought.

Joey swooped.

Aston's knife flickered as he raised it above his shoulder.

I've got it! Jamie said in Danny's mind and Danny felt the cool heat thrill of the crystal as behind him and Aston and the budgie, the boy's hands closed around it and lifted it.

The knife flew down at exactly the right moment and passed through the centre of the bird's body, cutting him from beak to tail into two perfect halves.

For an instant, Joey the budgie stood still in time, hanging in the air in two, surrounded by coloured fire and frantic electrical activity. There was no blood, no innards, just the searing light of its life.

What happened next reduced the plate glass window of the Fortune Shop into a bowing mosaic held in place only by the perfection of the fine fault lines that appeared in it. The whole Reading Room, from the point where the knife took Joey to the point where the hole in reality lay, became peppered with slanting holes which followed a straight line through the furniture and fittings, the walls, the floor, the ceiling and two of the upstairs rooms to the outside world.

As Joey the budgie exploded into a purple lotus-blossom with a blinding flash and a rumbling like thunder, the steak-knife vaporised. Joey's light and power were drawn instantly back into the yawning hole in reality, and the searing vapour of the knife followed it. But the hole was closed and gone long before the sheet of flame the knife had become arrived.

The stream of light from the crystal had vanished along with Joey. The room was filled with smoke.

And silence.

'I sent him back,' Aston said, turning back to Danny and grinning his freshly carved grin. 'He didn't take me. But I'm going to take *you!* And when I do, we can be like Jesus.'

Been like Jesus, Danny thought tiredly. *S'no great shakes. Too cold. Too cold.*

Aston pushed his forefinger against Danny's scar and Danny felt it open to accept him – and not just the psychic channel this time, either; the very flesh of the wound peeled itself open for him. Danny was very cold and very tired. He closed his eyes, distantly hoping he would die before Aston took him.

'I can see you in there, old Dan,' Aston said, leaning close enough for Danny to smell his breath.

'NO DON'T YOU!' Jamie screamed from beside him.

Danny opened his eyes. His vision was bleary. Up there, miles away, was a faded boy who was covered in blood, in pain and probably very close to dying. The boy was clutching the little glass bastard against the wound in his stomach as if hoping it would staunch the flow of his blood. Jamie looked very unsteady and very pale. *You got it, Jamie!* he thought. *You got it, but can you lift it now?*

A look of shocked bewilderment crossed Aston's bleeding face as he turned to face the boy.

Let him have it! Danny thought.

'Give him back to me!' Jamie said in a small voice.

Aston reached out for the crystal and Jamie tottered back a step, blinking hard.

Don't faint, Jamie, I need you! Danny thought.

I got it! Jamie said inside his head. *I got the crystal!*

Turn the lights on! Danny thought, willing strength into the boy. *Lift it high!*

Jamie's hands trembled.

'Give it to me!' Aston said.

And Jamie raised the crystal high over his head. Danny saw it start to glow. The glittering fog was forming inside it. *Who's doing this?* a part of him asked. *Me, Aston or Jamie?*

'Get off him!' Jamie said and a purple lotus-blossom of light formed inside the crystal. In that instant it had never looked more beautiful. Jamie grimaced. 'I got the birdy so get off him!'

And Danny felt Aston tense.

NOW! he thought.

And Jamie brought the crystal crashing down.

Chapter Twenty-Four
A Trip to the Telephone

1

It's a bit too late for that now, Danny thought sleepily as he found his right arm and clamped his left hand down on the jetting artery. *You've already bled most of the damn' stuff away, there's a hole in your face right down into your brain and everyone else is dead already, so it's a bit too late.*

But a part of him wouldn't let it be too late. A part of him wanted him to wake up and get tough and push away the dead body that lay on top of him, its cheek against his cheek as it leaked blood and brain into his face. This part of him would not believe. It wanted him to check Jamie, even though Jamie had keeled over and died shortly after bursting Aston's head open with the crystal.

Jamie had fallen to his knees after hitting Aston with the little glass bastard. He had wailed incoherently and tried to remove Aston's corpse from Danny's body then he had just keeled over, sighed and fallen silent. He was less than three feet away and Danny could not hear his breathing.

Which doesn't necessarily mean he's dead, his cry-baby complained. *And since you're the only remaining Hoodoo Man walking the face of the earth, get this guy off you and get some help. Jamie may not be dead and you're still alive, so get to the phone!*

Danny had embraced Aston in order to reach his bleeding arm. He let go now and summoned up all the energy he had to push the heavy body aside. All the energy he had was not enough. Danny simply wanted to sleep. He would soon be warm if he slept.

You won! You beat him! the cry-baby goaded. *So don't fall apart now. Wriggle out from under him!*

Danny wriggled. The jetting of his artery increased. Something warm and wet fell on to his face and he fought an urge to scream. A wave of cool darkness settled on him and Danny relaxed.

2

Wake up, you bastard!

Danny's eyes fluttered open. Everything was rimmed with black lines in exactly the way it had been during the week at nine twenty-one. He felt very weak and Aston was still on top of him. Danny did the wriggling exercise again and Aston's weight shifted. Did it again and the corpse slid off. Danny feebly kicked the tangle of heavy legs aside and pushed himself up to a sitting position. The gash across his chest and belly gaped and showed dark muscle tissue below. It hurt but not much. It was bleeding, but not badly. *Doesn't have much blood left to bleed with*, Danny thought stupidly. *It's all coming out of the arm instead*. He moved his head and the room spun, whitened and settled, looking horribly bleached. Danny looked at the gaping, jetting cut in his arm and felt sick.

Tourniquet! the cry-baby commanded. *Get a clamp on or you're going to die and there's no doubt about it, old Dan!*

Using his left hand, Danny tore away a strip of his tattered shirt and fumblingly arranged it around his arm, just above the bicep. The steak-knife's wooden handle was still clamped between Aston's fingers and fighting off the swooning feeling of falling, Danny leaned over and prised it away. He inserted the handle into the loop of material and twisted it as tightly as he could. The blood jetting from the gash subsided to a small irregular throb.

Now get to the phone!

Jamie lay nearby, sprawled into an approximation of the coma position. Danny watched him for a few seconds. He did not appear to be breathing. *You saved me from him*, Danny thought sadly. *You saved me but you died doing it.*

Danny could not stand up. He drew his tingling and (*empty . . . can legs be empty, old Dan?*) weak legs up and placed his hands on the floor to push himself up, but he didn't have the strength to stand and trying to force his muscles to work simply made him swoon.

Sitting down, he shuffled himself around so his back was facing the door and used what strength he had left and his legs to push him towards it in the same fashion as he'd travelled back up the stairs the other evening.

And this is not even as far as that! his cry-baby told him. *You did that and it was twice as far and uphill. All you have to do it's cross the hall, get into the other room and get to the phone. Easy-peasy!*

But the cry-baby was a liar. It wasn't easy-peasy lemon squeezy at all. Every foot covered was extremely fucking difficult and things were looking so bright and light with each movement that Danny didn't think he was going to make it at all.

3

The Reading Room door was the most difficult part of the operation. Danny could reach the handle from a sitting position, but the door opened inwards and couldn't be opened while you were sitting against it. He sat an inch away from it, tipped his light head back and stared up at the handle, surely a thousand miles away. His hand went up there into that huge distance where no man had reached before, found the cool metal of the handle then dropped away, plummeting back down to the distant floor where he sat.

Hickorydickorydickory! Joey trilled and Danny knew the distance between them was closing. Death was rolling steadily closer.

He reached for the handle again, found it, pulled it and moved the door towards him. His hand floated down and Danny went through the complicated manoeuvre of sliding away from the door, opening it towards him, then shuffling himself out into the hall where the sticky carpet gripped him, slowing his every movement. Too much time had passed. They weren't going to arrive in time to save him. Most of his rare B rhesus negative blood was decorating the Reading Room and even if they turned up before he was dead they certainly wouldn't be carrying any of *that* kind.

They'll most likely shove something up your arm that'll clump what blood you've got left, he thought. *It'll turn to treacle inside you! It'll probably hurt too. You'll spend your last moments writhing in agony!*

The door to the office-cum-lounge was closed too, but this one opened inwards. Danny whited-out as he reached up for the handle and the hall dissolved and Suzie's face appeared in front of him. *I can't find you!* she said. *Where are you, Danny? I can't find you!*

'I'm here!' he said, as the bleached hallway faded in again. 'I'm here and it's all over. I did it. I finished and I came out on top. It's all over!'

The door opened behind him. Leaving a trail of blood, Danny pushed himself across the floor and reached for the telephone.

'Emergency. Which service do you require?' the tinny voice bleated in his ear. Danny's mind blanked. His vision whited-out. The phone fell from his numb and tired hand. *Just let me sleep!* Danny thought. *It's too late!*

'Hello? Caller? Which service do you require?'

Danny's arms would not work. He leaned down towards the phone in his lap. 'Ambulance,' he gasped. 'Now. The Fortune Shop.'

'I can't hear you!'

Danny reached down for the phone with his fizzing left arm. He slid his fingers under it but they would not grip it. He lifted the handset and slammed it against his ear, holding there with his palm. 'Ambulance,' he said, 'I'm bleeding to death!'

Danny's vision began to tunnel. When he'd said his address, he sailed off into cool, white space.

4

Vinge arrived about ten seconds ahead of the ambulance, kicked the front door in and went straight into the Reading Room. 'Holy fucking Mary!' Danny heard him say. Then there was silence.

Then Vinge shook him gently and leaned into his restricted field of vision. 'Mr Stafford?'

'He got me,' Danny said. 'You happy?'

The ambulance men burst into the hall. 'Where are they?' a voice asked.

'Two dead in there,' Vinge called. 'One still alive in here. Quick!'

'Tell 'em,' Danny said as his vision faded into the cold falling whiteness. *Snow*, Danny thought. *It's snowing again.*

'What?' Vinge asked.

Danny had been going to ask him to tell them he was B rhesus negative but that didn't seem to matter any more. Only one thing mattered now.

'Tell 'em I love Suzie,' he said.

And Vinge might, or might not, have said, 'Okay.'

Chapter Twenty-Five
The Hoodoo Man's Last Reading

1

Two dead in there, one still alive in here!

Two dead in there!

Two dead!

Long after the confused and urgent call and response of all other voices had died away and long after the sensations of pain, movement and the dreadful thumping on his chest (which had turned to sharp needle strikes in his heart) had ceased, Vinge's voice echoed through the whiteness in Danny's mind like an announcement from the Tannoy of an empty station.

Two dead!

No Joey, fluttering away to Africa for the very last time. No cheerful budgie bickering. No screaming. No laughter. No dreams of mayhem, violence and murder. No visions of the Hoodoo Man. No pictures of Suzie, past present or future. No external stimulus at all. Only the constant echoing of the words Vinge had spoken.

Two dead.

2

The eyes of the only living Hoodoo Man currently on the face of the planet flicked open two days later in a bright hospital side-ward. For a moment there didn't seem to be any difference whatsoever. White became white.

Two dead! Vinge said inside Danny's head and the words brought the world crashing back into place. The soft nothingness instantly hardened into planes and angles, light and shade and textures which all screamed down his optic nerves and lit pain deep inside his brain.

Danny closed his eyes again and saw darkness against which blue and purple after-images swum. There had been a date-and-time clock on the far wall – the one his propped-up head was facing – and the time had been the magical moment of nine twenty-one. Lady Luck, it seemed, was now rubbing salt into the considerable wounds she had made.

Danny lay there, not thinking of the cold ache behind his eyes or how his chest and stomach hurt each time he inhaled the warm, disinfectant-tainted hospital air that was so familiar to him. The throbbing of his old bullet wound didn't matter; the fact that his right arm felt fat and heavy and would not move didn't matter; the pain in the splayed and tied fingers of his left hand was of little consequence. Because there were *two dead*. Not one, but *two*.

Danny's mind's eye showed him graphic pictures of Jamie: the terrified boy who had been forced into the Fortune Shop; his hilarity during the oft launched tickling attacks; the way he had held out his hand for Danny to hold; his big soppy grin. And then the boy raising the flickering crystal above his head while his blood soaked his shirt and trousers. The determination shining on his face as he yelled, *I got the birdy so get off him!* The way that face had blanked as Aston's head had shattered. The way Jamie's life had faded as the light in the crystal had faded and vanished.

Should have been you, old Dan, he told himself. *Not Jamie. It should have been you.*

Danny's eyes burned but they remained dry; no tears came this time. And not being able to cry for the boy who had sacrificed himself to save his life hurt more than all his other pains put together.

Two dead.

3

He's asking to see you! Come on, Danny, you were awake and talking a moment ago. He's still asking to see you!

Danny dreamed that Jamie was alive after all. Jamie was awake and talking a moment ago and asking to see him.

Danny's eyes flicked open and he looked up into the eyes of the nurse. 'Mary Taylor SRN', the badge said. Mary looked very familiar but Danny didn't remember being awake and talking to her before. But there were changes. His mouth was fresher and his pains were sharper. He now knew the extent of his injuries so he must have been awake and lucid at some point. There were a hundred and sixty-seven stitches in the wound that ran like a sash from his left shoulder to his right hip. He knew this without a shadow of a doubt. The index, middle and ring fingers of his left hand were broken and splinted and his right wrist was in plaster. He had taken six pints of blood during the operation to close the artery in his right arm. The surgeon, he knew, had also closed the hole in his cheekbone which had once been an old scar but was still puzzled as to how the hole had been made since it didn't look a bit like any of the weapon-wounds he'd seen before. The words 'spontaneous occurrence' and 'stigmata' had been bandied about in the theatre.

Danny's eyes flicked open again. The clock on the wall said nine twenty-three on the same date: 15 December. Two minutes had passed.

'Who's asking?' he said and his voice was little more than a hopeful croak.

'The detective,' Mary Taylor said, dashing that tiny hope. 'Mr Vinge.'

4

'What the fuck happened?' Vinge wanted to know, sitting down now that the nurse had left the room. 'And where's the shotgun? That must have been some fucking cartridge in there. It blew holes clean through the table, the floor, the ceiling and the damn' wall! Where's the gun?'

Vinge listened attentively while Danny haltingly told him everything he thought the man would believe. He left out the majority of the story, reducing it to a simple attack during which Jamie had saved his life.

'Three things,' Vinge said when he'd heard Danny's story. 'First, you'll be happy to know that it's official. You topped the right guy. His genetics check out with the semen samples from both crimes. Without a shadow of a doubt, Joseph Aston was the killer. We won't be charging you with his murder or even with manslaughter. Not after the mess he left you in.'

Danny summoned up a painful smile. 'Good,' he said thickly.

'Second: you never mentioned the gun.'

Danny's throat hurt and his mouth was dry. There was still a good quantity of dried blood plugging his nostrils and he was breathing through his mouth. The combination of this and the talking had made his tongue feel like a strip of dried leather. 'Drink,' he croaked, Vinge held the glass to his lips while he sipped. 'There wasn't a gun,' Danny said finally, shaking his head. 'There was a kind of explosion. Psychic origin. Short out.'

'Christ,' Vinge said unhappily, rolling his eyes. 'I should have known it'd be something like that. Charles Fort would have loved to have met you.'

'You did some research,' Danny said.

'Rains of frogs. Spontaneous human combustion. Out of body experiences. You name it, I've read about it. Believed it, no. Read about it, yes. And here's another one to add to my list of things that can't possibly happen: *a psychic explosion.*' Vinge shook his head. 'The forensic guys didn't like the shotgun theory, but they'll like yours even less.' He thought about it. 'There's gonna be an inquest, you know that, don't you?'

Danny nodded.

'We ought to make this a little more plausible for the coroner, I think. We can't hit 'em with the psychic stuff. I can't make myself believe it, and *I've* had demonstrations. Gas explosion maybe. I can probably talk forensic round. Okay?'

'Okay,' Danny said.

'I'll keep in touch. Let you know what I come up with.'

'Okay.'

Vinge got up. 'Better be going now. Duty calls.'

No apologies, Danny thought. *No sympathy. No thanks. No congratulations. No nothing.* In that moment it would have felt very good indeed to let Vinge have it in the mouth; to feel his teeth buckle the same way as the ace reporter Tim Gould's teeth had buckled against his fist.

'The third thing,' Danny grated as Vinge reached the door.

'What?' the detective asked, cocking his ear.

'The third thing. You said there were *three* things.'

Vinge came back, his brow furrowed while he tried to remember what the third thing was. 'Oh, yeah,' he said. 'The boy. I was going to ask you why you kept calling him Jamie, but it clicked anyway. Get stupid when I'm tired. The boy's name is Mark James. Jamie comes from the surname, right?'

Danny's heart leapt. '*Is*?' he said.

'What?'

'You said, *is*,' Danny said and waited, watching Vinge carefully. In the silence his mind spoke up: *Oh no, he didn't, old Dan. He didn't say* is *at all. That's just what you wanted to hear him say. What he* actually *said was*, was.

Vinge looked confused. Then his face cleared and he nodded his head as if he understood. 'Didn't they tell you?' he asked.

'What?' Danny half screamed.

'The boy's okay. He's out of intensive care, back on the ward, and he's been asking for you. They said they'd told you. Sorry, I thought you knew. He's alive, son. He's alive.'

5

Suzie was wrong, Danny thought in the taxi that was taking him home from the hospital. *Things don't always turn out for the bad in the end at all.*

It was snowing again out there on the empty roads, but the snow looked fresh and clean. Christmas had not been white, but it looked as if New Year would be. And the New Year seemed to hold a kind of magical promise.

While he was sitting beside his hospital bed on Christmas Day, clumsily (and somewhat painfully) spooning stringy turkey into his mouth, Danny had developed an idea. And the idea remained, even through the noisy visit from the whole James family and the small presents they'd bought for him. The idea burned brightly inside his head even when Jamie had whispered that there was a proper present waiting for him at home – a special one that could not be brought to the hospital.

And now he was out (and not just out of the hospital, but out of the itchy plaster cast and the finger splints and the hundred and sixty-seven stitches) in the quiet days between Christmas and New Year, the idea was still burning.

Things don't always have to turn out for the bad in the end, he told himself as he paid the taxi driver and gazed at the fine web of cracks in the bowed glass window of the Fortune Shop.

Someone – either the police or Lerner's gnome, Danny thought as he entered – had turned the heaters on and made a whole-hearted attempt at cleaning up the mess. The brown stains showed a trail down the sticky hall carpet from the Reading Room door to the office-cum-lounge, but the paintwork of both doors was clean. The Reading Room had been straightened and tidied. Someone had cut away and removed sections of the bloodstained carpet – the forensic people, Danny assumed – and a piece of hardboard had been crudely taped against the hole that went through the wall to the outside, but the chairs had been ranged neatly against the table and the little glass bastard stood in its place in the centre of the table, wrapped in its black velvet cloth.

One last time, Danny thought as he looked at the holes peppered through the wood of the table. *Just one last time*.

He turned on the uplighter and sat down in his seat at the table, not knowing if he could do it anymore. Things had been very normal since waking up in the hospital.

There had been no dreams, no visions, and not the faintest itch in the palms of his hands. The bullet-scar (now twice the size) had only throbbed while it was healing and there had been no further trouble with the blood-bag in his nose.

A part of Danny thought that there might no longer be any genuine Hoodoo Men walking the face of the planet these days. Joey Aston might well have taken the ability away from him.

Ignoring the tightness that still lingered across his body and the dull ache in his arm and fingers that he knew from experience would not go away without a great deal of physiotherapy, Danny reached out and took the velvet cloth from the crystal, thinking, *One last time*.

The crystal was merely an empty globe of glass. No dancing beams of light were contained within it or radiated from it. No mist sparkled gold inside and there was no thrill of cool heat as Danny placed his hands against it.

It was just cold, dead glass.

Which was cracked almost all the way through the centre. Danny turned it and the flaw caught the dim window light. It looked as if a sheet of ice had been inserted into the crystal. *You hit him hard, Jamie*, Danny thought. *Good boy*. And then he asked, *Can it still be done? Can you make it work, old Mystic of the West? Can you?*

And Danny thought he could.

He stared into the flawed globe, emptying his mind and letting himself relax. It still felt good and right. Even if the crystal didn't light; even if there was no physical sensation. *You can make it work*, he told himself.

And the crystal clouded with a fractured, twinkling mist.

6

Danny's link with the crystal was broken five minutes later by the frantic hammering on the front door. *You've never been wrong yet*, Danny told himself as he flooded back into reality from a hazy and distorted future whose events spun and rolled like a picture on a television with a bad aerial. *Trust yourself. You've never been wrong yet.*

'Shut your eyes, Danny!' Jamie yelled from outside when he saw Danny through the glass panel in the door. 'Shut your eyes and open the door!'

Smiling, because he believed what he'd seen in his last vision, Danny obeyed. He closed his eyes, opened the door and stood back.

'Your present,' Jamie announced excitedly. 'Your present I brought!'

'Is it big?' Danny asked.

'Hold you hands out,' the boy commanded. 'Wider.'

Danny held out his hands and heard the familiar rattle of metal wire as Jamie lifted the gift.

The proper present Jamie had spoken of so excitedly was light and its base was cool, flat metal. Danny thought he already knew what it was.

'Open!' Jamie said.

The bird cage contained a swing, a feeder, a water dispenser and a perch on which sat a fluffy blue budgerigar. It looked up at Danny with its beady black inquisitive eyes and began to chatter.

'He likes you, Danny!' Jamie chortled.

Tears filled Danny's eyes. '*Joey!*' the budgie chirruped. '*Joeyjoeyjoey*!'

Jamie grinned. 'He's called Joey! I choosed his name! We taught him to say it! He can talk!'

Danny put the cage on the floor, swept Jamie from the ground and hugged him. 'Thanks, Jamie,' he sobbed into the boy's ear. 'It's the best present I ever had!'

'Joeyjoeyjoey!' the budgie chirruped.

7

The taxi turned up at eleven-fifteen on the morning of New Year's Eve. Danny checked that the Fortune Shop door was locked behind him, picked up his case and the bird cage containing Joey and got into the taxi, his heart hammering and butterflies in his stomach.

Yesterday, after he had made a decision based on the last rolling vision he'd had using the crystal, he had gone to Jamie's house to say goodbye. Leaving Jamie had been the hardest part of what he intended to do. Danny had said his goodbyes, promised he would return soon and given the boy a present to remember him by.

The day after Jamie had given him the budgie, Danny had taken the crystal and tapped it gently with a hammer until it broke into two across the fault line.

The present was half the crystal. 'So we'll always be magically linked,' Danny had told the distraught Jamie, blinking away his own tears. 'You keep one half and I'll keep the other and together we'll make a whole one. And your half will call me back to you, soon.'

Jamie managed a sad smile. 'We'll be two Hoodoo Men,' he said.

'Two Hoodoo Men with one budgie named Joey,' Danny said.

'And we can bring back the birdy,' Jamie said.

'Whenever we want,' Danny had replied, holding the boy close. 'Whenever we want.'

'Joeyjoeyjoey!' the budgie said.

The taxi driver turned around, eyebrows raised.

'Christmas present,' Danny said, suddenly knowing the driver's name. He put it out of his mind.

The driver nodded, turned back and started the car.

You've never been wrong yet! Danny assured himself. *And you weren't wrong this time, even if the vision was faint and you don't know if it was future one or not.*

Danny settled back in his seat, no longer sure just *what* he believed.

The last vision he had forced from the crystal was imperfect and he hadn't checked it out with his life-charts, but Danny thought he'd somehow wiped his slate clean. Lady Luck had thrown everything she had at him and he had survived. Lerner had used him but now that part of his life seemed to be over too. He had returned from the cloudy vision with fresh hope, and his belief that things didn't always turn out for the bad in the end seemingly confirmed.

The last rolling vision of his own future had been of a wedding. Not of a white wedding in a large church, but of a small register office ceremony.

And the wedding was of the variety known as shotgun.

The bride, not blushing but smiling and showing a not yet large but already quite distinctive lump, had been Suzie Anderson. And the guy in the cheap suit had been the only living Hoodoo Man currently walking the face of the planet.

'What's the New Year gonna be holding in store for you then?' the taxi driver – whose name, Danny was trying hard to forget, was Alan Walker – asked.

Will she take you back, old Dan? Will she?

'I don't know,' Danny said truthfully. 'I have no idea how things will work out from now on.'

'Who does?' Alan Walker said philosophically. 'Who does?'

And in his cage on the seat beside Danny, Joey the budgie began to sing.